NGUIN BOOKS

ns and Lovers

David Herbert Lawrence was born into a miner's family in Eastwood, Nottinghamshire, in 1885, the fourth of five children. He attended Beauvale Board School and Nottingham High School, and trained as an elementary schoolteacher at Nottingham University College. He taught in Croydon from 1908. His first novel, *The White Peacock*, was published in 1911, just a few weeks after the death of his mother to whom he had been extraordinarily close. His career as a schoolteacher was ended by serious illness at the end of 1911.

In 1912 Lawrence went to Germany with Frieda Weekley, the German wife of the Professor of Modern Languages at the University College of Nottingham. They were married on their return to England in 1914. Lawrence had published *Sons and Lovers* in 1913; but *The Rainbow*, completed in 1915, was suppressed, and for three years he could not find a publisher for *Women in Love*, completed in 1917.

After the war Lawrence lived abroad, and sought a more fulfilling mode of life than he had so far experienced. With Frieda, he lived in Sicily, Sri Lanka, Australia, New Mexico and Mexico. They returned to Europe in 1925. His last novel, *Lady Chatterley's Lover*, was published in 1928 but was banned in England and America. In 1930 he died in Vence, in the south of France, at the age of forty-four.

Lawrence's life may have been short, but he lived it intensely. He also produced an amazing body of work: novels, stories, poems, plays, essays, travel books, translations, paintings and letters (over five thousand of which survive). After his death Frieda wrote, 'What he had seen and felt and known he gave in his writing to his fellow men, the splendour of living, the hope of more and more life . . . a heroic and immeasurable gift.'

Helen and Carl Baron met and married as research students in Cambridge in the late 1960s. It was Carl Baron's survey of Lawrence's manuscripts and proofs that persuaded CUP to undertake a scholarly edition of Lawrence's works. He became Senior Tutor at St Catharine's College and so Helen Baron, who had completed her Ph.D. on the manuscripts of

Sir Thomas Wyatt (1503–42), agreed to undertake the work of editing *Sons and Lovers*. Their intermittent joint discussion and planning sessions proved good practice for this critical introduction. Carl Baron became Academic Registrar at the University of Hull in 1996 and died in 1997. Helen Baron is now teaching in the English department of the University of Hull and is currently preparing an edition of the unpublished early versions of *Sons and Lovers*.

John Worthen is Advisory Editor for the works of D. H. Lawrence in Penguin. Currently Professor of D. H. Lawrence Studies at the University of Nottingham, he has published widely on Lawrence; his acclaimed biography, *D. H. Lawrence: The Early Years 1885–1912*, was published in 1991. He has also edited a number of volumes in the authoritative Cambridge Lawrence Edition, whose texts Penguin are reproducing.

D. H. LAWRENCE

SONS AND LOVERS

EDITED WITH AN INTRODUCTION AND
NOTES BY
HELEN BARON AND CARL BARON

PENGUIN BOOKS

PENGUIN BOOKS

Published by the Penguin Group
Penguin Books Ltd, 80 Strand, London WC2R 0RL, England
Penguin Putnam Inc., 375 Hudson Street, New York, New York 10014, USA
Penguin Books Australia Ltd, 250 Camberwell Road, Camberwell, Victoria 3124, Australia
Penguin Books Canada Ltd, 10 Alcorn Avenue, Toronto, Ontario, Canada M4V 3B2
Penguin Books India (P) Ltd, 11 Community Centre, Panchsheel Park, New Delhi – 110 017, India
Penguin Books (NZ) Ltd, Cnr Rosedale and Airborne Roads, Albany, Auckland, New Zealand
Penguin Books (South Africa) (Pty) Ltd, 24 Sturdee Avenue, Rosebank 2196, South Africa

Penguin Books Ltd, Registered Offices: 80 Strand, London WC2R 0RL, England

www.penguin.com

First published 1913
This edition published by Cambridge University Press 1992
Published in Penguin Books 1994
Reprinted in Penguin Classics 2000

13

Copyright © the Estate of Frieda Lawrence Ravagli, 1992
Editorial matter copyright © Helen Baron and Carl Baron, 1994
Chronology copyright © John Worthen, 1994

Contents

Note on the Penguin Lawrence Edition

D. H. Lawrence stands in the very front rank of English writers this century; unlike some other famous writers, however, he has always appealed to a large popular audience as well as to students of literature, and his work still arouses passionate loyalties and fervent disagreements. The available texts of his books have, nevertheless, been notoriously inaccurate. The Penguin Lawrence Edition uses the authoritative texts of Lawrence's work established by an international team of scholars engaged on the *Cambridge Edition of the Works of D. H. Lawrence* under its General Editors, Professor James T. Boulton and Professor Warren Roberts. Through rigorous study of surviving manuscripts, typescripts, proofs and early printings the Cambridge editors have provided texts as close as possible to those which Lawrence himself would have expected to see printed. Deletions deliberately made by printers, publishers or their editors, accidentally by typists and printers – at times removing whole pages of text – have been restored; while house-styling introduced by printers is removed as far as is possible. The Penguin Lawrence Edition thus offers both general readers and students the only texts of Lawrence which have any claim to be the authentic productions of his genius.

Acknowledgements

The editors would like to thank Cambridge University Press and the members of the D. H. Lawrence editorial board for help with the publication of the full text of *Sons and Lovers*. For encouragement, criticisms and suggestions for the present Introduction and Notes, we would like to thank first of all John Worthen, and also: Sylvia Adamson, Ian Alister, Michael Bell, Michael Black, Mac Daly, Simonetta de Filippis, David Hopkins, Nina Lavroukine, Peggy Needham, Christopher Ricks, Clementine Robert, Warren Roberts, Philippe Romanski and Julian Wynne.

Chronology

1885 David Herbert Richards Lawrence (hereafter DHL) born in Eastwood, Nottinghamshire, the fourth child of Arthur John Lawrence, collier, and Lydia, née Beardsall, daughter of a pensioned-off engine fitter.

1891–8 Attends Beauvale Board School.

1898–1901 Becomes first boy from Eastwood to win a County Council scholarship to Nottingham High School, which he attends until July 1901.

1901 Works three months as a clerk at Haywood's surgical appliances factory in Nottingham; severe attack of pneumonia.

1902 Begins frequent visits to the Chambers family at Haggs Farm, Underwood, and starts his friendship with Jessie Chambers.

1902–5 Pupil-teacher at the British School, Eastwood; sits the King's Scholarship exam in December 1904 and is placed in the first division of the first class.

1905–6 Works as uncertificated teacher at the British School; writes his first poems and starts his first novel *Laetitia* (later *The White Peacock*, 1911).

1906–8 Student at Nottingham University College following the normal course leading to a teacher's certificate; qualifies in July 1908. Wins *Nottinghamshire Guardian* Christmas 1907 short-story competition with 'A Prelude' (submitted under name of Jessie Chambers); writes second version of *Laetitia*.

1908–11 Elementary teacher at Davidson Road School, Croydon.

1909 Meets Ford Madox Hueffer (later Ford), who begins to publish his poems and stories in the *English Review* and recommends rewritten version of *The White Peacock* (1911) to William Heinemann; DHL writes *A Collier's Friday Night* (1934) and first version of 'Odour of Chrysanthemums' (1911); friendship with Agnes Holt.

1910   Writes *The Saga of Siegmund* (first version of *The Tres-passer*, 1912), based on the experiences of his friend, the Croydon teacher Helen Corke; starts affair with Jessie Chambers; writes first version of *The Widowing of Mrs. Holroyd* (1914); ends affair with Jessie Chambers but continues friendship; starts to write *Paul Morel* (later *Sons and Lovers*, 1913); death of Lydia Lawrence in December; gets engaged to his old friend Louie Burrows.

1911   Fails to finish *Paul Morel*; strongly attracted to Helen Corke; starts affair with Alice Dax, wife of an Eastwood chemist; meets Edward Garnett, publisher's reader for Duckworth, who advises him on writing and publication. In November falls seriously ill with pneumonia and has to give up school-teaching; *The Saga* accepted by Duck-worth; DHL commences its revision as *The Trespasser*.

1912   Convalesces in Bournemouth. Breaks off engagement to Louie; returns to Eastwood; works on *Paul Morel*; in March meets Frieda Weekley, wife of Ernest, Professor at the University College of Nottingham; ends affair with Alice Dax; goes to Germany on a visit to his relations on 3 May; travels, however, with Frieda to Metz. After many vicissitudes, some memorialized in *Look! We Have Come Through!* (1917), Frieda gives up her marriage and her children for DHL; in August they journey over the Alps to Italy and settle at Gargnano, where DHL writes the final version of *Sons and Lovers*.

1913   *Love Poems* published; writes *The Daughter-in-Law* (1965) and 200 pp. of *The Insurrection of Miss Houghton* (aban-doned); begins *The Sisters*, eventually to be split into *The Rainbow* (1915) and *Women in Love* (1920). DHL and Frieda spend some days at San Gaudenzio, then stay at Irschenhausen in Bavaria; DHL writes first versions of 'The Prussian Officer' and 'The Thorn in the Flesh' (1914). *Sons and Lovers* published in May. DHL and Frieda return to England in June, meet John Middleton Murry and Katherine Mansfield. They return to Italy (Fiascherino, near Spezia) in September; DHL revises *The Widowing of Mrs. Holroyd*; resumes work on *The Sisters*.

1914   Rewrites *The Sisters* (now called *The Wedding Ring*) yet again; agrees for Methuen to publish it; takes J. B. Pinker as agent. DHL and Frieda return to England in June, marry on 13 July. DHL meets Catherine Carswell and S. S. Koteliansky; compiles short-story collection *The Prussian Officer* (1914). Outbreak of war prevents DHL and Frieda returning to Italy; at Chesham he first writes *Study of Thomas Hardy* (1936) and then begins *The Rainbow*; starts important friendships with Ottoline Morrell, Cynthia Asquith, Bertrand Russell and E. M. Forster; grows increasingly desperate and angry about the war.

1915   Finishes *The Rainbow* in Greatham in March; plans lecture course with Russell; they quarrel in June. DHL and Frieda move to Hampstead in August; he and Murry bring out *The Signature* (magazine, three issues only). *The Rainbow* published by Methuen in September, suppressed at the end of October, prosecuted and banned in November. DHL meets painters Dorothy Brett and Mark Gertler; he and Frieda plan to leave England for Florida; decide to move to Cornwall instead.

1916   Writes *Women in Love* between April and October; publishes *Twilight in Italy* and *Amores*.

1917   *Women in Love* rejected by publishers; DHL continues to revise it. Makes unsuccessful attempts to go to America. Begins *Studies in Classic American Literature* (1923); publishes *Look! We Have Come Through!* In October he and Frieda evicted from Cornwall on suspicion of spying; in London he begins *Aaron's Rod* (1922).

1918   DHL and Frieda move to Hermitage, Berkshire, then to Middleton-by-Wirksworth; publishes *New Poems*; writes *Movements in European History* (1921), *Touch and Go* (1920) and the first version of 'The Fox' (1920).

1919   Seriously ill with influenza; moves back to Hermitage; publishes *Bay*. In the autumn, Frieda goes to Germany and then joins DHL in Florence; they visit Picinisco and settle in Capri.

1920   Writes *Psychoanalysis and the Unconscious* (1921). He and Frieda move to Taormina, Sicily; DHL writes *The Lost Girl* (1920), *Mr Noon* (1984), continues with *Aaron's Rod*; on summer visit to Florence has affair with Rosalind

Baynes; writes many poems from *Birds, Beasts and Flowers* (1923). *Women in Love* published.

1921   DHL and Frieda visit Sardinia and he writes *Sea and Sardinia* (1921); meets Earl and Achsah Brewster; finishes *Aaron's Rod* in the summer and writes *Fantasia of the Unconscious* (1922) and 'The Captain's Doll' (1923); plans to leave Europe and visit USA; puts together collection of stories *England, My England* (1922) and group of short novels *The Ladybird*, *The Fox* and *The Captain's Doll* (1923).

1922   DHL and Frieda leave for Ceylon, stay with Brewsters, then travel to Australia; he translates Verga. In Western Australia meets Mollie Skinner; at Thirroul, near Sydney, he writes *Kangaroo* (1923) in six weeks. Between August and September, he and Frieda travel to California via South Sea islands, and meet Witter Bynner and Willard Johnson; settle in Taos, New Mexico, at invitation of Mabel Dodge (later Luhan). In December, move up to Del Monte ranch, near Taos; DHL rewrites *Studies in Classic American Literature* (1923).

1923   Finishes *Birds, Beasts and Flowers*. He and Frieda spend summer at Chapala in Mexico where he writes *Quetzalcoatl* (first version of *The Plumed Serpent*, 1926). Frieda returns to Europe in August after serious quarrel with DHL; he journeys in USA and Mexico, rewrites Mollie Skinner's *The House of Ellis* as *The Boy in the Bush* (1924); arrives back in England in December.

1924   At dinner in Café Royal, DHL invites his friends to come to New Mexico; Dorothy Brett accepts and accompanies him and Frieda in March. Mabel Luhan gives Lobo (later renamed Kiowa) Ranch to Frieda; DHL gives her *Sons and Lovers* manuscript in return. During summer on the ranch he writes *St. Mawr* (1925), 'The Woman Who Rode Away' (1925) and 'The Princess' (1925); in August, suffers his first bronchial haemorrhage. His father dies in September; in October, he, Frieda and Brett move to Oaxaca, Mexico, where he starts *The Plumed Serpent* and writes most of *Mornings in Mexico* (1927).

1925   Finishes *The Plumed Serpent*, falls ill and almost dies of typhoid and pneumonia in February; in March diagnosed as suffering from tuberculosis. Recuperates at Kiowa ranch, writes *David* (1926) and compiles *Reflections on the Death of a Porcupine* (1925). He and Frieda return to Europe in September, spend a month in England and settle at Spotorno, Italy; DHL writes first version of *Sun* (1926); Frieda meets Angelo Ravagli.

1926   Writes *The Virgin and the Gypsy* (1930); serious quarrel with Frieda during visit from DHL's sister Ada. DHL visits Brewsters and Brett; has affair with Brett. Reconciled, DHL and Frieda move to Villa Mirenda, near Florence, in May and visit England (his last visit) in late summer. On return to Italy in October, he writes first version of *Lady Chatterley's Lover* (1944); starts second version in November. Friendship with Aldous and Maria Huxley; DHL starts to paint.

1927   Finishes second version of *Lady Chatterley's Lover* (1972); visits Etruscan sites with Earl Brewster; writes *Sketches of Etruscan Places* (1932) and the first part of *The Escaped Cock* (1928). In November, after meetings with Michael Arlen and Norman Douglas, works out scheme for private publication with Pino Orioli, and starts final version of *Lady Chatterley's Lover* (1928).

1928   Finishes *Lady Chatterley's Lover* and arranges for its printing and publication in Florence; fights many battles to ensure its despatch to subscribers in Britain and USA. In June writes second part of *The Escaped Cock* (1929). He and Frieda travel to Switzerland (Gsteig) and the island of Port Cros, then settle in Bandol, in the south of France. He writes many of the poems in *Pansies* (1929); *Lady Chatterley's Lover* pirated in Europe and USA.

1929   Visits Paris to arrange for cheap edition of *Lady Chatterley's Lover* (1929); unexpurgated typescript of *Pansies* seized by police; exhibition of his paintings in London raided by police. He and Frieda visit Majorca, France and Bavaria, returning to Bandol for the winter. He writes *Nettles* (1930), *Apocalypse* (1931) and *Last Poems* (1932); sees much of Brewsters and Huxleys.

1930   Goes into Ad Astra sanatorium in Vence at start of February; discharges himself on 1 March; dies at Villa

Robermond, Vence, on Sunday 2 March; buried on 4 March.

1935   Frieda sends Angelo Ravagli (now living with her at Kiowa Ranch – they marry in 1950) to Vence to have DHL exhumed, cremated, and his ashes brought back to the ranch.

1956   Frieda dies and is buried at Kiowa Ranch.

John Worthen, 1994

Introduction

APPROACHES AND INTERPRETATIONS

'If you try to nail anything down, in the novel, either it kills the novel, or the novel gets up and walks away with the nail,' wrote D. H. Lawrence in 'Morality and the Novel'.[1]

Sons and Lovers has received a great deal of critical attention, but it resists being pinned down to any single diagnostic account. It has been described in a variety of ways: as a record of working-class life, a successful (or failed) exercise in self-analysis, an illustration of one or other psychoanalytical theory, an exploration of admirable (or unattractive) role models for twentieth-century men and women, a critique of industrial capitalism, an example of powerful realism (or formlessness) in the modern novel. Readers will find at the back of this volume a list of critical accounts in which the abridged version of the novel has been interpreted according to one or more of these viewpoints.

This introduction will examine how it is that in *Sons and Lovers* Lawrence has written an apparently straightforward realistic novel in the late-nineteenth-century tradition, but has generalized and deepened the issues in ways that may not be immediately obvious, but which in effect make *Sons and Lovers* a twentieth-century novel. He has given the plot a highly patterned structure, introduced significant parallels between the characters and used narrative techniques that powerfully intensify the characters' consciousness of each other and of their surroundings.

THE PLACE OF *SONS AND LOVERS* IN LAWRENCE'S WORK

Sons and Lovers was Lawrence's third novel and one of the most highly acclaimed during his lifetime. It was published in May 1913 when he was twenty-seven, and although it did not make his fortune, it did establish his reputation as a novelist.

Lawrence had taken two years and four attempts to complete the book, starting again from the beginning each time. The first draft, of only 100 pages, was written in October and November 1910 while

Lawrence was working as a schoolteacher in Croydon. He wrote a second draft, which got a good deal further, from March to July 1911 and a third (this time complete) between November 1911 and June 1912. In August 1912 he decided to write the whole book yet again and in October he changed its title from *Paul Morel* to *Sons and Lovers*. Finally, in November 1912, he sent the fourth manuscript to the London publishing firm of Duckworth from northern Italy where he had gone to try to earn his living as a writer. Duckworth's literary adviser, Edward Garnett, who had befriended and encouraged Lawrence during his Croydon years, decided the manuscript was too long and crossed out eighty passages to make it a tenth shorter. That shortened text was the only version of the novel in print from 1913 to 1992.[2] All the passages cut by Garnett have been reinstated in this edition.

Now that it is possible for students to read the complete novel, one of the most widespread assumptions about *Sons and Lovers* must be challenged. It has been widely thought of as a simply and directly autobiographical novel by an author who invariably included in his fiction his own experiences and portraits of people he knew. Many commentators have assumed that Paul Morel is a direct self-portrait, and some have criticized Lawrence for identifying with Paul Morel at the expense of other characters, especially Miriam Leivers. Much is known about Lawrence's life, and although it is possible to see many similarities in the events and portraits in his fiction, responses to *Sons and Lovers* have been excessively preoccupied with such identifications. The many differences have been ignored; and an interest in the author has been allowed to dominate over an interest in the art that he produced. Now that a full and authoritative biography has been written about Lawrence's early years,[3] and now that the complete text of *Sons and Lovers* is available, the challenge facing readers is to respond to it as a free-standing novel and not as a slice of the author's life.

In fact, from the start Lawrence had not set out to write an autobiography: the second draft (most of which survives) has far fewer autobiographical elements than the third; and when Lawrence had rewritten the book for the fourth time he was convinced that, by his labour of 'pruning it and shaping it and filling it in', he had generalized his material to such a degree that he could call it 'a great tragedy ... the tragedy of thousands of young men in England'.[4]

THE RELATION OF *SONS AND LOVERS* TO
TRAGEDY AND OTHER LITERATURE

In claiming that it was a 'tragedy' Lawrence appears to have associated *Sons and Lovers* with tragic drama as well as fiction. When worried that his publisher was not enthusiastic enough about selling the book, he exclaimed, 'if *Hamlet* and *Œdipus* were published now, they wouldn't sell more than 100 copies, unless they were pushed'. This suggests that he saw *Sons and Lovers* as a modern successor to those supreme tragedies about the mother–son relationship.[5] He was, however, aware that the sons Oedipus and Hamlet had far more drastic fates than Paul Morel, for, two years after finishing *Sons and Lovers*, he set out his views on the different kinds of tragedy that confront characters in classic plays and modern novels, particularly novels by Thomas Hardy:

> Oedipus, Hamlet, Macbeth set themselves up against, or find themselves set up against the unfathomed moral forces of nature, and out of this unfathomed force comes their death. Whereas Anna Karenin, Eustacia, Tess, Sue and Jude find themselves up against the established system of human government and morality, they cannot detach themselves, and are brought down. Their real tragedy is that they are unfaithful to the greater unwritten morality . . .[6]

Lawrence saw Thomas Hardy as his chief forerunner in trying to transpose tragedy from drama to fiction, and he described the subject of Hardy's novels as 'the tragedy of those who, more or less pioneers, have died in the wilderness whither they had escaped for free action, after having left the walled security, and the comparative imprisonment, of the established convention'.[7]

But *Sons and Lovers* goes beyond this paradigm of an individual at odds with convention, for it is preoccupied with the breakup of the conventions themselves. In time and place it spans the transition in the English Midlands from a predominantly agricultural economy to an industrial one. The geographical survey of the opening pages is reminiscent of the first chapter of George Eliot's *The Mill on the Floss*, except that Lawrence has considerably subdued the personal voice and nostalgic tone of the narrator. But the ambitious scope of Lawrence's opening, with its broad historical perspective and its glance back to the arrival of the railways, seems to herald a work more in the manner of Geoge Eliot's *Middlemarch*, which portrays an earlier phase in these developments and contains a graphic description of the predicted impact of the railways on the rural landscape.[8]

Throughout *Sons and Lovers* there are indications of the pressure for change that existed from the last decades of the nineteenth century up to the outbreak of the First World War. (In Chapter Thirteen Paul Morel predicts the war (386:26–32).) The novel reflects many of the ways in which change affects people's sense of security as well as their feelings of imprisonment. For example, there are unsafe conditions and low pay in the mining community and the beginnings of organized strikes; the absence of state provision such as unemployment pay, sick benefit, maternity leave, facilities for childbirth, or schooling for children older than thirteen; the growing desire of women to move from the home to the workplace and to campaign for votes; increased class mobility; the decline in religious belief despite continued church attendance; the disruptive effect of evolutionary theory on many aspects of social and moral life; the beginnings of a willingness to talk about the taboo topic of sex; and the emergence of an interest in the 'unconscious', the nature of consciousness and individual identity.[9]

While, in its broad scope, *Sons and Lovers* reflects the problems of transition between the agricultural past and the industrial future, it also explores in detail those between one generation and the next, and more importantly between childhood and adolescence. In his focus on childhood Lawrence shows his debt to *The Mill on the Floss*, and in his analysis of adolescence he shows affinities with his contemporary, James Joyce, whose novel *A Portrait of the Artist as a Young Man* also survives in an early version named after its chief character (*Stephen Hero*). In making Paul Morel a painter Lawrence reveals, like Joyce, a preoccupation with the evolution of a *creative* individual, and this calls into question Lawrence's claim that *Sons and Lovers* is the tragedy 'of thousands of young men in England'. What difference would it make to the novel if Paul Morel were not an artist?

THE PATTERNED STRUCTURE OF THE PLOT

When Lawrence completed the fourth manuscript in November 1912 and sent it to Edward Garnett, he gave his own account of the plot:[10]

It follows this idea: a woman of character and refinement goes into the lower class, and has no satisfaction in her own life. She has had a passion for her husband, so the children are born of passion, and have heaps of vitality. But as her sons grow up she selects them as lovers – first the eldest, then the second. These sons are *urged* into life by their reciprocal love of their mother – urged on and on. But when they come to manhood, they can't love, because their mother is the strongest power in their lives, and holds them ... As soon as the young men come into contact with women, there's a split. William gives his sex to a fribble, and his mother holds his soul. But the split kills him, because he doesn't know where he is. The next son gets a woman who fights for his soul – fights his mother. The son loves the mother – all the sons hate and are jealous of the father. The battle goes on between the mother and the girl, with the son as object. The mother gradually proves stronger, because of the tie of blood. The son decides to leave his soul in his mother's hands, and, like his elder brother, go for passion. He gets passion. Then the split begins to tell again. But, almost unconsciously, the mother realises what is the matter, and begins to die. The son casts off his mistress, attends to his mother dying. He is left in the end naked of everything, with the drift towards death.

This has often been challenged as an adequate account of the novel; and indeed Lawrence himself stressed in his critical essays that it is important to attend to the 'tale' itself and not the author's account of it, or his propaganda within it. There is, of course, far more to the novel than the central triangle described here of mother, son(s) and girl-friend(s). But this selective account was chiefly designed to persuade Garnett to see how the novel hung together: 'I *have* patiently and laboriously constructed that novel.'[11] Garnett had criticized Lawrence for not adopting the carefully sculpted form of the novel used by the French writer Gustave Flaubert. Lawrence preferred, however, to claim a kind of natural, evolutionary or psychological shape for his novel: 'If *you* can't see the development – which is slow like growth – I can,' he told Garnett.[12]

Despite his organic metaphor, it is clear that Lawrence had given the plot an architectural symmetry. From early on in drafting the book he had divided it into two parts, which entrench its structural pattern. Even though Part II eventually became nearly twice as long as Part I, many symmetries are evident. Part I ends with the death of William and the 'taking on' of Paul as the centre of his mother's life, while Part II ends with the death of Mrs Morel and the 'release' of Paul from her control. (Near the end of each part, Paul *whimpers* 'Mother!' and is not heard (169:36, 464:30).) Part I follows Mrs Morel's relationships with Mr Morel, William and Paul, whereas Part II has the parallel pattern of Paul's relationships with Mrs Morel, Miriam and Clara. Part I traces the roots of Paul's psychology, while Part II follows the working-out of that psychological formation. There is also a balancing shift in style between the two parts: Part I is devoted to the minutely detailed evocation of objects and activities in the miner's home: the furniture and utensils, the fuse-making, cooking and meals, the gossip and quarrels. By contrast, in Part II the descriptions are frequently elaborated into a kind of symbolic imagery – such as the flowers Paul looks at when deciding to break off with Miriam (337:23–338:6), and the descent by Paul and Clara to a lower level at Clifton Grove (353:22–356:14) – while the conversations tend to become discussions of large moral and political issues.

Another way of examining the structure is to ask how the characters enter and leave the novel, and here another symmetry is found. Just as Paul is born into the book in the second chapter, Mrs Morel dies out of it in the second to last chapter. Mrs Morel is the first of the Morel family to appear: she enters a house which the narrator has prepared a paragraph before. The house is introduced after the historical and geographical panorama of the six opening paragraphs has narrowed its focus down to a *sight-seeing* tour of a block of miners' houses: 'one could walk all round, seeing . . . seeing . . . that was the view . . . facing inward . . . looking at . . .' But the resolute appeal to the reader's eye is starkly disillusioned: 'the actual conditions . . . that looked so nice, were quite unsavoury'. The bad smell of the outside lavatories ('ash-pits') leads to one of the narrator's most striking emotional interventions as he opens the house to Mrs Morel: 'the kitchens opened onto that nasty alley of ash-pits' (10:13–27).

At first Mrs Morel is described entirely in terms of her house. Then we see her briefly, but without colour or detail: 'A rather small woman, of delicate mould but resolute bearing' (10:37–8). Next, her husband explicitly does *not* appear: 'He went off early on the Monday morning' (11:3). We are not invited to see him. The first visual impression of him is provided by his son, William, who has seen him through holes in the tin covering over the window of the public house: he has his sleeves rolled up. Mrs Morel concludes that he has run out of money and is helping behind the bar to get an 'allowance' of beer. And in the next sentence the two key words, 'window' and 'allowance', are re-worked so that even this glimpse of the father's independent activity is recovered into Mrs Morel's control within the home: 'The children were allowed to sit at the window of their mother's bedroom' (13:6–13). (It is, we realize later, both parents' bedroom.) When Morel does enter the house, full of colour, his first words, 'Oh!—Oh!—waitin' for me lass?' have already been undercut by Mrs Morel's last disillusioned comment to herself, ten lines earlier: 'I wait, and what I wait for can never come' (14:29–30, 40).

William, too, begins the novel by leaving: 'William, a boy of seven, fled off immediately after breakfast' to roam the fairground, 'leaving Annie, who was only five, to whine all morning to go also' (11:5–7).

Paul is born into the book in Chapter Two – as an 'it': 'She looked at the child. It had blue eyes, and a lot of fair hair, and was bonny. Her love came up hot, in spite of everything. She had it in bed with her' (43:2–4). But as a child in the womb he has already taken part in the dramatic scene in Chapter One when Mrs Morel is locked out of the house at night by her husband after a quarrel, and has a strange swooning experience: 'her self melted out like scent . . . the child too melted with her in the mixing-pot of moonlight' (34:35–7).

Already, in the entrances made by these members of the family there is a microcosm of the plot: Mrs Morel has her house but cannot control the independent life outside it of Walter and William. Paul, however, is an object which she will keep close by her. Before he is even born he shares her strange experience of fusing with the surroundings, and this sensation will return to trouble and perplex him as he grows up.

Paul walks out of the book at the end, in what must have been one of the most open endings Lawrence's first readers had ever come across: 'He would not take that direction, to the darkness, to follow her. He walked towards the faintly humming, glowing town, quickly' (464:36–7). His direction is out of the book, as if leaving the darkness with the reader. The word 'quick' retained for Lawrence a strong flavour of the biblical meaning, 'alive'. Paul's 'drift towards death', which Lawrence had told Garnett was part of the novel's basic construction, is retrospectively de-constructed by the last two sentences. This teasing open-endedness resists a firm conclusion, but paradoxically confirms how carefully structured the book had been.

PARALLELS AMONG THE CHARACTERS

In one of Lawrence's few riddling titles, the 'Lovers' of the novel are Gertrude Morel's 'Sons', William and Paul. The novel's original title, 'Paul Morel', suggests that Lawrence thought of it as being about only one son, but from the third version onwards William's presence and significance were expanded, and in the final version he is an important role model for Paul. After William's death, Paul's relationship with their mother echoes his brother's in many respects: the bringing home of prizes for her, the flirting banter, the promises never to marry, the discussions about his unsatisfactory girl-friends, and so on.

In the summary of the novel's 'idea' that he wrote for Garnett, Lawrence associated Miriam Leivers with 'soul' and Clara Dawes with 'passion', as if they had very little in common, but in the novel they respond alike to Paul. Both love his quick movements (227:17–19, 308:38); both are hurt by his flirting with others and laughing in a way that they hate (290:34, 309:27); both want to embrace him when he does not want to be embraced (227:21, 399:20–28); both fix their eyes on him in moments of passion (328:29, 37, 399:24–5), wanting personal attention from him on the occasions that he offers them both impersonal passion (328:33, 38, 399:16).

'She wants to absorb him' is Mrs Morel's objection to Miriam as Paul's girl-friend (230:36–7) and she thinks 'he is just such a gaby as to let himself be absorbed' (196:27). Miriam 'loved him absorbedly', the narrator confirms (227:20), and Paul bitterly accuses Miriam of this desire to 'absorb' (258:1–4). But Paul has absorbed his mother's anxiety so profoundly that, despite his more successful passionate relationship with Clara, he also asks himself of Clara, 'Why does she absorb me' (402:14).

This interweaving of parallels and shared feelings among the characters makes the novel more complex than it appears in Lawrence's plot summary. In fact, the exploration of the central 'idea' relies so much on parallels and contrasts that, for example, even two minor characters, Arthur and Agatha, have comparable names and roles. One is Paul's younger brother, the other is Miriam's elder sister. They both make a success of their lives by getting away from their homes and rebelling against the ethos of their families: Agatha insisting on 'worldly values' in reaction to her mother's spirituality (207:23); Arthur running away to become a soldier, a career despised by his parents (219:33, 37, 220:36–9), and then marrying, at which point, unlike his father (22:38), he 'buckled to work, undertook his responsibilities' (300:39–40).

While the Morels' failed marriage and its cramping effect on their children's development holds centre-stage in the novel, the marriages of both the Leivers and the Dawes provide points of comparison. For example, when Paul is attacked by Baxter Dawes, it is as if he is forced to have with another rival, Dawes, the fight that both he and William longed to have with their father but were forbidden by their mother. In another example, the use of a similar phrase about childbirth suggests that Mrs Morel may be possessive in exactly the way that is attributed to Mrs Leivers. Mrs Morel reflects on her married life in the opening pages of the novel, and protests: 'What have I to do with all this. Even the child I am going to have! It doesn't seem as if *I* were taken into account' (14:23–5). Mrs Leivers is seen by Paul in comparable terms: 'nearly scared and shocked out of her virgin maidenhood, but not quite, in spite of her seven children. They had been born almost leaving her out of count, not of her, but upon her. So she could never let them go, because she never had possessed them' (323:35–9). The expression occurs again later in the novel, suggesting a deeper layer of interpretation, when Clara complains to Paul that their sexual relationship is a failure because he leaves her 'out of count' (407:36).

Once the patterning of the characters' experiences is identified, both in incident and in language, it becomes clear that patterning is a fundamental characteristic of the novel. Most important are the parallels in Paul's perceptions of his mother and his lovers, Miriam and Clara – but only occasionally does the novel bring his separate observations together for comparison. Paul takes all three of them on outings, pins flowers on them, observes their hands, notes the amount of mud that collects on their boots, sees how they climb over stiles and how they respond to gardens and wild flowers. He could also be said – at one time or another and in one sense or another – to go to 'bed' with each of them. For their part, they are all described as 'waiting' and they are all angry with men in their different ways. This leads to two of the fundamental questions posed by the novel:

What is it to be a man? What is it to be a woman? The apparently simple words 'man' and 'woman' are repeatedly made problematic and puzzling.

'BUT WHAT IS *SHE*?'

Miriam complains to Paul: 'Why should I, because I'm a girl, be kept at home and not allowed to be anything . . . Men have everything . . . Why *should* it be that I know nothing! . . . Why *shouldn't* I know mathematics!' (185:30–186:9). Miriam does not speculate on a possible distinction between the biological and social dimensions of female gender, but her complaint appears to be that women are denied adequate *social* provision, i.e. education, on false *biological* grounds. Paul immediately asks his mother, 'Did *you* want to be a man, mother?' and in the discussion that ensues (which Garnett cut: 186:19–36), Mrs Morel responds to Paul's question in terms that blur the distinction: 'I don't really want to be anything but myself, and never did . . . I thought I could make a great deal better job of it than most men do . . . anything that is natural is pleased to be itself. And when a woman wants very badly to be a man, you may back your life she's not much good as a woman.'

Like Miriam, Clara is angry at men, but in her case it is on grounds of economic inequality. She tells Paul that her work at home for the lace industry is 'sweated labour' and protests: 'Isn't *all* women's work? That's another trick the men have played, since we force ourselves into the labour market.' And again Lawrence immediately counterbalances the younger woman's protest with the response of a mother, Mrs Radford, who shifts the topic away from economics to personal relations: 'If the women wasn't fools the men wouldn't be bad uns' (303:33–6).

Mrs Radford and Mrs Morel seem secure in their battleground of the home, but the novel shows that their securities are under threat from their lack of economic power. In Chapter One Mrs Morel battles with her husband to win control of the home space, and after her victory he only feels at home in the pub and his fellow miners do not enter the house without her permission – even though his drinking companion, Jerry, stands in the doorway 'coolly asserting the rights of men and husbands' (28:39–40).

But in the central conflict of that first chapter, Walter Morel not only *locks* his wife out of their house, he also disowns the financial basis on which their division of labour in marriage is founded when he says, 'It's ma as brings th'money whoam, not thee. It's my house, not thine. Then ger out on't.' (33:8–10).[13] Even though this claim has already been weakened by the disclosure that the house belongs to his mother (21:9), this threat to his wife's security reverberates throughout the novel.

Equal pay for women is the tea-time topic of conversation at Willey Farm when Paul first meets Clara there – in another passage cut by Garnett (273:3–34). Clara argues that 'so much work should have so much pay, man or woman.' Paul argues for the *status quo*: 'And almost every man in the world, over thirty, supports a wife and family—and as a *rule*, the said wives are not wage-earners.' When rebuffed by Clara, he counters with a satirical version of male individualism which comes across as blatant sexism: 'Why should I be called "Men" when I'm only myself . . . And then . . . I'm made responsible for every sin in English history, from Queen Boadisca down to the Song of the Shirt. It's not fair.—I wish Man had a right to exist in modern society.' His other would-be witticisms at the expense of Clara's involvement with the suffrage movement are similarly placed by the novel as examples of boyish showing off.

In his bantering exchanges with his mother, Paul shows that he has learned from her habit of generalizing about men: 'just like a woman' (150:33), and 'a woman's whole doctrine for life—ease of soul and physical comfort' (299:26–7). At the height of his passionate relationship with Clara he shows a potential for growing out of these brittle stereotypes. He finds 'his own unconscious thoughts' asking, as Clara swims in the sea, 'But what is *she*?' He is at a loss: 'how little she is! . . . almost nothing among the morning . . . She represents something, like a bubble of foam represents the sea. But what is *she*? . . . But she is magnificent, and even bigger than the morning and the sea.—Is she?—is she?' (402:11–40). But as soon as Clara wants more of his attention than he is willing to give, he feels 'imprisoned', and 'as if he could not get a free deep breath, as if there were something on top of him' (403:15–17), and he reverts to the same sweeping generalizations about 'woman' that he had used in quarrels with his mother: 'That's just what a woman is. She thinks she knows what's good for a man, and she's going to see he gets it . . .' (404:26–8).

Introduction

'WHAT BEING A MAN MEANT'

The novel's probing of the other side of the gender question begins much earlier – in the flashback to Mrs Morel's youthful romance:

> 'But if you're a *man*—!' she had cried.
>
> 'Being a man isn't everything,' he replied, frowning with puzzled helplessness.
>
> Now, as she moved about her work at the Bottoms, with some experience of what being a man meant, she knew that it was *not* everything. (16:32–7)

Mrs Morel throws out the words 'man' and 'manly' repeatedly, and it seems to be a direct consequence of this that Paul is preoccupied with what being a woman means. When, in his final meeting with Miriam, he rejects one of the foundation stones of Miriam's hard-won independence, he says so in words that echo his mother's thoughts on men's freedom of action: 'you'll find earning your own living isn't everything' (460:15–16).

For Walter Morel, gender is a simple issue: he cuts off his one-year-old son's curls because 'Yer non want ter make a wench on 'im' (24:8).[14] Being a 'man' is not an abstract concept to Walter Morel until Jerry argues with him 'not to put up with a b— woman's domineering, what was he a man for?' When this stirs him to threaten his wife – 'I'll make you tremble at the sound of my footstep' (49:10–13) – she only laughs, as she does when Paul uses the same formula to persuade her of his authority in the factory: 'Oh but I *can* be impressive and boss people . . . I tell you my girls quake at my footstep' (346:14–19).

As the novel progresses Mrs Morel's reflections on masculinity, which she calls 'manliness', constantly undermine male domination. She finds her husband's fellow miner Barker 'manly' and at the same time a 'poor little fellow' (112:4–5, 13).[15] What is she admiring? In this case it is Barker's capacity to sympathize with her husband's pain after his mining accident. Later she tells her husband, 'Barker's little but he's ten times the man you are' (237:34) – because he does the family shopping on Friday nights. When William bullies and criticizes his fiancée, Lily, Mrs Morel's most severe rebuke is 'Why don't you be more manly' (163:26). For her, manliness is at the opposite end of the spectrum from bullying; it includes sympathy and supportiveness.

Clara also uses the word, when she returns to her husband after her affair with Paul and concludes that 'Her husband had more manly dignity' than Paul. What does she mean by this? 'Her husband at least was manly, and when he was beaten, gave in' (450:26, 31–2). Clara seems to have an even more emasculating attitude towards her husband than Mrs Morel. But earlier she had explained to Paul that she left Baxter after five years of marriage because he was degrading, bullying, dirty and brutal (318:7–14). When she first meets Paul she believes that a *horse* is probably 'More loving than most men' (276:13). Baxter Dawes, like Walter Morel, ends the novel weakened by his wife's rejection and by ill health. Baxter's typhoid leaves him with 'water' in his legs, and he laments that this means he is 'not much of a man' (448:32). It is this sense of defeat, and his fear of loneliness and death, that make him want to accept the relationship Clara offers, and her idea of manliness.

Thus, the novel's questions about what it is to be a man or a woman appear at first simply to reflect the social and cultural values of the period, but they are always directed towards the dimension of personal relationships. The issue becomes, in effect: why all this *strife* between men and women?

WHY ALL THIS STRIFE BETWEEN MEN AND WOMEN?

It is astonishing how often the word 'brutal' is used of men in the novel. But the reflections on male brutality are presented in terms of complex relationships. For example, Paul is said to realize that 'A good many of the nicest men he knew were like himself, bound in by their own virginity ... Being the sons of mothers whose husbands had blundered rather brutally through their feminine sanctities, they were themselves too diffident and shy' (323:3–9). But Paul is frequently brutally critical and angry with Miriam.[16] The word used of Paul's unkindness to Miriam is 'cruel' and it is invariably introduced by the narrator rather than by the characters (230:28–33, 258:5, 337:5–13). However, when Miriam is described as being afraid 'of the brute in him' (331:32) the reference is specifically to Paul's *sexual* approaches, as it appears to be when Clara uses the word 'brutal' of Baxter (318:14). Lawrence sometimes, therefore, associates the word 'brutal' with male sexuality, and 'cruel' with mental or emotional aggression.

The suggestion that male brutality is, paradoxically, caused by women is first made in a context which has no evident sexual connotations. The Leivers males are brutal because of Mrs Leivers's spirituality: 'The mother exalted everything, even a bit of housework, to the plane of a religious trust. The sons resented this; they felt themselves cut away underneath, and they answered with brutality' (177:35–8). Paul also 'seemed cut away underneath' when writing a birthday letter to Miriam (292:2). The idea is developed further when Paul tries to lay the blame on Clara for the brutality she attributed to her husband: 'Because I feel you did something to him – sort of broke his manliness ... I believe you did him as much damage, more than he did you, by sort of cutting him underneath, and making him feel ashamed' (320:7–16).[17]

These suggestions that male brutality is some kind of response to female 'cutting underneath', although made in relation to Mrs Leivers, Miriam and Clara, reflect indirectly on Mrs Morel. Lawrence seems to be using the expression to hint that the taboo, which was so powerful at the beginning of this century, against acknowledging human sexuality, damaged both men and women in ways that they often did not recognize or understand. The taboo against mentioning sexual activity prevented people from even thinking about it. When Paul asks Miriam why she is 'always clenched against' him, she explains that she is not used to the *thought* of sex, and adds, '. . . all my life.—Mother said to me—"there is one thing in marriage that is always dreadful, but you have to bear it"' (334:34, 36, 38–9). These are topics which it was very difficult for Lawrence to address explicitly at this stage in his career, but he tried. He wrote a scene of sexual reverence and healing between Paul and Clara, even though he feared that some of it would be censored before publication.[18] In addition, therefore, he developed narrative strategies which invite the reader to think more deeply about these problems of relationship and individual consciousness.

NARRATIVE STRATEGIES

From the beginning, the narrator moves *Sons and Lovers* forward in two ways: through generalization and dramatization. General descriptions of the historical situation, the patterns of mining life, regular meetings or habitual feelings, are interspersed with specific episodes. It may have been this narrative strategy which led some of the first reviewers to conclude that the novel had no plot! But the technique could be seen as an invitation to the reader to ponder the issues: not simply *what* is told, but *how*.

One intriguing place to consider that question is the episode in Chapter Four where Paul destroys his sister's doll, Arabella, in a ritual sacrifice (82:21–83:10). What effect does the inclusion of this episode have on the novel? When Paul accidentally smashes the wax face of the doll he is very young, but even so his reaction to his sister's grief is bizarre. He does not, for example, offer Annie something of his own, or ask his father to mend the doll or suggest buying a new one. Instead, the narrator offers the reader a brief reflection: the sacrifice 'disturbed Annie inwardly, although she could say nothing. He seemed to hate the doll so intensely, because he had broken it' (83:9–10).

Rather than interpret this episode by reference to ideas from outside the novel – such as psychological theories of what kinds of emotions children act out with dolls; or the likeness of the doll's unusual name, Arabella, to 'arable' or 'Annable';[19] or Thomas Hardy's use of the name Arabella in *Jude the Obscure*; or George Eliot's description of the 'fetish' doll on which Maggie Tulliver vented her feelings in *The Mill on the Floss*[20] – it is more helpful, for an understanding of how *Sons and Lovers* is narrated, to consider ways in which this episode resonates with other elements in the book. Three immediately come to mind.

Firstly, the identical emotion has already been attributed to Walter Morel: 'He dreaded his wife. Having hurt her, he hated her' (57:37–8). And later in the book Paul repeatedly has the same feeling towards Miriam (e.g. 261:15, 291:25–6). Secondly, there are occasions when Miriam, like Annie, *could say nothing* in the face of Paul's cruelty, and indeed, occasions when Mrs Morel insists that her protesting sons say nothing and even think no more about confronting their father over his brutality to her. Thirdly, in the episode that follows the sacrifice of Arabella, Paul arrives home one evening to find his father has hit his mother *in the face*. No backward reference is made to the doll's fate. The passages simply stand alongside each other with three short sentences of generalization sandwiched between. The two episodes, different in character and separated in time, are left to resonate against each other in the reader's mind.

This is a marked feature of the way the novel is narrated: episodes are placed side by side without any connecting argument or explanation. As readers, we are often hardly aware of how these strategies affect our reactions. Some episodes appear to hint at sexual undercurrents of which the characters themselves are unaware. For example, in the swing episode in Chapter Seven, Miriam's fear of swinging high when Paul pushes her, and of the strength and inevitability of each 'thrust', suggests her fear of sexuality. But then this suggestion is immediately complicated by the statement that when Paul himself was swinging he 'roused a warmth in her', and by the description of her walk two pages later: 'She walked with a swing' (182:3, 5, 11, 24, 184:23).

More obviously, Paul's sudden desire to put on Clara's stockings has strong but undefined sexual connotations (381:34–5).[21] It also reverberates retrospectively with an incident in Paul's childhood. Before leaving home to work in London, William reads out and burns his pile of love letters, including one from a girl he had met at a fancy-dress ball, who has written: 'I think I *never* saw anybody look so nice, with that *kilt* and those *stockings*' (80:7–8, cut by Garnett). This is a reference to an earlier scene in which William goes to a fancy-dress dance as a Highlander: Paul helps him dress, while William volubly admires his own legs and warns Paul he will never have the figure for a kilt (76:15–77:17). Meanwhile, Mrs Morel, who fears that William's dancing will make him become like his father, has 'put on her coat and bonnet' in preparation to leave the house. This makes William hesitate anxiously for a moment, but it is the 'sight of the Highland bonnet with its ribbons' that makes him forget his mother at once (76:3, 9). He is quite unaware that a *bonnet* and kilt are akin to what his mother is wearing, because he is obsessed with the prospect of parading his legs before the girls at the dance. The two incidents, so oddly about the brothers' legs and stockings, invite the reader to ponder Paul's complex inheritance in relation to the pursuit of women; the effect of his mother's possessiveness on him, not only directly but also through William, who is seven years his senior.

The narrator does not point out a connection but comments ambiguously on the outcome of William's fancy-dress ball: 'His mother was cool with him for a day or two. But he was so adorable—! And yet—a tinge of loneliness was creeping in again, between her and him' (77:20–22). The ambiguity is in the *point of view* being reported. The first sentence seems to report what William noticed, but to whom was he 'so adorable'? Surely, to Mrs Morel. And the third sentence seems to report both their feelings. This blending of the way people perceive each other occurs often in the narrative of *Sons and Lovers* and it invites the reader to notice how feelings are silently passed between people so that they are unconsciously affected by each other's emotions. The commentary by the narrator, which might be expected to clarify the relationships between individuals, frequently blurs the distinction between them.

NARRATIVE VOICE AND VIEWPOINT

In the late-nineteenth-century tradition of the novel which influenced Lawrence, there was a widely used convention by which the narrator could appear to reproduce directly the inner thoughts and feelings of a character. It is a blend of direct quotation and impersonal reporting which is known as 'free indirect style' or 'empathetic narrative'.[22] For example:

> She wondered what he was thinking of, as he stood suspended. His thick hair was tumbled over his forehead. Why might she not push it back for him, and remove the marks of Beatrice's comb? Why might she not press his body with her two hands. It looked so firm and every whit living. (246:19–23)

In the first sentence the narrator gives a reported version of: ' "What is he thinking of?" she wondered.' In the last three sentences the narrator appears to stand aside and allow Miriam's inner monologue to be heard direct. And yet, the actual words the reader imagines Miriam saying are different: 'Why may I not . . .? Why may I not . . . with my two hands. It looks so firm and every whit living.' The questions, exclamations ('so') and idioms ('every whit') of Miriam's 'direct speech' are reproduced within the narrator's 'reported speech', to give the reader the illusion of a privileged inside view of her emotions.

Normally, the context would show clearly whose thoughts were being reported by means of this narrative convention, but Lawrence also uses it unanchored. Not only do the narrator's frequent 'rather' and 'so' make the reader wonder who is exclaiming, there are many expressions of surprise which are not attributable to any specific character: 'the family was extraordinarily happy and peaceful' (112:36–7); 'The boys were amazingly superior. But Paul scarcely observed it' (156:9); 'Arthur was astonishingly handsome in his scarlet and yellow, and he knew it well, but was secretly ashamed of the uniform' (284:35–7). The impression is given of a narrator emotionally involved in the interplay between the characters.

It was customary to use this narrative style to report the inner thoughts or feelings of one character at a time. Lawrence exploits this aspect of the style, for example by sometimes alternating paragraphs of narration giving two characters' different points of view in a kind of silent dialogue. But he also disrupts the convention frequently by blurring or fusing the characters' viewpoints. For example, when Paul and Miriam are 'together' in Alfreton church (203:4–11) the paragraph moves so rapidly from one to the other describing their thoughts and actions that each appears to be involved in the other's feelings:

> In that atmosphere Miriam's soul came into a glow.[23] Paul was afraid of the things he mustn't do. And he was sensitive to the feel of the place. Miriam turned to him. He answered. They were together. He would not go beyond the communion rail. She loved him for that. Her soul expanded into prayer beside him. He felt the strange fascination of shadowy religious places. All his latent mysticism quivered into life. She was drawn to him. He was a prayer along with her.

Another technique is used to assimilate Mr and Mrs Morel to each other during their quarrel in Chapter One. They seem to be in very different states of mind, he tipsy and she responsible, but their separateness is modified by a narrative full of words about liquid. The reason for such words is, of course, his drunkenness and her activity of home-brewing but, at a less obvious level, the effect is to sweep them both into the same stream of emotion, a sort of intoxication of anger: 'pouring ... liquor pitched ... blood rose in a jet ... stirring ... continuing to stir ... boozing ... bezzle ... sponging ... swill ... guzzles and swills ... in the next wave ... she poured over him all her contempt ... shaken into tears ... drying into rage ... bursting full of blood ... dipped gradually into a stupor' (31:27–33:30). The sheer profusion of words suggesting liquid, together with the exploitation of multiple meanings ('sponging', 'poured', 'dipped'), adds to the intensity of the feelings described and also conveys an impression that people are affected by each other at a level of which they are unaware.

It is significant that this liquid imagery is physical and not mental. It does not describe the parents' conscious emotions. By contrast,

Paul's announcement to Miriam that he cannot love her (261:14) is followed by paragraphs of reaction in which, despite their opposition, they share the same range of emotionally charged vocabulary of conscious shame and humiliation: Miriam feels self-mistrust, deficiency, subtle shame; Paul, as seen by Miriam, grovels helplessly, flounders in a pitiable way, is humiliated; Paul calls himself deficient; Miriam sees him as shamefully clumsy. He finds the night jangled and hateful. When they next meet, a page later, Miriam feels ignominy and Paul is 'feeling humiliated' (262:30–31).

Lawrence uses an impressive number of different words to depict the same range of emotion. When simultaneously he exploits ambiguities, complex psychological layers can be suggested. For example, when Paul is ill as a child and watches his mother ironing, he feels sorry for her because 'she had never had her life's fulfilment', but the words used to describe his sympathy also undermine him personally: 'made his heart contract with love . . . It hurt the boy keenly . . . his own incapability to make up to her hurt him with a sense of impotence, yet made him patiently dogged inside. It was his childish aim' (90:39–91:5). The surface text tells us of his painfully intense love for his mother, but running counter to the surface meaning is an undercurrent which conveys the psychological damage Paul receives. For the secondary meanings of the words suggest that Paul's love for his mother makes him *contract* instead of develop; the *hurt* it does him in childhood will leave him *incapable* and *impotent* as he grows up; he will be *dogged* by it for life, and as long as he holds on to his aim of giving her her life's fulfilment he will remain *childish*.

Lawrence has inserted into a character's inner thoughts a degree of psychological complexity of which the character is unconscious. The young Paul's sense of his own emotions is so merged with his consciousness of his mother that he is unaware of the division and conflict within himself that that causes. Below the surface realism, the implied plot or 'idea' of the novel is whether Paul can become conscious of this division and free himself from his fusion with his mother. This is why *Sons and Lovers* is preoccupied with states of consciousness; the word occurs fifty-six times in its various forms: consciousness, conscious, unconscious, self-conscious and semi-conscious. Is this perhaps also why Lawrence made Paul Morel an artist?

THE PORTRAIT OF PAUL MOREL AS AN ARTIST

The connection between Paul's art, his mother and his *consciousness* is made in a significant pair of paragraphs near the beginning of Part II (190:12–24):

> For many hours she sat still, slightly conscious of him labouring away, whilst she worked or read her book. And he, with all his soul's intensity directing his pencil, could feel her warmth inside him like strength. They were both very happy so, and both unconscious of it. These times, that meant so much, and which were real living, they almost ignored.
>
> He was conscious only when stimulated. A sketch finished, he always wanted to take it to Miriam. Then he was stimulated into knowledge of the work he had produced unconsciously. In contact with Miriam, he gained insight, his vision went deeper. From his mother he drew the life warmth, the strength to produce; Miriam urged this warmth into intensity like a white light.

By this time, we are told, 'He was studying for his painting' (190:4). In the early chapters the picture of Paul as an artist is built up with slight touches, until he is compelled to look for a job at fourteen and realizes that his sole ambition in life is to 'have a cottage with his mother, paint and go out as he liked, and live happy ever after ... And he thought that *perhaps* he might also make a painter, the real thing. But that he left alone' (114:8–13). In comparison with his younger brother, Arthur, who gains a scholarship to the Grammar School in Nottingham, Paul is 'not brilliant. But still he stuck to his painting, and still he stuck to his mother. Everything he did, was for her' (142:21–3). On their walk to Willey Farm, Paul sketches a scene across the fields of a coal wagon being driven up a pit-hill, and they have their only discussion in the book about the subject-matter of his art. Her view is that 'The world is a wonderful place ... and wonderfully beautiful', but he asserts, 'I like the feel of *men* on things, while they're alive' (152:17–39).

After William's death, Paul's attack of pneumonia alters their relationship: Mrs Morel's life becomes rooted in him, but his sketches are for Miriam's family. The critical moment which bonds his mother to him, when he nearly dies, is described in terms of his consciousness and – significantly, given Paul's preoccupations as an artist – his awareness of his own body as an aggregation of *cells*: 'One night he tossed into consciousness, in the ghastly, sickly feeling of dissolution, when all the cells in the body seem in intense irritability to be breaking down, and consciousness makes a last flare of struggle, like madness' (171:21–4). Afterwards, when his mother takes him on holiday to help his recovery, it is to the Leivers family that he is 'anxious' to show his 'beloved sketches' of the coast: 'Almost they would interest Mrs Leivers more than they interested his mother. It was not his art Mrs Morel cared about, it was himself, and his achievement' (179:35–8).

From now on painting is a way of collecting rewards for his mother: her pride in his exhibition prizes, the prize-money, and the resulting opportunities for social climbing (222:1–28, 295–7). He feels his mother's silent presence as a warmth inside him while he paints, but the *content* of his art and his *thought* about it are for Miriam. This split in his consciousness leads him to extraordinary states of artistic perception which he describes to Miriam (232:27–36):

> I look at my hands, and wonder what they are doing there. That water there ripples right through me. I'm sure I am that rippling. It runs right through me, and I through it. There are no barriers between us ... A sort of disseminated consciousness, that's all there is of me. I feel as if my body were lying empty, as if I were in the other things—clouds and water—

The dispersal of his consciousness[24] into the surroundings is reminiscent of his mother's melting experience in the moonlight in Chapter One in which Paul, still in her womb, had shared. For her it is restful but for him it becomes a recurring nightmare. He experiences it in the dark, leaning against a stile and feeling so bewildered by the conflict between his mother and Miriam that 'the night and the space' seem to be 'breaking into him' (231:2–14).[25] And now it recurs in the daylight, as he holds forth to Miriam about Michelangelo, and the 'white intensity of his search' makes her feel that she is 'fingering the very quivering tissue, the very protoplasm of life' (232:6–7). This passage adds the suggestion that his states of disseminated consciousness are not only caused by his torn loyalties, but are bound up with his 'search' to perceive the smallest cell structures in nature. Earlier, he tries to reproduce 'protoplasm' in his art, in the first painting he discusses with Miriam: it is 'shimmery—as if I'd painted the shimmering protoplasm in the leaves and everywhere, and not the stiffness of the shape' (183:2–3).

In 'studying' for his art Paul reads about plant biology, as he explains cryptically to his mother in their climactic quarrel at the end of Chapter Eight, when he lists the things that he talks to Miriam about as painting and books and Herbert Spencer (251:17). Spencer's writings on the theory of evolution as applied to biology provide Paul not only with information about cell structure, but an important idea with which to control his extreme states of splitting and merging: 'proportion'. His reason for drawing roses as 'conventional studies' (that is, symmetrical designs) is based on a biological theory that he explains to Miriam: 'the theory that the force of gravitation is the great shaper, and that if it had all its own way, it would have a rose in correct geometrical line and proportion' (240:27–9, cut by Garnett).

Spencer's theory – that plants would be compelled by gravity to grow symmetrically if they were not also affected by other forces such as light and weather – was comparatively new when Lawrence was young. In replacing Spencer's word 'symmetry' with 'proportion', Lawrence is indicating Paul's quest for balance in his life as well as his art. The word 'balance' occurs in the novel as each of his relationships with women begins to founder. After the quarrel and reconciliation with his mother followed by the near-fight with his father in Chapter Eight, Paul makes his first attempt to end his relationship with Miriam, on the grounds that she loves him more than he can love her, or as he puts it to her, their friendship 'overbalances to one side—I hate a toppling balance' (260:23–4).[26] Again, later on, after his fight with Baxter Dawes in Chapter Thirteen, when he realizes that he no longer cares for Clara, we are told: 'He only knew that his life seemed unbalanced, as if it were going to smash into pieces' (412:24–5).

During Paul's transition from Miriam to Clara, his dawning awareness of sexual needs which Miriam cannot meet is indicated by the use of the word 'self-conscious'. It occurs three times in Chapter Nine to describe Paul, and on the third occurrence refers to his state of mind when writing the birthday letter to Miriam: 'Now he began to feel the torture of self-consciousness. He seemed cut away underneath, as if he could not stand on his feet, but must flounder and flounder' (292:1–3, cut by Garnett). The only other instance of the word 'consciousness' in Chapter Nine comes at the end: 'Often, as he talked to Clara Dawes, came that thickening and quickening of his blood, that peculiar concentration in the breast, as if something were alive there, a new self or a new centre of consciousness' (294:27–30).

Again, a new split occurs between Paul's artistic consciousness and his love life. His relationship with Clara is not intellectual and he does not expound his ideas on art to her as he had to Miriam. Yet he is still in search of a theory: 'He loved to paint large figures, full of light, but not merely made up of lights and cast shadows, like the impressionists; rather definite figures that had a certain luminous quality, like some of Michael Angelo's people. And these he fitted into a landscape, in what he thought true proportion' (345:10–14). He has left behind the shimmeriness of the impressionists with its hints of protoplasm; he has retained his interest in Michelangelo; and he is still in pursuit of 'proportion'. However, his interest in proportion is no longer focused on plant structure but on the relation of the individual to his environment.

This perspective is more readily aligned with the suffragette and socialist views of Clara Dawes; and when she and Paul stand on the Castle rock discussing the view down below, she comments, 'Yes—it is not necessary to get far off in order to see us proportionately' (313:21–2). The conversation that follows leads Paul, as his conversation with Miriam had once done, to a state of visionary reverie, but this time Paul does not feel threatened by his perception of things melting and merging (316:13–20):

> He was brooding now . . . The little, interesting diversity of shapes had vanished from the scene. All that remained was a vast, dark matrix of sorrow and tragedy, the same in all the houses and the river-flats and the people and the birds: they were only shapen differently. And now that the forms seemed to have melted away, there remained the mass from which all the landscape was composed, a dark mass of struggle and pain.

His artistic consciousness is active in Clara's company even though it remains unspoken, and in his dawning awareness of a physical attraction to Clara, he perceives her in terms that are reminiscent of the way he had felt his mother's 'warmth inside him like strength', when he used to sit painting in her company at home: 'He was filled with the warmth of her. In the glow, he could almost feel her as if she were present, her arms, her shoulders, her bosom, see them, feel them, almost contain them' (316:39–317:2).[27] This rapidly develops as a kind of reversal of the experience of being in the womb: 'he knew the curves of her breast and shoulders as if they had been moulded inside him' (319:14–15).

In making Paul's relationship with Clara different from that with Miriam in its absence of talk about art, Lawrence has set himself the difficult task of indicating by some other means that Paul's artistic vision does not somehow disappear during their affair. One of the ways he does this is by describing Paul's 'unconscious thoughts' about Clara on the Lincolnshire coast, when he watches her lose 'proportion' as she walks far across the sands to the sea and is 'dazzled out of sight' by the sun (402:3–40). Given Paul's preoccupation with 'proportion', his vision of her as minute, followed by his sense of her as huge when she is beside him again, must be significant. As in the case of the doll Arabella, a reader might usefully ask why Lawrence includes this episode. Why does he make Paul and Clara visit the sea? Is it an echo of Paul's childhood visit with his mother (179:32–6)? Is it an opportunity for further nakedness? Or is it to give Paul a special vision of man's relation to the universe?

> 'Look how little she is!' he said to himself. 'She's lost like a grain of sand in the beach—just a concentrated speck blown along—a tiny white foam-bubble—almost nothing among the morning. Why does she absorb me.' . . .
>
> . . . 'What is she after all?' he said to himself. 'Here's the sea-coast morning, big and permanent and beautiful. There she is, fretting, always unsatisfied, and temporary as a bubble of foam. What does she mean to me, after all? She represents something, like a bubble of foam represents the sea. But what is *she*! It's not her I care for—'

That Paul is shaken out of his stereotypes to wonder what Clara *is*, has been discussed before. But the whole passage gathers together more of Paul's emotional and intellectual life than this. The loss of proportion means becoming 'almost nothing'. The thought that a bubble of foam represents something is reminiscent of Paul's interest in protoplasm. The sense that the sea-coast morning with its 'immense, unbroken solitude' is the sole permanent thing in view relates to Paul's earlier effort to paint a true proportion between his luminous figures and their background.

More than this, Paul's thoughts about a human being's littleness in comparison with the immensity of the surrounding universe arise again after his mother's death, on the last page of the novel, where it is he himself who is 'almost nothing' (464:24). By now he cannot paint and has decided that 'Painting is not living' (456:23). But the artistic vision that he has struggled to develop enables him to stand in the 'immense night' and contemplate courageously his mother, 'intermingled herself', and 'himself, infinitesimal, at the core a nothingness, and yet not nothing' (464:12, 32, 29). The final page is a passage of poetic intensity which stands beside the greatest writing in English literature in its contemplation of the horror of man's littleness in comparison with the eternality of death and the immensity of the universe. Lawrence hardly explains to the reader what it is that enables Paul to resist his desire to follow his mother into the darkness, but he creates a powerful impression that it is Paul's prolonged quest for a proportionate vision which enables him to gaze at this overwhelming night without succumbing to it, and to arrive in the end at his grim determination to choose life, despite all the tragedy.

NOTES ON THE INTRODUCTION

1. D. H. Lawrence, *Study of Thomas Hardy and Other Essays*, ed. Bruce Steele (Cambridge University Press, 1985), 172:32–3.

2. D. H. Lawrence, *Sons and Lovers*, ed. Helen and Carl Baron (Cambridge University Press, 1992).

3. John Worthen, *D. H. Lawrence: The Early Years, 1885–1912* (Cambridge University Press, 1991).

4. James T. Boulton, ed., *The Letters of D. H. Lawrence*, volume I (Cambridge University Press, 1979), 477. (Hereafter referred to as *Letters*, i.)

5. *Letters*, i. 546. His remarks about Hamlet after seeing the play in January 1913 may reflect on his characterization of Paul Morel: 'He could not love, he could only judge' ('Italian Studies', *The English Review*, September 1913, 229).

6. *Study of Thomas Hardy*, 29:35–30:2. DHL wrote his *Study* from September to December 1914. The references are to *Anna Karenina* by Leo Tolstoy and *The Return of the Native, Tess of the D'Urbervilles* and *Jude the Obscure* by Thomas Hardy.

7. *Study of Thomas Hardy*, 21:18–21.

8. George Eliot, *The Mill on the Floss*, 1860; *Middlemarch*, 1871–2, Chapter Fifty-Six.

9. See Jose Harris, *Private Lives, Public Spirit, A Social History of Britain, 1870–1914* (Oxford University Press, 1993).

10. *Letters*, i. 476–7.

Introduction

11. *Letters*, i. 478.
12. *Letters*, i. 477.
13. 'It's me that brings the money home, not you. It's my house, not yours. Then get out of it.'
14. 'You don't want to make a girl of him.'
15. 'Little' is usually a word reserved (not only by Lawrence) for women: 149:3, 14, 31, 150:6, 151:35, 229:37, 286:22, 288:39, etc.
16. For example, 184:10–12, 188:34–189:26, 226:10–23, 256:19–258:4, etc.
17. Garnett left most of the conversation but cut Paul and Clara's eight exchanges on this topic, 320:5–17.
18. *Letters*, i. 478. In the end, the word 'naked' (382:28) and a whole paragraph (383:20–30) were removed from this scene, as well as other phrases elsewhere. Contrast Paul's delicacy in talking to Miriam of the risk of pregnancy as 'in the Gretchen way', which now seems merely coy (327:18).
19. The name of the gamekeeper in Lawrence's *The White Peacock*, ed. Andrew Robertson and Michael Black (Penguin Books, 1994).
20. George Eliot, *The Mill on the Floss*, Book I, Chapter Four.
21. Garnett did not cross this out in the manuscript, but it was censored on the proofs in 1913.
22. See: Geoffrey N. Leech and Michael H. Short, *Style in Fiction* (Longman, 1981), Chapter 10, pp. 318–51; and Sylvia Adamson, 'Empathetic Narrative: a literary and linguistic problem', *Literary Stylistics*, Chapter 6 (Cambridge University Press, to be published 1995).
23. A key word in their relationship. For example, when Miriam enters Bestwood library for her rendezvous with Paul (192:21–193:40), her face 'glowed' from her hard walk in the rain and her 'eyes met his'; before they part Paul's eyes 'gazed into hers' and they both went home 'glowing'.
24. The expression 'disseminated consciousness' also occurs in the poem 'Dolour of Autumn' (*The Complete Poems of D. H. Lawrence*, ed. Vivian de Sola Pinto and Warren Roberts, revised edn, Heinemann, 1972, pp. 107–8.) Lawrence may have registered the description of this state in *Lettres de mon Moulin* by Alphonse Daudet (1866, the chapter 'Le Phare des Sanguinaires'), a book which Clara reads. Lawrence wrote to a friend while his mother was dying, and described the 'peculiar fusion of soul' he had had with her, which 'seems to distribute one's consciousness far abroad from oneself, and one "understands"' (*Letters*, i. 190).
25. This motif is repeated on the last page of the book, where Paul leans against a stile to contemplate the 'Space' and the 'Night' but refuses to 'give in' (464:15, 19, 24, 34).
26. Seven pages earlier, Morel is described as 'toppling in his balance'

xl

(253:3), suggesting a connection between his drinking habit and his failed marital relationship.

27. In an earlier version, Lawrence had written here: 'He seemed to have in his chest and in his belly a consciousness of the woman . . .'

Note on the Text

This text of *Sons and Lovers* is based on Lawrence's complete final manuscript of the novel as it stood before Edward Garnett crossed out eighty passages, amounting to one tenth of the whole. Lawrence was sent two rounds of proofs and took the opportunity to make a small number of corrections and about 670 revisions varying in length from single words to several sentences. These revisions have been incorporated into the complete manuscript text.

Lawrence wrote the work from the beginning four times, and also made a thorough revision of the third manuscript. Not all the manuscripts are extant but there are a variety of survivals from the drafts; and it is possible to date most of them because Lawrence used the same supplies of paper for his letters and he dated his letters. The first version is lost. The second manuscript survives in large part (pp. 72–353), but has lost its beginning and ending. It is now located at the University of Texas at Austin (Roberts E373d). When Lawrence first began the third version he gave up after writing seven pages – these are now with the second manuscript. Of his second attempt at the third draft only 172 pages survive, which are dispersed. Lawrence transferred ninety-three pages of the third manuscript into the fourth as he wrote it, revising them slightly. A further fifty-six pages that he rejected from the opening chapters as he wrote the fourth version have survived and are kept with the fourth manuscript in the Bancroft Library, Berkeley, California (Roberts E373a,e). Finally, most of Chapter Nine from the third manuscript (which evolved into the 'Lad-and-Girl Love' chapter in the final manuscript) has survived because it was revised and criticized by Jessie Chambers, Lawrence's friend who was the model for Miriam Leivers (Roberts E373b, also at Austin, Texas).

Of the first proofs (galley proofs), unfortunately less than a tenth survive, but at least they are from the set that Lawrence corrected. Of the second proofs (page proofs), none that Lawrence checked survive but there is a complete uncorrected set.

The manuscripts, proofs and first editions are a rich mine of information about Lawrence's writing of *Sons and Lovers*, much of which is recorded in the Cambridge edition. Some examples can be briefly illustrated here. First, we discover that it was not until the final writing that Lawrence replaced many passages of explanation with dramatic exchanges between the characters, such as William's abrupt entry and demand for his lunch (11:10) and Walter Morel's exchange with his fellow miners at work in the pit (41:17–42:30).

Second, there are passages in the earlier drafts that show the seeds of Lawrence's later thinking. For example, the description of Mrs Morel's scolding of her husband, 'she wielded the lash unmercifully' (25:6), had originally been followed by some sentences which Lawrence deleted:

> No man can live unless his life is rooted in some woman: unless some woman believes in him, and so fixes his belief in himself. Otherwise he is like a water plant, whose root is detached: floating still, and apparently flourishing, upon the river of life, but really decaying slowly. Morel decayed slowly.
>
> It was a great tragedy, and it is the tragedy of many a man and woman.

The ideas in the first paragraph are more fully developed in *Women in Love* (1916). The second paragraph is a pre-echo of Lawrence's letter to Garnett of November 1912 in which he called *Sons and Lovers* 'a great tragedy'. But this passage was first written in November 1911 as part of the third manuscript.

Third, Garnett's editing of the final manuscript shows that among the eighty passages he crossed out were some instances of Mrs Morel's wit (72:1–73:2, 75:4–23, 150:19–151:9, 211:23–9, 213:39–214:6) and her outspokenness (44:19–45:11, 68:38–69:16, 164:8–18). There were also some examples of Paul's sensitivity towards Miriam (185:4–23, 188:14–33, 240:16–35, 263:10–37) as well as large chunks of his birthday letter to her and the whole of a four-page episode in which they meet at the library (190:30–194:18). In addition, Garnett censored minutely, removing the word 'natural' from 'He could smell her faint natural perfume' (375:30–31), and changing 'hips' to 'body' (333:32) and 'thighs' to 'limbs' (375:19). He also cut out disrespectful references to royalty (212:34–213:9).

Fourth, the proofs and first edition show that the printers altered Lawrence's punctuation on average every four or five lines, to fit the style that they normally used, and in a surprisingly large number of places they altered the meaning. Lawrence used dashes frequently to indicate hesitation, asides, second thoughts or changes of direction, but the printers altered many of them. For example, when Paul talks to Miriam about what he thinks is essential in marriage, Lawrence wrote that Miriam 'saw what he was seeking: a sort of baptism of fire in passion, it seemed to her ... Perhaps it was essential to him—as to some men to sow wild oats' (362:20–23). But the printers removed the dash so that passion and wild oats became the same thing: 'Perhaps it was essential to him, as to some men, to sow wild oats.' Similarly they removed many of Lawrence's commas, such as when Lawrence wrote of Clara: 'And she took him simply, because his need was bigger either than her or him' (397:38–9), which changed the meaning of 'simply' from 'in a simple way' to 'simply because'. Lawrence ended many questions with a full stop or an exclamation mark to indicate a character's confrontational attitude rather than a simple enquiry, but the printers put in the grammatically correct question marks. Thus Paul's reply to Baxter, as previously printed – 'Do you think so?' – suggests he is surprised and interested by Baxter's remark, whereas Lawrence had written a more hostile rejoinder:

> 'But perhaps even *then* you were a bigger fool,' said Dawes.
> There was a touch of triumph and malice in it.
> 'Do you think so!' said Paul. (447:40–448:2)

Fifth, the galley proofs show that when Lawrence received them they had already been further censored by Garnett, and in addition several passages had been marked with a query by the printer's proof-reader. Lawrence responded to some of these queries by changing his wording, for example changing 'It' in 'his experience had been It, and not Clara' to 'impersonal' (399:16). He also made unprompted revisions, adding phrases and rewriting sentences. For example, the passage, 'He talked to barmaids ... hunting something' (454:17–19) is Lawrence's handwritten revision of the galley text, which had read: 'He talked very gaily and gallantly to barmaids, to light women, till the intimacy got to a certain point; then he turned away, unable to go any farther. That also held nothing.' Two paragraphs later, he added the phrase 'when he lapsed from consciousness' (454:28).

Sixth, the laborious work of comparing the manuscript with all the proofs and first editions shows that some mistakes made by the printers had never been corrected until the Cambridge edition. For example, Lawrence wrote: 'Yet her soul seemed to be intensely supplicating the algebra book. She closed, shrinking, knowing he was angered' (188:10–12). But this was printed as: 'Yet her soul seemed to be intensely supplicating. The algebra book she closed . . .' And Lawrence's 'speck' (464:23) was printed as 'spark'.

Finally, mistakes which crept into later reprints from the 1930s onwards are now corrected, such as 'life' for 'file' (81:7), 'split' for 'spilt' (195:33) and 'whispered' for 'whimpered' (464:30).

Advisory Editor's Note

I would like to thank Professor James T. Boulton and Professor F. Warren Roberts, General Editors of the *Cambridge Edition of the Works of D. H. Lawrence*, for their advice and planning in the preparation of this edition.

John Worthen, 1994

SONS AND LOVERS

BY

D. H. LAWRENCE

AUTHOR OF

"LOVE POEMS," "THE WHITE PEACOCK," "THE TRESPASSER"

DESORMAIS

LONDON : DUCKWORTH & CO.

HENRIETTA STREET, COVENT GARDEN

1913

To Edward Garnett

Contents

PART I

CHAPTER I

The early married Life of the Morels

"The Bottoms" succeeded to "Hell Row." Hell Row was a block of thatched, bulging cottages that stood by the brook-side on Greenhill Lane. There lived the colliers who worked in the little gin-pits two fields away. The brook ran under the alder trees, scarcely soiled by these small mines, whose coal was drawn to the surface by donkeys that plodded wearily in a circle, round a gin. And all over the countryside were these same pits, some of which had been worked in the time of Charles II, the few colliers and the donkeys burrowing down like ants into the earth, making queer mounds and little black places among the corn-fields and the meadows. And the cottages of these coal-miners in blocks and pairs here and there, together with odd farms and homes of the stockingers, straying over the parish, formed the village of Bestwood.

Then, some sixty years ago, a sudden change took place. The gin-pits were elbowed aside by the large mines of the financiers. The coal and iron field of Nottinghamshire and Derbyshire was discovered. Carston, Waite and Co. appeared. Amid tremendous excitement, Lord Palmerston formally opened the company's first mine at Spinney Park, on the edge of Sherwood Forest.

About this time the notorious Hell Row, which through growing old had acquired an evil reputation, was burned down, and much dirt was cleansed away.

Carston, Waite and Co. found they had struck on a good thing, so, down the valleys of the brooks from Selby and Nuttall, new mines were sunk, until soon there were six pits working. From Nuttall, high up on the sandstone among the woods, the railway ran, past the ruined priory of the Carthusians and past Robin Hood's well, down to Spinney Park, then on to Minton, a large mine among corn-fields, from Minton across the farm-lands of the valley side to Bunker's Hill, branching off there, and running north to Beggarlee

9

and Selby, that looks over at Crich and the hills of Derbyshire; six mines like black studs on the countryside, linked by a loop of fine chain, the railway.

To accommodate the regiments of miners, Carston, Waite and Co. built the Squares, great quadrangles of dwellings on the hillside of Bestwood, and then, in the brook valley, on the site of Hell Row, they erected The Bottoms.

The Bottoms consisted of six blocks of miners' dwellings, two rows of three, like the dots on a blank-six domino, and twelve houses in a block. This double row of dwellings sat at the foot of the rather sharp slope from Bestwood, and looked out, from the attic windows at least, on the slow climb of the valley towards Selby.

The houses themselves were substantial and very decent. One could walk all round, seeing little front gardens with auriculas and saxifrage in the shadow of the bottom block, sweet williams and pinks, in the sunny top-block; seeing neat front windows, little porches, little privet hedges, and dormer windows for the attics. But that was outside; that was the view onto the uninhabited parlours of all the colliers' wives. The dwelling room, the kitchen, was at the back of the house, facing inward between the blocks, looking at a scrubby back-garden, and then at the ash-pits. And between the rows, between the long lines of ash-pits, went the alley, where the children played and the women gossiped and the men smoked. So, the actual conditions of living in the Bottoms, that was so well built, and that looked so nice, were quite unsavoury, because people must live in the kitchen, and the kitchens opened onto that nasty alley of ash-pits.

Mrs Morel was not anxious to move into the Bottoms, which was already twelve years old and on the downward path, when she descended to it from Bestwood. But it was the best she could do. Moreover, she had an end house in one of the top blocks, and thus had only one neighbour, on the other side an extra strip of garden. And, having an end house, she enjoyed a kind of aristocracy among the other women of the 'between' houses, because her rent was five shillings and sixpence instead of five shillings a week. But this superiority in station was not much consolation to Mrs Morel.

She was thirty-one years old, and had been married eight years. A rather small woman, of delicate mould but resolute bearing, she shrank a little from the first contact with the Bottoms women. She came down in the July, and in the September expected her third baby.

Her husband was a miner. They had only been in their new home three weeks, when the wakes or fair began. Morel, she knew, was sure to make a holiday of it. He went off early on the Monday morning, the day of the fair. The two children were highly excited. William, a boy of seven, fled off immediately after breakfast, to prowl round the wakes ground, leaving Annie, who was only five, to whine all morning to go also. Mrs Morel did her work. She scarcely knew her neighbours yet, and knew no-one with whom to trust the little girl. So she promised to take her to the wakes after dinner.

William appeared at half past twelve. He was a very active lad, fair haired, freckled, with a touch of the Dane or Norwegian about him.

"Can I have my dinner, mother?" he cried, rushing in with his cap on. " 'Cause it begins at half past one, the man says so."

"You can have your dinner as soon as it's done," replied the mother.

"Isn't it done?" he cried, his blue eyes staring at her in indignation. "Then I'm goin' be-out it."

"You'll do nothing of the sort. It will be done in five minutes. It is only half past twelve."

"They'll be beginnin'," the boy half cried, half shouted.

"You won't die if they do," said the mother. "Besides, it's only half past twelve, so you've a full hour."

The lad began hastily to lay the table, and directly the three sat down. They were eating batter pudding and jam, when the boy jumped off his chair and stood perfectly still. Some distance away could be heard the first small braying of a merry-go-round, and the tooting of a horn. His face quivered as he looked at his mother.

"I told you!" he said, running to the dresser for his cap.

"Take your pudding in your hand—and it's only five past one, so *you* were wrong—you haven't got your twopence," cried the mother in a breath.

The boy came back, bitterly disappointed, for his two-pence, then went off without a word.

"I want to go, I want to go," said Annie, beginning to cry.

"Well and you shall go, whining, wizzening little stick," said the mother. And later in the afternoon, she trudged up the hill under the tall hedge, with her child. The hay was gathered from the fields, and cattle were turned onto the eddish. It was warm, peaceful.

Mrs Morel did not like the wakes. There were two sets of horses, one going by steam, one pulled round by a pony; three organs were grinding, and there came odd cracks of pistol shots, fearful scree-ching of the cocoa-nut man's rattle, shouts of the Aunt Sally man, screams from the Peep-show lady. The mother perceived her son gazing enraptured outside the Lion Wallace booth, at the pictures of this famous lion that had killed a negro and maimed for life two white men. She left him alone, and went to get Annie a spin of toffee. Presently the lad stood in front of her, wildly excited.

"You never said you was coming—isn't the' a lot of things?—that lion's killed three men—I've spent my tuppence—an' look here—"

He pulled from his pocket two egg-cups with pink moss-roses on them.

"I got these from that stall where y'ave ter get them marbles in them holes—an' I got these two in two goes—'ae-penny a go—they've got moss-roses on, look here. I wanted these."

She knew he wanted them for her.

"Hm!" she said, pleased. "They *are* pretty!"

"Shall you carry 'em, 'cause I'm frightened o' breakin' 'em?"

He was tip-ful of excitement now she had come, led her about the ground, showed her everything. Then, at the peep-show, she explained the pictures, in a sort of story, to which he listened as if spell-bound. He would not leave her. All the time, he stuck close to her, bristling with a small boy's pride of her. For no other woman looked such a lady as she did, in her little black bonnet and her cloak. She smiled when she saw women she knew.

When she was tired, she said to her son:

"Well, are you coming now, or later?"

"Are you goin' a'ready?" he cried, his face full of reproach.

"'Already?'—It is past four, *I* know."

"What are you goin' a'ready for?" he lamented.

"You needn't come if you don't want," she said.

And she went slowly away with her little girl, whilst her son stood watching her, cut to the heart to let her go, and yet unable to leave the wakes. As she crossed the open ground, in front of the Moon and Stars, she heard men shouting, and smelled the beer, and hurried a little, thinking her husband was probably in the bar.

At about half past six her son came home, tired now, rather pale, and somewhat wretched.

"Well!" she said, pretending to be a bit cross with him, "if you'd been five minutes later, I should have cleared the things away. Another time, you'd have been famishing hours ago—"

And she gave him his tea. He was miserable, though he did not know it, because he had let her go alone. Since she had gone, he had not enjoyed his wakes.

"Has my dad been?" he asked.

"No," said the mother.

"He's helping to wait at the Moon and Stars. I see'd him through that black tin stuff wi' holes in, on the window, wi' his sleeves rolled up—"

"Ha!" exclaimed the mother, shortly. "He'd got no money. An' he'll be satisfied if he gets his 'lowance, whether they give him more or not."

The children were allowed to sit at the window of their mother's bedroom, and watch the folk coming home with toys from the bazaar, listen to the braying of the music, the shouting, the cracking of shots, the faint 'pang' of the thin iron target. Then at last they were tired, and went to bed.

When the light was fading, and Mrs Morel could see no more to sew, she rose and went to the door. Everywhere was the sound of excitement, the restlessness of the holiday, that at last infected her. She went out into the side garden. Women were coming home from the wakes, the children hugging a white lamb with green legs, or a wooden horse. Occasionally a man lurched past, almost as full as he could carry. Sometimes a good husband came along with his family, peacefully. But usually the women and children were alone. The stay-at-home mothers stood gossiping at the corners of the alley, as the twilight sank, folding their arms under their white aprons.

Mrs Morel was alone, but she was used to it. Her son and her little girl slept upstairs, so, it seemed, her home was there behind her, fixed and stable. But she felt wretched with the coming child. The world seemed a dreary place, where nothing else would happen for her—at least until William grew up. But for herself, nothing but this dreary endurance—till the children grew up. And the children! She could not afford to have this third. She did not want it. The father was serving beer in a public house, swilling himself drunk. She despised him, and was tied to him. This coming child was too much for her. If it were not for William and Annie, she was sick of it, the struggle with poverty and ugliness and meanness.

She went into the front garden, feeling too heavy to take herself out, yet unable to stay indoors. The heat suffocated her. And looking ahead, the prospect of her life made her feel as if she were buried alive.

The front garden was a small square with a privet hedge. There she stood, trying to soothe herself with the scent of flowers, and the fading, beautiful evening. Opposite her small gate was the stile that led uphill, under the tall hedge, between the burning glow of the cut pastures. The sky overhead throbbed and pulsed with light. The glow sank quickly off the field, the earth and the hedges smoked dusk. As it grew dark, a ruddy glare came out on the hill top, and out of the glare, the diminished commotion of the fair.

Sometimes, down the trough of darkness formed by the path under the hedges, men came lurching home. One young man lapsed into a run down the steep bit that ended the hill, and went with a crash into the stile. Mrs Morel shuddered. He picked himself up, swearing viciously, rather pathetically, as if he thought the stile had wanted to hurt him.

She went indoors, wondering if things were never going to alter. She was beginning by now to realise that they would not. She seemed so far away from her girlhood, she wondered if it were the same person walking heavily up the back garden at the Bottoms, as had run so lightly on the breakwater at Sheerness, ten years before.

"What have *I* to do with it!" she said to herself. "What have I to do with all this. Even the child I am going to have! It doesn't seem as if *I* were taken into account."

Sometimes life takes hold of one, carries the body along, accomplishes one's history, and yet is not real, but leaves one's self as it were slurred over.

"I wait," Mrs Morel said to herself. "I wait, and what I wait for can never come."

Then she straightened the kitchen, lit the lamp, mended the fire, looked out the washing for the next day, and put it to soak. After which she sat down to her sewing. Through the long hours, her needle flashed regularly through the stuff. Occasionally she sighed, moving to relieve herself. And all the time, she was thinking, how to make the most of what she had, for the children's sakes.

At half past eleven her husband came. His cheeks were very red and very shiny above his black moustache. His head nodded slightly. He was pleased with himself.

"Oh!—Oh!—waitin' for me lass? I've bin 'elpin' Anthony, an'

what's think he's gen me? Nowt b'r a lousy hae'f-crown, an' that's ivry penny—"

"He thinks you've made the rest up in beer," she said shortly.

"An' I 'aven't—that I 'aven't—you b'lieve me, I've 'ad very little this day, I have an' all." His voice went tender. "Here, an' I browt thee a bit o' brandysnap, an' a coconut for th' children." He laid the gingerbread and the cocoanut, a hairy object, on the table. "Nay, tha niver said thankyer for nowt i' thy life, did ter?"

As a compromise, she picked up the cocoa-nut and shook it, to see if it had any milk.

"It's a good 'un, you may back yer life o' that. I got it fra' Bill Hodgkisson. 'Bill,' I says, 'tha non wants them three nuts does ter?—arena ter for gi'ein' me one for my bit of a lad an' wench?' 'I ham, Walter, my lad,' 'e says, 'ta'e which on 'em ter's a mind.' An' so I took one, an' thanked 'im. I didn't like ter shake it afore 'is eyes, but 'e says 'Tha'd better ma'e sure it's a good un, Walt'—an' so, yer see, I knowed it was.—He's a nice chap, is Bill Hodgkisson, 'e's a nice chap!"

"A man will part with anything so long as he's drunk, and you're drunk along with him," said Mrs Morel.

"Eh tha mucky little 'ussy, who's drunk, I sh'd like ter know?" said Morel. He was extraordinarily pleased with himself, because of his day's helping to wait in the Moon and Stars. He chattered on.

Mrs Morel, very tired, and sick of his babble, went to bed as quickly as possible, while he raked the fire.

Mrs Morel came of a good old burgher family, famous independents who had fought with Colonel Hutchinson, and who remained stout Congregationalists. Her grandfather had gone bankrupt in the lace-market at a time when so many lace-manufacturers were ruined in Nottingham. Her father, George Coppard, was an engineer, a large, handsome, haughty man, proud of his fair skin and blue eyes, but more proud still of his integrity. Gertrude resembled her mother in her small build. But her temper, proud and unyielding, she had from the Coppards.

George Coppard was bitterly galled by his own poverty. He became foreman of the engineers in the dockyard at Sheerness. Mrs Morel—Gertrude—was the second daughter. She favoured her mother, loved her mother best of all: but she had the Coppards' clear, defiant blue eyes, and their broad brow. She remembered to have hated her father's overbearing manner towards her gentle, humorous, kindly-souled mother. She remembered running over the breakwater at Sheerness, and finding the boat. She remembered to have been petted and flattered by all the men when she had gone to the dockyard, for she was a delicate, rather proud child. She remembered the funny old mistress, whose assistant she had become, whom she had loved to help in the private school. And she still had the bible that John Field had given her. She used to walk home from chapel with John Field, when she was nineteen. He was the son of a well-to-do tradesman, had been to college in London, and was to devote himself to business.

She could always recall in detail a September Sunday afternoon, when they had sat under the vine at the back of her father's house. The sun came through the chinks in the vine-leaves, and made beautiful patterns, like a lace scarf falling on her and on him. Some of the leaves were clean yellow, like yellow flat flowers.

"Now sit still," he had cried. "Now your hair, I don't know what it *is* like! It's as bright as copper and gold, as red as burnt copper, and it has gold threads, where the sun shines on it. Fancy their saying it's brown. Your mother calls it mouse colour."

She had met his brilliant eyes, but her clear face scarcely showed the elation which rose within her.

"But you say you don't like business," she pursued.

"I don't—I hate it," he cried hotly.

"And you would *like* to go into the ministry," she half implored.

"I should—I should love it, if I thought I could make a first-rate preacher."

"Then why don't you—why *don't* you." Her voice rang with defiance. "If *I* were a man, nothing would stop me."

She held her head erect—he was rather timid before her.

"But my father's so stiff necked. He means to put me into the business, and I know he'll do it."

"But if you're a *man*—!" she had cried.

"Being a man isn't everything," he replied, frowning with puzzled helplessness.

Now, as she moved about her work at the Bottoms, with some experience of what being a man meant, she knew that it was *not* everything.

At twenty, owing to her health, she had left Sheerness. Her father had retired home to Nottingham. John Field's father had been ruined: the son had gone as a teacher in Norwood. She did not hear of him until, two years later, she made determined inquiry. He had married his landlady, a woman of forty, a widow with property.

And still Mrs Morel preserved John Field's bible. She did not now believe him to be—well, she understood pretty well what he might or might not have been. So she preserved his bible, and kept his memory intact in her heart, for her own sake. To her dying day, for thirty-five years, she did not speak of him.

When she was twenty three years old she met, at a christmas party, a young man from the Erewash Valley. Morel was then twenty-seven years old. He was well-set-up, erect and very smart. He had wavy, black hair that shone again, and a vigorous black beard that had never been shaved. His cheeks were ruddy, and his red, moist mouth was noticeable because he laughed so often and so heartily. He had that rare thing, a rich, ringing laugh. Gertrude Coppard had watched him fascinated. He was so full of colour and animation, his voice ran so easily into comic grotesque, he was so ready and so pleasant with everybody. Her own father had a rich fund of humour, but it was satiric. This man's was different: soft, non-intellectual, warm, a kind of gambolling.

She herself was opposite. She had a curious, receptive mind, which found much pleasure and amusement in listening to other folk. She was clever in leading folk on to talk. She loved ideas, and was considered very intellectual. What she liked most of all was an argument on religion or philosophy or politics, with some educated man. This she did not often enjoy. So she always had people tell her about themselves, finding her pleasure so.

In her person, she was rather small and delicate, with a large brow, and dropping bunches of brown silk curls. Her blue eyes were very straight, honest and searching. She had the beautiful hands of the Coppards. Her dress was always subdued. She wore dark blue silk, with a peculiar silver chain, of silver scallops. This, and a heavy brooch of twisted gold, was her only ornament. She was still perfectly intact, deeply religious, and full of beautiful candour.

Walter Morel seemed melted away before her. She was to the miner that thing of mystery and fascination, a lady. When she spoke to him, it was with a southern pronunciation and a purity of English which thrilled him to hear. She watched him. He danced well, as if it were natural and joyous in him to dance. His grandfather was a French refugee who had married an English barmaid—if it had been a marriage. Gertrude Coppard watched the young miner as he danced, a certain subtle exultation like glamour in his movement, and his face the flower of his body, ruddy, with tumbled black hair, and laughing alike whatever partner he bowed above. She thought him rather wonderful, never having met anyone like him. Her father was to her the type of all men. And George Coppard, proud in his bearing, handsome, and rather bitter; who preferred theology in reading, and who drew near in sympathy only to one man, the Apostle Paul; who was harsh in government, and in familiarity ironic; who ignored all sensuous pleasure—he was very different from the miner. Gertrude herself was rather contemptuous of dancing: she had not the slightest inclination towards that accomplishment, and had never learned even a Roger de Coverley. She was a puritan, like her father, high-minded, and really stern. Therefore the dusky, golden softness of this man's sensuous flame of life, that flowed from off his flesh like the flame from a candle, not baffled and gripped into incandescence by thought and spirit as her life was, seemed to her something wonderful, beyond her.

He came and bowed above her. A warmth radiated through her as if she had drunk wine.

"Now do come and have this one wi' me," he said, caressively. "It's easy, you know. I'm pining to see you dance."

She had told him before she could not dance. She glanced at his humility, and smiled. Her smile was very beautiful. It moved the man so that he forgot everything.

"No, I won't dance," she said softly. Her words came clean and ringing.

Not knowing what he was doing—he often did the right thing, by instinct—he sat beside her, inclining reverentially.

"But you mustn't miss your dance," she reproved.

"Nay, I don't want to dance that—it's not one as I care about."

"Yet you invited me to it."

He laughed very heartily at this.

"I never thought o' that. Tha'rt not long in taking the curl out of me."

It was her turn to laugh quickly.

"You don't look as if you'd come much uncurled," she said.

"I'm like a pig's tail, I curl because I canna help it," he laughed—rather boisterously.

"Aren't you having anythink to drink?" he asked.

"No thank you—I am not at all thirsty."

He hesitated—divined that she was a total abstainer—and felt a rebuff.

Then he pursued a number of quite polite, interested questions. She answered him brightly. He seemed quaint.

"And you are a miner!" she exclaimed in surprise.

"Yes. I went down when I was ten."

She looked at him in wondering dismay.

"When you were ten!—and wasn't it very hard?" she asked.

"You soon get used to it. You live like th' mice, an' you pop out at night to see what's going on."

"It makes me feel blind," she frowned.

"Like a moudiwarp!" he laughed. "Yi, an' there's some chaps as does go round like moudiwarps." He thrust his face forward in the blind, snout-like way of a mole, seeming to sniff and peer for direction. "They dun though!" he protested naïvely. "Tha niver seed such a way they get in. But tha mun let me ta'e thee down sometime, an' tha can see for thysen."

She looked at him startled. This was a new tract of life suddenly opened before her. She realised the life of the miners, hundreds of them toiling below earth and coming up at evening. He seemed to her noble. He risked his life daily, and with gaiety. She looked at him, with a touch of appeal in her pure humility.

"Shouldn't ter like it?" he asked tenderly. "'Appen not, it 'ud dirty thee."

She had never been "thee'd" and "thou'd" before.

The next Christmas they were married, and for three months she was perfectly happy: for six months she was very happy.

He had signed the pledge, and wore the blue ribbon of a teetotaller: he was nothing if not showy. They lived, she thought, in his own house. It was small, but convenient enough, and quite nicely furnished, with solid, worthy stuff that suited her honest soul. The women her neighbours were rather foreign to her, and Morel's mother and sisters were apt to sneer at her lady-like ways. But she could perfectly well live by herself, so long as she had her husband close.

Sometimes, when she herself wearied of love talk, she tried to open her heart seriously to him. She saw him listen deferentially, but without understanding. This killed her efforts at a finer intimacy, and she had flashes of fear. Sometimes he was restless of an evening: it was not enough for him just to be near her, she realised. She was glad when he set himself to little jobs.

He was a remarkably handy man, could make or mend anything. So she would say:

"I do like that coal-rake of your mother's—it is small and natty."

"Does ter, my wench. Well, I made that, so I can make thee one."

"What—why it's a steel one—!"

"An' what if it is!—tha s'lt ha'e one very similar, if not exactly same."

She did not mind the mess, nor the hammering and noise. He was busy and happy.

But in the seventh month, when she was brushing his Sunday coat, she felt papers in the breast pocket, and, seized with a sudden curiosity, took them out to read. He very rarely wore the frock coat he was married in: and it had not occurred to her before to feel curious concerning the papers. They were the bills of the household furniture, still unpaid.

"Look here," she said at night, after he was washed and had had his dinner. "I found these in the pocket of your wedding coat. Haven't you settled the bills yet?"

"No—I haven't had a chance."

"But you told me all was paid. I had better go into Nottingham on Saturday and settle them, I don't like sitting on another man's chairs, and eating from an unpaid table."

He did not answer.

"I can have your bank book, can't I?"

"Tha can ha'e it, for what good it'll be to thee."

"I thought— —" she began. He had told her he had a good bit of money left over. But she realised it was no use asking questions. She sat rigid with bitterness and indignation.

The next day, she went down to see his mother.

"Didn't you buy the furniture for Walter?" she asked.

"Yes, I did," tartly retorted the elder woman.

"And how much did he give you to pay for it?"

The elder woman was stung with fine indignation.

"Eighty pound, if you're so keen on knowin'," she replied.

"Eighty pounds! But there are forty two pounds still owing!"

"I can't help that."

"But where has it all gone?"

"You'll find all the papers, I think, if you look—beside ten pound as he owed me, an' six pound as the wedding cost down here."

"Six pounds!" echoed Gertrude Morel. It seemed to her monstrous that, after her own father had paid so heavily for her wedding, six pounds more should have been squandered in eating and drinking at Walter's parents' house, at his expense.

"And how much has he sunk in his houses?" she asked.

"His houses—which houses?"

Gertrude Morel went white to the lips. He had told her the house he lived in, and the next one, was his own.

"I thought the house we live in—" she began.

"They're my houses, those two," said the mother-in-law. "And not clear either. It's as much as I can do to keep the mortgage interest paid."

Gertrude sat white and silent. She was her father now.

"Then we ought to be paying you rent," she said coldly.

"Walter is paying me rent," replied the mother.

"And what rent?" asked Gertrude.

"Six-and-six a week," retorted the mother.

It was more than the house was worth. Gertrude held her head erect, looked straight before her.

"It is lucky to be you," said the elder woman bitingly, "to have a husband as takes all the worry of the money, and leaves you a free hand."

The young wife was silent.

She said very little to her husband, but her manner had changed towards him. Something in her proud, honorable soul had crystallised out hard as rock.

When October came in, she thought only of christmas. Two years ago, at Christmas, she had met him. Last Christmas she had married him. This Christmas she would bear him a child.

Being of a friendly disposition, she soon got to know her neighbours, and often stood talking with them, only afraid lest, because of the difference in speech, they should consider, as did his people, that she put on airs. They always gave her the first say, but they liked her.

"You don't dance yourself, do you Missis?" asked her nearest neighbour, in October, when there was great talk of opening a dancing class over the Brick and Tile Inn, at Bestwood.

"No—I never had the least inclination to," Mrs Morel replied.

"Fancy! An' how funny as you should ha' married your Mester. You know he's quite a famous one for dancing."

"I didn't know he was famous," laughed Mrs Morel.

"Yea, he is though! Why, he run that dancing class in the Miners' Arms Club-room for over five year."

"Did he?"

"Yes, he did." The other woman was defiant. "An' it was thronged every Tuesday, and Thursday, an' Sat'day—an' there *was* carryin's-on, accordin' to all accounts."

This kind of thing was gall and bitterness to Mrs Morel, and she had a fair share of it. The women did not spare her, at first; for she was superior, though she could not help it.

He began to be rather late in coming home.

"They're working very late now, aren't they?" she said to her washer woman.

"No later than they allers do, I don't think. But they stop to have their pint at Ellen's, an' they get talkin', an' there you are!—Dinner stone cold—an' it serves 'em right."

"But Mr Morel does not take any drink."

The woman dropped the clothes, looked at Mrs Morel, then went on with her work, saying nothing.

Gertrude Morel was very ill when the boy was born. Morel was good to her, as good as gold. But she felt very lonely, miles away from her own people. She felt lonely with him now, and his presence only made it more intense.

The boy was small and frail at first, but he came on quickly. He was a beautiful child, with dark gold ringlets, and dark blue eyes, which changed gradually to a clear grey. His mother loved him passionately. He came just when her own bitterness of disillusion was hardest to bear; when her faith in life was shaken, and her soul felt dreary and lonely. She made much of the child, and the father was jealous.

At last Mrs Morel despised her husband. She turned to the child, she turned from the father. He had begun to neglect her, the novelty of his own home was gone. He had no grit, she said bitterly to herself. What he felt just at the minute, that was all to him. He could not abide by anything. There was nothing at the back of all his show.

There began a battle between the husband and wife, a fearful, bloody battle that ended only with the death of one. She fought to make him undertake his own responsibilities, to make him fulfil his obligations. But he was too different from her. His nature was purely sensuous, and she strove to make him moral, religious. She tried to force him to face things. He could not endure it—it drove him out of his mind.

While the baby was still tiny, the father's temper had become so irritable that it was not to be trusted. The child had only to give a little trouble, when the man began to bully. A little more, and the hard hands of the collier hit the baby. Then Mrs Morel loathed her husband, loathed him for days: and he went out and drank: and she cared very little what he did. Only, on his return, she scathed him with her satire.

The estrangement between them caused him, knowingly or unknowingly, grossly to offend her where he would not have done. William, the baby, was just a year old, was just beginning to walk, and to say pretty things. He was a winsome child, still with a little mop of boy's curls, darkening now. He was fond of his father, who was very affectionate, indulgent and full of ingenuity to amuse the child, when it pleased him. The two played together, and Mrs Morel used to wonder which was the truer baby.

Morel always rose early, about five or six o'clock in the morning, whether holiday or work day. On Sunday morning he would get up and prepare breakfast. The fire was never let to go out. It was raked just at bed-time. That is, a great piece of coal, a raker, was placed so that it would be nearly burned through by morning. On Sunday mornings, the child would get up with his father, while the mother lay in bed for another hour or so. She was then more rested than at any other time: when father and child played and prattled together downstairs.

William was only one year old, and his mother was proud of him, he was so pretty. She was not well off now, but her sisters kept the boy in clothes. Then, with his little white hat curled with an ostrich feather, and his white coat, he was a joy to her, the twining wisps of hair clustering round his head. Mrs Morel lay listening, one Sunday morning, to the chatter of the two. Then she dozed off. When she came downstairs, a great fire glowed in the grate, the room was hot, the breakfast was roughly laid. And seated in his armchair, against the chimney piece, sat Morel, rather timid: and standing between his legs, the child—cropped like a sheep, with such an odd round poll—looking wondering at her: and on a newspaper spread out upon the hearth rug, a myriad of crescent-shaped curls, like the petals of a marigold scattered in the reddening firelight.

Mrs Morel stood still. It was her first baby. She went very white, and was unable to speak.

"What dost think on 'im?" Morel laughed uneasily.

She gripped her two fists, lifted them, and came forward. Morel shrank back.

"I could kill you, I could!" she said. She choked with rage, her two fists uplifted.

"Yer non want ter make a wench on 'im," Morel said, in a frightened tone, bending his head to shield his eyes from hers. His attempt at laughter had vanished.

The mother looked down at the jagged, close clipped head of her child. She put her hands on his hair, and stroked and fondled his head.

"Oh—my boy!—" she faltered. Her lip trembled, her face broke, and, snatching up the child, she buried her face in his shoulder and cried painfully. She was one of those women who cannot cry: whom it hurts as it hurts a man. It was like ripping something out of her, her sobbing. Morel sat with his elbows on his knees, his hands gripped together till the knuckles were white. He gazed in the fire, feeling almost stunned, as if he could not breathe.

Presently she came to an end, soothed the child—and cleared away the breakfast table. She left the newspaper littered with curls, spread upon the hearthrug. At last her husband gathered it up and put it at the back of the fire. She went about her work with closed mouth and very quiet. Morel was subdued. He crept about wretchedly, and his meals were a misery that day. She spoke to him civilly, and never alluded to what he had done. But he felt something final had happened.

Afterwards, she said she had been silly, that the boy's hair would have had to be cut, sooner or later. In the end, she even brought herself to say to her husband, it was just as well he had played barber when he did. But she knew, and Morel knew, that that act had caused something momentous to take place in her soul. She remembered the scene all her life, as one in which she had suffered the most intensely.

This act of masculine clumsiness was the spear through the side of her love for Morel. Before, while she had striven against him bitterly, she had fretted after him, as if he had gone astray from her. Now she ceased to fret for his love: he was an outsider to her. This made life much more bearable.

Nevertheless, she still continued to strive with him. She still had her high moral sense, inherited from generations of Puritans. It was now a religious instinct, and she was almost a fanatic with him, because she loved him, or had loved him. If he sinned, she tortured him. If he drank, and lied, was often a poltroon, sometimes a knave, she wielded the lash unmercifully.

The pity was, she was too much his opposite. She could not be content with the little he might be, she would have him the much that he ought to be. So, in seeking to make him nobler than he could be, she destroyed him. She injured and hurt and scarred herself, but she lost none of her worth. She also had the children.

He drank rather heavily, though not more than many miners, and always beer, so that whilst his health was affected, it was never injured. The week-end was his chief carouse. He sat in the Miners' Arms until turning out time every Friday, every Saturday, and every Sunday evening. On Monday and Tuesday he had to get up and reluctantly leave towards ten o'clock. Sometimes he stayed at home on Wednesday and Thursday evenings, or was only out for an hour. He practically never had to miss work owing to his drinking.

But although he was very steady at work, his wages fell off. He was blab-mouthed, a tongue-wagger. Authority was hateful to him, therefore he could only abuse the pit-managers. He would say, in the Palmerston:

"Th' gaffer come down to our stall this morning, an' 'e says: 'You know, Walter, this 'ere'll not do. What about these props!' An' I says to him, 'Why what art talkin' about? What d'st mean about th' props?' 'It'll niver do, this 'ere,' 'e says. 'You'll be havin' th' roof in, one o' these days.' An' I says, 'Tha'd better stan' on a bit o' clunch, then, an' hold it up wi' thy 'ead.' So 'e wor that mad, 'e cossed an' 'e swore, an' t'other chaps they did laugh." Morel was a good mimic. He imitated the manager's fat, squeaky voice, with its attempt at good English.

"'I shan't have it, Walter. Who knows more about it, me or you?' So I says 'I've niver fun out how much tha knows, Alfred. It'll 'appen carry thee ter bed an' back.'"

So Morel would go on, to the amusement of his boon companions. And some of this would be true. The pit-manager was not an educated man. He had been a boy along with Morel, so that, while the two disliked each other, they more or less took each other for granted. But Alfred Charlesworth did not forgive the butty these public-house sayings. Consequently, although Morel was a good miner, sometimes earning as much as five pounds a week when he married, he came gradually to have worse and worse stalls, where the coal was thin, and hard to get, and unprofitable.

A butty is a contractor. Two or three butties are given a certain length along a seam of coal, which they are to mine forward to a certain distance. They were paid something like 3/4 for every ton of coal they turned out. Out of this, they had to pay the men, holers and loaders, whom they hired by the day, and also for tools, powder, and so on. If their stall was a good one, and the pit was turning full time, then they got a hundred or two tons of coal out, and made good money. If their stall was a poor one, they might work just as hard, and earn very little. Morel, for thirty years of his life, never had a good stall. But, as his wife said, it was his own fault.

Also, in summer, the pits are slack. Often, on bright sunny mornings, the men are seen trooping home again at ten, eleven, or twelve-o'clock. No empty trucks stand at the pit mouth. The women on the hill side look across as they shake the hearthrug against the fence, and count the wagons the engine is taking along the line up the valley, to the pits.

"Seven," they say to each other, "either for Minton or Spinney Park. That's a fat lot to keep a pit going."

And the children, as they come from school at dinner-time, looking down the fields and seeing the wheels on the headstocks standing, say:

"Minton's knocked off. My dad'll be at home."

And there is a sort of shadow over all, women and children and men, because money will be short at the end of the week.

Morel was supposed to give his wife thirty shillings a week, to provide everything, rent, food, clothes, clubs, insurance, doctors. Occasionally, if he were flush, he gave her thirty five. But these occasions by no means balanced those when he gave her twenty five. In winter, with a decent stall, the miner might earn fifty or fifty five shillings a week. Then he was happy. On Friday night, Saturday, and Sunday, he spent royally, getting rid of his sovereign or thereabouts. And out of so much, he scarcely spared the children an extra penny, or bought them a pound of apples. It all went in drink. In the bad times, matters were more worrying, but he was not so often drunk, so that Mrs Morel used to say:

"I'm not sure I wouldn't rather be short, for when he's flush, there isn't a minute of peace."

If he earned forty shillings, he kept ten; from thirty five, he kept five; from thirty two, he kept four; from twenty eight, he kept three; from twenty four, he kept two; from twenty, he kept one and six; from eighteen, he kept a shilling; from sixteen, he kept sixpence. He never saved a penny, and he gave his wife no opportunity of saving; instead, she had occasionally to pay his debts; not public-house debts, for those never were passed on to the women, but debts when he had bought a canary, or a fancy walking-stick.

At the Wakes time, Morel was working badly, and Mrs Morel was trying to save against her confinement. So, it galled her bitterly to think he should be out taking his pleasure and spending money, whilst she remained at home, harassed. There were two days holiday. On the Tuesday morning, Morel rose early. He was in good spirits. Quite early, before six o'clock she heard him whistling away to himself downstairs. He had a pleasant way of whistling, lively and musical. He nearly always whistled hymns. He had been a choir-boy with a beautiful voice, and had taken solos in Southwell cathedral. His morning whistling alone betrayed it.

His wife lay listening to him tinkering away in the garden, his whistling ringing out as he sawed and hammered away. It always gave her a sense of warmth and peace to hear him thus as she lay in bed, the children not yet awake, in the bright early morning happy in his man's fashion.

At nine o'clock, while the children with bare legs and feet were sitting playing on the sofa, and the mother was washing up, he came in from his carpentry, his sleeves rolled up, his waistcoat hanging open. He was still a good looking man, with black, wavy hair, and a large black moustache. His face was perhaps too much inflamed, and there was about him a look almost of peevishness. But now he was jolly. He went straight to the sink where his wife was washing up.

"What, are thee there!" he said boisterously. "Sluther off an' let me wesh my-sen."

"You may wait till I've finished," said his wife.

"Oh mun I?—An' what if I shonna?"

This good-humoured threat amused Mrs Morel.

"Then you can go and wash yourself in the soft water tub."

"Ha! I can an' a', tha mucky little 'ussy."

With which he stood watching her a moment, then went away to wait for her.

When he chose, he could still make himself again a real 'gallant.' Usually he preferred to go out with a scarf round his neck. Now, however, he made a toilet. There seemed so much gusto in the way he puffed and swilled as he washed himself, so much alacrity with which he hurried to the mirror in the kitchen, and, bending because it was too low for him, scrupulously parted his wet black hair, that it irritated Mrs Morel. He put on a turn-down collar, a black bow, and wore his Sunday tail coat. As such, he looked spruce, and what his clothes would not do, his instinct for making the most of his good looks would.

At half-past nine Jerry Purdy came to call for his pal. Jerry was Morel's bosom friend, and Mrs Morel disliked him. He was a tall thin man, with a rather foxy face, the kind of face that seems to lack eyelashes. He walked with a stiff, brittle dignity, as if his head were on a wooden spring. His nature was cold and shrewd. Generous where he intended to be generous, he seemed to be very fond of Morel, and more or less to take charge of him.

Mrs Morel hated him. She had known his wife, who had died of consumption, and who had, at the end, conceived such a violent dislike of her husband, that if he came into her room it caused her hemorrhage. None of which Jerry had seemed to mind. And now his eldest daughter, a girl of fifteen, kept a poor house for him, and looked after the two younger children.

"A mean, wizzen-hearted stick!" Mrs Morel said of him.

"I've niver known Jerry mean in *my* life," protested Morel. "A opener-handed and more freer chap you couldn't find anywhere, accordin' to my knowledge."

"Open-handed to you," retorted Mrs Morel. "But his fist is shut tight enough to his children, poor things."

"Poor things!—and what for are they poor things, I should like to know."

But Mrs Morel would not be appeased on Jerry's score.

The subject of argument was seen, craning his thin neck over the scullery curtain. He caught Mrs Morel's eye.

"Mornin' missis!—mester in?"

"Yes—he is."

Jerry entered unasked and stood by the kitchen doorway. He was not invited to sit down, but stood there, coolly asserting the rights of men and husbands.

"A nice day," he said to Mrs Morel.

"Yes."

"Grand out this morning—grand for a walk."

"Do you mean *you're* going for a walk?" she asked.

"Yes. We mean walkin' to Nottingham," he replied.

"Hm!"

The two men greeted each other, both glad, Jerry however full of assurance, Morel rather subdued, afraid to seem too jubilant in presence of his wife. But he laced his boots quickly, with spirit. They were going for a ten mile walk across the fields to Nottingham. Climbing the hillside from the Bottoms, they mounted gaily into the morning. At the Moon and Stars they had their first drink, then on to the 'Old Spot.' Then a long five miles of drought, to carry them into Bulwell to a glorious pint of bitter. But they stayed in a field with some haymakers whose gallon bottle was full, so that, when they came in sight of the city, Morel was sleepy. The town spread upwards before them, smoking vaguely in the midday glare, fridging the crest away to the south with spires and factory bulks and chimneys. In the last field Morel lay down under an oak-tree and slept soundly for over an hour. When he rose to go forward, he felt queer.

The two had dinner in the Meadows, with Jerry's sister, then repaired to the 'Punch Bowl', where they mixed in the excitement of pigeon-racing. Morel never in his life played cards, considering them as having some occult, malevolent power: "the devil's pictures," he called them. But he was a master of skittles and of dominoes. He took a challenge from a Newark man, on skittles. All the men in the old, long bar took sides, betting either one way or the other. Morel took off his coat. Jerry held the hat containing the money. The men at the tables watched. Some stood with their mugs in their hands. Morel felt his big, wooden ball carefully, then launched it. He played havoc among the nine-pins, and won half-a-crown, which restored him to solvency.

By seven o'clock the two were in good condition. They caught the 7.30 train home.

Mrs Morel was depressed and wretched that day. She did what washing she could, but the ponching was too much for her. William tidied up the house for her.

"Should I do anything else, mother?" he asked.

"No, there's nothing for you to do—except take Annie out."

"I don't want to."

"Want or not want, you must."

So the child went out, hampered with his sister, while his mother worked. He was angry with her, for foisting the burden on him, and yet grieved for her, because he knew something was the matter. So, with his love for his mother vexing his young growth, he made the best of things.

In the afternoon, the Bottoms was intolerable. Every inhabitant remaining was out of doors. The women, in twos and threes, bare-headed and in white aprons, gossiped in the alley between the blocks. Men having a rest between drinks, sat on their heels and talked. The place smelled stale, the slate roofs glistered in the arid heat.

Mrs Morel took the little girl down to the brook, in the meadows which were not more than two hundred yards away. The water ran quickly over stones and broken pots. Mother and child leaned on the rail of the old sheep-bridge, watching. Up at the dipping-hole, at the other end of the meadow, Mrs Morel could see the naked forms of boys flashing round the deep yellow water, or an occasional bright figure dart glittering over the blackish, stagnant meadow. She knew William was at the dipping hole, and it was the dread of her life lest he should get drowned. Annie played under the tall old hedge, picking up alder cones, that she called currants. The child required much attention, and the flies were teasing.

The children were put to bed at seven o'clock. Then she worked awhile.

When Walter Morel and Jerry arrived at Bestwood, they felt a load off their minds: a railway journey no longer impended, so they could put the finishing touches to a glorious day. They entered the 'Nelson' with the satisfaction of returned travellers. Mrs Morel always said the after-life would hold nothing in store for her husband: he rose from the lower world into purgatory, when he came home from pit, and passed on to heaven in the Palmerston Arms.

As it grew cooler, the little garden at the Bottoms became fragrant. Mrs Morel went out to look at the flowers and to breathe the evening. Mrs Kirk, her neighbour, was not at home, or the two might have talked together. So she was alone. The black swifts, that the children call 'devilins,' darted to and fro like black arrow-heads just above her, veering round the corner of the house, flying in at the broad eaves, then slipping out again and darting down the air with little cries, that seem to come out of the light, not from the noiseless birds. Some one had trodden the stone-crop, that was littered over with fallen white rose-leaves. She stooped and brushed it up to raise its little yellow heads again.

The next day was a work-day, and the thought of it put a damper on the men's spirits. Most of them, moreover, had spent their money. Some were already rolling dismally home, to sleep in preparation for the morrow. Mrs Morel, listening to their mournful singing, went indoors. Nine o'clock passed, and ten, and still "the pair" had not returned. On a doorstep somewhere, a man was singing loudly, in a drawl, "Lead Kindly Light." Mrs Morel was always indignant with the drunken men, that they must sing that hymn when they got maudlin.

"As if 'Geneviève' weren't good enough," she said.

The kitchen was full of the scent of boiled herbs and hops. On the hob, a large black saucepan steamed slowly. Mrs Morel took a panchion, a great bowl of thick red earth, streamed a heap of white sugar into the bottom, and then, straining herself to the weight, was pouring in the liquor.

Just then, Morel came in. He had been very jolly in the 'Nelson', but coming home had grown irritable. He had not quite got over the feeling of irritability and pain, after having slept on the ground when he was so hot; and a bad conscience afflicted him as he neared the house. He did not know he was angry. But when the garden gate resisted his attempts to open it, he kicked it and broke the latch. He entered just as Mrs Morel was pouring the infusion of herbs out of the saucepan. Swaying slightly, he lurched against the table. The boiling liquor pitched. Mrs Morel started back.

"Good gracious," she cried, "coming home in his drunkenness!"

"Comin' home in his what——?" he snarled, his hat over his eye.

Suddenly her blood rose in a jet.

"Say you're *not* drunk!" she flashed.

She had put down her saucepan, and was stirring the sugar into the beer. He dropped his two hands heavily on the table, and thrust his face forward at her.

"'Say you're not drunk'" he repeated. "Why, nobody but a nasty little bitch like you 'ud 'ave such a thought."

"Well you've been boozing all day, so if you're not drunk by eleven o'clock at night——" she replied, continuing to stir.

31

"I've not been boozing all day—I've *not* been boozing all day—it's where you make your mistake," he said, snarling.

"It looks as if I made a mistake," she replied.

"Does it—does it—Oh—Oh indeed!—oh!"

"Goes out at nine in the morning, comes rolling home at midnight. Besides, we know well enough what you do when you go out with your beautiful Jerry."

"'Your beautiful Jerry'—what?—why wha 'r' yer talkin' about, woman—eh?—what?"

He thrust his face forward at her.

"There's money to bezzle with, if there's money for nothing else."

"I've not spent a two-shillin' bit this day," he said.

"You don't get as drunk as a lord on nothing," she replied. "And," she cried, flashing into sudden fury, "if you've been sponging on your beloved Jerry, why, let him look after his children, for they need it."

"'Let 'im look after his children'.—Why, what children's better looked after than hisn, I sh'd like to know."

"My sirs, not yours, if *you* had the looking after to do.—A man that can afford to swill his belly from morn till night—"

"It's a lie, it's a lie," he cried, breaking into rage and banging the table.

"—Can't afford to keep his children," she continued.

"What's it got to do wi' you?" he shouted.

"'Got to do with me?'—why, a good deal.—Gives me a miserable twenty-five shillings to do everything with, and goes jaunting off for the day, coming rolling home at midnight—"

"It's a lie, woman, it's a lie!"

"And thinks I'm going to go on scraping and pedgilling and contriving, while he guzzles and swills and jaunts to Nottingham carousing—"

"It's a lie, it's a lie—shut your face woman."

They were now at battle pitch. Each forgot everything save the hatred of the other, and the battle between them. She was fiery and furious as he. They went on till he called her a liar.

"No," she cried, starting up scarce able to breathe. "Don't call *me* that—you, the most despicable liar that ever walked in shoe-leather." She forced the last words out of suffocated lungs.

"You're a liar!" he yelled, banging the table with his fist. "You're a liar, you're a liar."

She stiffened herself, with clenched fists.

"I'd smite you down, you cowardly beast, if only I could," she said, in low, quivering tones.

Then, in the next wave, came out her passionate loathing of him. He raged at her, and banged the table till the house rang, while she poured over him all her contempt and hate of him.

"The house is filthy with you," she cried.

"Then get out on it—it's mine. Get out on it," he shouted. "It's ma as brings th' money whoam, not thee. It's my house, not thine. Then ger out on't—ger out on't!"

"And I would," she cried, suddenly shaken into tears of impotence. "Ah, wouldn't I, wouldn't I have gone long, long ago, but for those children. Ay, haven't I repented not going years ago, when I'd only the one—" suddenly drying into rage. "Do you think it's for *you* I stop—do you think I'd stop one minute for *you*—"

"Go then," he shouted, beside himself. "Go!"

"No!" she faced round. "No," she cried loudly, "you shan't have it *all* your own way: you shan't do *all* you like. I've got those children to see to. My word—" she laughed, "I should look well to leave them to you."

"Go," he cried thickly, lifting his fist. He was afraid of her. "Go!"

"I should be only too glad—I should laugh, laugh, my lord, if I could get away from you," she replied.

He came up to her, his red face, with its blood-shot eyes, thrust forward, and gripped her arms. She cried in fear of him, struggled to be free. Coming slightly to himself, panting, he pushed her roughly to the outer door, and thrust her forth, slotting the bolt behind her with a bang. Then he went back into the kitchen, dropped into his arm-chair, his head, bursting full of blood, sinking between his knees. Thus he dipped gradually into a stupor, from exhaustion and intoxication.

The moon was high and magnificent in the August night. Mrs Morel, seared with passion, shivered to find herself out there in a great, white light, that fell cold on her, and gave a shock to her inflamed soul. She stood for a few moments helplessly staring at the glistening great rhubarb leaves near the door. Then she got the air into her breast. She walked down the garden path, trembling in every limb, while the child boiled within her. For a while, she could not control her consciousness; mechanically she went over the last scene, then over it again, certain phrases, certain moments coming each time like a brand red hot, down on her soul: and each time she enacted again the past hour, each time the brand came down at the same points, till the mark was burnt in, and the pain burnt out, and at last she came to herself. She must have been half an hour in this delirious condition. Then the presence of the night came again to her. She glanced round in fear. She had wandered to the side garden, where she was walking up and down the path beside the currant bushes under the long wall. The garden was a narrow strip, bounded from the road that cut transversely between the blocks, by a thick thorn hedge.

She hurried out of the side garden to the front, where she could stand as if in an immense gulf of white light, the moon streaming high in face of her, the moonlight standing up from the hills in front, and filling the valley where the Bottoms crouched, almost blindingly. There, panting and half weeping in reaction from the stress, she murmured to herself over and again: "The nuisance!—the nuisance!"

She became aware of something about her. With an effort, she roused herself, to see what it was that penetrated her consciousness. The tall white lilies were reeling in the moonlight, and the air was charged with their perfume, as with a presence. Mrs Morel gasped slightly in fear. She touched the big, pallid flowers on their petals, then shivered. They seemed to be stretching in the moonlight. She put her hand into one white bin: the gold scarcely showed on her fingers by moonlight. She bent down, to look at the bin-ful of yellow pollen: but it only appeared dusky. Then she drank a deep draught of the scent. It almost made her dizzy.

She looked round her. The privet hedge had a faint glitter among its blackness. Various white flowers were out. In front, the hill rose into indistinctness, barred by high black hedges, and nervous with cattle moving in the dim moonlight. Here and there the moonlight seemed to stir and ripple.

Mrs Morel leaned on the garden gate, looking out, and she lost herself awhile. She did not know what she thought. Except for a slight feeling of sickness, and her consciousness in the child, her self melted out like scent into the shiny, pale air. After a time, the child too melted with her in the mixing-pot of moonlight, and she rested with the hills and lilies and houses, all swum together in a kind of swoon.

When she came to herself, she was tired for sleep. Languidly, she looked about her; the clumps of white phlox seemed like bushes spread with linen; a moth ricochetted over them, and right across the garden. Following it with her eye roused her. A few whiffs of the raw strong scent of phlox invigorated her. She passed along the path hesitating at the white rose-bush. It smelled sweet and simple. She touched the white ruffles of the roses. Their fresh scent and cool, soft leaves reminded her of the morning-time and sunshine. She was very fond of them. But she was tired and wanted to sleep. In the mysterious out-of-doors she felt forlorn.

There was no noise anywhere. Evidently the children had not been wakened, or had gone to sleep again. A train, three miles away, roared across the valley. The night was very large, and very strange, stretching its hoary distances infinitely. And out of the silver-grey fog of darkness came sounds vague and hoarse: a corncrake not far off, sound of a train like a sigh, and distant shouts of men.

Her quietened heart beginning to beat quickly again, she hurried down the side garden to the back of the house. Softly, she lifted the latch: the door was still bolted, shut hard against her. She rapped gently, waited, then rapped again. She must not rouse the children, nor the neighbours. He must be asleep, and he would not wake easily. Her heart began to burn to be indoors. She clung to the door-handle. Now, it was cold: she would take a chill, and in her present condition!

Putting her apron over her head and her arms, she hurried again to the side garden, to the window of the kitchen. Leaning on the sill, she could just see, under the blind, her husband's arms spread out on the table, and his black head on the board. He was sleeping with his face lying on the table. Something in his attitude made her feel tired of things. The lamp was burning smokily, she could tell by the copper colour of the light. She tapped at the window more and more noisily. Almost it seemed as if the glass would break. Still he did not wake up.

After vain efforts, she began to shiver, partly from contact with the stone, and from exhaustion. Fearful always for the unborn child, she wondered what she could do for warmth. She went down to the coal-house, where was an old hearth-rug she had carried out for the rag-man the day before. This she wrapped over her shoulders. It was warm, if grimy. Then she walked up and down the garden path, peeping every now and then under the blind, knocking, and telling herself that in the end the very strain of his position must wake him.

35

At last, after about an hour, she rapped long and low at the window. Gradually the sound penetrated to him. When in despair she had ceased to tap, she saw him stir, then lift his face blindly. The labouring of his heart hurt him into consciousness. She rapped imperatively at the window. He started awake. Instantly she saw his fists set and his eyes glare. He had not a grain of physical fear. If it had been twenty burglars, he would have gone blindly for them. He glared round, bewildered, but prepared to fight.

"Open the door Walter," she said coldly.

His hands relaxed—it dawned on him what he had done. His head dropped, sullen and dogged. She saw him hurry to the door, heard the bolt chock. He tried the latch. It opened—and there stood the silver grey night, fearful to him, after the tawny light of the lamp. He hurried back.

When Mrs Morel entered, she saw him almost running through the door to the stairs. He had ripped his collar off his neck, in his haste to be gone ere she came in, and there it lay with bursten button-holes. It made her angry.

She warmed and soothed herself. In her weariness forgetting everything, she moved about at the little tasks that remained to be done, set his breakfast, rinsed his pit-bottle, put his pit-clothes on the hearth to warm, set his pit-boots beside them, put him out a clean scarf and snap-bag and two apples, raked the fire and went to bed. He was already dead asleep. His narrow black eyebrows were drawn up in a sort of peevish misery, into his forehead, while his cheek's downstrokes, and his sulky mouth, seemed to be saying: "I don't care who you are nor what you are, I *shall* have my own way."

Mrs Morel knew him too well to look at him. As she unfastened her brooch at the mirror, she smiled faintly to see her face all smeared with the yellow dust of lilies. She brushed it off, and at last lay down. For some time her mind continued snapping and jetting sparks, but she was asleep before her husband awoke from the first sleep of his drunkenness.

CHAPTER II

The Birth of Paul, and another Battle

After such a scene as the last, Walter Morel was for some days abashed and ashamed, but he soon regained his old bullying indifference. Yet there was a slight shrinking, a diminishing in his assurance. Physically even, he shrank, and his fine full presence waned. He never grew in the least stout, so that, as he sank from his erect, assertive bearing, his physique seemed to contract along with his pride and moral strength.

But now he realised how hard it was for his wife to drag about at her work and, his sympathy quickened by penitence, hastened forward with his help. He came straight home from the pit, and stayed in at evening—till Friday, and then he could not remain at home. But he was back again by ten o'clock, almost quite sober.

He always made his own breakfast. Being a man who rose early and had plenty of time, he did not, as some miners do, drag his wife out of bed at six o'clock. At five, sometimes earlier, he woke, got straight out of bed and went downstairs. When she could not sleep, his wife lay waiting for this time, as for a period of peace. The only real rest seemed to be when he was out of the house.

He went downstairs in his shirt, and then struggled into his pit-trousers, which were left on the hearth to warm all night. There was always a fire, because Mrs Morel raked. And the first sound in the house was the bang, bang of the poker against the raker, as Morel smashed the remainder of the coal to make the kettle, which was filled and left on the hob, finally boil. His cup and knife and fork, all he wanted except just the food, was laid ready on the table on a newspaper. Then he got his breakfast, made the tea, packed the bottom of the doors with rugs to shut out the draught, piled a big fire, and sat down to an hour of joy. He toasted his bacon on a fork and caught the drops of fat on his bread. Then he put the rasher on his thick slice of bread, and cut off chunks with a clasp knife, poured his tea into his saucer, and was happy. With his family about, meals were never so pleasant. He loathed a fork. It is a modern introduction which has still scarcely reached the common people. What

37

Morel preferred was a clasp knife. Then, in solitude, he ate, and drank, often sitting, in cold weather, on a little stool with his back to the warm chimney piece, his food on the fender, his cup on the hearth. And then he read the last night's newspaper, what of it he could, spelling it over laboriously. He preferred to keep the blinds down and the candle lit, even when it was daylight. It was the habit of the mine.

At a quarter to six he rose, cut two thick slices of bread and butter, and put them in the white calico snap-bag. He filled his tin bottle with tea. Cold tea without milk or sugar was the drink he preferred for the pit. Then he pulled off his shirt, and put on his pit-singlet, a vest of thick flannel cut low round the neck, and with short sleeves like a chemise.

Then he went upstairs to his wife, with a cup of tea because she was ill, and because it occurred to him.

"I've browght thee a sup o' tea, lass," he said.

"Well you needn't, for you know I don't like it," she replied.

"Drink it up, it'll pop thee off to sleep again."

She accepted the tea. It pleased him to see her take it and sip it.

"I'll back my life there's no sugar in," she said.

"Yi—there's one big un," he replied, injured.

"It's a wonder," she said, sipping again.

She had a winsome face when her hair was loose. He loved her to grumble at him in this manner. He looked at her again, and went, without any sort of leave taking. He never took more than two slices of bread and butter to eat in the pit, so an apple or an orange was a treat to him. He always liked it when she put one out for him. He tied a scarf round his neck, put on his great, heavy boots, his coat with the big pocket that carried his snap-bag and his bottle of tea, and went forth into the fresh, morning air, closing without locking the door behind him. He loved the early morning. He always left the house at six, though the men were not turned down till about seven, and he had only a half hour's walk. Usually he went over the fields, and often, in summer, would look in the gin-close for mushrooms, straying through the thick wet grass in his pit-boots, looking for the lurking, white-fleshed things. If he found any, he stowed them carefully in his pocket. It scarcely seemed hard to him, to leave the fresh, cool air of morning, and go down. He was so used to it, it came simply and naturally. So he appeared at the pit top, often with a stalk from the hedge between his teeth, which he chewed all day to keep his mouth moist, down the mine, feeling quite as happy as when he was in the field.

Later, when the time for the baby grew nearer, he would bustle round in his slovenly fashion, poking out the ashes, rubbing the fire-place, sweeping the house before he went to work. Then, feeling very self-righteous, he went upstairs.

"Now I'n cleaned up for thee: that's no 'casions ter stir a peg all day, but sit and read thy books."

Which made her laugh, in spite of her indignation.

"And the dinner cooks itself?" she answered.

"Eh, I know nowt about th' dinner."

"You'd know if there weren't any."

"Ay, 'appen so," he answered, departing.

When she got downstairs, she would find the house tidy, but dirty. She could not rest until she had thoroughly cleaned. As she went down to the ash-pit with her dust-pan, Mrs Kirk, spying her, would contrive to have to go to her own coal-place at that minute. Then, across the wooden fence, she would call:

"So you keep wagging on then?"

"Ay," answered Mrs Morel, deprecatingly. "There's nothing else for it."

Mrs Kirk was a thin, nervous woman, apt to be hysterical. Mrs Morel liked her. The two women came together, one on either side of the fence, each holding her dust-pan, and they talked for awhile. Then:

"You may go on till you drop," said Mrs Kirk. "Won't your mester do a bit for you? Tom's not bad that way."

"Ay," answered the neighbour, "he came up this morning to tell me he'd cleaned up, so I'd nothing to do all day but sit and read."

"Eh, but isn't men great gawps!" exclaimed Mrs Kirk.

"And I found the fire-place thick with silt, and all th' dirt under the hearthrug."

Mrs Kirk laughed, her thin face showing her teeth.

"It's allers alike," she said. "They smarm a brush an' a duster across, an' bless you, it'll do for them."

"They don't care how they pig it," said Mrs Morel.

"They don't. Our Tom's just the same."

"All alike," said Mrs Morel.

"You've 'eered about Mrs Allsop?"

"No."

"Not?—her's has come."

"You don't mean it! When?"

"Night afore last—after that thunderstorm—"

"What—!"

And both women laughed heartily.

. . . . .

"Have you seen Hose," called a very small woman from across the road. It was Mrs Anthony, a black haired, strange little body, who always wore a brown velvet dress, tight fitting.

"I haven't," said Mrs Morel.

"Eh, I wish he'd come. I've got a copperful of clothes, an' I'm sure I heered his bell."

"Hark—he's at the end."

The two women looked down the Alley. At the end of the Bottoms a man stood in a sort of old-fashioned trap, bending over bundles of cream-coloured stuff, while a cluster of women held up their arms to him, some with bundles. Mrs Anthony herself had a heap of creamy, undyed stockings hanging over her arm.

"I've done ten dozen this week," she said proudly to Mrs Morel.

"T-t-t!" went the other. "I don't know how you can find time."

"Eh!" said Mrs Anthony. "You can find time if you make time."

"I don't know how you do it," said Mrs Morel. "And how much shall you get for those many?"

"Tuppence-ha'penny a dozen," replied the other.

"Well!" said Mrs Morel, "I'd starve before I'd sit down and seam twenty four stockings for twopence ha'penny."

"Oh I don't know," said Mrs Anthony. "You can rip along with 'em."

. . . . .

'Hose' was coming along, ringing his bell. Women were waiting at the yard-ends with their seamed stockings hanging over their arms. The man, a common fellow, made jokes with them, tried to swindle them, and bullied them. Mrs Morel went up her yard disdainfully.

It was an understood thing that if one woman wanted her neighbour, she should put the poker in the fire and bang at the back of the fire-place, which, as the fires were back to back, would make a great noise in the adjoining house. One morning Mrs Kirk, mixing a pudding, nearly started out of her skin as she heard the thud, thud, in her grate. With her hands all floury, she rushed to the fence.

"Did you knock, Mrs Morel?"

"If you wouldn't mind, Mrs Kirk."

Mrs Kirk climbed onto her copper, got over the wall onto Mrs Morel's copper, and ran in to her neighbour.

"Eh dear, how are you feeling?" she cried in concern.

"You might fetch Mrs Bower," said Mrs Morel.

Mrs Kirk went into the yard, lifted up her strong, shrill voice, and called:

"Ag-gie—Ag-gie!"

The sound was heard from one end of the Bottoms to the other. At last, Aggie came running up, and was sent for Mrs Bower, whilst Mrs Kirk left her pudding and stayed with her neighbour.

Mrs Morel went to bed. Mrs Kirk had Annie and William for dinner. Mrs Bower, fat and waddling, bossed the house.

"Hash some cold meat up for the master's dinner, and make him an apple-charlotte pudding," said Mrs Morel.

"He may go without pudding *this* day," said Mrs Bower.

Morel was not as a rule one of the first to appear at the bottom of the pit, ready to come up. Some men were there before four o'clock, when the whistle blew loose-all. But Morel, whose stall, a poor one, was at this time about a mile and a half away from the bottom, worked usually till the first mate stopped, then he finished also. This day, however, the miner was sick of the work. At two o'clock he looked at his watch, by the light of the green candle—he was in a safe working—and again at half past two. He was hewing at a piece of rock that was in the way for the next day's work. As he sat on his heels, or kneeled, giving hard blows with his pick, 'Uszza—uszza!' he went.

"Shall ter finish, *Sorry?" cried Barker, his fellow butty.

"Finish—niver while the world stands!" growled Morel.

And he went on striking. He was tired.

"It's a heart-breaking job," said Barker.

But Morel was too exasperated, at the end of his tether, to answer. Still he struck and hacked with all his might.

"Tha might as well leave it, Walter," said Barker. "It'll do tomorrow, without thee hackin' thy guts out."

"I s'll lay no b— finger on this tomorrow, Isr'el," cried Morel.

"Oh well, if tha wunna, someb'dy else'll ha'e to," said Israel.

Then Morel continued to strike.

"Hey-up theer—*loose-a*'," cried the men, leaving the next stall.

* ('Sorry' is a common form of address. It is perhaps a corruption of 'Sirrah'.)

Morel continued to strike.

"Tha'll happen catch me up," said Barker, departing.

When he had gone, Morel, left alone, felt savage. He had not finished his job. He had overworked himself into a frenzy. Rising, wet with sweat, he threw his tool down, pulled on his coat, blew out his candle, took his lamp and went. Down the main road, the lights of the other men went swinging. There was a hollow sound of many voices. It was a long, heavy tramp underground.

He sat at the bottom of the pit, where the great drops of water fell plash. Many colliers were waiting their turns to go up, talking noisily. Morel gave his answers short and disagreeable.

"It's rainin', Sorry," said old Giles, who had had the news from the top. Morel found one comfort. He had his old umbrella, which he loved, in the lamp cabin. At last he took his stand on the chair, and was at the top in a moment. Then he handed in his lamp and got his umbrella, which he had bought at an auction for one-and-six. He stood on the edge of the pit-bank for a moment, looking out. Over the fields, grey rain was falling. The trucks stood full of wet, bright coal. Water ran down the sides of the wagons, over the white C. W. & Co. Colliers, walking indifferent to the rain, were streaming down the line and up the field, a grey, dismal host. Morel put up his umbrella, and took pleasure from the peppering of the drops thereon.

All along the road to Bestwood, the miners tramped, wet and grey and dirty, but their red mouths talking with animation. Morel also walked with a gang, but he said nothing. He frowned peevishly as he went. Many men passed into the Prince of Wales, or into Ellen's. Morel, feeling sufficiently disagreeable to resist temptation, trudged along under the dripping trees that overhung the park wall, and down the mud of Greenhill Lane.

Mrs Morel lay in bed, listening to the rain, and the feet of the colliers from Minton, their voices, and the bang! bang!! of the gates as they went through the stile up the field.

"There's some herb beer behind the pantry door," she said. "Th' master 'll want a drink, if he doesn't stop."

But he was late, so she concluded he had called for a drink, since it was raining. What did he care about the child or her.

She was very ill when her children were born.

"What is it?" she asked, feeling sick to death.

"A boy."

And she took consolation in that. The thought of being the mother of men was warming to her heart. She looked at the child. It had blue eyes, and a lot of fair hair, and was bonny. Her love came up hot, in spite of everything. She had it in bed with her.

Morel, thinking nothing, dragged his way up the garden path, wearily, and angrily. He closed his umbrella, and stood it in the sink. Then he sluthered his heavy boots into the kitchen. Mrs Bower appeared in the inner doorway.

"Well," she said, "she's about as bad as she can be.—It's a boy-childt."

The miner grunted, put his empty snap-bag and his tin bottle on the dresser, went back into the scullery and hung up his coat, then came and dropped into his chair.

"Han yer got a drink?" he asked.

The woman went into the pantry. There was heard the pop of a cork. She set the mug with a little, disgusted rap, on the table before Morel. He drank, gasped, wiped his big moustache on the end of his scarf, drank, gasped, and lay back in his chair. The woman would not speak to him again—she set his dinner before him, and went upstairs.

"Was that the master?" asked Mrs Morel.

"I've gave him his dinner," replied Mrs Bower.

After he had sat with his arms on the table—he resented the fact that Mrs Bower put no cloth on for him, and gave him a little plate, instead of a full sized dinner-plate—he began to eat. The fact that his wife was ill, that he had another boy, was nothing to him at that moment. He was too tired, he wanted his dinner, he wanted to sit with his arms lying on the board, he did not like having Mrs Bower about. The fire was too small to please him.

After he had finished his meal, he sat for twenty minutes. Then he stoked up a big fire. Then, in his stocking feet, he went reluctantly upstairs. It was a struggle to face his wife at this moment, and he was tired. His face was black, and smeared with sweat. His singlet had dried again, soaking the dirt in. He had a dirty woollen scarf round his throat. So, he stood at the foot of the bed.

"Well, how are ter then?" he asked.

"I s'll be all right," she answered.

"Hm!"

He stood at a loss what to say next. He was tired, and this bother was rather a nuisance to him, and he didn't quite know where he was.

"A lad, tha says," he stammered.

She turned down the sheet and showed the child.

"Bless him!" he murmured. Which made her laugh, because he blessed by rote—pretending paternal emotion, which he did not feel just then.

"Go now," she said.

"I will my lass," he answered, turning away.

Dismissed, he wanted to kiss her, but he dared not. She half wanted him to kiss her, but could not bring herself to give any signs. She only breathed freely when he was gone out of the room again, leaving behind him a faint smell of pit-dirt.

Mrs Morel had a visit every day from the Congregational clergyman. Mr Heaton was young, and very poor. His wife had died at the birth of his first baby, so he remained alone in the manse. He was a Bachelor of Arts of Cambridge, very shy, and no preacher. Mrs Morel was fond of him, and he depended on her. For hours, he talked to her, when she was well. He became the god-parent of the child.

The mother lay in bed thinking of her children. As she had no life of her own, but was busy from morning till night cleaning, cooking, nursing, and sewing, she had to put her own living aside, put it in the bank, as it were, of her children. She thought and waited for them, dreamed what they would do, with herself behind them as motor force, when they grew up. Already William was a lover to her. If she had neuralgia, from which she suffered badly at times, and she was pale and silent at her work:

"Have you got toothache mother?" he asked.

"Yes."

"Is it awful?"

She laughed, in spite of the pain. But sometimes, when she was suckling the baby, it was so bad she could scarcely move. Then her eldest son would be found lying weeping bitterly to himself in the front room, and when his father asked:

"Whativer's a matter, my duckie?" he replied:

"My mother's got toothache."

"Well," Mrs Morel would say, when she heard him, "*you* haven't got it, silly, so what are you crying for?"

Then he did not like the new baby.

"He looks nasty, mother," he said.

"Why?" asked the mother.

"He scowls," said William.

Then Mrs Morel kissed the baby quickly. It had a peculiar pucker on the forehead, as if something had startled its tiny consciousness before birth. When Mrs Morel looked at the infant, something hurt her, inside. But the baby was good. Often she sat singing nursery rhymes to it.

"He can't understand you, what do you sing to him for?" said William.

"Well, he likes the noise, I'm sure," said the mother, laughing with her rare warmth shining in her blue eyes, at the baby, worrying the tiny fingers with her lips; while William stood aside and fumed.

Occasionally the minister stayed to tea with Mrs Morel. Then she laid the cloth early, got out her best cups, with a little green rim, and hoped Morel would not come too soon. Indeed, if he stayed for a pint, she would not mind this day. She had always two dinners to cook, because she believed children should have their chief meal at mid-day, whereas Morel needed his at five o'clock. So Mr Heaton would hold the baby, whilst Mrs Morel beat up a batter pudding or peeled the potatoes, and he, watching her all the time, would discuss his next sermon. His ideas were quaint and fantastic, she brought him judiciously to earth. It was a discussion of the Wedding at Cana.

"When He changed the water into wine at Cana," he said, "that is a symbol, that the ordinary life, even the blood, of the married husband and wife, which had before been uninspired, like water, became filled with the spirit, and was as wine, because, when love enters, the whole spiritual constitution of a man changes, is filled with the Holy Ghost, and almost his form is altered."

Mrs Morel thought to herself:

"Yes, poor fellow, his young wife is dead; that is why he makes his love into the Holy Ghost."

"No," she said aloud, "don't make things into symbols. Say: 'It was a wedding, and the wine ran out. Then the father-in-law was put about, because there was nothing to offer the guests, except water—there was no tea, no coffee, in those days, only wine. And how would he like to see all the people sitting with glasses of water in front of them. The host and his wife were ashamed, the bride was miserable, and the bridegroom was disagreeable. And Jesus saw them whispering together, and looking worried. And He knew they were poor. They were only, perhaps, farm-labouring people. So He thought to himself "What a shame!—all the wedding spoiled." And so He made wine, as quickly as he could.'—You can say, wine isn't beer, not so intoxicating—and people in the East never get drunk. It's getting drunk makes beer so bad."

The poor man looked at her. He wanted badly to say how human love is the presence of the Holy Ghost, making the lovers divine and immortal. Mrs Morel insisted on his making the bible real to the people, and on his having only bits of his own stuff in between. They both were very excited, and very happy. Suddenly William appeared.

"Goodness!" exclaimed Mrs Morel, "is it so late?"

She popped the kettle on, and hurried with the only clean cloth, hoping her husband would not be early. William and Annie, with a piece of bread and butter each, went to play in the street. There were radishes and jam and marmalade for tea. Everything looked clean and pretty. Mrs Morel was happy, bullying her clergyman over his sermons, sitting at tea with a gentleman, who passed her the bread and butter, who waited for her to begin.

They were half way down their first cup of tea when they heard the sluther of pit-boots.

"Good gracious!" exclaimed Mrs Morel, in spite of herself.

The minister looked rather scared. Morel entered. He was feeling rather savage. He nodded a 'How d'yer do' to the clergyman, who rose to shake hands with him.

"Nay," said Morel, showing his hand, "look thee at it! Tha niver wants ter shake hands wi' a hand like that, does ter? There's too much pick-haft and shovel dirt on it."

The minister flushed with confusion, and sat down again. Mrs Morel rose, carried out the steaming saucepan. Morel took off his coat, dragged his arm-chair to table, and sat down, heavily.

"Are you tired?" asked the clergyman.

"Tired—I ham that," replied Morel. "*You* don't know what it is to be tired, as *I'm* tired."

"No," replied the clergyman.

"Why look yer 'ere," said the miner, showing the shoulders of his singlet. "It's a bit dry now, but it's wet as a clout with sweat even yet. Feel it."

"Goodness!" cried Mrs Morel. "Mr Heaton doesn't want to feel your nasty singlet."

The clergyman put out his hand gingerly.

"No, perhaps he doesn't," said Morel. "But it's all come out of *me*, whether or not. An' iv'ry day alike my singlet's wringing wet.— 'Aven't you got a drink, Missis, for a man when he comes home barkled up from the pit."

"You know you drank all the beer,' said Mrs Morel, pouring out his tea.

"An' was there no more to be got?"—turning to the clergyman. "A man gets that caked up wi' th' dust, you know, that clogged up, down a coal mine, he *needs* a drink when he comes home."

"I am sure he does," said the clergyman.

"But it's ten to one if there's owt for him."

"There's water—and there's tea," said Mrs Morel.

"Water—it's not water as'll clear his throat."

He poured out a saucerful of tea, blew it, and sucked it up through his great black moustache, sighing afterwards. Then he poured out another saucerful, and stood his cup on the table.

"My cloth!" said Mrs Morel, putting it on a plate.

"A man as comes home as I do 's too tired to care about cloths," said Morel.

"Pity!" exclaimed his wife, sarcastically.

The room was full of the smell of meat and vegetables, and pit-clothes.

He leaned over to the minister, his great moustache thrust forward, his mouth very red in his black face.

"Mr Heaton," he said, "a man as has been down the black hole all day, dingin' away at a coal face, yi, a sight harder than that wall—"

"Needn't make a moan of it," put in Mrs Morel.

"Needn't he—oh needn't 'e! We know *you'd* rather not hear." Then he turned away from her to the clergyman again. "—he comes home that tired he doesn't know what to do with himself." He looked at his dinner, which stood before him. "Yi, he's too tired to eat his dinner, that he is." Whereupon he laid his arms, black with coal dust, on the white cloth.

"Goodness man, it's a clean cloth!" exclaimed Mrs Morel involuntarily. It was the only clean cloth.

"Am I to have my dinner in the yard, like a dog?" he shouted.

"There was no question of the yard," replied his wife coldly.

He kept his arms on the table cloth.

"When a man's been drivin' a pick into 'ard rock all day, Mister Heaton, his arms is that tired, 'e doesn't know what to do with 'em."

"I can understand it," said the clergyman.

The miner was a sort of strange beast to him.

"There are arms to your chair," said Mrs Morel.

"Yer'd 'ave ter put *your* spoke in, would yer!" her husband said.

She would have scorned to say, how *she* must work and slave. The miner ate with his knife, shovelling the food into his mouth noisily. It made his wife's flesh creep. He was quite regardless of anyone's feelings. After a while he laid his knife down.

"Mester Heaton," he said, "can yer tell me owt for my 'ead?"

"I find cascara—" faltered the minister.

"Tell him to drink less beer and keep his liver in order," said Mrs Morel.

" 'Drink less beer!' " Morel repeated. "Oh!—oh!—everything's the *beer*!—A man happens to drink a glass, Mester Heaton, an' he never hears the last of it."

"I'm glad he drinks a glass," said Mrs Morel.

She hated her husband, because, whenever he had an audience, he whined and played for sympathy. William, sitting nursing the baby, hated him with a boy's hatred for false sentiment, and for the stupid treatment of his mother. Annie had never liked him: she merely avoided him.

When the minister had gone, Mrs Morel looked at her cloth.

"A fine mess!" she said.

"Dos't think I'm goin' to sit wi' my arms danglin', cos tha's got a parson for tea wi' thee?" he bawled.

They were both angry, but she said nothing. The baby began to cry, and Mrs Morel, picking up a saucepan from the hearth, accidentally knocked Annie on the head, whereupon the girl began to whine, and Morel to shout at her. In the midst of this pandemonium, William looked up at the big, glazed text over the mantelpiece and read, distinctly:

"God Bless Our Home."

Whereupon Mrs Morel, trying to soothe the baby, jumped up, rushed at him, boxed his ears, saying:

"What are *you* putting in for?"

And then she sat down and laughed, till tears ran over her cheeks, while William kicked the stool he had been sitting on, and Morel growled:

"I canna see what there is so much to laugh at."

It was about this time Mrs Morel was destroying her husband's authority. Until now, she had felt too much alone to stand away from him. But William was growing up, and all his young soul was his mother's. Annie too was against her father. Finally, there was this last baby. Mrs Morel had hated her husband during the year before it was born. They were poor, and Morel was mean. He had got in with a gang of pals, of whom one was Jerry, who insisted that a man did the work and should have the money wherewith to enjoy himself. They discussed the various degrees of subjection in which their wives were held. Morel found his wife was not sufficiently subdued. After one inflamed evening, when Jerry had been telling him 'not to put up with any b— woman's domineering, what was he a man for?', he shouted at her:

"I'll make you tremble at the sound of my footstep."

It was a historical phrase in her life. She had sat down and laughed till she was quite good-humoured and merry at the idea. He had stood bursting with fury and ignominy. And, by giving her as little money as possible, by drinking much and going out with men who brutalised him and his idea of women, he paid her back. Then she thought, he was taking his pleasure out of the lives of the children, so she threw herself on their side against him.

One evening directly after the parson's visit, feeling unable to bear herself after another display from her husband, she took Annie and the baby and went out. Morel had kicked William, and the mother would never forgive him.

She went over the sheep-bridge and across a corner of the meadow to the cricket ground. The meadows seemed one space of ripe, evening light, whispering with the distant mill-race. She sat on a seat under the alders in the cricket ground, and fronted the evening. Before her, level and solid, spread the big green cricket-field, like the bed of a sea of light. Children played in the bluish shadow of the pavilion. Many rooks, high up, came cawing home across the softly woven sky. They stooped in a long curve down into the golden glow, concentrating, cawing, wheeling like black flakes on a slow vortex, over a tree-clump that made a dark boss among the pasture.

A few gentlemen were practising, and Mrs Morel could hear the chock of the ball, and the voices of men suddenly roused; could see the white forms of men shifting silently over the green, upon which already the under-shadows were smouldering. Away at the grange, one side of the hay-stacks was lit up, the other sides blue-grey. A wagon of sheaves rocked small across the melting yellow light.

The sun was going down. Every open evening, the hills of Derbyshire were blazed over with red sunset. Mrs Morel watched the sun sink from the glistening sky, leaving a soft flower-blue overhead, while the western space went red, as if all the fire had swum down there, leaving the bell cast flawless blue. The mountain-ash berries across the field stood fierily out from the dark leaves, for a moment. A few shocks of corn in a corner of the fallow stood up as if alive: she imagined them bowing: perhaps her son would be a Joseph. In the east, a mirrored sunset floated pink opposite the west's scarlet. The big haystacks on the hill-side that butted into the glare, went cold.

With Mrs Morel, it was one of those still moments when the small frets vanish, and the beauty of things stands out, and she had the peace and the strength to see herself. Now and again, a swallow cut close to her. Now and again, Annie came up with a handful of alder currants. The baby was restless on his mother's knee, clambering with his hands at the light.

Mrs Morel looked down at him. She had dreaded this baby like a catastrophe, because of her feeling for her husband. And now, she felt strangely towards the infant. Her heart was heavy because of the child, almost as if it were unhealthy, or malformed. Yet it seemed quite well. But she noticed the peculiar knitting of the baby's brows, and the peculiar heaviness of its eyes, as if it were trying to understand something that was pain. She felt, when she looked at the child's dark, brooding pupils, as if a burden were on her heart.

"He looks as if he was thinking about something—quite sorrowful," said Mrs Kirk.

Suddenly, looking at him, the heavy feeling at the mother's heart melted into passionate grief. She bowed over him, and a few tears shook swiftly out of her very heart. The baby lifted his fingers.

"My lamb!" she cried, softly.

And at that moment she felt, in some far inner place of her soul, that she and her husband were guilty.

The baby was looking up at her. It had blue eyes like her own, but its look was heavy, steady, as if it had realised something that had stunned some point of its soul.

In her arms lay the delicate baby. Its deep blue eyes, always looking up at her unblinking, seemed to draw her innermost thoughts out of her. She no longer loved her husband; she had not wanted this child to come, and there it lay in her arms and pulled at her heart. She felt as if the navel string that had connected its frail little body with hers had not been broken. A wave of hot love went over her to the infant. She held it close to her face and breast. With all her force, with all her soul she would make up to it for having brought it into the world unloved. She would love it all the more now it was here, carry it in her love. Its clear, knowing eyes gave her pain and fear. Did it know all about her? When it lay under her heart, had it been listening then? Was there a reproach in the look? She felt the marrow melt in her bones, with fear, and pain.

Once more she was aware of the sun lying red on the rim of the hill opposite. She suddenly held up the child in her hands.

"Look!" she said. "Look, my pretty!"

She thrust the infant forward to the crimson, throbbing sun, almost with relief. She saw him lift his little fist. Then she put him to her bosom again, ashamed almost of her impulse to give him back again whence he came.

"If he lives," she thought to herself, "what will become of him—what will he be?"

Her heart was anxious.

"I will call him 'Paul'," she said, suddenly, she knew not why.

After a while, she went home. A fine shadow was flung over the deep green meadow, darkening all.

As she expected, she found the house empty. But Morel was home by ten o'clock, and that day at least ended peacefully.

Walter Morel was, at this time, exceedingly irritable. His work seemed to exhaust him. When he came home, he did not speak civilly to anybody. If the fire were rather low, he bullied about that; he grumbled about his dinner; if the children made a chatter, he shouted at them in a way that made their mother's blood boil, and made them hate him.

"You have no need to shout their heads off," Mrs Morel would say. "We are none of us hard of hearing."

"I'll put my foot through 'em," he bawled.

If, whilst he was washing in the scullery, anyone entered or left the house:

"Shut that doo-er!" he shouted, so that he could be heard down the Bottoms.

"It's a pity, poor nesh creature!" Mrs Morel said quietly.

"I shonna ha'e my ribs blowed out o' my sides wi' that draught, for nob'dy!" he would shout. Whenever he was angry, he bawled.

"Goodness me man," said Mrs Morel at last. "There isn't a bit of peace while you're in the house."

"No, I know that. I know you're niver right till I'm out o' your sight."

"True," she said calmly to herself.

"Oh I know—I know what yer chunterin' 's about. You're niver satisfied till I'm down pit, none on yer. They ought ter keep me theer, like one o' th' 'osses."

"True," said Mrs Morel again, under her breath, as she turned with a tight-shut mouth.

He hurried to escape from the house, thrusting his head forward in determined rage.

"I'll pay the b— out!" he said to himself, meaning his wife.

He was not home by eleven o'clock. The baby was unwell, and was restless, crying if he were put down. Mrs Morel, tired to death, and still weak, was scarcely under control.

"I wish the nuisance would come," she said wearily to herself.

The child at last sank down to sleep in her arms. She was too tired to carry him to the cradle.

"But I'll say nothing, whatever time he comes," she said. "It only works me up, I won't say anything." She did not trust herself, however. Time after time she had said the same, determined to refrain, and then her sudden anger had flashed out. She wished, with the loathing of weariness, that she might be spared seeing him when he came home. The reason she would not go to bed and leave him to come in when he liked—let any woman tell.

"I know if he does anything, it'll make my blood boil," she said pitiably to herself.

She sighed, hearing him coming, as if it were something she could not bear. He, taking his revenge, was nearly drunk. She kept her head bent over the child as he entered, not wishing to see him. But it went through her like a flash of hot fire when, in passing, he lurched against the dresser, setting the tins rattling, and clutched at the white pot knobs for support. He hung up his hat and coat, then returned, stood glowering from a distance at her, as she sat bowed over the child.

"Is there nathing to eat in the house?" he asked, insolently, as if to a servant. In certain stages of his intoxication he affected the clipped, mincing speech of the towns. Mrs Morel hated him most in this condition.

"You know what there is in the house," she said, so coldly, it sounded impersonal.

He stood and glared at her without moving a muscle.

"I asked a civil question, and I expect a civil answer," he said, affectedly.

"And you got it," she said, still ignoring him.

He glowered again. Then he came unsteadily forward. He leaned on the table with one hand, and with the other jerked at the table drawer to get a knife to cut bread. The drawer stuck, because he pulled sideways. In a temper, he dragged at it so that it flew out bodily, and spoons, forks, knives, a hundred metallic things splashed with a clatter and a clang upon the brick floor. The baby gave a little convulsed start.

"What are you doing, clumsy drunken fool?" the mother cried.

"Then tha should get the flamin' thing thysen. Tha should get up like other women have to, an' wait on a man."

"Wait on you—wait on *you*!" she cried. "Yes, I see myself."

"Yis, an' I'll learn thee tha's got to. Wait on *me*, yes, tha sh'lt wait on *me*—"

"Never, milord. I'd wait on a dog at the door first."

"What—what?"

He was trying to fit in the drawer. At her last speech, he turned round. His face was crimson, his eyes bloodshot. He stared at her one silent second, in threat.

"P-h!" she went quickly, in contempt.

He jerked at the drawer in his excitement. It fell, cut sharply on his shin, and on the reflex, he flung it at her.

One of the corners caught her brow as the shallow drawer crashed into the fireplace. She swayed, almost fell stunned from her chair. To her very soul she was sick; she clasped the child tightly to her bosom. A few moments elapsed. Then, with an effort, she brought herself to. The baby was crying plaintively. Her left brow was bleeding rather profusely. As she glanced down at the child, her brain reeling, some drops of blood soaked into its white shawl. But the baby was at least not hurt. She balanced her head to keep equilibrium, so that the blood ran into her eye.

Walter Morel remained as he had stood, leaning on the table with

53

one hand, looking blank. When he was sufficiently sure of his balance, he went across to her, swayed, caught hold of the back of her rocking-chair, almost tipping her out. Then, leaning forward over her and swaying as he spoke, he said, in a tone of wondering concern:

"Did it catch thee?"

He swayed again, as if he would pitch onto the child. With the catastrophe, he had lost all balance.

"Go away!" she said, struggling to keep her presence of mind.

He hiccoughed. "Let's—let's look at it," he said, hiccoughing again.

"Go away," she cried.

"Lemme—lemme look at it lass."

She smelled him of drink, felt the unequal pull of his swaying grasp on the back of her rocking-chair.

"Go away," she said, and weakly she pushed him off.

He stood, uncertain in balance, gazing upon her.

Summoning all her strength, she rose, the baby on one arm. By a cruel effort of will, moving as if in sleep, she went across to the scullery, where she bathed her eye for a minute in cold water. But she was too dizzy. Afraid lest she should swoon, she returned to her rocking-chair, trembling in every fibre. By instinct, she kept the baby clasped.

Morel, bothered, had succeeded in pushing the drawer back into its cavity, and was on his knees, groping with numb paws for the scattered spoons.

Her brow was still bleeding. Presently Morel got up and came craning his neck towards her.

"What has it done to thee, lass?" he asked, in a very wretched, humble tone.

"You can see what it's done," she answered.

He stood bending forward, supported on his hands, which grasped his legs just above the knee. He peered to look at the wound. She drew away from the thrust of his face, with its great moustache, averting her own face as much as possible. As he looked at her, who was cold and impassive as stone, with mouth shut tight, he sickened with feebleness and hopelessness of spirit. He was turning drearily away, when he saw a drop of blood fall from the averted wound into the baby's fragile, glistening hair. Fascinated, he watched the heavy dark drop hang in the glistening cloud, and pull down the gossamer. Another drop fell. It would soak through to the baby's scalp. He watched fascinated, feeling it soak in. Then, finally, his manhood broke.

"What of this child?" was all his wife said to him. But her low, intense tones brought his head lower. She softened:

"Get me some wadding out of the middle drawer," she said.

He stumbled away very obediently, presently returning with a pad, which she singed before the fire, then put on her forehead, as she sat with the baby on her lap.

"Now that clean pit-scarf."

Again he rummaged and fumbled in the drawer, returning presently with a red, narrow scarf. She took it, and with trembling fingers proceeded to bind it round her head.

"Let me tie it for thee," he said humbly.

"I can do it myself," she replied.

When it was done she went upstairs, telling him to rake the fire and lock the door.

In the morning, Mrs Morel said:

"I knocked against the latch of the coal-place, when I was getting a raker in the dark, because the candle blew out." Her two small children looked up at her with wide, dismayed eyes. They said nothing, but their parted lips seemed to express the unconscious tragedy they felt.

Walter Morel lay in bed next day until nearly dinner time. He did not think of the previous evening's work. He scarcely thought of anything, but he would not think of that. He lay and suffered like a sulking dog. He had hurt himself most. And he was the more damaged, because he would never say a word to her, or express his sorrow. He tried to wriggle out of it.

"It was her own fault," he said to himself. Nothing, however, could prevent his inner consciousness inflicting on him the punishment which ate into his spirit like rust, and which he could only alleviate by drinking.

He felt as if he had not the initiative to get up, or to say a word, or to move, but could only lie like a log. Moreover he had himself violent pains in the head. It was Saturday. Towards noon he rose, cut himself food in the pantry, ate it with his head dropped, then pulled on his boots and went out, to return at three o'clock, slightly tipsy, and relieved; then once more straight to bed. He rose again at six in the evening, had tea, and went straight out.

Sunday was the same: bed till noon, the 'Palmerston Arms' till 2.30, dinner and bed; scarcely a word spoken. When Mrs Morel went upstairs, towards four o'clock, to put on her Sunday dress, he was fast asleep. She would have felt sorry for him, if he had once said: "Wife, I'm sorry." But no, he insisted to himself it was her fault. And so he broke himself. So she merely left him alone. There was this deadlock of passion between them, and she was stronger.

The family began tea. Sunday was the only day when all sat down to meals together.

"Isn't my father going to get up?" asked William.

"Let him lie," the mother replied.

There was a feeling of misery over all the house. The children breathed the air that was poisoned, and they felt dreary. They were rather disconsolate, did not know what to do, what to play at.

Immediately Morel woke he got straight out of bed. That was characteristic of him, all his life. He was all for activity. The prostrated inactivity of two mornings was stifling him.

It was near six o'clock when he got down. This time he entered without hesitation, his wincing sensitiveness having hardened again. He did not care any longer what the family thought or felt.

The tea-things were on the table. William was reading aloud from *The Child's Own*, Annie listening and asking eternally 'Why?' Both children hushed into silence as they heard the approaching thud of their father's stockinged feet, and shrank as he entered. Yet he was usually indulgent to them.

Morel made the meal alone, brutally. He ate and drank more noisily than he had need. No one spoke to him. The family life withdrew, shrank away and became hushed as he entered. But he cared no longer about his alienation.

Immediately he had finished tea he rose with alacrity to go out. It was this alacrity, this haste to be gone, which so sickened Mrs Morel. As she heard him sousing heartily in cold water, heard the eager scratch of the steel comb on the side of the bowl, as he wetted his hair, she closed her eyes in disgust. As he bent over, lacing his boots, there was a certain vulgar gusto in his movement that divided him from the reserved, watchful rest of the family. He always ran away from the battle with himself. Even in his own heart's privacy, he excused himself, saying, 'If she hadn't said so-and-so, it would never have happened. She asked for what she's got.' The children waited in restraint during his preparations. When he had gone, they sighed with relief.

He closed the door behind him, and was glad. It was a rainy evening. The 'Palmerston' would be the cosier. He hastened forward in anticipation. All the slate roofs of the Bottoms shone black with wet. The roads, always dark with coal dust, were full of blackish mud. He hastened along. The Palmerston windows were steamed over. The passage was paddled with wet feet. But the air was warm, if foul, and full of the sound of voices and the smell of beer and smoke.

"What shollt ha'e, Walter?" cried a voice, as soon as Morel appeared in the doorway.

"Oh, Jim, my lad, wheriver has thee sprung fro'?"

The men made a seat for him, and took him in warmly. He was glad. In a minute or two, they had thawed all responsibility out of him, all shame, all trouble, and he was clear as a bell, for a jolly night.

But the next evening, as he was sitting on his heels at the garden gate, smoking, and calling across to the miners on the other side the alley, watching the youths, still unwashed from the pit, playing football, Mrs Kirk came out of her yard.

"Evenin' Missis!" said Morel, in his gallant, hearty fashion.

"You lookin' well, aren't yer?" said Mrs Kirk.

"Why, what's amiss?" cried Morel.

"Lettin' your Missis split 'er 'ead open like she has done," said Mrs Kirk.

"Yes, it was a nasty accident," said Morel, only thankful his wife had not told her neighbours.

"I can't think how she did it," said Mrs Kirk.

"No, nor me," answered Morel.

"At any rate, she'll be scarred for life."

"Ay it was a nasty bang," said Morel. "Yes—it's a great pity! I want her to go to th' doctor with it, but she won't."

"Your mester says he wants you to go to the doctor's with that eye of yours," said Mrs Kirk to Mrs Morel.

"Does he?" answered Mrs Morel.

On the Wednesday following, Morel was penniless. He dreaded his wife. Having hurt her, he hated her. He did not know what to do with himself that evening, having not even twopence with which to go to the Palmerston, and being already rather deeply in debt. So, while his wife was down the garden with the child, he hunted in the top drawer of the dresser where she kept her purse, found it, and looked inside. It contained a half crown, two halfpennies, and a sixpence. So he took the sixpence, put the purse carefully back, and went out.

The next day, when she wanted to pay the greengrocer, she looked in the purse for her sixpence, and her heart sank to her shoes. Then she sat down and thought: "*Was* there a sixpence?—I hadn't spent it, had I?—and I hadn't left it anywhere else?"

She was much put about. She hunted round everywhere for it. And, as she sought, the conviction came into her heart that her husband had taken it. What she had in her purse was all the money she possessed. But that he should sneak it from her thus was unbearable. He had done so twice before. The first time, she had not accused him, and at the week end he had put the shilling again into her purse. So that was how she had known he had taken it. The second time he had not paid back.

This time, she felt it was too much. When he had had his dinner—he came home early that day—she said to him coldly:

"Did you take sixpence out of my purse last night?"

"Me!" he said, looking up in an offended way, "No, I didna! I niver clapped eyes on your purse."

But she could detect the lie.

"Why you know you did," she said quietly.

"I tell you I didna," he shouted. "Yer at me again, are yer? I've had about enough on't."

"So you filch sixpence out of my purse while I'm taking the clothes in."

"I'll may yer pay for this," he said, pushing back his chair in desperation. He bustled and got washed, then went determinedly upstairs. Presently he came down dressed, and with a big bundle in a blue-checked enormous handkerchief.

"And now," he said, "you'll see me again when you do."

"It'll be before I want to," she replied, and at that, he marched out of the house with his bundle. She sat trembling slightly, but her heart brimming with contempt. What would she do if he went to some other pit, obtained work, and got in with another woman? But she knew him too well—he couldn't. She was dead sure of him. Nevertheless her heart was gnawed inside her.

"Where's my Dad?" said William, coming in from school.

"He says he's run away," replied the mother.

"Where to?"

"Eh, I don't know. He's taken a bundle in the blue handkerchief, and says he's not coming back."

"What shall we do?" cried the boy.

"Eh never trouble, he won't go far."

"But if he doesn't come back," wailed Annie.

And she and William retired to the sofa and wept. Mrs Morel sat and laughed.

"You pair of gabeys!" she exclaimed. "*You'll* see him before the night's out."

But the children were not to be consoled. Twilight came on. Mrs Morel grew anxious from very weariness. One part of her said, it would be a relief to see the last of him: another part fretted because of keeping the children: and inside her, as yet, she could not quite let him go. At the bottom, she knew very well he could *not* go.

When she went down to the coal-place at the end of the garden, however, she felt something behind the door. So she looked. And there in the dark lay the big blue bundle. She sat on a piece of coal, in front of the bundle, and laughed. Every time she saw it, so fat and yet so ignominious, slunk into its corner in the dark, with its ends flopping like dejected ears from the knots, she laughed again.

She went up with her coal to the house. Annie and William were having a fresh weep because she had gone out.

"Silly pair of babies," she said. "Go down to the coalplace and look behind the door, and *then* you'll see how far he's gone."

"What?" exclaimed William, rather pathetically.

"Go and see," said his mother.

And he slunk out, followed by Annie, who trotted sniffing up her tears. Directly he reappeared in great excitement, hugging the bundle.

"He won't go now, will he mother?" he cried.

"No—and I knew he never would.—My only fear was that he'd pawn something. But take it back—go and put it where you found it."

"But—!" faltered William. "What's in it?"

"Go and put it back!" she insisted, "and never mind."

The boy lugged the fat bundle down the yard again, and dropped it behind the coal-place door. Then, relieved but not yet at ease, the children went to bed.

Mrs Morel sat waiting. He had not any money, she knew, so if he stopped, he was running up a bill. She was very tired of him, tired to death. He had not even the courage to carry his bundle beyond the yard end.

As she meditated, at about nine o'clock, he opened the door and came in, slinking, and yet sulky. She said not a word. He took off his coat and slunk to his arm-chair, where he began to take off his boots.

"You'd better fetch your bundle before you take your boots off," she said, quietly.

"You may thank your stars I've come back tonight," he said, looking up from under his dropped head, sulkily, trying to be impressive.

"Why where should you have gone? You daren't even get your parcel through the yard-end," she said.

He looked such a fool she was not even angry with him. He continued to take his boots off and prepare for bed.

"I don't know what's in your blue handkerchief," she said. "But if you leave it the children shall fetch it in the morning."

Whereupon he got up and went out of the house, returning presently and crossing the kitchen with averted face, hurrying upstairs. As Mrs Morel saw him slink quickly through the inner doorway, holding his bundle, she laughed to herself—but her heart was bitter, because she had loved him.

CHAPTER III

The Casting off of Morel, the Taking on of William

During the next week Morel's temper was almost unbearable. Like all miners, he was a great lover of medicines, which, strangely enough, he would often pay for himself.

"You mun get me a drop o' laxy vitral," he said. "It's a winder as we canna ha'e a sup i' th'ouse."

So Mrs Morel bought him elixir of vitriol, his favourite first medicine. And he made himself a jug of wormwood tea. He had hanging in the attic great bunches of dried herbs: wormwood, rue, horehound, elder-flowers, parsley-purt, marsh-mallow, hyssop, dandelion and centaury. Usually there was a jug of one or other decoction standing on the hob, from which he drank largely.

"Grand!" he said, smacking his lips after wormwood. "Grand!" And he exhorted the children to try.

"It's better than any of your tea or your cocoa stews," he vowed. But they were not to be tempted.

This time, however, neither pills nor vitriol nor all his herbs would shift the "nasty peens in his head." He was sickening for an attack of an inflammation of the brain. He had never been well since his sleeping on the ground when he went with Jerry to Nottingham. Since then he had drunk and stormed. Now he fell seriously ill, and Mrs Morel had him to nurse. He was one of the worst patients imaginable. But, in spite of all, and putting aside the fact that he was bread-winner, she never quite wanted him to die. Still there was one part of her wanted him for herself.

The neighbours were very good to her: occasionally some had the children in to meals, occasionally some would do the downstairs work for her, one would mind the baby for a day. But it was a great drag, nevertheless. It was not every day the neighbours helped. Then she had nursing of baby and husband, cleaning and cooking, everything to do. She was quite worn out, but she did what was wanted of her.

And the money was just sufficient. She had seventeen shillings a week from clubs, and every Friday, Barker and the other butty put by a portion of the stall's profits for Morel's wife. And the neighbours made broths, and gave eggs, and such invalids' trifles. If they had not helped her so generously in those times, Mrs Morel would never have pulled through, without incurring debts that would have dragged her down.

The weeks passed, Morel, almost against hope, grew better. He had a fine constitution, so that, once on the mend, he went straight forward to recovery. Soon he was pottering about downstairs. During his illness his wife had spoilt him a little. Now he wanted her to continue. He often put his hand to his head, pulled down the corners of his mouth, and shammed pains he did not feel. But there was no deceiving her. At first she merely smiled to herself. Then she scolded him sharply.

"Goodness man, don't be so lachrymose."

That wounded him slightly, but still he continued to feign sickness.

"I wouldn't be such a mardy baby," said his wife shortly.

Then he was indignant, and cursed under his breath, like a boy. He was forced to resume a normal tone, and to cease to whine.

Nevertheless, there was a state of peace in the house for some time. Mrs Morel was more tolerant of him, and he, depending on her almost like a child, was rather happy. Neither knew that she was more tolerant because she loved him less. Up till this time, in spite of all, he had been her husband, and her man. She had felt that, more or less, what he did to himself he did to her. Her living depended on him. There were many, many stages in the ebbing of her love for him, but it was always ebbing.

Now, with the birth of this third baby, her self no longer set towards him, helplessly, but was like a tide that scarcely rose, standing off from him. After this she scarcely desired him. And standing more aloof from him, not feeling him so much part of herself, but merely part of her circumstances she did not mind so much what he did, could leave him alone.

There was the halt, the wistfulness about the ensuing year, which is like autumn in a man's life. His wife was casting him off, half regretfully, but relentlessly; casting him off and turning now for love and life to the children. Henceforward he was more or less a husk. And he half acquiesced, as so many men do, yielding their place to their children.

During his recuperation, when it was really over between them, both made an effort to come back somewhat to the old relationship of the first months of their marriage. He sat at home, and, when the children were in bed, and she was sewing—she did all her sewing by hand, made all shirts and children's clothing—he would read to her from the newspaper, slowly pronouncing and delivering the words like a man pitching quoits. Often she hurried him on, giving him a phrase in anticipation. And then he took her words humbly.

The silences between them were peculiar. There would be the swift, slight 'cluck' of her needle, the sharp 'pop' of his lips as he let out the smoke, the warmth, the sizzle on the bars as he spat in the fire. Then her thoughts turned to William. Already he was getting a big boy. Already he was top of the class, and the master said he was the smartest lad in the school. She saw him a man, young, full of vigour, making the world glow again for her.

And Morel sitting there, quite alone, and having nothing to think about, would be feeling vaguely uncomfortable. His soul would reach out in its blind way to her, and find her gone. He felt a sort of emptiness, almost like a vacuum in his soul. He was unsettled and restless. Soon he could not live in that atmosphere, and he affected his wife. Both felt an oppression on their breathing, when they were left together for some time. Then he went to bed, and she settled down to enjoy herself alone, working, thinking, living.

So, having to get into an atmosphere where he could live, not being able to acquiesce in his own obliteration, Morel faltered back to the Palmerston and to Jerry, and his wife, in her heart of hearts, was relieved to have him go.

He had lost his game now. Though, of course, he recurred again and again to his old selves, still had his moments of dominance and authority and pride. But they were like echoes. The baby Paul, towards whom he also felt strangely moved, would not be touched by him. The infant had a gathering in the ear, when he was eight months old, and was very fretful. Morel wanted to hold the child, to soothe him. It would have done the man good to be able to nurse his sick baby. But the child would not be nursed by him. It would stiffen in his arms, and, although usually a quiet baby, would scream, draw back from the father's hands. And Morel, seeing the small fists clenched, the baby face averted, the wet blue eyes turned frantically to the mother, would say in a kind of impatient despair:

"Here, come an' ta'e him!"

"It's your moustache frightens him," she replied, as she took the child and pressed it to her bosom. Nevertheless her heart hurt with pain. And Morel was afraid of the child.

Meanwhile another infant was coming, fruit of this little peace and tenderness between the separating parents. Paul was seventeen months old when the new baby was born. He was then a plump, pale child, quiet, with heavy blue eyes and still the peculiar slight knitting of the brows. The last child was also a boy, fair and bonny. Mrs Morel was sorry when she knew she was with child, both for economic reasons, and because she did not love her husband; but not for the sake of the infant.

They called the baby Arthur. He was very pretty, with a mop of gold curls, and he loved his father from the first. Mrs Morel was glad this child loved the father. Hearing the miner's footsteps, the baby would put up his arms and crow. And if Morel were in a good temper, he called back immediately, in his hearty, mellow voice:

"What then, my beauty—I sh'll come to thee, in a minute."

And as soon as he had taken off his pitcoat, Mrs Morel would put an apron round the child, and give him to his father.

"What a sight the lad looks!" she would exclaim sometimes, taking back the baby, that was smutted on the face from his father's kisses and play. Then Morel laughed joyfully.

"He's a little collier, bless his bit o' mutton," he exclaimed. And these were the happy moments of her life now, when the children included the father in her heart.

Meanwhile William grew bigger and stronger and more active, while Paul, always rather delicate and quiet, got slimmer, and trotted after his mother like her shadow. He was usually active and interested, but sometimes he would have fits of depression. Then the mother would find the boy of three or four crying on the sofa.

"What's the matter?" she asked, and got no answer.

"What's the matter?" she insisted, getting cross.

"I don't know," sobbed the child.

So she tried to reason him out of it, or to amuse him, but without effect. It made her feel beside herself. Then the father, always impatient, would jump from his chair and shout:

"If he doesn't stop I'll smack him till he does."

"You'll do nothing of the sort," said the mother coldly.

And then she carried the child into the yard, plumped him into his little chair, and said:

"Now cry there, Misery!"

And then a butterfly on the rhubarb leaves perhaps caught his eye, or at last he cried himself to sleep. These fits were not often, but they caused a shadow in Mrs Morel's heart, and her treatment of Paul was different from that of the other children.

One morning Mrs Morel, hearing 'Barm-O', went down into the alley with her mug. 'Barm-O' was not yet up to her gate, so she stood waiting, listening to the snatches of hymns the man was singing as he dipped the can into his barrels and filled the pots the women gave him. He was a cheerful old man, with a rather bulbous comic face surrounded with white whiskers. In his decrepit old cart were two barrels of brewer's yeast, covered with a wet sack. As he went along, he sang snatches of hymns, since he had been converted three months before.

> "We shall meet beyond the river,
> Where the surges cease to roll—Barm-O!"

came his big, half wicked cry down the alley. And he chaffed the women as he served them their ha'porths of barm. Suddenly Mrs Morel heard a voice calling her. It was the thin little Mrs Anthony in brown velvet.

"Here, Mrs Morel, I want to tell you about your Willie."

"Oh do you?" replied Mrs Morel.

Mrs Anthony did not come close, but stood and shouted across the alley.

"D'you reckon he's got any right to rip our Alfie's collar off'n his back?"

"Why, has he done?" Mrs Morel called back. Both women scorned to go near each other.

"He has that—and if you don't believe me, I'll go an' fetch it you."

"I think you've no need," said Mrs Morel. "But how do you know our William did it?"

"What, do you think our Alfie doesn't tell the truth then? There isn't a more truthful spoken lad in the Bottoms. All right, ask Annie Bower an' a lot more of 'em. He got hold of my lad's collar an' ripped it clean off his back. And *I* can't afford to buy new collars when their own's ripped up by folks—."

"I know you can't," said Mrs Morel.

"An' what I say," said Mrs Anthony, hotly, "is, he ought to have a good thrashing, that's what he ought."

"'At the Cross at the cross, where I found—' Barm-O!—Barm-OO!—How much this dip Missis?"

"A ha-porth 'll do," said Mrs Morel, handing up her mug.

"A ha-porth in this mug, an' 'ere you are, all fresh an' drippin', an' God's blessin' on you," replied Barm-O. He and his cart stood between the two women.

"'Consider the lilies how they grow'—Yes Mrs Anthony—a ha-porth. All ha'porths! Never mind. 'They toil not neither do they spin. Yet not even Solerman—' Thank yer—"

He moved on, having made not the slightest impression on the two women. Mrs Anthony was rather more indignant than ever.

"—A lad as gets 'old of another an' rips his clothes off'n 'is back," she repeated.

"Your Alfred's as old as my William," said Mrs Morel.

"'Appen 'e is, but that doesn't give him a right to get hold of the boy's collar, an' fair rip it clean off his back."

"Well," said Mrs Morel, "I don't thrash my children, and even if I did, I should want to hear their side of the tale."

"They'd happen be a bit better if they did get a good hiding," retorted Mrs Anthony, "when it comes ter rippin' a lad's clean collar off'n 'is back a purpose—"

"I'm sure he didn't do it on purpose," said Mrs Morel.

"Make me a liar!" shouted Mrs Anthony.

Mrs Morel moved away and closed her gate. Her hand trembled as she held her mug of barm.

"But I s'll let your mester know," Mrs Anthony cried after her.

At dinner time, when William had finished his meal and wanted to be off again—he was then eleven years old—his mother said to him:

"What did you tear Alfred Anthony's collar for?"

"When did I tear his collar?"

"I don't know when, but his mother says you did."

"Why—it was yesterday—an' it was torn a'ready."

"But you tore it more."

"Well, I'd got a cobbler as 'ad licked seventeen—an' Alfy Ant'ny 'e says:

> 'Adam an' Eve an' Pinch-me,
> Went down to a river to bade.
> Adam an' Eve got drownded,
> Who d'yer think got saved—?'

An' so I says 'Oh, Pinch-*you*', an' so I pinched 'im, an' 'e was mad, an' so he snatched my cobbler an' run off with it. An' so I run after 'im, an' when I was gettin' hold of him, 'e dodged an' it ripped 'is collar. But I got my cobbler—"

He pulled from his pocket a black old horse-chestnut hanging on a string. This old cobbler had 'cobbled'—hit and smashed—seventeen other cobblers on similar strings. So the boy was proud of his veteran.

"Well," said Mrs Morel, "you know you've got no right to rip his collar."

"Well our mother!" he answered. "I never meant tr'a done it—an' it was on'y an old indirrubber collar as was torn a'ready."

"Next time," said his mother, "*you* be more careful. I shouldn't like it if you came home with *your* collar torn off."

"I don't care, our mother, I never did it a-purpose."

The boy was rather miserable at being reprimanded.

"No—well you be more careful."

William fled away, glad to be exonerated. And Mrs Morel, who hated any bother with the neighbours, thought she would explain to Mrs Anthony, and the business would be over.

But that evening, Morel came in from the pit looking very sour. He stood in the kitchen and glared round, but did not speak for some minutes. Then:

"Wheer's that Willy?" he asked.

"What do you want *him* for?" asked Mrs Morel, who had guessed.

"I'll let 'im know when I get him," said Morel, banging his pit-bottle onto the dresser.

"I suppose Mrs Anthony's got hold of you and been yarning to you about their Alfy's collar," said Mrs Morel, rather sneering.

"Niver mind who's got hold of me," said Morel. "When I get hold of 'im I'll make his bones rattle."

"It's a poor tale," said Mrs Morel, "that you're so ready to side with any snipey vixen who likes to come telling tales against your own children."

"I'll learn 'im!" said Morel. "It none matters to me whose lad 'e is, 'e's none goin' rippin' an' tearin' about just as he's a mind."

"'Ripping and tearing about!'" repeated Mrs Morel.—"He was running after that Alfy, who'd taken his cobbler, and he accidentally got hold of his collar—because the other dodged—as an Anthony would."

"I know—" shouted Morel, threateningly.

"You would, before you're told," replied his wife bitingly.

"Niver you mind," stormed Morel. "I know my business."

"That's more than doubtful," said Mrs Morel, "supposing some loud-mouthed creature had been getting you to thrash your own children."

"I know," repeated Morel.

And he said no more, but sat and nursed his bad temper.

Suddenly William ran in, saying:

"Can I have my tea mother?"

"Tha can ha'e more than that," shouted Morel.

"Hold your noise man," said Mrs Morel. "And don't look so ridiculous."

"He'll look ridiculous before I've done wi' him!" shouted Morel, rising from his chair and glaring at his son. William, who was a tall lad for his years, but very sensitive, had gone pale and was looking in a sort of horror at his father.

"Go out!" Mrs Morel commanded her son.

William had not the wit to move. Suddenly Morel clenched his fist, and crouched.

"I'll *gi'e* him go out!" he shouted, like an insane thing.

"What!" cried Mrs Morel, panting with rage. "You shall not touch him for *her* telling, you shall not."

"Shonna I?" shouted Morel. "Shonna I?"

And, glaring at the boy, he ran forward. Mrs Morel sprang in between them, with her fist lifted.

"Don't you *dare*!" she cried.

"What!" he shouted, baffled for the moment. "What!"

She spun round to her son.

"*Go* out of the house!" she commanded him in fury. The boy, as if hypnotised by her, turned suddenly and was gone. Morel rushed to the door, but was too late. He returned, pale under his pit-dirt with fury. But now his wife was fully roused.

"Only dare!" she said, in a loud, ringing voice. "Only dare, milord, to lay a finger on that child. You'll regret it for ever."

He was afraid of her. In a towering rage, he sat down.

"No, you've done it before, but you shall do it no more!" she began suddenly, after a pause. "I don't forget the time you kicked him, and made great bruises on him, because of old Mother Sharp's spite against him—you shall do it no more," she panted. She was quite breathless with passion.

"Shonna I? Shonna I?" repeated Morel.

"You bully, you miserable coward and bully!" she cried. "Haven't you more stomach than to be ordered about by any common cat like that Anthony, when she comes bidding you to thrash your children. Is *she* to decide for you, when you're to come home and knock the lad about?—and you to do it, you coward, and you bully!—No, not while I'm here!"

"Tha'lt see what'll 'appen while tha'rt here," threatened Morel.

"Never again, milord, never again do you lay a finger on my children."

"Oh!—Oh!!" he snarled.

And that night he went out and got drunk, and that week-end he did not give William his weekly penny.

"You are better without it," said Mrs Morel to her son.

When the children were old enough to be left, Mrs Morel joined the Women's Guild. It was a little club of women attached to the Co-operative Wholesale Society, which met on Monday night in the long room over the grocery shop of the Bestwood "Co-op." The women were supposed to discuss the benefits to be derived from Co-operation, and other social questions. Sometimes Mrs Morel read a paper. It seemed queer to the children to see their mother, who was always busy about the house, sitting writing in her rapid fashion, thinking, referring to books, and writing again. They felt for her on such occasions the deepest respect.

But they loved the 'Guild.' It was the only thing to which they did not grudge their mother: and that partly because she enjoyed it, partly because of the treats they derived from it. The guild was called by some hostile husbands, who found their wives getting too independent, the "clat-fart" shop: that is, the gossip shop. It is true, from off the basis of the guild, the women could look at their homes, at the conditions of their own lives, and find fault. So, the colliers found their women had a new standard of their own, rather disconcerting. And also, Mrs Morel always had a lot of news on Monday nights, so that the children liked William to be in when their mother came home, because she told him things.

Then, when the lad was thirteen, she got him a job in the Co-op. office. He was a very clever boy, frank, with rather rough features and real viking blue eyes.

"What dost want ter ma'e a stool-harsed Jack on 'im for?" said Morel. "All he'll do is to wear his britches behind out an' earn nowt. What's 'e startin' wi'?"

"It doesn't matter what he's starting with," said Mrs Morel.

"It wouldna! Put 'im i' th' pit wi' me, an' 'e'll earn a easy ten shillin' a wik from th' start. But six shillin' wearin' his truck-end out on a stool's better than ten shillin' i' th' pit wi' me, I know."

"He is *not* going in the pit," said Mrs Morel, "and there's an end of it."

"It wor good enough for me, but it's non good enough for 'im."

"If your mother put you in the pit at twelve, it's no reason why I should do the same with my lad."

"Twelve!—it wor a sight afore that!"

"Whenever it was," said Mrs Morel.

She was very proud of her son. He went to the night-school, and learned shorthand, so that by the time he was sixteen, he was the best short-hand clerk and book-keeper on the place, except one. Then he taught in the nightschools. But he was so fiery, that only his good-nature and his size protected him.

All the things that men do—the decent things—William did. He could run like the wind. When he was twelve, he won a first prize in a race: an inkstand of glass, shaped like an anvil. It stood proudly on the dresser, and gave Mrs Morel a keen pleasure. The boy only ran for her. He flew home with his anvil, breathless, with a:

"Look mother!"

That was the first real tribute to herself. She took it like a queen.

"How pretty!" she exclaimed.

The children of the Bottoms, playing round the stile, used to shout, as William came along:

"Jump it Willy—jump it."

And he would leap over the fence, some four or five feet, grandly.

"Sithee at that!" the small boys shouted.

He also could throw farther than any youth in Bestwood. His comrades and rivals were very jealous of these feats, and they vowed that his stones were not those that lay furthest, beyond the hedge. So William disdainfully marked them with a W.M.

When he was seventeen, he won a bicycle race at Ilkeston. Morel, in one of his bursts of bragging, had challenged his son against any champion there in the public house. William felt it his duty to fulfil his father's boasts. Mrs Morel did not approve.

"See me lick 'em, mother!" he cried, smacking the calves of his legs. All that day Mrs Morel sat in suspense and misery. He might be killed or hurt. She was sure his heart was not strong enough for cycle-racing. Then he came home at night with a little oak writing desk.

"Here you are, mother!" he said. "Didn't I tell you I'd bring it you?"

But she made him promise not to enter a cycle-race again.

He had pupils, and taught short-hand at home. But he was so furious and fiery, that only the youths who were students by nature, could stand him. He and his pupil sat at the table in the kitchen. It was warm and lamp-lit, and very still. The red chintz cushions on the sofa were soft, the red cotton table-cloth seemed cosy. As a rule, the pupil, a lad of thirteen or fourteen, sat anxiously, while William, rapid and energetic, corrected the exercise. There were snorts of impatience and disgust from the teacher. Then suddenly he would cry:

"Why you doddering blockhead, you had it right in the last sentence, and now—"

The poor pupil blew his nose nervously on his red handkerchief as he peered over William's elbow. Sometimes Mrs Morel sat sewing in her rocking-chair. Then the lesson-proper began. William grew more and more impatient, until he burst forth:

"You great booby, you block-head, you thundering idiot and fool, what have I told you a thousand times—?"

"William! William!" cried his mother. "Be ashamed of yourself! I wonder anyone puts up with you.—Take no notice of him Robert, it's his own impatience that's the matter, not you. *You're* quick enough." And Robert would give a glance of shame and gratitude at Mrs Morel, while William continued:

"Come on—and for Goodness sake don't be a blockhead. Look—!"

At last Mrs Morel made it a rule, always to go out of the house when these lessons took place, in order to spare the feelings of the poor lads.

William had to be at his office at eight, so his mother got up at seven o'clock to prepare him. He was usually late, or on the verge of lateness. But nothing could hurry him. He loved these breakfasts alone with his mother. Then, being jolly, he rattled away to her, and teased her.

One morning he asked her for his clean shirt. He stood on the hearthrug as she gave it him. Then she sat down to her cup of tea. He held up the woollen shirt, that was largely patched, open in front of him.

"What do you call this, mother?" he asked.

"A shirt," she replied, beginning to laugh.

"'A rose would smell as sweet—'!" he quoted, whimsically.

"Well—you're such a rip—and I'd no more stuff like the shirt—besides, who'll see it?"

"Are you sure it won't show through my breeks—I feel as if it would shine through," he said, still surveying the shirt doubtfully.

"Put it on—look at the time!" she commanded, laughing in spite of herself, as she sat in her rocking-chair, sipping her tea. He stood just before her, a big, strong youth, holding out his patchwork-shirt.

"My Joseph's-Coat!" he addressed it, "I don't think anybody'll be jealous of you—one, two, three, four—which is the original stuff, mother?"

"Put it on!" commanded his mother.

"But suppose I have an accident, and am taken to the hospital, and recover consciousness to see four nurses holding out the tail of my shirt—" he grumbled.

"They will say what good looking-after you have," she laughed.

He struggled into the shirt, saying, with his face yet muffled up: "'Not even Solomon in all his glory—'"

"No," laughed Mrs Morel, "I don't suppose anybody would put as many stitches in for Solomon—."

William peered over his shoulder quizzically:

"My tail of woe!" he lamented.

Mrs Morel was now shaking with laughter. She struggled with herself, recovered sufficiently to bang the table with her fist, and cry:

"*Will* you get dressed, sir! There it is a quarter to eight."

"You don't expect me to hurry, clad about with all these patches, do you mother?"

"Oh you looney and gabey!" she cried. "You'll go breaking your neck on that bicycle—"

"Yes, if I were dead I shouldn't be ashamed of my shirt," he interrupted.

She jumped up, seized the hair-brush, and rapped his head with it.

"Brush that hair of yours," she commanded.

They left each other glowing warm: he made her feel warm inside, and she him.

Then he began to get ambitious. He gave all his money to his mother. When he earned fourteen shillings a week, she gave him back two for himself, and, as he never drank, he felt himself rich. He went about with the bourgeois of Bestwood. The townlet contained nothing higher than the clergyman. Then came the bank-manager, then the doctors, then the tradespeople, and after that, the hosts of colliers. William began to consort with the sons of the chemist, the schoolmaster, and the tradesmen. He played billiards in the Mechanics' Hall. Also he danced, this in spite of his mother. All the life that Bestwood offered, he enjoyed, from the sixpenny-hops down Church Street, to sports and billiards.

"Waltz!" exclaimed his father. "Dost reckon *tha* can waltz? When I was a bit nimbler, I could turn on a threp'ny bit."

"I'll bet you could," said William sceptically.

"I could an' all!" protested Morel, with pride.

"Go on then—let's have a look at you."

But Morel was afraid to dance before his children.

"Nay, that I niver sholl! It's a fool's game altogether, an' I canna see what good it'll do thee."

"You see I'm following in my father's footsteps," he said.

"An' more fool thee," said his father, "if iver tha does that."

"That's all right when you're too stiff to dance any more," said William.

"I've niver danced for twenty year," cried Morel hotly.

"An' I'll bet you found it hard work to give it up."

But William persisted. He was a great favourite with the ladies.

"'Postle," he used to say to his brother Paul, after a dance, as the two lay in bed together. "'Postle—a girl in white satin—d'yer hear, white satin down to her slippers—lives at Sutton—dead gone on me! I'm going to see her tomorrow."

After a fortnight Paul would ask of him:

"What about that white-satin lady?"

"Don't care for her 'Postle—no cop! But there's a little gem from Ripley—faintly scented with cherry-blossom—fair as a lily—"

Paul was treated to dazzling descriptions of all kinds of flower-like ladies, most of whom lived like cut blooms in William's heart, for a brief fortnight.

Occasionally some flame would come in pursuit of her errant

swain. Mrs Morel would find a strange girl at the door, and immediately she sniffed the air.

"Is Mr Morel in?" the damsel would ask appealingly.

"My husband is at home," Mrs Morel replied.

"I—I mean *young* Mr Morel," repeated the maiden, painfully.

"Which one—there are several?"

Whereupon much blushing and stammering from the fair one.

"I—I met Mr Morel—at Ripley," she explained.

"Oh—at a dance!"

"Yes."

"I don't approve of the girls my son meets at dances. And he is *not* at home."

Mrs Morel hated the cheap dances her son went to.

"Do you think," she said to him, "I don't know the brazen hussies that go there?"

"Well mother, *I'm* not brazen, as you see."

"I'm not so sure," laughed his mother.

"You don't think I shall fall in love with 'em, do you? I shan't. I only want a bit of fun with them."

"But they don't merely want a bit of fun with *you*. And it is not right."

"Why? I shan't get married. Don't you fret, Mater, I shan't get married till I meet a woman like you—an' that'll be a long time first.—And then—I s'll get married at thirty, when I'm sick of romping about."

"We s'll see, my son," replied his mother.

Then he came home angry with his mother for having turned the girl away so rudely. He was a careless, yet eager-looking fellow, who walked with long strides, sometimes frowning, often with his cap pushed jollily to the back of his head. Now he came in frowning. He threw his cap onto the sofa, and took his strong jaw in his hand, and glared down at his mother. She was small, with her hair taken straight back from her forehead. She had a quiet air of authority, and yet of rare warmth. Knowing her son was angry, she trembled inwardly.

"Did a lady call for me yesterday, mother?" he asked.

"I don't know about a lady—there was a girl came."

"And why didn't you tell me?"

"Because I forgot, simply."

He fumed a little.

"A good-looking girl—seemed a lady?"

"I didn't look at her."

"Big brown eyes—!"

"Yes."

Again he fumed.

"And what did you tell her?"

"That you were not at home."

"And what else?"

"Merely that I didn't approve of girls you had met once coming to your mother's house for you."

"Well you needn't have said that," he replied. "Her father's well off—they keep two servants—"

"They weren't with her, so I didn't know."

"But why need you be nasty—there was no wrong in her coming, was there."

"I thought she was a brazen hussy."

"She wasn't—she wasn't—her father—"

"Keeps two servants," chimed in Mrs Morel.

"No—he's the vet for Woodlinton—besides mother—"

"She was a brazen hussy."

"She wasn't.—And she *was* pretty, wasn't she?"

"I didn't look."

"But you must have done—own up—"

"I did *not* look. And tell your girls, my son, that when they're running after you, they're not to come and ask your mother for you—tell them that—brazen baggages you meet at dancing classes."

"I'm sure she was a nice girl—"

"And I'm sure she wasn't."

There ended the altercation. Over the dancing there was a great strife between the mother and the son. The grievance reached its height when William said he was going to Hucknall Torkard—considered a low town—to a fancy dress ball. He was to be a Highlander. There was a dress he could hire, which one of his friends had had, and which fitted him perfectly. The Highland suit came home. Mrs Morel received it coldly, and would not unpack it.

"My suit come?" cried William.

"There's a parcel in the front room."

He rushed in and cut the string.

"How do you fancy your son in this!" he said enraptured, showing her the suit.

"You know I don't want to fancy you in it."

On the evening of the dance, when he had come home to dress, Mrs Morel put on her coat and bonnet.

"Aren't you going to stop and see me, mother?" he asked.

"No—I don't want to see you," she replied.

She was rather pale, and her face was closed and hard. She was afraid of her son's going the same way as his father. He hesitated a moment, and his heart stood still with anxiety. Then he caught sight of the Highland bonnet with its ribbons. He picked it up gleefully, forgetting her. She went out.

He never knew how disappointed he was. The excitement of the moment, and of anticipation, was enough to carry him through the present. But all his pride was built on *her* seeing him. And afterwards, it always hurt him to think back on this ball.

However, he went upstairs in great excitement. Paul helped him to dress.

"This is a fancy dress set 'Postle," he said. "Give me those things." He struggled into a pair of black, tight drawers, very short. Then he stood in front of his mother's looking glass with glee.

"See me in my black shorts!" he said, twisting round. Then he added: "You see, 'Postle, a real Highlander doesn't wear drawers—he covers his nakedness with a kilt. But if I happened to kick rather high, and all those ladies there—why—it wouldn't do!"

The small boy thought it wouldn't, though it didn't seem to him as serious as all that.

"Fine pair of legs there, 'Postle! Fine legs! They've won four prizes in running for me, and two bicycle races. Not a bad pair!" He slapped his strong young thighs. "Muscle, my lad!—There's one fault though, I can't quite make my knees touch. I'm a smite bandy, 'Postle. But it makes for strength.—Nicholas Nickleby—he had fine legs—he could make his knees touch, according to the picture. And I guess, so could Mr Good. Was it Mr Good who had the 'beautiful white legs' in *King Solomon's Mines*. Fasten me that. This suit doesn't half look well on me, does it 'Postle?"

"No," said Paul, reverently.

"A real Highlander," continued William, "has to fold his kilt. I wish this was one of that sort—I should like to have a go at arranging it. You see, 'Postle, I can wear a kilt, because I'm a tidy size round where it sits. You'd be no good—as flat as [a] box-lid.

You must pray to the Lord for development in that quarter, or you'll never be able to wear a kilt."

Paul wondered vaguely why he should ever want to wear a kilt. He could not aspire to his brother's brawn and stature, being slight and small himself.

"Now how do my knees look!—all right, don't they? Ripping knees they are—ripping knees—legs altogether! The chaps had a bet on the other day in the office, that I was padded. So Vickers crept up while I was writing and stuck a pin in. I nearly yelled the ceiling down, and I jumped and punched his head, I can tell you.—I wish I hadn't knocked that bit of skin off with my bike."

"Happen you could put a bit of your pink toothpowder on," suggested Paul.

"Happen I could—it says antiseptic—but will it give me gyp! You know, I've a real highland figure—ginger hair, blue eyes, and fierce, 'Postle, fierce—besides brawn to back it up.—If ever I enlisted it'ud be in the Black Watch.—That tooth-powder's a nobby idea—."

When he was dressed, a tribe of children came in to see him, and several neighbours. Then he set off. He had a high good time; and yet, when he remembered it, it seemed a pain. His mother was cool with him for a day or two. But he was so adorable—! And yet—a tinge of loneliness was creeping in again, between her and him.

About this time he began to study. With a friend of his, he set off to learn French and Latin, and other things. Soon he grew pale. After the office, he would go to Fred Simpson's house, and the two would work together until midnight, almost till one o'clock. Mrs Morel remonstrated, got violently angry, implored him to take more care of his health.

"When we're at it," he says, "I can*not* remember the time—neither of us can—till Fred's mother shouts downstairs."

These nights of study were mixed with 'soirées' and dances. As he grew older, he got leaner, and the carelessness went out of his eyes.

His mother, watching for him and waiting for him, felt a little chill at her heart. Was he going to 'come off'? A grain of anxiety mingled with her pride in him. And she had waited so long for him, she could not bear it if he failed. She did not know what she wanted him to do. Perhaps she only wanted him to be himself, to develop and bring to fruit all that she had put into him. In him, she wanted to see her life's fruition, that was all. And with all the strength of her soul she tried to keep him strong and balanced and moving straight forwards. But he was baffling, without clarity of purpose. Sometimes he lapsed and was purely like his father. It made her heart sink with dismay and apprehension.

He had had dozens of flirtations, but not anything approaching a love affair. She did not mind flirtations, so long as he went straight forward with his career. But she dreaded lest he should come a cropper over some shallow hussy.

When he was nineteen, he suddenly left the 'Co-op' office, and got a situation in Nottingham. In his new place he had thirty shillings a week, instead of eighteen. This was indeed a rise. His mother and his father were brimmed up with pride. Everybody praised William. It seemed he was going to get on rapidly. Mrs Morel hoped, with his aid, to help her younger sons. Annie was now studying to be a teacher. Paul, also very clever, was getting on well, having lessons in French and German from his Godfather, the clergyman who was still a friend to Mrs Morel. Arthur, a spoilt and very good-looking boy, was at the board school, but there was talk of his trying to get a Scholarship for the High School in Nottingham.

William remained a year at his new post in Nottingham. He was studying hard, and growing serious. Something seemed to be fretting him. Still he went out to the dances and the river parties. He did not drink. The children were all rabid teetotallers. He came home very late at night, and sat yet longer studying. His mother implored him to take more care, to do one thing or another.

"Dance if you want to dance, my son, but don't think you can work in the office, and then amuse yourself, and *then* study on top of all. You can't, the human frame won't stand it. Do one thing or the other—amuse yourself or learn Latin—but don't try to do both."

Then he got a place in London, at a hundred and twenty a year. This seemed a fabulous sum. His mother doubted almost whether to rejoice or to grieve.

"They want me in Lime Street on Monday week, mother," he cried, his eyes blazing, as he read the letter. Mrs Morel felt everything go silent inside her. He read the letter. "—'and will you reply by Thursday whether you accept—Yours faithfully—' —they want me, mother, at a hundred and twenty a year, and don't even ask to see me. Didn't I tell you I could do it! Think of me in London!—And I can give you twenty pounds a year, Mater—we s'll all be rolling in money."

"We shall, my son," she answered sadly.

It never occurred to him that she might be more hurt at his going away, than glad of his success. Indeed, as the days drew near for his departure, her heart began to close and grow dreary with despair. She loved him so much. More than that, she hoped in him so much. Almost she lived by him. She liked to do things for him: she liked to put a cup for his tea and to iron his collars, of which he was so proud. It was a joy to her to have him proud of his collars. There was no laundry. So she used to rub away at them with her little convex iron, to polish them, till they shone from the sheer pressure of her arm. Now she would not do it for him. Now he was going away. She felt almost as if he were going as well out of her heart. He did not seem to leave her inhabited with himself. That was the grief and the pain to her. He took nearly all himself away.

A few days before his departure—he was just twenty—he burned his love-letters. They had hung on a file at the top of the kitchen cupboard. From some of them he had read extracts to his mother. Some of them she had taken the trouble to read herself. But most were too trivial.

Now, on the Saturday morning he said:

"Come on, 'Postle, let's go through my letters, and you can have the birds and flowers."

Mrs Morel had done her Saturday's work on the Friday, because he was having a last day's holiday. She was making him a rice cake, which he loved, to take with him. He was scarcely conscious that she was so miserable.

He took the first letter off the file. It was mauve-tinted, and had purple and green thistles. William sniffed the page:

"Nice scent—smell—!"

And he thrust the sheet under Paul's nose.

"Um!" said Paul, breathing in. "What d'you call it?"

"That's Jockey Club," said William, though he did not know in the least.

"It couldn't be thistle," said Paul, "because thistles don't smell."

"Listen—'Dear One—' —hark Mater."

"I dont want to hear the silly hussies," said Mrs Morel.

"Listen though! 'Dear One—You *did not* tell me your first name, so I can only call you what you *are*. I have to write to you, or I think I shall go off my head—' think of that, Mater."

"Yes the silly lunatics! It's little head they've got, to *go* off.—And they don't know what a rod they're making for their backs puffing you up."

"That's not puffing me up. She *was* gone on me."

"And if she was, is it anything to be proud of? A silly thing!"

"You shouldn't say 'puffing him up to make a rod for her own back,' mother," interrupted Paul.

"*You* would be right, of course," laughed his mother.

"'I fairly *love* Scotch things since I saw you in that kilt. It suited you *awfully*. I think I *never* saw anybody look so nice, with that *kilt* and those *stockings*—' It's my knees—I know it's my knees Mater. They can't escape 'em."

"They can't, if they're common cats."

"Clip the thistle out, Postle. It's a nice one, isn't it?"

Paul loved the pretty little embellishments to the love-letters. William burned the letter. The next was pink, with cherry blossom in the corner.

"Cherry blossom!" said Paul, sniffing deeply. "Grand—smell mother."

His mother ducked her small, fine nose down to the paper.

"*I* don't want to smell their rubbish," she said, sniffing.

"This girl's father," said William, "is as rich as Crœsus. He owns property without end.—She calls me Lafayette, because I know French.—'You will see, I've forgiven you.'—I like *her* forgiving me.—'I told mother about you this morning, and she will have much pleasure if you come to tea on Sunday, but she will have to get father's consent also. I sincerely hope he will agree. I will let you know how it transpires. If however you—'"

"'Let you know how it' what?" interrupted Mrs Morel.

"'Transpires'—oh yes!"

"'Transpires!'" repeated Mrs Morel, mockingly. "I thought she was so well-educated!"

William felt slightly uncomfortable, and abandoned this maiden, giving Paul the corner with the cherry-blossom. He continued to read extracts from his letters, some of which amused his mother, some of which saddened her and made her anxious for him.

"My lad," she said, "they're very wise. They know they've only got to flatter your vanity, and you press up to them like a dog that has its head scratched."

"Well, they can't go on scratching for ever," he replied. "And when they've done, I trot away."

"But one day you'll find a string round your neck, that you can't pull off," she answered.

"Not me! I'm equal to any of 'em, Mater, they needn't flatter themselves."

"You flatter *yourself*," she said quietly.

Soon there was a heap of twisted black pages, all that remained of the file of scented letters: except that Paul had thirty or forty pretty tickets from the corners of the notepaper, swallows and forget-me-nots and ivy sprays. And William went to London, to start a new file.

CHAPTER IV

The young Life of Paul

Paul would be built like his mother, slightly, and rather small. His fair hair went reddish, and then dark brown: his eyes were grey. He was a pale, quiet child, with eyes that seemed to listen, and with a full, dropping underlip.

As a rule, he seemed old for his years. He was so conscious 'of what other people felt, particularly his mother. When she fretted, he understood, and could have no peace. His soul seemed always attentive to her.

As he grew older, he became stronger. William was too far removed from him to accept him as a companion. So the smaller boy belonged at first almost entirely to Annie. She was a tom-boy and a 'flybie-skybie,' as her mother called her. But she was intensely fond of her second brother. So Paul was towed round at the heels of Annie, sharing her game. She raced wildly at lerky, with the other young wild-cats of the Bottoms. And always Paul flew beside her, living her share of the game, having as yet no part of his own. He was quiet and not noticeable. But his sister adored him. He always seemed to care for things if she wanted him to.

She had a big doll of which she was fearfully proud, though not so fond. So she laid the doll on the sofa, and covered it with an antimacassar, to sleep. Then she forgot it. Meantime Paul must practise jumping off the sofa arm. So he jumped crash into the face of the hidden doll. Annie rushed up, uttered a loud wail, and sat down to weep a dirge. Paul remained quite still.

"You couldn't tell it was there, mother: you couldn't tell it was there," he repeated over and over. So long as Annie wept for the doll he sat helpless with misery. Her grief wore itself out. She forgave her brother, he was so much upset. But a day or two afterwards she was shocked.

"Let's make a sacrifice of Arabella," he said. "Let's burn her." She was horrified, yet rather fascinated. She wanted to see what the boy would do. He made an altar of bricks, pulled some of the shavings out of Arabella's body, put the waxen fragments into the hollow face, poured on a little paraffin, and set the whole thing alight. He watched with wicked satisfaction the drops of wax melt off the broken forehead of Arabella, and drop like sweat into the flame. So long as the stupid big doll burned, he rejoiced in silence. At the end, he poked among the embers with a stick, fished out the arms and legs, all blackened, and smashed them under stones.

"That's the sacrifice of Missis Arabella," he said. "An' I'm glad there's nothing left of her."

Which disturbed Annie inwardly, although she could say nothing. He seemed to hate the doll so intensely, because he had broken it.

All the children, but particularly Paul, were peculiarly *against* their father, along with their mother. Morel continued to bully and to drink. He had periods, months at a time, when he made the whole life of the family a misery. Paul never forgot coming home from the Band of Hope, one Monday evening, and finding his mother with her eye swollen and discoloured, his father standing on the hearth-rug, feet astride, his head down, and William, just home from work, glaring at his father. There was a silence as the young children entered, but none of the elders looked round.

William was white to the lips, and his fists were clenched. He waited until the children were silent, watching with children's rage and hate, then he said:

"You coward, you daren't do it when I was in."

But Morel's blood was up. He swung round on his son. William was bigger, but Morel was hard-muscled, and mad with fury.

"Dossn't I?" he shouted. "Dossn't I? Ha'e much more o' thy chelp, my young jockey, an' I'll rattle my fist about thee. Ay an' I sholl that, dost see."

Morel crouched at the knees and showed his fist in an ugly, almost beast-like fashion. William was white with rage.

"Will yer!" he said, quiet and intense. "It'ud be the last time, though."

Morel danced a little nearer, crouching, drawing back his fist to strike. William put his fists ready. A light came into his blue eyes, almost like a laugh. He watched his father. Another word, and the men would have begun to fight. Paul hoped they would. The three children sat pale on the sofa.

"Stop it both of you," cried Mrs Morel, in a hard voice. "We've had enough for *one* night.—And *you*," she said, turning onto her husband, "look at your children."

Morel glanced at the sofa.

"Look at the children, you nasty little bitch," he sneered, "why what have *I* done to the children, I should like to know. But they're like yourself—you've put 'em up to your own tricks and nasty ways—you've learned 'em in it, you 'ave."

She refused to answer him. No one spoke. After a while, he threw his boots under the table and went to bed.

"Why didn't you let me have a go at him," said William, when his father was upstairs. "I could easily have beaten him."

"A nice thing, your own father," she replied.

"'*Father*!'" repeated William. "Call *him my* father!"

"Well he is—and so—"

"But why don't you let me settle him, I could do easily."

"The idea!" she cried. "It hasn't come to *that* yet."

"No," he said, "it's come to worse—look at yourself. *Why* didn't you let me give it him."

"Because I couldn't bear it, so never think of it," she cried quickly.

And the children went to bed, miserably.

When William was growing up, the family moved from the Bottoms to a house on the brow of the hill, commanding a view of the valley, which spread out like a convex cockle shell, or a clamp shell, before it. In front of the house was a huge old ash-tree. The west wind, sweeping from Derbyshire, caught the houses with full force, and the tree shrieked again. Morel liked it.

"It's music," he said. "It sends me to sleep."

But Paul and Arthur and Annie hated it. To Paul, it became almost a demoniacal noise. The winter of their first year in the new house, their father was very bad. The children played in the street, on the brim of the wide dark valley, until eight o'clock. Then they went to bed. Their mother sat sewing below. Having such a great space in front of the house gave the children a feeling of night, of vastness, and of terror. This terror came in from the shrieking of the tree and the anguish of the home discord. Often Paul would wake up, after he had been asleep a long time, aware of thuds downstairs. Instantly he was wide awake. Then he heard the booming shouts of his father, come home nearly drunk, then the sharp replies of his mother, then the bang, bang of his father's fist on the table, and the nasty snarling shout as the man's voice got higher. And then the whole was drowned in a piercing medley of shrieks and cries from the great, wind-swept ash-tree. The children lay silent in suspense, waiting for a lull in the wind to hear what their father was doing. He might hit their mother again. There was a feeling of horror, a kind of bristling in the darkness, and a sense of blood. They lay with their hearts in the grip of an intense anguish. The wind came through the tree fiercer and fiercer. All the cords of the great harp hummed, whistled, and shrieked. And then, came the horror of the sudden silence: silence everywhere, outside, and downstairs. What was it?—was it a silence of blood? What had he done.

The children lay and breathed the darkness. And then, at last, they heard their father throw down his boots and tramp upstairs in his stocking feet. Still they listened. Then at last, if the wind allowed, they heard the water of the tap drumming into the kettle, which their mother was filling for morning, and they could go to sleep in peace.

So they were happy in the morning, happy, very happy, playing, dancing at night round the lonely lamppost in the midst of the darkness. But they had one tight place of anxiety in their hearts, one darkness in their eyes, which showed all their lives.

Paul hated his father. As a boy, he had a fervent private religion.

"Make him stop drinking," he prayed every night.

"Lord, let my father die," he prayed very often.

"Let him be killed at pit," he prayed when, after tea, the father did not come home from work.

That was another time when the family suffered intensely. The children came from school and had their teas. On the hob, the big black saucepan was simmering, the stew-jar was in the oven, ready for Morel's dinner. He was expected at five o'clock. But, for months, he would stop and drink every night on his way from work.

In the winter nights, when it was cold, and grew dark early, Mrs Morel would put a brass candlestick on the table, light a tallow candle to save the gas. The children finished their bread and butter, or dripping, and were ready to go out to play. But if Morel had not come, they faltered. The sense of his sitting in all his pit-dirt, drinking, after a long day's work, not coming home and eating and washing, but sitting getting drunk on an empty stomach, made Mrs Morel unable to bear herself. From her, the feeling was transmitted to the children. She never suffered alone any more: the children suffered with her.

Paul went out to play with the rest. Down in the great trough of twilight, tiny clusters of lights burned where the pits were. A few last colliers straggled up the dim field-path. The lamp-lighter came along. No more colliers came. Darkness shut down over the valley, work was gone, it was night.

Then Paul ran anxiously into the kitchen. The one candle still burned on the table, the big fire glowed red, Mrs Morel sat alone. On the hob the saucepan steamed: the dinner plate lay waiting on the table. All the room was full of the sense of waiting, waiting, for the man who was sitting in his pit-dirt, dinnerless, some mile away from home, across the darkness, drinking himself drunk. Paul stood in the doorway.

"Has my Dad come?" he asked.

"You can see he hasn't," said Mrs Morel, cross with the futility of the question.

Then the boy dawdled about, near his mother. They shared the same anxiety. Presently Mrs Morel went out and strained the potatoes.

"They're ruined and black," she said, "but what do I care." Not many words were spoken. Paul almost hated his mother for suffering because his father did not come home from work.

"What do you bother yourself for?" he said. "If he wants to stop and get drunk, why don't you let him?"

"Let him!" flashed Mrs Morel. "You may well say 'let him.'" She knew that the man who stops on the way home from work is on a quick way to ruining himself and his home. The children were yet young, and depended on the bread-winner. William gave her the sense of relief, providing her at last with someone to turn to, if Morel failed. But the tense atmosphere of the room on these waiting evenings was the same.

The minutes ticked away. At six o'clock, still the cloth lay on the table, still the dinner stood waiting, still the same sense of anxiety and expectation in the room. The boy could not stand it any longer. He could not go out and play. So he ran in to Mrs Inger, next door but one, for her to talk to him. She had no children. Her husband was good to her, but he was in a shop, and came home late. So, when she saw the lad at the door, she called:

"Come in, Paul."

The two sat talking for some time, when suddenly the boy rose, saying:

"Well, I'll be going and seeing if my mother wants an errand doing."

He pretended to be perfectly cheerful, and did not tell his friend what ailed him. Then he ran indoors.

Morel, at these times, came in churlish and hateful.

"This is a nice time to come home," said Mrs Morel.

"Wha's it matter to yo', what time I come whoam," he shouted.

And everybody in the house was still, because he was dangerous. He ate his food in the most brutal manner possible, and when he had done, pushed all the pots in a heap away from him, to lay his arms on the table. Then, he went to sleep.

Paul hated his father so. The collier's small, mean head with its black hair slightly soiled with grey, lay on the bare arms, and the face, dirty and inflamed, with a fleshy nose and thin, paltry brows, was turned sideways, asleep with beer and weariness and nasty temper. If anyone entered suddenly, or a noise were made, the man looked up and shouted:

"I'll lay my fist about thy y'ead, I'm tellin' thee, if tha doesna stop that clatter. Dost hear!"

And the two last words, shouted in a bullying fashion, usually at Annie, made the family writhe with hate of the man.

He was shut out from all family affairs. No one told him anything. The children, alone with their mother, told her all about the day's happenings, everything. Nothing had really taken place in them, until it was told to their mother. But as soon as the father came in, everything stopped. He was like the scotch in the smooth, happy machinery of the home. And he was always aware of this fall of silence on his entry, the shutting off of life, the unwelcome. But now it was gone too far to alter.

He would dearly have liked the children to talk to him, but they could not. Sometimes Mrs Morel would say:

"You ought to tell your father."

Paul won a prize in a competition in a child's paper. Everybody was highly jubilant.

"Now you'd better tell your father when he comes in," said Mrs Morel. "You know how he carries on and says he's never told anything."

"All right," said Paul. But he would almost rather have forfeited the prize than have to tell his father.

"I've won a prize in a competition, Dad," he said.

Morel turned round to him.

"Have you, my boy—what sort of a competition?"

"Oh nothing—about famous women."

"And how much is the prize, then, as you've got?"

"It's a book."

"Oh indeed!"

"About birds."

"Hm—hm!"

And that was all. Conversation was impossible between the father and any other member of the family. He was an outsider. He had denied the God in him.

The only times when he entered again into the life of his own people was when he worked, and was happy at work. Sometimes, in the evening, he cobbled the boots or mended the kettle or his pit-bottle. Then he always wanted several attendants, and the children enjoyed it. They united with him in the work, in the actual doing of something, when he was his real self again.

He was a good workman, dexterous, and one who, when he was in a good humour, always sang. He had whole periods, months, almost years, of friction and nasty temper. Then sometimes he was jolly again. It was nice to see him run with a piece of red-hot iron into the scullery, crying:

"Out of my road, out of my road!"

Then he hammered the soft, red-glowing stuff on his iron goose, and made the shape he wanted. Or he sat absorbed for a moment, soldering. Then the children watched with joy as the metal sank suddenly molten, and was shoved about against the nose of the soldering iron, while the room was full of a scent of burnt resin and hot tin, and Morel was silent and intent for a minute. He always sang when he mended boots, because of the jolly sound of hammering. And he was rather happy when he sat putting great patches on his moleskin pit trousers, which he would often do, considering them too dirty, and the stuff too hard, for his wife to mend.

But the best time for the young children was when he made fuses. Morel fetched a sheaf of long sound wheat straws from the attic. These he cleaned with his hand, till each one gleamed like a stalk of gold. After which he cut the straws into lengths of about six inches, leaving if he could a notch at the bottom of each piece. He always had a beautifully sharp knife, that could cut a straw clean without hurting it. Then he set in the middle of the table a heap of gunpowder, a little pile of black grains upon the white-scrubbed board. He made and trimmed the straws while Paul and Annie filled and plugged them. Paul loved to see the black grains trickle down a crack in his palm, into the mouth of the straw, peppering jollily downwards till the straw was full. Then he bunged up the mouth with a bit of soap—which he got on his thumb nail from a pat in a saucer—and the straw was finished.

"Look Dad!" he said.

"That's right, my beauty," replied Morel, who was peculiarly lavish of endearments to his second son. Paul popped the fuse into the powder tin, ready for the morning, when Morel would take it to the pit, and use it to fire a shot that would blast the coal down.

Meantime Arthur, still fond of his father, would lean on the arm of Morel's chair and say:

"Tell us about down-pit, Daddy."

This Morel loved to do.

"Well, there's one little 'oss, we call 'im Taffy," he would begin. "An' he's a fawce un!"

Morel had a warm way of telling a story. He made one feel Taffy's cunning.

"He's a brown un," he would answer, "an' not very high. Well, he comes i' th' stall wi' a rattle, an' then yo' 'ear 'im sneeze.

''Ello Taff,' you say, 'what art sneezin' for. Bin ta'ein' some snuff?'

An' e sneezes again. Then he slives up an' shoves 'is 'ead on yer, that cadin'.

'What's want, Taff?' yo' say."

"And what does he?" Arthur always asked.

"He wants a bit o' bacca, my duckey."

This story of Taffy would go on interminably, and everybody loved it.

Or sometimes it was a new tale.

"An' what dost think, my darlin'. When I went to put my coat on at snap time, what should go runnin' up my arm but a mouse.

'Hey up, theer!' I shouts.

An' I wor just in time ter get 'im by th' tail."

"And did you kill it?"

"I did, for they're a nuisance. The place is fair snied wi' 'em."

"An' what do they live on?"

"The corn as the 'osses drops—an' they'll get in your pocket an' eat your snap, if you'll let 'em—no matter where yo' hing your coat—the slivin' nibblin' little nuisances, for they are—"

These happy evenings could not take place unless Morel had some job to do. And then, he always went to bed very early, often before the children. There was nothing remaining for him to stay up for, when he had finished tinkering, and had skimmed the head lines of the newspaper.

And the children felt secure when their father was in bed. They lay and talked softly awhile. Then they started as the lights went suddenly sprawling over the ceiling, from the lamps that swung in the hands of the colliers tramping by outside, going to take the nine o'clock shift. They listened to the voices of the men, imagined them dipping down into the dark valley. Sometimes they went to the window and watched the three or four lamps growing tinier and tinier, swaying down the fields in the darkness. Then it was a joy to rush back to bed and cuddle closely in the warmth.

Paul was rather a delicate boy, subject to bronchitis. The others were all quite strong, so this was another reason for his mother's difference in feeling for him. One day he came home at dinner time feeling ill. But it was not a family to make any fuss.

"What's the matter with *you*?" his mother asked sharply.

"Nothing," he replied.

But he ate no dinner.

"If you eat no dinner you're not going to school," she said.

"Why?" he asked.

"That's why."

So after dinner he lay down on the sofa, on the warm chintz cushions the children loved. Then he fell into a kind of doze. That afternoon, Mrs Morel was ironing. She listened to the small, restless noise the boy made in his throat, as she worked. Again rose in her heart the old, almost weary feeling towards him. She had never expected him to live. And yet he had a great vitality in his young body. Perhaps it would have been a little relief to her if he had died. She always felt a mixture of anguish in her love for him.

He, in his semi-conscious sleep, was vaguely aware of the clatter of the iron on the iron-stand, of the faint thud, thud on the ironing-board. Once, roused, he opened his eyes to see his mother standing on the hearthrug with the hot iron near her cheek, listening as it were to the heat. Her still face, with the mouth closed tight from suffering and disillusion and self-denial, and her nose the smallest bit on one side, and her blue eyes so young, quick, and warm, made his heart contract with love. When she was quiet, so, she looked brave and rich with life, but as if she had been done out of her rights. It hurt the boy keenly, this feeling about her, that she had never had her life's fulfilment: and his own incapability to make up to her hurt him with a sense of impotence, yet made him patiently dogged inside. It was his childish aim.

She spat on the iron, and a little ball of spit bounded, raced off the dark glossy surface. Then, kneeling, she rubbed the iron on the sack lining of the hearthrug, vigorously. She was warm in the ruddy firelight. Paul loved the way she crouched and put her head on one side. Her movements were light and quick. It was always a pleasure to watch her. Nothing she ever did, no movement she ever made, could have been found fault with by her children.—The room was warm, and full of the scent of hot linen. Later on, the clergyman came and talked softly with her.

Paul was laid up with an attack of bronchitis. He did not mind much. What happened, happened, and it was no good kicking against the pricks. He loved the evenings, after eight o'clock, when the light was put out, and he could watch the fire flames spring over the darkness of the walls and ceiling; could watch huge shadows waving and tossing, till the room seemed full of men who battled silently.

On retiring to bed, the father would come into the sick-room. He was always very gentle if anyone were ill. But he disturbed the atmosphere for the boy.

"Are ter asleep, my darlin'?" Morel asked softly.

"No—is my mother comin'?"

"She's just finishin' foldin' the clothes. Do you want anything?" Morel rarely "thee'd" his son.

"I don't want nothing.—But how long will she be?"

"Not long, my duckie."

The father waited undecidedly on the hearthrug for a moment or two. He felt his son did not want him. Then he went to the top of the stairs and said to his wife:

"This childt's axin' for thee—how long art goin' to be?"

"Until I've finished, good gracious! Tell him to go to sleep."

"She says you're to go to sleep," the father repeated gently to Paul.

"Well, I want *her* to come," insisted the boy.

"He says he can't go off till you come," Morel called downstairs.

"Eh dear! I shan't be long. And do stop shouting downstairs. There's the other children—"

Then Morel came again, and crouched before the bedroom fire. He loved a fire dearly.

"She says she won't be long," he said.

He loitered about indefinitely. The boy began to get feverish with irritation. His father's presence seemed to aggravate all his sick impatience. At last Morel, after having stood looking at his son awhile, said softly:

"Goodnight my darling."

"Goodnight," Paul replied, turning round in relief to be alone.

Paul loved to sleep with his mother. Sleep is still most perfect, in spite of hygienists, when it is shared with a beloved. The warmth, the security and peace of soul, the utter comfort from the touch of the other, knits the sleep, so that it takes the body and soul completely in its healing. Paul lay against her and slept, and got better;—whilst she, always a bad sleeper, fell later on into a profound sleep that seemed to give her faith.

In convalescence he would sit up in bed, see the fluffy horses feeding at the troughs in the field, scattering their hay on the trodden yellow snow; watch the miners troop home, small, black figures trailing slowly in gangs across the white field. Then the night came up in dark blue vapor from the snow.

In convalescence everything was wonderful. The snowflakes, suddenly arriving on the window pane, clung there a moment like swallows, then were gone, and a drop of water was crawling down the glass. The snowflakes whirled round the corner of the house, like pigeons dashing by. Away across the valley, the little black train crawled doubtfully over the great whiteness.

While they were so poor, the children were delighted if they could do anything to help, economically. Annie and Paul and Arthur went out early in the morning, in summer, looking for mushrooms, hunting through the wet grass, from which the larks were rising, for the white skinned, wonderful naked bodies crouched secretly in the green. And if they got half a pound, they felt exceedingly happy: there was the joy of finding something, the joy of accepting something straight from the hand of nature, and the joy of contributing to the family exchequer.

But the most important harvest, after gleaning for frumenty, was the blackberries. Mrs Morel must buy fruit for puddings, on the Saturdays; also she liked blackberries. So Paul and Arthur scoured the coppices and woods and old quarries, so long as a blackberry was to be found, every week end going on their search. In that region of mining villages, blackberries became a comparative rarity. But Paul hunted far and wide. He loved being out in the country, among the bushes. But he also could not bear to go home to his mother empty. That, he felt, would disappoint her, and he would have died rather.

"Good gracious!" she would exclaim as the lads came in, late, and tired to death, and hungry. "Wherever have you been ?"

"Well," replied Paul, "there wasn't any, so we went over Misk Hills.—And look here, our mother."

She peeped into the basket.

"Now those are fine ones," she exclaimed.

"And there's over two pounds—isn't there over two pounds?"

She tried the basket.

"Yes," she answered, doubtfully.

Then Paul fished out a little spray. He always brought her one spray, the best he could find.

"Pretty!" she said, in a curious tone, of a woman accepting a love-token.

The boy walked all day, went miles and miles, rather than own himself beaten, and come home to her empty-handed. She never realised this, whilst he was young. She was a woman who waited for her children to grow up. And William occupied her chiefly.

But when William went to Nottingham, and was not so much at home, the mother made a companion of Paul. The latter was unconsciously jealous of his brother, and William was jealous of him. At the same time, they were good friends.

Mrs Morel's intimacy with her second son was more subtle and fine, perhaps not so passionate as with her eldest. It was the rule that Paul should fetch the money on Friday afternoons. The colliers of the five pits were paid on Fridays, but not individually. All the earnings of each stall were put down to the chief butty, as contractor, and he divided the wages again, either in the public house, or in his own home. So that the children could fetch the money, school closed early on Friday afternoons. Each of the Morel children, William, then Annie, then Paul, had fetched the money on Friday afternoons, until they went themselves to work. Paul used to set off at half past three, with a little calico bag in his pocket. Down all the paths, women, girls, children and men were seen trooping to the Offices.

These offices were quite handsome: a new, red-brick building, almost like a mansion, standing in its own well-kept grounds at the end of Greenhill Lane. The waiting room was the hall, a long, bare room paved with blue brick, and having a seat all round, against the wall. Here sat the colliers in their pit-dirt. They had come up early. The women and children usually loitered about on the red gravel paths. Paul always examined the grass border, and the big grass bank, because in it grew tiny pansies and tiny forget me nots. There was a sound of many voices. The women had on their Sunday hats. The girls chattered loudly. Little dogs ran here and there. The green shrubs were silent all around.

Then, from inside came the cry "Spinney Park—Spinney Park." All the folk for Spinney Park trooped inside. When it was time for Bretty to be paid, Paul went in among the crowd. The pay-room was quite small. A counter went across, dividing it into half. Behind the counter stood two men, Mr Braithwaite and his clerk, Mr Winterbottom. Mr Braithwaite was large, somewhat of the stern patriarch in appearance, having a rather thin white beard. He was usually muffled in an enormous silk neckerchief, and right up to the hot summer, a huge fire burned in the open grate. No window was open. Sometimes in winter, the air scorched the throats of the people, coming in from the freshness.—Mr Winterbottom was rather small and fat and very bald. He made remarks that were not witty, whilst his chief launched forth patriarchal admonitions against the colliers.

The room was crowded with miners in their pit dirt, men who had been home and changed, and women, and one or two children, and usually a dog. Paul was quite small, so it was often his fate to be jammed behind the legs of the men, near the fire which scorched him. He knew the order of the names—they went according to stall number.

"Holliday," came the ringing voice of Mr Braithwaite. Then Mrs Holliday stepped silently forward, was paid, drew aside.

"Bower—John Bower."

A boy stepped to the counter. Mr Braithwaite, large and irascible, glowered at him over his spectacles.

"John Bower!" he repeated.

"It's me," said the boy.

"Why you used to 'ave a different nose than that," said glossy Mr Winterbottom, peeering over the counter. The people tittered, thinking of John Bower senior.

"How is it your father's not come?" said Mr Braithwaite, in a large and magisterial voice.

"He's badly," piped the boy.

"You should tell him to keep off the drink," pronounced the great cashier.

"An' niver mind if he puts his foot through yer," said a mocking voice from behind.

All the men laughed. The large and important cashier looked down at his next sheet.

"Fred Pilkington!" he called, quite indifferent.

Mr Braithwaite was an important shareholder in the firm.

Paul knew his turn was next but one, and his heart began to beat. He was pushed against the chimney piece. His calves were burning. But he did not hope to get through the wall of men.

"Walter Morel!" came the ringing voice.

"Here!" piped Paul, small and inadequate.

"Morel—Walter Morel!" the cashier repeated, his finger and thumb on the invoice, ready to pass on.

Paul was suffering convulsions of self consciousness, and could not or would not shout. The backs of the men obliterated him. Then Mr Winterbottom came to the rescue.

"He's here—where is he! Morel's lad?"

The fat, red, bald little man peered round with keen eyes. He pointed at the fireplace. The colliers looked round, moved aside, and disclosed the boy.

"Here he is!" said Mr Winterbottom.

Paul went to the counter.

"'Seventeen pounds eleven and fivepence'—Why don't you shout up when you're called?" said Mr Braithwaite. He banged onto the invoice a five pound bag of silver, then, in a delicate and pretty movement, picked up a little ten-pound column of gold, and plumped it beside the silver. The gold slid in a bright stream over the paper. The cashier finished counting off the money, the boy dragged the whole down the counter to Mr Winterbottom, to whom the stoppages for rent, and tools, must be paid. Here he suffered again.

"Sixteen an' six," said Mr Winterbottom.

The lad was too much upset to count. He pushed forward some loose silver and half a sovereign.

"How much do you think you've given me?" asked Mr Winterbottom.

The boy looked at him, but said nothing. He had not the faintest notion.

"Haven't you got a tongue in your head?"

Paul bit his lip and pushed forward some more silver.

"Don't they teach you to count at the Board School?" he asked.

"Nowt but algibbra an' French," said a collier.

"An' cheek an' impidence," said another.

Paul was keeping someone waiting. With trembling fingers he got his money into the bag, and slid out. He suffered the tortures of the damned on these occasions.

His relief, when he got outside, and was walking along the Mansfield Road, was infinite. On the Park Wall the mosses were green. There were some gold and some white fowls pecking under the apple trees of an orchard. The colliers were walking home in a stream. The boy went near the wall, self consciously. He knew many of the men, but could not recognise them in their dirt. And this was a new torture to him.

When he got down to the New Inn, at Bretty, his father was not yet come. Mrs Wharmby, the landlady, knew him. His grandmother, Morel's mother, had been Mrs Wharmby's friend.

"Your father's not come yet," said the landlady, in the peculiar half scornful, half patronising voice of a woman who talks chiefly to grown men. "Sit you down."

Paul sat down on the edge of the bench in the bar. Some colliers were "reckoning"—sharing out their money—in a corner; others came in. They all glanced at the boy, without speaking. At last Morel came: brisk and with something of an air, even in his blackness.

"Hello," he said, rather tenderly, to his son. "Have you bested me? Shall you have a drink of something?"

Paul, and all the children, were bred up fierce anti-alcoholists. And he would have suffered more in drinking a lemonade before all the men, than in having a tooth drawn.

The landlady looked at him *de haut en bas*, rather pitying, and at the same time resenting his clear, fierce morality. Paul went home, glowering. He entered the house silently. Friday was baking day, and there was usually a hot bun. His mother put it before him.

Suddenly he turned on her in a fury, his eyes flashing.

"I'm *not* going to the Office any more," he said.

"Why, what's the matter?" his mother asked in surprise. His sudden rages rather amused her.

"I'm *not* going any more," he declared.

"Oh very well, tell your father so."

He chewed his bun as if he hated it.

"I'm not—I'm not going to fetch the money."

"Then one of Carlin's children can go. They'd be glad enough of the sixpence," said Mrs Morel.

This sixpence was Paul's only income. It mostly went in buying birthday presents. But it *was* an income, and he treasured it. But:

"They can have it then!" he said. "I don't want it."

"Oh very well," said his mother. "But you needn't bully *me* about it."

"They're hateful, and common, and hateful, they are, and I'm not going any more. Mr Braithwaite drops his 'h's', an' Mr Winterbottom says 'you was'."

"And is that why you won't go any more?" smiled Mrs Morel.

The boy was silent for some time. His face was pale, his eyes dark and furious. His mother moved about at her work, taking no notice of him.

"They always stan' in front of me, so's I can't get out," he said.

"Well my lad, you've only to *ask* them," she replied.

"An' then Alfred Winterbottom says 'What do they teach you at the board school?'"

"They never taught *him* much," said Mrs Morel, "that is a fact—neither manners nor wit—and his cunning he was born with."

"An' they say 'Nowt but algibbra an' French.' They *don't* teach me French at the board school."

"And if they did," smiled his mother, "you needn't get into a state about it.—You're such a baby, my boy, if anyone says a word."

"Well—!"—he looked at her almost in tears, and still with more rage and hate than grief.

"You're such a silly," she said. "You can't simply say 'it's my turn now', you let yourself be passed over, and then get into a fury. It's all your own fault."

So, in her own way, she soothed him. His ridiculous hypersensitiveness made her heart ache. And sometimes, the fury in his eyes roused her, made her sleeping soul lift up its head a moment, surprised.

"What was the cheque?" she asked.

"Seventeen pounds eleven and fivepence, and sixteen and six

stoppages," replied the boy. "It's a good week, and only five shillings stoppages for my father."

So she was able to calculate how much her husband had earned, and could call him to account if he gave her short money. Morel always kept to himself the secret of the week's amount.

Friday was baking night and market night. It was the rule that Paul should stay at home and bake. He loved to stop in and draw or read: he was very fond of drawing. Annie always "gallivanted" on Friday nights, Arthur was enjoying himself as usual. So the boy remained alone.

Mrs Morel loved her marketing. In the tiny market-place on the top of the hill, where four roads, from Nottingham and Derby, Ilkeston and Mansfield meet, many stalls were erected. Brakes ran in from surrounding villages. The market-place was full of women, the streets packed with men. It was amazing to see so many men everywhere in the streets. Mrs Morel usually quarrelled with her lacewoman, sympathised with her fruit man, who was a gabey, but his wife was a bad un, laughed with the fish man, who was a scamp but so droll, put the linoleum man in his place, was cold with the odd-wares man, and only went to the crockery man when she was driven—or drawn by the cornflowers on a little dish. Then she was coldly polite.

"I wondered how much that little dish was," she said.

"Sevenpence to you."

"Thank you."

She put the dish down and walked away. But she could not leave the market place without it. Again she went by where the pots lay coldly on the floor, and she glanced at the dish, furtively, pretending not to.

She was a little woman in a bonnet and a black costume. Her bonnet was in its third year; it was a great grievance to Annie.

"Mother!" the girl implored, "don't wear that nubbly little bonnet."

"Then what else shall I wear," replied the mother, tartly. "And I'm sure it's right enough."

It had started with a tip: then had had flowers: now was reduced to black lace and a bit of jet.

"It looks rather come down," said Paul. "Couldn't you give it a pick me up."

"I'll jowl your head for impudence," said Mrs Morel, and she tied the strings of the black bonnet valiantly under her chin.

She glanced at the dish again. Both she and her enemy, the pot-man, had an uncomfortable feeling, as if there were something between them. Suddenly he shouted:

"Do you want it for fivepence?"

She started. Her heart hardened. But then she stooped and took up her dish.

"I'll have it," she said.

"Yer'll do me the favour, like?" he said. "Yer'd better spit in it, like yer do when y'ave something give yer."

Mrs Morel paid him the fivepence in a cold manner.

"I don't see you give it me," she said. "You wouldn't let me have it for fivepence if you didn't want to."

"In this flamin' scrattlin' place you may count yerself lucky if you can give your things away," he growled.

"Yes, there are bad times, and good," said Mrs Morel.

But she had forgiven the pot man. They were friends. She dare now finger his pots. So she was happy.

Paul was waiting for her. He loved her homecoming. She was always her best so, triumphant, tired, laden with parcels, feeling rich in spirit. He heard her quick light step in the entry and looked up from his drawing.

"Oh!" she sighed, smiling at him from the doorway.

"My word you *are* loaded!" he exclaimed, putting down his brush.

"I am!" she gasped. "That brazen Annie said she'd meet me. *Such* a weight!"

She dropped her string bag, and her packages, on the table.

"Is the bread done?" she asked, going to the oven.

"The last one is soaking," he replied. "You needn't look, I've not forgotten it."

"Oh that pot man!" she said, closing the oven door. "You know what a wretch I've said he was. Well, I don't think he's quite so bad."

"Don't you?"

The boy was attentive to her. She took off her little black bonnet.

"No—I think he can't make any money—well, it's everybody's cry alike nowadays—and it makes him disagreeable."

"It would *me*," said Paul.

"Well, one can't wonder at it.—And he let me have—how much do you think he let me have *this* for?"

She took the dish out of its rag of newspaper, and stood looking on it with joy.

"Show me!" said Paul.

The two stood together gloating over the dish.

"I *love* cornflowers on things," said Paul.

"Yes, and I thought of the teapot you bought me—"

"One and three," said Paul.

"Fivepence!"

"It's not enough, mother."

"No. Do you know, I fairly sneaked off with it. But I'd been extravagant, I couldn't afford any more. And he needn't have let me have it if he hadn't wanted to."

"No, he needn't, need he," said Paul, and the two comforted each other from the fear of having robbed the pot-man.

"We c'n have stewed fruit in it," said Paul.

"Or custard, or a jelly," said his mother.

"Or radishes and lettuce," said he.

"Don't forget that bread," she said, her voice bright with glee.

Paul looked in the oven—tapped the loaf on the base.

"It's done," he said, giving it to her.

She tapped it also.

"Yes," she replied, going to unpack her bag.—"Oh, and I'm a wicked extravagant woman—I know I s'll come to want."

He hopped to her side eagerly, to see her latest extravagance. She unfolded another lump of newspaper and disclosed some roots of pansies and of crimson daisies.

"Four penn'orth!" she moaned.

"How *cheap*!" he cried.

"Yes, but I couldn't afford it *this* week of all weeks."

"But lovely!" he cried.

"Aren't they!" she exclaimed, giving way to pure joy. "Paul—look at this yellow one—isn't it—!—and a face just like an old man!"

"Just!" cried Paul, stooping to sniff. "And smells that nice! But he's a bit splashed."

He ran in the scullery, came back with the flannel, and carefully washed the pansy.

"*Now* look at him now he's wet!" he said.

"Yes!" she exclaimed, brimful of satisfaction.

The children of Scargill Street felt quite select. At the end where the Morels lived, there were not many young things. So the few were more united. Boys and girls played together, the girls joining in the fights and the rough games, the boys taking part in the dancing games and rings and make belief of the girls.

Annie and Paul and Arthur loved the winter evenings, when it was not wet. They stayed indoors till the colliers were all gone home, till it was thick dark, and the street would be deserted. Then they tied their scarves round their necks, for they scorned overcoats, as all the colliers' children did, and went out. The entry was very dark, and at the end, the whole great night opened out, in a hollow, with a little tangle of lights below where Minton pit lay, and another far away opposite, for Selby. The farthest tiny lights seemed to stretch out the darkness forever. The children looked anxiously down the road at the one lamp-post, which stood at the end of the field path. If the little, luminous space were deserted, the two boys felt genuine desolation. They stood with their hands in their pockets under the lamp, turning their backs on the night, quite miserable, watching the dark houses. Suddenly a pinafore under a short coat was seen, and a long legged girl came flying up.

"Wheer's Billy Pillins an' your Annie an' Eddie Dakin?"

"I don't know."

But it did not matter so much—there were three now. They set up a game round the lamp-post, till the others rushed up yelling. Then the play went fast and furious.

There was only this one lamp-post. Behind, was the great scoop of darkness, as if all the night were there. In front, another wide, dark way opened over the hill brow. Occasionally somebody came out of this way and went into the field down the path. In a dozen yards, the night had swallowed them. The children played on.

They were brought exceedingly close together, owing to their isolation. If a quarrel took place, the whole play was spoilt. Arthur was very touchy, and Billy Pillins, really Philips, was worse. Then Paul had to side with Arthur, and on Paul's side went Alice, while Billy Pillins always had Emmie Limb and Eddie Dakin to back him up. Then the six would fight, hate with a fury of hatred, and flee home in terror. Paul never forgot, after one of these fierce internecine fights, seeing a big red moon lift itself up, slowly, between the waste road over the hill-top; steadily, like a great bird. And he thought of the bible, that the moon should be turned to blood. And the next day he made haste to be friends with Billy Pillins. And then the wild, intense games went on again under the lamp post, surrounded by so much darkness. Mrs Morel, going into her parlour, would hear the children singing away:

> "My shoes are made of Spanish leather
>   My socks are made of silk;
> I wear a ring on every finger
>   I wash myself in milk."

They sounded so perfectly absorbed in the game, as their voices came out of the night, that they had the feel of wild creatures singing. It stirred the mother. And she understood when they came in at eight o'clock, ruddy, with brilliant eyes, and quick passionate speech.

They all loved the Scargill Street house for its openness, for the great scallop of the world it had in view. On summer evenings, the women would stand against the field fence, gossiping, facing the west, watching the sunsets flare quickly out, till the Derbyshire hills ridged across the crimson, far away, like the black crest of a newt.

In this summer season, the pits never turned full time, particularly the soft coal. Mrs Dakin, who lived next door to Mrs Morel, going to the field fence to shake her hearth-rug, would spy men coming slowly up the hill. She saw at once they were colliers. Then she waited, a tall, thin, shrew faced woman, standing on the hill brow almost like a menace to the poor colliers who were toiling up. It was only eleven o'clock. From the far-off, wooded hills the haze that hangs like fine black crape at the back of a summer morning had not yet dissipated. The first man came to the stile. 'Chock-chock!' went the gate under his thrust.

"What, han' yer knocked off?" cried Mrs Dakin.

"We han, Missis."

"It's a pity as they letn yer goo," she said, sarcastically.

"It is that," replied the man.

"Nay, you know you're flig to come up again," she said.

And the man went on. Mrs Dakin, going up her yard, spied Mrs Morel taking the ashes to the ash-pit.

"I reckon Minton's knocked off, Missis," she cried.

"Isn't it sickenin'!" exclaimed Mrs Morel in wrath.

"Ha!—But I'n just seed Jont Hutchly."

"They might as well have saved their shoe-leather," said Mrs Morel, and both women went indoors disgusted.

The colliers, their faces scarcely blackened, were trooping home again. Morel hated to go back. He loved the sunny morning. But he had gone to pit to work, and to be sent home again spoilt his temper.

"Good gracious, at this time!" exclaimed his wife, as he entered.

"Can I help it woman!" he shouted.

"And I've not done half enough dinner."

"Then I'll eat my bit o' snap as I took with me," he bawled, pathetically. He felt ignominious and sore.

And the children coming home from school, would wonder to see their father eating with his dinner the two thick slices of rather dry and dirty bread and butter, that had been to pit and back.

"What's my Dad eating his snap for now?" asked Arthur.

"I should ha'e it holled at me if I didna," snorted Morel.

"What a story!" exclaimed his wife.

"An' is it goin' to be wasted?" said Morel. "I'm not such an extravagant mortal as you lot, with your waste. If I drop a bit of bread at pit, in all the dust an' dirt, I pick it up an' eat it."

"The mice would eat it," said Paul. "It wouldn't be wasted."

"Good bread an' butter's not for mice, neither," said Morel. "Dirty or not dirty, I'd eat it rather than it should be wasted."

"You might leave it for the mice and pay for it out of your next pint," said Mrs Morel.

"Oh might I!" he exclaimed.

They were very poor that autumn. William had just gone away to London, and his mother missed his money. He sent ten shillings once or twice, but he had many things to pay for at first. His letters came regularly, once a week. He wrote a good deal to his mother, telling her all his life, how he made friends, and was exchanging lessons with a Frenchman, how he enjoyed London. His mother felt again he was remaining to her just as when he was at home. She wrote to him every week her direct, rather witty letters. All day long, as she cleaned the house, she thought of him. He was in London: he would do well. Almost, he was like her knight who wore *her* favour in the battle.

He was coming at Christmas for five days. There had never been such preparations. Paul and Arthur scoured the land for holly and evergreens. Annie made the pretty paper hoops in the old-fashioned way. And there was unheard-of extravagance in the larder. Mrs Morel made a big and magnificent cake. Then, feeling queenly, she showed Paul how to blanche almonds. He skinned the long nuts reverently, counting them all, to see not one was lost. It was said that eggs whisked better in a cold place. So the boy stood in the scullery, where the temperature was nearly at freezing point, and whisked and whisked, and flew in excitement to his mother as the white of egg grew stiffer and more snowy.

"Just look, mother—isn't it lovely?"

And he balanced a bit on his nose, then blew it in the air.

"Now don't waste it," said the mother.

Everybody was mad with excitement. William was coming on Christmas Eve. Mrs Morel surveyed her pantry. There was a big plum cake, and a rice cake: jam tarts, lemon tarts, and mince pies, two enormous dishes. She was finishing cooking:—Spanish tarts and cheese-cakes. Everywhere was decorated. The kissing-bunch, of berried holly hung with bright and glittering things, spun slowly over Mrs Morel's head as she trimmed her little tarts in the kitchen. A great fire roared. There was a scent of cooked pastry. He was due at seven o'clock, but he would be late. The three children had gone to meet him. She was alone. But at a quarter to seven, Morel came in again. Neither wife nor husband spoke. He sat in his arm-chair, quite awkward with excitement, and she quietly went on with her baking. Only by the careful way in which she did things could it be told how much moved she was. The clock ticked on.

"What time dost say he's coming?" Morel asked, for the fifth time.

"The train gets in at half past six," she replied, emphatically.

"Then he'll be here at ten past seven."

"Eh bless you, it'll be hours late, on the Midland," she said, indifferently. But she hoped, by expecting him late, to bring him early. Morel went down the entry to look for him. Then he came back.

"Goodness man!" she said. "You're like an ill-sitting hen."

"Hadna you better be gettin' him summat t'eat ready?" asked the father.

"There's plenty of time," she answered.

"There's not so much as *I* can see on," he answered, turning crossly in his chair. She began to clear her table. The kettle was singing. They waited and waited.

Meantime the three children were on the platform at Lethley Bridge, on the Midland main line, two miles from home. They waited one hour. A train came—he was not there. Down the line the red and green lights shone. It was very dark and very cold.

"Ask him if the London train's come," said Paul to Annie, when they saw a man in a tip cap.

"I'm not," said Annie. "You be quiet—he might send us off."

But Paul was dying for the man to know they were expecting someone by the London train: it sounded so grand. Yet he was much too much scared of broaching any man, let alone one in a peaked cap, to dare to ask. The three children could scarcely go into the waiting room, for fear of being sent away, and for fear something should happen whilst they were off the platform. Still they waited in the dark and cold.

"It's an hour an' a half late," said Arthur, pathetically.

"Well," said Annie, "it's Christmas eve."

They all grew silent. He wasn't coming. They looked down the darkness of the railway. There was London! It seemed the uttermost of distance. They thought, anything might happen, if one came from London. They were all too troubled to talk. Cold, and unhappy, and silent, they huddled together on the platform.

At last, after more than two hours, they saw the lights of an engine veering round, away down the darkness. A porter ran out. The children drew back with beating hearts. A great train, bound for Manchester, drew up. Two doors opened—and from one of them, William. They flew to him. He handed parcels to them cheerily, and immediately began to explain that this great train had stopped for *his* sake, at such a small station as Lethley Bridge: it was not booked to stop.

Meanwhile the parents were getting anxious. The table was set, the chop was cooked, everything was ready. Mrs Morel put on her black apron. She was wearing her best dress. Then she sat, pretending to read. The minutes were a torture to her.

"Hm!" said Morel. "It's an hour an' a ha'ef."

"And those children waiting!" she said.

"Th' train canna ha' come in yit," he said.

"I tell you, on Christmas Eve they're *hours* wrong."

They were both a bit cross with each other, so gnawed with anxiety. The ash-tree moaned outside in a cold, raw wind. And all that space of night from London home! Mrs Morel suffered. The slight click of the works inside the clock irritated her: it was getting so late: it was getting unbearable.

At last there was a sound of voices, and a footstep in the entry.

"He's here!" cried Morel, jumping up.

Then he stood back. The mother ran a few steps towards the door, and waited. There was a rush and a patter of feet, the door burst open, William was there. He dropped his gladstone bag and took his mother in his arms.

"Mater!" he said.

"My boy!" she cried.

And for two seconds, no longer, she clasped him and kissed him. Then she withdrew and said, trying to be quite normal:

"But how late you are!"

"Aren't I!" he cried, turning to his father.

"Well Dad!"

The two men shook hands.

"Well my lad!"

Morel's eyes were wet.

"We thought tha'd niver be commin'," he said.

"Oh I'd come," exclaimed William.

Then the son turned round to his mother.

"But you look well," she said proudly, laughing.

"Well!" he exclaimed. "I should think so—coming home."

He was a fine fellow, big, straight, and fearless looking. He looked round, at the evergreens and the kissing bunch and the little tarts that lay in their tins on the hearth.

"By jove, mother, it's not different," he said, as if in relief.

Everybody was still for a second. Then he suddenly sprang forward, picked a tart from the hearth, and pushed it whole into his mouth.

"Well did iver you see such a parish oven!" the father exclaimed.

He had brought them endless presents. Every penny he had, he had spent on them. There was a sense of luxury overflowing in the house. For his mother, there was an umbrella with gold on the pale handle. She kept it to her dying day, and would have lost anything rather than that. Everybody had something gorgeous, and besides, there were pounds of unknown sweets: Turkish delight, crystallised pineapple, and such like things which, the children thought, only the splendour of London could provide. And Paul boasted of these sweets among his friends.

"Real pineapple, cut off in slices, and then turned into crystal—fair grand!"

Everybody was mad with happiness in the family. Home was home, and they loved it with a passion of love, whatever the suffering had been. There were parties, there were rejoicings. People came in to see William, to see what difference London had made to him. And they all found him "such a gentleman, and *such* a fine fellow, my word!"

When he went away again the children retired to various places to weep alone, Morel went to bed in misery, and Mrs Morel felt as if she were numbed by some drug, as if her feelings were paralysed. She loved him passionately.

He was in the office of a lawyer connected with a large shipping firm, and at the midsummer, his chief offered him a trip in the Mediterranean, on one of the boats, for quite a small cost. Mrs Morel wrote: "Go, go, my boy, you may never have a chance again, and I should love to think of you cruising there in the Mediterranean almost better than to have you at home." But William came home for his fortnight's holiday. Not even the Mediterranean, which pulled at all his young man's desire to travel, and at his poor man's wonder at the glamorous south, could take him away when he might come home. That compensated his mother for much.

CHAPTER V

Paul Launches into Life

Morel was rather a heedless man, careless of danger. So, he had endless accidents. Now, when Mrs Morel heard the rattle of an empty coal-cart cease at her entry-end, she ran into the parlour to look, expecting almost to see her husband seated in the wagon, his face grey under his dirt, his body limp and sick with some hurt or other. If it were he she would run out to help.

About a year after William went to London, and just after Paul had left school, before he got work, Mrs Morel was upstairs and her son was painting in the kitchen—he was very clever with his brush—when there came a knock at the door. Crossly, he put down his brush to go. At the same moment his mother opened a window upstairs and looked down.

A pit lad in his dirt stood on the threshold.

"Is this Walter Morel's?" he asked.

"Yes!" said Mrs Morel. "What is it?"

But she had guessed already.

"Your mester's got hurt," he said.

"Eh dear me!" she exclaimed. "It's a wonder if he hadn't, lad. And what's he done this time?"

"I don't know for sure, but it's 'is leg somewhere. They ta'ein' 'im ter th'ospital."

"Good gracious me!" she exclaimed. "Eh dear, what a one he is! There's not five minutes of peace, I'll be hanged if there is! His thumb's nearly better, and now—Did you see him?"

"I seed him at th' bottom. An' I seed 'em bring 'im up in a tub, an' 'e wor in a dead faint. But he shouted like anythink when Doctor Fraser examined him i'th' lamp cabin—an' cossed an' swore—an' said as 'e wor goin' to be ta'en whoam—'e worn't goin' ter th'ospital—!" The boy faltered to an end.

"He *would* want to come home, so that I can have all the bother.—Thank you, my lad.—Eh dear, if I'm not sick--sick and surfeited, I am!"

She came downstairs. Paul had mechanically resumed his painting.

"And it must be pretty bad if they've taken him to the hospital," she went on. "But what a *careless* creature he is! *Other* men don't have all these accidents.—Yes, he *would* want to put all the burden on me.—Eh dear, just as we *were* getting easy a bit at last.—Put those things away, there's no time to be painting now.—What time is there a train? I know I s'll have to go trailing to Keston.—I s'll have to leave that bedroom."

"I can finish it," said Paul.

"You needn't—I shall catch the seven o'clock back, I should think.—Oh my blessed heart, the fuss and commotion he'll make! And those granite setts at Tinder Hill—he might well call them kidney pebbles—they'll jolt him almost to bits. I wonder why they can't mend them, the state they're in, an' all the men as go across in that ambulance.—You'd think they'd have a hospital here.—The men bought the ground, and, my Sirs, there'd be accidents enough to keep it going. But no, they must trail them ten miles in a slow ambulance, to Nottingham. It's a crying shame!—Oh and the fuss he'll make, I know he will! I wonder who's with him—Barker, I s'd think. Poor beggar, he'll wish himself anywhere rather. But he'll look after him, I know. Now there's no telling how long he'll be stuck in that hospital—and *won't* he hate it! But if it's only his leg it's not so bad."

All the time, she was getting ready. Hurriedly taking off her bodice, she crouched at the boiler while the water ran slowly into her lading can.

"I wish this boiler was at the bottom of the sea!" she exclaimed, wriggling the handle impatiently. She had very handsome, strong arms, rather surprising on a smallish woman.

Paul cleared away, put on the kettle, and set the table.

"There isn't a train till four-twenty," he said. "You've time enough."

"Oh no I haven't!" she cried, blinking at him over the towel as she wiped her face.

"Yes you have—you must drink a cup of tea at any rate. Should I come with you to Keston?"

"Come with me, what for I should like to know!—Now what have I to take him? Eh dear!—His clean shirt—and it's a blessing it *is* clean. But it had better be aired—and stockings—he won't want them—and a towel, I suppose—and handkerchiefs—now what else?"

"A comb, a knife and fork and spoon," said Paul. His father had been in the hospital before.

"Goodness knows what sort of state his feet were in," continued Mrs Morel, as she combed her long brown hair, that was fine as silk, and was touched now with grey. "He's very particular to wash himself to the waist, but below he thinks doesn't matter. But there, I suppose they see plenty like it."

Paul had laid the table. He cut his mother one or two pieces of very thin bread and butter.

"Here you are," he said, putting her cup of tea in her place.

"I can't be bothered," she exclaimed, crossly.

"Well you've got to, so there, now it's put out ready," he insisted.

So she sat down and sipped her tea, and ate a little, in silence. She was thinking.

In a few minutes she was gone, to walk the two and a half miles to Keston Station. All the things she was taking him she had in her bulging string bag. Paul watched her go up the road between the hedges, a little, quick-stepping figure, and his heart ached for her, that she was thrust forward again into pain and trouble. And she, tripping so quickly in her anxiety, felt at the back of her her son's heart waiting on her, felt him bearing what part of the burden he could, even supporting her. And when she was at the hospital, she thought, "It *will* upset that lad when I tell him how bad it is—I'd better be careful." And when she was trudging home again, she felt she was coming to share her burden.

"Is it bad?" asked Paul, as soon as she entered the house.

"It's bad enough," she replied.

"What?"

She sighed and sat down, undoing her bonnet strings. Her son watched her face as it was lifted, and her small, work-hardened hands fingering at the bow under her chin.

"Well," she answered, "it's not really dangerous—but the nurse says it's a dreadful smash. You see, a great piece of rock fell on his leg—here—and it's a compound fracture—there are pieces of bone sticking through—"

"Ugh—how horrid!" exclaimed the children.

"And," she continued, "of course he says he's going to die—it wouldn't be him if he didn't. 'I'm done for, my lass!' he said, looking at me. 'Don't be so silly,' I said to him. 'You're not going to die of a broken leg, however badly it's smashed.'—'I s'll niver come out of 'ere but in a wooden box,' he groaned. 'Well!' I said, 'if you want them to carry you into the garden in a wooden box, when you're better, I've no doubt they will.'—'If we think it's good for him'—said the Sister. She's an awfully nice Sister, but rather strict."

Mrs Morel took off her bonnet. The children waited in silence.

"Of course he *is* bad," she continued, "and he will be. It's a great shock, and he's lost a lot of blood—and of course, it *is* a very dangerous smash. It's not at all sure that it will mend so easily. And then there's the fever and the mortification—if it took bad ways he'd quickly be gone—. But there, he's a clean blooded man, with wonderful healing flesh, and so I see no reason why it *should* take bad ways.—Of course, there's a wound—"

She was pale now with emotion and anxiety. The three children realised that it was very bad for their father, and the house was silent, anxious.

"But he always gets better," said Paul, after a while.

"That's what I tell him," said the mother.

Everybody moved about in silence.

"And he really looked nearly done for," she said. "But the Sister says that is the pain."

Annie took away her mother's coat and bonnet.

"And he looked at me when I came away—! I said 'I s'll have to go now, Walter, because of the train—and the children—' —and he looked at me.—It seems hard—"

Paul took up his brush again and went on painting. Arthur went outside for some coal. Annie sat looking dismal. And Mrs Morel, in her little rocking-chair, that her husband had made for her when the first baby was coming, remained motionless, brooding. She was grieved, and bitterly sorry for the man who was hurt so much. But still, in her heart of hearts, where the love should have burned, there was a blank. Now, when all her woman's pity was roused to its full extent, when she would have slaved herself to death to nurse him and to save him, when she would have taken the pain herself, if she could, somewhere far away inside her she felt indifferent to him and to his suffering. It hurt her most of all, this failure to love him, even when he roused her strong emotions. She brooded awhile.

"And there!" she said suddenly, "when I'd got half way to Keston, I found I'd come out in my working boots—and *look* at them." They were an old pair of Paul's, brown and rubbed through at the toes. "I didn't know what to do with myself, for shame," she added.

In the morning, when Annie and Arthur were at school, Mrs Morel talked again to her son, who was helping her with her house-work.

"I found Barker at the hospital. He did look bad, poor little fellow. 'Well,' I said to him, 'what sort of a journey did you have with him?' 'Dunna ax me, missis!' he said. 'Ay,' I said, 'I know what he'd be.'—'But it *wor* bad for him, Mrs Morel, it *wor* that!' he said. 'I know,' I said. 'At ivry jolt I thought my 'eart would ha' flown clean out o' my mouth,' he said. 'An' the scream 'e give sometimes—missis, not for a fortune would I go through wi' it again.' 'I can quite understand it,' I said. 'It's a nasty job, though,' he said, 'an' one as'll be a long while afore it's right again.' 'I'm afraid it will,' I said. I like Mr Barker—I *do* like him. There's something so manly about him."

Paul resumed his task silently.

"And of course," Mrs Morel continued, "for a man like your father, the hospital *is* hard. He *can't* understand rules and regulations. And he won't let anybody else touch him, not if he can help it. When he smashed the muscles of his thigh, and it had to be dressed four times a day, *would* he let anybody but me or his mother do it—he wouldn't. So of course he'll suffer in there, with the nurses.—And I didn't like leaving him. I'm sure, when I kissed him an' came away, it seemed a shame—"

So she talked to her son, almost as if she were thinking aloud to him, and he took it in as best he could, by sharing her trouble to lighten it. And in the end, she shared almost everything with him, without knowing.

Morel had a very bad time; for a week he was in a critical condition. Then he began to mend. And then, knowing he was going to get better, the whole family sighed with relief, and proceeded to live happily.

They were not badly off whilst Morel was in the hospital. There were fourteen shillings a week from the pit, ten shillings from the sick club, and five shillings from the Disability Fund; and then every week the butties had something for Mrs Morel, five or seven shillings, so that she was quite well to do. And whilst Morel was progressing favourably in the hospital, the family was extraordinarily happy and peaceful. On Saturdays and Wednesdays Mrs Morel went to Nottingham to see her husband. Then she always brought back some little thing: a small tube of paints, for Paul, or some thick paper—a couple of post-cards for Annie, that the whole family rejoiced over for days before the girl was allowed to send them away—or a fret-saw for Arthur, or a bit of pretty wood. She described her adventures into the big shops with joy. Soon the folk in the picture shop knew her, and knew about Paul. The girl in the book shop took a keen interest in her. Mrs Morel was full of information when she got home from Nottingham. The three sat round till bed-time, listening, putting-in, arguing. Then Paul often raked the fire.

"I'm the man in the house now," he used to say to his mother, with joy. They learned how perfectly peaceful the home could be. And they almost regretted—though none of them would have owned to such callousness—that their father was soon coming back.

Paul was now fourteen, and was looking for work. He was a rather small and rather finely-made boy, with dark brown hair and light blue eyes. His face had already lost its youthful chubbiness, and was becoming somewhat like William's, rough-featured, almost rugged, and it was extraordinarily mobile. Usually he looked as if he saw things, was full of life, and warm; then his smile, like his mother's, came suddenly and was very lovable; and then, when there was any clog in his soul's quick running, his face went stupid and ugly. He was the sort of boy that becomes a clown and a lout as soon as he is not understood, or feels himself held cheap; and again is adorable at the first touch of warmth.

He suffered very much from the first contact with anything. When he was seven, the starting school had been a nightmare and a torture to him. But afterwards he liked it. And now that he felt he had to go out into life, he went through agonies of shrinking self consciousness. He was quite a clever painter, for a boy of his years. And he knew some French and German and mathematics, that Mr Heaton had taught him. But nothing he had was of any commercial value. He was not strong enough for heavy manual work, his mother said. He did not care for making things with his hands, preferred racing about, or making excursions into the country, or reading, or painting.

"What do you want to be?" his mother asked.

He had not the faintest notion. He would have liked to go on painting, but that never occured to him, since it was impossible. He quite strongly did not want to do anything. But it was urgent now that he should begin to earn. And since he did not feel that he was of high monetary value in the world, and since he knew that at any job a man makes thirty shillings or thirty five shillings a week, he invariably replied:

"Anything."

"That is no answer," said Mrs Morel.

But it was quite truthfully the only answer he could give. His ambition, as far as this world's gear went, was quietly to earn his thirty or thirty-five shillings a week, somewhere near home, and then, when his father died, have a cottage with his mother, paint and go out as he liked, and live happy ever after. That was his programme as far as doing things went. But he was proud within himself, measuring people against himself, and placing them, inexorably. And he thought that *perhaps* he might also make a painter, the real thing. But that he left alone.

"Then," said his mother, "you must look in the paper for the advertisements."

He looked at her. It seemed to him a bitter humiliation and an anguish to go through. But he said nothing. When he got up in the morning, his whole being was knotted up over this one thought:

"I've got to go and look for advertisements for a job."

It stood in front of the morning, that thought, killing all joy and even life, for him. His heart felt like a tight knot.

And then, at ten o'clock, he set off. He was supposed to be a queer, quiet child. Going up the sunny street of the little town, he felt as if all the folk he met said to themselves: "He's going to the Co-op Reading Room to look in the papers for a place. He can't get a job. I suppose he's living on his mother." Then he crept up the stone stairs behind the drapery shop at the Co-op, and peeped in the reading room. Usually one or two men were there, either old useless fellows, or colliers 'on the club.' So he entered, full of shrinking and suffering when they looked up, seated himself at the table, and pretended to scan the news. He knew they would think, "What does a lad of thirteen want in a reading room, with a newspaper," and he suffered.

Then he looked wistfully out of the window. Already he was a prisoner of industrialism. Large sunflowers stared over the old red wall of the garden opposite, looking in their jolly way down on the women who were hurrying with something for dinner. The valley was full of corn, brightening in the sun. Two collieries, among the fields, waved their small white plumes of steam. Far-off on the hills were the woods of Aldersley, dark and fascinating. Already his heart went down. He was being taken into bondage. His freedom in the beloved home valley, was going now.

The brewers' wagons came rolling up from Keston, with enormous barrels, four a side, like beans in a burst bean-pod. The wagoner, throned aloft, rolling massively in his seat, was not so much below Paul's eye. The man's hair, on his small, bullet head, was bleached almost white by the sun, and on his thick red arms, rocking idly on his sack apron, the white hairs glistened. His red face shone and was almost asleep with sunshine. The horses, handsome and brown, went on by themselves, looking by far the masters of the show.

Paul wished he were stupid. "I wish," he thought to himself, "I was fat like him, and like a dog in the sun. I wish I was a pig, and a brewer's wagoner."

Then, the room being at last empty, he would hastily copy an advertisement on a scrap of paper, then another, and slip out in immense relief. His mother would scan over his copies.

"Yes," she said, "you may try."

William had written out a letter of application, couched in admirable business language, which Paul copied, with variations. The boy's handwriting was execrable, so that William, who did all things well, got into a fever of impatience.

The elder brother was becoming quite swanky. In London, he found that he could associate with men far above his Bestwood friends in station. Some of the clerks in the office had studied for the law, and were more or less going through a kind of apprenticeship. William always made friends among men, wherever he went, he was so jolly. Therefore he was soon visiting and staying in houses of men who, in Bestwood, would have looked down on the unapproachable Bank Manager, and would merely have called indifferently on the Rector. So he began to fancy himself as a great gun. He was indeed rather surprised at the ease with which he became a gentleman.

His letters to his mother often ran in a pleased vein.

> "'The Myrmidons'
> Limpsfield

My dear Mater,

It is one o'clock, a.m. Imagine your son seated on an ancient oak chair, with a latest pattern electric lamp in front of him, on the table, writing to you. He is wearing evening clothes, and the gold studs you gave him for his 21st, and he thinks no end of himself. He only wishes you could see him. Solomon in all his glory must have felt dowdy in comparison.

I am staying the week-end with Loosemore, and seize this opportunity of writing to you.— —"

His mother was glad, he seemed so pleased. And his lodging in Walthamstow was so dreary. But now there seemed to come a kind of fever into the young man's letters. He was unsettled by all the change, he did not stand firm on his own feet, but seemed to spin rather giddily on the quick current of the new life. His mother was anxious for him. She could feel him losing himself. He had danced and gone to the theatre, boated on the river, been out with friends; and she knew he sat up afterwards in his cold bedroom, grinding away at Latin, because he intended to get on in his office, and in the Law as much as he could. He never sent his mother any money now. It was all taken, the little he had, for his own life. And she did not want any, except sometimes, when she was in a tight corner, and when ten shillings would have saved her much worry. She still dreamed of William, and of what he would do, with herself behind him. Never for a minute would she admit to herself, how heavy and anxious her heart was because of him.

Also he talked a good deal now of a girl he had met at a dance, a handsome brunette, quite young, and a lady, after whom the men were running thick and fast.

"I wonder if you would run my boy," his mother wrote to him, "unless you saw all the other men chasing her too. You feel safe enough and vain enough in a crowd. But take care, and see how you feel when you find yourself alone, and in triumph—"

William resented these things, and continued the chase. He had taken the girl on the river—"if you saw her, mother, you would know how I feel. Tall, and elegant, with the clearest of clear transparent olive complexions, hair as black as jet, and such grey eyes, bright, mocking, like lights on water at night. It is all very well to be a bit satirical, till you see her. And she dresses as well as any woman in London. I tell you your son doesn't half put his head up, when she goes walking down Piccadilly with him."

Mrs Morel wondered, in her heart, if her son did not go walking down Piccadilly with an elegant figure and fine clothes, rather than with a woman who was near to him. But she congratulated him, in her doubtful fashion. And, as she stood over the washing tub, the mother brooded over her son. She saw him saddled with an elegant and expensive wife, earning little money, dragging along and getting draggled in some small ugly house in a suburb. "But there," she told herself, "I am very likely a silly—meeting trouble half way." Nevertheless, the load of anxiety scarcely ever left her heart, lest William should do the wrong thing by himself.

Presently, Paul was bidden call upon Thomas Jordan, manufacturer of surgical appliances, at 21 Spaniel Row, Nottingham. Mrs Morel was all joy.

"There you see!" she cried, her eyes shining. "You've only written four letters, and the third is answered. You're lucky, my boy, as I always said you were."

Paul looked at the picture of a wooden leg, adorned with elastic stockings and other appliances, that figured on Mr Jordan's notepaper, and he felt alarmed. He had not known that elastic stockings existed. And he seemed to feel the business world, with its regulated system of values, and its impersonality, and he dreaded it. It seemed monstrous also that a business could be run on wooden legs.

Mother and son set off together one Tuesday morning. It was August and blazing hot. Paul walked with something screwed up tight inside him. He would have suffered much physical pain rather than this unreasonable suffering at being exposed to strangers to be accepted or rejected. Yet he chattered away with his mother. He would never have confessed to her how he suffered over these things, and she only partly guessed. She was gay, like a sweetheart. She stood in front of the ticket office at Bestwood, and Paul watched her take from her purse the money for the tickets. As he saw her hands in their old, black kid gloves, getting the silver out of the worn purse, his heart contracted with pain of love of her.

She was quite excited, and quite gay. He suffered because she *would* talk aloud in presence of the other travellers.

"Now look at that silly cow!" she said. "Careering round as if it thought it was a circus."

"It's most likely a bott fly," he said, very low.

"A what?" she asked, brightly, and unashamed.

They thought awhile. He was sensible all the time of having her opposite him. Suddenly their eyes met, and she smiled to him, a rare, intimate smile, beautiful with brightness and love. Then each looked out of the window.

And suddenly she turned to him and said, distinctly:

"And I really think you'll get it.—And if you don't, well, you can't grumble if you don't get the *third* place you apply for, can you? But I think you will. You are lucky, though you don't deserve to be."—She *would* talk so that the other people could hear!

The sixteen slow miles of railway journey passed. The mother and son walked down Station Street, feeling the excitement of lovers having an adventure together. In Carrington Street they stopped to hang over the parapet and look at the barges on the canal below.

"It's just like Venice," he said, seeing the sunshine on the water, that lay between high factory walls.

"Perhaps," she answered, smiling.

They enjoyed the shops immensely.

"Now you see that blouse," she would say, "wouldn't that just suit our Annie?—And for one and eleven three. Isn't that cheap!"

"And made of needlework as well," he said.

"Yes."

They had plenty of time, so they did not hurry. The town was strange and delightful to them. But the boy was tied up inside in a knot of apprehension. He dreaded the interview with Thomas Jordan.

It was nearly eleven o'clock by St. Peter's Church. They turned up a narrow street that led to the Castle. It was gloomy and old-fashioned, having low dark shops and dark-green house-doors with brass knockers, and yellow ochred doorsteps projecting onto the pavement, then another old shop whose small window looked like a cunning, half-shut eye. Mother and son went cautiously, looking everywhere for 'Thomas Jordan and Son.' It was like hunting in some wild place. They were on tiptoe of excitement.

Suddenly they spied a big dark archway, in which were names of various firms, Thomas Jordan among them.

"Here it is," said Mrs Morel. "But now *where* is it?"

They looked round. On one side was a queer, dark cardboard-factory, on the other a Commercial Hotel.

"It's up the entry," said Paul.

And they ventured under the archway, as into the jaws of the dragon. They emerged into a wide yard, like a well, with buildings all round. It was littered with straw and boxes and cardboard. The sunshine actually caught one crate whose straw was streaming onto the yard like gold. But elsewhere the place was like a pit. There were several doors, and two flights of steps. Straight in front, on a dirty glass door at the top of a staircase, loomed the ominous words

"Thomas Jordan and Son—Surgical Appliances." Mrs Morel went first, her son followed her. Charles the First mounted his scaffold with a lighter heart than had Paul Morel as he followed his mother up the dirty steps to the dirty door.

She pushed open the door, and stood in pleased surprise. In front of her was a big warehouse, with creamy paper parcels everywhere, and clerks with their shirt sleeves rolled back, were going about in an at-home sort of way. The light was subdued, the glossy cream parcels seemed luminous, the counters were of dark brown wood. All was quiet and very homely. Mrs Morel took two steps forward, then waited. Paul stood behind her. She had on her Sunday bonnet and a black veil, he wore a boy's broad white collar and a norfolk suit.

One of the clerks looked up. He was thin and tall, with a small face. His way of looking was alert. Then he glanced round to the other end of the room, where was a glass office. And then he came forward. He did not say anything, but leaned in a gentle, inquiring fashion towards Mrs Morel.

"Can I see Mr Jordan?" she asked.

"I'll fetch him," answered the young man.

He went down to the glass office. A red faced, white whiskered old man looked up. He reminded Paul of a pomeranian dog. Then the same little man came up the room. He had short legs, was rather stout, and wore an alpaca jacket. So, with one ear up, as it were, he came stoutly and inquiringly down the room.

"Goodmorning!" he said, hesitating before Mrs Morel, in doubt as to whether she were a customer or not.

"Goodmorning—I came with my son, Paul Morel—you asked him to call this morning."

"Come this way," said Mr Jordan, in a rather snappy little manner intended to be business like.

They followed the manufacturer into a grubby little room, uphol-stered in black American leather, glossy with the rubbing of many customers. On the table was a pile of trusses, yellow wash-leather hoops tangled together. They looked new and living. Paul sniffed the odor of new wash-leather. He wondered what the things were. By this time he was so much stunned that he only noticed the outside things.

"Sit down!" said Mr Jordan, irritably pointing Mrs Morel to a horse hair chair. She sat on the edge, in an uncertain fashion. Then the little old man fidgeted, and found a paper.

"Did you write this letter?" he snapped, thrusting what Paul recognised as his own note-paper in front of him.

"Yes," he answered.

At that moment, he was occupied in two ways: first, in feeling guilty for telling a lie, since William had composed the letter, second, in wondering why his letter seemed so strange and different, in the fat, red hand of the man, from what it had been when it lay on the kitchen table. It was like part of himself, gone astray. He resented the way the man held it.

"Where did you learn to write?" said the old man, crossly.

Paul merely looked at him shamedly, and did not answer.

"He *is* a bad writer," put in Mrs Morel, apologetically. Then she pushed up her veil. Paul hated her for not being prouder with this common little man, and he loved her face, clear of the veil.

"And you say you know French?" inquired the little man, still sharply.

"Yes," said Paul.

"What school did you go to?"

"The board school."

"And did you learn it there?"

"No—I—" the boy went crimson, and got no further.

"His god-father gave him lessons," said Mrs Morel, half pleading, and rather distant.

Mr Jordan hesitated. Then, in his irritable manner—he always seemed to keep his hands ready for action—he pulled another sheet of paper from his pocket, unfolded it. The paper made a crackling noise. He handed it to Paul.

"Read that," he said.

It was a note in French, in thin, flimsy foreign handwriting that the boy could not decipher. He stared blankly at the paper.

"'Monsieur,'" he began, then looked in great confusion at Mr Jordan.

"It's the—it's the— —."

He wanted to say 'handwriting', but his wits would no longer work even sufficiently to supply him with the word. Feeling an utter fool, and hating Mr Jordan, he turned desperately to the paper again.

"'Sir—Please send me'—er—er—I can't tell the— —er—'two pairs—*gris fil bas*—grey thread stockings—er—er—*sans*—without—' er I can't tell the words—er—'doigts—fingers'—er—I can't tell the— —"

He wanted to say handwriting, but the word still refused to come. Seeing him stuck, Mr Jordan snatched the paper from him.

"'Please send by return two pairs grey thread stockings without *toes*—'"

"Well," flashed Paul, "'doigts' mean fingers—as well—as a rule—"

The little man looked at him. He did not know whether 'doigts' meant 'fingers', he knew that for all *his* purposes, it meant 'toes.'

"Fingers to stockings!" he snapped.

"Well it *does* mean fingers," the boy persisted.

He hated the little man, who made such a clod of him. Mr Jordan looked at the pale, stupid, defiant boy, then at the mother, who sat quiet and with that peculiar shut-off look of the poor who have to depend on the favour of others.

"And when could he come?" he asked.

"Well," said Mrs Morel, "as soon as you wish. He has finished school now."

"He would live in Bestwood?"

"Yes—but he could be in—at the station—at quarter to eight—"

"Hm!"

It ended by Paul's being engaged as junior spiral clerk, at eight shillings a week. The boy did not open his mouth to say another word, after having insisted that 'doigts' meant 'fingers'. He followed his mother down the stairs. She looked at him with her bright blue eyes full of love and joy.

"I think you'll like it," she said.

"'Doigts' does mean 'fingers', mother—and it was the writing—I couldn't read the writing."

"Never mind, my boy.—I'm sure he'll be all right, and you won't see much of him.—Wasn't that first young fellow nice—I'm sure you'll like them."

"But wasn't Mr Jordan common, mother? Does he own it all?"

"I suppose he was a workman, who has got on," she said. "You mustn't mind people so much. They're not being disagreeable to *you*—it's their way—you always think people are meaning things for you. But they don't."

It was very sunny. Over the big, desolate space of the market-place, the blue sky shimmered, and the granite cobbles of the paving glistened. Shops down the Long Row were deep in obscurity, and the shadow was full of colour. Just where the horse trams trundled across the market, was a row of fruit stalls, with fruit blazing in the sun, apples and piles of reddish oranges, small greengage plums, and bananas. There was a warm scent of fruit as mother and son passed. Gradually his feeling of ignominy and of rage sank.

"Where should we go for dinner?" asked the mother.

"Should we buy something, and eat it in the Arboretum?"

"No, we shan't."

"Should we go to Morley's?"

"Their tea's stewed. No—you've got the place—we'll go and have some proper dinner."

It was felt to be a reckless extravagance. Paul had only been in an eating house once or twice in his life, and then only to have a cup of tea and a bun. Most of the people of Bestwood considered that tea and bread and butter, and perhaps potted beef, was all they could afford to eat in Nottingham. Real cooked dinner was considered great extravagance. Paul felt rather guilty.

They found a place that looked quite cheap. But when Mrs Morel scanned the bill of fare, her heart was heavy, things were so dear. So she ordered kidney pies and potatoes, as the cheapest available dish.

"We oughtn't to have come here, mother," said Paul.

"Never mind," she said. "We won't come again."

She insisted on his having a small currant tart, because he liked sweets.

"I don't want it, mother," he pleaded.

"Yes," she insisted, "you'll have it."

And she looked round for the waitress. But the waitress was busy, and Mrs Morel did not like to bother her then. So the mother and son waited for the girl's pleasure, whilst she flirted among the men.

"Brazen hussy," said Mrs Morel to Paul. "Look now, she's taking that man *his* pudding, and he came long after us."

"It doesn't matter mother," said Paul.

Mrs Morel was angry. But she was too poor, and her orders were too meagre, so that she had not the courage to insist on her rights just then. They waited and waited.

"Should we go, mother?" he said.

Then Mrs Morel stood up. The girl was passing near.

"Will you bring one currant tart," said Mrs Morel clearly.

The girl looked round insolently.

"Directly," she said.

"We have waited quite long enough," said Mrs Morel.

In a moment the girl came back with the tart. Mrs Morel asked coldly for the bill. Paul wanted to sink through the floor. He marvelled at his mother's hardness. He knew that only years of battling had taught her to insist even so little on her rights. She shrank as much as he.

"It's the last time I go *there* for anything!" she declared, when they were outside the place, thankful to be clear.

"We'll go," she said, "and look at Keep's, and Boot's, and one or two places, shall we?"

They had discussions over the pictures, and Mrs Morel wanted to buy him a little sable brush, that he hankered after. But this indulgence he refused. He stood in front of milliners' shops, and drapers' shops, almost bored, but content for her to be interested. They wandered on.

"Now just look at those black grapes!" she said. "They make your mouth water.—I've wanted some of those for years, but I s'll have to wait a bit before I get them."

Then she rejoiced in the florist's, standing in the doorway, sniffing.

"Oh!—Oh!—isn't it simply lovely!"

Paul saw, in the darkness of the shop, an elegant young lady in black peering over the counter curiously.

"They're looking at you," he said, trying to draw his mother away.

"But what *is* it?" she exclaimed, refusing to be moved.

"Stocks!" he answered, sniffing hastily. "Look, there's a tub-ful."

"So there is—red and white!—but really, I never knew stocks to smell like it!" And, to his great relief, she moved out of the doorway, but only to stand in front of the window.

"Paul!" she cried to him, who was trying to get out of sight of the elegant young lady in black, the shop-girl. "Paul! Just look here!"

He came reluctantly back.

"Now, just look at that fuchsia!" she exclaimed, pointing.

"Hm!"—he made a curious, interested sound. "You'd think every second as the flowers was going to fall off, they hang so big an' heavy."

"And such an abundance!" she cried.

"And the way they drop downwards with their threads and knots—!"

"Yes!" she exclaimed. "Lovely!"

"I wonder who'll buy it!" he said.

Sons and Lovers

"I wonder!" she answered. "Not us."

"It would die in our parlour."

"Yes, beastly cold sunless hole, it kills every bit of a plant you put in—and the kitchen chokes them to death—"

They bought a few things, and set off towards the station. Looking up the canal, through the dark pass of the buildings, they saw the Castle on its bluff of brown, green-bushed rock, in a positive miracle of delicate sunshine.

"Won't it be nice for me to come out at dinner-times!" said Paul. "I can go all round here and see everything. I s'll love it."

"You will," assented his mother.

He had spent a perfect afternoon with his mother. They arrived home in the mellow evening, happy, and glowing, and tired. In the morning he filled in the form for his season ticket, and took it to the station. When he got back, his mother was just beginning to wash the floor. He sat crouched up on the sofa.

"He says it'll be here by Saturday," he said.

"And how much will it be?"

"About one pound eleven," he said.

She went on washing her floor in silence.

"Is it a lot?" he asked.

"It's no more than I thought," she answered.

"An' I s'll earn eight shillings a week," he said.

She did not answer, but went on with her work. At last she said:

"That William promised me, when he went to London, as he'd give me a pound a month. He has given me ten shillings—twice: and now I know he hasn't a farthing if I asked him. Not that I want it. Only just now, you'd think he might be able to help with this ticket, which I'd never expected."

"He earns a lot," said Paul.

"He earns a hundred and thirty pounds. But they're all alike. They're large in promises, but it's precious little fulfilment you get."

"He spends over fifty shillings a week on himself," said Paul.

"And I keep this house on less than thirty," she replied, "and am supposed to find money for extras. But they don't care about helping you, once they've gone. He'd rather spend it on that dressed-up creature."

"She should have her own money, if she's so grand," said Paul.

"She should, but she hasn't. I asked him.—And *I* know he

124

doesn't buy her a gold bangle for nothing. I wonder who ever bought *me* a gold bangle."

"Well, you never wanted one."

"No, I didn't—but it would have been all the same if I had."

"Didn't my father ever buy you things?"

"Yes—one half-pound of apples—and that was all—every penny he spent on me, before we were married."

"Why?"

"Because I was silly, and when he said 'What should I buy thee?' I told him 'Nothing'. But bring me anything!—it never occurred to him. And William wouldn't buy gold bangles, except for a fol-de-lol who makes great pretensions."

"And I'll bet she'd got plenty," said the boy.

"Got plenty, ay! But he'd have to give her another, to seem grand as well. What does he care, really! I can keep him while he's earning a few shillings, and then, as soon as his money is anything like, and one might feel a bit of peace and security, he goes away, and it's the same struggle over again, nowhere to turn to when there's anything needed, nobody to do you a hand's turn."

"You should ask him."

"Yes, and he'd have to borrow it. I could borrow it myself, if it came to that. I'm sure I'm not going to be beholden to him for anything I have to ask him for. He needn't write to me, singing her praises, and saying the operas they've been to. I don't want to hear. A fat lot of thought he has for me, I must say.—But there, they don't care! They've got their own lives to live, and their own way to go, and what am I to him. But a nuisance I will never be, nor ask him for anything.—And I hope your father will live long enough, till I'm gone. For it's a poor tale, if you have to be dependent on your children."

"Well mother—I s'll be earning soon—an' you can always have my money, 'cause I s'll never get married."

"It's an old tale, and one William was always preaching. Wait a bit, and your tune will alter."

"It won't."

"Very well."

She went on washing her floor of red brick, in silence.

"What shall you do?" asked Paul.

"I suppose I s'll have to draw out of the Co-op—and that'll break into my share, so I shan't get full dividend. And I *didn't* want to break into it again."

The boy was very miserable, rather angry. It was for him the money was needed, and it galled him.

"Well," he said, "I s'll soon get a raise, and you can have all my money."

"That's all very well," she said. "But that doesn't provide thirty shillings for Saturday morning."

William was succeeding with his "Gipsy", as he called her. He asked the girl—her name was Louisa Lily Denys Western—for a photograph to send to his mother. The photo came—a handsome brunette, taken in profile, smirking slightly—and, it might be, quite naked, for on the photograph not a scrap of clothing was to be seen, only a naked bust.

"Yes," wrote Mrs Morel to her son, "the photograph of Louie is very striking, and I can see she must be attractive. But do you think, my boy, it was very good taste of a girl, to give her young man that photo to send to his mother, the first. Certainly the shoulders are beautiful, as you say. But I hardly expected to see so much of them at the first view—."

Morel found the photograph standing on the chiffonnier in the parlour. He came out with it between his thick thumb and finger.

"Who dost reckon this is?" he asked of his wife.

"It's the girl our William is going with," replied Mrs Morel.

"Hm! 'Er's a bright spark, from th' look on 'er—an' one as wunna do him owermuch good neither.—Who is she?"

"Her name is Louisa Lily Denys Western."

"An' come again tomorrer!" exclaimed the miner. "An' is 'er an actress?"

"She is not. She's supposed to be a lady."

"I'll bet," he exclaimed, still staring at the photo. "A lady, is she? An' how much does she reckon ter keep up this sort o' game on?"

"On nothing—she lives with an old aunt, whom she hates, and takes what bit of money's given her."

"Hm!" said Morel, laying down the photograph. "Then he's a fool to ha' ta'en up wi' such a one as that."

"Dear Mater," William replied. "I'm sorry you didn't like the photograph. It never occurred to me, when I sent it, that you mightn't think it decent. However, I told Gyp that it didn't quite suit your prim and proper notions, so she's going to send you another, that I hope will please you better. She's always being photographed. In fact, the photographers *ask* her if they may take her, for nothing."

Presently the new photograph came, with a little silly note from the girl. This time the young lady was seen in a black satin evening bodice, cut square, with little puff sleeves, and black lace hanging down her beautiful arms.

"I wonder if she ever wears anything except evening clothes," said Mrs Morel sarcastically. "I'm sure I *ought* to be impressed."

"You *are* disagreeable, mother," said Paul. "I think the first one with bare shoulders is lovely."

"Do you," answered his mother. "Well, I don't."

On the Monday morning, the boy got up at six, to start work. He had the season-ticket which had cost such bitterness, in his waist-coat pocket. He loved it, with its bars of yellow across. His mother packed his dinner in a small, shut up basket, and he set off at a quarter to seven to catch the 7.15 train. Mrs Morel came to the entry end to see him off.

It was a perfect morning. From the ash-tree, the slender green fruits that the children call 'pigeons' were twinkling gaily down on a little breeze, into the front gardens of the houses. The valley was full of a lustrous dark haze, through which the ripe corn shimmered, and in which the steam from Minton pit melted swiftly. Puffs of wind came. Paul looked over the high woods of Aldersley, where the country gleamed, and home had never pulled at him so powerfully.

"Goodmorning mother," he said, smiling, but feeling very unhappy.

"Goodmorning," she replied, cheerfully and tenderly.

She stood in her white apron on the open road, watching him as he crossed the field. He had a small, compact body, that looked full of life. She felt, as she saw him trudging over the field, that where he determined to go, he would get. She thought of William. He would have leaped the fence, instead of going round to the stile. He was away in London, doing well. Paul would be working in Nottingham. Now she had two sons in the world. She could think of two places, great centres of industry, and feel that she had put a man into each of them, that these men would work out what *she* wanted; they were derived from her, they were of her, and their works also would be hers. All the morning long she thought of Paul.

At eight o'clock he climbed the dismal stairs of Jordan's Surgical Appliance Factory, and stood helplessly against the first great parcel-rack, waiting for somebody to pick him up. The place was still not awake. Over the counters were great dust sheets. Two men only had arrived, and were heard talking in a corner, as they took off their coats and rolled up their shirt sleeves. It was ten past eight. Evidently there was no rush of punctuality. Paul listened to the voices of the two clerks. Then he heard someone cough, and saw in the office at the end of the room, an old, decaying clerk in a round smoking cap of black velvet embroidered with red and green, opening letters. He waited and waited. One of the junior clerks went to the old man, greeted him cheerily and loudly. Evidently the old 'chief' was deaf. Then the young fellow came striding importantly down to his counter. He spied Paul.

"Hello!" he said. "You the new lad?"

"Yes," said Paul.

"Hm! What's your name?"

"Paul Morel."

"Paul Morel?—All right, you come on round here."

Paul followed him round the rectangle of counters. The room was second storey. It had a great hole in the middle of the floor, fenced as with a wall of counters, and down this wide shaft the lifts went, and the light for the bottom storey. Also there was a corresponding big, oblong hole in the ceiling, and one could see above, over the fence of the top floor, some machinery. And right away overhead was the glass roof, and all light for the three storeys came downwards, getting dimmer, so that it was always night on the ground floor, and rather gloomy on the second floor. The factory was the top floor, the warehouse the second, the storehouse the ground floor. It was an insanitary ancient place.

Paul was led round to a very dark corner.

"This is the 'Spiral' corner," said the clerk. "You're Spiral, with Pappleworth. He's your boss, but he's not come yet. He doesn't get here till half past eight. So you can fetch the letters, if you like, from Mr Melling down there."

The young man pointed to the old clerk in the office.

"All right," said Paul.

"Here's a peg to hang your cap on—here are your entry ledgers—Pappleworth won't be long."

And the thin young man stalked away with long, busy strides, over the hollow wooden floor.

After a minute or two, Paul went down and stood in the door of the glass office. The old clerk in the smoking cap looked down over the rim of his spectacles.

"Good—morning," he said, kindly and impressively. "You want the letters for the Spiral department, Thomas?"

Paul resented being called Thomas. But he took the letters and returned to his dark place, where the counter made an angle, where the great parcel-rack came to an end, and where there were three doors in the corner. He sat on a high stool and read the letters, those whose handwriting was not too difficult. They ran as follows:

"Will you please send me at once a pair of lady's silk, spiral thigh hose, without feet, such as I had from you last year—length—thigh to knee— —etc"

or "Major Chamberlain wishes to repeat his previous order for a silk, non-elastic suspensory bandage."

Many of these letters, some of them in French or Norwegian, were a great puzzle to the boy. He sat on his stool nervously awaiting the arrival of his "boss." He suffered tortures of shyness when, at half past eight, the factory girls for upstairs trooped past him.

Mr Pappleworth arrived chewing a chlorodyne gum, at about twenty to nine, when all the other men were at work. He was a thin, sallow man with a red nose, quick, staccato, and smartly but stiffly dressed. He was about thirty six years old. There was something rather 'doggy', rather 'smart', rather 'cute and shrewd, and something warm, and something slightly contemptible about him.

"You my new lad?" he said.

Paul stood up and said he was.

"Fetched the letters?"

Mr Pappleworth gave a chew to his gum.

"Yes."

"Copied 'em?"

"No."

"Well come on then, let's look slippy. Changed your coat?"

"No."

"You want to bring an old coat, and leave it here"—he pronounced the last words with the chlorodyne gum between his side teeth. He vanished into darkness behind the great parcel rack, re-appeared coatless, turning up a smart striped shirt cuff over a thin and hairy arm. Then he slipped into his coat. Paul noticed how thin he was, and that his trousers were in folds behind. He seized a stool, dragged it beside the boy's, and sat down.

"Sit down," he said. Paul took a seat. Mr Pappleworth was very close to him. The man seized the letters, snatched a long entry book out of a rack in front of him, flung it open, seized a pen, and said:

"Now look here—you want to copy these letters in here."

He sniffed twice, gave a quick chew at his gum, stared fixedly at a letter, then went very still and absorbed, and wrote the entry rapidly, in a beautiful flourishing hand. He glanced quickly at Paul.

"See that?"

"Yes."

"Think you can do it all right?"

"Yes."

"All right then—let's see you."

He sprang off his stool. Paul took a pen. Mr Pappleworth disappeared. Paul rather liked copying the letters, but he wrote slowly, laboriously, and exceedingly badly. He was doing the fourth letter, and feeling quite busy and happy, when Mr Pappleworth reappeared.

"Now then—how'r'yer getting on—done'em?"

He leaned over the boy's shoulder, chewing, and smelling of chlorodyne.

"Strike my bob, lad, but you're a beautiful writer!" he exclaimed, satirically. "Ne'er mind, how many h'yer done? Only three! I'd 'a eaten 'em. Get on, my lad, an' put numbers on 'em—here look! Get on!"

Paul ground away at the letters, whilst Mr Pappleworth fussed over various jobs. Suddenly the boy started as a shrill whistle sounded near his ear. Mr Pappleworth came, took a plug out of a pipe, and said, in an amazingly cross and bossy voice:

"Yes!"

Paul heard a faint voice, like a woman's, out of the mouth of the tube. He gazed in wonder, never having seen a speaking tube before.

"Well," said Mr Pappleworth, disagreeably, into the tube, "you'd better get some of your back work done then."

Again the woman's tiny voice was heard, sounding pretty and cross.

"I've not time to stand here while you talk," said Mr Pappleworth, and he pushed the plug into the tube.

"Come my lad," he said, imploringly, to Paul, "there's Polly crying out for them orders. Can't you buck up a bit? Here—come out."

He took the book, to Paul's immense chagrin, and began the

copying himself. He worked quickly and well. This done, he seized some strips of long yellow paper, about three inches wide, and made out the day's orders for the work girls.

"You'd better watch me," he said to Paul, working all the while rapidly. Paul watched the weird little drawings of legs and thighs and ankles, with the strokes across and the numbers, and the few brief directions, which his chief made upon the yellow paper. Then Mr Pappleworth finished and jumped up.

"Come on with me," he said, and, the yellow papers flying in his hands, he dashed through a door and down some stairs, into the basement where the gas was burning. They crossed the cold, damp store-room, then a long dreary room with a long table on trestles, into a smaller cosy apartment, not very high, which had been built-on to the main building. In this room a small woman with a red serge blouse, and her black hair done on top of her head, was waiting like a proud little bantam.

"Here y'are!" said Pappleworth.

"I think it is 'here you are'!" exclaimed Polly. "The girls have been here nearly half an hour waiting. Just think of the time wasted!"

"*You* think of getting your work done and not talking so much," said Mr Pappleworth. "You could ha' been finishing off."

"You know quite well we finished everything off on Saturday," cried Polly, flying at him, her dark eyes flashing.

"Tu-tu-tu-tu-terterter!" he mocked. "Here's your new lad. Don't ruin him as you did the last."

"'As we did the last!'" repeated Polly. "Yes, *we* do a lot of ruining, we do. My word, a lad would *take* some ruining after he'd been with you."

"It's time for work now, not for talk," said Mr Pappleworth severely and coldly.

"It was time for work some time back," said Polly, marching away with her head in the air. She was an erect little body of forty.

In that room were two round spiral machines on the bench under the window. Through the inner doorway was another, longer room, with six more machines. A little group of girls, nicely dressed and in white aprons, stood talking together.

"Have you nothing else to do but talk?" said Mr Pappleworth.

"Only wait for you," said one handsome girl, laughing.

"Well, get on, get on," he said. "Come on my lad. You'll know your road down here again."

And Paul ran upstairs after his chief. He was given some checking and invoicing to do. He stood at the desk, labouring in his execrable handwriting: Presently Mr Jordan came strutting down from the glass office, and stood behind him, to the boy's great discomfort. Suddenly a red and fat finger was thrust on the form he was filling in.

"*Mr* J.A.Bates Esquire!" exclaimed the cross voice just behind his ear.

Paul looked at "Mr J.A.Bates Esquire," in his own vile writing, and wondered what was the matter now.

"Didn't they teach you any better than *that* while they were at it. If you put 'Mr' you don't put 'Esquire'—a man can't be both at once."

The boy regretted his too-much generosity in disposing of honors, hesitated, and with trembling fingers, scratched out the "Mr." Then all at once Mr Jordan snatched away the invoice.

"Make another! Are you going to send *that* to a gentleman?" and he tore up the blue form irritably.

Paul, his ears red with shame, began again. Still Mr Jordan watched.

"I don't know what they *do* teach in school. You'll have to write better than that. Lads learn nothing nowadays, but how to recite poetry and play the fiddle.—Have you seen his writing?" he asked of Mr Pappleworth.

"Yes—prime, isn't it?" replied Mr Pappleworth indifferently. "He'll come on all right."

Mr Jordan gave a little grunt, not unamiable. Paul divined that his master's bark was worse than his bite. Indeed, the little manufacturer, although he spoke bad English, was quite gentleman enough to leave his men alone, and to take no notice of trifles. But he knew he did not look like the boss and owner of the show, so he had to play his rôle of proprietor at first, to put things on a right footing.

"Let's see, *what's* your name?" asked Mr Pappleworth of the boy.

"Paul Morel."

It is curious that children suffer so much at having to pronounce their own names.

"Paul Morel is it! All right, you Paul-Morel through them things there, and then—"

Mr Pappleworth subsided onto a stool, and began writing. A girl came up from out of a door just behind, put some newly pressed elastic web appliances on the counter, and returned. Mr Pappleworth picked up the whitey-blue knee-band, examined it and its yellow order-paper quickly, and put it on one side. Next was a flesh-pink 'leg'. He went through the few things, wrote out a couple of orders, and called to Paul to accompany him. This time they went through the door whence the girl had emerged. There Paul found himself at the top of a little wooden flight of steps, and below him saw a room with windows round two sides, and at the further end, half a dozen girls sitting bending over the benches, in the light from the window, sewing. They were singing together "Two Little Girls in Blue." Hearing the door opened, they all turned round, to see Mr Pappleworth and Paul looking down on them from the far end of the room. They stopped singing.

"Can't you make a bit less row?" said Mr Pappleworth. "Folk'll think we keep cats."

A hunchback woman on a high stool turned her long, rather heavy face towards Mr Pappleworth and said, in a contralto voice:

"They're all tom-cats then."

In vain Mr Pappleworth tried to be impressive for Paul's benefit. He descended the steps into the finishing-off room, and went to the hunchback Fanny. She had such a short body, on her high stool, that her head, with its great bands of bright brown hair, seemed over large, as did her pale, heavy face. She wore a dress of green-black cashmere, and her wrists, coming out of the narrow cuffs, were thin and flat, as she put down her work nervously. He showed her something that was wrong with a knee-cap.

"Well," she said, "you needn't come blaming it onto me—it's not my fault." Her colour mounted to her cheek.

"I never said it *was* your fault—will you do as I tell you!" replied Mr Pappleworth shortly.

"You don't say it's my fault, but you'd like to make out as it was," the hunch-back woman cried, almost in tears. Then she snatched the knee-cap from her "boss," saying: "Yes, I'll do it for you, but you needn't be snappy."

"Here's your new lad," said Mr Pappleworth.

Fanny turned, smiling very gently on Paul.

"Oh!" she said.

"Yes—don't make a softy of him between you."

"It's not us as 'ud make a softy of him," she said indignantly.

"Come on then Paul," said Mr Pappleworth.

"*Au revoy*, Paul," said one of the girls.

There was a titter of laughter. Paul went out, blushing deeply, not having spoken a word.

The day was very long. All morning, the work people were coming to speak to Mr Pappleworth, Paul was writing, or learning to make up parcels, ready for the mid-day post. At one o'clock, or rather at a quarter to one, Mr Pappleworth disappeared to catch his train: he lived in the suburbs. At one o'clock, Paul, feeling very lost, took his dinner basket down into the stack room in the basement, that had the long table on trestles, and ate his meal hurriedly, alone in that cellar of gloom and desolation. Then he went out of doors. The brightness and the freedom of the streets made him feel adventurous and happy. But at two o'clock he was back in the corner of the big room. Soon the work girls went trooping past, making remarks. It was the commoner girls, who worked upstairs at the heavy tasks of truss-making and the finishing of artificial limbs. He waited for Mr Pappleworth, not knowing what to do, sitting scribbling on the yellow order paper. Mr Pappleworth came at twenty minutes to three. Then he sat and gossiped with Paul, treating the boy entirely as an equal, even in age.

In the afternoon there was never very much to do, unless it were near the week end, and the accounts had to be made up. At five o'clock all the men went down into the dungeon with the table on trestles, and there they had tea, eating bread and butter on the bare, dirty boards, talking with the same kind of ugly haste and slovenliness with which they ate their meal. And yet upstairs the atmosphere among them was always jolly and clear. The cellar and the trestles affected them.

After tea, when all the gases were lighted, work went more briskly. There was the big evening post to get off. The hose came up warm and newly pressed from the workrooms. Paul had made out the invoices. Now he had the packing up and addressing to do, then he had to weigh his stack of parcels on the scales. Everywhere voices were calling weights, there was the chink of metal, the rapid snapping of string, the hurrying to old Mr Melling for stamps. And at last the postman came with his sack, laughing and jolly. Then everything slacked off, and Paul took his dinner basket, and ran to the station to catch the eight twenty train. The day in the factory was just twelve hours long.

His mother sat waiting for him rather anxiously. He had to walk from Keston, so was not home until about twenty past nine. And he left the house before seven in the morning. Mrs Morel was rather anxious about his health. But she herself had had to put up with so much, that she expected her children to take the same odds. They must go through with what came. And Paul stayed at Jordan's, although all the time he was there, his health suffered from the darkness, and lack of air, and the long hours.

He came in pale and tired. His mother looked at him. She saw he was rather pleased, and her anxiety all went.

"Well, and how was it?" she asked.

"Ever so funny, mother," he replied. "You don't have to work a bit hard, and they're nice with you."

"And did you get on all right?"

"Yes—they only say my writing's bad. But Mr Pappleworth—he's my man, said to Mr Jordan I should be all right. I'm Spiral, mother. You must come and see. It's ever so nice.— —"

He told her everything, all he had observed, all he thought, giving her every scrap of his experience. The only thing he hid from her was the fact that he had put "Mr J.A.Bates Esquire." Of that he would have been very much ashamed, if she had known. And he never told her anything disagreeable that was said to him, only the nice things, trying always to make her believe he was happy and well-liked, and that the world went well with him—which as a rule it did. He brought her everything, except his small shames or ignominies; he could never have borne to make her feel ashamed or ignominious for him.

Soon he liked Jordan's. Mr Pappleworth, who had a certain 'saloon bar' flavour about him, was always natural, and treated him as if he had been a comrade. Sometimes the 'Spiral boss' was irritable, and chewed more lozenges than ever. Even then, however, he was not offensive, but one of those people who hurt themselves by their own irritability, more than they hurt other people.

"Haven't you done that *yet*?" he would cry. "Go on, be a month of Sundays."

Again, and Paul could understand him least then, he was jocular and in high spirits.

"I'm going to bring my little Yorkshire terrier bitch tomorrow," he said jubilantly to Paul.

"What's a Yorkshire terrier?"

"*Don't* know what a Yorkshire terrier is?—*don't know* a *Yorkshire*—!" Mr Pappleworth was aghast.

"Is it a little silky one—colours of iron and rusty silver?"

"*That's* it my lad. She's a gem. She's had five pounds' worth of pups already, and she's worth over seven pounds herself: and she doesn't weigh twenty ounces—."

The next day the bitch came. She was a shivering miserable morsel. Paul did not care for her, she seemed so like a wet rag that would never dry. Then a man called for her, and began to make coarse jokes. But Mr Pappleworth nodded his head in the direction of the boy, and the talk went on sotto voce.

Mr Jordan only made one more excursion to watch Paul, and then the only fault he found was, seeing the boy lay his pen on the counter:

"Put your pen in your ear, if you're going to be a clerk. Pen in your ear!"

And one day he said to the lad:

"*Why* don't you hold your shoulders straighter? Come down here." When he took him into the glass office and fitted him with special braces for keeping the shoulders square.

But Paul liked the girls best. The men seemed common and rather dull. He liked them all, but they were uninteresting. Polly, the little brisk overseer downstairs, finding Paul eating in the cellar, asked him if she could cook him anything on her little stove. Next day his mother gave him a dish that could be heated up. He took it into the pleasant, clean room, to Polly. And very soon it grew to be an established custom that he should have dinner with her. When he came in at eight in the morning he took his basket to her, and when he came down at one o'clock, she had his dinner ready.

He was not very tall, and pale, with thick chestnut hair, irregular features, and a wide full mouth. She was like a small bird. He often called her a 'robinet.' Though naturally rather quiet, he would sit and chatter with her for hours, telling her about his home. The girls all liked to hear him talk. They often gathered in a little circle, while he sat on a bench, and held forth to them, laughing. Some of them regarded him as a curious little creature, so serious, yet so bright and jolly, and always so delicate in his way with them. They all liked him, and he adored them. Polly he felt he belonged to. Then Connie, with her mane of red hair, her face of apple-blossom, her murmuring voice, such a lady in her shabby black frock, appealed to his romantic side.

"When you sit winding," he said, "it looks as if you were spinning at a spinning-wheel—it looks ever so nice. You remind me of Elaine in the *Idylls of the King*. I'd draw you if I could." And she glanced at him, blushing shyly. And later on, he had a sketch he prized very much: Connie sitting on the stool before the wheel, her flaming mane of red hair on her rusty black frock, her red mouth shut and serious, running the scarlet thread off the hank onto the reel.

With Louie, handsome and brazen, who always seemed to thrust her hip at him, he usually joked.

"What are you making?"

"What do you want to know for?" she replied, putting her head up mockingly.

"Because I don't believe you know yourself."

"Why not?" She found him piquant.

"Because you don't look as if you do."

"How do I look then?"

"You look as if you were thinking of something. What were you thinking about?"

She looked at him sideways, burst into a laugh, saying:

"You'd like to know, wouldn't you!"

"Come out," he said, "let's give your stocking a turn."

And he seized the handle of her machine and began to grind.

She suddenly snatched him away.

"It'll be wrong," she cried.

They looked at each other, laughing.

Emma was rather plain, rather old, and condescending. But to condescend to him made her happy, and he did not mind.

"How do you put needles in?" he asked.

"Go away and don't bother."

"But I ought to know how to put needles in."

She ground at her machine all the while, steadily.

"There are many things you ought to know," she replied.

"Tell me then how to stick needles in the machine."

"Oh, the boy, what a nuisance he is!—Why, *this* is how you do it—"

He watched her attentively. Suddenly a whistle piped. Then Polly appeared, and said in a clear voice:

"Mr Pappleworth wants to know how much longer you're going to be down here playing with the girls, Paul."

Paul flew upstairs, calling "Goodbye!", and Emma drew herself up:

"It wasn't *me* who wanted him to play with the machine," she said.

"What yer been doin'?" asked Mr Pappleworth, as the boy appeared.

"Just talking to Emma, and learning how to set needles."

"You'd better take your work an' go an' live down there."

"Well, there's nothing particular to do, is there?"

"Th' boss was looking for you a minute since. You'll catch it! And what about this ledger?"

Paul buckled to work quite cheerfully.

As a rule, when all the girls came back, at two o'clock, he ran upstairs to Fanny, the hunchback, in the finishing-off room. Mr Pappleworth did not appear till twenty to three, and he often found his boy sitting beside Fanny, talking, or drawing, or singing with the girls.

"Come Paul, my darling," Fanny would cry. "We thought you wasn't coming today. We thought you was going to stop down there, because we wasn't good enough for you."

"I've been in the town."

"What have you been in the town for, my duck?"

"For a keg of cranberries for my mother."

"And did you get it?"

Then the talk had started, and it went on endlessly. He was very fond of Fanny, and the hunchback loved him. She was twenty nine years old, and had suffered too much. He loved to sit beside her looking out of her window and making sketches of all the weird jungle of chimney pots and roof-ridges, ancient and peaked, that filled the prospect. Then he would say:

"Sing Fanny."

"Now look here, you don't want me to sing," she answered, as she stitched rapidly and nervously with her thin hands. "You only want to make game of me."

"Why I don't! I was only telling my mother how you could sing—."

"I don't know what your mother'd think of *me*, Paul, if she saw me. She'd think it was a monkey on a stick."

"She knows what you're like, because I've told her. And she likes you. Sing 'There is a Tavern—.' This is going to be a grand sketch I'm doing."

Then, after a minute's hesitation, Fanny would begin to sing. She had a fine contralto voice. Everybody joined in the chorus, and it went well. Paul was not at all embarrassed, sitting in the room with the half dozen work-girls.

At the end of the song Fanny would say:

"I know you've been laughing at me."

"Don't be so soft, Fanny!" cried one of the girls.

Once there was mention of Connie's red hair.

"Fanny's is better, to my fancy," said Emma.

"You needn't try to make a fool of me," said Fanny, flushing deeply.

"No but she has, Paul, she's got beautiful hair."

"It's a treat of a colour," said he. "That coldish colour, like earth, and yet shiny. It's like bog-water."

"Goodness me!" exclaimed one girl, laughing.

"How I do but get criticised," said Fanny.

"But you should see it down, Paul," cried Emma earnestly. "It's simply beautiful. Put it down for him, Fanny, if he wants something to paint."

Fanny would not. And yet she wanted to.

"Then I'll take it down myself," said the lad.

"Well, you can if you like," said Fanny.

And he carefully took the pins out of the knot, and the rush of hair, of uniform dark brown, slid over the humped back.

"What a lovely lot!" he exclaimed.

The girls watched. There was silence. The youth shook the hair loose from the coil.

"It's splendid," he said, smelling its perfume. "I'll bet it's worth pounds."

"I'll leave it you when I die, Paul," said Fanny, half joking.

"You look just like anybody else, sitting drying their hair," said one of the girls to the long-legged hunch-back.

Poor Fanny was morbidly sensitive, always imagining insults. Polly was curt and business like. The two departments were for ever at war, and Paul was always finding Fanny in tears. Then he was made the recipient of all her woes, and he had to plead her cause with Polly.

Mr Jordan's daughter was a painter. She had Connie for a model. Connie told her about Paul, and Miss Jordan asked to see some of his sketches. Then she came to see him. She was dry and business-like, but she took some interest in the boy.

So the time went along happily enough. The factory had a homely feel. No one was rushed or driven. Paul always enjoyed it when the work got faster, towards post-time, and all the men united in labour. He liked to watch his fellow clerks at work. The man was the work, and the work was the man, one thing, for the time being. It was different with the girls. The real woman never seemed to be there at the task, but as if left out, waiting.

From the train going home at night, he used to watch the lights of the town, sprinkled thick on the hills, fusing together in a blaze in the valleys. He felt rich in life and happy. Drawing further off, there was a patch of lights at Bulwell, like myriad petals shaken to the ground from the shed stars; and beyond was the red glare of the furnaces, playing like hot breath on the clouds.

He had to walk two and more miles from Keston home, up two long hills, down two short hills. He was often tired, and he counted the lamps climbing the hill above him, how many more to pass. And from the hill-top, on pitch dark nights, he looked round on the villages five or six miles away, that shone like swarms of glittering living things, almost a heaven against his feet. Marlpool and Heanor scattered the far off darkness with brilliance. And occasionally, the black valley space between was traced, violated by a great train rushing south to London, or north to Scotland. The trains roared by like projectiles level on the darkness, fuming and burning, making the valley clang with their passage. They were gone, and the lights of the towns and villages glittered in silence.

And then he came to the corner at home, which faced the other side of the night. The ash tree seemed a friend now. His mother rose with gladness as he entered. He put his eight shillings proudly on the table.

"It'll help, mother?" he asked, wistfully.

"There's precious little left," she answered, "after your ticket and dinners and such are taken off."

Then he told her the budget of the day. His life-story, like an *Arabian Nights*, but much duller, was told night after night to his mother. It was almost as if it were her own life.

CHAPTER VI

Death in the Family

Arthur Morel was growing up. He was a quick, careless, impulsive boy, a good deal like his father. He hated study, made a great moan if he had to work, and escaped as soon as possible to his sport again.

In appearance, he remained the flower of the family, being well made, graceful, and full of life. His dark brown hair and fresh colouring, and his exquisite dark blue eyes shaded with long lashes, together with his generous manner and fiery temper, made him a favourite. But as he grew older his temper became uncertain. He flew into rages over nothing, seemed unbearably raw and irritable.

His mother, whom he loved, wearied of him sometimes. He thought only of himself. When he wanted amusement, all that stood in his way he hated, even if it were she. When he was in trouble, he moaned to her ceaselessly.

"Goodness boy," she said, when he groaned about a master who, he said, hated him, "if you don't like it, alter it, and if you can't alter it, put up with it."

And his father, whom he had loved and who had worshipped him, he came to detest. As he grew older, Morel fell into a slow ruin. His body, which had been beautiful in movement and in being, shrank, did not seem to ripen with the years, but to get mean and rather despicable. There came over him a look of meanness, and of paltriness. And when the mean-looking elderly man bullied or ordered the boy about, Arthur was furious. Moreover, Morel's manners got worse and worse, his habits somewhat disgusting. When the children were growing up, and in the crucial stage of adolescence, the father was like some ugly irritant to their souls. His manners in the house were the same as he used among the colliers down pit.

"Dirty nuisance!" Arthur would cry, jumping up and going straight out of the house, when his father disgusted him.

And Morel persisted the more, because his children hated it. He seemed to take a kind of satisfaction in disgusting them, and driving them nearly mad, while they were so irritably sensitive, at the age of fourteen or fifteen. So that Arthur, who was growing up when his father was degenerate and elderly, hated him worst of all.

Then, sometimes, the father would seem to feel the contemptuous hatred of his children.

"There's not a man tries harder for his family," he would shout. "He does his best for them, and then gets treated like a dog.—But I'm not going to stand it, I tell you!"

But for the threat, and the fact that he did not try so hard as he imagined, they would have felt sorry. As it was, the battle now went on nearly all between father and children, he persisting in his dirty and disgusting ways, just to assert his independence. They loathed him.

Arthur was so inflamed and irritable at last that, when he won a scholarship for the Grammar School in Nottingham, his mother decided to let him live in town, with one of her sisters, and only come home at week-ends.

Annie was still a junior teacher in the Board School, earning about four shillings a week. But soon she would have fifteen shillings, since she had passed her examination, and there would be financial peace in the house.

Mrs Morel clung now to Paul. He was quiet and not brilliant. But still he stuck to his painting, and still he stuck to his mother. Everything he did, was for her. She waited for his coming home in the evening, and then she unburdened herself of all she had pondered or of all that had occurred to her during the day. He sat and listened with his earnestness. The two shared lives.

William was engaged now to his brunette, and had bought her an engagement ring that cost eight guineas. The children gasped at such a fabulous price.

"Eight guineas!" said Morel. "More fool him!—If he'd gen me some on't, it 'ud ha' looked better on 'im."

"Given *you* some of it," cried Mrs Morel. "Why give *you* some of it!"

She remembered he had bought no engagement ring at all, and she preferred William, who was not mean, if he were foolish. But now the young man talked only of the dances to which he went with his betrothed, and the different resplendent clothes she wore; or he told his mother with glee, how they went to the theatre, like great swells.

He wanted to bring the girl home. Mrs Morel said she should

come at the Christmas. This time, William arrived with a lady, but with no presents. Mrs Morel had prepared supper. Hearing footsteps she rose and went to the door. William entered.

"Hello mother!"—he kissed her hastily, then stood aside, to present a tall, handsome girl, who was wearing a costume of fine black-and-white check, and furs.

"Here's Gyp!"

Miss Western held out her hand and she showed her teeth in a small smile.

"Oh, how do you do, Mrs Morel!" she exclaimed.

"I am afraid you will be hungry," said Mrs Morel.

"Oh no, we had dinner in the train.—Have you got my gloves, Chubby?"

William Morel, big and raw-boned, looked at her quickly.

"How should I?" he said.

"Then I've lost them. Don't be cross with me—."

A frown went over his face, but he said nothing. She glanced round the kitchen. It was small and curious to her, with its glittering kissing-bunch, its evergreens behind the pictures, its wooden chairs and little deal table. At that moment Morel came in.

"Hello Dad!"

"Hello my son—tha's let on me!"

The two shook hands, and William presented the lady. She gave the same smile that showed her teeth.

"How do you do, Mr Morel?"

Morel bowed obsequiously.

"I'ne very well, and I hope so are you.—You must make yourself very welcome."

"Oh thank you," she replied, rather amused.

"You will like to go upstairs," said Mrs Morel.

"If you don't mind—but not if it is any trouble to you."

"It is no trouble—Annie will take you.—Walter, carry up this box."

"And don't be an hour dressing yourself up," said William to his betrothed.

Annie took a brass candlestick, and, too shy almost to speak, preceded the young lady to the front bedroom, which Mr and Mrs Morel had vacated for her. It too was small, and cold by candlelight. The colliers' wives only lit fires in bedrooms, in case of extreme illness.

"Shall I unstrap the box?" asked Annie.

"Oh thank you very much!"

Annie played the part of maid, then went downstairs for hot water.

"I think she's rather tired, mother," said William. "It's a beastly journey, and we had such a rush."

"Is there anything I can give her?" asked Mrs Morel.

"Oh no—she'll be all right."

But there was a chill in the atmosphere. After half an hour, Miss Western came down, having put on a purplish coloured dress, very fine for the collier's kitchen.

"I told you you'd no need to change," said William to her.

"Oh Chubby!—" then she turned with that sweetish smile to Mrs Morel. "Don't you think he's always grumbling, Mrs Morel?"

"Is he?" said Mrs Morel. "That's not very nice of him."

"It isn't, really!"

"You are cold," said the mother, "won't you come near the fire."

Morel jumped out of his arm-chair.

"Come and sit you here," he cried, "come and sit you here."

"No Dad—keep your own chair—sit on the sofa, Gyp," said William.

"No no!" cried Morel. "This cheer's warmest. Come and sit here, Miss Wesson."

"Thank you *so* much," said the girl, seating herself in the collier's arm-chair, the place of honor. She shivered, feeling the warmth of the kitchen penetrate her.

"Fetch me a hanky, Chubby dear!" she said, putting up her mouth to him, and using the same intimate tone, as if they were alone: which made the rest of the family feel as if they ought not to be present. The young lady evidently did not realise them as people: they were creatures to her, for the present. William winced.

In such a household, in Streatham, Miss Western would have been a lady condescending to her inferiors. These people were, to her, certainly clownish—in short, the working classes. How was she to adjust herself?

"I'll go," said Annie.

Miss Western took no notice, as if a servant had spoken. But when the girl came downstairs again with the handkerchief, she said:

"Oh thank you," in a gracious way.

She sat and talked: about the dinner on the train, which had been so poor; about London, about dances. She was really very nervous, and chattered from fear. Morel sat all the time smoking his thick-twist tobacco, watching her, and listening to her glib London speech, as he puffed. Mrs Morel, dressed up in her best black-silk blouse, answered quietly and rather briefly. The three children sat round in silence and admiration. Miss Western was the princess. Everything of the best was got out for her: the best cups, the best spoons, the best table-cloth, the best coffee-jug. The children thought she must find it quite grand. She felt strange, not able to realise the people, not knowing how to treat them. William joked, and was slightly uncomfortable.

At about ten o'clock, he said to her:

"Aren't you tired, Gyp?"

"Rather, Chubby," she answered, at once in the intimate tones, and putting her head slightly on one side.

"I'll light her the candle, mother?" he said.

"Very well," replied the mother.

Miss Western stood up, held out her hand to Mrs Morel.

"Goodnight, Mrs Morel," she said.

Paul sat at the boiler, letting the water run from the tap into a stone beer-bottle. Annie swathed the bottle in an old flannel pit singlet, and kissed her mother goodnight. She was to share the room with the lady, because the house was full.

"You wait a minute," said Mrs Morel to Annie. And Annie sat nursing the hot water bottle. Miss Western shook hands all round, to everybody's discomfort, and took her departure, preceded by William. In five minutes he was downstairs again. His heart was rather sore, he did not know why. He talked very little till everybody had gone to bed but himself and his mother. Then he stood with his legs apart, in his old attitude on the hearth-rug, and said hesitatingly:

"Well mother?"

"Well, my son!"

She sat in the rocking-chair, feeling somehow hurt and humiliated, for his sake.

"Do you like her?"

"Yes," came the slow answer.

"She's shy yet, mother—she's not used to it. It's different from her Aunt's house, you know."

"Of course it is, my boy—and she must find it difficult."

"She does." Then he frowned swiftly. "If only she wouldn't put on her *blessed* airs!"

"It's only her first awkwardness, my boy. She'll be all right."

"That's it, mother," he replied, gratefully. But his brow was gloomy. "You know she's not like you, mother—she's not serious—and she can't think."

"She's young, my boy."

"Yes!—And she's had no sort of show. Her mother died when she was a child. Since then she's lived with her aunt, whom she can't bear. And her father was a rake.—She's had no love."

"No!—Well, you must make up to her."

"And so—you have to forgive her a lot of things."

"*What* do you have to forgive her, my boy?"

"I dunno—when she seems shallow, you have to remember she's never had anybody to bring her deeper side out.—And she's *fearfully* fond of me."

"Anybody can see that."

"But you know mother—she's—she's different from us. Those sort of people, like those she lives amongst—they don't seem to have the same principles."

"You mustn't judge too hastily," said Mrs Morel.

But he seemed uneasy within himself.

In the morning, however, he was up singing and larking round the house.

"Hello!" he called, sitting on the stairs. "Are you getting up?"

"Yes," her voice called, faintly.

"Merry Christmas!" he shouted to her.

Her laugh, pretty and tinkling, was heard in the bedroom. She did not come down in half an hour.

"Was she *really* getting up when she said she was?" he asked of Annie.

"Yes, she was," replied Annie.

He waited awhile, then went to the stairs again.

"Happy New Year!" he called.

"Thank you Chubby Dear!" came the laughing voice, far away.

"Buck up!" he implored.

It was nearly an hour, and still he was waiting for her. Morel, who always rose before six, looked at the clock.

"Well it's a winder!" he exclaimed.

Death in the Family

The family had breakfasted, all but William. He went to the foot of the stairs.

"Shall I have to send you an Easter Egg up there?" he called, rather crossly. She only laughed. The family expected, after that time of preparation, something like magic. At last she came, looking very nice in a blouse and skirt.

"Have you *really* been all this time getting ready?" he asked.

"Chubby dear!—That question is not permitted, is it, Mrs Morel?"

She played the grand lady at first. When she went with William to Chapel, he in his frock coat and silk hat, she in her furs and London-made costume, Paul and Arthur and Annie expected everybody to bow to the ground in admiration. And Morel, standing in his Sunday Suit at the end of the road, watching the gallant pair go, felt he was the father of princes and princesses.

And yet she was not so grand. For a year now, she had been a sort of secretary, or clerk, in a London office.

But while she was with the Morels she queened it: she sat and let Annie or Paul wait on her as if they were her servants. She treated Mrs Morel with a certain glibness, and Morel with patronage. But after a day or so, she began to change her tune.

William always wanted Paul, or Annie, to go along with them on their walks. It was so much more interesting. And Paul really *did* admire 'Gypsy,' whole heartedly. In fact, his mother scarcely forgave the boy for the adulation with which he treated the girl.

On the second day, when Lily said:

"Oh Annie, do you know where I left my muff?"

William replied:

"You know it is in your bedroom. Why do you ask Annie?"

And Lily went upstairs, with a cross, shut mouth. But it angered the young man, that she made a servant of his sister.

On the third evening, William and Lily were sitting together in the parlour, by the fire, in the dark. At a quarter to eleven, Mrs Morel was heard raking the fire. William came out to the kitchen, followed by his beloved.

"Is it as late as that, mother?" he said. She had been sitting alone.

"It is not *late*, my boy—but it is as late as I usually sit up."

"Won't you go to bed, then?" he asked.

"And leave you two?—No, my boy, I don't believe in it."

"Can't you trust us, mother?"

"Whether I can or not, I won't do it.—You can stay till eleven if you like, and I can read."

"Go to bed, Gyp," he said to his girl. "We won't keep Mater waiting."

"Annie has left the candle burning, Lily," said Mrs Morel. "I think you will see."

"Yes thank you. Goodnight, Mrs Morel."

William kissed his sweetheart at the foot of the stairs, and she went. He returned to the kitchen.

"Can't you trust us, mother?" he repeated, rather offended.

"My boy, I tell you I don't *believe* in leaving two young things like you alone downstairs, when everyone else is in bed."

And he was forced to take this answer. He kissed his mother goodnight.

At Easter, he came over alone. And then he discussed his sweetheart endlessly, with his mother.

"You know mother—when I'm away from her, I don't care for her a bit—I shouldn't care if I never saw her again.—But then when I'm with her in the evenings, I am awfully fond of her."

"It's a queer sort of love, to marry on," said Mrs Morel. "If she holds you no more than that!"

"It *is* funny!" he exclaimed. It worried and perplexed him. "But yet—there's so much between us now—I couldn't give her up."

"You know best," said Mrs Morel. "But if it is as you say, I wouldn't call it *love*—at any rate it doesn't look much like it."

"Oh I don't know, mother. She's an orphan, and—."

They never came to any sort of conclusion. He seemed puzzled, and rather fretted. She was rather reserved. All his strength and money went in keeping this girl. He could scarcely afford to take his mother to Nottingham, when he came over.

Paul's wages had been raised at Christmas to ten shillings, to his great joy. He was quite happy at Jordan's, but his health suffered from the long hours and the confinement. His mother, to whom he became more and more significant, thought how to help.

His half-day holiday was on Monday afternoon. On a Monday morning in May, as the two sat alone at breakfast, she said:

"I think it will be a fine day."

He looked up in surprise. This meant something.

"You know Mr Leivers has gone to live on a new farm. Well he asked me last week if I wouldn't go and see Mrs Leivers, and I promised to bring you on Monday, if it's fine. Shall we go?"

"I say, little woman, how lovely!" he cried. "And we'll go this afternoon?"

"If you won't be too tired—it's a long way."

"How far?"

"Four miles."

"Pooh—it's not me that'll be tired with walking four miles, it's you. Can you do it?"

"Of course I can."

"Jolly—jolly!" he cried. "I'll make haste home. And is it pretty?"

"He says so—you must see for yourself."

"I don't know Mrs Leivers, mother—do you?"

"Why you do know her—a little pathetic woman with great brown eyes, used to sit opposite us in Chapel."

"I can't remember."

"I should have thought you could remember her hat, if nothing else,—for she never had a new one all the six years *I've* known her: a little black object with a scrap of lace stuck on it by accident: I'm sure, when I used to see it perched on her head, Sunday after Sunday, and still it came again, I used to feel as if I could pull it off. Yet he's so smart, and a good looking man."

"She was happen poor," said Paul.

"And if she was! *I* know she was no worse off than *I* was. But she *wouldn't* have anything new, because she wouldn't."

"But is she nice?"

"Yes, I *always* liked her—except that she *won't* manage to make herself look decent for that man.—And it's pride that does it, nothing else."

"Why?"

"Well, she's a little, delicate, refined woman, with great pathetic brown eyes—rather soulful. And *I* know she's had a hard, dragging time, with seven children and Alfred Leivers' bit of money. I think *he* doesn't like hard work—though perhaps—. But so, because she's come down, and is made a veritable drudge of, she's too proud to keep up appearances level with any other ordinary woman, she must go about an old fashioned object—yet she's pretty."

"Is she proud, mother?"

"Well no, not to other people. But to herself, she's as proud as they're made. Her poverty and drudging galls her soul, so she sticks to that bit of a black hat, to spite her poverty—or him—Goodness knows. But *you'll* like her—and *I* like her."

"Well," said Paul, "if we go to see her in a farm, she won't have a hat on at all."

"Let's hope not," said Mrs Morel. "Not but what it's a scandal and a shame to put such a burden on a little body like her, but then she needn't make a fright of herself, for spite. How he must feel—!"

Paul hurried off to the station, jubilant. Down Derby Road was a cherry tree that glistened. The old brick wall by the Statutes ground burned scarlet, spring was a very flame of green. And the steep swoop of highroad lay, in its cool morning dust, splendid with patterns of sunshine and shadow, perfectly still. The trees sloped their great green shoulders proudly. And inside the warehouse all morning, the boy had a vision of spring outside.

When he came home at dinner-time, his mother was rather excited.

"Are we going?" he asked.

"When I'm ready," she replied.

"But you've done your work?"

"Yes."

He sat down to dinner. She took the frying pan.

"Now what business had you to be making rhubarb fritters," he said to her, "when you've no time?"

"Because I choose to make fritters," she said. "And I shall be ready as soon as you are."

She made the fritters because he was only home for dinner this one week-day, and he liked them.

"No you won't—go away and let me do them," he said.

He got up, tried to take the handle of the frying-pan from her.

"I shall do nothing of the sort!" she said, waving her fork. "I shall be in plenty of time."

He retired discomfited to his dinner, whilst she went on cooking.

"It's just like a woman," he said, "to go dabbling in the frying pan when she ought to be getting ready to go somewhere."

"And it's just like a boy, to think he knows everything," she said. She put the sweets in front of him.

"And you've burned your face like one-o'clock," he said; "and you know what a rising sun you'll look by the time you get there."

"Then I shan't ask *you* to look at me."

"I wouldn't if you did ask me," he said.

"Ingratitude!"

"Red-face!"

She sniffed, and drew herself up, in the way he called "turtling."

"Are you washed?" he asked.

"Yes I am."

"Well you don't look it, for you've got a smut on your nose as usual."

She went to the glass to see.

"What a nuisance!" she exclaimed.

Presently he got up.

"Go and get dressed while I wash up," he said.

She did so. He washed the pots, straightened, and then took her boots. They were quite clean. Mrs Morel was one of those naturally exquisite people who can walk in mud without dirtying their shoes. But Paul had to clean them for her. They were kid boots at eight shillings a pair. He however, thought them the most dainty boots in the world, and he cleaned them with as much reverence as if they had been flowers.

Suddenly she appeared in the inner doorway, rather shyly. She had got a new cotton blouse on. Paul jumped up and went forward.

"Oh my stars!" he exclaimed, "what a bobby-dazzler!"

She sniffed in a little, haughty way, and put her head up.

"It's not a bobby dazzler at all!" she replied. "It's very quiet."

She walked forward, whilst he hovered round her.

"Well," she asked, quite shy, but pretending to be high and mighty. "Do you like it?"

"Awfully! You *are* a fine little woman, to go jaunting out with!"

He went and surveyed her from the back.

"Well!" he said, "if I was walking down the street behind you, I should say: 'Doesn't *that* little person fancy herself.'"

"Well she doesn't," replied Mrs Morel. "She's not sure it suits her."

"Oh no!—she wants to be in dirty black, looking as if she was wrapped in burnt paper. It *does* suit you, and *I* say you look nice."

She sniffed in her little way, pleased, but pretending to know better.

"Well," she said, "it's cost me just three shillings. You couldn't have got it ready made for that price, could you?"

"I should think you couldn't," he replied.

"And you know, it's good stuff."

151

"Awfully pretty," he said.

The blouse was white, with a little sprig of heliotrope and black.

"Too young for me, though, I'm afraid," she said.

"Too young for you!" he exclaimed in disgust. "Why don't you buy some false white hair, and stick it on your head."

"I s'll soon have no need," she replied. "I'm going white fast enough."

"Well, you've no business to," he said. "What do I want with a white haired mother."

"I'm afraid you'll have to put up with one, my lad," she said, rather strangely.

They set off in great style, she carrying the umbrella William had given her, because of the sun. Paul was considerably taller than she, though he was not big. He fancied himself.

On the fallow land the young wheat shone silkily. Minton pit waved its plumes of white steam, coughed and rattled hoarsely.

"Now look at that!" said Mrs Morel. Mother and son stood on the road to watch. Along the ridge of the great pit-hill crawled a little group in silhouette against the sky, a horse, a small truck, and a man. They climbed the incline against the heavens: at the end the man tipped the wagon; there was an undue rattle as the waste fell down the sheer slope of the enormous bank.

"You sit a minute, mother," he said, and she took a seat on a bank, whilst he sketched rapidly. She was silent whilst he worked, looking round at the afternoon, the red cottages shining among their greenness.

"The world is a wonderful place," she said, "and wonderfully beautiful."

"And so's the pit," he said. "Look how it heaps together, like something alive, almost—a big creature that you don't know."

"Yes," she said. "Perhaps!"

"And all the trucks standing waiting, like a string of beasts to be fed," he said.

"And very thankful I am they *are* standing," she said, "for that means they'll turn middling time this week."

"But I like the feel of *men* on things, while they're alive. There's a feel of men about trucks, because they've been handled with men's hands, all of them."

"Yes," said Mrs Morel.

They went along under the trees of the high road. He was

constantly informing her, but she was interested. They passed the end of Nethermere, that was tossing its sunshine like petals lightly in its lap. Then they turned on a private road, and in some trepidation approached a big farm. A dog barked furiously. A woman came out to see.

"Is this the way to Willey Farm?" Mrs Morel asked.

Paul hung behind, in terror of being sent back. But the woman was amiable, and directed them. The mother and son went through the wheat and oats, over a little bridge into a wild meadow. Peewits with their white breasts glistening wheeled and screamed about them. The lake was still and blue. High overhead a heron floated. Opposite, the wood heaped on the hill, green and still.

"It's a wild road, mother," said Paul. "Just like Canada."

"Isn't it beautiful!" said Mrs Morel, looking round.

"See that heron—see—see her legs?"

He directed his mother, what she must see, and what not. And she was quite content.

"But now," she said, "which way?—He told me, through the wood." The wood, fenced and dark, lay on their left.

"I can feel a bit of a path this road," said Paul. "You've got town feet, somehow or other, you have."

They found a little gate, and soon were in a broad green alley of the wood, with a new thicket of fir and pine on one hand, an old oak glade, dipping down on the other. And among the oaks the bluebells stood in pools of azure, under the new green hazels, upon a pale fawn floor of oak-leaves. He found flowers for her.

"Here's a bit of new-mown hay," he said, then again he brought her forgetmenots. And again his heart hurt with love, seeing her hand, used with work, holding the little bunch of flowers he gave her. She was perfectly happy.

But at the end of the riding was a fence to climb. Paul was over in a second.

"Come," he said, "let me help you."

"No—go away. I will do it in my own way."

He stood below, with his hands up ready to help her. She climbed cautiously.

"What a way to climb!" he exclaimed scornfully, when she was safely to earth again.

"Hateful stiles!" she cried.

"Duffer of a little woman," he replied, "who can't get over 'em."

In front, along the edge of the wood, was a cluster of low, red farm buildings. The two hastened forward. Flush with the wood was the apple-orchard, where blossom was falling on the grind stone. The pond was deep under a hedge, and overhanging oak-trees. Some cows stood in the shade. The farm and buildings, three sides of a quadrangle, embraced the sunshine towards the wood. It was very still.

Mother and son went into the small railed garden, where was a scent of red gillivers. By the open door were some floury loaves, put out to cool. A hen was just coming to peck them. Then, in the doorway suddenly appeared a girl in a dirty apron. She was about fourteen years old, had a rosy dark face, a bunch of short black curls, very fine and free, and dark eyes; shy, questioning, a little resentful of the strangers. She disappeared. In a minute another figure appeared, a small, frail woman, rosy, with great dark brown eyes.

"Oh!" she exclaimed, smiling with a little glow, "you've come then. I *am* glad to see you." Her voice was intimate, and rather sad.

The two women shook hands.

"Now are you sure we're not a bother to you?" said Mrs Morel. "I know what a farming life is."

"Oh no. We're only too thankful to see a new face, it's so lost up here."

"I suppose so," said Mrs Morel.

They were taken through into the parlour, a long, low room, with a great bunch of guelder-roses in the fire-place. There the women talked, whilst Paul went out to survey the land. He was in the garden smelling the gillivers and looking at the plants, when the girl came out quickly to the heap of coal which stood by the fence.

"I suppose these are cabbage roses," he said to her, pointing to the bushes along the fence. She looked at him with startled, big brown eyes.

"I suppose they are cabbage roses, when they come out?" he said.

"I don't know," she faltered. "They're white, with pink middles."

"Then they're maiden-blush."

Miriam flushed. She had a beautiful warm colouring.

"I don't know," she said.

"You don't have *much* in your garden," he said.

"This is our first year here," she answered, in a distant, rather superior way, drawing away and going indoors. He did not notice, but went his round of exploration. Presently his mother came out, and they went through the buildings. Paul was hugely delighted.

"And I suppose you have the fowls and calves and pigs to look after?" said Mrs Morel to Mrs Leivers.

"No," replied the little woman. "I can't find time to look after cattle, and I'm not used to it. It's as much as I can do to keep going in the house."

"Well, I suppose it is," said Mrs Morel.

Presently the girl came out.

"Tea is ready, mother," she said, in a musical, quiet voice.

"Oh thank you, Miriam, then we'll come," replied her mother, almost ingratiatingly. "Would you *care* to have tea now, Mrs Morel?"

"Of course," said Mrs Morel. "Whenever it's ready."

Paul and his mother and Mrs Leivers had tea together. Then they went out into the wood, that was flooded with bluebells, while fumy forgetmenots were in the paths. The mother and son were in ecstasy together.

When they got back to the house, Mr Leivers and Edgar, the eldest son, were in the kitchen. Edgar was about eighteen. Then Geoffrey and Maurice, big lads of twelve and thirteen were in from school. Mr Leivers was a good-looking man in the prime of life, with a golden-brown moustache and blue eyes screwed up against the weather.

"Have you had a look round?" he asked of Paul, heartily.

"Not everywhere," the boy replied.

Then he went out with Geoffrey and Maurice.

"Where do *you* work?" asked Geoffrey of Paul. They were all three shy.

"In Jordan's Surgical Appliance Factory in Nottingham."

"And what do you do there?"

"I'm a clerk."

"And what do you do?"

"I copy the letters, and make orders, and make out invoices."

"What sort of letters do you copy?"

"Oh—any sort—mostly orders for elastic stockings."

"Elastic stockings!—what's them?"

There followed many explanations.

"And some of the letters are from France, and other places," said Paul.

"And do you copy them?"

"Yes."

"In French?"

"No—translate them."

"Why, do you reckon *you* know French?"

"I know some—and German as well."

"Why who learnt you that?"

"My Godfather—and algebra and Euclid."

"I don't want *my* 'ead full of that stuff," said Geoffrey.

The boys were amazingly superior. But Paul scarcely observed it. They went round for eggs, scrambling into all sorts of places. As they were feeding the fowls, Miriam came out. The boys took no notice of her. One hen with her yellow chickens was in a coop. Maurice took his hand full of corn and let the hen peck from it.

"Durst you do it?" he asked of Paul.

"Let's see," said Paul.

He had a small hand, warm, and rather capable-looking. Miriam watched. He held the corn to the hen. The bird eyed it with her hard bright eye, and suddenly made a peck into his hand. He started, and laughed. 'Rap-rap-rap!' went the bird's beak in his palm. He laughed again, and the other boys joined.

"She knocks you, and nips you, but she never hurts," said Paul, when the last corn had gone.

"Now Miriam," said Maurice, "you come an' 'ave a go."

"No," she cried, shrinking back.

"Ha! Baby. The mardy-kid!" said her brothers.

"It doesn't hurt a bit," said Paul. "It only just nips rather nicely."

"No," she still cried, shaking her black curls and shrinking.

"She dursn't," said Geoffrey. "She niver durst do anything except recite poitry."

"Dursn't jump off a gate—dursn't tweedle—dursn't go on a slide—dursn't stop a girl hittin' her—she can do nowt but go about thinkin' herself somebody—'The Lady of the Lake'—yah!" cried Maurice.

Miriam was crimson with shame and misery.

"I dare do more than you," she cried. "You're never anything but cowards and bullies."

"Oh 'cowards and bullies!'" they repeated, mincingly mocking her speech.

> "'Not such a clown shall anger me
> A boor is answered silently'"

he quoted against her, shouting with laughter.

She went indoors. Paul went with the boys into the orchard, where they had rigged up a parallel bar. They did feats of strength. He was more agile than strong, but it served. He fingered a piece of apple-blossom, that hung low on a swinging bough.

"I wouldn't get the apple-blossom," said Edgar, the eldest brother. "There'll be no apples next year."

"I wasn't going to get it," replied Paul, going away.

The boys felt hostile to him. They were more interested in their own pursuits. He wandered back to the house to look for his mother. As he went round the back, he saw Miriam kneeling in front of the hen coop, some maize in her hand, biting her lip, and crouching in an intense attitude. The hen was eyeing her wickedly. Very gingerly she put forward her hand. The hen bobbed for her. She drew back quickly with a cry, half of fear, half of chagrin.

"It won't hurt you," said Paul.

She flushed crimson and started up.

"I only wanted to try," she said, in a low voice.

"See, it doesn't hurt," he said, and, putting only two corns in his palm, he let the hen peck, peck, peck at his bare hand. "It only makes you laugh," he said.

She put her hand forward, and dragged it away, tried again, and started back with a cry. He frowned.

"Why I'd let her take corn from my face," said Paul, "only she bumps a bit. She's ever so neat. If she wasn't, look how much ground she'd peck up every day."

He waited grimly, and watched. At last Miriam let the bird peck from her hand. She gave a little cry, fear, and pain because of fear, rather pathetic. But she had done it, and she did it again.

"There you see," said the boy. "It doesn't hurt, does it."

She looked at him with dilated dark eyes.

"No," she laughed, trembling.

Then she rose and went indoors. She seemed to be in some way resentful of the boy.

"He thinks I'm only a common girl," she thought, and she wanted to prove she was a grand person like the 'Lady of the Lake.'

Paul found his mother ready to go home. She smiled on her son. He took the great bunch of flowers. Mr and Mrs Leivers walked down the fields with them. The hills were golden with evening: deep in the wood showed the darkening purple of bluebells: it was everywhere perfectly still, save for the rustling of leaves and birds.

"But it is a beautiful place," said Mrs Morel.

"Yes," answered Mr Leivers. "It's a nice little place, if only it weren't for the rabbits. The pasture's bitten down to nothing. I dunno if ever I s'll get the rent off it."

He clapped his hands, and the field broke into motion, near the woods, brown rabbits hopping everywhere.

"Would you believe it!" exclaimed Mrs Morel.

She and Paul went on alone together.

"Wasn't it lovely, mother?" he said, quietly. A thin moon was coming out. His heart was full of happiness till it hurt. His mother had to chatter, because she too wanted to cry with happiness.

"Now *wouldn't* I help that man!" she said. "*Wouldn't* I see to the fowls and the young stock. And *I'd* learn to milk, and *I'd* talk with him, and *I'd* plan with him. My word, if I were his wife, the farm would be run, I know.—But there, she hasn't the strength—she simply hasn't the strength. She ought never to have been burdened like it, you know. I'm sorry for her, and I'm sorry for him too. My word if *I'd* had him, I shouldn't have thought him a bad husband.—Not that she does either.—And she's very lovable."

William came home again with his sweetheart at the Whitsuntide. He had one of his week's holidays then. It was beautiful weather. As a rule, William and Lily and Paul went out in the morning together, for a walk. William did not talk to his beloved much, except to tell her things from his boyhood. Paul talked endlessly to both of them. They lay down, all three, in a meadow by Minton Church. On one side, by the Castle farm, was a beautiful quivering screen of poplars. Hawthorn was dropping from the hedges: penny daisies and ragged robin were in the field, like laughter. William, a big fellow of twenty three, thinner now and even a bit gaunt, lay back in the sunshine and dreamed, while she fingered with his hair. Paul went gathering the big daisies. She had taken off her hat. Her hair was black as a horse's mane. Paul came back and threaded daisies in her jet black hair, big spangles of white and yellow, and just a pink touch of ragged robbin.

"Now you look like a young witch-woman," the boy said to her. "Doesn't she William?"

Lily laughed. William opened his eyes and looked at her. In his gaze was a certain baffled look of misery and fierce appreciation.

"Has he made a sight of me?" she asked, laughing down on her lover.

"That he has!" said William, smiling. And as he lay he continued to look at her. His eyes never sought hers. He did not want to meet her eyes. He only wanted to look at her, not to come together with her in her gaze. And the fact that he wanted to avoid her was in his eyes like misery. He turned away again. She let her slim dark hand, whereon the diamonds sparkled, stray in his hair a moment longer. Then she said:

"Paul knows how to do things."

"All right," said he. "So long as he makes you happy. He'll do for mornings, and I for evenings."

She turned laughing to the boy.

"I want to put three more over your ear," he said, standing above her. "Then you'll be finished."

She submitted. He threaded in the daisies.

"Can't you smell the sun on your hair?" he said. "Now, that's how you ought to go to a ball."

"Thank you," she laughed.

Presently they rose to go.

"Don't wear a hat yet," said Paul.

"Shall I?" she asked of William. "May I go like this."

William looked at her again. Her beauty seemed to hurt him. He glanced at her flower-decked head and frowned.

"You look nice enough, if that's what you want to know," he said.

And she walked without her hat. In a little while, William recovered, and was rather tender to her. Coming to a bridge, he carved her initials, and his, in a heart.

She watched his strong, nervous hand, with its glistening hairs and freckles, as he carved, and she seemed fascinated by it.

All the time, there was a feeling of sadness, and warmth, and a certain tenderness in the house, whilst William and Lily were at home. But often he got irritable. She had brought, for an eight days' stay, five dresses and six blouses.

"Oh would you mind," she said to Annie, "washing me these two blouses—and these things."

And Annie stood washing when William and Lily went out, the next morning. Mrs Morel was furious. And sometimes the young man, catching a glimpse of his sweetheart's attitude towards his sister, hated her.

On Sunday morning she looked very beautiful, in a dress of

foulard, silky and sweeping, and blue as a jay-bird's feather, and in a large cream hat covered with many roses, mostly crimson. Nobody could admire her enough. But in the evening, when she was going out, she asked again:

"Chubby, have you got my gloves?"

"Which?" asked William.

"My new black suède?"

"No."

There was a hunt. She had lost them.

"Look here, mother," said William. "That's the fourth pair she's lost since Christmas—at five shillings a pair."

"You only gave me *two* of them," she remonstrated.

And in the evening, after supper, he stood on the hearth-rug, whilst she sat on the sofa, and he seemed to hate her. In the afternoon he had left her, whilst he went to see some old friend. She had sat looking at a book. After supper, William wanted to write a letter.

"Here is your book, Lily," said Mrs Morel. "Would you care to go on with it for a few minutes?"

"No thank you," said the girl. "I will sit still."

"But it is so dull—"

William scribbled irritably at a great rate. As he sealed the envelope, he said:

"Read a book!—Why she's never read a book in her life."

"Oh go along!" said Mrs Morel, cross with the exaggeration.

"It's true mother—she hasn't," he cried, jumping up and taking his old position on the hearthrug. "She's never read a book in her life."

"'Er's like me," chimed in Morel. "'Er canna see what there is i' books, ter sit borin' your nose in 'em for, nor more can I!"

"But you shouldn't say these things," said Mrs Morel to her son.

"But it's true mother—she *can't* read—what did you give her?"

"Well I gave her a little thing of Annie Swan's. Nobody wants to read dry stuff on Sunday afternoon."

"Well I'll bet she didn't read ten lines of it."

"You are mistaken," said his mother.

All the time, Lily sat miserably on the sofa. He turned to her swiftly.

"*Did* you read any?" he asked.

"Yes, I did," she replied.

"How much?"

"I don't know how many pages—"

"Tell me *one thing* you read."

She could not.

"Be quiet, William," said his mother. "The very idea!"

"But she can't mother!" he cried, bitterly. "She can't take it in, when she reads. She can't read, and she can't talk. There's not a thing you can talk to her about. She only thinks in frocks and how folk admire her."

"Take no notice of him, Lily," said Mrs Morel.

"It's only fools as sits wi' their noses stuck i' books, that's what *I* say," added Morel.

And the poor girl remained in ignominy. He seemed to hate her. Later Mrs Morel found her a very simple book, and it was pathetic to see her, on a wet afternoon, wading in misery through a few lines. She never got beyond the second page. He read a great deal, and had a quick, active intelligence. She could understand nothing but love making and chatter. He was accustomed to having all his thoughts sifted through his mother's mind. So, when he wanted companionship, and was asked in reply to be the billing and twittering lover, he hated his betrothed.

"You know, mother," he said, when he was alone with her at night, "she's no idea of money, she's so wessel-brained. When she's paid, she'll suddenly buy such rot as *marrons glacés*. And then *I* have to buy her season-ticket, and her extras, even her underclothing. And she wants to get married—And I think myself we might as well get married next year. But at this rate—!"

"A fine mess of a marriage it would be," replied his mother. "I should consider it again, my boy."

"Oh well—I've gone too far to break off now," he said. "And so I shall get married as soon as I can."

"Very well, my boy. If you will you will, and there's no stopping you.—But I tell you, *I* can't sleep when I think about it."

"Oh, she'll be all right, mother. We shall manage."

"And she lets you buy her underclothing?" asked the mother.

"Well," he began, apologetically. "She didn't ask me. But one morning—and it *was* cold—I found her on the station, shivering, not able to keep still. So I asked her if she was well wrapped up. She said, 'I think so.' So I said 'Have you got warm underthings on?' And she said, no, they were cotton. I asked her why on earth she hadn't got something thicker on, in weather like that, and she said, because she *had* nothing. And there she is a bronchial subject!—I *had* to take her and get some warm things.—Well mother, I shouldn't mind the money, if we had any.—And you know, she *ought* to keep enough to pay for her season ticket. But no—she comes to me about that, and I have to find the money—"

"It's a poor look-out," said Mrs Morel bitterly.

He was pale, and his rugged face, that used to be so perfectly careless and laughing, was stamped with conflict and despair.

"But I can't give her up, now, it's gone too far," he said. "And besides, for *some* things, I couldn't do without her—."

"My boy, remember you're taking your life in your hands," said Mrs Morel. "*Nothing* is as bad as a marriage that's a hopeless failure. Mine was bad enough, God knows, and ought to teach you something.—But it might have been worse by a long chalk."

He leaned with his back against the side of the chimney piece, his hands in his pockets. He was a big, raw-boned man, who looked as if he would go to the world's end, if he wanted to. But she saw the despair on his face.

"I couldn't give her up now," he said.

"Well," she said. "Remember there are worse wrongs than breaking off an engagement."

They remained in silence, he staring across the room. Only his mother could help him now. And yet, he would not let her decide for him. He stuck to what he had done.

"And of course," added Mrs Morel, "there's a great deal more nobility in breaking off in order to avoid doing more wrong, than in keeping on because you've said you would."

He was stock still, staring across the room.

"I can't give her up *now*," he said.

The clock ticked on. Mother and son remained in silence, a conflict between them. But he would say no more. At last she said:

"Well, go to bed, my son—you'll feel better in the morning—and perhaps you'll know better."

He kissed her, and went. She raked the fire. Her heart was heavy now as it had never been. Before, with her husband, things had seemed to be breaking down in her, but they did not destroy her power to live. Now, her soul felt lamed in itself. It was her hope that was struck.

And so often, William manifested the same hatred towards his betrothed. On the last evening at home, he was railing against her.

"Well," he said, "if you don't believe me, what she's like, would you believe she has been confirmed three times!"

"Nonsense," laughed Mrs Morel.

"Nonsense or not, she *has*! That's what confirmation means for her—a bit of a theatrical show where she can cut a figure."

"I haven't, Mrs Morel," cried the girl. "I haven't. It is not true."

"What!" he cried, flashing round on her. "Once in Bromley, once in Beckenham, and once somewhere else."

"Nowhere else!" she said, in tears. "Nowhere else."

"It *was*! And if it wasn't, why were you confirmed *twice*?"

"Once I was only fourteen, Mrs Morel," she pleaded, tears in her eyes.

"Yes," said Mrs Morel. "I can quite understand it, child. Take no notice of him. You ought to be ashamed, William, saying such things."

"But it's true. She's religious—she has blue velvet prayerbooks—and she's not as much religion, or anything else, in her than that table leg. Gets confirmed three times, for show, to show herself off. And that's how she is in *everything*, *everything*!"

The girl sat on the sofa, crying. She was not strong.

"As for *love*!" he cried. "You might as well ask a fly to love you. It'll love settling on you—"

"Now say no more," commanded Mrs Morel. "If you want to say these things, you must find another place than this. I am ashamed of you, William. Why don't you be more manly. To do nothing but find fault with a girl—and then pretend you're engaged to her—!" Mrs Morel subsided in wrath and indignation.

William was silent. And later he repented, kissed and comforted the girl. Yet it was true, what he had said. He hated her.

When they were going away, Mrs Morel accompanied them as far as Nottingham. It was a long way to Keston station.

"You know mother," he said to her, "Gyp's shallow—nothing goes deep with her."

"William I *wish* you wouldn't say these things," said Mrs Morel, very uncomfortable for the girl who walked beside her.

"But it doesn't mother.—She's very much in love with me *now*.—But if I died, she'd have forgotten me in three months."

Mrs Morel was afraid. Her heart beat furiously, hearing the quiet bitterness of her son's last speech.

"How do you know!" she replied. "You *don't* know—and therefore you've no right to say such a thing."

"He's always saying these things!" cried the girl.

"In three months after I was buried, you'd have somebody else, and I should be forgotten," he said. "And that's your love!"

Mrs Morel saw them into the train in Nottingham, then she returned home.

"You know," she said pathetically to Paul, "it's no good, and it never will be any good. What it will be like if ever they *do* marry, is too much for me to think of. If *only* he'd let her go, he wouldn't torment her half so much, I'm sure. But they'll hang on to each other till they kill each other. And I felt, when he said *that*, going to Keston, as if I couldn't walk another stride. Poor thing, I'm sorry for her. But she's not fit for him, she isn't. I'm sure, it seems a wicked thing to say, but she's delicate, and I'd rather she died than he married her."

All summer long Mrs Morel thought about her son. He seemed now to be making a ruin of his life. But still the marriage was a long way off.

"There's one comfort," she said to Paul, "he'll never have any money to marry on, that I *am* sure of. And so she'll save him that way."

So she took cheer. Matters were not yet very desperate. She firmly believed William would never marry his Gipsy. She waited, and she kept Paul near to her.

All summer long William's letters had a feverish tone. He seemed unnatural and intense. Sometimes he was exaggeratedly jolly, usually he was flat and bitter in his letter.

"Ay," his mother said, "I'm afraid he's ruining himself against that creature, who isn't worthy of his love, no, no more than a rag doll."

He wanted to come home. The midsummer holiday was gone. It was a long while to Christmas. He wrote in wild excitement saying he could come for Saturday and Sunday at Goose Fair, the first week in October.

"You are not well, my boy," said his mother when she saw him. She was almost in tears at having him to herself again.

"No, I've not been well," he said, "I've seemed to have a dragging cold all the last month. But it's going, I think."

It was sunny October weather. He seemed wild with joy like a schoolboy escaped. Then again he was silent, and reserved. He was more gaunt than ever, and there was a haggard look in his eyes.

"You are doing too much," said his mother to him.

He was doing extra work, trying to make some money to marry on, he said. He only talked to his mother once, on the Saturday night. Then he was sad and tender about his beloved.

"And yet, you know mother, for all that, if I died she'd be broken-hearted for two months, and then she'd start to forget me. You'd see, she'd never come home here to look at my grave, not even once."

"Why William," said his mother, "you're not going to die, so why talk about it."

"But whether or not—" he replied.

"And she can't help it—she is like that—and if you choose her, well, you can't grumble," said his mother.

On the Sunday morning, as he was putting his collar on:

"Look," he said to his mother, holding up his chin, "what a rash my collar's made under my chin!"

Just at the junction of chin and throat was a big red inflammation.

"It ought not to do that," said his mother. "Here, put a bit of this soothing ointment on. You should wear different collars."

He went away on Sunday midnight, seeming better and more solid for his two days at home.

On Tuesday morning came a telegram from London, that he was ill. Mrs Morel got off her knees from washing the floor, read the telegram, called a neighbour, went to her landlady and borrowed a sovereign, put on her things and set off. She hurried to Keston, caught an express for London in Nottingham. She had to wait in Nottingham nearly an hour. A small figure in her black bonnet, she was anxiously asking the porters, if they knew how to get to Elmers End. The journey was three hours. She sat in her corner in a kind of stupor, never moving. At King's Cross still no one could tell her how to get to Elmers End.—Carrying her string bag, that contained her nightdress, comb and brush, she went from person to person. At last they sent her underground to Cannon Street.

It was six o'clock when she arrived at William's lodging. The blinds were not down.

"How is he?" she asked.

"No better," said the landlady.

She followed the woman upstairs. William lay on the bed, with blood-shot eyes, his face rather discoloured. The clothes were tossed about, there was no fire in the room, a glass of milk stood on the stand at his bedside. No one had been with him.

"Why, my son!" said the mother bravely.

He did not answer. He looked at her, but did not see her.

Then he began to say, in a dull voice, as if repeating a letter from dictation: "Owing to a leakage in the hold of the vessel, the sugar had set, and become converted into rock. It needed hacking—"

He was quite unconscious. It had been his business to examine some such cargo of sugar in the Port of London.

"How long has he been like this?" the mother asked the landlady.

"He got home at six o'clock on Monday morning, and he seemed to sleep all day. Then in the night we heard him talking, and this morning he asked for you. So I wired, and we fetched the doctor."

"Will you have a fire made?"

Mrs Morel tried to soothe her son, to keep him still.

The doctor came. It was pneumonia, and, he said, a peculiar erysipelas, which had started under the chin where the collar chafed, and was spreading over the face. He hoped it would not get to the brain.

Mrs Morel settled down to nurse. She prayed for William, prayed that he would recognise her. But the young man's face grew more discoloured. In the night she struggled with him. He raved, and raved, and would not come to consciousness. At two o'clock, in a dreadful paroxysm, he died.

Mrs Morel sat perfectly still for an hour, in the lodging bedroom. Then she roused the house-hold.

At six o'clock, with the aid of the char-woman, she laid him out. Then she went round the dreary London village, to the registrar and the doctor.

At nine o'clock, to the cottage on Scargill Street, another wire. "William died last night. Let father come—bring money."

Annie, Paul, and Arthur were at home. Mr Morel was gone to work. The three children said not a word. Annie began to whimper with fear. Paul set off for his father.

It was a beautiful day. At Bretty pit the white steam melted slowly in the sunshine of a soft blue sky, the wheels of the headstocks twinkled high up, the screen, shuffling its coal into the trucks, made a busy noise.

"I want my father—he's got to go to London," said the boy to the first man he met on the bank.

"Tha wants Walter Morel?—Go in theer an' tell Joe Ward."

Paul went into the little top office.

"I want my father—he's got to go to London."

"Thy feyther—is he down—what's his name?"

"Mr Morel."

"What, Walter? Is owt amiss?"

"He's got to go to London."

The man went to the telephone and rang up the bottom office.

"Walter Morel's wanted—Number 42 Hard. Summat's amiss—there's his lad here."

Then he turned round to Paul.

"He'll be up in a few minutes," he said.

Paul wandered out to the pit top. He watched the chair come up, with its wagon of coal. The great iron cage sank back on its rests, a full carfle was hauled off, an empty tram run onto the chair, a bell 'ting-ed' somewhere, the chair heaved, then dropped like a stone.

Paul did not realise William was dead—it was impossible, with such a bustle going on. The puller-off swung the small truck onto the turn-table, another man ran with it along the bank, down the curving lines. "And William is dead, and my mother's in London, and what will she be doing?" The boy asked himself, as if it were a conundrum.

He watched chair after chair come up, and still no father. At last, standing beside a wagon, a man's form! The chair sank on its rests, Morel stepped off. He was slightly lame from an accident.

"Is it thee Paul!—is 'e worse?"

"You've got to go to London."

The two walked off the pit bank, where men were watching curiously. As they came out, and went along the railway, with the sunny autumn field on one side, and a wall of trucks on the other, Morel said, in a frightened voice:

"'E's niver gone, child?"

"Yes."

"When wor't?"

The miner's voice was terrified.

"Last night—we had a telegram from my mother."

Morel walked on a few strides, then leaned up against a truck side, his hand over his eyes. He was not crying. Paul stood looking round, waiting. On the weighing machine a truck trundled slowly. Paul saw everything, except his father leaning against the truck as if he were tired.

Morel had only once before been to London. He set off, scared and peaked, to help his wife. That was on Tuesday. The children were left alone in the house. Paul went to work, Arthur went to school, and Annie had in a friend to be with her.

On Saturday night, as Paul was turning the corner, coming home from Keston, he saw his mother and father, who had come to Lethley Bridge station. They were walking in silence in the dark, tired, straggling apart. The boy waited.

"Mother!" he said, in the darkness.

Mrs Morel's small figure seemed not to observe. He spoke again.

"Paul!" she said, uninterestedly. She let him kiss her, but she seemed unaware of him.

In the house she was the same, small, white, and mute. She noticed nothing, she said nothing, only:

"The coffin will be here tonight, Walter. You'd better see about some help." Then, turning to the children. "We're bringing him home."

Then she relapsed into the same mute looking into space, her hands folded on her lap. Paul, looking at her, felt he could not breathe. The house was dead silent.

"I went to work, mother," he said, plaintively.

"Did you," she answered, dully.

After half an hour, Morel, troubled and bewildered, came in again.

"Wheer s'll we ha'e him when he *does* come?" he asked his wife.

"In the front room."

"Then I'd better shift th'table?"

"Yes."

"An' ha'e him across th' chairs?"

"You know there—yes—I suppose so."

Morel and Paul went, with a candle, into the parlour. There was no gas there. The father unscrewed the top of the big, mahogany, oval table, and cleared the middle of the room. Then he arranged six chairs opposite each other, so that the coffin could stand on their beds.

"You niver seed such a length as he is!" said the miner, watching anxiously as he worked.

Paul went to the bay window and looked out. The ash-tree stood monstrous and black, in front of the wide darkness. It was a faintly luminous night. Paul went back to his mother.

At ten o'clock, Morel called:

"He's here!"

Everyone started. There was a noise of unbarring and unlocking the front door, which opened straight from the night into the room.

"Bring another candle," called Morel.

Annie and Arthur went. Paul followed with his mother. He stood with his arm round her waist, in the inner doorway. Down the middle of the cleared room waited six chairs, face to face. In the window, against the lace curtains, Arthur held up one candle—and by the open door, against the night, Annie stood leaning forward, her brass candlestick glittering.

There was the noise of wheels. Outside in the darkness of the street below, Paul could see horses and a black vehicle, one lamp, and a few pale faces. Then some men, miners, all in their shirt sleeves, seemed to struggle in the obscurity. Presently, two men appeared, bowed beneath a great weight. It was Morel and his neighbour.

"Steady!" called Morel, out of breath.

He and his fellow mounted the steep garden step, heaved into the candle light with their gleaming coffin-end. Limbs of other men were seen struggling behind. Morel and Burns, in front, staggered. The great, dark weight swayed.

"Steady, steady!" cried Morel, as if in pain.

All the six bearers were up in the small garden, holding the great coffin aloft. There were three more steps to the door. The yellow lamp of the carriage shone alone down in the black road.

"Now then!" said Morel.

The coffin swayed, the men began to mount the three steps with their load. Annie's candle flickered, and she whimpered as the first men appeared, and the limbs and bowed heads of six men struggled to climb into the room, bearing the coffin that rode like sorrow on their living flesh.

"Oh my son—my son!" Mrs Morel sang softly. And each time the coffin swung to the unequal climbing of the men:

"Oh my son—my son—my son!"

"Mother!" Paul whimpered, his hand round her waist. "Mother!"

She did not hear.

"Oh my son, my son!" she repeated.

Paul saw drops of sweat fall from his father's brow. Six men were in the room, six coatless men with yielding, struggling limbs filling the room and knocking against the furniture. The coffin veered, and was gently lowered onto the chairs. The sweat fell from Morel's face on its boards.

"My word, he's a weight!" said a man, and the five miners sighed, bowed, and trembling with the struggle, descended the steps again, closing the door behind them.

The family was alone in the parlour, with the great polished box, William, when laid out, was six feet four inches long. Like a monument lay the bright brown, ponderous coffin. Paul thought it would never be got out of the room again. His mother was stroking the polished wood.

They buried him, on the Monday, in the little cemetery on the hillside, that looks over the fields at the big church and the houses. It was sunny, and the white chrysanthemums frilled themselves in the warmth.

Mrs Morel could not be persuaded, after this, to talk and take her old bright interest in life. She remained shut off. All the way home, in the train, she had said to herself: "If only it could have been me."

When Paul came home at night, he found his mother sitting, her day's work done, with hands folded in her lap, upon her coarse apron. She always used to have changed her dress, and put on a black apron, before. Now Annie set his supper, and his mother sat looking blankly in front of her, her mouth shut tight. Then he beat his brains for news to tell her.

"Mother, Miss Jordan was down today, and she said my sketch of a colliery at work was beautiful—"

But Mrs Morel took no notice. Night after night he forced himself to tell her things, although she did not listen. It drove him almost insane to have her thus. At last:

"What's a-matter, mother?" he asked. She did not hear.

"What's a-matter?" he persisted. "Mother, what's a-matter?"

"You know what's the matter," she said, irritably, turning away. The lad—he was sixteen years old, went to bed drearily. He was cut off and wretched through October, November, and December. His mother tried, but she could not rouse herself. She could only brood on her dead son. He had been let to die so cruelly.

At last, on the 23rd of December, with his five shillings Christmas box in his pocket, Paul wandered blindly home. His mother looked at him, and her heart stood still.

"What's the matter?" she asked.

"I'm badly, mother!" he replied. "Mr Jordan gave me five shillings for a Christmas box."

He handed it to her with trembling hands. She put it on the table.

"You aren't glad," he reproached her.

But he trembled violently.

"Where hurts you?" she said, unbuttoning his overcoat.

It was the old question.

"I feel badly, mother."

She undressed him and put him to bed. He had pneumonia, dangerously, the doctor said.

"Might he never have had it if I'd kept him at home, not let him go to Nottingham?" was one of the first things she asked.

"He might not have been so bad," said the doctor.

Mrs Morel stood condemned on her own ground.

"I should have watched the living, not the dead," she told herself.

Paul was very ill. His mother lay in bed at nights with him. They could not afford a nurse. He grew worse, and the crisis approached. One night he tossed into consciousness, in the ghastly, sickly feeling of dissolution, when all the cells in the body seem in intense irritability to be breaking down, and consciousness makes a last flare of struggle, like madness.

"I s'll die, mother!" he cried, heaving for breath on the pillow.

She lifted him up, crying in a small voice:

"Oh, my son, my son!"

That brought him to. He realised her. His whole will rose up and arrested him. He put his head on her breast, and took ease of her, for love.

"For some things," said his aunt, "it was a good thing Paul was ill that Christmas. I believe it saved his mother."

Paul was in bed for seven weeks. He got up white and fragile. His father had bought him a pot of scarlet and gold tulips. They used to flame in the window, in the March sunshine, as he sat on the sofa chattering to his mother. The two knitted together in perfect intimacy. Mrs Morel's life now rooted itself in Paul.

William had been a prophet. Mrs Morel had a little present and a letter from Lily at Christmas. Mrs Morel's sister had a letter at the New Year.

"I was at a ball last night. Some delightful people were there and I enjoyed myself thoroughly," said the letter. "I had every dance—did not sit out one—"

Mrs Morel never heard any more of her.

Morel and his wife were gentle with each other for some time after the death of their son. He would go into a kind of daze, staring wide-eyed and blank across the room. Then he got up suddenly and hurried out to the "Three Spots," returning in his normal state. But never in his life would he go for a walk up Shepstone, past the office where his son had worked, and he always avoided the cemetery.

PART II

CHAPTER VII

Lad-and-Girl Love

Paul had been many times up to Willey Farm, during the Autumn. He was friends with the two younger boys. Edgar, the eldest, would not condescend at first. And Miriam also refused to be approached. She was afraid of being set at nought, as by her own brothers. The girl was romantic in her soul. Everywhere was a Walter Scott heroine being loved by men with helmets or with plumes in their caps. She herself was something of a princess turned into a swine girl, in her own imagination. And she was afraid lest this boy, who nevertheless looked something like a Walter Scott hero, who could paint and speak French and knew what algebra meant, and who went by train to Nottingham every day, might consider her simply as the swine girl, unable to perceive the princess beneath, so she held aloof.

Her great companion was her mother. They were both brown-eyed and inclined to be mystical, such women as treasure religion inside them, breathe it in their nostrils, and see the whole of life in a mist thereof. So, to Miriam Christ and God made one great figure, which she loved tremblingly and passionately when a tremendous sunset burned out the western sky; and Ediths and Lucys and Rowenas, Brian de Bois Guilberts, Rob Roys and Guy Mannerings rustled the sunny leaves in the morning, or sat in her bedroom, aloft, alone, when it snowed. That was life to her. For the rest, she drudged in the house, which work she would not have minded had not her clean red floor been mucked-up immediately by the trampling farm-boots of her brothers; she madly wanted her little brother of four to let her swathe him and stifle him in her love; she went to church, reverently, with bowed head, and quivered in anguish from the vulgarity of the other choir-girls, and from the common-sounding voice of the curate; she fought with her brothers, whom she considered brutal louts; and she held not her father in too high

173

esteem, because he did not carry any mystical ideals cherished in his heart, but only wanted to have as easy a time as he could, and his meals when he was ready for them.

She hated her position as swine-girl. She wanted to be considered. She wanted to learn, thinking that if she could read, as Paul said he could read, 'Colomba' or the *Voyage Autour de ma Chambre*, the world would have a different face for her, and a deepened respect. She could not be princess by wealth or standing. So, she was mad to have learning whereon to pride herself. For she was different from other folk, and must not be scooped up among the common fry. Learning was the only distinction to which she thought to aspire.

Her beauty, that of a shy, wild, quiveringly sensitive thing, seemed nothing to her. Even her soul, so strong for rhapsody, was not enough. She must have something to reinforce her pride, because she felt different from other people. Paul she eyed rather wistfully. On the whole she scorned the male sex. But here was a new specimen, quick, light, graceful, who could be gentle and who could be sad, and who was clever and who knew a lot, and who had a death in the family. The boy's poor morsel of learning exalted him almost sky-high in her esteem. Yet she tried hard to scorn him, because he would not see in her the princess, but only the swinegirl.

And he scarcely observed her.

Then he was so ill, and she felt he would be weak. Then she would be stronger than he. Then she could love him. If she could be mistress of him in his weakness, take care of him, if he could depend on her, if she could, as it were, have him in her arms, how she would love him!

As soon as the skies brightened, and plum blossom was out, Paul drove off in the milk-man's heavy float up to Willey Farm. Mr Leivers shouted in a kindly fashion at the boy, then clicked to the horse as they climbed the hill, slowly, in the freshness of the morning. White clouds went on their way, crowding to the back of the hills that were rousing in the springtime. The water of Nethermere lay below, very blue against the seared meadows and the thorn trees.

It was four and a half miles' drive. Tiny buds on the hedges, vivid as copper-green, were opening into rosettes, and thrushes called, and black-birds shrieked and scolded. It was a new, glamorous world.

Miriam, peeping through the kitchen window, saw the horse walk through the big white gate into the farmyard that was backed by the oak-wood, still bare. Then a youth, in a heavy overcoat, climbed down. He put up his hands for the whip and the rug, that the good-looking ruddy farmer handed down to him.

Miriam appeared in the doorway. She was nearly sixteen, very beautiful, with her warm colouring, her gravity, her eyes dilating suddenly like an ecstasy.

"I say," said Paul, turning shyly aside, "your daffodils are nearly out. Isn't it early? But don't they look cold?"

"Cold!" said Miriam, in her musical, caressing voice.

"The green on their buds—" and he faltered into silence, timidly.

"Let me take the rug," said Miriam, over gently.

"I can carry it," he answered, rather injured. But he yielded it to her.

Then Mrs Leivers appeared.

"I'm sure you're tired and cold," she said. "Let me take your coat. It *is* heavy—you mustn't walk far in it."

She helped him off with his coat. He was quite unused to such attention. She was almost smothered under its weight.

"Why mother," laughed the farmer, as he passed through the kitchen swinging the great milk churns: "You've got almost more than you can manage there." She beat up the sofa cushions for the youth.

The kitchen was very small and irregular. The farm had been originally a laborer's cottage. And the furniture was old and battered. But Paul loved it, loved the sack bag that formed the hearthrug, and the funny little corner under the stairs, and the small window deep in the corner, through which, bending a little, he could see the plum-trees in the back garden, and the lovely round hills beyond.

"Won't you lie down?" said Mrs Leivers.

"Oh no—I'm not tired," he said. "Isn't it lovely coming out, don't you think? I saw a sloe-bush in blossom, and a lot of celandines. I'm glad it's sunny."

"Can I give you anything to eat or to drink?"

"No thank you."

"How's your mother?"

"I think she's tired now—I think she's had too much to do. Perhaps in a little while she'll go to Skegness with me. Then she'll be able to rest. I s'll be glad if she can."

"Yes," replied Mrs Leivers. "It's a wonder she isn't ill herself."

Miriam was moving about preparing dinner. Paul watched everything that happened. His face was pale and thin, but his eyes were quick and bright with life as ever. He watched the strange, almost rhapsodic way in which the girl moved about, carrying a great stew-jar to the oven, or looking in the saucepan. The atmosphere was different from that of his own home, where everything seemed so ordinary. When Mr Leivers called loudly outside to the horse, that was reaching over to feed on the rose bushes in the garden, the girl started, looking round with dark eyes, as if something had come breaking in on her world. There was a sense of silence inside the house and out. Miriam seemed as in some dreamy tale, a maiden in bondage, her spirit dreaming in a land far away and magical. And her discoloured, old blue frock, and her broken boots, seemed only like the romantic rags of King Cophetua's beggar maid.

She suddenly became aware of his keen blue eyes upon her, taking her all in. Instantly her broken boots and her frayed old frock hurt her. She resented his seeing everything. Even he knew that her stocking was not pulled up. She went into the scullery, blushing deeply. And afterwards her hands trembled slightly at her work, she nearly dropped all she handled. When her inside dream was shaken, her body quivered with trepidation. She resented that he saw so much.

Mrs Leivers sat for some time talking to the boy, although she was needed at her work. She was too polite to leave him. Presently she excused herself, and rose. After a while she looked into the tin saucepan:

"Oh *dear* Miriam," she cried, "these potatoes have boiled dry!"

Miriam started as if she had been stung.

"*Have* they mother!" she cried.

"I shouldn't care Miriam," said the mother, "if I hadn't trusted them to you." She peered into the pan.

The girl stiffened as if from a blow. Her dark eyes dilated, she remained standing in the same spot.

"Well," she answered, gripped tight in self-conscious shame, "I'm sure I looked at them five minutes since."

"Yes," said the mother. "I know it's easily done."

"They're not much burned," said Paul. "It doesn't matter, does it?"

Mrs Leivers looked at the youth with her brown, hurt eyes.

"It wouldn't matter but for the boys," she said to him. "Only Miriam knows what a trouble they make if the potatoes are caught."

"Then," thought Paul to himself, "you shouldn't let them make a trouble."

After a while, Edgar came in. He wore leggings, and his boots were covered with earth. He was rather small, rather formal for a farmer. He glanced at Paul, nodded to him distantly, and said:

"Dinner ready?"

"Nearly Edgar," replied the mother apologetically.

"I'm ready for mine," said the young man, taking up the news-paper and reading. Presently the rest of the family trooped in. Dinner was served. The meal went rather brutally. The over gentleness and apologetic tone of the mother brought out all the brutality of manners in the sons. Edgar tasted the potatoes, moved his mouth quickly like a rabbit, looked indignantly at his mother, and said:

"These potatoes are burnt, mother!"

"Yes Edgar—I forgot them for a minute. Perhaps you'll have bread if you can't eat them."

Edgar looked in anger across at Miriam.

"What was Miriam doing that she couldn't attend to them?" he said.

Miriam looked up. Her mouth opened, her dark eyes blazed and winced, but she said nothing. She swallowed her anger and her shame, bowing her dark head.

"I'm sure she was trying hard," said the mother.

"She hasn't got sense even to boil the potatoes," said Edgar. "What is she kept at home for?"

"On'y for eating everything that's left in th' pantry," said Maurice.

"They don't forget that potato-pie against our Miriam," laughed the father. She was utterly humiliated. The mother sat in silence, suffering, like some saint out of place at the brutal board.

It puzzled Paul. He wondered vaguely why all this intense feeling went running because of a few burnt potatoes. The mother exalted everything, even a bit of housework, to the plane of a religious trust. The sons resented this; they felt themselves cut away underneath, and they answered with brutality, and also with a sneering super-ciliousness.

Paul was just opening out from childhood into manhood. This

atmosphere, where everything took a religious value, came with a subtle fascination to him. There was something in the air. His own mother was logical. Here there was something different, something he loved, something that at times he hated.

Miriam quarrelled with her brothers, fiercely. Later in the afternoon, when they had gone away again, her mother said:

"You disappointed me at dinner-time, Miriam."

The girl dropped her head.

"They are such *brutes!*" she suddenly cried, looking up with flashing eyes.

"But hadn't you promised not to answer them?" said the mother. "And I believed in you. I *can't* stand it, when you wrangle."

"But they're so hateful!" cried Miriam. "And—and *low*."

"Yes dear. But how often have I asked you not to answer Edgar back. Can't you let him say what he likes?"

"But why should he say what he likes!"

"Aren't you strong enough to bear it, Miriam, if even for my sake. Are you so weak that you must wrangle with them."

Mrs Leivers stuck unflinchingly to this doctrine of "the other cheek." She could not instil it at all into the boys. With the girls she succeeded better, and Miriam was the child of her heart. The boys loathed the other cheek when it was presented to them. Miriam was often sufficiently lofty to turn it. Then they spat on her and hated her. But she walked in her proud humility, living within herself.

There was always this feeling of jangle and discord in the Leivers family. Although the boys resented so bitterly the eternal appeal to their deeper feelings of resignation and proud humility, yet it had its effect on them. They could not establish between themselves and an outsider just the ordinary human feeling, and unexaggerated friendship: they were always restless for the something deeper. Ordinary folk seemed shallow to them, trivial and inconsiderable. And so they were unaccustomed, painfully uncouth in the simplest social intercourse, suffering, and yet insolent in their superiority. Then beneath was the yearning for the soul intimacy to which they could not attain, because they were too dumb, and every approach to close connexion was blocked by their clumsy contempt of other people. They wanted genuine intimacy, but they could not get even normally near to anyone, because they scorned to take the first steps, they scorned the triviality which forms common human intercourse.

Paul fell under Mrs Leivers' spell. Everything had a religious and intensified meaning, when he was with her. His soul, hurt, highly developed, sought her as if for nourishment. Together, they seemed to sift the vital fact from an experience.

Miriam was her mother's daughter. In the sunshine of the afternoon, mother and daughter went down the fields with him. They looked for nests. There was a jenny wren's in the hedge by the orchard.

"I *do* want you to see this," said Mrs Leivers.

He crouched down, and carefully put his finger through the thorns into the round door of the nest.

"It's almost as if you were feeling inside the live body of the bird," he said, "it's so warm. They say a bird makes its nest round like a cup with pressing its breast on it. Then how did it make the ceiling round, I wonder." The nest seemed to start into life for the two women. After that, Miriam came to see it every day. It seemed so close to her. Again, going down the hedge side with the girl, he noticed the celandines, scalloped splashes of gold, on the side of the ditch.

"I like them," he said, "when their petals go flat back with the sunshine. They seem to be pressing themselves at the sun." And then the celandines ever after drew her with a little spell. Anthropomorphic as she was, she stimulated him into appreciating things thus, and then they lived for her. She seemed to need things kindling in her imagination or in her soul, before she felt she had them. And she was cut off from ordinary life, by her religious intensity, which made the world for her either a nunnery garden, or a Paradise where sin and knowledge were not, or else an ugly, cruel thing.

So it was in this atmosphere of subtle intimacy, this meeting in their common feeling for some thing in nature, that their love started.

Personally, he was a long time before he realised her. For ten months he had to stay at home, after his illness. For a while he went to Skegness with his mother, and was perfectly happy. But even from the seaside he wrote long letters to Mrs Leivers, about the shore and the sea. And he brought back his beloved sketches of the flat Lincoln coast, anxious for them to see. Almost, they would interest the Leivers more than they interested his mother. It was not his art Mrs Morel cared about, it was himself, and his achievement. But Mrs Leivers, and her children, were almost his disciples. They kindled him, and made him glow to his work, whereas his mother's influence was to make him quietly determined, patient, dogged, unwearied.

He soon was friends with the boys, whose rudeness was only superficial. They had all, when they could trust themselves, a strange gentleness and loveableness.

"Will you come with me onto the fallow?" asked Edgar, rather hesitatingly. Paul went joyfully, and spent the afternoon helping to hoe, or to single turnips, with his friend. He used to lie with the three brothers on the hay piled up in the barn, and tell them about Nottingham and about Jordan's. In return they taught him to milk, and let him do little jobs, chopping hay or pulping turnips, just as much as he liked. At midsummer he worked all through hay harvest with them, and then he loved them. The family was so cut off from the world, actually. They seemed somehow like 'les derniers fils d'une race épuisée.' Though the lads were strong and healthy, yet they had all that over-sensitiveness and hanging-back which made them so lonely, yet also such close, delicate friends once their intimacy was won. Paul loved them dearly, and they him.

Miriam came later. But he had come into her life before she made any mark on his. One dull afternoon, when the men were on the land, and the rest at school, only Miriam and her mother at home, the girl said to him, after having hesitated for some time:

"Have you seen the swing?"

"No," he answered. "Where?"

"In the cowshed," she replied.

She always hesitated to offer or to show him anything. Men have such different standards of worth from women, and her dear things, the valuable things to her, her brothers had so often mocked or flouted.

"Come on then," he replied, jumping up.

There were two cowsheds, one on either side of the barn. In the lower, darker shed, there was standing for four cows. Hens flew scolding over the manger wall as the youth and girl went forward for the great thick rope which hung from the beam in the darkness overhead, and was pushed back over a peg in the wall.

"It's something like a rope!" he exclaimed, appreciatively, and he sat down in it, anxious to try it. Then immediately he rose.

"Come on then, and have first go," he said to the girl.

"See," she answered, going into the barn, "we put some bags on the seat." And she made the swing comfortable for him. That gave her pleasure. He held the rope.

"Come on then," he said to her.

"No, I won't go first," she answered.

She stood aside in her still, aloof fashion.

"Why?"

"You go," she pleaded.

Almost for the first time in her life, she had the pleasure of giving-up to a man, of spoiling him. Paul looked at her.

"All right," he said, sitting down. "Mind out!"

He set off with a spring, and in a moment was flying through the air, almost out of the door of the shed, the upper half of which was open, showing outside the drizzling rain, the filthy yard, the cattle standing disconsolate against the black cart-shed, and at the back of all, the grey-green wall of the wood. She stood below in her crimson tam-o'-shanter, and watched. He looked down at her, and she saw his blue eyes sparkling.

"It's a treat of a swing," he said.

"Yes."

He was swinging through the air, every bit of him swinging, like a bird that swoops for joy of movement. And he looked down at her. Her crimson cap hung over her dark curls, her beautiful warm face, so still in a kind of brooding, was lifted towards him. It was dark and rather cold in the shed. Suddenly a swallow came down from the high roof, and darted out of the door.

"I didn't know a bird was watching," he called.

He swung negligently. She could feel him falling and lifting through the air, as if he were lying on some force.

"Now I'll die," he said, in a detached, dreamy voice, as though he were the dying motion of the swing. She watched him fascinated. Suddenly he put on the brake and jumped out.

"I've had a long turn," he said. "But it's a treat of a swing, it's a real treat of a swing."

Miriam was amused that he took a swing so seriously, and felt so warmly over it.

"No, you go on," she said.

"Why—don't you want one?" he asked, astonished.

"Well—not much. I'll have just a little."

She sat down, whilst he kept the bags in place for her.

"It's so ripping," he said, setting her in motion. "Keep your heels

181

up or they'll bang the manger wall."

She felt the accuracy with which he caught her, exactly at the right moment, and the exactly proportionate strength of his thrust, and she was afraid. Down to her bowels went the hot wave of fear. She was in his hands. Again, firm and inevitable came the thrust at the right moment. She gripped the rope, almost swooning.

"Ha!" she laughed in fear. "No higher!"

"But you're not a *bit* high," he remonstrated.

"But no higher."

He heard the fear in her voice and desisted. Her heart melted in hot pain when the moment came for him to thrust her forward again. But he left her alone. She began to breathe.

"Won't you really go any further?" he asked. "Should I keep you there?"

"No, let me go by myself," she answered.

He moved aside and watched her.

"Why you're scarcely moving," he said.

She laughed silently with shame, and in a moment got down.

"They say if you can swing you won't be sea-sick," he said as he mounted again. "I don't believe I should ever be sea sick."

Away he went. There was something fascinating to her in him. For the moment he was nothing but a piece of swinging stuff, not a particle of him that did not swing. She could never lose herself so, nor could her brothers. It roused a warmth in her. It were almost as if he were a flame that had lit a warmth in her, whilst he swung in the middle air.

And gradually, the intimacy with the family concentrated for Paul on three persons: the mother, Edgar, and Miriam. To the mother he went for that sympathy and that appeal which seemed to draw him out. Edgar was his very close friend. And to Miriam he more or less condescended, because she seemed so humble.

But the girl gradually sought him out. If he brought up his sketch book, it was she who pondered longest over the last picture. Then she would look up at him. Suddenly, her dark eyes alight like water that shakes with a stream of gold in the dark, she would ask:

"Why do I like this so?"

Always something in his breast shrank from these close, intimate dazzled looks of hers.

"Why *do* you?" he asked.

"I don't know—it seems so true."

"It's because—it's because there is scarcely any shadow in it—it's more shimmery—as if I'd painted the shimmering protoplasm in the leaves and everywhere, and not the stiffness of the shape. That seems dead to me. Only this shimmeriness is the real living. The shape is a dead crust. The shimmer is inside, really."

And she, with her little finger in her mouth, would ponder these sayings. They gave her a feeling of life again, and vivified things which had meant nothing to her. She managed to find some meaning in his struggling, abstract speeches. And they were the medium through which she came distinctly at her beloved objects.

Another day she sat at sunset whilst he was painting some pine-trees which caught the red glare from the west. He had been quiet.

"There you are!" he said suddenly. "I wanted that. Now look at them and tell me, are they pine trunks or are they red coals, standing-up pieces of fire in that darkness. There's God's burning bush, for you, that burned not away."

Miriam looked, and was frightened. But the pine trunks were wonderful to her, and distinct. He packed his box and rose. Suddenly he looked at her.

"Why are you always sad?" he asked her.

"Sad!" she exclaimed, looking up at him with startled, wonderful brown eyes.

"Yes," he replied. "You are always, always sad."

"I am not—Oh, not a bit!" she cried.

"But even your joy is like a flame coming off of sadness," he persisted. "You're never jolly, or even just all right."

"No," she pondered. "I wonder—why—."

"Because you're not—because you're different inside—like a pine tree—and then you flare up—but you're not just like an ordinary tree, with fidgety leaves and jolly—"

He got tangled up in his own speech; but she brooded on it, and he had a strange, roused sensation, as if his feelings were new. She got so near him. It was a strange stimulant.

Then sometimes he hated her. Her youngest brother was only five. He was a frail lad, with immense brown eyes in his quaint, fragile face; one of Reynolds' 'Choir of Angels,' with a touch of elf. Often Miriam knelt to the child, and drew him to her.

"Eh my Hubert!" she sang, in a voice heavy and surcharged with love. "Eh my Hubert!"

And folding him in her arms, she swayed slightly from side to side with love, her face half lifted, her eyes half closed, her voice drenched with love.

"Don't!" said the child, uneasy. "Don't Miriam."

"Yes you love me, don't you!" she murmured deep in her throat, almost as if she were in a trance, and swaying also as if she were swooned in an ecstasy of love.

"Don't!" repeated the child, a frown on his clear brow.

"You love me, don't you?" she murmured.

"What do you make such a *fuss* for!" cried Paul, all in suffering because of her extreme emotion. "Why can't you be ordinary with him?"

She let the child go, and rose, and said nothing. Her intensity, which would leave no emotion on a normal plane, irritated the youth into a frenzy. And this fearful naked contact of her soul on small occasions, shocked him. He was used to his mother's reserve. And on such occasions, he was thankful in his heart and soul, that he had his mother, so sane and wholesome.

All the life of Miriam's body was in her eyes, which were usually dark as a dark church, but could flame with light like a conflagration. Her face scarcely ever altered from its look of brooding. She might have been one of the women who went with Mary when Jesus was dead. Her body was not flexible and living. She walked with a swing, rather heavily, her head bowed forward, pondering. She was not clumsy, and yet none of her movements seemed quite *the* movement. Often, when wiping the dishes, she would stand in bewilderment and chagrin, because she had pulled in two halves a cup or a tumbler. It was as if, in her fear and self mistrust, she put too much strength into the effort. There was no looseness or abandon about her. Everything was gripped stiff with intensity, and her effort, overcharged, closed in on itself.

She rarely varied from her swinging, forward, intense walk. Occasionally she ran with Paul down the fields. Then her eyes blazed naked in a kind of ecstasy, that frightened him. But she was physically afraid. If she were getting over a stile, she gripped his hands in a little hard anguish, and began to lose her presence of mind. And he could not persuade her to jump from even a small height. Her eyes dilated, became exposed and palpitating.

"No!" she cried half laughing in terror, "No!"

"You shall!" he cried once, and, jerking her forward, he brought her falling from the fence. But her wild "Ah!" of pain, as if she were losing consciousness, cut him. She landed on her feet safely, and afterwards, had courage in this respect.

Often they walked together, Paul and Miriam, down the fields to Nethermere. He was naturally agile and very active. He went dancing from one thing to another. But she kept her regular course, almost unmovable. And gradually he fell in beside her, took her pace, and walked head-down with her. Till they came to the water. The margin of the lake was littered with white feathers from the swans. They sat on a pebbly bank. Suddenly he caught sight of a nice flat stone, and, jumping up, began to make ducks and drakes on the water.

"Can *you* skim?" he asked.

"Not very well," she replied, shaking her head. She remained seated, watching him.

"See that!" he cried. "Four hops!"

"Yes," she said, commending him. "That was very good." But soon he desisted, came and sat down again beside her.

"Why don't *you* want to do ducks and drakes as well?" he asked.

"I don't know," she replied.

"You never want to *do* things," he said.

"Well, you see, I have to work in the house."

He did not continue the argument. They fell into a discussion of books.

She was very much dissatisfied with her lot.

"Don't you like being at home?" Paul asked her, surprised.

"Who would!" she answered, low and intense. "What is it! I'm all day cleaning what the boys make just as bad in five minutes. I don't *want* to be at home."

"What do you want then?"

"I want to do something. I want a chance like anybody else. Why should I, because I'm a girl, be kept at home and not allowed to be anything. What chance *have* I?"

"Chance of what?"

"Of knowing anything—of learning—of doing anything. It's not fair, because I'm a woman."

She seemed very bitter. Paul wondered. In his own home, Annie was almost glad to be a girl. She had not so much responsibility, things were lighter for her. She never wanted to be other than a girl. But Miriam almost fiercely wished she were a man. And yet she hated men, at the same time.

"But it's as well to be a woman as a man," he said, frowning.

"Ha!—is it! Men have everything."

"I should think women ought to be as glad to be women, as men are to be men," he answered.

"No!" she shook her head. "No! Everything, the men have."

"But what do you want?" he asked.

"I want to learn. Why *should* it be that I know nothing!"

"What—such as mathematics and French—?"

"Why *shouldn't* I know mathematics!—Yes!" she cried, her eyes expanding in a kind of defiance.

"Well you can learn as much as I know," he said. "I'll teach you if you like."

Her eyes dilated. She mistrusted him as teacher.

"Would you?" he asked.

Her head had dropped and she was sucking her finger broodingly.

"Yes," she said, hesitatingly.

He used to tell his mother all these things.

"Did *you* want to be a man, mother?" he asked.

"Sometimes I have—but it's silly—and no, I don't really want to be anything but myself, and never did."

"What did you want to be a man for, even sometimes?"

"Well my boy," she laughed, "I thought I could make a great deal better job of it than most men do—which isn't to be wondered at."

"I don't want to be a woman," he replied thoughtfully. "And I don't think I could be a woman better than a woman is one herself."

"No," laughed his mother. "I don't suppose you could.—But it makes us sometimes feel that we could do better than men."

"Perhaps you could, mother," he said.

"Well—!" she replied, with her little amused sniff—"And my boy," she continued, "anything that is natural is pleased to be itself. And when a woman wants very badly to be a man, you may back your life she's not much good as a woman."

"I hate it when a woman wants to be a man," he said.

"It shows her pride as a woman is pretty low," she answered. He always came to his mother, making her the touchstone.

"I'm going to teach Miriam algebra," he said.

"Well," replied Mrs Morel. "I hope she'll get fat on it."

When he went up to the farm on the Monday evening, it was drawing twilight. Miriam was just sweeping up the kitchen, and was kneeling at the hearth when he entered. Everyone was out but her. She looked round at him, flushed, her dark eyes shining, her fine hair falling about her face.

"Hello," she said, soft and musical, "I knew it was you."

"How?"

"I knew your step. Nobody treads so quick and firm."

He sat down, sighing.

"Ready to do some algebra?" he asked, drawing a little book from his pocket.

"But—!" He could feel her backing away.

"You said you wanted," he insisted.

"Tonight though—?" she faltered.

"But I came on purpose. And if you want to learn it, you must begin."

She took up her ashes in the dustpan, and looked at him, half tremulously laughing.

"Yes but—tonight!—you see I haven't thought of it."

"Well my goodness—take the ashes, and come."

He went and sat on the stone bench in the back yard, where the big milk cans were standing, tipped up, to air. The men were in the cowsheds. He could hear the little sing song of the milk spurting into the pails. Presently she came, bringing some big greenish apples.

"You know you like them," she said.

He took a bite.

"Sit down," he said with his mouth full.

She was short sighted, and peered over his shoulder. It irritated him. He gave her the book quickly.

"Here," he said. "It's only letters for figures. You put down *a* instead of '2' or '6.' "

They worked, he talking, she with her head down on the book. He was quick and hasty. She never answered. Occasionally when he demanded of her:

"Do you see?"

She looked up at him, her eyes wide with the half laugh that comes of fear.

"Don't you!" he cried.

He had been too fast. But she said nothing. He questioned her more, then got hot. It made his blood rouse to see her there, as it were at his mercy, her mouth open, her eyes dilated with laughter that was afraid, apologetic, ashamed. Then Edgar came along with two buckets of milk.

"Hello!" he said. "What are you doing?"

"Algebra," replied Paul.

"Algebra!" repeated Edgar, curiously. Then he passed on with a laugh. Paul took a bite at his forgotten apple, looked at the miserable cabbages in the garden, pecked into lace by the fowls, and he wanted to pull them up. Then he glanced at Miriam. She was poring over the book, seemed absorbed in it, yet trembling lest she could not get at it. It made him cross. She was ruddy and beautiful. Yet her soul seemed to be intensely supplicating the algebra book. She closed, shrinking, knowing he was angered. And at the same instant he grew gentle, seeing her hurt because she did not understand.

"Tell me what seems hard?" he asked, tenderly.

The new note made her look at him suddenly, with dark eyes that seemed to try so hard. It hurt him, and a wave of tenderness went over him.

"You see it seems easy to me," he said. "I'm used to it, and I forget. See——"

Then patiently, gently, he went over it again. Edgar had come and was standing behind him. Miriam's dark head was beneath Paul's eyes. She had a small head, with black curls floating short like silk. She seemed to try so hard. His voice was a caress all the time.

"I see!" exclaimed Edgar suddenly from behind. "But—this—"

And his thick forefinger came down on the book. Miriam winced away. Paul looked round at his friend. Edgar was good-looking, and his brown eyes, sound and healthy, looked interested. It was like breathing fresh air, to explain to him.

Paul taught Miriam regularly. The lessons usually took place in the parlour. There the youth began brightly. She always had learned and knew what task he had set from the week before. Often, she knew it more accurately than he. But things came slowly to her. And when she held herself in a grip, seemed so utterly humble before the lesson, it made his blood rouse. He stormed at her, got ashamed, continued the lesson, and grew furious again, abusing her. She listened in silence. Occasionally, very rarely, she defended herself. Her liquid dark eyes blazed at him.

"You don't give me time to learn it," she said.

"All right," he answered, throwing the book on the table, and lighting a cigarette. Then after a while he went back to her repentant. So the lessons went. He was always either in a rage, or very gentle.

"What do you tremble your *soul* before it for?" he cried. "You don't learn algebra with your blessed soul. Can't you look at it with your clear simple wits?"

Often, when he went again into the kitchen, Mrs Leivers would look at him reproachfully, saying:

"Paul, don't be so hard on Miriam. She may not be quick—but I'm sure she tries."

"I can't help it," he said, rather pitiably. "I go off like it."

"You don't mind me, Miriam, do you?" he asked of the girl, later.

"No," she reassured him, in her beautiful deep tones. "No, I don't mind."

"Don't mind me, it's my fault."

But in spite of himself, his blood began to boil with her. It was strange that no-one else made him in such fury. He flared against her. Once he threw the pencil in her face. There was a silence. She turned her face slightly aside.

"I didn't—" he began, but got no further, feeling weak in all his bones. She never reproached him, or was angry with him. He was often cruelly ashamed. But still again his anger burst like a bubble surcharged. And still, when he saw her eager, silent, as it were blind face, he felt he wanted to throw the pencil in it. And still, when he saw her hand trembling and her mouth parted with suffering, his heart was scalded with pain for her. And because of the intensity to which she roused him, he sought her.

Then he often avoided her and went with Edgar. Miriam and her brother were naturally antagonistic. Edgar was a rationalist, who was curious, and had a sort of scientific interest in life. It was a great bitterness to Miriam to see herself deserted by Paul for Edgar, who seemed so much lower. But the youth was very happy with her elder brother. The two men spent afternoons together on the land, or in the loft, doing carpentry when it rained. And they talked together, or Paul taught Edgar the songs he himself had learned from Annie at the piano. And often all the men, Mr Leivers as well, had bitter debates on the nationalising of the land, and similar problems. Paul had already heard his mother's views, and as these were as yet his own, he argued for her. Miriam attended and took part, but was all the time waiting until it should be over, and a personal communication might begin.

"After all," she said within herself, "if the land were nationalised, Edgar and Paul and I would be just the same."

So she waited for the youth to come back to her.

He was studying for his painting. He loved to sit at home, alone with his mother at night, working and working. She sewed or read. Then, looking up from his task, he would rest his eyes for a moment on her face, that was bright with living warmth, and he returned gladly to his work.

"I can do my best things when you sit there in your rocking-chair, mother," he said.

"I'm sure!" she exclaimed, sniffing with mock scepticism. But she felt it was so, and her heart quivered with brightness. For many hours she sat still, slightly conscious of him labouring away, whilst she worked or read her book. And he, with all his soul's intensity directing his pencil, could feel her warmth inside him like strength. They were both very happy so, and both unconscious of it. These times, that meant so much, and which were real living, they almost ignored.

He was conscious only when stimulated. A sketch finished, he always wanted to take it to Miriam. Then he was stimulated into knowledge of the work he had produced unconsciously. In contact with Miriam, he gained insight, his vision went deeper. From his mother he drew the life warmth, the strength to produce; Miriam urged this warmth into intensity like a white light.

When he returned to the factory the conditions of work were better. He had Wednesday afternoon off to go to the Art School—Miss Jordan's provision—returning in the evening. Then the factory closed at six instead of at eight on Thursday and Friday evenings.

In Bestwood was a decent little library, the subscription to which was only four-and-six a year. Mrs Morel and Mrs Leivers had both joined when their children were growing up. The library was open in two rooms in the Mechanics Hall, on Thursday evenings from 7.0 till 9.0. Paul always fetched the books for his mother, who read a considerable amount, and Miriam trudged down with five or six volumes, for her family. It became the custom for the two to meet in the library.

Paul knew the two small rooms, with books all round the walls. It was warm with a great fire in the corner. Mr Sleath, the librarian, had white whiskers round his child-like face. He was tall and inquisitive, but very affectionate, knew everybody and everybody's affairs. Mr Smedley was plump and bald and knowing.

Paul stood waiting whilst Mr Sleath finished his gossip with the last subscriber. Then he plumped his books onto the counter. Mr Sleath looked at him with lively but unseeing old blue eyes.

"Twenty-two fifty seven," said Paul.

The librarian—who was one of the chief clerks of the Colliery Company, and quite a gentleman in comparison with the youth, repeated the numbers cheerily, turning the leaves of his great ledger.

"Ha!—Ha!" he exclaimed, glancing at the page. Then he looked warmly and welcoming at the youth, rubbed his hands, and said:

"Ha!—Well Paul!—Ha! How's your mother?"

"Very well," replied Paul. "Thank you."

"That's right! She wasn't at chapel on Sunday night."

"No, she had an inflammation in her eyes."

"Oh dear—oh dear—sorry to hear that!"

"I thought you said," put in Mr Smedley, "that she was very well." Paul did not answer, or look at the little man behind the counter. Mr Sleath was ticking off the books in his great ledger. Mr Smedley put some more coal on the fire. Several folk were talking freely as they stood about the shelves. Their heels clicked as they walked on the paddled brick floor.

"But she'll be able to get out this week-end?" asked Mr Sleath, having ticked off the books.

"Yes," said Paul.

"That's right—that's right. I wondered where she could be."

It was an understood thing that folk should enquire after his mother, but his father was never mentioned.

He moved away to the book-shelves. Folk kept coming in, putting their umbrellas in the passage, exchanging pleasant greetings. The youth knew everybody, and everybody's history. They did not interest him. Perhaps Miriam would not come, because of the rain. He gazed at the book in his hand, did not see it for some moments, thinking of her, then saw it again. The time went by like a sleep. There were noises of people going, but no one entered. If she did not come? Then at the thought, he could see the night ahead, dreary and profitless. But she would come. It still felt warm and rich, just in front, and night went no further than the moment when she would arrive.

"Nasty night, Alfred, nasty night," said Mr Sleath, turning round for someone to talk to. The library was empty.

"Seems like it," replied Mr Smedley.

Then Mr Sleath caught sight of Paul.

"Hello Paul!" he exclaimed. "Not found what you want yet, eh?"

"It's not books as Paul's waiting for, I think," said Mr Smedley.

"Oh—oh—!" exclaimed Mr Sleath.

"I think there's a young lady at the back of it," said Mr Smedley. "But it's a bad night to come from Willey Woods."

A footstep was heard in the passage. The young man listened. It was not she. A boy entered. When Paul saw the lad in the doorway where she should have been, he hated him. Yet she would come. She was so dependable. One of her great charms for the youth, was that she was not held by conventions. If she wanted to come, she would come in spite of rain. And it was not so very bad. He listened for the sound of the weather. He heard the boy say that it was pouring. The boy was objectionable. She *would* come, in spite of him. He clung to the hope of her. He could feel her, across the night, wanting to come. And she never failed him. With her, the inner life counted for everything, the outer for nothing.

He heard her step in the hall and his suspense relaxed. He watched. In the doorway she hung back a moment. Her red cap was glistening with rain, her hair was revelling in dewy curliness, her face glowed. She was searching anxiously for him. Then her short-sighted eyes met his. A flame came up in her that burned him too. She went, satisfied, to the counter. He turned his back to her.

Then she came hesitatingly forward.

"Am I late?" she asked.

"As usual," he replied. "Are you wet?"

"No—nothing."

"Did you come down the railway?" he said.

"Yes. Were you afraid I shouldn't come?"

"A bit."

He gave her a little smile.

"Come and see what books I found you," he said. She followed him implicitly. Books did not matter to her. But he insisted on her approving. She gazed over his arm, not seeing. But she touched him.

"Will it do?" he asked.

"Yes," she answered.

Then, when her books were entered, the two went quickly out of the library. They rejoiced in the darkness. They were excitedly happy. Paul had a great black mackintosh, under the cape of which he carried the books. They walked side by side down Mansfield road, in the rainy darkness, under the dripping trees.

The conversation started quick and vigorous, and immediately it was a discussion of a book. He held forth passionately, she listened and her soul expanded. From the book, they inevitably came to a discussion of beliefs, very intimate.

"It seems as if it didn't matter, one more or less, among the lot," he said.

"No," she replied, gravely, questioning.

"I used to believe that about a sparrow falling—and hairs of the head—"

"Yes," she said. "And now?"

"Now I think that the race of sparrows matters, but not one sparrow: all my hair, but not one hair."

"Yes," she said, questioningly.

"And people matter. But *one* isn't so very important. Look at William."

"Yes," she pondered.

"I call it only wasted," he said. "Waste, no more."

"Yes," she said, very low.

It was her belief that the more people there were, the less they mattered. But to hear him talk was like life to her: like starting the breathing in a new-born baby.

"Yet," he said, "I reckon we've got a proper way to go—and if we go it, we're all right—and if we go near it. But if we go wrong, we die. I'm sure our William went wrong somewhere."

"And if we follow the course of our lives, we don't die?" she asked.

"No we don't. What we are inside makes us so that we ought to go one particular way, and no other."

"But do we know when we're following the true course?" she asked.

"Yes! *I* do. I know I'm following mine."

"You do?" she asked.

"Yes—I'm certain."

He had stood under a lamp to think. His mackintosh shone wet. She looked at his face. His eyes, so certain and so steady, gazed into hers. He was quite firm. It fascinated her. She went on home, her heart glowing.

But when he turned round to go back, he forgot her in the knowledge that his mother would be angry with him for walking so far and getting wet. He hurried home, glowing nevertheless from the contact with Miriam. He had got some satisfaction from the night.

"Do you mean to say you've been walking home with Miriam Leivers on a night like this?" asked his mother, looking up suddenly at him, a minute after he had been in the house.

"I stopped in the library ever such a long time," replied Paul.

"What, she came did she!" exclaimed Mrs Morel, quietly, scathingly. Paul winced.

"She has nothing to read all week if she doesn't come," he said.

"I don't know what her mother's doing, to let her trapse about ten miles in the pouring rain."

"It doesn't rain much," he said. "Not hard."

"I've only to look at your mackintosh and boots," she answered.

"Look what I brought you," he said, but she was too cross to condescend.

One evening in the summer Miriam and he went over the fields by Herod's Farm on their way from the library home. So, it was only three miles to Willey Farm. There was a yellow glow over the mowing grass, and the sorrel heads burned crimson. Gradually as they walked along the high land the gold in the west sank down to red, the red to crimson, and then the chill blue crept up against the glow.

They came out upon the high-road to Alfreton, which ran white between the darkening fields. There Paul hesitated. It was two miles home for him, one mile forward for Miriam. They both looked up the road, that ran in shadow right under the glow of the north-west sky. On the crest of the hill Selby with its stark houses and the up-pricked headstocks of the pit stood in black silhouette small against the sky.

He looked at his watch.

"Nine o'clock!" he said.

The pair stood loth to part, hugging their books.

"The wood is so lovely now," she said. "I wanted you to see it."

He followed her slowly across the road to the white gate.

"They grumble so if I'm late," he said.

"But you're not doing anything wrong," she answered, impatiently. He followed her across the nibbled pasture in the dusk. There was a coolness in the wood, a scent of leaves, of honeysuckle, and a twilight. The two walked in silence. Night came wonderfully there, among the throng of dark tree-trunks. He looked round, expectant.

She wanted to show him a certain wild-rose bush she had discovered. She knew it was wonderful. And yet, till he had seen it, she felt it had not come into her soul. Only he could make it her own, immortal. She was dissatisfied.

Dew was already on the paths. In the old oak-wood a mist was rising and he hesitated, wondering whether one whiteness were a strand of fog or only campion flowers, pallid in a cloud.

By the time they came to the pine-trees Miriam was getting very eager, and very tense. Her bush might be gone. She might not be able to find it. And she wanted it so much. Almost passionately, she wanted to be with him when she stood before the flowers. They were going to have a communion together, something that thrilled her, something holy. He was walking beside her in silence. They were very near to each other. She trembled, and he listened, vaguely anxious.

Coming to the edge of the wood, they saw the sky in front like mother-of-pearl, and the earth growing dark. Somewhere on the outermost branches of the pine-wood the honeysuckle was streaming scent.

"Where?" he asked.

"Down the middle path," she murmured, quivering.

When they turned the corner of the path she stood still. In the wide walk between the pines, gazing rather frightened, she could distinguish nothing for some moments, the greying light robbed things of their colour. Then she saw her bush.

"Ah!" she cried, hastening forward.

It was very still. The tree was tall and straggling. It had thrown its briars over a hawthorn bush, and its long streamers trailed thick, right down to the grass, splashing the darkness everywhere with great spilt stars, pure white. In bosses of ivory and in large splashed stars the roses gleamed on the darkness of foliage and stems and grass. Paul and Miriam stood close together, silent, and watched. Point after point, the steady roses shone out to them, seeming to kindle something in their souls. The dusk came like smoke around, and still did not put out the roses.

Paul looked into Miriam's eyes. She was pale and expectant with wonder, her lips were parted, and her dark eyes lay open to him. His look seemed to travel down into her. Her soul quivered. It was the communion she wanted. He turned aside, as if pained. He turned to the bush.

"They seem as if they walk like butterflies, and shake themselves," he said.

She looked at her roses. They were white, some incurved and holy, others expanded in an ecstasy. The tree was dark as a shadow. She lifted her hand impulsively to the flowers, she went forward and touched them in worship.

"Let us go," he said.

There was a cool scent of ivory roses, a white, virgin scent. Something made him feel anxious and imprisoned. The two walked in silence.

"Till Sunday," he said quietly, and left her, and she walked home slowly, feeling her soul satisfied with the holiness of the night. He stumbled down the path. And as soon as he was out of the wood, in the free open meadow where he could breathe, he started to run as fast as he could. It was like a delicious delirium in his veins.

Always, when he went with Miriam, and it grew rather late, he knew his mother was fretting and getting angry about him, why he could not understand. As he went into the house, flinging down his cap, his mother looked up at the clock. She had been sitting, thinking, because the chill to her eyes prevented her reading. She could feel Paul being drawn away by this girl. And she did not care for Miriam. "She is one of those who will want to suck a man's soul out till he has none of his own left," she said to herself, "and he is just such a gaby as to let himself be absorbed. She will never let him become a man, she never will." So, while he was away with Miriam, Mrs Morel grew more and more worked up.

She glanced at the clock, and said, coldly, and rather tired:

"You have been far enough tonight."

His soul, warm and exposed from contact with the girl, shrank.

"You must have been right home with her," his mother continued.

He would not answer. Mrs Morel, looking at him quickly, saw his hair was damp on his forehead with haste, saw him frowning in his heavy fashion, resentfully.

"She must be wonderfully fascinating, that you can't get away from her, but must go trailing eight miles at this time of night."

He was hurt between the past glamour with Miriam and the

knowledge that his mother fretted. He had meant not to say anything, to refuse to answer. But he could not harden his heart to ignore his mother.

"I *do* like to talk to her," he answered irritably.

"Is there nobody else to talk to?"

"You wouldn't say anything if I went with Edgar."

"You know I should. You know, whoever you went with, I should say it was too far for you to go trailing, late at night, when you've been to Nottingham.—Besides—" her voice suddenly flashed into anger and contempt, "it is disgusting, bits of lads and girls courting."

"It is *not* courting," he cried.

"I don't know what else you call it."

"It's not! Do you think we *spoon* and do? We only talk."

"Till Goodness knows what time and distance," was the sarcastic rejoinder. Paul snapped at the laces of his boots, angrily.

"What are you so mad about?" he asked. "Because you don't like her."

"I don't say I don't like her. But I don't hold with children keeping company, and never did."

"But you don't mind our Annie going out with Jim Inger."

"They've more sense than you two."

"Why?"

"Our Annie's not one of the deep sort."

He failed to see the meaning of this remark. But his mother looked tired. She was never so strong after William's death. And her eyes hurt her.

"Well," he said, "it's so pretty in the country.—Mr Sleath asked about you. He said he'd missed you.—Are you a bit better?"

"I ought to have been in bed a long time ago," she replied.

"Why mother, you know you wouldn't have gone before quarter past ten."

"Oh yes I should!"

"Oh little woman, you'd say anything now you're disagreeable with me, wouldn't you?"

He kissed her forehead, that he knew so well: the deep marks between the brows, the rising of the fine hair, greying now, and the proud setting of the temples. His hand lingered on her shoulder after his kiss. Then he went slowly to bed. He had forgotten Miriam; he only saw how his mother's hair was lifted back from her warm, broad brow. And somehow, she was hurt.

Then the next time he saw Miriam, he said to her:

"Don't let me be late tonight—not later than ten o'clock. My mother gets so upset."

Miriam dropped her head, brooding.

"Why does she get upset?" she asked.

"Because she says I oughtn't to be out late when I have to get up early."

"Very well!" said Miriam, rather quietly, with just a touch of a sneer. He resented that. And he was usually late again.

That there was any love growing between him and Miriam, neither of them would have acknowledged. He thought he was too sane for such sentimentality, and she thought herself too lofty. They both were late in coming to maturity, and psychical ripeness was much behind even the physical. Miriam was exceedingly sensitive, as her mother had always been. The slightest grossness made her recoil almost in anguish. Her brothers were brutal, but never coarse in speech. The men did all the discussing of farm matters outside. But, perhaps because of the continual business of birth and of begetting which goes on upon every farm, Miriam was the more hypersensitive to the matter, and her blood was chastened almost to disgust of the faintest suggestion of such intercourse. Paul took his pitch from her, and their intimacy went on in an utterly blanched and chaste fashion. It could never be mentioned that the mare was in foal.

When he was nineteen, he was earning only twenty shillings a week, but he was happy. His painting went well, and life went well enough. On the Good Friday he organised a walk to the Hemlock Stone. There were three lads of his own age, then Annie and Arthur, Miriam and Geoffrey. Arthur, apprenticed as an electrician in Nottingham, was home for the holiday. Morel, as usual, was up early, whistling and sawing in the yard. At seven o'clock the family heard him buy three-pennyworth of hot cross buns, he talked with gusto to the little girl who brought them, calling her 'my darling'. He turned away several boys who came with more buns, telling them they had been "kested" by a little lass. Then Mrs Morel got up, and the family straggled down. It was an immense luxury to everybody, this lying in bed just beyond the ordinary time, on a week-day. And Paul and Arthur read before breakfast, and had the meal unwashed, sitting in their shirt sleeves. This was another holiday luxury. The room was warm. Everything felt free of care and anxiety. There was a sense of plenty in the house.

While the boys were reading, Mrs Morel went into the garden. They were now in another house, an old one, near the Scargill street home, which had been left soon after William had died. Directly came an excited cry from the garden:

"Paul—Paul—come and look!"

It was his mother's voice. He threw down his book and went out. There was a long garden that ran to a field. It was a grey, cold day with a sharp wind blowing out of Derbyshire. Two fields away Bestwood began, with a jumble of roofs and red house-ends, out of which rose the church tower and the spire of the congregational chapel. And beyond went woods and hills, right away to the pale grey heights of the Pennine Chain.

Paul looked down the garden for his mother. Her head appeared among the young currant bushes.

"Come here!" she cried.

"What for?" he answered.

"Come and see."

She had been looking at the buds on the currant trees. Paul went up.

"To think," she said, "that here I might never have seen them!"

Her son went to her side. Under the fence, in a little bed, was a ravel of poor grassy leaves, such as come from very immature bulbs, and three scillas in bloom. Mrs Morel pointed to the deep blue flowers.

"Now just see those!" she exclaimed. "I was looking at the currant bushes, when thinks I to myself 'there's something very blue—is it a bit of sugar-bag?' And there behold you! Sugar-bag! Three Glories of the Snow, and *such* beauties! But where on earth did they come from?"

"*I* don't know," said Paul.

"Well that's a marvel now! I *thought* I knew every weed and blade in this garden. But *haven't* they done well? You see that gooseberry bush just shelters them. Not nipped, not touched!"

He crouched down and turned up the bells of the blue little flowers.

"They're a glorious colour!" he said.

"Aren't they!" she cried. "I guess they come from Switzerland where they say they have such lovely things. Fancy them against the snow! But where have they come from? They can't have *blown* here, can they?"

Then he remembered having set here a lot of little trash of bulbs, to mature.

"And you never told me," she said.

"No, I thought I'd leave it till they might flower."

"And now you see! I might have missed them. And I've never had a Glory of the Snow in my garden in my life."

She was full of excitement and elation. The garden was an endless joy to her. Paul was thankful for her sake at last to be in a house with a long garden that went down to the field. Every morning after breakfast she went out and was happy pottering about in it. And it was true, she knew every weed and blade.

Everybody turned up for the walk. Food was packed, and they set off, a merry, delighted party. They hung over the wall of the mill race, dropped paper in the water on one side the tunnel and watched it shoot out on the other. They stood on the footbridge over Boathouse Station, and looked at the metals gleaming coldly.

"You should see the Flying Scotchman come through at half past six," said Leonard, whose father was a signalman. "Lad, but she doesn't half buzz!" And the little party looked up the lines one way, to London, and the other way, to Scotland, and they felt the touch of these two magical places.

In Ilkeston the colliers were waiting in gangs for the public houses to open. It was a town of idleness and lounging. At Stanton Gate the iron foundry blazed. Over everything there were great discussions. At Trowell they crossed again from Derbyshire into Nottinghamshire. They came to the Hemlock Stone at dinner time. Its field was crowded with folk from Nottingham and Ilkeston.

They had expected a venerable and dignified monument. They found a little, gnarled, twisted stump of rock, something like a decayed mushroom, standing out pathetically on the side of a field. Leonard and Dick immediately proceeded to carve their initials, L.W. and R.P., in the old red sandstone, but Paul desisted, because he had read in the newspaper satirical remarks about initial-carvers who could find no other road to immortality. Then all the lads climbed to the top of the rock to look round.

Everywhere in the field below, factory girls and lads were eating lunch or sporting about. Beyond was the garden of an old manor. It had yew hedges, and thick clumps and borders of yellow crocuses round the lawn.

"See," said Paul to Miriam, "what a quiet garden."

She saw the dark yews and the golden crocuses, then she looked at him gratefully. He had not seemed to belong to her among all these others; he was different then, not her Paul who understood the slightest quiver of her innermost soul, but something else, speaking another language than hers. How it hurt her and deadened her very perceptions. Only when he came right back to her, leaving his other, his lesser self as she thought, would she feel alive again. And now he asked her to look at this garden wanting the contact with her again. Impatient of the set in the field, she turned to the quiet lawn surrounded by sheaves of shut-up crocuses. A feeling of stillness, almost of ecstasy came over her. It felt almost as if she were alone with him in this garden.

Then he left her again, and joined the others. Soon they started home. Miriam loitered behind, alone. She did not fit in with the others; she could very rarely get into human relations with anyone: so her friend, her companion, her lover was nature. She saw the sun declining wanly. In the dusky, cold hedgerows were some red leaves. She lingered to gather them, tenderly, passionately. The love in her finger-tips caressed the leaves, the passion in her heart came to a glow upon the leaves.

Suddenly she realised she was alone in a strange road, and she hurried forward. Turning a corner in the lane, she came upon Paul who stood bent over something, his mind fixed on it, working away steadily, patiently, a little hopelessly. She hesitated in her approach, to watch.

He remained concentrated in the middle of the road. Beyond, one rift of rich gold in that colourless grey evening seemed to make him stand out in dark relief. She saw him slender and firm, as if the setting sun had given him to her. A deep pain took hold of her, and she knew she must love him. And she had discovered him, discovered in him a rare potentiality, discovered his loneliness. Quivering as at some 'Annunciation', she went slowly forward.

At last he looked up.

"Why," he exclaimed gratefully, "have you waited for me!"

She saw a deep shadow in his eyes.

"What is it?" she asked.

"The spring broken here."

And he showed her where his umbrella was injured. Instantly, with some shame, she knew he had not done the damage himself, but that Geoffrey was responsible.

"It is only an old umbrella, isn't it?" she asked.

She wondered why he, who did not usually trouble over trifles, made such a mountain of this molehill.

"But it was William's—an' my mother can't help but know," he said quietly, still patiently working at the umbrella. The words went through Miriam like a blade. This then was the confirmation of her vision of him! She looked at him. But there was about him a certain reserve, and she dared not comfort him, not even speak softly to him.

"Come on," he said. "I can't do it."

And they went in silence along the road.

That same evening they were walking along under the trees by Nether Green. He was talking to her, fretfully, seemed to be struggling to convince himself.

"You know," he said, with an effort, "if one person loves, the other does."

"Ah!" she answered, "like mother said to me when I was little: 'Love begets love'."

"Yes—something like that—I think it *must* be."

"I hope so—because if it were not, love might be a very terrible thing," she said.

"Yes but it *is*—at least with most people," he answered.

And Miriam, thinking he had assured himself, felt strong in herself. She always regarded that sudden coming upon him in the lane as a revelation. And this conversation remained graven in her mind, as one of the letters of the Law.

Now she stood with him and for him. When, about this time, he outraged the family feeling at Willey Farm, by some overbearing insult, she stuck to him and believed he was right.

And at this time she dreamed dreams of him, vivid, unforgettable. These dreams came again later on, developed to a more subtle psychological stage.

On the Easter Monday the same party took an excursion to Wingfield Manor. It was great excitement to Miriam to catch a train at Lethley Bridge, amid all the bustle of the Bank Holiday crowd. They left the train at Alfreton. Paul was interested in the street, and in the colliers with their dogs. Here was a new race of miners. Miriam did not live till they came to the church. They were all rather timid of entering, with their bags of food, for fear of being turned out. Leonard, a comic, thin fellow, went first, Paul, who would have died rather than be sent back, went last. The place was decorated for Easter. In the font hundreds of white narcissi seemed to be growing. The air was dim, and coloured from the windows, and thrilled with a subtle scent of lilies and narcissi. In that atmosphere Miriam's soul came into a glow. Paul was afraid of the things he mustn't do. And he was sensitive to the feel of the place. Miriam turned to him. He answered. They were together. He would not go beyond the communion rail. She loved him for that. Her soul expanded into prayer beside him. He felt the strange fascination of shadowy religious places. All his latent mysticism quivered into life. She was drawn to him. He was a prayer along with her.

In the church-yard daffodils and jonquils were out, and so bright in the sunshine that they seemed to flutter. Lambs in the park were making the air tremble with their many tiny bleats. Leonard and Dick went into a public-house for a drink, much to the disgust of Paul and Annie.

"What did you go in a pub for?" asked Paul, crossly.

"Well," laughed Dick. "We only went for a lemonade."

"Even then you could have got it in a shop," said Annie.

"Shop!" cried Leonard. "Can you see our stout British hearts drinking lemonade in a shop?"

"No," said Paul, "but I can see your stout British mug."

"What's my mug done amiss?" said Leonard, wiping his wide mouth.

Miriam very rarely talked to the other lads. They at once became awkward in conversation with her. So usually she was silent.

It was past mid-day when they climbed the steep path to the manor. All things shone softly in the sun, which was wonderfully warm and enlivening. Celandines and violets were out. Everybody was tip-top full with happiness. The glitter of the ivy, the soft, atmospheric grey of the castle walls, the gentleness of everything near the ruin was perfect.

The manor is of hard, pale-grey stone, and the outer walls are blank and calm. The young folk were in raptures. They went in trepidation, almost afraid that the delight of exploring this ruin might be denied them. In the first courtyard, within the high, broken walls, were farm-carts with their shafts lying idle on the ground, the tyres of the wheels brilliant with gold-red rust. It was very still.

All eagerly paid their sixpences, and went timidly through the fine clean arch of the inner courtyard. They were shy. Here on the pavement where the hall had been, an old thorn-tree was budding. All kinds of strange openings and broken rooms were in the shadow around them.

"Isn't this all right!" exclaimed Leonard.

"Isn't it just!" added Paul.

And they rushed off to explore.

"Lad!" cried Leonard. "Here's an oven for you!"

And he promptly crept in the cavern. Dick and Paul crawled in after him, and the three sat and bellowed as if from the bowels of the earth.

"They could cook an ox or two in here," said Dick.

"*And* a deer or two," added Paul.

"*And* a hass or two," added Leonard.

Whereupon he brayed loudly, while the other two punched him. Paul made a dive for the open air, and the exploration continued. At last they came upon Geoffrey and the girls again. Geoffrey was eating.

"I reckon it *is* about snap-time," said Leonard.

"I've begun," said Geoffrey. He had been eating, more or less, since the party set out.

"Where shall we sit?" asked Miriam.

"Let's go in the banqueting chamber," said Paul.

"How d'you know it's a banqueting chamber?" asked Leonard.

"Because I saw it on a picture."

"Right then, we'll banquet," said Leonard.

In the big, ruined apartment, with its raw edges high up against the blue sky, they sat in the sunshine to eat, looking up at the birds that twittered in the tracery of the big window.

"Now Lord Fuzzball," said Leonard to Paul, "willst thou partake of this venison pasty?"

"No, Sir Staybone," replied Paul. "I will e'en have of this haunch of bread and cheese."

"And prithee," said Geoffrey, "hutch up an' make a bit more room."

"A million pardons, Gracious Sir," said Leonard. "Thou sprottlest so."

"Paul," said Annie, "here's your hard-boiled egg."

"Today we have, my hearty nobles, a feast of phœnix eggs, laid by our only phœnix, and bearing all our crest, as printed there by our most accommodating fowl—" said Paul.

"Namely, a bit of dirt," said Leonard.

"Which has been our proud crest for generations Amen!" said Annie.

"A smut rampant," added Paul, which made Miriam laugh.

After lunch, they set off once more to explore the ruin. This time the girls went with the boys, who could act as guides and expositors. There was one tall tower in a corner, rather tottering, where they say Mary Queen of Scots was imprisoned.

"Think of the queen going up here," said Miriam, in a low voice, as she climbed the hollow stairs.

"If she could get up," said Paul, "for she had rheumatism like anything. I reckon they treated her rottenly."

"You don't think she deserved it?" asked Miriam.

"No I don't. She was only lively."

They continued to mount the winding stair-case. A high wind blowing through the loopholes went rushing up the shaft and filled the girl's skirts like a balloon, so that she was ashamed, until he took the hem of her dress, and held it down for her. He did it perfectly simply, as he would have picked up her glove. She remembered this always.

Round the broken top of the tower the ivy bushed out, old and handsome. Also there were a few chill gillivers, in pale cold bud. Miriam wanted to lean over for some ivy, but he would not let her. Instead she had to wait behind him, and take from him each spray as he gathered it and held it to her, each one separately, in the purest manner of chivalry. The tower seemed to rock in the wind. They looked over miles and miles of wooded country, and country with gleams of pasture.

The crypt underneath the manor was beautiful and in perfect preservation. Paul made a drawing. Miriam stayed with him. She was thinking of Mary Queen of Scots looking with her strained hopeless eyes, that could not understand misery, over the hills where no help came, or sitting in this crypt being told of a God as cold as the place she sat in.

They set off again gaily, looking round on their beloved manor that stood so clean and big on its hill.

"Supposing you could have *that* farm," said Paul to Miriam.

"Yes!"

"Wouldn't it be lovely to come and see you!"

They were now in the bare country of stone walls, which he loved.

and which, though only ten miles from home, seemed so foreign to Miriam. The party was straggling now. As they were crossing a large meadow that sloped away from the sun, along a path embedded with innumerable tiny glittering points, Paul, walking alongside, laced his fingers in the strings of the bag Miriam was carrying, and instantly she felt Annie behind, watchful and jealous. But the meadow was bathed in a glory of sunshine, and the path was jewelled, and it was seldom that he gave her any sign. She held her fingers very still among the strings of the bag, his fingers touching. And the place was golden as a vision.

At last they came into the straggling grey village of Crich, that lies high. Beyond the village was the famous Crich Stand, that Paul could see from the garden at home. The party pushed on. Great expanse of country spread around and below. The lads were eager to get to the top of the hill. It was capped by a round knoll, half of which was by now cut away, and on the top of which stood an ancient monument, sturdy and squat, for signalling in old days far down into the level lands of Nottinghamshire and Leicestershire.

It was blowing so hard, high up there in the exposed place, that the only way to be safe was to stand nailed by the wind to the wall of the tower. At their feet fell the precipice where the limestone was quarried away. Below was a jumble of hills and tiny villages— Matlock, Ambergate, Stoney Middleton. The lads were eager to spy out the Church of Bestwood, far away among the rather wooded country on the left. They were disgusted that it seemed to stand on a plain. They saw the hills of Derbyshire fall into the monotony of the midlands, that swept away south.

Miriam was somewhat scared by the wind, but the lads enjoyed it. They went on, miles and miles, to Whatstandwell. All the food was eaten, everybody was hungry and there was very little money to get home with. But they managed to procure a loaf and a currant loaf, which they hacked into pieces with shut-knives, and ate sitting on the wall near the bridge, watching the bright Derwent rushing by, and the brakes from Matlock pulling up at the inn.

Paul was now pale with weariness. He had been responsible for the party all day, and now he was done. Miriam understood, and kept close to him, and he left himself in her hands.

They had an hour to wait at Ambergate station. Trains came, crowded with excursionists, returning to Manchester, Birmingham and London.

"We might be going there—folk easily might think we're going that far," said Paul.

They got back rather late. Miriam, walking home with Geoffrey, watched the moon rise big and red and misty. She felt something was fulfilled in her.

She had an elder sister Agatha, who was a school-teacher. Between the two girls was a feud. Miriam considered Agatha worldly. And she wanted herself to be a school-teacher.

One Saturday afternoon Agatha and Miriam were upstairs dressing. Their bedroom was over the stable. It was a low room, not very large, and bare. Miriam had nailed on the wall a reproduction of Veronese's "St. Catherine." She loved the woman who sat in the window, dreaming. Her own windows were too small to sit in. But the front one was dripped over with honeysuckle and virginia creeper, and looked upon the tree-tops of the oak-wood across the yard, while the little back window, no bigger than a handkerchief, was a loop-hole to the east, to the dawn beating up against the beloved round hills.

The two sisters did not talk much to each other. Agatha, who was fair and small and determined, had rebelled against the home atmosphere, against the doctrine of "the other cheek." She was out in the world now, in a fair way to be independent. And she insisted on worldly values, on appearance, on manners, on position, which Miriam would fain have ignored.

Both girls liked to be upstairs, out of the way, when Paul came. They preferred to come running down, open the stairfoot door, and see him watching, expectant of them. Miriam stood painfully pulling over her head a rosary he had given her. It caught in the fine mesh of her hair. But at last she had it on, and the red-brown wooden beads looked well against her cool-brown neck. She was a well-developed girl, and very handsome. But in the little looking glass nailed against the white-washed wall, she could only see a fragment of herself at a time. Agatha had bought a little mirror of her own, which she propped up to suit herself. Miriam was near the window. Suddenly she heard the well-known click of the chain, and she saw Paul fling open the gate, push his bicycle into the yard. She saw him look at the house, and she shrank away. He walked in a nonchalant fashion, and his bicycle went with him as if it were a live thing.

"Paul's come!" she exclaimed.

"Aren't you glad?" said Agatha cuttingly.

Miriam stood still in amazement and bewilderment.

"Well, aren't you?" she asked.

"Yes, but I'm not going to let him see it, and think I wanted him."

Miriam was startled. She heard him putting his bicycle in the stable underneath, and talking to Jimmy, who had been a pit-horse, and who was seedy.

"Well Jimmy my lad, how are ter? Nobbut sick an' sadly, like? Why then it's a shame, my owd lad!"

She heard the rope run through the hole as the horse lifted its head from the lad's caress. How she loved to listen, when he thought only the horse could hear. But there was a serpent in her Eden. She searched earnestly in herself to see if she wanted Paul Morel. She felt there would be some disgrace in it. Full of twisted feeling, she was afraid she did want him. She stood selfconvicted. Then came an agony of new shame. She shrank within herself in a coil of torture. Did she want Paul Morel, and did he know she wanted him? What a subtle infamy upon her! She felt as if her whole soul coiled into knots of shame.

Agatha was dressed first and ran downstairs. Miriam heard her greet the lad gaily, knew exactly how brilliant her grey eyes became with that tone. She herself would have felt it bold to have greeted him in such wise. Yet there she stood under the self-accusation of wanting him, tied to that stake of torture. In bitter perplexity, she kneeled down and prayed:

"Oh Lord, let me not love Paul Morel. Keep me from loving him, if I ought not to love him."

Something anomalous in the prayer arrested her. She lifted her head and pondered. How could it be wrong to love him? Love was God's gift. And yet it caused her shame. That was because of him, Paul Morel. But then, it was not his affair, it was her own, between herself and God. She was to be a sacrifice. But it was God's sacrifice, not Paul Morel's or her own. After a few minutes she hid her face in the pillow again, and said:

"But, Lord, if it is Thy will that I should love him, make me love him—as Christ would, who died for the souls of men. Make me love him splendidly, because he is Thy son."

She remained kneeling for some time, quite still, and deeply moved, her black hair against the red squares, and the lavender sprigged squares of the patchwork quilt. Prayer was almost essential to her. Then she fell into that rapture of self-sacrifice, identifying herself with a God who was sacrificed, which gives to so many human souls their deepest bliss.

When she went downstairs, Paul was lying back in an arm-chair, holding forth with much vehemence to Agatha, who was scorning a little painting he had brought to show her. Miriam glanced at the two, and avoided their levity. She went into the parlour, to be alone.

It was tea-time before she was able to speak to Paul, and then her manner was so distant, he thought he had offended her.

Miriam discontinued her practice of going each Thursday evening to the library in Bestwood. After calling for Paul regularly during the whole spring, a number of trifling incidents and tiny insults from his family awakened her to their attitude towards her, and she decided to go no more. So she announced to Paul one evening she would not call at his house again for him on Thursday nights.

"Why?" he asked, very short.

"Nothing. Only I'd rather not."

"Very well."

"But," she faltered, "if you'd care to meet me, we could still go together."

"Meet you where?"

"Somewhere—where you like."

"I shan't meet you anywhere. I don't see why you shouldn't keep calling for me. But if you won't, I don't want to meet you."

So the Thursday evenings, which had been so precious to her, and to him, were dropped. He worked instead. Mrs Morel sniffed with satisfaction at this arrangement.

He would not have it that they were lovers. The intimacy between them had been kept so abstract, such a matter of the soul, all thought and weary struggle into consciousness, that he saw it only as a Platonic friendship. He stoutly denied there was anything else between them. Miriam was silent, or else she very quietly agreed. He was a fool who did not know what was happening to himself. By tacit agreement they ignored the remarks and insinuations of their acquaintances.

"We aren't lovers, we are friends," he said to her. "*We* know it. Let them talk. What does it matter, what they say."

Sometimes, as they were walking together, she slipped her arm timidly into his. But he always resented it, and she knew it. It caused a violent conflict in him. With Miriam he was always on the high plane of abstraction, when his natural fire of love was transmitted into the fine steam of thought. She would have it so. If he were jolly and, as she put it, flippant, she waited till he came back to her, till the change had taken place in him again, and he was wrestling with his own soul, frowning, passionate in his desire for understanding. And in this passion for understanding her soul lay close to his, she had him all to herself. But he must be made abstract first.

Then, if she put her arm in his, it caused him almost torture. His consciousness seemed to split. The place where she was touching him ran hot with friction. He was one internecine battle, and he became cruel to her because of it.

One evening in midsummer Miriam called at the house, warm from climbing. Paul was alone in the kitchen, his mother could be heard moving about upstairs.

"Come and look at the sweet-peas," he said to the girl.

They went into the garden. The sky behind the townlet and the church was orange-red, the flower garden was flooded with a strange warm light that lifted every leaf into significance. Paul passed along a fine row of sweet-peas, gathering a blossom here and there, all cream and pale blue. Miriam followed, breathing the fragrance. To her flowers appealed with such strength she felt she must make them part of herself. When she bent and breathed a flower, it was as if she and the flower were loving each other. Paul hated her for it. There seemed a sort of exposure about the action, something too intimate.

When he had got a fair bunch, they returned to the house. He listened for a moment to his mother's quiet movement upstairs, then he said:

"Come here, and let me pin them in for you."

He arranged them two or three at a time in the bosom of her dress, stepping back now and then to see the effect.

"You know," he said, taking the pin out of his mouth, "a woman ought always to arrange her flowers before her glass."

Miriam laughed. She thought flowers ought to be pinned in one's dress without any care. That Paul should take pains to fix her flowers for her was his whim.

He was rather offended at her laughter.

"Some women do—those who look decent," he said.

Miriam laughed again, but mirthlessly, to hear him thus mix her up with women in a general way. From most men she would have ignored it. But from him, it hurt her.

He had nearly finished arranging the flowers when he heard his mother's footstep on the stairs. Hurriedly he pushed in the last pin and turned away.

"Don't let mater know," he said.

Miriam picked up her books and stood in the doorway, looking with chagrin at the beautiful sunset. She would call for Paul no more, she said.

"Goodevening, Mrs Morel," she said, in a deferential way. She sounded as if she felt she had no right to be there.

"Oh is it you Miriam!" replied Mrs Morel coolly.

But Paul insisted on everybody's accepting his friendship with the girl, and Mrs Morel was too wise to have any open rupture.

It was not till he was twenty years old that the family could ever afford to go away for a holiday. Mrs Morel had never been away for a holiday, except to see her sister, since she had been married. Now at last Paul had saved enough money, and they were all going. There was to be a party: some of Annie's friends, one friend of Paul's, a young man in the same office where William had previously been, and Miriam.

It was great excitement writing for rooms. Paul and his mother debated it endlessly between them. They wanted a furnished cottage for two weeks. She thought one week would be enough, but he insisted on two. He went out before the post came in the morning. So, when he came home, his mother's first words to him were:

"Paul, you know that cat at Skegness—she only wants four guineas a week for her measly bungalow."

"Then let her whistle for it," said Paul.

"I should think so," replied his mother, indignantly. Then that evening, he wrote another letter. At last they got an answer from Mablethorpe, a cottage such as they wished for thirty shillings a week. There was immense jubilation. Paul was wild with joy for his mother's sake. She would have a real holiday now. He and she sat at evening picturing what it would be like. Annie came in, and Leonard, and Alice, and Kitty. There was wild rejoicing and anticipation. Paul told Miriam. She seemed to brood with joy over it. But the Morels' house rang with excitement.

They were to go on Saturday morning by the seven train. Paul suggested that Miriam should sleep at his house, because it was so far for her to walk. She came down for supper. Everybody was so excited that even Miriam was accepted with warmth. But almost as soon as she entered, the feeling in the family became close and tight. He had discovered a poem by Jean Ingelow which mentioned Mablethorpe, and so he must read it to Miriam. He would never have got so far in the direction of sentimentality as to read poetry to his own family. But now they condescended to listen. Miriam sat on the sofa, absorbed in him. She always seemed absorbed in him and by him, when he was present. Mrs Morel sat jealously in her own chair. She was going to hear also. And even Annie and the father attended, Morel with his head cocked on one side, like somebody listening to a sermon and feeling conscious of the fact. Paul ducked his head over the book. He had got now all the audience he cared for. And Mrs Morel and Annie almost contested with Miriam who should listen best and win his favour. He was in very high feather.

"But," interrupted Mrs Morel, "what *is* the 'Bride of Enderby', that the bells are supposed to ring."

"It's an old tune they used to play on the bells for a warning against water. I suppose the Bride of Enderby was drowned in a flood," he replied. He had not the faintest knowledge what it really was, but he would never have sunk so low as to confess that to his women-folk. They listened and believed him. He believed himself.

"And the people knew what that tune meant?" said his mother.

"Yes—just like the Scotch when they heard 'The Flowers o' the Forest'—and when they used to ring the bells backward for alarm."

"How!" said Annie. "A bell sounds the same whether it's rung backwards or forwards."

"But," he said, "if you start with the deep bell and ring up to the high one—der—der—der—der—der—der—der—der!"

He ran up the scale. Everybody thought it clever. He thought so too. Then, waiting a minute, he continued the poem.

"Hm!" said Mrs Morel, curiously, when he finished. "But I wish everything that's written weren't so sad."

"*I* canna see what they want drownin' theirselves for," said Morel. There was a pause. Annie got up to clear the table.

"I think 'Elizabeth' is a beautiful name," said Miriam, in a low voice. " 'My son's wife Elizabeth—' "

"Yes," said Paul.

"Yes," said his mother. "But I don't like 'Lizzie', and 'Liza' I abominate."

It didn't appear, either to Paul or Miriam, that 'Lizzie' and 'Liza' had anything to do with it.

"But 'Elizabeth'!" murmured Miriam.

"And Queen Elizabeth was awfully fond of being called 'Great Eliza'," said Paul.

"And come again tomorrow!" ejaculated Morel.

Mrs Morel laughed—so did Paul.

"I'll bet 'er wor a toe-rag," said Morel, following up his joke.

"Don't you be so cheeky about a queen," said Annie.

"Queens!" said Morel. "Why what's a' on you but queens? You've nowt to do but sit i' your grandeur."

Miriam rose to help with the pots.

"Let *me* help to wash up," she said.

"Certainly not," cried Annie. "You sit down again. There aren't many."

And Miriam, who could not be familiar and insist, sat down again to look at the book with Paul.

He was master of the party—his father was no good. And great tortures he suffered lest the tin box should be put out at Firsby instead of at Mablethorpe. And he wasn't equal to getting a carriage. His bold little mother did that.

"Here!" she cried to a man, "Here!"

Paul and Annie got behind the rest, convulsed with shamed laughter.

"How much will it be to drive to Brook Cottage?" said Mrs Morel.

"Two shillings."

"Why how far is it?"

"A good way."

"I don't believe it," she said.

But she scrambled in. There were eight crowded in one old sea-side carriage.

"You see," said Mrs Morel, "it's only threepence each, and if it were a tram car—"

They drove along. Each cottage they came to, Mrs Morel cried: "Is it this?—now this is it!"

Everybody sat breathless. They drove past. There was a universal sigh.

"I'm thankful it wasn't that brute," said Mrs Morel. "I *was* frightened."

They drove on and on.

"That stinking hussy said ten minutes to the sea—!" exclaimed Mrs Morel.

"An' hour if it's a minute," replied Morel.

And everybody fell on him in fury.

"Are we *never* going to get there!" cried Mrs Morel.

"Don't shout so mother," said Annie. "Whatever will he think?"

Mrs Morel looked up quizzically at the driver.

"I'm sure I couldn't say. But not much, from the look of him."

At last they descended at a house that stood alone over the dyke by the high road. There was wild excitement because they had to cross a little bridge to get into the front garden. But they loved the house, that lay so solitary, with a sea-meadow on one side, and immense expanse of land patched in white barley, yellow oats, red wheat, and green root-crops, flat and stretching level to the sky.

Paul kept accounts. He and his mother ran the show. The total expenses, lodging, food everything, was sixteen shillings a week per person. He and Leonard went bathing in the morning. Morel was wandering abroad quite early.

"You Paul," his mother called from the bedroom. "Eat a piece of bread and butter."

"All right," he answered.

And when he got back, he saw his mother presiding in state at the breakfast table. The woman of the house was young. Her husband was blind, and she did laundry work. So Mrs Morel always washed the pots in the kitchen and made the beds.

"But you said you'd have a real holiday," said Paul, "and now you work."

"Work!" she exclaimed. "What are you talking about!"

He loved to go with her across the fields to the village and the sea. She was afraid of the plank bridges, and he abused her for being a baby. On the whole, he stuck to her as if he were *her* man.

Miriam did not get much of him—except, perhaps, when all the others went to the 'Coons.' Coons were insufferably stupid to Miriam, so he thought they were to himself also, and he preached priggishly to Annie about the fatuity of listening to them. Yet he too knew all their songs, and sang them along the roads, roisterously. And if he found himself listening, the stupidity pleased him very much. Yet to Annie he said:

"Such rot!—there isn't a grain of intelligence in it. Nobody with more gumption than a grasshopper could go and sit and listen." And to Miriam he said, with much scorn, of Annie and the others:

"I suppose they're at the Coons."

It was queer to see Miriam singing Coon songs. She had a straight chin, that went in a perpendicular line from the lower lip to the turn. She always reminded Paul of some sad Botticelli angel when she sang, even when it was:

"Come down Lover's Lane
For a walk with me, talk with me—"

Only when he sketched, or at evening when the others were at the Coons, she had him to herself. He talked to her endlessly about his love of horizontals: how they, the great levels of sky and land in Lincolnshire meant to him the eternality of the will: just as the bowed Norman arches of the church, repeating themselves, meant the dogged leaping forward of the persistent human soul, on and on, nobody knows where: in contradiction to the perpendicular lines, and to the gothic arch, which, he said, leapt up at heaven and touched the ecstasy and lost itself in the divine. Himself, he said, was Norman, Miriam was Gothic. She bowed in consent even to that.

One evening, he and she went up the great, sweeping shore of sand towards Theddlethorpe. The long breakers plunged and ran in a hiss of foam along the coast. It was a warm evening. There was not a figure but themselves on the far reaches of sand, no noise but the sound of the sea. Paul loved to see it clanging at the land. He loved to feel himself between the noise of it and the silence of the sandy shore. Miriam was with him. Everything grew very intense. It was quite dark when they turned again. The way home was through a gap in the sand hills, and then along a raised grass road between two dykes. The country was black and still. From behind the sandhills came the whisper of the sea. Paul and Miriam walked in silence. Suddenly he started. The whole of his blood seemed to burst into flame, and he could scarcely breathe. An enormous orange moon was staring at them from the rim of the sand hills. He stood still, looking at it.

"Ah!" cried Miriam, when she saw it.

He remained perfectly still, staring at the immense and ruddy moon, the only thing in the far-reaching darkness of the level. His heart beat heavily, the muscles of his arms contracted.

"What is it?" murmured Miriam, waiting for him.

He turned and looked at her. She stood beside him, for ever in shadow. Her face, covered with the darkness of her hat, was watching him unseen. But she was brooding. She was slightly afraid—

deeply moved and religious. That was her best state. He was impotent against it. His blood was concentrated like a flame in his chest. But he could not get across to her. There were flashes in his blood. But somehow she ignored them. She was expecting some religious state in him. Still yearning, she was half aware of his passion, and gazed at him, troubled.

"What is it?" she murmured again.

"It's the moon," he answered, frowning.

"Yes," she assented. "Isn't it wonderful?" She was curious about him. The crisis was past.

He did not know himself what was the matter. He was naturally so young, and their intimacy was so abstract, he did not know he wanted to crush her onto his breast to ease the ache there. He was afraid of her. The fact that he might want her as a man wants a woman had in him been suppressed into a shame. When she shrank in her convulsed, coiled torture from the thought of such a thing, he had winced to the depths of his soul. And now this 'purity' prevented even their first love kiss. It was as if she could scarcely stand the shock of physical love, even a passionate kiss, and then he was too shrinking and sensitive to give it.

As they walked along the dark fen-meadow, he watched the moon, and did not speak. She plodded beside him. He hated her, for she seemed, in some way, to make him despise himself. Looking ahead, he saw the one light in the darkness, the window of their lamp-lit cottage.

He loved to think of his mother, and the other jolly people.

"Well, everybody else has been in long ago!" said his mother as they entered.

"What does that matter!" he cried irritably. "I can go a walk if I like, can't I?"

"And I should have thought you could get in to supper with the rest," said Mrs Morel.

"I shall please myself," he retorted. "It's not *late*. I shall do as I like."

"Very well," said his mother, cuttingly, "then *do* as you like."

And she took no further notice of him that evening. Which he pretended neither to notice nor to care about, but sat reading. Miriam read also, obliterating herself. Mrs Morel hated her for making her son like this. She watched Paul growing irritable, priggish, and melancholic. For this she put the blame on Miriam.

Annie, and all her friends joined against the girl. Miriam had no friend of her own, only Paul. But she did not suffer so much, because she despised the triviality of these other people.

And Paul hated her because, somehow, she spoilt his ease and naturalness. And he writhed himself with a feeling of humiliation.

CHAPTER VIII

Strife in Love

Arthur finished his apprenticeship, and got a job on the electrical plant at Minton pit. He earned very little, but had a good chance of getting on. But he was wild and restless. He did not drink, nor gamble. Yet he somehow contrived to get into endless scrapes, always through some hot-headed thoughtlessness. Either he went rabbiting in the woods, like a poacher, or he stayed in Nottingham all night instead of coming home, or he miscalculated his dive into the canal at Bestwood, and scored his chest into one mass of wounds on the raw stones and tins at the bottom.

He had not been at his work many months, when again he did not come home one night.

"Do you know where Arthur is?" asked Paul at breakfast.

"I do not," replied his mother.

"He is a fool," said Paul. "And if he *did* anything I shouldn't mind! But no, he simply can't come away from a game of whist, or else he must see a girl home from the skating rink—quite proprietously—and so can't get home. He's a fool."

"I don't know that it would make it any better if he did something to make us all ashamed," said Mrs Morel.

"Well I should respect him more," said Paul.

"I very much doubt it," said his mother coldly.

They went on with breakfast.

"Are you fearfully fond of him?" Paul asked his mother.

"What do you ask that for?"

"Because they say a woman always likes the youngest best."

"She may do—but I don't.—No, he wearies me."

"And you'd actually rather he was good?"

"I'd rather he showed some of a man's common-sense."

Paul was raw and irritable. He also wearied his mother very often. She saw the sunshine going out of him, and she resented it.

As they were finishing breakfast, came the postman with a letter from Derby. Mrs Morel screwed up her eyes to look at the address.

"Give it here, blind eye!" exclaimed her son, snatching it away from her. She started and almost boxed his ears.

"It's from your son Arthur," he said.

"What now—!" cried Mrs Morel.

"'My dearest Mother,'" Paul read. "'I don't know what made me such a fool. I want you to come and fetch me back from here. I came with Jack Bredon yesterday, instead of going to work, and enlisted. He said he was sick of wearing the seat of a stool out, and like the idiot you know I am, I came away with him.

I have taken the King's Shilling, but perhaps if you came for me they would let me go back with you. I was a fool when I did it. I don't want to be in the army. My dear mother, I am nothing but a trouble to you. But if you get me out of this, I promise I will have more sense and consideration.——'"

Mrs Morel sat down in her rocking-chair.

"Well *now*," she cried, "let him stop!"

"Yes," said Paul. "Let him stop."

There was silence. The mother sat with her hands folded in her apron, her face set, thinking.

"If I'm not *sick*!" she cried suddenly. "Sick!!"

"Now!" said Paul, beginning to frown, "you're not going to worry your soul out about this, do you hear."

"I suppose I'm to take it as a blessing," she flashed, turning on her son.

"You're not going to mount it up to a tragedy, so there," he retorted.

"The *fool*!—the young fool!" she cried.

"He'll look well in uniform," said Paul, irritatingly.

His mother turned on him like a fury.

"Oh will he!" she cried. "Not in my eyes—!"

"He should get in a cavalry regiment—he'll have the time of his life, and will look an awful swell."

"Swell!—*swell*!!—a mighty swell indeed!—a common soldier!"

"Well," said Paul, "what am I but a common clerk?"

"A good deal, my boy," cried his mother, stung.

"What?"

"At any rate, a *man*, and not a thing in a red coat."

"I shouldn't mind being in a red coat—or dark blue, that would suit me better—if they didn't boss me about too much."

But his mother had ceased to listen.

"Just as he was getting on, or might have been getting on at his job—a young nuisance—here he goes and ruins himself for life. What good will he be, do you think, after *this*?"

"It may lick him in to shape beautifully," said Paul.

"Lick him into shape!—lick what marrow there *was* out of his bones. A *soldier*!—a common *soldier*!!—nothing but a body that makes movements when it hears a shout! It's a fine thing!"

"I can't understand why it upsets you," said Paul.

"No, perhaps you can't. But *I* understand," and she sat back in her chair, her chin in one hand, holding her elbow with the other, brimmed up with wrath and chagrin.

"And shall you go to Derby?" asked Paul.

"Yes."

"It's no good."

"I'll see for myself."

"And why on earth don't you let him stop. It's just what he wants."

"Of course," cried the mother, "*you* know what he wants."

She got ready and went by the first train to Derby, where she saw her son and the sergeant. It was however no good.

When Morel was having his dinner in the evening, she said suddenly:

"I've had to go to Derby today."

The miner turned up his eyes, showing the whites in his black face.

"Has ter lass—what took thee there?"

"That Arthur!"

"Oh—an' what's agate now?"

"He's only enlisted."

Morel put down his knife and leaned back in his chair.

"Nay," he said, "that he niver 'as!"

"And is going down to Aldershot tomorrow."

"Well!" exclaimed the miner. "That's a winder."

Morel considered it a moment, said "Hm!", and proceeded with his dinner. Suddenly his face contracted with wrath.

"I hope he may never set foot i' my house again," he said.

"The idea!" cried Mrs Morel. "Saying such a thing!"

"I do," repeated Morel. "A fool as runs away for a soldier—let 'im look after 'issen—I s'll do no more for 'im."

"A fat sight you have done as it is," she said.

And Morel was almost ashamed to go to his public house that evening.

"Well did you go?" said Paul to his mother when he came home.

"I did."

"And could you see him?"

"Yes."

"And what did he say?"

"He blubbered when I came away."

"Hm!"

"And so did I, so you needn't 'hm!'."

Mrs Morel fretted after her son. She knew he would not like the army. He did not. The discipline was intolerable to him.

"But the doctor," she said with some pride, to Paul, "said he was perfectly proportioned—almost exactly, all his measurements were correct. He *is* good-looking, you know."

"He's awfully nice looking. But he doesn't fetch the girls like William, does he?"

"No—it's a different character. He's a good deal like his father, irresponsible."

To console his mother, Paul did not go much to Willey Farm at this time. And in the autumn exhibition of Students' Work in the Castle, he had two studies, a landscape in water colour and a still-life in oil, both of which had first prize awards. He was highly excited.

"What do you think I've got for my pictures mother?" he asked, coming home one evening. She saw by his eyes he was glad. Her face flushed.

"Now how should I know, my boy!"

"A first prize for those glass jars—"

"Hm!"

"And a first prize for that sketch up at Willey Farm."

"Both first?"

"Yes."

"Hm!"

There was a rosy, bright look about her, though she said nothing.

"It's nice," he said, "isn't it?"

"It is."

"Why don't you praise me up to the skies?"

She laughed.

"I should have the trouble of dragging you down again," she said.

But she was full of joy nevertheless. William had brought her his sporting trophies. She kept them still: and she did not forgive his death. Arthur was handsome, at least a good specimen, and warm and generous, and probably would do well in the end. But Paul was going to distinguish himself. She had a great belief in him, the more because he was unaware of his own powers. There was so much to come out of him. Life for her was rich with promise. She was to see herself fulfilled. Not for nothing had been her struggle.

Several times during the exhibition, Mrs Morel went to the Castle, unknown to Paul. She wandered down the long room looking at the other exhibits. Yes, they were good. But they had not in them a certain something, which she demanded for her satisfaction. Some made her jealous, they were so good. She looked at them a long time trying to find fault with them. Then suddenly she had a shock that made her heart beat. There hung Paul's picture! She knew it as if it were printed on her heart.

"Name—Paul Morel—First Prize."

It looked so strange, there in public, on the walls of the Castle gallery, where in her life-time she had seen so many pictures. And she glanced round to see if anyone had noticed her again in front of the same sketch.

But she felt a proud woman. When she met well-dressed ladies going home to the Park, she thought to herself:

"Yes, you look very well—but I wonder if *your* son has two first prizes in the Castle."

And she walked on, as proud a little woman as any in Nottingham. And Paul felt he had done something for her, if only a trifle. All his work was hers.

One day, as he was going up Castle Gate, he met Miriam. He had seen her on the Sunday, and had not expected to meet her in town. She was walking with a rather striking woman, blonde, with a sullen expression, and a defiant carriage. It was strange how Miriam, in her bowed, meditative bearing, looked dwarfed, beside this woman with the handsome shoulders. Miriam watched Paul searchingly. His gaze was on the stranger, who ignored him. The girl saw his masculine spirit rear its head.

"Hello!" he said. "You didn't tell me you were coming to town."

"No," replied Miriam, half apologetically. "I drove in to Cattle Market with father."

He looked at her companion.

"I've told you about Mrs Dawes," said Miriam, huskily. She was nervous. "Clara, do you know Paul?"

"I think I've seen him before," replied Mrs Dawes indifferently, as she shook hands with him. She had scornful grey eyes, a skin like white honey, and a full mouth with a slightly lifted upper lip, that did not know whether it was raised in scorn of all men, or out of eagerness to be kissed, but which believed the former. She carried her head back, as if she had drawn away in contempt, perhaps from men also. She wore a large, dowdy hat of black beaver, and a sort of slightly-affected simple dress that made her look rather sack-like. She was evidently poor and had not much taste. Miriam usually looked nice.

"Where have you seen me?" Paul asked of the woman.

She looked at him as if she would not trouble to answer. Then: "Walking with Louie Travers," she said.

Louie was one of the Spiral girls.

"Why do you know her?" he asked.

She did not answer. He turned to Miriam.

"Where are you going?" he asked.

"To the Castle."

"What train are you going home by?"

"I am driving with father. I wish you could come too. What time are you free?"

"You know not till eight tonight, damn it."

And directly the two women moved on.

Paul remembered that Clara Dawes was the daughter of an old friend of Mrs Leivers. Miriam had sought her out because she had once been Spiral overseer at Jordan's, and because her husband, Baxter Dawes, was smith for the factory, making the irons for cripple instruments, and so on. Through her, Miriam felt she got into direct contact with Jordan's, and could estimate better Paul's position. But Mrs Dawes was separated from her husband, and had taken up women's rights. She was supposed to be clever. It interested Paul.

Baxter Dawes he knew and disliked. The smith was a man of thirty one or two. He came occasionally through Paul's corner: a big, well set man, also striking to look at, and handsome. There was a peculiar similarity between himself and his wife. He had the same white skin with a clear, golden tinge. His hair was soft brown, his moustache was golden. And he had a similar defiance in his bearing and manner. But then came the difference. His eyes, dark brown and quick-shifting, were dissolute. They protruded very slightly, and his eyelids hung over them in a way that was half hate. His mouth too was sensual. His whole manner was of cowed defiance, as if he were ready to knock anybody down who disapproved of him—perhaps because he really disapproved of himself.

From the first day he had hated Paul. Finding the lad's impersonal, deliberate gaze of an artist on his face, he got into a fury.

"What are yer lookin' at?" he sneered, bullying.

The boy glanced away. But the smith used to stand behind the counter and talk to Mr Pappleworth. His speech was dirty, with a kind of rottenness. Again he found the youth with his cool, critical gaze fixed on his face. The smith started round as if he had been stung.

"What'r yer lookin' at, three hap'orth o' pap?" he snarled.

The boy shrugged his shoulders slightly.

"Why yer—!" shouted Dawes.

"Leave him alone," said Mr Pappleworth, in that insinuating voice which means, 'he's only one of your good little sops who can't help it.'

Since that time the boy used to look at the man every time he came through, with the same curious criticism, glancing away before he met the smith's eye. It made Dawes furious. They hated each other in silence.

Clara Dawes had no children. When she had left her husband, the home had been broken up, and she had gone to live with her mother. Dawes lodged with his sister. In the same house was a sister-in-law and somehow Paul knew that this girl, Louie Travers, was now Dawes' woman. She was a handsome, insolent hussy, who mocked at the youth, and yet flushed if he walked along to the station with her as she went home.

The next time he went to see Miriam, it was Saturday evening. She had a fire in the parlour and was waiting for him. The others, except her father and mother and the young children, had gone out so the two had the parlour together. It was a long, low warm room. There were three of Paul's small sketches on the wall, and his photo was on the mantel-piece. On the table, and on the high old rose-wood piano were bowls of coloured leaves. He sat in the arm-chair, she crouched on the hearthrug near his feet. The glow was warm on her handsome, pensive face as she kneeled there like a devotee.

"What did you think of Mrs Dawes?" she asked, quietly.

"She doesn't look very amiable," he replied.

"No, but don't you think she's a fine woman?" she said, in a deep tone.

"Yes—in stature. But without a grain of taste. I like her for some things. *Is* she disagreeable?"

"I don't think so. I think she's dissatisfied."

"What with?"

"Well—how would *you* like to be tied for life to a man like that?"

"Why did she marry him then, if she was to have revulsions so soon?"

"Ay, why did she!" repeated Miriam bitterly.

"And I should have thought she had enough fight in her to match him," he said.

Miriam bowed her head.

"Ay?" she queried satirically. "What makes you think so?"

"Look at her mouth—made for passion—and the very set-back of her throat—"

He threw his head back in Clara's defiant manner.

Miriam bowed a little lower.

"Yes," she said.

There was a silence for some moments, while he thought of Clara.

"And what were the things you liked about her?" she asked.

"I don't know—her skin and the texture of her—and her—I don't know—there's a sort of fierceness somewhere in her.—I appreciate her as an artist, that's all."

"Yes."

He wondered why Miriam crouched there brooding in that strange way. It irritated him.

"You don't really like her, do you?" he asked the girl.

She looked at him with her great, dazzled dark eyes.

"I do," she said.

"You don't—you can't—not really."

"Then what?" she asked, slowly.

"Eh I don't know—perhaps you like her because she's got a grudge against men."

That was more probably one of his own reasons for liking Mrs Dawes, but this did not occur to him. They were silent. There had come into his forehead a knitting of the brows which was becoming habitual with him, particularly when he was with Miriam. She longed to smooth it away, and she was afraid of it. It seemed the stamp of a man who was not her man in Paul Morel.

There were some crimson berries among the leaves in the bowl. He reached over and pulled out a bunch.

"If you put red berries in your hair," he said, "why would you look like some witch or priestess, and never like a reveller."

She laughed with a naked, painful sound.

"I don't know," she said.

His vigorous, warm hands were playing excitedly with the berries.

"Why can't you laugh?" he said. "You never laugh laughter. You only laugh when something is odd or incongruous, and then it almost seems to hurt you."

She bowed her head as if he were scolding her.

"I wish you could laugh at me just for one minute—just for a minute. I feel as if it would set something free."

"But!"—and she looked up at him with eyes frightened and struggling—"I do laugh at you—I *do*."

"Never! There's always a kind of intensity. When you laugh I could always cry, it seems as if it shows up your suffering. Oh, you make me knit the brows of my very soul and cogitate."

Slowly she shook her head, despairingly.

"I'm sure I don't want to," she said.

"I'm so damned spiritual with *you* always," he cried.

She remained silent, thinking 'Then why don't you be otherwise.' But he saw her crouching, brooding figure, and it seemed to tear him in two.

"But there, it's autumn," he said, "and everybody feels like a disembodied spirit then."

There was still another silence. This peculiar sadness between them thrilled her soul. He seemed so beautiful, with his eyes gone dark, and looking as if they were deep as the deepest well.

"You make me so spiritual!" he lamented. "And I don't want to be spiritual."

She took her finger from her mouth with a little pop, and looked up at him almost challenging. But still her soul was naked in her great dark eyes, and there was the same yearning appeal upon her. If he could have kissed her in abstract purity he would have done so. But he could not kiss her thus—and she seemed to leave no other way. And she yearned to him.

He gave a brief laugh.

"Well," he said, "get that French and we'll do some—some Verlaine."

"Yes," she said, in a deep tone, almost of resignation. And she rose and got the books. And her rather red, nervous hands looked so pitiful, he was mad to comfort her and kiss her. But then he dared not—or could not. There was something prevented him. His kisses were wrong for her. They continued the reading, till ten o'clock, when they went into the kitchen and Paul was natural and jolly again with the father and mother. His eyes were dark and shining, there was a kind of fascination about him.

When he went into the barn for his bicycle, he found the front wheel punctured.

"Fetch me a drop of water in a bowl," he said to her. "I shall be late, and then I s'll catch it."

He lighted the hurricane lamp, took off his coat, turned up the bicycle and set speedily to work. Miriam came with the bowl of water and stood close to him, watching. She loved to see his hands doing things. He was slim and vigorous, with a kind of easiness even in his most hasty movements. And busy at his work, he seemed to forget her. She loved him absorbedly. She wanted to run her hands down his sides. She always wanted to embrace him, so long as he did not want her.

"There!" he said, rising suddenly. "Now could you have done it quicker?"

"No!" she laughed.

He straightened himself. His back was towards her. She put her two hands on his sides, and ran them quickly down.

"You are so *fine*!" she said.

He laughed, hating her voice, but his blood roused to a wave of flame by her hands. She did not seem to realise *him* in all this. He might have been an object. She never realised the male he was.

He lighted his bicycle lamp, bounced the machine on the barn floor to see that the tyres were sound, buttoned his coat.

"That's all right!" he said.

She was trying the brakes, that she knew were broken.

"Did you have them mended?" she asked.

"No!"

"But why didn't you?"

"The back one goes on a bit."

"But it's not safe."

"I can use my toe."

"I wish you'd had them mended," she murmured.

"Don't worry—come to tea tomorrow, with Edgar."

"Shall we?"

"Do—about four—I'll come to meet you."

"Very well."

She was pleased. They went across the dark yard to the gate. Looking across, he saw through the uncurtained window of the kitchen, the heads of Mr and Mrs Leivers, in the warm glow. It looked very cosy. The road, with pine-trees, was quite black in front.

"Till tomorrow," he said, jumping on his bicycle.

"You'll take care, won't you?" she pleaded.

"Yes."

His voice already came out of the darkness. She stood a moment watching the light from his lamp race into obscurity along the ground. She turned very slowly indoors. Orion was wheeling up over the wood, his dog twinkling after him, half smothered. For the rest, the world was full of darkness, and silent, save for the breathing of cattle in their stalls. She prayed earnestly for his safety that night. When he left her, she often lay in anxiety, wondering if he had got home safely.

He dropped down the hills on his bicycle. The roads were greasy, so he had to let it go. He felt a pleasure as the machine plunged over the second, steeper drop in the hill. "Here goes!" he said. It was risky, because of the curve in the darkness at the bottom, and because of the brewer's wagons with drunken wagoners asleep. His bicycle seemed to fall beneath him, and he loved it. Recklessness is almost a man's revenge on his woman. He feels he is not valued, so he will risk destroying himself to deprive her altogether.

The stars on the lake seemed to leap like grasshoppers silver upon the blackness, as he spun past. Then there was the long climb home.

"See mother!" he said, as he threw her the berries and leaves onto the table.

"Hm!" she said, glancing at them, then away again. She sat reading, alone, as she always did.

"Aren't they pretty?"

"Yes."

He knew she was cross with him. After a few minutes he said:

"Edgar and Miriam are coming to tea tomorrow."

She did not answer.

"You don't mind?"

Still she did not answer.

"Do you?" he asked.

"You know whether I mind or not."

"I don't see why you should—I have plenty of meals there."

"You do."

"Then why do you begrudge them tea?"

"I begrudge whom tea?"

"What are you so horrid for?"

"Oh say no more! You've asked her to tea, it's quite sufficient. She'll come."

He was very angry with his mother. He knew it was merely Miriam she objected to. He flung off his boots and went to bed.

Paul went to meet his friends the next afternoon. He was glad to see them coming. They arrived home at about four o'clock. Everywhere was clean and still for Sunday afternoon. Mrs Morel sat in her black dress and black apron. She rose to meet the visitors. With Edgar she was cordial, but with Miriam cold and rather grudging. Yet Paul thought the girl looked so nice in her brown cashmere frock.

He helped his mother to get tea ready. Miriam would have gladly proffered, but was afraid. He was rather proud of his home. There was about it now, he thought, a certain distinction. The chairs were only wooden, and the sofa was old. But the hearthrug and cushions were cosy, the pictures were prints in good taste, there was a simplicity in everything, and plenty of books. He was never ashamed in the least of his home, nor was Miriam of hers, because both were what they should be and warm. And then, he was proud of the table; the china was pretty, the cloth was fine: it did not matter that the spoons were not silver, nor the knives ivory-handled; everything looked nice. Mrs Morel had managed wonderfully, while her children were growing up, so that nothing was out of place.

Miriam talked books a little. That was her unfailing topic. But Mrs Morel was not cordial, and turned soon to Edgar.

At first Edgar and Miriam used to go into Mrs Morel's pew. Morel never went to chapel, preferring the public house. Mrs Morel, like a little champion, sat at the head of her pew, Paul at the other end; and at first Miriam sat next to him. Then the chapel was like home. It was a pretty place, with dark pews, and slim, elegant pillars, and flowers. And the same people had sat in the same places ever since he was a boy. It was wonderfully sweet and soothing to sit there for an hour and a half, next to Miriam, and near to his mother, uniting his two loves under the spell of the place of worship. Then he felt warm and happy and religious at once. And after chapel he walked home with Miriam, whilst Mrs Morel spent the rest of the evening with her old friend Mrs Burns. He was keenly alive on his walks on Sunday nights with Edgar and Miriam. He never went past the pits at night, by the lighted lamp-house, the tall black head-stocks and lines of trucks, past the fans spinning slowly like shadows, without the feeling of Miriam returning to him keen and almost unbearable.

She did not very long occupy the Morels' pew. Her father took one for themselves once more. It was under the little gallery, oppo-site the Morels'. When Paul and his mother came in the chapel, the Leivers' pew was always empty. He was anxious for fear she would not come: it was so far and there were so many rainy Sundays. Then, often very late indeed, she came in with her long stride, her head bowed, her face hidden under her hat of dark green velvet. Her face as she sat opposite was always in shadow. But it gave him a very keen feeling, as if all his soul stirred within him, to see her there. It was not the same glow, happiness and pride, that he felt in having his mother in charge: something more wonderful, less human, and tinged to intensity by a pain, as if there were something he could not get to.

At this time, he was beginning to question the orthodox creed. He was twenty one and she was twenty. She was beginning to dread the spring: he became so wild and hurt her so much. All the way he went cruelly smashing her beliefs. Edgar enjoyed it. He was by nature critical and rather dispassionate. But Miriam suffered exquisite pain, as, with an intellect like a knife, the man she loved examined her religion in which she lived and moved and had her being. But he did not spare her. He was cruel. And when they went alone he was even more fierce, as if he would kill her soul. He bled her beliefs till she almost lost consciousness.

"She exults—she exults as she carries him off from me," Mrs Morel cried in her heart, when Paul had gone. "She's not like an ordinary woman, who can leave me my share in him. She wants to absorb him. She wants to draw him out and absorb him till there is nothing left of him, even for himself. He will never be a man on his own feet—she will suck him up." So the mother sat and battled and brooded bitterly.

And he, coming home from his walks with Miriam, was wild with torture. He walked biting his lips and with clenched fists, going at a great rate. Then, brought up against a stile, he stood for some minutes and did not move. There was a great hollow of darkness fronting him, and on the black upslopes, patches of tiny lights, and in the lowest trough of the night, a flare of the pit. It was all weird and dreadful. Why was he torn so, almost bewildered and unable to move? Why did his mother sit at home and suffer? He knew she suffered badly. But why should she? And why did he hate Miriam, and feel so cruel towards her, at the thought of his mother? If Miriam caused his mother suffering then he hated her. And he easily hated her. Why did she make him feel as if he were uncertain of himself, insecure, an indefinite thing, as if he had not sufficient sheathing to prevent the night and the space breaking into him? How he hated her! And then, what a rush of tenderness and humility!

Suddenly he plunged on again, running home. His mother saw on him the marks of some agony, and she said nothing. But he had to make her talk to him. Then she was angry with him for going so far with Miriam.

"Why don't you like her, mother?" he cried in despair.

"I don't know, my boy," she replied piteously. "I'm sure I've tried to like her, I've tried and tried—but I can't, I can't—."

And he felt dreary and hopeless, between the two.

Spring was the worst time. He was changeable and intense and cruel. So he decided to stay away from her. Then came the hours when he knew Miriam was expecting him. His mother watched him growing restless. He could not go on with his work. He could do nothing. It was as if something were drawing his soul out, towards Willey Farm. Then he put on his hat and went, saying nothing. And his mother knew he was gone. And as soon as he was on the way, he sighed with relief. And when he was with her, he was cruel again.

One day in March, he lay on the bank of Nethermere, with Miriam sitting beside him. It was a glistening, white and blue day. Big clouds, so brilliant, went by overhead, while shadows stole along on the water. The clear spaces in the sky were of clean, cold blue. Paul lay on his back in the old grass, looking up. He could not bear to look at Miriam. She seemed to want him, and he resisted. He resisted all the time. He wanted now to give her passion and tenderness, and he could not. He felt that she wanted the soul out of his body, and not him. All his strength and energy she drew into herself through some channel which united them. She did not want to meet him, so that there were two of them, man and woman together. She wanted to draw all of him into her. It urged him to an intensity like madness. Which fascinated him, as drug taking might.

He was discussing Michael Angelo. It felt to her as if she were fingering the very quivering tissue, the very protoplasm of life, as she heard him. It gave her her deepest satisfaction. And in the end it frightened her. There he lay in the white intensity of his search, and his voice gradually filled her with fear, so level it was, almost inhuman as if in a trance.

"Don't talk any more," she pleaded softly, laying her hand on his forehead. He lay quite still, almost unable to move. His body was somewhere discarded.

"Why not—are you tired?"

"Yes, and it wears you out."

He laughed shortly, realising.

"Yet you always make me like it," he said.

"I don't wish to," she said, very low.

"Not when you've gone too far, and you feel you can't bear it. But your unconscious self always asks it of me. And I suppose I want it."

"Then how can I help it?"

"I suppose you can't. Yet you always do it. You switch me off somewhere, and project me out of myself. I am quite ghostish, disembodied."

"Don't!" she pleaded.

"Even now," he continued. "Even now, I look at my hands, and wonder what they are doing there. That water there ripples right through me. I'm sure I am that rippling. It runs right through me, and I through it. There are no barriers between us."

"But—!" she stumbled.

"A sort of disseminated consciousness, that's all there is of me. I feel as if my body were lying empty, as if I were in the other things—clouds and water—"

She looked at him, and saw in him that strange look, as if he were a thing and not a person, which fascinated her so, and which she feared. Yet, because she feared, she must have more. But now she wanted him to stop.

"You see," he went on, "the individual bodily me is discarded. But if so then I am not alive here. I'm sure it would destroy me.

What you want to do is to make me fat, and normal, not shadowy. You want to fix my soul well in its sheath. It'll slip out, like the sword that slipped out of a loose scabbard and fell into the sea, one of these days."

Miriam pondered bitterly. Suddenly she lifted her head and looked at him with shining eyes.

"Then let me be the sheath to you," she said.

Her hands fluttered towards him.

"If you could," he said. "But you are what your unconscious self makes you, not so much what you want to be. We're neither of us quite normal—but now I want to be, and I don't think you do. You want to be nothing ordinary."

"I don't," she cried. But there was fear again in her voice.

"At any rate," he went on, in his dead fashion, "not now. You can't take me that way now. Because both you and me are only souls this minute, bloodless. And it would set up another vibration that would criss-cross with this like veritable torture.—If only you could want *me*, and not want what I can reel off for you!"

"I!" she cried bitterly. "I! Why when would you let me take you?"

"Then it's my fault," he said, and gathering himself together, he got up and began to talk trivialities. He felt insubstantial. In a vague way, he hated her for it. And he knew he was as much to blame himself. This however, did not prevent his hating her.

One evening about this time he had walked along the home road with her. They stood by the pasture leading down to the wood, unable to part. As the stars came out the clouds closed. They had glimpses of their own constellation, Orion, towards the west. His jewels glimmered for a moment, his dog ran low, struggling with difficulty through the spume of cloud.

Orion was for them chief in significance among the constellations. They had gazed at him in their strange, surcharged hours of feeling, until they seemed themselves to live in every one of his stars. This evening Paul had been moody and perverse. Orion had seemed just an ordinary constellation to him. He had fought against his glamour and fascination. Miriam was watching her lover's mood carefully. But he said nothing that gave him away, till the moment came to part, when he stood frowning gloomily at the gathered clouds, behind which the great constellation must be striding still.

There was to be a little party at his house the next day, at which she was to attend.

"I shan't come and meet you," he said.

"Oh very well—it's not very nice out," she replied slowly.

"It's not that—only they don't like me to. They say I care more for you than for them. And you understand, don't you?—you know it's only friendship."

Miriam was astonished and hurt for him. It had cost him an effort. She left him, wanting to spare him any further humiliation. A fine rain blew in her face as she walked along the road. She was hurt deep down. And she despised him, for being blown about by any wind of authority. And in her heart of hearts, unconsciously, she felt that he was trying to get away from her. This she would never have acknowledged. She pitied him.

At this time Paul became an important factor in Jordan's warehouse. Mr Pappleworth left to set up a business of his own, and Paul remained with Mr Jordan as Spiral Overseer. His wages were to be raised to thirty shillings at the year end, if things went well.

Still on Friday night Miriam often came down for her French lesson. Paul did not go so frequently to Willey Farm, and she grieved at the thought of her education's coming to an end; moreover they both loved to be together, in spite of discords. So they read Balzac, and did compositions, and felt highly cultured.

Friday night was reckoning night for the miners. Morel 'reckoned'—shared up the money of the stall—either in the New Inn at Bretty, or in his own house, according as his fellow butties wished. Barker had turned a non-drinker, so now the men reckoned at Morel's house.

Annie, who had been teaching away, was at home again. She was still a tomboy. And she was engaged to be married. Paul was studying design.

Morel was always in good spirits on Friday evening, unless the week's earnings were small. He bustled immediately after his dinner, prepared to get washed. It was decorum for the women to absent themselves while the men reckoned. Women were not supposed to spy into such a masculine privacy as the butties' reckoning—nor were they to know the exact amount of the week's earnings. So, whilst her father was spluttering in the scullery, Annie went out to spend an hour with a neighbour. Mrs Morel attended to her baking.

"Shut that doo-er!" bawled Morel furiously.

Annie banged it behind her and was gone.

"If tha oppens it again while I'm weshin' me, I'll ma'e thy jaw rattle," he threatened, from the midst of his soapsuds. Paul and the mother frowned to hear him.

Presently he came running out of the scullery with the soapy water dripping from him, dithering with cold.

"Oh my sirs!" he said. "Wheer's my towel?"

It was hung on a chair to warm before the fire, otherwise he would have bullied and blustered. He squatted on his heels before the hot baking-fire, to dry himself.

"F-ff-f!" he went, pretending to shudder with cold.

"Goodness man, don't be such a kid!" said Mrs Morel. "It's *not* cold."

"Thee strip thysen stark nak'd to wesh thy flesh i' that scullery," said the miner, as he rubbed his hair; "nowt b'r a h'ice-'ouse!"

"And I shouldn't make that fuss," replied his wife.

"No, tha'd drop down stiff, as dead as a door-knob, wi' thy nesh sides."

"Why is a door-knob deader than anything else?" asked Paul, curious.

"Eh I dunno—that's what they say," replied his father. "But there's that much draught i' yon scullery, as it blows through your ribs like through a five-barred gate."

"It would have some difficulty in blowing through yours," said Mrs Morel.

Morel looked down ruefully at his sides.

"Me!" he exclaimed. "I'm nowt b'r a skinned rabbit. My bones fair juts out on me."

"I should like to know where," retorted his wife.

"Iv'ry-wheer! I'm nobbut a sack o' faggots."

Mrs Morel laughed. He had still a wonderfully young body, muscular, without any fat. His skin was smooth and clear. It might have been the body of a man of twenty eight, except that there were perhaps too many blue scars, like tattoo marks, where the coal-dust remained under the skin, and that his chest was too hairy. But he put his hands on his sides ruefully. It was his fixed belief that, because he did not get fat, he was as thin as a starved rat.

Paul looked at his father's thick, brownish hands, all scarred, with broken nails, rubbing the fine smoothness of his sides, and the incongruity struck him. It seemed strange they were the same flesh.

"I suppose," he said to his father, "you had a good figure once."

"Eh!" exclaimed the miner, glancing round startled and timid, like a child.

"He had," exclaimed Mrs Morel. "If he didn't hurtle himself up as if he was trying to get in the smallest space he could."

"Me!" exclaimed Morel. "Me a good figure! I wor niver much more n'r a skeleton."

"Man!" cried his wife, "don't be such a pulamiter!"

"'Strewth!" he said. "Tha's niver knowed me but what I looked as if I wor goin' off in a rapid decline."

She sat and laughed.

"You've had a constitution like iron," she said. "And never a man had a better start, if it was body that counted. You should have seen him as a young man—" she cried suddenly to Paul, drawing herself up to imitate her husband's once handsome bearing. Morel watched her shyly. He saw again the passion she had had for him. It blazed upon her for a moment. He was shy, rather scared, and humble. Yet again he felt his old glow. And then, immediately, he felt the ruin he had made during these years. He wanted to bustle about, to run away from it.

"Gi'e my back a bit of a wesh," he asked her.

His wife brought a well-soaped flannel and clapped it on his shoulders. He gave a jump.

"Eh tha mucky little 'ussy!" he cried. "Cowd as death!"

"You ought to have been a salamander," she laughed, washing his back. It was very rarely she would do anything so personal for him. The children did those things.

"The next world won't be half hot enough for you," she added.

"No," he said, "tha'lt see as it's draughty for me."

But she had finished. She wiped him in a desultory fashion and went upstairs, returning immediately with his shifting-trousers. When he was dried he struggled into his shirt. Then, ruddy and shiny, with hair on end, and his flannelette shirt hanging over his pit-trousers, he stood warming the garments he was going to put on. He turned them, he pulled them inside out, he scorched them.

"Goodness man," cried Mrs Morel, "get dressed!"

"Should thee like to clap thysen into britches as cowd as a tub o' watter!" he said.

At last he took off his pit trousers and donned decent black. He did all this on the hearthrug, as he would have done if Annie and her familiar friends had been present.

Mrs Morel turned the bread in the oven. Then from the red earthenware panchion of dough that stood in a corner she took another handful of paste, worked it to the proper shape, and dropped it into a tin. As she was doing so Barker knocked and entered. He was a quiet, compact little man who looked as if he would go through a stone wall. His black hair was cropped short, his head was bony. Like most miners, he was pale, but healthy and taut.

"Evenin' Missis," he nodded to Mrs Morel, and he seated himself with a sigh.

"Good evening," she replied cordially.

"Tha's made thy heels crack," said Morel.

"I dunno as I have," said Barker.

He sat, as the men always did in Mrs Morel's kitchen, effacing himself rather.

"How's Missis?" she asked of him.

He had told her some time back:—

"We're expectin' us third just now, you see—"

"Well," he answered, rubbing his head, "she keeps pretty middlin' I think."

"Let's see, when—?" asked Mrs Morel.

"Well—I shouldn't be surprised any time now—"

"Ah! And she's kept fairly?"

"Yes—tidy!"

"That's a blessing, for she's none too strong."

"No.—An' I've done another silly trick."

"What's that?"

Mrs Morel knew Barker wouldn't do anything very silly.

"I'n come be-out th' market bag."

"You can have mine."

"Nay, you'll be wantin' that yourself."

"I shan't—I take a string bag—always."

She saw the determined little collier buying in the week's groceries and meat on the Friday nights, and she admired him. 'Barker's little, but he's ten times the man you are,' she said to her husband.

Just then Wesson entered. He was thin, rather frail looking, with a boyish ingenuousness and a slightly foolish smile, despite his seven children. But his wife was a passionate woman.

"I see you've kested me," he said, smiling rather vapidly.

"Yes," replied Barker.

The newcomer took off his cap and his big woollen muffler. His nose was pointed and red.

"I'm afraid you're cold, Mr Wesson," said Mrs Morel.

"It's a bit nippy," he replied.

"Then come to the fire."

"Nay, I s'll do wheer I am."

Both colliers sat away back. They could not be induced to come onto the hearth. The hearth is sacred to the family.

"Go thy ways i' th' armchair," cried Morel, cheerily.

"Nay, thank yer, I'm very nicely here."

"Yes, come of course," insisted Mrs Morel.

He rose and went awkwardly. He sat in Morel's armchair awkwardly. It was too great a familiarity. But the fire made him blissfully happy.

"And how's that chest of yours?" demanded Mrs Morel.

He smiled again, with his blue eyes rather sunny.

"Oh, it's very middlin'," he said.

"Wi' a rattle in it like a kettle-drum," said Barker shortly.

"T-t-t-t!" went Mrs Morel rapidly with her tongue. "Did you have that flannel singlet made?"

"Not yet," he smiled.

"Then why didn't you?" she cried.

"It'll come," he smiled.

"Ah, an' Doomsday!" exclaimed Barker.

Barker and Morel were both impatient of Wesson. But then they were both as hard as nails, physically.

When Morel was nearly ready, he pushed the bag of money to Paul.

"Count it, boy," he asked, humbly.

Paul impatiently turned from his books and pencil, tipped the bag upside down on the table. There was a £5 bag of silver, sovereigns, and loose money. He counted quickly, referred to the checks, the written papers giving amount of coal, put the money in order. Then Barker glanced at the checks.

Mrs Morel went upstairs, and the three men came to table. Morel, as master of the house, sat in his arm-chair with his back to the hot fire. The two butties had cooler seats. None of them counted the money.

"What did we say Simpson's was?" asked Morel, and the butties cavilled for a minute over the day-man's earnings. Then the amount was put aside.

"An' Bill Naylor's?"

This money also was taken from the pack.

Then, because Wesson lived in one of the company's houses, and his rent had been deducted, Morel and Barker took four-and-six each. And because Morel's coals had come, and the leading was stopped, Barker and Wesson took four shillings each. Then it was plain sailing. Morel gave each of them a sovereign till there were no more sovereigns: each half a crown till there were no more half crowns: each a shilling till there were no more shillings. If there was anything at the end that wouldn't split, Morel took it and stood drinks.

Then the three men rose and went. Morel scuttled out of the house before his wife came down. She heard the door close, and descended. She looked hastily at the bread in the oven. Then, glancing on the table, she saw her money lying. Paul had been working all the time. But now he felt his mother counting the week's money, and her wrath rising.

"T-t-t-t-t!" went her tongue.

He frowned. He could not work when she was cross. She counted again.

"A measly twenty-five shillings!" she exclaimed. "How much was the cheque?"

"Ten pounds eleven," said Paul, irritably. He dreaded what was coming.

"And he gives me a scrattlin' twenty five, an' his club this week! But I know him—he thinks because *you're* earning, he needn't keep the house any longer. No, all he has to do with his money is to guttle it. But I'll show him—"

"Oh mother don't!" cried Paul.

"Don't what, I should like to know?" she exclaimed.

"Don't carry on again—I can't work."

She went very quiet.

"Yes it's all very well," she said. "But how do you think I'm going to manage?"

"Well, it won't make it any better to whittle about it."

"I should like to know what you'd do if you had it to put up with!"

"It won't be long—you can have my money—let him go to Hell."

He went back to his work, and she tied her bonnet strings grimly. When she was fretted he could not bear it. But now he began to insist on her recognising him.

"The two loaves at the top," she said, "will be done in twenty minutes. Don't forget them."

"All right," he answered, and she went to market.

He remained alone working. But his usual intense concentration became unsettled. He listened for the yard gate. At a quarter past seven came a low knock, and Miriam entered.

"All alone?" she said.

"Yes."

As if at home, she took off her tam o'shanter and her long coat, hanging them up. It gave him a thrill. This might be their own house, his and hers.

Then she came back and peered over his work.

"What is it?" she asked.

"Still design—for decorating stuffs, and for embroidery."

She bent short-sightedly over the drawings.

"And you like it?" she asked.

"I love it. I've got a passion for conventionalising things just now."

"Yes."

She did not care for conventional studies. But she thought he knew best about those things. They were men's things, that did not belong to her. And yet—she would know why he had a passion for conventionalising things. What was there in the conventional to fascinate him?

"What makes you like this?" she asked, poring.

He began the old attempt to justify himself. Struggling, he tried to expound to her the theory that the force of gravitation is the great shaper, and that if it had all its own way, it would have a rose in correct geometrical line and proportion—and so on. This created in her some sort of feeling for a conventional drawing, which had before seemed a mere lie to her. At last he scooped all the books away.

"Should I—?" he said, balanced, hesitating.

"What?"

"Show you?—I meant not to till it was done."

He could not keep from her anything he did. He went into the parlour and returned with a bundle of brownish linen. Carefully unfolding it, he spread it on the floor. It proved to be a curtain or portière, beautifully stencilled with a design on roses.

"Ah, how beautiful!" she cried.

The spread cloth with its wonderful reddish roses and dark green stems, all so simple, and somehow so wicked looking, lay at her feet. She went on her knees before it, her dark curls dropping. He saw her crouched voluptuously before his work, and his heart beat quickly. Suddenly she looked up at him.

"Why does it seem cruel?" she asked.

"What?"

"There seems a feeling of cruelty about it," she said.

"It's jolly good, whether or not," he replied, folding up his work with a lover's hands. She rose slowly, pondering.

"And what will you do with it?" she asked.

"Send it to Liberty's. I did it for my mother—but I think she'd rather have the money."

"Yes," said Miriam. He had spoken with a touch of bitterness, and Miriam sympathised. Money would mean nothing to *her*.

He took the cloth back into the parlour. When he returned he threw to Miriam a smaller piece. It was a cushion cover with the same design.

"I did that for you," he said.

She fingered the work with trembling hands, and did not speak. He became embarrassed.

"By Jove, the bread!" he cried.

He took the top loaves out, tapped them vigorously. They were done. He put them on the hearth to cool. Then he went to the scullery, wetted his hands, scooped the last white dough out of the panchion, and dropped it in a baking tin. Miriam was still bent over her painted cloth. He stood rubbing the bits of dough from his hands.

"You do like it?" he asked.

She looked up at him with her dark eyes one flame of love. He laughed uncomfortably. Then he began to talk about the design. There was for him the most intense pleasure in talking about his work to Miriam. All his passion, all his wild blood went into this intercourse with her, when he talked and conceived his work. She brought forth to him his imaginations. She did not understand, any more than a woman understands when she conceives a child in her womb. But this was life for her, and for him.

While they were talking, a young woman of about twenty two, small and pale, hollow eyed, yet with a relentless look about her, entered the room. She was a friend at the Morels'.

241

"Take your things off," said Paul.

"No—I'm not stopping."

She sat down in the arm-chair opposite Paul and Miriam, who were on the sofa. Miriam moved a little further from him. The room was hot, with a scent of new bread. Brown, crisp loaves stood on the hearth.

"I shouldn't have expected to see you here tonight, Miriam Leivers," said Beatrice, wickedly.

"Why not?" murmured Miriam huskily.

"Why let's look at your shoes."

Miriam remained uncomfortably still.

"If tha doesna tha durs'na," laughed Beatrice.

Miriam put her feet from under her dress. Her boots had that queer, irresolute, rather pathetic look about them, which showed how self-conscious and self-mistrustful she was. And they were covered with mud.

"Glory—you're a positive muck-heap!" exclaimed Beatrice. "Who cleans your boots?"

"I clean them myself."

"Then you wanted a job," said Beatrice. "It would ha' taken a lot of men to ha' brought me down here tonight.—But love laughs at sludge—doesn't it, 'Postle my duck?"

"Inter alia," he said.

"Oh Lord, are you going to spout foreign languages!—What does it mean, Miriam?"

There was a fine sarcasm in the last question, but Miriam did not see it.

"'Among other things,' I believe," she said, humbly.

Beatrice put her tongue between her teeth, and laughed wickedly.

"'Among other things,' 'Postle?" she repeated. "Do you mean love laughs at mothers and fathers and sisters and brothers and men friends and lady friends, and even at the b'lovèd himself?"

She affected a great innocence.

"In fact it's one big smile," he replied.

"Up its sleeve, 'Postle Morel—you believe me," she said.

And she went off into another burst of wicked, silent laughter.

Miriam sat silent, withdrawn into herself. Every one of Paul's friends delighted in taking sides against her, and he left her in the lurch, seemed almost to have a sort of revenge upon her then.

"Are you still at school?" asked Miriam of Beatrice.

"Yes."

"You've not had your notice then?"

"I expect it at Easter."

"Isn't it an awful shame, to turn you off merely because you didn't pass the exam!"

"I don't know," said Beatrice, coldly.

"Agatha says you're as good as any teacher anywhere. It seems to me ridiculous. I wonder why you didn't pass!"

"Short of brains, eh 'Postle?" said Beatrice, briefly.

"Only brains to bite with," replied Paul, laughing.

"Nuisance!" she cried, and springing from her seat, she rushed and boxed his ears. She had beautiful small hands. He held her wrists whilst she wrestled with him. At last she broke free and seized two handfuls of his thick, dark brown hair, which she shook.

"Beat," he said, as he pulled his hair straight with his fingers. "I hate you."

She laughed with glee.

"Mind!" she said. "I want to sit next to you."

"I'd as lief be neighbours with a vixen," he said, nevertheless making place for her between him and Miriam.

"Did it ruffle his pretty hair then!" she cried, and, with her hair comb, she combed him straight.

"And his nice little moustache!" she exclaimed. She tilted his head back, and combed his young moustache.

"It's a wicked moustache, 'Postle," she said. "It's a red for danger.—Have you got any of those cigarettes?"

He pulled his cigarette case from his pocket. Beatrice looked inside it.

"None of those nice little whiffs that Connie gave you?" she asked.

"There's one somewhere—."

Rummaging in his pocket, he found a little box. Beatrice took it.

"Oh yes, just one!" she said. "But Miriam ought to have this. Have Connie's remaining fag, Miriam?"

"No thanks," replied Miriam. "Who is Connie?"

"Hasn't he told you?" cried Beatrice, in great surprise. "Well 'Postle Morel, I don't think it's fair to keep a poor girl in the dark."

"Will you try a smoke?" asked Paul of Miriam.

"You know I won't," she answered.

"And fancy me having Connie's last cig.," said Beatrice, putting the thing between her teeth. He held a lit match to her, and she puffed daintily.

"Thanks so much darling," she said, mockingly.

It gave her a wicked delight.

"Don't you think he does it nicely Miriam?" she asked.

"Oh very!" said Miriam.

He took a cigarette for himself.

"Light, old boy?" said Beatrice, tilting her cigarette at him.

He bent forward to her to light his cigarette at hers. She was winking at him as he did so. Miriam saw his eyes trembling with mischief, and his full, almost sensual mouth quivering. He was not himself, and she could not bear it. As he was now, she had no connection with him, she might as well not have existed. She saw the cigarette dancing on his full red lips. She hated his thick hair for being tumbled loose on his forehead.

"Sweet boy!" said Beatrice, tipping up his chin and giving him a little kiss on the cheek.

"I s'll kiss thee back, Beat," he said.

"Tha wunna!" she giggled, jumping up and going away. "Isn't he shameless, Miriam?"

"Quite!" said Miriam. "By the way, aren't you forgetting the bread?"

"By Jove!" he cried, flinging open the oven door. Out puffed the bluish smoke, and a smell of burned bread.

"Oh Golly!" cried Beatrice, coming to his side. He crouched before the oven, she peered over his shoulder. "This is what comes of the oblivion of love my boy."

Paul was ruefully removing the loaves. One was burnt black on the hot side, another was hard as a brick.

"Poor mater!" said Paul.

"You want to grate it," said Beatrice. "Fetch me the nutmeg grater."

She arranged the bread in the oven. He brought the grater, and she grated the bread onto a newspaper on the table. He set the doors open to blow away the smell of burned bread. Beatrice grated away, puffing her cigarette, knocking the charcoal off the poor loaf.

"My word Miriam, you're in for it this time," said Beatrice.

"I!" exclaimed Miriam in amazement.

"You'd better be gone when his mother comes in.—*I* know why

King Alfred burned the cakes. Now I see it. 'Postle would fix up a
tale about his work making him forget, if he thought it would wash.
If that old woman had come in a bit sooner, she'd have boxed the
brazen thing's ears who made the oblivion, instead of poor
Alfred's—"

She giggled as she scraped the loaf. Even Miriam laughed in spite
of herself. Paul mended the fire, ruefully.

The garden gate was heard to bang.

"Quick!" cried Beatrice, giving Paul the scraped loaf. "Wrap it up
in a damp towel."

Paul disappeared into the scullery. Beatrice hastily blew her
scrapings into the fire, and sat down innocently. Annie came bursting in. She was an abrupt, quite smart young woman. She blinked in
the strong light.

"Smell of burning!" she exclaimed.

"It's the cigarettes," replied Beatrice demurely.

"Where's Paul?"

Leonard had followed Annie. He had a long, comic face and blue
eyes very sad.

"I suppose he's left you to settle it between you," he said.

He nodded sympathetically to Miriam, and became gently sarcastic to Beatrice.

"No," said Beatrice, "he's gone off with number nine."

"I just met number five inquiring for him," said Leonard.

"Yes—we're going to share him up like Solomon's baby," said
Beatrice.

Annie laughed.

"Oh ay?" said Leonard. "And which bit should you have?"

"I don't know," said Beatrice. "I'll let all the others pick first."

"An' you'd have the leavings, like?" said Leonard, twisting up a
comic face.

Annie was looking in the oven. Miriam sat ignored. Paul entered.

"This bread's a fine sight, our Paul," said Annie.

"Then you should stop an' look after it," said Paul.

"You mean *you* should do what you're reckoning to do," replied
Annie.

"He should, shouldn't he!" cried Beatrice.

"I s'd think he'd got plenty on hand," said Leonard.

"You had a nasty walk, didn't you Miriam?" said Annie.

"Yes—but I'd been in all week—"

245

Sons and Lovers

"And you wanted a bit of a change, like," insinuated Leonard kindly.

"Well, you can't be stuck in the house for ever," Annie agreed. She was quite amiable. Beatrice pulled on her coat, and went out with Leonard and Annie. She would meet her own boy.

"Don't forget that bread, our Paul," cried Annie. "Goodnight Miriam, I don't think it will rain."

When they had all gone, Paul fetched the swathed loaf, unwrapped it, and surveyed it sadly.

"It's a mess!" he said.

"But," answered Miriam impatiently, "what is it, after all—twopence ha'penny."

"Yes but—it's the mater's precious baking, and she'll take it to heart.—However, it's no good bothering."

He took the loaf back into the scullery. There was a little distance between him and Miriam. He stood balanced opposite her for some moments, considering, thinking of his behaviour with Beatrice. He felt guilty inside himself, and yet glad. For some inscrutable reason, it served Miriam right. He was not going to repent. She wondered what he was thinking of, as he stood suspended. His thick hair was tumbled over his forehead. Why might she not push it back for him, and remove the marks of Beatrice's comb? Why might she not press his body with her two hands. It looked so firm and every whit living. And he would let other girls, why not her?

Suddenly he started into life. It made her quiver almost with terror as he quickly pushed the hair off his forehead and came towards her.

"Half past eight!" he said. "We'd better buck up. Where's your French?"

Miriam shyly and rather bitterly produced her exercise book. Every week she wrote for him a sort of diary of her inner life, in her own French. He had found this was the only way to get her to do compositions. And her diary was mostly a love-letter. He would read it now; she felt as if her soul's history were going to be desecrated by him in his present mood. He sat beside her. She watched his hand, firm and warm, rigorously scoring her work.

He was reading only the French, ignoring her soul that was there. But gradually his hand forgot its work. He read in silence, motionless. She quivered.

"Ce matin les oiseaux m'ont éveillé," he read. "Il faisait encore

246

un crépuscule. Mais la petite fenêtre de ma chambre était blême, et
puis, jaûne, et tous les oiseaux du bois éclatèrent dans un chanson
vif et résonnant. Toute l'aûbe tressaillit. J'avais rêvé de vous. Est-ce
que vous voyez aussi l'aûbe? Les oiseaux m'éveillent presque tous
les matins, et toujours il y a quelque chose de terreur dans le cri des
grives. Il est si clair— —"

Miriam sat tremulous, half ashamed. He remained quite still,
trying to understand. He only knew she loved him. He was afraid of
her love for him. It was too good for him, and he was inadequate.
His own love was at fault, not hers. Ashamed, he corrected her work,
humbly writing above her words.

"Look," he said quietly, "the past participle conjugated with
'avoir' agrees with the direct object when it precedes."

She bent forward, trying to see and to understand. Her free, fine
curls tickled his face. He started as if they had been red hot,
shuddering. He saw her peering forward at the page, her red lips
parted piteously, the black hair springing in fine strands across her
tawny ruddy cheek. She was coloured like a pomegranate for rich-
ness. His breaths came short as he watched her. Suddenly she
looked up at him. Her dark eyes were naked with their love, afraid,
and yearning. His eyes too were dark, and they hurt her. They
seemed to master her. She lost all her self control, was exposed in
fear. And he knew, before he could kiss her, he must drive something out of himself. And a touch of hate for her crept back again
into his heart. He returned to her exercise.

Suddenly he flung down the pencil, and was at the oven in a leap,
turning the bread. For Miriam he was too quick. She started
violently, and it hurt her with real pain. Even the way he crouched
before the oven hurt her. There seemed to her something cruel in it,
something cruel in the swift way he pitched the bread out of the tins,
caught it up again. If only he had been gentle in his movements, she
would have felt so rich and warm. As it was, she was hurt.

He returned and finished the exercise.

"You've done well this week," he said.

She saw he was flattered by her diary. It did not repay her entirely.

"You really do blossom out sometimes," he said. "You ought to
write poetry."

She lifted her head with joy, then she shook it mistrustfully.

"I don't trust myself," she said.

"You should try!"

Again she shook her head.

"Shall we read, or is it too late?" he asked.

"It is late—but we can read just a little," she pleaded.

She was really getting now the food for her life during the next week. He made her copy Baudelaire's 'Le Balcon.' Then he read it for her. His voice was soft and caressing, but growing almost brutal. He had a way of lifting his lips and showing his teeth, passionately and bitterly, when he was much moved. This he did now. It made Miriam feel as if he were trampling on her. She dared not look at him, but sat with her head bowed. She could not understand why he got into such a tumult and fury. It made her wretched. She did not like Baudelaire, on the whole—nor Verlaine.

> "Behold her singing in the field
> Yon solitary highland lass—"

That nourished her heart—so did 'Fair Ines.' And:

> "It was a beauteous evening, calm and pure,
> And breathing holy quiet like a nun—"

These were like herself. And there was he, saying in his throat, bitterly:

> "Tu te rappelleras la beauté des caresses."

The poem was finished, he took the bread out of the oven, arranging the burnt loaves at the bottom of the panchion, the good ones at the top. The desiccated loaf remained swathed up in the scullery.

"Mater needn't know till morning," he said. "It won't upset her so much then, as at night."

Miriam looked in the book-case, saw what postcards and letters he had received, saw what books were there. She took one that had interested him. Then he turned down the gas and they set off. He did not trouble to lock the door.

He was not home again until a quarter to eleven. His mother was seated in the rocking-chair. Annie, with a rope of hair hanging down her back, remained sitting on a low stool before the fire, her elbows on her knees, gloomily. On the table stood the offending loaf, unswathed. Paul entered rather breathless. No one spoke. His mother was reading the little local newspaper. He took off his coat, and went to sit down on the sofa. His mother moved curtly aside to let him pass. No one spoke. He was very uncomfortable. For some minutes he sat pretending to read a piece of paper he found on the table. Then:

"I forgot that bread mother," he said.

There was no answer from either woman.

"Well," he said, "it's only two-pence ha'penny. I can pay you for that."

Being angry, he put three pennies on the table and slid them towards his mother. She turned away her head. Her mouth was shut tightly.

"Yes," said Annie, "you don't know how badly my mother is!"

The girl sat staring glumly into the fire.

"Why is she badly?" asked Paul, in his overbearing way.

"Well!" said Annie. "She could scarcely get home."

He looked closely at his mother. She looked ill.

"*Why* could you scarcely get home?" he asked her, still sharply. She would not answer.

"I found her as white as a sheet, sitting here," said Annie, with a suggestion of tears in her voice.

"Well *why*?" insisted Paul. His brows were knitting, his eyes dilating passionately.

"It was enough to upset anybody," said Mrs Morel; "hugging those parcels—meat, and green-groceries and a pair of curtains——"

"Well, why *did* you hug them, you needn't have done."

"Then who would?"

"Let Annie fetch the meat."

"Yes, and I *would* fetch the meat, but how was I to know. You were off with Miriam, instead of being in when my mother came."

"And what was the matter with you?" asked Paul of his mother.

"I suppose it's my heart," she replied. Certainly she looked bluish round the mouth.

"And have you felt it before?"

"Yes—often enough."

"Then why haven't you told me, and why haven't you seen a doctor?"

Mrs Morel shifted in her chair, angry with him for his hectoring.

"You'd never notice anything," said Annie. "You're too eager to be off with Miriam."

"Oh am I—and any worse than you with Leonard?"

"*I* was in at a quarter to ten."

There was silence in the room for a time.

"I should have thought," said Mrs Morel bitterly, "that she wouldn't have occupied you so entirely, as to burn a whole ovenful of bread."

"Beatrice was here as well as she."

"Very likely. But we know why the bread is spoilt."

"Why?" he flashed.

"Because you were engrossed with Miriam," replied Mrs Morel hotly.

"Oh very well—then it was *not!*" he replied angrily.

He was distressed and wretched. Seizing a paper, he began to read. Annie, her blouse unfastened, her long ropes of hair twisted into a plait, went up to bed, bidding him a very curt goodnight.

Paul sat pretending to read. He knew his mother wanted to upbraid him. He also wanted to know what had made her ill, for he was troubled. So, instead of running away to bed, as he would have liked to do, he sat and waited. There was a tense silence. The clock ticked loudly.

"You'd better go to bed before your father comes in," said the mother, harshly. "And if you're going to have anything to eat, you'd better get it."

"I don't want anything."

It was his mother's custom to bring him some trifle for supper on Friday night, the night of luxury for the colliers. He was too angry now to go and find it in the pantry this night. This insulted her.

"If I *wanted* you to go to Selby on Friday night, I can imagine the scene," said Mrs Morel. "But you're never too tired to go if *she* will come for you. Nay, you neither want to eat nor drink then."

"I can't let her go alone."

"Can't you—and why does she come?"

"Not because I ask her."

"She doesn't come without you want her—"

"Well, what if I *do* want her—!" he replied.

"Why, nothing, if it was sensible or reasonable. But to go trapseing up there miles and miles in the mud, coming home at midnight, and got to go to Nottingham in the morning—"

"If I hadn't, you'd be just the same."

"Yes I should, because there's no sense in it. Is she *so* fascinating, that you must follow her all that way—?" Mrs Morel was bitterly sarcastic. She sat still, with averted face, stroking with a rhythmic, jerked movement, the black sateen of her apron. It was a movement that hurt Paul to see.

"I do like her," he said, "but——."

"*Like* her!" said Mrs Morel, in the same biting tones. "It seems to me you like nothing and nobody else. There's neither Annie, nor me, nor anyone now for you."

"What nonsense, mother—you know I don't love her—I—I tell you I *don't* love her—she doesn't even walk with my arm, because I don't want her to."

"Then why do you fly to her so often?"

"I *do* like to talk to her—I never said I didn't. But I *don't* love her."

"Is there nobody else to talk to?"

"Not about the things we talk of. There's lots of things that you're not interested in, that——"

"What things—?"

Mrs Morel was so intense that Paul began to pant.

"Why—painting—and books. *You* don't care about Herbert Spencer."

"No," was the sad reply. "And *you* won't at my age."

"Well, but I do now—and Miriam does——"

"And how do you know," Mrs Morel flashed defiantly, "that *I* shouldn't. Do you ever try me—!"

"But you don't, mother, you know you don't care whether a picture's decorative or not—you don't care what *manner* it is in."

"How do you know I don't care—do you ever try me? Do you ever talk to me about these things, to try?"

"But it's not that that matters to you mother, you know it's not."

"What is it then—what is it then that matters to me," she flashed. He knitted his brows with pain.

"You're old, mother, and we're young."

He only meant that the interests of *her* age, were not the interests of his. But he realised the moment he had spoken, that he had said the wrong thing.

"Yes, I know it well—I am old! And therefore I may stand aside, I have nothing more to do with you. You only want me to wait on you—the rest is for Miriam."

He could not bear it. Instinctively, he realised that he was life to her. And after all she was the chief thing to him, the only supreme thing.

"You know it isn't, mother, you know it isn't."

She was moved to pity by his cry.

"It looks a great deal like it," she said, half putting aside her despair.

"No mother—I really *don't* love her. I talk to her—but I want to come home to you."

He had taken off his collar and tie, and rose, bare-throated, to go to bed. As he stooped to kiss his mother, she threw her arms round his neck, hid her face on his shoulder, and cried, in a whimpering voice, so unlike her own that he writhed in agony:

"I can't bear it. I could let another woman—but not her—she'd leave me no room, not a bit of room—"

And immediately he hated Miriam bitterly.

"And I've never—you know, Paul—I've never had a husband—not really—"

He stroked his mother's hair, and his mouth was on her throat.

"And she exults so in taking you from me—she's not like ordinary girls."

"Well, I don't love her, mother," he murmured, bowing his head and hiding his eyes on her shoulder in misery. His mother kissed him a long, fervent kiss:

"My boy!" she said, in a voice trembling with passionate love. Without knowing, he gently stroked her face.

"There," said his mother, "now go to bed. You'll be *so* tired in the morning."

As she was speaking, she heard her husband coming.

"There's your father—now go.—" Suddenly she looked at him almost as if in fear. "Perhaps I'm selfish. If you want her, take her, my boy."

His mother looked so strange, Paul kissed her, trembling.

"Ha—mother!" he said softly.

Morel came in, walking unevenly. His hat was over one corner of his eye. He balanced in the doorway.

"At your mischief again?" he said, venomously.

Mrs Morel's emotion turned into sudden hate of the drunkard who had come in thus upon her.

"At any rate, it is sober," she said.

"Hm—hm! hm—hm!" he sneered.

He went into the passage, hung up his hat and coat. Then they heard him go down three steps to the pantry. He returned with a piece of pork-pie in his fist. It was what Mrs Morel had bought for her son.

"Nor was that bought for you. If you can give me no more than twenty five shillings, I'm sure I'm not going to buy you pork-pie to stuff, after you've swilled a belly-ful of beer."

"Wha-at—wha-at!" snarled Morel, toppling in his balance. "Wha-at—not for me?" He looked at the piece of meat and crust, and suddenly, in a vicious spurt of temper, flung it into the fire.

Paul started to his feet.

"Waste your own stuff," he cried.

"What—what!!" suddenly shouted Morel, jumping up and clenching his fist. "I'll show yer yer young jockey—!"

"All right!" said Paul viciously, putting his head on one side. "Show me—!"

He would at that moment dearly have loved to have a smack at something. Morel was half crouching, fists up, ready to spring. The young man stood, smiling with his lips.

"—Ussha!" hissed the father, swiping round with a great stroke, just past his son's face. He dared not, even though so close, really touch the young man, but swerved an inch away.

"Right!" said Paul, his eyes upon the side of his father's mouth, where in another instant his fist would have hit. He ached for that stroke. But he heard a faint moan from behind. His mother was deadly pale, and dark at the mouth. Morel was dancing up to deliver another blow.

"Father!" said Paul, so that the word rang.

Morel started, and stood at attention.

"Mother!" moaned the boy. "Mother!"

She began to struggle with herself. Her open eyes watched him, although she could not move. Gradually she was coming to herself. He laid her down on the sofa, ran upstairs for a little whiskey, which at last she could sip. The tears were hopping down his face. As he knelt in front of her, he did not cry, but the tears ran down his face quickly. Morel, on the opposite side of the room, sat with his elbows on his knees, glaring across.

"What's a-matter with 'er?" he asked.

"Faint!" replied Paul.

"Hm!"

The elderly man began to unlace his boots. He stumbled off to bed. His last fight was fought in that home.

Paul knelt there, stroking his mother's hand.

"Don't be poorly, mother—don't be poorly!" he said, time after time.

"It's nothing, my boy," she murmured.

At last he rose, fetched in a large piece of coal, and raked the fire. Then he cleared the room, put everything straight, laid the things for breakfast, and brought his mother's candle.

"Can you go to bed, mother?"

"Yes, I'll come."

"Sleep with Annie, mother, not with him."

"No, I'll sleep in my own bed."

"Don't sleep with him, mother."

"I'll sleep in my own bed."

She rose, and he turned out the gas, then followed her closely up stairs, carrying her candle. On the landing he kissed her close.

"Goodnight mother."

"Goodnight!" she said.

He pressed his face upon the pillow in a fury of misery. And yet, somewhere in his soul, he was at peace because still he loved his mother best. It was the bitter peace of resignation.

The efforts of his father to conciliate him next day were a great humiliation to him.

Everybody tried to forget the scene.

CHAPTER IX

Defeat of Miriam

Paul was dissatisfied with himself and with everything. The deepest of his love belonged to his mother. When he felt he had hurt her, or wounded his love for her, he could not bear it. Now it was spring and there was battle between him and Miriam. This year he had a good deal against her. She was vaguely aware of it. The old feeling that she was to be a sacrifice to this love, which she had had when she prayed, was mingled in all her emotions. She did not at the bottom believe she ever would have him. She did not believe in herself, primarily: doubted whether she could ever be what he would demand of her. Certainly she never saw herself living happily through a life-time with him. She saw tragedy, sorrow, and sacrifice ahead. And in sacrifice she was proud, in renunciation she was strong; for she did not trust herself to support everyday life. She was prepared for the big things and the deep things, like tragedy. It was the sufficiency of the small day-life she could not trust.

The Easter holidays began happily. Paul was his own frank self. Yet she felt it would go wrong. On the Sunday afternoon she stood at her bedroom window, looking across at the oak-trees of the wood, in whose branches a twilight was tangled, below the bright sky of the afternoon. Grey-green rosettes of honeysuckle leaves hung before the window, some already, she fancied, showing bud. It was spring, which she loved and dreaded.

Hearing the clack of the gate, she stood in suspense. It was a bright grey day. Paul came into the yard with his bicycle, which glittered as he walked. Usually he rang his bell and laughed towards the house. Today he walked with shut lips, and cold, cruel bearing, that had something of a slouch and a sneer in it. She knew him well by now, and could tell from that keen-looking, aloof young body of his what was happening inside him. There was a cold correctness in the way he put his bicycle in its place, that made her heart sink.

She came downstairs nervously. She was wearing a new net blouse, that she thought became her. It had a high collar with a tiny ruff, reminding her of Mary Queen of Scots, and making her, she thought, look wonderfully a woman, and dignified. At twenty, she was full-breasted and luxuriously formed. Her face was still like a soft rich mask, unchangeable. But her eyes, once lifted, were wonderful. She was afraid of him. He would notice her new blouse.

He, being in a hard, ironical mood, was entertaining the family to a description of a service given in the Primitive Methodist Chapel, conducted by one of the well-known preachers of the sect. He sat at the head of the table, his mobile face, with the eyes that could be so beautiful, shining with tenderness or dancing with laughter, now taking on one expression and then another, in imitation of various people he was mocking. His mockery always hurt her—it was too near the reality. He was too clever and cruel. She felt that when his eyes were like this, hard with mocking hate, he would spare neither himself nor anybody else. But Mrs Leivers was wiping her eyes with laughter, and Mr Leivers, just awake from his Sunday nap, was rubbing his head in amusement. The three brothers sat with ruffled, sleepy appearance, in their shirt sleeves, giving a guffaw from time to time. The whole family loved a "take-off" more than anything.

He took no notice of Miriam. Later, she saw him remark her new blouse, saw that the artist approved, but it won from him not a spark of warmth. She was nervous, could hardly reach the tea-cups from the shelves.

When the men went out to milk, she ventured to address him personally.

"You were late," she said.

"Was I?" he answered.

There was silence for awhile.

"Was it rough riding?" she asked.

"I didn't notice it."

She continued quickly to lay the table. When she had finished,

"Tea won't be for a few minutes. Will you come and look at the daffodils?" she said.

He rose without answering. They went out into the back garden, under the budding damson trees. The hills and the sky were clean and cold. Everything looked washed, rather hard. Miriam glanced at Paul. He was pale and impassive. It seemed cruel to her that his eyes and brows, which she loved, could look so hurting.

"Has the wind made you tired?" she asked.

She detected an underneath feeling of weariness about him.

"No, I think not," he answered.

"It must be rough on the road—the wood moans so."

"You can see by the clouds it's a south-west wind: that helps me here."

"You see I don't cycle, so I don't understand," she murmured.

"Is there need to cycle to know that?" he said.

She thought his sarcasms were unnecessary. They went forward in silence. Round the wild, tussocky lawn at the back of the house was a thorn hedge, under which daffodils were craning forward from among their sheaves of grey-green blades. The cheeks of the flowers were greenish with cold. But still some had burst, and their gold ruffled and glowed. Miriam went on her knees before one cluster, took a wild looking daffodil between her hands, turned up its face of gold to her, and bowed down, caressing it with her mouth and cheeks and brow. He stood aside with his hands in his pockets, watching her. One after another she turned up to him the faces of the yellow, bursten flowers, appealingly, fondling them lavishly all the while.

"Aren't they magnificent?" she murmured.

"Magnificent!—it's a bit thick!—they're pretty!"

She bowed again to her flowers at his censure of her praise. He watched her crouching, sipping the flowers with fervid kisses.

"Why must you always be fondling things!" he said, irritably.

"But I love to touch them," she replied, hurt.

"Can you never like things without clutching them as if you wanted to pull the heart out of them? Why don't you have a bit more restraint or reserve or something?"

She looked up at him, full of pain, then continued slowly to stroke her lips against a ruffled flower. Their scent, as she smelled it, was so much kinder than he, it almost made her cry.

"You wheedle the soul out of things," he said. "I would never wheedle—at any rate I'd go straight."

He scarcely knew what he was saying. These things came from him mechanically. She looked at him. His body seemed one weapon, firm and hard against her.

"You're always begging things to love you," he said, "as if you were a beggar for love. Even the flowers, you have to fawn on them—"

Rhythmically, Miriam was swaying and stroking the flower with her mouth, inhaling the scent which ever after made her shudder as it came to her nostrils.

"You don't want to love—your eternal and abnormal craving is to be loved. You aren't positive, you're negative. You absorb, absorb, as if you must fill yourself up with love, because you've got a shortage somewhere."

She was stunned by his cruelty, and did not hear. He had not the faintest notion of what he was saying. It was as if his fretted, tortured soul, run hot by thwarted passion, jetted off these sayings like sparks from electricity. She did not grasp anything he said. She only sat crouched beneath his cruelty and his hatred of her. She never realised in a flash. Over everything she brooded and brooded.

After tea he stayed with Edgar and the brothers, taking no notice of Miriam. She, extremely unhappy on this looked-for holiday, waited for him. And at last he yielded and came to her. She was determined to track this mood of his to its origin. She counted it not much more than a mood.

"Shall we go through the wood a little way?" she asked him, knowing he never refused a direct request.

They went down to the warren. On the middle path they passed a trap, a narrow horse-shoe hedge of small fir-boughs, baited with the guts of a rabbit. Paul glanced at it frowning. She caught his eye.

"Isn't it dreadful?" she asked.

"I don't know! Is it worse than a weasel with its teeth in a rabbit's throat?—One weasel or many rabbits?—One or the other must go—!"

He was taking the bitterness of life badly. She was rather sorry for him.

"We will go back to the house," he said. "I don't want to walk out."

They went past the lilac-tree, whose bronze leaf-buds were coming unfastened. Just a fragment remained of the haystack, a monument squared and brown, like a pillar of stone. There was a little bed of hay from the last cutting.

"Let us sit here a minute," said Miriam.

He sat down, against his will, resting his back against the hard wall of hay. They faced the amphitheatre of round hills, that glowed with sunset, tiny white farms standing out, the meadows golden, the woods dark and yet luminous, tree-tops folded over tree-tops, distinct in the distance. The evening had cleared, and the east was tender with a magenta flush, under which the land lay still and rich.

"Isn't it beautiful?" she pleaded.

But he only scowled. He would rather have had it ugly just then.

At that moment a big bull terrier came rushing up, open mouthed, pranced his two paws on the youth's shoulders, licking his face. Paul drew back, laughing. Bill was a great relief to him. He pushed the dog aside, but it came leaping back.

"Get out," said the lad, "or I'll dot thee one."

But the dog was not to be pushed away. So Paul had a little battle with the creature, pitching poor Bill away from him, who however only floundered tumultuously back again, wild with joy. The two fought together, the man laughing grudgingly, the dog grinning all over. Miriam watched them. There was something pathetic about the man. He wanted so badly to love, to be tender. The rough way he bowled the dog over was really loving. Bill got up, panting with happiness, his brown eyes rolling in his white face, and lumbered back again. He adored Paul. The lad frowned.

"Bill, I've had enough o' thee," he said.

But the dog only stood with two heavy paws, that quivered with love, upon his thigh, and flickered a red tongue at him. He drew back.

"No," he said. "No—I've had enough."

And in a minute the dog trotted off, happily, to vary the fun.

He remained staring miserably across at the hills, whose still beauty he begrudged. He wanted to go and cycle with Edgar. Yet he had not the courage to leave Miriam.

"Why are you sad?" she asked, humbly.

"I'm not sad, why should I be," he answered. "I'm only normal."

She wondered why he always claimed to be normal when he was disagreeable.

"But what is the matter?" she pleaded, coaxing him soothingly.

"Nothing!"

"Nay!" she murmured.

He picked up a stick and began to stab the earth with it.

"You'd far better not talk," he said.

"But I wish to know——" she replied.

He laughed resentfully.

"You always do," he said.

"It's not fair to me," she murmured.

He thrust, thrust, thrust at the ground with the pointed stick, digging up little clods of earth, as if he were in a fever of irritation. She gently and firmly laid her hand on his wrist.

259

"Don't!" she said. "Put it away."

He flung the stick into the currant bushes, and leaned back. Now he was bottled up.

"What is it?" she pleaded softly.

He lay perfectly still, only his eyes alive, and they full of torment.

"You know," he said at length, rather wearily, "you know—we'd better break off."

It was what she dreaded. Swiftly, everything seemed to darken before her eyes.

"Why!" she murmured. "What has happened?"

"Nothing has happened.—We only realise where we are.—It's no good—."

She waited in silence, sadly, patiently. It was no good being impatient with him. At any rate he would tell her now what ailed him.

"We agreed on friendship," he went on, in a dull, monotonous voice, "How often *have* we agreed for friendship!—And yet—it neither stops there, nor gets anywhere else."

He was silent again. She brooded. What did he mean? He was so wearying. There was something he would not yield. Yet she must be patient with him.

"I can only give friendship—it's all I'm capable of—it's a flaw in my make-up.—The thing overbalances to one side—I hate a toppling balance—let us have done."

There was warmth of fury in his last phrases. He meant she loved him more than he her. Perhaps he could not love her. Perhaps she had not in herself that which he wanted. It was the deepest motive of her soul, this self-mistrust. It was so deep she dared neither realise nor acknowledge it. Perhaps she was deficient. Like an infinitely subtle shame, it kept her always back. If it were so, she would do without him. She would never let herself want him. She would merely see.

"But what has happened?" she said.

"Nothing—it's all in myself—it only comes out just now.—We're always like this towards Easter time."

He grovelled so helplessly, she pitied him. At least she never floundered in such a pitiable way. After all, it was he who was chiefly humiliated.

"What do you want?" she asked him.

"Why—I mustn't come often—that's all. Why should I monopolise you, when I'm not—. You see, I'm deficient in something with regard to you—."

He was telling her he did not love her, and so ought to leave her a chance with another man. How foolish and blind and shamefully clumsy he was! What were other men to her! What were men to her at all! But he, ah, she loved his soul. Was *he* deficient in something? Perhaps he was.

"But I don't understand," she said huskily. "Yesterday—."

The night was turning jangled and hateful to him as the twilight faded. And she bowed under her suffering.

"I know," he cried, "you never will. You'll never believe that I can't—can't physically, any more than I can fly up like a skylark—"

"What?" she murmured. Now she dreaded.

"Love you."

He hated her bitterly at that moment, because he made her suffer. Love her! She knew he loved her. He really belonged to her. This about not loving her, physically, bodily, was a mere perversity on his part, because he knew she loved him. He was stupid like a child. He belonged to her. His soul wanted her. She guessed somebody had been influencing him. She felt upon him the hardness, the foreignness of another influence.

"What have they been saying at home?" she asked.

"It's not that," he answered.

And then she knew it was. She despised them for their commonness, his people. They did not know what things were really worth.

He and she talked very little more that night. After all he left her to cycle with Edgar.

He had come back to his mother. Hers was the strongest tie in his life. When he thought round, Miriam shrank away. There was a vague, unreal feel about her. And nobody else mattered. There was one place in the world that stood solid and did not melt into unreality: the place where his mother was. Everybody else could grow shadowy, almost non-existent to him, but she could not. It was as if the pivot and pole of his life, from which he could not escape, was his mother.

And in the same way, she waited for him. In him was established her life now. After all, the life beyond offered very little to Mrs Morel. She saw that our chance for *doing* is here, and doing counted with her. Paul was going to prove that she had been right: he was going to make a man whom nothing should shift off his feet, he was going to alter the face of the earth, in some way which mattered.

Wherever he went, she felt her soul went with him. Whatever he did, she felt her soul stood by him, ready, as it were, to hand him his tools. She could not bear it when he was with Miriam. William was dead. She would fight to keep Paul.

And he came back to her. And in his soul was a feeling of the satisfaction of self-sacrifice because he was faithful to her. She loved him first, he loved her first. And yet it was not enough. His new, young life, so strong and imperious, was urged towards something else. It made him mad with restlessness. She saw this, and wished bitterly that Miriam had been a woman who could take this new life of his, and leave her the roots. He fought against his mother almost as he fought against Miriam.

It was a week before he went again to Willey Farm. Miriam had suffered a great deal, and was afraid to see him again. Was she now to endure the ignominy of his abandoning her? That would only be superficial and temporary. He would come back. She held the keys to his soul. But meanwhile, how he would torture her with his battle against her. She shrank from it.

However, the Sunday after Easter he came to tea. Mrs Leivers was glad to see him. She gathered something was fretting him, that he found things hard. He seemed to drift to her for comfort. And she was good to him. She did him that great kindness of treating him almost with reverence.

He met her with the young children in the front garden.

"I'm glad you've come," said the mother, looking at him with her great, appealing brown eyes. "It is such a sunny day.—I was just going down the fields, for the first time this year."

He felt she would like him to come. That soothed him. They went, talking simply, he gentle and humble. He could have wept with gratitude that she was deferential to him. He was feeling humiliated.

At the bottom of the mow close they found a thrush's nest.

"Shall I show you the eggs?" he said.

"Do!" replied Mrs Leivers. "They seem *such* a sign of spring, and so hopeful."

He put aside the thorns and took out the eggs, holding them in the palm of his hand.

"They are quite hot—I think we frightened her off them," he said.

"Ay, poor thing," said Mrs Leivers.

Miriam could not help touching the eggs, and his hand, which, it seemed to her, cradled them so well.

"Isn't it a strange warmth!" she murmured, to get near him.

"Blood heat," he answered.

She watched him putting them back, his body pressed against the hedge, his arm reaching slowly through the thorns, his hand folded carefully over the eggs. He was concentrated on the act. Seeing him so, she loved him, he seemed so simple and sufficient to himself. And she could not get to him.

Over tea he discussed with Mrs Leivers the Good Friday sermon. It was too far for the mother to get to Chapel now: and she liked almost better to have the sermon through Paul, with his comments and arguments. The others listened. Even the big, rough lads were attentive, interested, gathering food from the discourse.

"He took," said Paul, "that Chapter—'Who hath believed our report'—I like it."

Mrs Leivers' large brown eyes flushed with light at the thought of it.

"And he spoilt it altogether—he spoilt it."

He glanced suddenly at Miriam, for her to be with him now.

"He said—."

Paul, earnest and wrathful, gave the sermon over again. It was thus Miriam loved him. She watched him, and was filled with deep satisfaction. She loved him in the same way that Mary loved at Bethany. Only when the man came up in him was there war between them. And which was stronger in him, the Disciple or the man. She believed the former, and by the former she held him.

When she was clearing the tea-table he said, in rather a forced tone:

"We'll go out when you've done."

And he helped her to wipe the pots in the scullery. She quivered slightly in apprehension. But she knew she had no cause for fear from his resentment that night.

"Shall we take a book?" she said, laying her fingers on her favourite Palgrave's *Golden Treasury*. He was his best with her when they read poetry.

"Not that," he said.

Her heart sank. She stood hesitating at the book-shelf. He took *Tartarin de Tarascon*. Again they sat on the bank of hay at the foot of the stack. He read a couple of pages, but without any heart for it. Again the dog came racing up, to repeat the fun of the other day. He shoved his muzzle in the man's chest. Paul fingered his ear for a moment. Then he pushed him away.

"Go away, Bill," he said. "I don't want you."

Bill slunk off, and Miriam wondered, and dreaded what was coming. There was a silence about the youth that made her still with apprehension. It was not his furies, but his quiet resolutions that she feared.

Turning his face a little to one side, so that she could not see him, he began, speaking slowly and painfully:

"Do you think—if I didn't come up so much—you might get to like somebody else—another man—?"

So this was what he was still harping on.

"But I don't know any other men—why do you ask?" she replied, in a low tone that should have been a reproach on him.

"Why," he blurted, "because they say I've no right to come up like this—without we mean to marry—"

Miriam was indignant at anybody's forcing the issues between them. She had been furious with her own father for suggesting to Paul, laughingly, that he knew why he came so much.

"Who says?" she asked, wondering if her people had anything to do with it. They had not.

"Mother—and the others. They say, at this rate, everybody will consider me engaged, and I ought to consider myself so, because it's not fair to you.—And I've tried to find out—and I don't think I love you as a man ought to love his wife.—What do *you* think about it?"

Miriam bowed her head moodily. She was angry at having this struggle. People should leave him and her alone.

"I don't know," she murmured.

"Do you think we love each other enough to marry?" he asked, definitely. It made her tremble.

"No," she answered, truthfully. "I don't think so—we're too young."

"I thought perhaps," he went on miserably, "that you, with your intensity in things, might have given me more—than I could ever make up to you.—And even now—if you think it better—we'll be engaged."

Now Miriam wanted to cry. And she was angry too. He was always such a child, for people to do as they liked with.

"No, I don't think so," she said firmly.

He pondered a minute.

"You see," he said, "with me—I don't think one person would ever monopolise me—be everything to me—I think never."

This she did not consider.

"No," she murmured. Then after a pause, she looked at him and her dark eyes flashed:

"This is your mother," she said. "I know she never liked me."

"No no, it isn't," he said hastily. "It was for your sake she spoke this time. She only said, if I was going on, I ought to consider myself engaged." There was a silence.—"And if I ask you to come down any time, you won't stop away, will you?"

She did not answer. By this time she was very angry.

"Well, what shall we do?" she said shortly. "I suppose I'd better drop French. I was just beginning to get on with it.—But I suppose I can go on alone."

"I don't see that we need," he said. "I can give you a French lesson, surely."

"Well—and there are Sunday nights. I shan't stop coming to chapel, because I enjoy it, and it's all the social life I get. But you've no need to come home with me. I can go alone."

"All right," he answered, rather taken aback. "But if I ask Edgar, he'll always come with us, and then they can say nothing."

There was silence. After all then, she would not lose much. For all their talk down at his home, there would not be much difference. She wished they would mind their own business.

"And you won't think about it, and let it trouble you, will you?" he asked.

"Oh no," replied Miriam, without looking at him.

He was silent. She thought him unstable. He had no fixity of purpose, no anchor of righteousness that held him.

"Because," he continued, "a man gets across his bicycle—and goes to work—and does all sorts of things. But a woman broods."

"No, I shan't bother," said Miriam. And she meant it.

It had gone rather chilly. They went indoors.

"How white Paul looks!" Mrs Leivers exclaimed. "Miriam, you shouldn't have let him sit out of doors.—Do you think you've taken cold Paul?"

"Oh no!" he laughed.

But he felt done up. It wore him out, the conflict in himself. Miriam pitied him now. But quite early, before nine o'clock, he rose to go.

"You're not going home, are you?" asked Mrs Leivers anxiously.

"Yes," he replied. "I said I'd be early."

He was very awkward.

"But this *is* early," said Mr Leivers.

Miriam sat in the rocking-chair, and did not speak. He hesitated, expecting her to rise and go with him to the barn as usual for his bicycle. She remained as she was. He was at a loss.

"Well—goodnight all!" he faltered.

She spoke her goodnight along with all the others. But as he went past the window, he looked in. She saw him pale, his brows knit slightly in a way that had become constant with him, his eyes dark with pain.

She rose and went to the doorway to wave goodbye to him as he passed through the gate. He rode slowly under the pine trees, feeling a cur and a miserable wretch. His bicycle went tilting down the hills at random. He thought it would be a relief to break one's neck.

Two days later he sent her up a book and a little note, urging her to read and be busy.

And yet, he was different afterwards. He had seen the position. He knew he did *not* want to marry her. The reasons why he loved her were not reasons why he should want to marry her; that he had decided upon. And his mother had dinned it into him that this present situation could not go on for ever, and was grossly unfair to the girl. So he tried to put as much distance between him and her, as he could. He was cold and hard to her. She felt it all bitterly, ascribed it to his mother, and waited. She knew he could not leave her alone. But he seemed to be trying to throw up barriers between them, him and her, behind which he could retreat, away from her. She suffered rather badly.

At this time, he gave all his friendship to Edgar. He loved the family so much, he loved the farm so much, it was the dearest place on earth to him. His home was not so lovable. It was his mother. But then he would have been just as happy with his mother anywhere. Whereas Willey Farm he loved passionately. He loved the little, pokey kitchen, where men's boots tramped and the dog slept with one eye open, for fear of being trodden on: where the lamp hung over the table at night, and everything was so silent. He loved Miriam's long, low parlour, with its atmosphere of romance, its flowers, its books, its high rosewood piano. He loved the gardens and the buildings, that stood with their scarlet roofs on the naked edges of the fields, crept towards the wood as if for cosiness, the wild country scooping down a valley and up the uncultured hills of the other side. Only to be there was an exhilaration and a joy to him. He loved Mrs Leivers, with her unworldliness and her quaint cynicism; he loved Mr Leivers, so warm and young and lovable; he loved Edgar, who lit up when he came, and the boys and the children and Bill—even the sow Circe and the Indian game cock called Tippoo. All this besides Miriam. He could not give it up.

So he went as often, but he was usually with Edgar. Only, all the family, including the father, joined in charades and games at evening. And later, Miriam drew them together, and they read *Macbeth* out of penny books, taking parts. It was great excitement. Miriam was glad, and Mrs Leivers was glad, and Mr Leivers enjoyed it. Then they all learned songs together, from tonic solfa, singing in a circle round the fire. But now, Paul was very rarely alone with Miriam. She waited. When she and Edgar and he walked home together from Chapel or from the literary society in Bestwood, she knew his talk, so passionate and so unorthodox nowadays, was for her. She did envy Edgar, however, his cycling with Paul, his Friday nights, his days working in the fields. For her Friday nights and her French lessons were gone. She was nearly always alone, walking pondering in the wood, reading, studying, dreaming, waiting. And he wrote to her frequently.

One Sunday evening they attained to their old, rare harmony. Edgar had stayed to Communion—he wondered what it was like— with Mrs Morel. So Paul came on alone with Miriam to his home. He was more or less under her spell again. As usual, they were discussing the sermon. He was setting now full sail towards Agnosticism, but such a religious Agnosticism that Miriam did not suffer so badly. They were at the Renan *Vie de Jésus* stage. Miriam was the threshing floor on which he threshed out all his beliefs. While he trampled his ideas upon her soul, the truth came out for him. She alone was his threshing floor. She alone helped him towards realisation. Almost impassive, she submitted to his argument and expounding. And somehow, because of her, he gradually realised where he was wrong. And what he realised, she realised. She felt he could not do without her.

They came to the silent house. He took the key out of the scullery window, and they entered. All the time, he went on with his discussion. He lit the gas, mended the fire, and brought her some cakes from the pantry. She sat on the sofa, quietly, with a plate on her knee. She wore a large white hat with some pinkish flowers. It was a cheap hat, but he liked it. Her face beneath was still and pensive, golden brown and ruddy. Always her ears were hid in her short curls. She watched him.

She liked him on Sundays. Then he wore a dark suit that showed the lithe movement of his body. There was a clean, clear-cut look about him. He went on with his thinking to her. Suddenly he reached for a bible. Miriam liked the way he reached up, so sharp, straight to the mark. He turned the pages quickly, and read her a chapter of St. John. As he sat in the arm-chair, reading, intent, his voice only thinking, she felt as if he were using her unconsciously, as a man uses his tools at some work he is bent on. She loved it. And the wistfulness of his voice was like a reaching to something, and it was as if she were what he reached with. She sat back on the sofa, away from him, and yet feeling herself the very instrument his hand grasped. It gave her great pleasure.

Then he began to falter, and to get self-conscious. And when he came to the verse: "A woman, when she is in travail, hath sorrow because her hour is come," he missed it out. Miriam had felt him growing uncomfortable. She shrank when the well-known words did not follow. He went on reading, but she did not hear. A grief and shame made her bend her head. Six months ago, he would have read it simply. Now there was a scotch in his running with her. Now she felt there was really something hostile between them, something of which they were ashamed.

She ate her cake mechanically. He tried to go on with his argument, but could not get back the right note. Soon Edgar came in. Mrs Morel had gone to her friend's. The three set off to Willey Farm.

Miriam brooded over his split with her. There was something else he wanted. He could not be satisfied, he could give her no peace. There was between them now always a ground for strife. She wanted to prove him. She believed that his chief need in life was herself. If she could prove it, both to herself and to him, the rest might go, she could simply trust to the future.

So, in May, she asked him to come to Willey Farm and meet Mrs Dawes. There was something he hankered after. She saw him, whenever they spoke of Clara Dawes, rouse and get slightly angry.

He said he did not like her. Yet he was keen to know about her. Well, he should put himself to the test. She believed that there were in him desires for higher things, and desires for lower, and that the desire for the higher would conquer. At any rate, he should try. She forgot that her 'higher' and 'lower' were arbitrary.

He was rather excited at the idea of meeting Clara at Willey Farm. Mrs Dawes came for the day. Her heavy, dun-coloured hair was coiled on top of her head. She wore a white blouse and navy skirt, and somehow, wherever she was, seemed to make things look paltry and insignificant. When she was in the room, the kitchen seemed too small and mean altogether. Miriam's beautiful twilighty parlour looked stiff and stupid. All the Leivers were eclipsed like candles. They found her rather hard to put up with. Yet she was perfectly amiable, but indifferent, and rather hard.

Paul did not come till afternoon. He was early. As he swung off his bicycle, Miriam saw him look round at the house, eagerly. He would be disappointed if the visitor had not come. Miriam went out to meet him, bowing her head because of the sunshine. Nasturtiums were coming out crimson under the cool green shadow of their leaves. The girl stood dark haired, glad to see him.

"Hasn't Clara come?" he asked.

"Yes," replied Miriam, in her musical tone. "She's reading."

He wheeled his bicycle into the barn. He had put on a handsome tie, of which he was rather proud, and socks to match.

"She came this morning?" he asked.

"Yes," replied Miriam, as she walked at his side. "You said you'd bring me that letter from the man at Liberty's. Have you remembered?"

"Oh dash, no!" he said. "But nag at me till you get it."

"I don't like to nag at you."

"Do it whether or not. And is she any more agreeable?" he continued.

"You know I always think she is quite agreeable."

He was silent. Evidently his eagerness to be early today had been the new-comer. Miriam already began to suffer. They went together towards the house. He took the clips off his trousers, but was too lazy to brush the dust from his shoes, in spite of the socks and tie.

Clara sat in the cool parlour, reading. He saw the nape of her white neck, and the fine hair lifted from it. She rose, looking at him indifferently. To shake hands, she lifted her arm straight in a

269

manner that seemed at once to keep him at a distance, and yet to fling something to him. He noticed how her breasts swelled inside her blouse, and how her shoulder curved handsomely under the thin muslin at the top of her arm.

"You have chosen a fine day," he said.

"It happens so," she said.

"Yes," he said, "I am glad."

She sat down, not thanking him for his politeness.

"What have you been doing all morning?" asked Paul of Miriam.

"Well you see," said Miriam, coughing huskily, "Clara only came with father—and so—she's not been here very long."

Clara sat leaning on the table, holding aloof. He noticed her hands were large but well kept. And the skin on them seemed almost coarse, opaque and white, with fine golden hairs. She did not mind if he observed her hands. She intended to scorn him. Her heavy arm lay negligently on the table. Her mouth was closed as if she were offended, and she kept her face slightly averted.

"You were at Margaret Bonford's meeting the other evening," he said to her. Miriam did not know this courteous Paul. Clara glanced at him:

"Yes," she said.

"Why," asked Miriam, "how do you know?"

"I went in for a few minutes before the train came," he answered.

Clara turned away again rather disdainfully.

"I think she's a lovable little woman," said Paul.

"Margaret Bonford!" exclaimed Clara. "She's a great deal cleverer than most men."

"Well, I didn't say she wasn't," he said, deprecating. "She's lovable for all that."

"And of course that is all that matters," said Clara witheringly.

He rubbed his head, rather perplexed, rather annoyed.

"I suppose it matters more than her cleverness," he said; "—which after all would never get her to heaven."

"It's not heaven she wants to get—it's her fair share on earth," retorted Clara. She spoke as if he were responsible for some deprivation which Miss Bonford suffered.

"Well," he said, "I thought she was warm, and awfully nice—only too frail. I wished she was sitting comfortably in peace—"

"'Darning her husband's stockings'," said Clara, scathingly.

"I'm sure she wouldn't mind darning even my stockings," he said.

"And I'm sure she'd do them well.—Just as I wouldn't mind blacking her boots, if she wanted me to."

But Clara refused to answer this sally of his. He talked to Miriam for a little while. The other woman held aloof.

"Well," he said, "I think I'll go and see Edgar. Is he on the land?"

"I believe," said Miriam, "he's gone for a load of coal. He should be back directly."

"Then," he said, "I'll go and meet him."

Miriam dared not propose anything for the three of them. He rose and left them.

On the top road, where the gorse was out, he saw Edgar walking lazily beside the mare, who nodded her white-starred forehead as she dragged the clanking load of coal. The young farmer's face lighted up as he saw his friend. Edgar was good-looking, with dark warm eyes. His clothes were old and rather disreputable, and he walked with considerable pride.

"Hello!" he said, seeing Paul bareheaded. "Where are you going?"

"Came to meet you. Can't stand 'Nevermore'."

Edgar's teeth flashed in a laugh of amusement.

"Who is 'Nevermore'?" he asked.

"The lady—Mrs Dawes—it ought to be Mrs the Raven that quothed 'Nevermore'."

Edgar laughed with glee.

"Don't you like her?" he asked.

"Not a fat lot," said Paul. "Why, do you?"

"No!" The answer came with a deep ring of conviction. "No!" Edgar pursed up his lips. "I can't say she's much in my line." He mused a little. Then: "But why do you call her 'Nevermore'?" he asked.

"Well," said Paul. "If she looks at a man, she says haughtily 'Nevermore,' and if she looks at herself in the looking-glass she says disdainfully 'Nevermore,' and if she thinks back she says it in disgust, and if she looks forward she says it cynically—"

Edgar considered this speech, failed to make much out of it, and said, laughing:

"You think she's a man-hater?"

"*She* thinks she is," replied Paul.

"But you don't think so?"

"No," replied Paul.

"Wasn't she nice with you then?"

"Could you imagine her *nice* with anybody?" asked the young man.

Edgar laughed. Together they unloaded the coal in the yard. Paul was rather self-conscious because he knew Clara could see if she looked out of the window. She didn't look.

On Saturday afternoons the horses were brushed down, and groomed. Paul and Edgar worked together, sneezing with the dust that came from the pelts of Jimmy and Flower.

"Do you know a new song to teach me?" said Edgar.

He continued to work all the time. The back of his neck was sun-red, when he bent down, and his fingers that held the brush were thick. Paul watched him sometimes.

"'Mary Morrison'?" suggested the younger.

Edgar agreed. He had a good tenor voice, and he loved to learn all the songs his friend could teach him, so that he could sing whilst he was carting. Paul had a very indifferent baritone voice, but a good ear. However, he sang softly, for fear of Clara. Edgar repeated the line in a clear tenor. At times they both broke off to sneeze, and first one, then the other, abused his horse.

Miriam was impatient of men. It took so little to amuse them— even Paul. She thought it anomalous in him that he could be so thoroughly absorbed in a triviality.

It was tea-time when they had finished.

"What song was that?" asked Miriam.

Edgar told her. The conversation turned to singing.

"We have such jolly times," Miriam said to Clara.

Mrs Dawes ate her meal in a slow, dignified way. Whenever the men were present, she grew distant.

"Do you like singing?" Miriam asked her.

"If it is good," she said.

Paul, of course, coloured.

"You mean if it is high-class, and trained?" he said.

"I think a voice needs training before the singing is anything," she said.

"You might as well insist on having people's voices trained before you allowed them to talk," he replied. "Really, people sing for their own pleasure, as a rule."

"And it may be for other people's discomfort."

"Then the other people should have flaps to their ears," he replied.

The boys laughed. There was a silence. He flushed deeply and ate in silence.

The conversation turned again on the point whether women's wages should be equal with those of men. Mrs Leivers upheld that men had families to keep; Clara said, so much work should have so much pay, man or woman. Mr Leivers was inclined to agree with her. Whatever Mrs Dawes had said, Paul would have taken sides against her. He argued that a woman was only an accessory in the labour market, and that, in the majority of cases she was a transitory thing, supporting herself alone for a year or two. Clara quoted the number of women who supported father, mother, sisters etc.

"And almost every man in the world, over thirty, supports a wife and family—and as a *rule*, the said wives are not wage-earners," he replied.

"I think my friend," said Clara very coldly, "that I have met your sort before: the young man who thinks he knows everything—."

"And you are the young woman who thinks I know nothing," he retorted.

"Oh yes—you know how to make yourself heard," she said.

He was furious. Then he burst into a laugh.

"Sounds like a suffragette meeting," he said, "you on the platform."

And then Clara coloured to the roots of her hair.

"Why should I be called 'Men' when I'm only myself," he continued.

"As if that weren't enough," laughed Edgar.

"And then," Paul resumed, "I'm made responsible for every sin in English history, from Queen Boadisca down to the Song of the Shirt. It's not fair.—I wish Man had a right to exist in modern society—any corner in which to lay his head."

"Why," jested Mrs Leivers, "when all comes to all, his place remains very much the same, while we're made as we are."

But this joke was too subtle for all but Clara. She was indignant.

After tea, when all the men had gone but Paul, Mrs Leivers said to Clara:

"And you find life happier now?"

"Infinitely."

"And you are satisfied?"

"So long as I can be free and independent."

273

"And you don't *miss* anything in your life?" asked Mrs Leivers gently.

"I've put all that behind me."

Paul had been feeling uncomfortable during this discourse. He got up:

"You'll find you're always tumbling over the things you've put behind you," he said. Then he took his departure to the cowsheds. He felt he had been witty, and his manly pride was high. He whistled as he went down the brick track.

Miriam came for him a little later to know if he would go with Clara and her for a walk. They set off down to Strelley Mill farm. As they were going beside the brook, on the Willey Water side, looking through the brake at the edge of the wood, where pink campions glowed under a few sunbeams, they saw, beyond the tree trunks and the thin hazel-bushes, a man leading a great bay horse through the gullies. The big, red beast seemed to dance romantically through that dimness of green hazel-drift, away there where the air was shadowy as if it were in the past, among the fading bluebells that might have bloomed for Deirdre or Iseult.

The three stood charmed.

"What a treat to be a knight," he said, "and to have a pavilion here."

"And to have us shut up safely?" replied Clara.

"Yes," he answered, "singing with your maids at your broidery. I would carry your banner of white and green and heliotrope. I would have W.S.P.U. emblazoned on my shield, beneath a woman rampant—."

"I have no doubt," said Clara, "that you would much rather fight for a woman than let her fight for herself."

"I would! When she fights for herself she seems like a dog before a looking glass, gone into a mad fury with its own shadow."

"And *you* are the looking-glass?" she asked, with a curl of the lip.

"Or the shadow," he replied.

"I am afraid," she said, "that you are too clever."

"Well, I leave it to you to be *good*," he retorted, laughing. "Be good, sweet maid, and just let *me* be clever."

But Clara wearied of his flippancy. Suddenly, looking at her, he saw that the upward lifting of her face was misery and not scorn. His heart grew tender for everybody. He turned and was gentle with Miriam, whom he had neglected till then.

At the wood's edge, they met Limb, a thin, swarthy man of forty, tenant of Strelley Mill, which he ran as a cattle raising farm. He held the halter of the powerful stallion indifferently, as if he were tired. The three stood to let him pass over the stepping stones of the first brook. Paul admired that so large an animal should walk on such springy toes, with an endless excess of vigour. Limb pulled up before them.

"Tell your father, Miss Leivers," he said, in a peculiar piping voice, "that his young beas'es 'as broke that bottom fence three days an' runnin'."

"Which?" asked Miriam, tremulous.

The great horse breathed heavily, shifting round its red flanks, and looking suspiciously with its wonderful big eyes, upwards from under its lowered head and falling mane.

"Come along a bit," replied Limb, "an' I'll show you."

The man and the stallion went forward. It danced sideways, shaking its white fetlocks, and looking frightened as it felt itself in the brook.

"No hanky-pankyin'," said the man affectionately to the beast.

It went up the bank in little leaps, then splashed finely through the second brook. Clara, walking with a kind of sulky abandon, watched it half fascinated, half contemptuous. Limb stopped and pointed to the fence under some willows.

"There, you see where they got through," he said. "My man's druv 'em back three times."

"Yes," answered Miriam, colouring as if she were at fault.

"Are you comin' in?" asked the man.

"No thanks—but we should like to go by the pond."

"Well just as you've a mind," he said.

The horse gave little whinneys of pleasure at being so near home.

"He is glad to be back," said Clara, who was interested in the creature.

"Yes—'e's been a tidy step today."

They went through the gate, and saw approaching them from the big farm-house a smallish dark, excitable-looking woman of about thirty five. Her hair was touched with grey, her dark eyes looked wild. She walked with her hands behind her back. Her brother went forward. As it saw her, the big bay stallion whinneyed again. She came up excitedly.

"Are you home again, my boy!" she said tenderly, to the horse, not to the man. The great beast shifted round to her, ducking his head. She smuggled into his mouth the wrinkled yellow apple she had been hiding behind her back, then she kissed him near the eyes. He gave a big sigh of pleasure. She held his head in her arms, against her breast.

"Isn't he splendid!" said Miriam to her.

Miss Limb looked up. Her dark eyes glanced straight at Paul.

"Oh good evening, Miss Leivers," she said. "It's ages since you've been down."

Miriam introduced her friends.

"Your horse *is* a fine fellow!" said Clara.

"Isn't he!" Again she kissed him. "As loving as any man!"

"More loving than most men, I should think," replied Clara.

"He's a nice boy!" cried the woman, again embracing the horse.

Clara, fascinated by the big beast, went up to stroke his neck.

"He's quite gentle," said Miss Limb. "Don't you think big fellows are?"

"He's a beauty!" replied Clara.

She wanted to look in his eyes. She wanted him to look at her.

"It's a pity he can't talk," she said.

"Oh but he can, all but," replied the other woman.

Then her brother moved on with the horse.

"Are you coming in?—*do* come in Mr—I didn't catch it—"

"Morel!" said Miriam. "No—we won't come in, but we should like to go by the mill-pond."

"Yes—yes do. Do you fish Mr Morel?"

"No," said Paul.

"Because if you do you might come and fish any time," said Miss Limb. "We scarcely see a soul from week's end to week's end. I should be thankful."

"What fish are there in the pond?" he asked.

They went through the front garden, over the sluice, and up the steep bank to the pond, which lay in shadow, with its two wooded islets. Paul walked with Miss Limb.

"I shouldn't mind swimming here," he said.

"Do," she replied. "Come when you like. My brother will be awfully pleased to talk with you. He is so quiet, because there is no one to talk to. Do come and swim."

Clara came up.

"It's a fine depth," she said, "and so clear."

"Yes," said Miss Limb.

"Do you swim?" said Paul. "Miss Limb was just saying we could come when we liked."

"Of course there's the farm-hands," said Miss Limb.

They talked a few moments, then went on up the wild hill, leaving the lonely, haggard-eyed woman on the bank.

The hillside was all ripe with sunshine. It was wild and tussocky, given over to rabbits. The three walked in silence. Then:

"She makes me feel uncomfortable," said Paul.

"You mean Miss Limb?" asked Miriam. "Yes!"

"What's a matter with her? Is she going dotty with being too lonely?"

"Yes," said Miriam. "It's not the right sort of life for her. I think it's cruel to bury her there. *I* really ought to go and see her more. But—she upsets me."

"She makes me feel sorry for her—yes and she bothers me—" he said.

"I suppose," blurted Clara suddenly, "she wants a man."

The other two were silent for a few moments.

"But it's the loneliness sends her cracked," said Paul.

Clara did not answer, but strode on uphill. She was walking with her head hanging, her legs swinging as she kicked through the dead thistles and the tussocky grass, her arms hanging loose. Rather than walking, her handsome body seemed to be blundering up the hill. A hot wave went over Paul. He was curious about her. Perhaps life had been cruel to her. He forgot Miriam, who was walking beside him talking to him. She glanced at him, finding he did not answer her. His eyes were fixed ahead on Clara.

"Do you still think she is disagreeable?" she asked.

He did not notice that the question was sudden. It ran with his thoughts.

"Something's the matter with her," he said.

"Yes," answered Miriam.

They found at the top of the hill a hidden wild field, two sides of which were backed by the wood, the other sides by high loose hedges of hawthorn and elder-bushes. Between these overgrown bushes were gaps that the cattle might have walked through, had there been any cattle now. There the turf was smooth as velveteen, padded and holed by the rabbits. The field itself was coarse, and crowded with tall big cowslips, that had never been cut. Clusters of strong flowers rose everywhere above the coarse tussocks of bent. It was like a roadstead crowded with tall fairy-shipping.

"Ah!" cried Miriam, and she looked at Paul, her dark eyes dilating. He smiled. Together they enjoyed the field of flowers. Clara, a little way off, was looking at the cowslips, disconsolately. Paul and Miriam stayed close together, talking in subdued tones. He kneeled on one knee, quickly gathering the best blossoms, moving from tuft to tuft restlessly, talking softly all the time. Miriam plucked the flowers lovingly, lingering over them. He always seemed to her too quick and almost scientific. Yet his bunches had a natural beauty more than hers. He loved them, but as if they were his and he had a right to them. She had more reverence for them: they held something she had not.

The flowers were very fresh and sweet. He wanted to drink them. As he gathered them, he ate the little yellow trumpets. Clara was still wandering about disconsolately. Going towards her, he said:

"Why don't you get some?"

"I don't believe in it. They look better growing."

"But you'd like some?"

"They want to be left."

"I don't believe they do."

"I don't want the corpses of flowers about me," she said.

"That's a stiff artificial notion," he said. "They don't die any quicker in water than on their roots.—And besides, they *look* nice in a bowl, they look jolly. And you only call a thing a corpse because it looks corpse-like."

"Whether it is one or not?" she argued.

"It isn't one to me. A dead flower isn't a corpse of a flower."

Clara now ignored him.

"And even so—what right have you to pull them?" she asked.

"Because I like them, and want them—and there's plenty of them."

"And that is sufficient?"

"Yes—why not. I'm sure they'd smell nice in your room in Nottingham."

"And I should have the pleasure of watching them die."

"But then—it does not matter if they do die."

Whereupon he left her, and went stooping over the clumps of tangled flowers, which thickly sprinkled the field like pale, luminous foam-clots. Miriam had come close. Clara was kneeling breathing some scent from the cowslips.

"I think," said Miriam, "if you treat them with reverence—you don't do them any harm—it is the spirit you pluck them in that matters."

"Yes," he said. "But no, you get 'em because you want 'em, and that's all." He held out his bunch.

Miriam was silent. He picked some more.

"Look at these!" he continued; "sturdy and lusty like little trees and like boys with fat legs—"

Clara's hat lay on the grass not far off. She was kneeling, bending forward still to smell the flowers. Her neck gave him a sharp pang, such a beautiful thing, yet not proud of itself just now. Her breasts swung slightly in her blouse. The arching curve of her back was beautiful and strong: she wore no stays. Suddenly, without knowing, he was scattering a handful of cowslips over her hair and neck, saying:

> "Ashes to ashes and dust to dust
> If the Lord won't have you the devil must."

The chill flowers fell on her neck. She looked up at him, with almost pitiful, scared grey eyes, wondering what he was doing. Flowers fell on her face and she shut her eyes.

Suddenly, standing there above her, he felt awkward.

"I thought you wanted a funeral," he said, ill at ease.

Clara laughed strangely, and rose, picking the cowslips from her hair. She took up her hat and pinned it on. One flower had remained tangled in her hair. He saw, but would not tell her. He gathered up the flowers he had sprinkled over her.

At the edge of the wood the bluebells had flowed over into the field and stood there like flood-water. But they were fading now. Clara strayed up to them. He wandered after her. The bluebells pleased him.

"Look how they've come out of the wood!" he said.

Then she turned with a flash of warmth and of gratitude.

"Yes!" she smiled.

His blood beat up.

"It makes me think of the wild men of the woods, how terrified they would be when they got breast to breast with the open space."

"Do you think they were?" she asked.

"I wonder which was more frightened, among old tribes: those bursting out of their darkness of woods upon all the space of light, or those from the open tip-toeing into the forests."

"I should think the second," she answered.

"Yes, you *do* feel like one of the open space sort—trying to force yourself into the dark—don't you?"

"How should I know?" she answered, queerly.

The conversation ended there.

The evening was deepening over the earth. Already the valley was full of shadow. One tiny square of light stood opposite at Crossleigh Bank Farm. Brightness was swimming on the tops of the hills. Miriam came up slowly, her face in her big, loose bunch of flowers, walking ankle deep through the scattered froth of the cowslips. Beyond her, the trees were coming into shape, all shadow.

"Shall we go?" she asked.

And the three turned away. They were all silent. Going down the path, they could see the light of home right across, and on the ridge of the hill, a thin dark outline with little lights, where the colliery village touched the sky.

"It has been nice, hasn't it?" he asked.

Miriam murmured assent. Clara was silent.

"Don't you think so?" he persisted.

But she walked with her head up, and still did not answer. He could tell by the way she moved, as if she didn't care, that she suffered.

At this time Paul took his mother to Lincoln. She was bright and enthusiastic as ever, but as he sat opposite her in the railway carriage, she seemed to look frail. He had a momentary sensation as if she were slipping away from him. Then he wanted to get hold of her, to fasten her, almost to chain her. He felt he must keep hold of her with his hand.

They drew near to the city. Both were at the window looking for the cathedral.

"There she is, mother!" he cried.

They saw the great cathedral lying couchant above the plain.

"Ah!" she exclaimed. "So she is!"

He looked at his mother. Her blue eyes were watching the cathedral quietly. She seemed again to be beyond him. Something in the eternal repose of the uplifted cathedral, blue and noble against the sky, was reflected in her, something of the fatality. What was, *was!*—with all his young will he could not alter it. He saw her face, the skin still fresh and pink and downy, but crow's-feet near her eyes, her eyelids steady, sinking a little, her mouth always closed with disillusion; and there was on her the same eternal look, as if she knew fate at last. He beat against it with all the strength of his soul.

"Look mother how big she is above the town! Think, there are streets and streets below her: she looks bigger than the city altogether."

"So she does!" exclaimed his mother, breaking bright into life again. But he had seen her sitting, looking steady out of the window at the cathedral, her face and eyes fixed, reflecting the relentlessness of life. And the crow's-feet near her eyes, and her mouth shut so hard, made him feel he would go mad.

They ate a meal that she considered wildly extravagant.

"Don't imagine I like it," she said, as she ate her cutlet. "I *don't* like it, I really don't! Just *think* of your money wasted!"

"You never mind my money," he said. "You forget I'm a fellow taking his girl for an outing."

And he bought her some blue violets.

"Stop it at once, Sir!" she commanded. "How can I do it?"

"You've got nothing to do! Stand still."

And in the middle of the High Street, he stuck the flowers in her coat.

"An old thing like me!" she said, sniffing.

"You see," he said, "I want people to think we're awful swells. So look ikey."

"I'll jowl your head," she laughed.

"Strut," he commanded. "Be a fantail pigeon."

It took him an hour to get her through the street. She stood above Glory Hole, she stood before Stone Bow, she stood everywhere, and exclaimed. A man came up, took off his hat and bowed to her:

"Can I show you the town, Madam?"

"No thank you," she answered. "I've got my son."

Then Paul was cross with her for not answering with more dignity.

"You go away with you," she exclaimed. "Ha—that's the Jew's House! Now do you remember that lecture, Paul———"

But she could scarcely climb the Cathedral hill. He did not notice. Then suddenly he found her unable to speak. He took her into a little public house, where she rested.

"It's nothing!" she said. "My heart is only a bit old; one must expect it."

He did not answer, but looked at her. Again his heart was crushed in a hot grip. He wanted to cry, he wanted to smash things in fury.

They set off again, pace by pace, so slowly. And every step seemed like a weight on his chest. He felt as if his heart would burst. At last they came to the top. She stood enchanted, looking at the castle gate, looking at the Cathedral front. She had quite forgotten herself.

"Now *this* is better than I thought it could be!" she cried.

But he hated it. Everywhere he followed her, brooding. They sat together in the Cathedral. They attended a little service in the choir. She was timid.

"I suppose it is open to anybody?" she asked him.

"Yes," he replied. "Do you think they'd have the damned cheek to send us away."

"Well I'm, sure!" she exclaimed; "they would if they heard your language."

Her face seemed to shine again with joy and peace, during the service. And all the time he was wanting to rage and smash things and cry.

Afterwards, when they were leaning over the wall, looking at the town below, he blurted suddenly:

"Why can't a man have a *young* mother? What is she old for?"

"Well," his mother laughed, "she can scarcely help it."

"And why wasn't I the oldest son! Look—they say the young ones have the advantage—but look, *they* had the young mother. You should have had me for your eldest son."

"*I* didn't arrange it," she remonstrated. "Come to consider, you're as much to blame as me."

He turned on her, white, his eyes furious.

"What are you old for!" he said, mad with his impotence. "*Why* can't you walk? *Why* can't you come with me to places?"

"At one time," she replied, "I could have run up that hill a good deal better than you."

"What's the good of that to *me*?" he cried, hitting his fist on the wall. Then he became plaintive. "It's too bad of you to be ill, Little, it is—."

"Ill!" she cried. "I'm a bit old, and you'll have to put up with it, that's all."

They were quiet. But it was as much as they could bear. They got jolly again over tea. As they sat by Brayford, watching the boats, he told her about Clara. His mother asked him innumerable questions.

"Then who does she live with?"

"With her mother, on Bluebell Hill."

"And have they enough to keep them?"

"I don't think so: I think they do lace work."

"And wherein lies her charm, my boy?"

"I don't know that she's charming, mother. But she's nice. And she seems straight, you know—not a bit deep, not a bit."

"But she's a good deal older than you."

"She's thirty, I'm going of twenty-three."

"You haven't told me what you like her for."

"Because I don't know—a sort of defiant way she's got—a sort of angry way—"

Mrs Morel considered. She would have been glad now for her son to fall in love with some woman who would—she did not know what. But he fretted so, got so furious suddenly, and again was melancholic. She wished he knew some nice woman—. She did not know what she wished, but left it vague. At any rate she was not hostile to the idea of Clara.

Annie too was getting married. Leonard had gone away to work in Birmingham. One week-end when he was home, she had said to him:

"You don't look very well, my lad."

"I dunno," he said. "I feel anyhow or nohow, Ma."

He called her Ma already, in his boyish fashion.

"Are you sure they're good lodgings?" she asked.

"Yes—yes. Only—it's a winder when you have to pour your own tea out—an' nobody to grouse if you team it in your saucer and sup it up. It somehow takes a' th' taste out of it."

Mrs Morel laughed.

"And so it knocks you up?" she said.

"I dunno.—I want to get married," he blurted, twisting his fingers, and looking down at his boots. There was a silence.

"But," she exclaimed, "I thought you said you'd wait another year."

"Yes, I did say so," he replied stubbornly.

Again she considered.

"And you know," she said, "Annie's a bit of a spendthrift. She's saved no more than eleven pounds—and I know, lad, you haven't had much chance."

He coloured up to the ears.

"I've got twenty three quid," he said.

"It doesn't go far," she answered.

He said nothing, but twisted his fingers.

"And you know," she said, "I've nothing—."

"I didn't want, Ma—!" he cried, very red, suffering, and remonstrating.

"No my lad, I know.—I was only wishing I had.—And take away five pounds for the wedding and things—it leaves twenty nine pounds—you won't do much on that—"

He twisted still, impotent, stubborn, not looking up.

"But do you really want to get married?" she asked. "Do you feel as if you ought?"

He gave her one straight look from his blue eyes.

"Yes!" he said.

"Then," she replied, "we must all do the best we can for it, lad."

The next time he looked up there were tears in his eyes.

"I don't want Annie to feel handicapped—!" he said, struggling.

"My lad," she said, "you're steady—you've got a decent place. If a man had *needed* me, I'd have married him on his last week's wages. She may find it a bit hard, to start humbly. Young girls *are* like that. They look forward to the fine home they think they'll have. But *I* had expensive furniture! It's not everything."

So the wedding took place almost immediately. Arthur came home, and was splendid in uniform. Annie looked nice in a dove-grey dress that she could take for Sundays. Morel called her a fool for getting married, and was cool with his son-in-law. Mrs Morel had white tips in her bonnet, and some white on her blouse, and was teased by both her sons for fancying herself so grand. Leonard was jolly and cordial, and felt a fearful fool. Paul could not quite see what Annie wanted to get married for. He was fond of her, and she of him. Still, he hoped rather lugubriously that it would turn out all right. Arthur was astonishingly handsome in his scarlet and yellow, and he knew it well, but was secretly ashamed of the uniform. Annie cried her eyes up in the kitchen, on leaving her mother. Mrs Morel cried a little, then patted her on the back and said:

"But don't cry, child, he'll be good to you."

Morel stamped and said she was a fool to go and tie herself up. Leonard looked white and overwrought. Mrs Morel said to him:

"I s'll trust her to you, my lad, and hold you responsible for her."

"You can," he said, nearly dead with the ordeal. And it was all over.

When Morel and Arthur were in bed, Paul sat talking, as he often did, with his mother.

"You're not sorry she's married, mother, are you?" he asked.

"I'm not sorry she's married—but—it seems strange that she should go from me. It even seems to me hard that she can prefer to go with her Leonard. That's how mothers are—I know it's silly."

"And shall you be miserable about her?"

"When I think of my own wedding day," his mother answered, "I can only hope her life will be different."

"But you can trust him to be good to her?"

"Yes. Yes! They say he's not good enough for her. But I say if a man is *genuine*, as he is, and a girl is fond of him—then—it should be all right—he's as good as she."

"So you don't mind?"

"I would *never* have let a daughter of mine marry a man I didn't *feel* to be genuine through and through.—And yet, there's the gap now she's gone—"

They were both miserable, and wanted her back again. It seemed to Paul, his mother looked lonely, in her new black silk blouse with its bit of white trimming.

"At any rate, mother, I s'll never marry," he said.

"Ay, they all say that, my lad. You've not met the one yet. Only wait a year or two."

"But I shan't marry mother—I shall live with you, and we'll have a servant."

"Ay my lad—it's easy to talk. We'll see when the time comes."

"What time? I'm nearly twenty three."

"Yes—you're not one that would marry young. But in three years' time—"

"I shall be with you just the same."

"We'll see, my boy, we'll see."

"But you don't want me to marry?"

"I shouldn't like to think of you going through your life without anybody to care for you and do—no—."

"And you think I ought to marry?"

"Sooner or later, every man ought."

"But you'd rather it were later."

"It would be hard—and very hard. It's as they say:

'A son's my son till he takes him a wife,
But my daughter's my daughter the whole of my life.'"

"And you think I'd let a wife take me from you?"

"Well, you wouldn't ask her to marry your mother as well as you," Mrs Morel smiled.

"She could do what she liked—she wouldn't have to interfere."

"She wouldn't—till she'd got you—and then you'd see."

"I never will see. I'll never marry while I've got you—I won't."

"But I shouldn't like to leave you with nobody, my boy," she cried.

"You're not going to leave me. What are you—fifty three! I'll give you till seventy five. There you are, I'm fat and forty four. Then I'll marry a staid body. See—!"

His mother sat and laughed.

"Go to bed," she said, "go to bed."

"And we'll have a pretty house, you and me, and a servant, and it'll be just all right.—I s'll perhaps be rich with my painting."

"Will you go to bed!"

"And then you s'll have a pony carriage. See yourself, a little Queen Victoria trotting round."

"I tell you to go to bed," she laughed.

He kissed her, and went. His plans for the future were always the same.

Mrs Morel sat brooding, about her daughter, about Paul, about Arthur. She fretted at losing Annie. The family was very closely bound. And she felt she *must* live now, to be with her children. Life was so rich for her. Paul wanted her, and so did Arthur. Arthur never knew how deeply he loved her. He was a creature of the moment. Never yet had he been forced to realise himself. The army had disciplined his body, but not his soul. He was in perfect health, and very handsome. His dark, vigorous hair sat close to his smallish head. There was something childish about his nose, something almost girlish about his dark blue eyes. But he had the full, red mouth of a man under his brown moustache, and his jaw was strong. It was his father's mouth, it was the nose and eyes of her own mother's people, good-looking, weak-principled folk. Mrs

Morel was anxious about him. Once he had really run the rig he was safe. But how far would he go?

The army had not really done him any good. He resented bitterly the authority of the petty officers. He hated having to obey as if he were an animal. But he had too much sense to kick. So he turned his attention to getting the best out of it. He could sing, he was a boon-companion. Often he got into scrapes, but they were the manly scrapes that are easily condoned. So he made a good time out of it, whilst his self-respect was in suppression. He trusted to his good looks and handsome figure, his refinement, his decent education, to get him most of what he wanted, and he was not disappointed. Yet he was restless. Something seemed to gnaw him inside. He was never still, he was never alone. With his mother he was rather humble. Paul he admired and loved and despised slightly. And Paul admired and loved and despised him slightly.

Mrs Morel had had a few pounds left to her by her father, and she decided to buy her son out of the army. He was wild with joy. Now he was like a lad taking a holiday.

He had always been fond of Beatrice Wyld, and during his furlough he picked up with her again. She was stronger and better in health. The two often went long walks together, Arthur taking her arm in soldier's fashion, rather stiffly. And she came to play the piano whilst he sang. Then Arthur would unhook his tunic collar. He grew flushed, his eyes were bright, he sang in a manly tenor. Afterwards they sat together on the sofa. He seemed to flaunt his body: she was aware of him so, the strong chest, the sides, the thighs in their close-fitting trousers.

He liked to lapse into the dialect when he talked to her. She would sometimes smoke with him. Occasionally she would only take a few whiffs at his cigarette.

"Nay," he said to her one evening, when she reached for his cigarette: "Nay tha doesna. I'll gi'e thee a smoke kiss if ter's a mind."

"I wanted a whiff, no kiss at all," she answered.

"Well—an' tha s'lt ha'e a whiff," he said, "along wi' t' kiss."

"I want a draw at thy fag," she cried, snatching for the cigarette between his lips.

He was sitting with his shoulder touching her. She was small and quick as lightning. He just escaped.

"I'll gi'e thee a smoke kiss," he said.

"Tha'rt a knivey nuisance, Arty Morel," she said, sitting back. "Ha'e a smoke kiss!"

The soldier leaned forward to her, smiling. His face was near hers.

"Shonna!" she replied, turning away her head.

He took a draw at his cigarette, and pursed up his mouth, and put his lips close to her. His dark-brown, cropped moustache stood out like a brush. She looked at the puckered crimson lips, then suddenly snatched the cigarette from his fingers and darted away. He, leaping after her, seized the comb from her back hair. She turned, threw the cigarette at him. He picked it up, put it in his mouth, and sat down.

"Nuisance!" she cried. "Give me my comb!"

She was afraid that her hair, specially done for him, would come down. She stood with her hands to her head. He hid the comb between his knees.

"I'n non got it,' he said.

The cigarette trembled between his lips with laughter, as he spoke.

"Liar!" she said.

"'S true as I'm here!" he laughed, showing his hands.

"You brazen imp!" she exclaimed, rushing and scuffling for the comb, which he had under his knees. As she wrestled with him, pulling at his smooth, tight-covered thighs, he laughed till he lay back on the sofa shaking with laughter. The cigarette fell from his mouth, almost singeing his throat. Under his delicate tan, the blood flushed up, and he laughed till his blue eyes were blinded, his throat swollen almost to choking. Then he sat up. Beatrice was putting in her comb.

"Tha tickled me, Beat," he said thickly.

Like a flash, her small white hand went out and smacked his face. He started up, glaring at her. They stared at each other. Slowly the flush mounted her cheek, she dropped her eyes, then her head. He sat down sulkily. She went into the scullery to adjust her hair. In private there she shed a few tears, she did not know what for.

When she returned, she was pursed up close. But it was only a film over her fire. He, with ruffled hair, was sulking upon the sofa. She sat down opposite, in the arm-chair, and neither spoke. The clock ticked in the silence, like blows.

"You are a little cat, Beat," he said at length, half apologetically.

"Well, you shouldn't be brazen," she replied.

There was again a long silence. He whistled to himself, like a man much agitated, but defiant. Suddenly she went across to him and kissed him.

"Did it, pore fing?" she mocked.

He lifted his face, smiling curiously.

"Kiss?" he invited her.

"Daren't I?" she asked.

"Go on!" he challenged, his mouth lifted to her.

Deliberately, and with a peculiar quivering smile, that seemed to overspread her whole body, she put her mouth on his. Immediately his arms folded round her. As soon as the long kiss was finished, she drew back her head from him, put her delicate fingers on his neck, through the open collar. Then she closed her eyes, giving herself up again in a kiss.

She acted of her own free will. What she would do, she did, and made nobody responsible.

Paul felt life changing around him. The conditions of youth were gone. Now, it was a home of grown-up people. Annie was a married woman, Arthur was following his own pleasure, in a way unknown to his folk. For so long, they had all lived at home, and gone out to pass their time. But now, for Annie and Arthur, life lay outside their mother's house. They came home for holiday and for rest. So there was that strange, half empty feeling about the house, as if the birds had flown. Paul became more and more unsettled. Annie and Arthur had gone. He was restless to follow. Yet home was for him beside his mother. And still, there was something else, something outside, something he wanted.

He grew more and more restless. Miriam did not satisfy him. His old mad desire to be with her grew weaker. Sometimes he met Clara in Nottingham, sometimes he went to meetings with her, sometimes he saw her at Willey Farm. But on these last occasions, the situation became strained. There was a triangle of antagonism between Paul and Clara and Miriam. With Clara, he took on a smart, worldly, mocking tone very antagonistic to Miriam. It did not matter what went before. She might be intimate and sad with him. Then as soon as Clara appeared, it all vanished, and he played to the newcomer.

Miriam had one beautiful evening with him in the hay. He had been on the horse-rake, and, having finished, came to help her to put the hay in cocks. Then he talked to her of his hopes and despairs, and his whole soul seemed to lie bare before her. She felt as if she watched the very quivering stuff of life in him. The moon came out: they walked home together: he seemed to have come to her because he needed her so badly, and she listened to him, gave him all her love and her faith. It seemed to her, he brought her the best of himself to keep, and that she would guard it all her life. Nay, the sky did not cherish the stars more surely and eternally than she would guard the good in the soul of Paul Morel. She went on home alone feeling exalted, glad in her faith.

And then, the next day, Clara came. They were to have tea in the hayfield. Miriam watched the evening drawing to gold and shadow. And all the time, Paul was sporting with Clara. He made higher and higher heaps of hay, that they were jumping over. Miriam did not care for the game, and stood aside. Edgar and Geoffrey and Maurice and Clara and Paul jumped. Paul won, because he was light. Clara's blood was roused. She could run like an Amazon. Paul loved the determined way she rushed at the hay-cock and leaped, landed on the other side, her breasts shaken, her thick hair coming undone.

"You touched!" he cried, "you touched."

"No!" she flashed, turning to Edgar. "I didn't touch, did I? Wasn't I clear?"

"I couldn't say," laughed Edgar.

None of them could say.

"But you touched," said Paul, "you're beaten."

"I did *not* touch," she cried.

"As plain as anything," said Paul.

"Box his ears for me," she cried to Edgar.

"Nay," Edgar laughed, "I daren't. You must do it yourself."

"And nothing can alter the fact that you touched," laughed Paul.

She was furious with him. Her little triumph before these lads and men was gone. She had forgotten herself in the game. Now he was to humble her.

"I think you are despicable!" she said.

And again he laughed, in a way that tortured Miriam.

"And I *knew* you couldn't jump that heap," he teased.

She turned her back on him. Yet, everybody could see, that the only person she listened to, or was conscious of, was he, and he of her. It pleased the men to see this battle between them. But Miriam was tortured.

Paul could choose the lesser in place of the higher, she saw. He could be unfaithful to himself, unfaithful to the real, deep Paul Morel. There was a danger of his becoming frivolous, of his running after his satisfactions like any Arthur, or like his father. It made Miriam bitter, to think that he should throw away his soul for this flippant traffic of triviality with Clara. She walked in bitterness and silence, while the other two rallied each other, and Paul sported.

And afterwards, he would not own it, but he was rather ashamed of himself, and prostrated himself before Miriam. Then again he rebelled.

"It's not religious to be religious," he said. "I reckon a crow is religious when it sails across the sky. But it only does it because it feels itself carried to where it's going, not because it thinks it is being eternal."

But Miriam knew that one should be religious in everything, have God, whatever God He might be, present in everything.

"I don't believe God knows such a lot about himself," he cried. "God doesn't *know* things, he *is* things—and I'm sure he's not soulful."

And then it seemed to her that Paul was arguing God onto his own side, because he wanted his own way, and his own pleasure. There was a long battle between him and her. He was utterly unfaithful to her even in her own presence; then he was ashamed, then repentant; then he hated her and went off again. Those were the ever-recurring conditions.

She fretted him to the bottom of his soul. There she remained, sad, pensive, a worshipper. And he caused her sorrow. Half the time he grieved for her, half the time he hated her. She was his conscience; and he felt, somehow, he had got a conscience that was too much for him. He could not leave her, because in one way she did hold the best of him. He could not stay with her because she did not take the rest of him, which was three quarters. So he chafed himself into rawness over her.

When she was twenty-one, he wrote her a letter which could only have been written to her.

"Must I write you a birthday letter?—It seems a pernicious thing to do deliberately, don't you think? Because I'm sure to get flatulent and sententious." Then followed a certain amount of flatulence.

"My last letter prepared you, did it not, to rejoice over your coming of age. Do you not feel like an heiress being installed into her heritage? For now you come publicly into full possession of yourself. Would you have more than yourself?—Impossible!"

Now he began to feel the torture of self-consciousness. He seemed cut away underneath, as if he could not stand on his feet, but must flounder and flounder.

"—May I speak of our old, worn love, this last time. It too is changing, is it not? Say, has not the body of that love died, and left you its invulnerable soul! You see, I can give you a spirit love, I have given it you this long, long time: but not embodied passion. See, you are a nun. I have given you what I would give a holy nun—as a mystic monk to a mystic nun: surely you esteem it best. Yet you regret—no, have regretted—the other. In all our relations, no body enters. I do not talk to you through the senses—rather through the spirit. That is why we cannot love in the common sense. When I talk to you, I do not look at you, often, for, can you understand, I do not talk to your eyes, though they are dark and fine, nor to your ears, hidden under a graceful toss of silky hair—but to you away inside, beyond. So I shall continue to do a whole life-time, if fate does not intervene. Do you see? And do you understand now why I only kiss you under the mistletoe. Do you understand?—and do I?—and is it better, think you? I think I am too refined, too civilised. I think many folk are.

You have a place in my nature which no one else could fill. You have played a fundamental part in my development. And this grief, which has been like a cloud between our two souls, does it not begin to dissipate? Ours is not an everyday affection. As yet, we are mortal, and to live side by side with one another would be dreadful, for somehow, with you I cannot long be trivial, and, you know, to be always beyond this mortal state would be to lose it. If people marry, they must live together as affectionate humans who may be commonplace with each other without feeling awkward—not as two souls. So I feel it.

I might marry in the years to come. It would be a woman I could kiss and embrace, whom I could make the mother of my children, whom I could talk to playfully, trivially, earnestly, but never with this dreadful seriousness. See how fate has disposed things. You, you might marry, a man who would not pour himself out like fire before you. I wonder if you understand—I wonder if I understand myself. But you do know that these things make me sick, and now here is an end of our talk on the matter. Forgive me for all this—it is unnatural, I know—and burn this letter, and do not think of it, or make me think of it, and so help us to bear the burden of ourselves.

How will you like a *Manual of Ethics*? You will like it, and we can talk about that, and learn—oh yes. And you will be richer. Is it not so?—You see our intimacy would have been all beautiful, but for one little mistake.

And you are twenty one. I am so glad you are an independent woman now. You are as strong as I, are you not?—yes stronger. Oh, if we are to live, we must be wise, and not drive ourselves too far. We must be trivial, and we must seek beauty, and not pain, or else we are in a quandary. Mind, mind, not a word on the sensitive places yet.

Oh we will be gay at your party on Saturday. I am not sad, not a bit sad, now, in my heart.

Ought I to send this letter—I doubt it. But there—it is best to understand.—Au revoir—"

Miriam read this letter twice, after which she sealed it up. A year later she broke the seal to show her mother the letter.

"You are a nun—you are a nun"—the words went into her heart again and again. Nothing he ever had said, had gone into her so deeply, fixedly, like a mortal wound.

She answered him two days after the party. "'Our intimacy would have been all beautiful, but for one little mistake,'" she quoted. "Was the mistake mine?"

Almost immediately, he replied to her from Nottingham, sending her at the same time a little *Omar Khayyam*.

"—You will find a good deal between the flimsy covers of this little book, but the lesson that we should drink the red wine of life and let it make us glad awhile is the reason why I got it. Also I want to bring you *The Blessed Damosel*, to spend an evening with you and Rossetti.

'The little mistake was yours?' you ask? Why, whoever erred alone! Your share of the mistake was glorious, making for immortality. But mine was an unflagging recognition of the clay of the pot—brittle—rigid—confining. And I alternately hated and loved the earthy stuff of myself. When I loved it I was cruel to you, when I hated it I was cruel to myself, and everything. Have I not a faculty for being very cruel?

If on your birthday I was still somewhat stormy, it was because I recognised in your sun of Wednesday the washed brightness of your long day of sleet on Tuesday. I do not sit down and fight my battles out as you do. I shake my enemy by the throat and tell him he's a villain and a dog. With that I bid him go, and for a while, I am free.

Then I say he was a weakling farce, and I laugh. After awhile, I am plunged again into blackness on finding he is not gone or dead—when this is unbearable I have another wild fling at him. By such guerilla warfares I succeed, or I do not succeed. No triumphs, no Waterloos. Thus I do not suffer so keenly, and am less stable. After all, it is a joke, this of 'us', is it not?

I am glad you answered—you are so calm and natural you put me to shame. What a ranter I am! I must play though——. You do not understand how I must dance round my enemies, howling at them and spying them out, playing with anything that comes my way, having occasional tussles. If I closed with everything, and kept my sorrow hugged in my breast as you do, I should die of exhaustion. In these things our natures are radically different.

So we are often out of sympathy. But in fundamentals, we may always be together, I think.

I must thank you for your sympathy with my painting and drawing. Many a sketch is dedicated to you. I do look forward to your criticisms, which, to my shame and glory, are always grand appreciations. It is a lovely joke that.

Au revoir. Now I must balance up a damned dry account. I hope you burn these letters. It is my rule to burn all—for none are so nice but what I can recall the pleasure they refer to, and most are full of lurking tears which I must run away from——"

This was the end of the first phase of Paul's love affair. He was now about twenty-three years old, and, though still virgin, the sex instinct that Miriam had over refined for so long now grew particularly strong. Often, as he talked to Clara Dawes, came that thickening and quickening of his blood, that peculiar concentration in the breast, as if something were alive there, a new self or a new centre of consciousness, warning him that sooner or later he would have to ask one woman or another. But he belonged to Miriam. Of that she was so fixedly sure, that he allowed her right.

CHAPTER X
Clara

When he was twenty-three years old Paul sent in a landscape to the winter exhibition at Nottingham Castle. Miss Jordan had taken a good deal of interest in him, had invited him to her house, where he met other artists. He was beginning to grow ambitious.

One morning the postman came just as he was washing in the scullery. Suddenly he heard a wild noise from his mother. Rushing into the kitchen he found her standing on the hearth-rug wildly waving a letter and crying 'Hurray!' as if she had gone mad. He was shocked and frightened.

"Why mother!" he exclaimed.

She flew to him, flung her arms round him for a moment, then waved the letter crying:

"Hurray, my boy—I knew we should do it!"

He was afraid of her, the small, severe woman with greying hair suddenly bursting out in such frenzy. The postman came running back, afraid something had happened. They saw his tipped cap over the short curtain. Mrs Morel rushed to the door.

"His picture's got first prize, Fred," she cried, "and is sold for twenty guineas."

"My word, that's somethink like!" said the young postman, whom they had known all his life.

"And Major Moreton has bought it," she cried.

"It looks like meanin' somethink, that does, Mrs Morel," said the postman, his blue eyes bright. He was glad to have brought such a lucky letter. Mrs Morel went indoors and sat down, trembling. Paul was afraid lest she might have mis-read the letter, and might be disappointed after all. He scrutinised it once, twice. Yes, he became convinced it was true. Then he sat down, his heart beating with joy.

"Mother!" he exclaimed.

"Didn't I *say* we should do it?" she said, pretending she was not crying.

He took the kettle off the fire and mashed the tea.

"You didn't think, mother—" he began, tentatively.

"No my son—not so much—but I expected a good deal."

"But not so much," he said.

"No—no—but I knew we should do it."

And then she recovered her composure, apparently at least. He sat with his shirt turned back, showing his young throat almost like a girl's, and the towel in his hand, his hair sticking up wet.

"Twenty guineas, mother! That's just what you wanted to buy Arthur out. Now you needn't borrow any. It'll just do."

"Indeed I shan't take it all!" she said.

"But why?"

"Because I shan't."

"Well—you have twelve pounds, I'll have nine."

They cavilled about sharing the twenty guineas. She wanted only to take the five pounds she needed. He would not hear of it. So they got over the stress of emotion by quarrelling.

Morel came home at night from the pit saying:

"They tell me Paul's got first prize for his picture, and sold it to Lord Henry Bentley for fifty pound."

"Oh what stories people do tell!" she cried.

"Ha!" he answered. "I said I wor sure it wor a lie. But they said tha'd told Fred Hodgkisson."

"As if I would tell him such stuff!"

"Ha!" assented the miner.

But he was disappointed nevertheless.

"It's true he has got the first prize—" said Mrs Morel.

The miner sat heavily in his chair.

"He has beguy!" he exclaimed.

He stared across the room fixedly.

"But as for fifty pounds, such nonsense!" She was silent awhile. "Major Moreton bought it for twenty guineas, that's true—."

"Twenty guineas! Tha niver says!" exclaimed Morel.

"Yes, and it was worth it."

"Ay!" he said. "I don't misdoubt it.—But twenty guineas for a bit of a paintin' as he knocked off in an hour or two—!" he was silent with conceit of his son. Mrs Morel sniffed, as if it were nothing.

"And when does he handle th'money?" asked the collier.

"That I couldn't tell you—when the picture is sent home, I suppose."

There was silence. Morel stared at the sugar basin instead of eating his dinner. His black arm, with the hand all gnarled with work, lay on the table. His wife pretended not to see him rub the back of his hand across his eyes, nor the smear in the coal-dust on his black face.

"Yes, an' that other lad 'ud 'a done as much, if they hadna ha' killed 'im," he said, quietly.

The thought of William went through Mrs Morel like a cold blade. It left her feeling she was tired, and wanted rest.

Paul was invited to dinner at Mr Jordan's. Afterwards he said:

"Mother, I want an evening suit."

"Yes, I was afraid you would," she said. She was glad. There was a moment or two of silence. "There's that one of William's," she continued, "that I know cost four pounds ten, and which he'd only worn three times—."

"Should you like me to wear it, mother?" he asked.

"Yes. I think it would fit you—at least the coat. The trousers would want shortening."

He went upstairs and put on the coat and vest. Coming down, he looked strange, in a flannel collar, and a flannel shirtfront, with an evening coat and vest. It was rather large.

"The tailor can make it right," she said, smoothing her hand over his shoulder. "It's beautiful stuff. I never could find in my heart to let your father wear the trousers, and very glad I am now."

And as she smoothed her hand over the silk collar, she thought of her eldest son. But this son was living enough inside the clothes. She passed her hand down his back to feel him. He was alive and hers. The other was dead.

He went out to dinner several times in his evening suit that had been William's. Each time his mother's heart was firm with pride and joy. He was started now. The studs she and the children had bought for William were in his shirt front: he wore one of William's dress shirts. But he had an elegant figure. His face was rough, but warm-looking and rather pleasing. He did not look particularly a gentleman, but she thought he looked quite a man.

He told her everything that took place, everything that was said. It was as if she had been there. And he was dying to introduce her to these new friends who had dinner at 7.30 in the evening.

"Go along with you," she said. "What do they want to know me for?"

"They do!" he cried indignantly. "If they want to know me, and they say they do, then they want to know you—because you're quite as clever as I am."

"Go along with you, child," she laughed.

But she began to spare her hands. They too were workgnarled now. The skin was shiny with so much hot water, the knuckles rather swollen. But she began to be careful to keep them out of soda. She regretted what they had been, so small and exquisite. And when Annie insisted on her having more stylish blouses to suit her age, she submitted. She even went so far as to allow a black velvet bow to be placed on her hair. Then she sniffed in her sarcastic manner, and was sure she looked a sight. But she looked a lady, Paul declared, as much as Mrs Major Moreton, and far, far nicer. The family was coming on. Only Morel remained unchanged, or rather, lapsed slowly.

Paul and his mother now had long discussions about life. Religion was fading into the background. He had shovelled away all the beliefs that would hamper him, had cleared the ground, and come more or less to the bedrock of belief, that one should feel inside oneself for right and wrong, and should have the patience to gradually realise one's God. Now life interested him more.

"You know," he said to his mother, "I don't want to belong to the well-to-do middle class. I like my common people best. I belong to the common people."

"But if anyone else said so, my son, wouldn't you be in a tear. *You* know you consider yourself equal to any gentleman."

"In myself," he answered, "not in my class or my education or my manners. But in myself, I am."

"Very well then—then why talk about the common people."

"Because—the difference between people isn't in their class, but in themselves.—Only from the middle classes, one gets ideas, and from the common people—life itself, warmth. You feel their hates and loves—"

"It's all very well, my boy—but then why don't you go and talk to your father's pals?"

"But they're rather different."

"Not at all. They're the common people. After all, whom do you mix with now, among the common people? Those that exchange ideas, like the middle classes. The rest don't interest you."

"But—there's the life—"

"I don't believe there's a jot more life from Miriam than you could get from any educated girl—say Miss Moreton. It is *you* who are snobbish about class."

She frankly *wanted* him to climb into the middle classes, a thing not very difficult, she knew. And she wanted him in the end to marry a lady.

Now she began to combat him in his restless fretting. He still kept up his connection with Miriam, could neither break free nor go the whole length of engagement. And this indecision seemed to bleed him of his energy. Moreover his mother suspected him of an unrecognised leaning towards Clara, and, since the latter was a married woman, she wished he would fall in love with one of the girls in a better station of life. But he was stupid, and would refuse to love or even to admire a girl much, just because she was his social superior.

"My boy," said his mother to him, "all your cleverness, your breaking away from old things and taking life in your own hands, doesn't seem to bring you much happiness."

"What is happiness!" he cried. "It's nothing to me! How *am* I to be happy?"

The plump question disturbed her.

"That's for you to judge, my lad. But if you could meet some *good* woman who would *make* you happy—and you began to think of settling your life—when you have the means—so that you could work without all this fretting—it would be much better for you."

He frowned. His mother caught him on the raw of his wound of Miriam. He pushed the tumbled hair off his forehead, his eyes full of pain and fire.

"You mean easy, mother," he cried. "That's a woman's whole doctrine for life—ease of soul and physical comfort. And I do despise it."

"Oh do you!" replied his mother. "And do you call yours a divine discontent?"

"Yes—I don't care about its divinity. But damn your happiness! So long as life's full, it doesn't matter whether it's happy or not. I'm afraid your happiness would bore me."

"You never give it a chance," she said. Then suddenly all her passion of grief over him broke out. "But it does matter!" she cried, "And you *ought* to be happy, you ought to try to be happy, to live to be happy. How could I bear to think your life wouldn't be a happy one!"

"Your own's been bad enough, mater, but it hasn't left you so much worse off than the folk who've been happier. I reckon you've done well. And I am the same. Aren't I well enough off?"

"You're not, my son. Battle—battle—and suffer, it's about all you do, as far as I can see."

"But why not, my dear? I tell you it's the best—."

"It isn't!—and one *ought* to be happy, one *ought*."

By this time Mrs Morel was trembling violently. Struggles of this kind often took place between her and her son, when she seemed to fight for his very life, against his own will to die. He took her in his arms. She was ill, and pitiful.

"Never mind, Little!" he murmured. "So long as you don't feel life's paltry, and a miserable business, the rest doesn't matter, happiness or unhappiness."

She pressed him to her.

"But I want you to be happy," she said, pathetically.

"Eh my dear—say rather you want me to live."

Mrs Morel felt as if her heart would break for him. At this rate, she knew he would not live. He had that poignant carelessness about himself, his own suffering, his own life, which is a form of slow suicide. It almost broke her heart. With all the passion of her strong nature, she hated Miriam, for having in this subtle way undermined his joy. It did not matter to her that Miriam could not help it. Miriam did it, and she hated her.

She wished so much he would fall in love with a girl equal to be his mate—educated and strong. But he would not look at anybody above him in station. He seemed to like Mrs Dawes. At any rate that feeling was wholesome. His mother prayed and prayed for him, that he might not be wasted. That was all her prayer—not for his soul or his righteousness, but that he might not be wasted. And while he slept, for hours and hours, she thought and prayed for him.

He drifted away from Miriam imperceptibly, without knowing he was going. Arthur only left the army to be married. The baby was born six months after his wedding. Mrs Morel got him a job under the firm again, at twenty one shillings a week. She furnished for him, with the help of Beatrice's mother, a little cottage of two rooms. He was caught now. It did not matter how he kicked and struggled, he was fast. For a time he chafed, was irritable with his young wife, who loved him; he went almost distracted when the baby, which was delicate, cried or gave trouble. He grumbled for hours to his mother. She only said "Well, my lad, you did it yourself, now you must make the best of it." And then the grit came out in him. He buckled to work, undertook his responsibilities, acknowledged that he belonged to his wife and child, and did make a good best of it. He had never been very closely inbound into the family. Now he was gone altogether.

The months went slowly along. Paul had more or less got into connection with the socialist, suffragette, unitarian people in Nottingham, owing to his acquaintance with Clara. One day a friend of his and of Clara's, in Bestwood, asked him to take a message to Mrs Dawes. He went in the evening across Sneinton Market to Bluebell Hill. He found the house in a mean little street paved with granite cobbles, and having causeways of dark blue, grooved bricks. The front door went up a step from off this rough pavement where the feet of the passers-by rasped and clattered. The brown paint on the door was so old that the naked wood showed between the rents. He stood on the street below, and knocked. There came a heavy footstep; a large, stout woman of about sixty towered above him. He looked up at her from the pavement. She had a rather severe face.

She admitted him into the parlour, which opened onto the street. It was a small, stuffy, defunct room, of mahogany and deathly enlargements of photographs of departed people, done in carbon. Mrs Radford left him. She was stately, almost martial. In a moment Clara appeared. She flushed deeply, and he was covered with confusion. It seemed as if she did not like being discovered in her home circumstances.

"I thought it couldn't be your voice," she said.

But she might as well be hung for a sheep as for a lamb. She invited him out of the mausoleum of a parlour into the kitchen.

That was a little, darkish room too, but it was smothered in white lace. The mother had seated herself again by the cupboard, and was drawing thread from a vast web of lace. A clump of fluff and ravelled cotton was at her right hand, a heap of three-quarter-inch lace lay on her left, whilst in front of her was the mountain of the lace web, piling the hearthrug. Threads of curly cotton, pulled out from beneath the lengths of lace, strewed over the fender and the fireplace. Paul dared not go forward, for fear of treading on piles of white stuff.

On the table was a jenny for carding the lace. There was a pack of brown cardboard squares, a pack of cards of lace, a little box of pins. And on the sofa lay a heap of drawn lace.

The room was all lace—and it was so dark and warm, that the white, snowy stuff seemed the more distinct.

"If you're coming in you won't have to mind the work," said Mrs Radford. "I know we're about blocked up. But sit you down."

Clara, much embarrassed, gave him a chair against the wall opposite the white heaps. Then she herself took her place on the sofa, shamedly.

"Will you drink a bottle of stout?" Mrs Radford asked. "Clara, get him a bottle of stout."

He protested, but Mrs Radford insisted.

"You look as if you could do with it," she said. "Haven't you never any more colour than that?"

"It's only a thick skin I've got, that doesn't show the blood through," he answered.

Clara, ashamed and chagrined, brought him a bottle of stout and a glass. He poured out some of the black stuff.

"Well," he said, lifting the glass, "here's health!"

"And thank you," said Mrs Radford.

He took a drink of stout.

"And light yourself a cigarette, so long as you don't set the house on fire," said Mrs Radford.

"Thank you," he replied.

"Nay, you needn't thank me," she answered. "I s'll be glad to smell a bit of smoke in th'ouse again. A house o' women is as dead as a house wi' no fire, to my thinkin'. I'm not a spider as likes a corner to myself. I like a man about, if he's only something to snap at."

Clara began to work. Her jenny spun with a subdued buzz, the white lace hopped from between her fingers onto the card. It was filled, she snipped off the length and pinned the end down to the banded lace. Then she put a new card in her jenny. Paul watched her. She sat square and magnificent. Her throat and arms were bare. The blood still mantled below her ears, she bent her head in shame of her humility. Her face was set on her work. Her arms were creamy and full of life, beside the white lace; her large, well-kept hands worked with a balanced movement, as if nothing would hurry them. He, not knowing, watched her all the time. He saw the arch of her neck from the shoulder, as she bent her head; he saw the coil of dun hair; he watched her moving, gleaming arms.

"I've heard a bit about you from Clara," continued the mother. "You're in Jordan's, aren't you?" She drew her lace unceasing.

"Yes."

"Ay, well and I can remember when Thomas Jordan used to ask *me* for one of my toffies."

"Did he?" laughed Paul. "And did he get it?"

"Sometimes he did, sometimes he didn't—which was latterly. For he's the sort that takes all and gives naught, he is—or used to be."

"I think he's very decent," said Paul.

"Yes, well I'm glad to hear it."

Mrs Radford looked across at him steadily. There was something determined about her that he liked. Her face was falling loose, but her eyes were calm, and there was something strong in her that made it seem she was not old, merely her wrinkles and loose cheeks were an anachronism. She had the strength and *sang froid* of a woman in the prime of life. She continued drawing the lace, with slow, dignified movements. The big web came up inevitably over her apron, the length of lace fell away at her side. Her arms were finely shapen, but glossy and yellow as old ivory. They had not the peculiar dull gleam that made Clara's so fascinating to him.

"And you've been going with Miriam Leivers?" the mother asked him.

"Well—" he answered.

"Yes, she's a nice girl," she continued. "She's very nice, but she's a bit too much above this world to suit my fancy."

"She is a bit like that," he agreed.

"She'll never be satisfied till she's got wings and can fly over everybody's head, she won't," she said.

Clara broke in, and he told her his message. She spoke humbly to him. He had surprised her in her drudgery. To have her humble made him feel as if he were lifting his head in expectation.

"Do you like jennying?" he asked.

"What can a woman do!" she replied bitterly.

"Is it sweated?"

"More or less. Isn't *all* women's work? That's another trick the men have played, since we force ourselves into the labour market."

"Now then, you shut up about the men," said her mother. "If the women wasn't fools the men wouldn't be bad uns, that's what I say.—No man was ever that bad wi' me, but what he got it back again.—Not but what they're a lousy lot, there's no denying it."

"But they're all right really, aren't they?" he asked.

"Well—they're a bit different from women," she answered.

"Would you care to be back at Jordan's?" he asked Clara.

"I don't think so," she replied.

"Yes she would!" cried her mother; "thank her stars if she could get back. Don't you listen to her. She's forever on that 'igh horse of hers. An' its back's that thin an' starved, it'll cut her i' two one of these days."

Clara suffered badly from her mother. Paul felt as if his eyes were coming very wide open. Wasn't he to take Clara's fulminations so seriously, after all? She spun steadily at her work. He experienced a thrill of joy, thinking she might need his help. She seemed denied and deprived of so much. And her arm moved mechanically, that should never have been subdued to a mechanism, and her head was bowed to the lace, that never should have been bowed. She seemed to be stranded there, among the refuse that life has thrown away, doing her jennying. It was a bitter thing to her to be put aside by life, as if it had no use for her. No wonder she protested.

She came with him to the door. He stood below in the mean street, looking up at her. So fine she was in her stature and her bearing, she reminded him of Juno dethroned. As she stood in the doorway, she winced from the street, from her surroundings.

"And you will go with Mrs Hodgkinson to Hucknall?"

He was talking quite meaninglessly, only watching her. Her grey eyes at last met his. They looked dumb with humiliation, pleading with a kind of captive misery. He was shaken and at a loss. He had thought her high and mighty.

When he left her he wanted to run. He went to the station in a sort of dream, and was at home without realising he had moved out of her street.

He had an idea that Susan, the overseer of the Spiral girls, was about to be married. He asked her the next day.

"I say Susan, I heard a whisper of your getting married. What about it?"

Susan flushed red.

"Who's been talking to you?" she replied.

"Nobody—I merely heard a whisper that you *were* thinking— —"

"Well I am—though you needn't tell anybody. What's more I wish I wasn't—!"

"Nay Susan, you won't make me believe that."

"Shan't I? You *can* believe it though. I'd rather stop here a thousand times."

Paul was perturbed.

"Why, Susan?"

The girl's colour was high, and her eyes flashed.

"That's why!"

"And must you?"

For answer, she looked at him. There was about him a candour, and gentleness, which made the women trust him. He understood.

"Ah, I'm sorry," he said. Tears came to her eyes.

"But you'll see it'll turn out all right. You'll make the best of it," he continued, rather wistfully.

"There's nothing else for it."

"Yea, there's making the worst of it. Try and make it all right."

He soon made occasion to call again on Clara.

"Would you," he said, "care to come back to Jordan's?"

She put down her work, laid her beautiful arms on the table, and looked at him for some moments without answering. Gradually the flush mounted her cheek.

"Why?" she asked.

Paul felt rather awkward.

"Well—because Susan is thinking of leaving," he said.

Clara went on with her jennying. The white lace leaped in little jumps and bounds onto the card. He waited for her. Without raising her head, she said at last, in a peculiar low voice:

"Have you said anything about it?"

"Except to you, not a word."

There was again a long silence.

"I will apply when the advertisement is out," she said.

"You will apply before that. I will let you know exactly when."

She went on spinning her little machine, and did not contradict him.

Clara came to Jordan's. Some of the older hands, Fanny among them, remembered her earlier rule, and cordially disliked the memory. Clara had always been 'ikey'—reserved and superior. She had never mixed with the girls as one of themselves. If she had occasion to find fault, she did it coolly and with perfect politeness: which the defaulter felt to be a bigger insult than crossness. Towards Fanny, the poor, overstrung hunchback, Clara was unfailingly compassionate, and gentle, as a result of which Fanny shed more bitter tears than ever the rough tongues of the other overseers had caused her.

There was something in Clara that Paul disliked, and much that piqued him. If she were about, he always watched her strong throat, or her neck upon which the blonde hair grew low and fluffy. There was a fine down, almost invisible, upon the skin of her face and arms, and when once he had perceived it, he saw it always.

When he was at his work, painting in the afternoon, she would come and stand near to him, perfectly motionless. Then he felt her, though she neither spoke nor touched him. Although she stood a yard away, he felt as if he were pressed against her, and was full of her warmth. Then he could paint no more. He flung down the brushes, and turned to talk to her.

Sometimes she praised his work, sometimes she was critical and cold.

"You are affected in that piece," she would say, and, as there was an element of truth in her condemnation, his blood boiled with anger.

Again: "What of this?" he would ask enthusiastically.

"Hm!" She made a small, doubtful sound. "It doesn't interest me much."

"Because you don't understand it," he retorted.

"Then why ask me about it?"

"Because I thought you would understand."

She would shrug her shoulders, in scorn of his work. She maddened him—he was furious. Then he abused her, and went into passionate exposition of his stuff. This amused and stimulated her. But she never owned that she had been wrong.

During the ten years that she had belonged to the women's movement, she had acquired a fair amount of education. And having had some of Miriam's passion to be instructed, had taught herself French, and could read in that language with a struggle. She considered herself as a woman apart, and particularly apart from her class. The girls in the spiral department were all of good homes. It was a small, special industry, and had a certain distinction. There was an air of refinement in both rooms. But Clara was aloof also from her fellow workers.

None of these things, however, did she reveal to Paul. She was not the one to give herself away. There was a sense of mystery about her. She was so reserved, he felt she had much to reserve. Her history was open on the surface, but its inner meaning was hidden from everybody. It was exciting. And then sometimes he caught her looking at him from under her brows, with an almost furtive, sullen scrutiny, which made him move quickly. Often she met his eyes. But then her own were, as it were, covered over, revealing nothing. She gave him a little, lenient smile. She was to him extraordinarily provocative, because of the knowledge she seemed to possess, and gathered fruit of experience he could not attain.

One day he picked up a copy of *Lettres de mon Moulin* from her work-bench.

"You read French, do you?" he cried.

Clara glanced round negligently. She was making an elastic stocking of heliotrope silk, turning the spiral-machine with slow, balanced regularity, occasionally bending down to see her work, or to adjust the needles: then her magnificent neck, with its down and fine pencils of hair shone white against the lavender, lustrous silk. She turned a few more rounds, and stopped.

"What did you say?" she asked, smiling sweetly.

Paul's eyes glittered at her insolent indifference to him.

"I did not know you read French," he said, very polite.

"Did you not?" she replied, with a faint, sarcastic smile.

"Rotten swank!" he said, but scarcely loud enough to be heard.

He shut his mouth angrily, as he watched her. She seemed to scorn the work she mechanically produced. Yet the hose she made were as nearly perfect as possible.

"You don't like spiral work," he said.

"Oh well, all work is work," she answered, as if she knew all about it. He marvelled at her coldness. He had to do everything hotly. She must be something special.

"What would you prefer to do?" he asked.

She laughed at him, indulgently, as she said:

"There is so little likelihood of my ever being given a choice, that I haven't wasted time considering."

"Pah!" he said, contemptuous on his side now. "You only say that, because you're too proud to own up what you want and can't get."

"You know me very well," she replied, coldly.

"I know you think you're terrific great shakes, and that you live under the eternal insult of working in a factory—." He was very angry, and very rude. She merely turned away from him in disdain. He walked whistling down the room, flirted and laughed with Hilda.

Later on, he said to himself:

"What was I so impudent to Clara for?" He was rather annoyed with himself, at the same time glad.

"Serve her right—she stinks with silent pride," he said to himself angrily.

For several days he avoided seeing her at all. At last, however, he had to go down and discuss an order with her. Upon the surface of all his wrath and discomfort, he was gay and pleasant as ever.

"You are wearing a flower," he said. "I thought that was against your rule."

"I have no *rule*," she said, gently raising the head of a rather bruised red rose.

"No; of course; only a preference. But you don't as a rule, I believe, *choose* to wear the languishing heads of decapitated flowers, on your bosom."

She let fall the rose with a sharp movement.

"This," she said, "is a flower I found in the street."

"Jetsam of lost ladies," he said—"I'd hold a conversation with it, if I were you:—'The Rose and the Tomb.'—Know that poem?"

"I do not," she said.

"I thought you were a French scholar," he mocked. The blood came up in her cheek. She was going to be nasty, but he forestalled her.

"You might learn it," he said, grinning, "and then we'd act it. I'll ventriloquise the rose, and you do the tomb."

"I think," she said, "you should learn manners."

"I will, when it'll profit me anything." He began to lose his head. "And I don't want *all* the virtues to be on my side.—And besides, you'd do the tomb so well. Everybody feels as if they want a gleg at the skeleton in your vault."

Now he had lost his head, and gone too far.

"But I beg your pardon," he said, pulling up.

She turned coldly aside. He fled upstairs.

"Paul's sat on a cinder," said the other girls.

In the afternoon he came down. There was a certain weight on his heart, which he wanted to remove. He thought to do it by offering her chocolates.

"Have one?" he said. "I bought a handful to sweeten me up."

To his great relief, she accepted. He sat on the work-bench beside her machine, twisting a piece of silk round his finger. She loved him for his quick, unexpected movements, like a young animal. His feet swung as he pondered. The sweets lay strewn on the bench. She bent over her machine, grinding rhythmically, then stooping to see the stocking that hung beneath, pulled down by the weight. He watched the handsome crouching of her back, and the apron strings curling on the floor.

"There is always about you," he said, "a sort of waiting. Whatever I see you doing, you're not really there, you are waiting—like Penelope when she did her weaving." He could not help a spurt of wickedness. "I'll call you Penelope," he said.

"Would it make any difference?" she said, carefully removing one of her needles.

"That doesn't matter, so long as it pleases me.—Here, I say, you seem to forget I'm your boss. It just occurs to me."

"And what does that mean?" she asked coolly.

"It means I've got a right to boss you."

"Is there anything you want to complain about?"

"Oh I say, you needn't be nasty," he said angrily.

"I don't know what you want," she said, continuing her task.

"I want you to treat me nicely and respectfully."

"Call you 'Sir', perhaps?" she asked quietly.

"Yes, call me Sir. I should love it."

"Then I wish you would go upstairs, Sir."

His mouth closed, and a frown came on his face. He jumped suddenly down.

"You're too blessed superior for anything," he said.

And he went away to the other girls. He felt he was being angrier than he had any need to be. In fact, he doubted slightly that he was showing off. But if he were, then he would. Clara heard him laughing, in a way she hated, with the girls down the next room.

When at evening he went through the department after the girls had gone, he saw his chocolates lying untouched in front of Clara's machine. He left them. In the morning they were still there, and Clara was at work. Later on, Minnie, a little brunette they called Pussy, called to him:

"Hey, haven't you got a chocolate for anybody?"

"Sorry Pussy," he replied. "I meant to have offered them, then I went and forgot 'em."

"I think you did," she answered.

"I'll bring you some this afternoon. You don't want them after they've been lying about, do you?"

"Oh I'm not particular," smiled Pussy.

"Oh no," he said. "They'll be dusty."

He went up to Clara's bench.

"Sorry I left these things littering about," he said.

She flushed scarlet. He gathered them together in his fist.

"They'll be dirty now," he said. "You should have taken them. I wonder why you didn't. I meant to have told you I wanted you to."

He flung them out of the window, into the yard below. He just glanced at her. She winced from his eyes.

In the afternoon he brought another packet.

"Will you take some," he said, offering them first to Clara. "These are fresh."

She accepted one, and put it onto the bench.

"Oh, take several, for luck," he said.

She took a couple more, and put them on the bench also. Then she turned in confusion to her work. He went on up the room.

"Here you are Pussy," he said. "Don't be greedy!"

"Are they all for her?" cried the others, rushing up.

"Of course they're not," he said.

The girls clamoured round. Pussy drew back from her mates.

"Come out!" she cried. "I can have first pick, can't I Paul?"

"Be nice with 'em," he said, and went away.

"You *are* a dear," the girls cried.

"Tenpence," he answered.

He went past Clara without speaking. She felt the three chocolate creams would burn her if she touched them. It needed all her courage to slip them into the pocket of her apron.

The girls loved him and were afraid of him. He was so nice while he was nice, but if he were offended, so distant, treating them as if they scarcely existed, or not more than the bobbins of thread. And then, if they were impudent, he said quietly: "Do you mind going on with your work," and stood and watched.

When he celebrated his twenty third birthday, the house was in trouble. Arthur was just going to be married. His mother was not well. His father, getting an old man, and lame from his accidents, was given a paltry, poor job. Miriam was an eternal reproach. He felt he owed himself to her, yet could not give himself. The house moreover needed his support. He was pulled in all directions. He was not glad it was his birthday. It made him bitter.

He got to work at eight o'clock. Most of the clerks had not turned up. The girls were not due till 8.30. As he was changing his coat, he heard a voice behind him say:

"Paul, Paul, I want you."

It was Fanny, the hunch-back, standing at the top of her stairs, her face radiant with a secret. Paul looked at her in astonishment.

"I want you," she said. He stood at a loss.

"Come on," she coaxed. "Come before you begin of the letters."

He went down the half dozen steps into her dry, narrow 'finishing-off' room. Fanny walked before him: her black bodice was so short, the waist was under her arm-pits; and her green-black cashmere skirt seemed very long, as she strode with big strides before the young man, himself so graceful. She went to her seat at the narrow end of the room, where the window opened onto chimney pots. Paul watched her thin hands and her flat red wrists as she excitedly twitched her white apron, which was spread on the bench in front of her. She hesitated.

"You didn't think we'd forgot you," she asked, reproachful.

"Why?" he asked. He had forgotten his birthday himself.

"'Why', he says! 'Why!' Why, look here!" She pointed to the calendar, and he saw, surrounding the big black numbers '21', hundreds of little crosses in black-lead.

"Oh, kisses for my birthday," he laughed. "How did you know?"

"Yes, you want to know, don't you," Fanny mocked, hugely delighted. "There's one from everybody—except Lady Clara—and two from some. But I shan't tell you how many *I* put."

"Ah, I know you're spooney," he said.

"There you *are* mistaken," she cried, indignant. "I could never be so soft." Her voice was strong and contralto.

"You always pretend to be such a hard-hearted hussy," he laughed. "And you know you're as sentimental— — —"

"I'd rather be called sentimental than frozen meat," Fanny blurted. Paul knew she referred to Clara, and he smiled.

"Do you say such nasty things about me?" he laughed.

"No, my duck," the hunchback woman answered, lavishly tender. She was thirty nine. "No my duck, because you don't think yourself a fine figure in marble and us nothing but dirt. I'm as good as you, aren't I, Paul?" and the question delighted her.

"Why, we're not better than one another, are we?" he replied.

"But I'm as good as you, aren't I, Paul?" she persisted daringly.

"Of course you are. If it comes to goodness, you're better."

She was rather afraid of the situation. She might get hysterical.

"I thought I'd get here before the others—won't they say I'm deep!—Now shut your eyes—" she said.

"'And open your mouth, and see what God sends you'," he continued, suiting action to words, and expecting a piece of chocolate. He heard the rustle of the apron, and a faint clink of metal.

"I'm going to look," he said.

He opened his eyes. Fanny, her long cheeks flushed, her blue eyes shining, was gazing at him. There was a little bundle of paint tubes on the bench before him. He turned pale.

"No Fanny," he said quickly.

"From us all," she answered hastily.

"No but— —"

"Are they the right sort?" she asked, rocking herself with delight.

"Jove!—they're the best in the catalogue—"

"But they're the right sorts—?" she cried.

"They're off the little list I'd made, to get when my ship came in." He bit his lip.

Fanny was overcome with emotion. She must turn the conversation.

"They was all on thorns to do it, they all paid their shares, all except the Queen of Sheba."

The Queen of Sheba was Clara.

"And wouldn't she join?" Paul asked.

"She didn't get the chance—we never told her—we wasn't going to have *her* bossing *this* show. We didn't *want* her to join."

Paul laughed at the woman. He was much moved. At last he must go. She was very close to him. Suddenly she flung her arms round his neck and kissed him vehemently.

"I can give you a kiss today," she said, apologetically. "You've looked so white, it's made my heart ache."

Paul kissed her, and left her. Her arms were so pitifully thin, that his heart ached also.

That day, he met Clara as he ran downstairs to wash his hands at dinner time.

"You have stayed to dinner!" he exclaimed. It was unusual for her.

"Yes—and I seem to have dined on old surgical-appliance stock. I *must* go out now, or I shall feel stale india-rubber right through."

She lingered. He instantly caught at her wish.

"You are going anywhere?" he asked.

They went together up to the Castle. Out-doors she dressed very plainly, down to ugliness. Indoors she always looked nice. She walked with hesitating steps alongside Paul, bowing and turning away from him. Dowdy in dress, and drooping, she showed to great disadvantage. He could scarcely recognise her strong form, that seemed to slumber with power. She appeared almost insignificant, drowning her stature in her stoop, as she shrank from the public gaze.

The Castle grounds were very green and fresh. Climbing the precipitous ascent, he laughed and chattered, but she was silent, seeming to brood over something. There was scarcely time to go inside the squat, square building that crowns the bluff of rock. They leaned upon the wall where the cliff runs sheer down to the Park. Below them, in their holes in the sandstone, pigeons preened themselves and cooed softly. Away down upon the boulevard at the foot of the rock, tiny trees stood in their own pools of shadow, and tiny people went scurrying about in almost ludicrous importance.

"You feel as if you could scoop up the folk like tadpoles, and have a handful of them," he said.

She laughed, answering:

"Yes—it is not necessary to get far off in order to see us proportionately. The trees are much more significant."

"Bulk only," he said.

She laughed cynically.

Away beyond the boulevard, the thin stripes of the metals showed upon the railway track, whose margin was crowded with little stacks of timber, beside which smoking toy engines fussed. Then the silver string of the canal lay at random among the black heaps. Beyond, the dwellings, very dense on the river flats, looked like black, poisonous herbage, in thick rows and crowded beds, stretching right away, broken now and then by taller plants, right to where the river glistened in a hieroglyph across the country. The steep scarp cliffs across the river looked puny. Great stretches of country, darkened with trees and faintly brightened with corn-land, spread towards the haze, where the hills rose blue beyond grey.

"It is comforting," said Mrs Dawes, "to think the town goes no further. It is only a *little* sore upon the country yet."

"A little scab," Paul said.

She shivered. She loathed the town. Looking drearily across at the country which was forbidden her, her impassive face pale and hostile, she reminded Paul of one of the bitter, remorseful angels.

"But the town's all right," he said. "It's only temporary. This is the crude, clumsy make-shift we've practised on, till we find out what the idea is. The town will come all right."

"The optimist by intention!" she smiled, sarcastic.

"Perhaps so. But I don't hate the town. It's only a clumsy effort. We haven't learned to live together yet."

"But do we want to learn that?" she replied.

"Are you always like this?" he asked. "Loathing the very flesh on your bones, and the words of your mouth."

"It's only the unnatural things," she replied. "When things are natural they are beautiful."

"And what isn't natural?" he asked.

"Everything man has made," she answered, "including himself."

"But his women made him," he replied. "Besides, wasn't Dawes natural?"

She coloured deeply, looked away from him.

"We will not discuss it," she said.

"All right—But I think he's a bit *too* natural: a bit too near the native beast."

"You can spoil an animal," she said.

"Quite so. He'd be all right in his place. We're only mixed up: seven million stages, from the chimpanzee to me then to the poets and the christs. Dawes suits Hilda."

"I think you have not yet learned respect for another person's feelings," she said, coldly. He laughed.

"I am reprimanded," he said, continuing, "But what does it matter! I think about it—I only say it because I'm interested. And at the present moment, we're 'up above the world so high, like two cherubs in the sky'—and goodness, if that man was Dawes, that strutty little object down there, shouldn't you feel he was little enough for a subject of discussion?"

The blithe ignorance in which he trespassed through her private places disarmed her anger. She smiled at him, inwardly. He was an interesting, but such a young boy.

"I shall soon be constrained to call you the 'enfant terrible'," she said, smiling. She had got something of a platform trick of speech.

"Call me what you like," he replied. "'A rose would smell as sweet etc'."

314

The pigeons in the pockets of rock, among the perched bushes, cooed comfortably. To the left, the large church of St. Mary's rose into space, to keep close company with the Castle, above the heaped rubble of the town. Mrs Dawes smiled brightly as she looked across the country.

"I feel better," she said.

"Thank you," he replied. "Great compliment!"

"Oh, my brother!" she laughed.

"Hm!—that's snatching back with the left hand what you gave with the right, and no mistake," he said.

She laughed in amusement at him.

"But what was the matter with you?" he asked. "I know you were brooding something special. I can see the stamp of it on your face yet."

"I think I will not tell you," she said.

"All right—hug it," he answered.

She flushed and bit her lip.

"No," she said, "it was the girls."

"What about 'em?" Paul asked.

"They have been plotting something for a week now, and today they seem particularly full of it. All alike, they insult me with their secrecy."

"Do they?" he asked in concern.

"I should not mind," she went on, in the metallic, angry tone, "if they did not thrust it into my face, the fact that they have a secret."

"Just like women," said he.

"It is hateful, their mean gloating," she said intensely.

Paul was silent. He knew what the girls gloated over. He was sorry to be the cause of this new dissension.

"They can have all the secrets in the world," she went on, brooding bitterly. "But they might refrain from glorying in them, and making me feel more out of it than ever. It is—it is almost unbearable."

Paul thought for a few minutes. He was much perturbed.

"I will tell you what it's all about," he said, pale and nervous. "It's my birthday, and they've bought me a fine lot of paints, all the girls. They're jealous of you—."

He felt her stiffen coldly at the word 'jealous.'

"—merely because I sometimes bring you a book," he added slowly. "But—you see—it's only a trifle. Don't bother about it, will you—because—" he laughed quickly, "—well—what would they say if they saw us here, now, in spite of their victory— —!"

She was angry with him for his clumsy reference to their present intimacy. It was almost insolent of him. Yet he was so quiet, she forgave him, although it cost her an effort.

Their two hands lay on the rough stone parapet of the castle wall. He had inherited from his mother, a fineness of mould, so that his hands were small and vigorous. Hers were large, to match her large limbs, but white and powerful looking. As Paul looked at them he knew her. "She is wanting somebody to take her hands—for all she is so contemptuous of us," he said to himself. And she saw nothing but his two hands, so warm and alive, which seemed to live for her. He was brooding now, staring out over the country from under sullen brows. The little, interesting diversity of shapes had vanished from the scene. All that remained was a vast, dark matrix of sorrow and tragedy, the same in all the houses and the river-flats and the people and the birds: they were only shapen differently. And now that the forms seemed to have melted away, there remained the mass from which all the landscape was composed, a dark mass of struggle and pain. The factory, the girls, his mother, the large uplifted church, the thicket of the town, merged into one atmosphere, dark, brooding and sorrowful, every bit.

"Is that two o'clock striking?" Mrs Dawes said in surprise.

Paul started, and everything sprang into form, regained its individuality and its forgetfulness, its cheerfulness.

They hurried back to work.

When he was in the rush of preparing for the night's post, examining the work up from Fanny's room, which smelt of ironing, the evening postman came in.

"'Mr Paul Morel'," he said smiling, handing Paul a package. "A lady's handwriting! Don't let the girls see it."

The postman, himself a favourite, was pleased to make fun of the girls' affection for Paul.

It was a volume of verse with a brief note: "You will allow me to send you this, and so spare me my isolation. I also sympathise and wish you well. C.D." Paul flushed hot.

"Good Lord—Mrs Dawes! She can't afford it. Good Lord—who ever'd have thought it!"

He was suddenly, intensely moved. He was filled with the warmth of her. In the glow, he could almost feel her as if she were present, her arms, her shoulders, her bosom, see them, feel them, almost contain them.

This move on the part of Clara brought them into closer intimacy. The other girls noticed that, when Paul met Mrs Dawes, his eyes lifted and gave that peculiar bright greeting which they could interpret. Knowing he was unaware, Clara made no sign, save that occasionally she turned aside her face from him when he came upon her.

They walked out together very often at dinner-time. It was quite open, quite frank. Everybody seemed to feel that he was quite unaware of the state of his own feeling, and that nothing was wrong. He talked to her now with some of the old fervour with which he had talked to Miriam, but he cared less about the talk; he did not bother about his conclusions.

One day in October they went out to Lambley for tea. Suddenly they came to a halt on top of the hill. He climbed and sat on a gate, she sat on the stile. The afternoon was perfectly still, with a dim haze, and yellow sheaves glowing through. They were quiet.

"How old were you when you married?" he asked, quietly.

"Twenty two."

Her voice was subdued, almost submissive. She would tell him now.

"It is eight years ago?"

"Yes."

"And when did you leave him?"

"Three years ago."

"Five years!—Did you love him when you married him?"

She was silent for some time. Then she said slowly:

"I thought I did—more or less. I didn't think much about it. And he wanted me. I was very prudish then."

"And you sort of walked into it without thinking?"

"Yes! I seem to have been asleep nearly all my life."

"Somnambule?—But—when did you wake up?"

"I don't know that I ever did, or ever have—since I was a child."

"You went to sleep as you grew to be a woman? How queer! And he didn't wake you?"

"No—he never got there—" she replied, in a monotone.

The brown birds dashed over the hedges where the rose-hips stood naked and scarlet.

"Got where?" he asked.

"At me. He never really mattered to me."

The afternoon was so gently warm and dim. Red roofs of the cottages burned among the blue haze. He loved the day. He could feel, but he could not understand what Clara was saying.

"But why did you leave him?—was he horrid to you?"

She shuddered lightly.

"He—he sort of degraded me. He wanted to bully me, because he hadn't got me. And then I felt as if I wanted to run, as if I was fastened and bound up. And he seemed dirty."

"I see."

He did not at all see.

"And was he always dirty?" he asked.

"A bit," she replied, slowly. "And then he seemed as if he couldn't get *at* me, really. And then he got brutal—he *was* brutal!"

"And why did you leave him finally?"

"Because—because he was unfaithful to me—."

They were both silent for some time. Her hand lay on the gate-post as she balanced. He put his own over it. His heart beat thickly.

"But did you—were you ever—did you ever give him a chance?"

"Chance?—how?"

"To come near to you."

"I married him—and I was willing—"

They both strove to keep their voices steady.

"I believe he loves you," he said.

"It looks like it," she replied.

He wanted to take his hand away, and could not. She saved him by removing her own. After a silence, he began again:

"Did you leave him out of count all along?"

"He left me," she said.

"And I suppose he couldn't *make* himself mean everything to you?"

"He tried to bully me into it."

But the conversation had got them both out of their depth. Suddenly Paul jumped down.

"Come on," he said. "Let's go and get some tea."

They found a cottage, where they sat in the cold parlour. She poured out his tea. She was very quiet. He felt she had withdrawn again from him. After tea, she stared broodingly into her tea-cup, twisting her wedding ring all the time. In her abstraction, she took the ring off her finger, stood it up and spun it upon the table. The gold became a diaphanous, glittering globe. It fell, and the ring was quivering upon the table. She spun it again and again. Paul watched fascinated.

But she was a married woman, and he believed in simple friendship. And he considered that he was perfectly honorable with regard to her. It was only a friendship between man and woman, such as any civilised persons might have.

He was like so many young men of his own age. Sex had become so complicated in him that he would have denied that he ever could want Clara or Miriam or any woman whom he *knew*. Sex desire was a sort of detached thing, that did not belong to a woman. He loved Miriam with his soul. He grew warm at the thought of Clara, he battled with her, he knew her curves of her breast and shoulders as if they had been moulded inside him. And yet he did not positively desire her. He would have denied it for ever. He believed himself really bound to Miriam. If ever he should marry, some time in the far future, it would be his duty to marry Miriam. That he gave Clara to understand, and she said nothing, but left him to his courses. He came to her, Mrs Dawes, whenever he could. Then he wrote frequently to Miriam, and visited the girl occasionally. So he went on through the winter. But he seemed not so fretted. His mother was easier about him. She thought he was getting away from Miriam.

Miriam knew now how strong was the attraction of Clara for him. But still she was certain that the best in him would triumph. His feeling for Mrs Dawes—who moreover was a married woman—was shallow and temporal, compared with his love for herself. He would come back to her, she was sure; with some of his young freshness gone, perhaps, but cured of his desire for the lesser things which other women than herself could give him. She could bear all if he were inwardly true to her, and must come back.

He saw none of the anomaly of his position. Miriam was his old friend, lover, and she belonged to Bestwood and home and his youth. Clara was a newer friend, and she belonged to Nottingham, to life, to the world. It seemed to him quite plain.

Mrs Dawes and he had many periods of coolness, when they saw little of each other. But they always came together again.

"Were you horrid with Baxter Dawes?" he asked her. It was a thing that seemed to trouble him.

"In what way?"

"Oh I don't know. But weren't you horrid with him? Didn't you do something that knocked him to pieces?"

"What pray?"

"I tell you I don't know."

"Then why invent things!"

"Because I feel you did something to him—sort of broke him—broke his manliness. What did you do?"

"If I broke his manliness, it must have been a very easy thing to break."

"Easier than you, I guess.—But you were superior, I know you were superior with him. You are superior with me, but I don't care."

"When am I superior with you?"

"Now for instance. But it doesn't matter. I believe you did him as much damage, more than he did you, by sort of cutting him underneath, and making him feel ashamed."

"He looks ashamed, doesn't he!" she sneered.

"Making him feel as if he were nothing—*I* know," Paul declared.

"You are so clever, my friend," she said coolly.

The conversation broke off there. But it made her cool with him for some time.

She very rarely saw Miriam now. The friendship between the two women was not broken off, but considerably weakened.

"Will you come in to the concert on Sunday afternoon?" Clara asked him just after Christmas.

"I promised to go up to Willey Farm," he replied.

"Oh very well."

"You don't mind, do you?" he asked.

"Why should I?" she answered.

Which almost annoyed him.

"You know," he said, "Miriam and I have been a lot to each other ever since I was sixteen—that's seven years now."

"It's a long time," Clara replied.

"Yes. But somehow she—it doesn't go right—"

"How?" asked Clara.

"She seems to draw me and draw me, and she wouldn't leave a single hair of me free to fall out and blow away—she'd keep it."

"But you like to be kept."

"No," he said, "I don't. I wish it could be normal give and take—like me and you. I want a woman to keep me, but not in her pocket."

"But if you love her, it couldn't be normal, like me and you."

"Yes—I should love her better then. She sort of wants me so much, that I can't give myself."

"Wants you how?"

"Wants the soul out of my body. I can't help shrinking back from her."

"And yet you love her?"

"No, I don't love her. I never even kiss her."

"Why not?" Clara asked.

"I don't know."

"I suppose you're afraid," she said.

"I'm not. Something in me shrinks from her like hell—she's so good, when I'm not good."

"How do you know what she is?"

"I do! I know she wants a sort of soul union."

"But how do you know what she wants?"

"I've been with her for seven years."

"And you haven't found out the very first thing about her."

"What's that?"

"That she doesn't want any of your soul communion. That's your own imagination. She wants you."

He pondered over this. Perhaps he was wrong.

"But she seems——" he began.

"You've never tried," she answered.

CHAPTER XI

The Test on Miriam

With the spring came again the old madness and battle. Now he knew he would have to go to Miriam. But what was his reluctance? He told himself it was only a sort of overstrong virginity in her and him, which neither could break through. He might have married her. But his circumstances at home made it difficult, and moreover, he did not want to marry. Marriage was for life, and because they had become close companions, he and she, he did not see that it should inevitably follow they should be man and wife. He did not feel that he wanted marriage with Miriam. He wished he did. He would have given his head to have felt a joyous desire to marry her and to have her. Then why couldn't he bring it off? There was some obstacle. And what was the obstacle? It lay in the physical bondage. He shrank from the physical contact. But why? With her he felt bound up inside himself. He could not go out to her. Something struggled in him, but he could not get to her. Why? She loved him. Clara said she even wanted him. Then why couldn't he go to her, make love to her, kiss her? Why, when she put her arm in his, timidly, as they walked, did he feel he would burst forth in brutality and recoil? He owed himself to her. He wanted to belong to her. Perhaps the recoil and the shrinking from her was love in its first fierce modesty. He had no aversion for her. No, it was the opposite: it was a strong desire battling with a still stronger shyness and virginity. It seemed as if virginity were a positive force, which fought and won in both of them. And with her he felt it so hard to overcome. Yet he was nearest to her, and with her alone could he deliberately break through. And he owed himself to her.—Then, if they could get things right, they could marry. But he would not marry unless he could feel strong in the joy of it—never. He could not have faced his mother. It seemed to him that to sacrifice himself in a marriage he did not want would be degrading, and would undo all his life, make it a nullity. He would try what he *could* do.

And he had a great tenderness for Miriam. Always, she was sad, dreaming her religion. And he was nearly a religion to her. He could not bear to fail her. It would all come right if they tried.

He looked round. A good many of the nicest men he knew were like himself, bound in by their own virginity, which they could not break out of. They were so sensitive to their women, that they would go without them for ever rather than do them a hurt, an injustice. Being the sons of mothers whose husbands had blundered rather brutally through their feminine sanctities, they were themselves too diffident and shy. They could easier deny themselves than incur any reproach from a woman. For a woman was like their mother, and they were full of the sense of their mother. They preferred themselves to suffer the misery of celibacy, rather than risk the other person.

All the talk, all the abstraction that went on between him and Miriam, all the cleverness and the realisation, what was it but the kisses that should have been given, translated into terms of consciousness, the warmth with which he would have held her in his arms turned to the purpose of thinking and philosophising. And what was thought, realisation?—it only wasted him away. It was not life, fruition. It was a form of death: living impulse turned into an abstraction. He would stop now. They would stop these abstractions, he and Miriam.

He went back to her. Something in her, when he looked at her, brought the tears almost to his eyes. One day he stood behind her as she sang. Annie was playing a song on the piano. As Miriam sang her mouth seemed hopeless. She sang like a nun singing to heaven. It reminded him so much of the mouth and eyes of one who sings beside a Botticelli Madonna, so spiritual. Again, hot as steel came up the pain in him. Why must he ask her for the other thing? Why was there his blood battling with her? If only he could have been always gentle, tender with her, breathing with her the atmosphere of reverie and religious dreams, he would give his right hand. It was not fair to hurt her. There seemed an eternal maidenhood about her. And when he thought of her mother, he saw the great brown eyes of a maiden who was nearly scared and shocked out of her virgin maidenhood, but not quite, in spite of her seven children. They had been born almost leaving her out of count, not of her, but upon her. So she could never let them go, because she never had possessed them.

Mrs Morel saw him going again frequently to Miriam, and was

astonished. He said nothing to his mother. He did not explain nor excuse himself. If he came home late, and she reproached him, he frowned and turned on her in an overbearing way:

"I shall come home when I like," he said, "I am old enough."

"Must she keep you till this time?"

"It is I who stay," he answered.

"And she lets you—but very well," she said.

And she went to bed, leaving the door unlocked for him. But she lay listening until he came, often long after. It was a great bitterness to her that he had gone back to Miriam. She recognised, however, the uselessness of any further interference. He went to Willey Farm as a man now, not as a youth. She had no right over him. There was a coldness between him and her. He hardly told her anything. Discarded, she waited on him, cooked for him still, and loved to slave for him. But her face closed again like a mask. There was nothing for her to do now but the housework. For all the rest he had gone to Miriam. She could not forgive him. Miriam killed the joy and the warmth in him. He had been such a jolly lad, and full of the warmest affection. Now he grew colder, more and more irritable and gloomy. It reminded her of William. But Paul was worse. He did things with more intensity, and more realisation of what he was about. His mother knew how he was suffering for want of a woman, and she saw him going to Miriam. If he had made up his mind, nothing on earth would alter him. Mrs Morel was tired. She began to give up at last. She had finished. She was in the way.

He went on determinedly. He realised more or less what his mother felt. It only hardened his soul. He made himself callous towards her. But it was like being callous to his own health. It undermined him quickly. Yet he persisted.

He lay back in the rocking-chair at Willey Farm one evening. He had been talking to Miriam for some weeks, but had not come to the point. Now he said suddenly:

"I am twenty four, almost."

She had been brooding. She looked up at him suddenly in surprise.

"Yes!—What makes you say it?"

There was something in the charged atmosphere that she dreaded.

"Sir Thomas More says one can marry at twenty four."

She laughed quaintly, saying:

"Does it need Sir Thomas More's sanction?"

"No—but one ought to marry about then."

"Ay!" she answered, broodingly; and she waited.

"I can't marry you," he continued slowly, "not now, because we've no money—and they depend on me at home."

She sat half guessing what was coming.

"But I want to marry now—"

"You want to marry—?" she repeated.

"A woman—you know what I mean."

She was silent.

"Now, at last, I must," he said.

"Ay," she answered.

"And you love me?"

She laughed bitterly.

"Why are you ashamed of it," he answered. "You wouldn't be ashamed before your God, why are you before people?"

"Nay," she answered deeply, "I am not ashamed."

"You are!" he replied, bitterly. "And it's my fault. But you know I can't help being—as I am—don't you?"

"I know you can't help it," she replied.

"I love you an awful lot—then there is something short."

"Where?" she answered, looking at him.

"Oh in me! It is I who ought to be ashamed—like a spiritual cripple. And I am ashamed. It is misery. Why is it?"

"I don't know," replied Miriam.

"And I don't know," he repeated. "Don't you think we have been too fierce in our, what they call purity? Don't you think that to be so much afraid and averse is a sort of dirtiness?"

She looked at him with startled dark eyes.

"You recoiled away from anything of the sort, and I took the motion from you, and recoiled also—perhaps worse—."

There was silence in the room for some time.

"Yes," she said, "it is so."

"There is between us," he said, "all these years of intimacy. I feel naked enough before you: do you understand?"

"I think so," she answered.

"And you love me?"

She laughed.

"Don't be bitter," he pleaded.

She looked at him, and was sorry for him: his eyes were dark with torture. She was sorry for him: it was worse for him to have this deflected love, than for herself, who could never be properly mated. He was restless, forever urging forward and trying to find a way out. He might do as he liked, and have what he liked of her.

"Nay," she said softly, "I am not bitter."

She felt she could bear anything for him, she would suffer for him. She put her hand on his knee as he leaned forward in his chair. He took it and kissed it. But it hurt to do so. He felt he was putting himself aside. He sat there sacrificed to her purity, which felt more like nullity. How could he kiss her hand passionately, when it would drive her away, and leave nothing but pain? Yet slowly he drew her to him and kissed her.

They knew each other too well to pretend anything. As she kissed him, she watched his eyes. They were staring across the room, with a peculiar dark blaze in them, that fascinated her. He was perfectly still. She could feel his heart throbbing heavily in his breast.

"What are you thinking about?" she asked.

The blaze in his eyes shuddered, became uncertain.

"I was thinking, all the while, I love you. I have been obstinate."

She sank her head on his breast.

"Yes?" she answered.

"That's all," he said, and his voice seemed sure, and his mouth was kissing her throat.

Then she raised her head and looked into his eyes with her full gaze of love. The blaze struggled, seemed to try to get away from her, and then was quenched. He turned his head quickly aside. It was a moment of anguish.

"Kiss me," she whispered.

He shut his eyes, and kissed her, and his arms folded her closer and closer.

When she walked home with him over the fields, he said:

"I am glad I came back to you. I feel so simple with you—as if there was nothing to hide. We will be happy?"

"Yes," she murmured, and the tears came to her eyes.

"Some sort of perversity in our souls," he said, "makes us not want, get away from, the very thing we want. We have to fight against that."

"Yes," she said, and she felt stunned.

As she stood under the drooping thorn-tree, in the darkness by the roadside, he kissed her, and his fingers wandered over her face.

In the darkness, where he could not see her, but only feel her, his passion flooded him. He clasped her very close.

"Sometime you will have me?" he murmured, hiding his face on her shoulder, it was so difficult.

"Not now," she said.

His hopes and his heart sank. A dreariness came over him.

"No," he said.

His clasp of her slackened.

"I love to feel your arm *there*!" she said, pressing his arm against her back, where it went round her waist. "It rests me so."

He tightened the pressure of his arm upon the small of her back, to rest her.

"We belong to each other," he said.

"Yes."

"Then why shouldn't we belong to each other all together?"

"But—" she faltered.

"I know it's a lot to ask," he said. "But there's not much risk for you really—not in the Gretchen way. You can trust me there?"

"Oh I can trust you!" The answer came quick and strong. "It's not that—it's not that at all—but—"

"What?"

She hid her face in his neck with a little cry of misery.

"I don't know," she cried.

She seemed slightly hysterical, but with a sort of horror. His heart died in him.

"You don't think it ugly?" he asked.

"No—not now. You have *taught* me it isn't."

"You are afraid?"

She calmed herself hastily.

"Yes, I am only afraid," she said.

He kissed her tenderly.

"Never mind," he said. "You shall please yourself."

Suddenly she gripped her arms round him, and clenched her body stiff.

"You *shall* have me," she said, through her shut teeth.

His heart beat up again like fire. He folded her close, and his mouth was on her throat. She could not bear it. She drew away. He disengaged her.

"Won't you be late?" she asked, gently.

He sighed, scarcely hearing what she said. She waited, wishing he would go. At last he kissed her quickly and climbed the fence. Looking round he saw the pale blotch of her face down in the darkness under the hanging tree. There was no more of her but this pale blotch.

"Goodbye!" she called softly. She had no body, only a voice and a dim face. He turned away and ran down the road, his fists clenched. And when he came to the wall over the lake he leaned there, almost stunned, looking up the black water.

Miriam plunged home over the meadows. She was not afraid of people, what they might say. But she dreaded the issue with him. Yes, she would let him have her, if he insisted. And then, when she thought of afterwards, her heart went down. He would be disappointed, he would find no satisfaction, and then he would go away. Yet he was so insistent. And over this, which did not seem so all-important to her, was their love to break down. After all, he was only like other men, seeking his satisfaction. Oh but there was something more in him, something deeper! She could trust to it, in spite of all desires. He said that possession was a great moment in life. All strong emotions concentrated there. Perhaps it was so. There was something divine in it. Then she would submit, religiously, to the sacrifice. He should have her. And at the thought her whole body clenched itself involuntarily, hard, as if against something. But Life forced her through this gate of suffering too, and she would submit. At any rate, it would give him what he wanted, which was her deepest wish. She brooded and brooded and brooded herself towards accepting him.

He courted her now like a lover. Often, when he grew hot, she put his face from her, held it between her hands, and looked in his eyes. He could not meet her gaze. Her dark eyes, full of love, earnest and searching, made him turn away. Not for an instant would she let him forget. Back again he had to torture himself, into a sense of his responsibility and hers. Never any relaxing, never any leaving himself to the great hunger and impersonality of passion. He must be brought back to a deliberate, reflective creature. As if from a swoon of passion, she called him back to the littleness, the personal relationship. He could not bear it. 'Leave me alone—leave me alone!' he wanted to cry. But she wanted him to look at her with eyes full of love. His eyes, full of the dark, impersonal fire of desire, did not belong to her.

There was a great crop of cherries at the farm. The trees at the back of the house, very large and tall, hung thick with scarlet and crimson drops, under the dark leaves. Paul and Edgar were gathering the fruit one evening. It had been a hot day, and now the clouds were rolling in the sky, dark and warm. Paul climbed high in the tree, above the scarlet roofs of the buildings. The wind, moaning steadily, made the whole tree rock with a subtle, thrilling motion that stirred the blood. The young man, perched insecurely in the slender branches, rocked till he felt slightly drunk, reached down the boughs, where the scarlet beady cherries hung thick underneath, and tore off handful after handful of the sleek, cool-fleshed fruit. Cherries touched his ears and his neck as he stretched forward, their chill finger-tips sending a flash down his blood. All shades of red, from a golden vermilion to a rich crimson, glowed and met his eyes, under a darkness of leaves.

The sun, going down, suddenly caught the broken clouds. Immense piles of gold flared out in the south-east, heaped in soft, glowing yellow right up the sky. The world, till now dusk and grey, reflected the gold glow, astonished. Everywhere the trees, and the grass, and the far-off water, seemed roused from the twilight, and shining.

Miriam came out wondering.

"Oh!" Paul heard her mellow voice call: "isn't it wonderful!"

He looked down. There was a faint gold glimmer on her face, that looked very soft, turned up to him.

"How high you are!" she said.

Beside her, on the rhubarb leaves, were four dead birds, thieves that had been shot. Paul saw some cherry-stones hanging quite bleached, like skeletons, picked clear of flesh. He looked down again to Miriam.

"Clouds are on fire!" he said.

"Beautiful," she cried.

She seemed so small, so soft, so tender down there. He threw a handful of cherries at her. She was startled and frightened. He laughed with a low, chuckling sound, and pelted her. She ran for shelter, picking up some cherries. Two fine red pairs she hung over her ears, then she looked up again.

"Haven't you got enough?" she asked.

"Nearly. It is like being on a ship, up here."

"And how long will you stay?"

"While the sunset lasts."

She went to the fence and sat there, watching the gold clouds fall to pieces, and go in immense, rose coloured ruin towards the darkness. Gold flamed to scarlet, like pain in its intense brightness. Then the scarlet sank to rose, and rose to crimson, and quickly the passion went out of the sky. All the world was dark grey. Paul scrambled quickly down with his basket, tearing his shirt-sleeve as he did so.

"They are lovely," said Miriam, fingering the cherries.

"I've torn my sleeve," he answered.

She took the three-cornered rip, saying:

"I shall have to mend it."

It was near the shoulder. She put her fingers through the tear.

"How warm!" she said.

He laughed. There was a new, strange note in his voice, one that made her pant.

"Shall we stay out?" he said.

"Won't it rain?" she asked.

"No, let us walk a little way."

They went down the fields, and into the thick plantation of fir-trees and pines.

"Shall we go in among the trees?" he asked.

"Do you want to?"

"Yes."

It was very dark among the firs, and the sharp spines pricked her face. She was afraid. Paul was silent and strange.

"I like the darkness," he said. "I wish it were thicker—good, thick darkness."

He seemed to be almost unaware of her, as a person: she was only to him then, a woman. She was afraid.

He stood against a pine-tree trunk and took her in his arms. She relinquished herself to him—but it was a sacrifice, in which she felt something of horror. This thick-voiced, oblivious man was a stranger to her.

Later it began to rain. The pine-trees smelled very strong. Paul lay with his head on the ground, on the dead pine needles, listening to the sharp hiss of the rain, a steady keen noise. His heart was down, very heavy. Now he realised that she had not been with him all the time, that her soul had stood apart, in a sort of horror. He was physically relieved, but no more. Very dreary at heart, very sad, and very tender, his fingers wandered over her face pitifully. Now again she loved him deeply. He was tender and beautiful.

"The rain!" he said.

"Yes—is it coming on you?"

She put her hands over him, on his hair, on his shoulders, to feel if the raindrops fell on him. She loved him dearly. He, as he lay with his face on the dead pine-leaves, felt extraordinarily quiet. He did not mind if the rain-drops came on him: he would have lain and got wet through: he felt as if nothing mattered, as if his living were smeared away into the beyond, near and quite lovable. This strange, gentle reaching-out to death was new to him.

"We must go," said Miriam.

"Yes," he answered, but did not move.

To him now life seemed a shadow, day a white shadow, night, and death, and stillness, and inaction, this seemed like *being*. To be alive, to be urgent, and insistent, that was *not-to-be*. The highest of all was, to melt out into the darkness and sway there, identified with the great Being.

"The rain is coming in on us," said Miriam.

He rose, and assisted her.

"It is a pity," he said.

"What?"

"To have to go. I feel so still."

"Still!" she repeated.

"Stiller than I have ever been in my life."

He was walking with his hand in hers. She pressed his fingers, feeling a slight fear. Now he seemed beyond her: she had a fear lest she should lose him.

"The fir-trees are like presences on the darkness: each one only a presence."

She was afraid, and said nothing.

"A sort of hush: the whole night, wondering, and asleep: I suppose that's what we do in death: sleep on wonder."

She had been afraid before of the brute in him: now of the mystic. She trod beside him in silence. The rain fell with a heavy 'Hush!' on the trees. At last they gained the cart-shed.

"Let us stay here awhile," he said.

There was a sound of rain everywhere, smothering everything.

"I feel so strange and still," he said; "along with everything."

"Ay," she answered patiently.

He seemed again unaware of her, though he held her hand close.

"To be rid of our individuality, which is our will, which is our effort—to live effortless, a kind of conscious sleep—that is very beautiful, I think—that is our after-life—our immortality."

"Yes?"

"Yes—and very beautiful to have."

"You don't usually say that."

"No."

In a while, they went indoors. Everybody looked at them curiously. He still kept the quiet, heavy look in his eyes, the stillness in his voice. Instinctively, they all left him alone.

About this time Miriam's grandmother, who lived in a tiny cottage in Woodlinton, fell ill, and the girl was sent to keep house. It was a beautiful little place. The cottage had a big garden in front, with red brick walls against which the plum-trees were nailed. At the back another garden was separated from the fields by a tall old hedge. It was very pretty. Miriam had not much to do, so she found time for her beloved reading, and for writing little introspective pieces which interested her.

At the holiday time her grandmother, being better, was driven to Derby to stay with her daughter for a day or two. She was a crotchety old lady, and might return the second day, or the third. So Miriam stayed alone in the cottage—which also pleased her.

Paul used often to cycle over, and they had as a rule peaceful and happy times. He did not embarrass her much. But then on the Monday of the holiday he was to spend a whole day with her.

It was perfect weather. He left his mother, telling her where he was going. She would be alone all the day. It cast a shadow over him. But he had three days that were all his own, when he was going to do as he liked. It was sweet to rush through the morning lanes on his bicycle.

He got to the cottage at about eleven o'clock. Miriam was busy preparing dinner. She looked so perfectly in keeping with the little kitchen, ruddy and busy. He kissed her and sat down to watch. The room was small and cosy. The sofa was covered all over with a sort of linen in squares of red and pale blue, old, much washed, but pretty. There was a stuffed owl in a case over a corner cupboard. The sunlight came through the leaves of the scented geraniums in the window. She was cooking a chicken in his honor. It was their cottage for the day, and they were man and wife. He beat the eggs for her and peeled the potatoes. He thought she gave a feeling of home almost like his mother. And no one could look more beautiful, with her tumbled curls, when she was flushed from the fire.

The dinner was a great success. Like a young husband, he carved. They talked all the time with unflagging zest. Then he wiped the dishes she had washed, and they went out down the fields. There was a bright little brook that ran into a bog at the foot of a very steep bank. Here they wandered, picking still a few marsh marigolds, and many big, blue forgetmenots. Then she sat on the bank with her hands full of flowers, mostly golden water-blobs. As she put her face down into the marigolds it was all overcast with a yellow shine.

"Your face is bright," he said, "like a transfiguration."

She looked at him questioning. He laughed pleadingly to her, laying his hand on hers. Then he kissed her fingers, then her face.

The world was all steeped in sunshine, and quite still, yet not asleep, but quivering with a kind of expectancy.

"I have never seen anything more beautiful than this," he said. He held her hand fast all the time.

"And the water singing to itself as it runs—do you love it?"

She looked at him full of love. His eyes were very dark, very bright.

"Don't you think it's a great day?" he asked.

She murmured her assent. She *was* happy, and he saw it.

"And our day—just between us," he said.

They lingered a little while. Then they stood up upon the sweet thyme, and he looked down at her simply.

"Will you come?" he asked.

They went back to the house, hand in hand, in silence. The chickens came scampering down the path to her. He locked the door, and they had the little house to themselves.

He never forgot seeing her as she lay naked on the bed, when he was unfastening his collar. First he saw only her beauty, and was blind with it. She had the most beautiful hips he had ever imagined. He stood unable to move or speak, looking at her, his face half smiling with wonder. And then he wanted her, and threw off his things. And then, as he went forward to her, her hands lifted in a little pleading movement, and he looked at her face, and stopped. Her big brown eyes were watching him, still and resigned and loving; she lay as if she had given herself up to sacrifice: there was her body for him; but the look at the back of her eyes, like a creature awaiting immolation, arrested him, and all his blood fell back.

"You are sure you want me?" he asked, as if a cold shadow had come over him.

"Yes, quite sure."

She was very quiet, very calm. She only realised that she was doing something for him. He could hardly bear it. She lay to be sacrificed for him, because she loved him so much. And he had to sacrifice her. For a second, he wished he were sex-less, or dead. Then he shut his eyes again to her, and his blood beat back again.

And afterwards he loved her, loved her to the last fibre of his being. He loved her. But he wanted, somehow, to cry. There was something he could not bear, for her sake. He stayed with her till quite late at night. As he rode home he felt that he was finally initiated. He was a youth no longer. But why had he the dull pain in his soul? Why did the thought of death, the after-life, seem so sweet and consoling?

He spent the week with Miriam, and wore her out with his passion before it was gone. He had always, almost wilfully, to put her out of count, and act from the brute strength of his own feelings. And he could not do it very often, and there remained afterwards always the sense of failure and of death. If he were really with her, he had to put aside himself and his desire. If he would have her, he had to put her aside.

"When I come to you," he asked her, his eyes dark with pain and shame, "you don't really want me, do you?"

"Ah yes!" she replied quickly.

He looked at her.

"Nay," he said.

She began to tremble.

"You see," she said, taking his face and shutting it out against her shoulder; "you see—as we are—how can I get used to you?—It would come all right if we were married."

He lifted his head and looked at her.

"You mean now, it is always too much shock?"

"Yes—and—"

"You are always clenched against me."

She was trembling with agitation.

"You see," she said, "I'm not used to the thought—"

"You are lately," he said.

"But all my life.—Mother said to me—'there is one thing in marriage that is always dreadful, but you have to bear it.' And I believed it."

334

"And still believe," he said.

"No!" she cried, hastily. "I believe as you do, that loving, even in *that* way, is the high-water mark of living."

"That doesn't alter the fact that you never *want* it."

"No," she said, taking his head in her arms and rocking in despair. "Don't say so! You don't understand." She rocked with pain. "Don't I want your children?"

"But not me."

"How can you say so? But we must be married to have children—"

"Shall we be married then? *I* want you to have my children."

He kissed her hand, reverently. She pondered sadly, watching him.

"We are too young," she said at length.

"Twenty four and twenty three—"

"Not yet," she pleaded, as she rocked herself in distress.

"When you will," he said.

She bowed her head gravely. The tone of hopelessness in which he said these things grieved her deeply. It had always been a failure between them. Tacitly, she acquiesced in what he felt.

And after a week of love, he said to his mother suddenly, one Sunday night just as they were going to bed:

"I shan't go so much to Miriam's, mother."

She was surprised. But she would not ask him anything.

"You please yourself," she said.

So he went to bed. But there was a new quietness about him which she had wondered at. She almost guessed. She would leave him alone, however. Precipitation might spoil things. She watched him in his loneliness, wondering where he would end. He was sick, and much too quiet for him. There was a perpetual little knitting of his brows, such as she had seen when he was a small baby, and which had been gone for many years. Now it was the same again. And she could do nothing for him. He had to go on alone, make his own way.

He continued faithful to Miriam. For one day he had loved her, utterly. But it never came again. The sense of failure grew stronger. At first it was only a sadness. Then he began to feel he could not go on. He wanted to run, to go abroad, anything. Gradually, he ceased to ask her to have him. Instead of drawing them together, it put them apart. And then he realised, consciously, that it was no good.—It was useless trying: it would never be a success between them.

For some months he had seen very little of Clara. They had

occasionally walked out for half an hour at dinner-time. But he always reserved himself for Miriam. With Clara, however, his brow cleared and he was gay again. She treated him indulgently, as if he were a child. He thought he did not mind. But deep below the surface it piqued him.

Sometimes Miriam said:

"What about Clara? I hear nothing of her lately."

"I walked with her about twenty minutes yesterday," he replied.

"And what did she talk about?"

"I don't know. I suppose I did all the jawing, I usually do.—I think I was telling her about the strike, and how the women took it."

"Yes."

So he gave the account of himself.

But insidiously, without his knowing it, the warmth he felt for Clara drew him away from Miriam, for whom he felt responsible, and to whom he felt he belonged. He thought he was being quite faithful to her. It is not easy to estimate exactly the strength and warmth of one's feelings for a woman, till they have run away with one.

He began to give more time to his men friends. There was Jessop, at the Art School, Swain who was chemistry demonstrator at the University, Newton who was a teacher: besides Edgar and Miriam's younger brothers. Pleading work, he sketched and studied with Jessop. He called in the University for Swain, and the two went 'down town' together. Having come home in the train with Newton, he called and had a game of billiards with him in the 'Moon and Stars.' If he gave to Miriam the excuse of his men friends, he felt quite justified. His mother began to be relieved. He always told her where he had been.

During the summer, Clara wore sometimes a dress of soft cotton stuff with loose sleeves. When she lifted her hands, her sleeves fell back, and her beautiful strong arms shone out.

"Half a minute," he cried. "Hold your arm still."

He made sketches of her hand and arm, and the drawings contained some of the fascination the real thing had for him. Miriam, who always went scrupulously through his books and papers, saw the drawings.

"I think Clara has such beautiful arms," he said.

"Yes! When did you draw them?"

"On Tuesday, in the work-room. You know I've got a corner

where I can work. Often I can do every single thing they need in the department before dinner. Then I work for myself in the afternoon, and just see to things at night."

"Yes," she said, turning the leaves of his sketch-book.

Frequently he hated Miriam. He hated her as she bent forward and pored over his things. He hated her way of patiently casting him up, as if he were an endless psychological account. When he was with her, he hated her for having got him, and yet not got him, and he tortured her. She took all and gave nothing, he said. At least, she gave no living warmth. She was never alive, and giving off life. Looking for her was like looking for something which did not exist. She was only his conscience, not his mate. He hated her violently, and was more cruel to her. They dragged on till the next summer. He saw more and more of Clara.

At last he spoke. He had been sitting working at home one evening. There was between him and his mother a peculiar condition of people frankly finding fault with each other. Mrs Morel was strong on her feet again. He was not going to stick to Miriam. Very well, then she would stand aloof till he said something. It had been coming a long time, this bursting of the storm in him, when he would come back to her. This evening there was between them a peculiar condition of suspense. He worked feverishly and mechanically, so that he could escape from himself. It grew late. Through the open door, stealthily, came the scent of madonna lilies, almost as if it were prowling abroad. Suddenly he got up and went out of doors.

The beauty of the night made him want to shout. A half moon, dusky gold, was sinking behind the black sycamore at the end of the garden, making the sky dull purple with its glow. Nearer, a dim white fence of lilies went across the garden, and the air all round seemed to stir with scent, as if it were alive. He went across the bed of pinks, whose keen perfume came sharply across the rocking, heavy scent of the lilies, and stood alongside the white barrier of flowers. They flagged all loose, as if they were panting. The scent made him drunk. He went down to the field to watch the moon sink under.

A corn-crake in the hay-close called insistently. The moon slid quite quickly downwards, growing more flushed. Behind him, the great flowers leaned as if they were calling. And then, like a shock, he caught another perfume, something raw and coarse. Hunting round, he found the purple iris, touched their fleshy throats, and their dark, grasping hands. At any rate he had found something. They stood stiff in the darkness. Their scent was brutal. The moon was melting down upon the crest of the hill. It was gone, all was dark. The corncrake called still.

Breaking off a pink he suddenly went indoors.

"Come my boy," said his mother. "I'm sure it's time you went to bed."

He stood with the pink against his lips.

"I shall break off with Miriam, mother," he answered calmly.

She looked up at him over her spectacles. He was staring back at her, unswerving. She met his eyes for a moment, then took off her glasses. He was white. The male was up in him, dominant. She did not want to see him too clearly.

"But I thought—" she began.

"Well," he answered. "I don't love her—I don't want to marry her—so, I shall have done."

"But—!" exclaimed his mother, amazed. "I thought lately you had made up your mind to have her, and so I said nothing."

"I had—I wanted to—but now I don't want. It's no good. I shall break off on Sunday. I ought to, oughtn't I?"

"You know best. You know I said so long ago."

"I can't help that now. I shall break off on Sunday."

"Well," said his mother, "I think it will be best. But lately I decided you had made up your mind to have her, so I said nothing, and should have said nothing. But I say as I have always said, I *don't* think she is suited to you."

"On Sunday I break off," he said, smelling the pink. He put the flower in his mouth. Unthinking, he bared his teeth, closed them on the blossom slowly, and had a mouthful of petals. These he spat into the fire, kissed his mother, and went to bed.

On Sunday he went up to the farm in the early afternoon. He had written Miriam that they would walk over the fields to Hucknall. His mother was very tender with him. He said nothing. But she saw the effort it was costing. The peculiar set look on his face stilled her.

"Never mind, my son," she said. "You will be so much better when it is all over."

Paul glanced swiftly at his mother, in surprise and resentment. He did not want sympathy.

Miriam met him at the lane end. She was wearing a new dress of

338

figured muslin, that had short sleeves. Those short sleeves, and Miriam's brown-skinned arms beneath them, such pitiful, resigned arms, gave him so much pain that they helped to make him cruel. She had made herself look so beautiful and fresh, for him. She seemed to blossom for him alone. Every time he looked at her, a mature young woman now, and beautiful in her new dress, it hurt so much that his heart seemed almost to be bursting with the restraint he put on it. But he had decided, and it was irrevocable.

On the hills, they sat down, and he lay with his head in her lap, whilst she fingered his hair. She knew that 'he was not there', as she put it. Often, when she had him with her, she looked for him, and could not find him. But this afternoon she was not prepared.

It was nearly five o'clock when he told her. They were sitting on the bank of a stream, where the lip of turf hung over a hollow bank of yellow earth, and he was hacking away with a stick, as he did when he was perturbed, and cruel.

"I have been thinking," he said, "we ought to break off."

"Why?" she cried in surprise.

"Because it's no good going on."

"Why is it no good?"

"It isn't. I don't want to marry. I don't want ever to marry. And if we're not going to marry it's no good going on."

"But why do you say this now?"

"Because I've made up my mind."

"And what about these last months, and the things you told me then?"

"I can't help it—I don't want to go on."

"You don't want any more of me?"

"I want us to break off—you be free of me, I free of you."

"And what about these last months?"

"I don't know. I've not told you anything but what I thought was true—"

"Then why are you different now?"

"I'm not—I'm the same—only I know it's no good going on."

"You haven't told me why it's no good."

"Because I don't want to go on—and I don't want to marry."

"How many times have you offered to marry me—and I wouldn't?"

"I know—but I want us to break off."

There was silence for a moment or two, while he dug viciously at

339

the earth. She bent her head, pondering. He was an unreasonable child. He was like an infant which, when it has drunk its fill, throws away and smashes the cup. She looked at him feeling she could get hold of him and *wring* some consistency out of him. But she was helpless. Then she cried:

"I have said you were only fourteen—you are only *four*!"

He still dug at the earth viciously. He heard.

"You are a child of four," she repeated in her anger.

He did not answer, but said in his heart 'All right, if I'm a child of four, what do you want me for. *I* don't want another mother.' But he said nothing to her, and there was silence.

"And have you told your people?" she asked.

"I have told my mother."

There was another long interval of silence.

"Then what do you *want*?" she asked.

"Why—I want us to separate. We have lived on each other all these years—now let us stop. I will go my own way, without you, and you will go your way, without me. You will have an independent life of your own then."

There was in it some truth that, in spite of her bitterness, she could not help registering. She knew she felt in a sort of bondage to him, which she hated because she could not control it. She had hated her love for him from the moment it grew too strong for her. And, deep down, she had hated him because she loved him and he dominated her. She had resisted his domination. She had fought to keep herself free of him, in the last issue. And she *was* free of him, even more than he of her.

"And," he continued, "we shall always be more or less each other's work. You have done a lot for me, I for you. Now let us start and live by ourselves."

"What do you want to do?" she asked.

"Nothing, only be free," he answered.

She, however, knew in her heart that Clara's influence was over him to liberate him. But she said nothing.

"And what have I to tell my mother?" she asked.

"I told my mother," he answered, "that I was breaking off—clean and altogether."

"I shall not tell them at home," she said.

Frowning, "You please yourself," he said.

He knew he had landed her in a nasty hole, and was leaving her in the lurch. It angered him.

The Test on Miriam

"Tell them you wouldn't and won't marry me, and have broken off," he said. "It's true enough."

She bit her finger moodily. She thought over their whole affair. She had known it would come to this: she had seen it all along. It chimed with her bitter expectation.

"Always, it has always been so!" she cried. "It has been one long battle between us—you fighting away from me."

It came from her unawares, like a flash of lightning. The man's heart stood still. Was this how she saw it?

"But we've had *some* perfect hours, *some* perfect times, when we were together," he pleaded.

"Never!" she cried, "never! It has always been you fighting me off."

"Not always—not at first," he pleaded.

"Always—from the very beginning—always the same."

She had finished—but she had done enough. He sat aghast. He had wanted to say 'It has been good, but it is at an end.' And she, she whose love he had believed in when he had despised himself, denied that their love had ever been love. 'He had always fought away from her?' Then it had been monstrous. There had never been anything really between them—all the time he had been imagining something where there was nothing. And she had known. She had known so much, and had told him so little. She had known all the time. All the time this was at the bottom of her!

He sat silent in bitterness. At last, the whole affair appeared in a cynical aspect to him. She had really played with him, not he with her. She had hidden all her condemnation from him, had flattered him, and despised him. She despised him now. He grew intellectual and cruel.

"You ought to marry a man who worships you," he said. "Then you could do as you liked with him. Plenty of men will worship you, if you get on the private side of their natures. You ought to marry one such. They would never fight you off."

"Thank you," she said. "But don't advise me to marry someone else any more. You've done it before."

"Very well," he said, "I will say no more."

He sat still, feeling as if he had had a blow, instead of giving one. Their eight years of friendship and love, *the* eight years of his life, were nullified.

"When did you think of this?" she asked.

"I thought definitely on Thursday night."

"I knew it was coming," she said.

That pleased him bitterly. 'Oh very well, if she knew, then it doesn't come as a surprise to her', he thought.

"And have you said anything to Clara?" she asked.

"No—but I shall tell her now."

There was a silence.

"Do you remember the things you said this time last year—in my grandmother's house—nay, last month even?"

"Yes," he said. "I do! And I meant them. I can't help that it's failed."

"It has failed because you want something else."

"It would have failed whether or not. *You* never believed in me."

She laughed strangely.

He sat in silence. He was full of a feeling that she had deceived him. She had despised him when he thought she worshipped him. She had let him say wrong things, and had not contradicted him. She had let him fight alone. But it stuck in his throat, that she had despised him whilst he thought she worshipped him. She should have told him when she found fault with him. She had not played fair. He hated her. All these years, she had treated him as if he were a hero, and thought of him secretly as an infant, a foolish child. Then why had she left the foolish child to his folly. His heart was hard against her.

She sat full of bitterness. She had known—oh well she had known. All the time he was away from her, she had summed him up, seen his littleness, his meanness, and his folly. Even she had guarded her soul against him. She was not overthrown, nor prostrated, not even much hurt. She had known. Only why, as he sat there, had he still this strange dominance over her. His very movements fascinated her as if she were hypnotised by him. Yet he was despicable, false, inconsistent, and mean. Why this bondage for her? Why was it the movement of his arm stirred her as nothing else in the world could? Why was she fastened to him? Why even now, if he looked at her and commanded her, would she have to obey? She would obey him in his trifling commands. But once he was obeyed, then she had him in her power, she knew, to lead him where she would. She was sure of herself. Only, this new influence! Ah, he was not a man, he was a baby that cries for the newest toy. And all the attachment of his soul would not keep him. Very well, he would have to go. But he would come back, when he had tired of his new sensation.

He hacked at the earth till she was fretted to death. She rose. He sat flinging lumps of earth in the stream.

"We will go and have tea here?" he asked.

"Yes," she answered.

They chattered over irrelevant subjects during tea. He held forth on the love of ornament—the cottage parlour moved him thereto—and its connection with aesthetics. She was cold and quiet. As they walked home, she asked:

"And we shall not see each other?"

"No—or rarely," he answered.

"Nor write?" she asked, almost sarcastically.

"As you will," he answered. "We're not strangers—never should be, whatever happened. I will write to you now and again. You please yourself."

"I see," she answered, cuttingly.

But he was at that stage at which nothing else hurts. He had made a great cleavage in his life. He had had a great shock, when she had told him their love had been always a conflict. Nothing more mattered. If it never had been much, there was no need to make a fuss that it was ended.

He left her at the lane-end. As she went home, solitary, in her new frock, having her people to face at the other end, he stood still with shame and pain in the highroad, thinking of the suffering he caused her.

In a reaction towards restoring his self esteem, he went into the Willow Tree for a drink. There were four girls who had been out for the day, drinking a modest glass of port. They had some chocolates on the table. Paul sat near, with his whiskey. He noticed the girls whispering and nudging. Presently one, a bonny dark hussy, leaned to him and said:

"Have a chocolate?"

The others laughed loudly at her impudence.

"All right," said Paul. "Give me a hard one—nut. I don't like creams."

"Here you are then," said the girl. "Here's an almond for you."

She held the sweet between her fingers. He opened his mouth. She popped it in, and blushed.

"You *are* nice," he said.

"Well," she answered, "we thought you looked overcast, and they dared me offer you a chocolate."

"I don't mind if I have another—another sort," he said.

And presently they were all laughing together.

It was nine o'clock when he got home, falling dark. He entered the house in silence. His mother, who had been waiting, rose anxiously.

"I told her," he said.

"I'm glad!" replied the mother, with great relief.

He hung up his cap wearily.

"I said we'd have done altogether," he said.

"That's right, my son," said the mother. "It's hard for her now, but best in the long run. I know. You weren't suited for her."

He laughed shakily as he sat down.

"I've had such a lark with some girls in a pub," he said.

His mother looked at him. He had forgotten Miriam now. He told her about the girls in the Willow Tree. Mrs Morel looked at him. It seemed unreal, his gaiety. At the back of it was too much horror and misery.

"Now have some supper," she said, very gently.

Afterwards, he said wistfully:

"She never thought she'd have me, mother, not from the first—and so she's not disappointed."

"I'm afraid," said his mother, "she doesn't give up hopes of you yet."

"No," he said, "perhaps not."

"You'll find it's better to have done," she said.

"*I* don't know," he said desperately.

"Well, leave her alone," replied his mother.

So he left her, and she was alone. Very few people cared for her, and she for very few people. She remained alone with herself, waiting.

CHAPTER XII

Passion

He was gradually making it possible to earn a livelihood by his art. Liberty's had taken several of his painted designs on various stuffs, and he could sell designs for embroideries, for altar-cloths, and similar things, in one or two places. It was not very much he made at present, but he might extend it. He also had made friends with the designer for a pottery firm, and was gaining some knowledge of his new acquaintance's art. The applied arts interested him very much. At the same time he laboured slowly at his pictures. He loved to paint large figures, full of light, but not merely made up of lights and cast shadows, like the impressionists; rather definite figures that had a certain luminous quality, like some of Michael Angelo's people. And these he fitted into a landscape, in what he thought true proportion. He worked a great deal from memory, using everybody he knew. He believed firmly in his work, that it was good and valuable. In spite of fits of depression, shrinking, everything, he believed in his work.

He was twenty four when he said his first confident thing to his mother.

"Mother," he said, "I s'll make a painter that they'll attend to."

She sniffed in her quaint fashion. It was like a half-pleased shrug of the shoulders.

"Very well, my boy, we'll see," she said.

"You shall see, my pigeon. You see if you're not swanky one of these days."

"I'm quite content my boy," she smiled.

"But you'll have to alter. Look at you with Minnie."

Minnie was the small servant, a girl of fourteen.

"And what about Minnie?" asked Mrs Morel with dignity.

"I heard her this morning: 'Eh Mrs Morrel, I was going to do that', when you went out in the rain for some coal," he said. "That looks a lot like *your* being able to manage servants."

"Well—it was only the child's niceness," said Mrs Morel.

"And you apologising to her: 'You can't do two things at once, can you?'"

"She *was* busy washing up," replied Mrs Morel.

"And what did she say? 'It could easy have waited a bit. Now look how your feet paddle!'"

"Yes, brazen young baggage!" said Mrs Morel, smiling.

"And then you talk of being swanky."

Mrs Morel sniffed.

"Your servants would be so good to you," he said, "you wouldn't dare to move for fear they should be after you."

"Come to that," cried his mother suddenly, "I heard *you* yesterday, when you were going in the passage: 'Eh, don't go in there,' said Minnie. 'Why not?' you said. 'I've just washed it.' And you said: 'Well, I can jump to the mat.' And so, sir, what room have *you* to talk to me?"

"Oh but I *can* be impressive and boss people."

His mother burst out laughing.

"I'll guarantee," she mocked.

"I can, you should see me," he insisted.

"I should," she laughed.

"I tell you my girls quake at my footstep. But a boss of a million girls wouldn't wash with *you*."

She only laughed at him.

"But won't it be fine, when you sit in the dining room and ring when you want your boots to go out."

"It *will*!" she said sceptically.

"But it *will* be, you see. You shall have a real Turkey carpet."

"Very well—very well, my boy. But I'll wait till I get it. Besides, you'll want it for your own home."

"Which home—*this* is my home!"

"It won't always be."

"It *will* I tell you."

"Ah wait a bit!"

"Oh yes, I'll wait. I'll wait till the Venus of Milo comes walking along my way."

"What, would you like a woman like the Venus of Milo?" laughed his mother.

"She *might* want somebody grander," he said. "She'd make a good match with Mr Gladstone."

"And think of poor Mrs Gladstone!" laughed Mrs Morel; "so nice!"

"Yes—yes—she worshipped him—he'd have to have a wife who

346

worshipped him. Lady Venus de Milo wouldn't. I *might* like her. But she's rather old. At any rate, I'll see when she comes."

He looked at his mother, laughing. She was quite warm and rosy again with love of him. It seemed as if all the sunshine were on her for a moment. He continued his work gladly. She seemed so well when she was happy, that he forgot her grey hair.

And that year she went with him to the Isle of Wight for a holiday. It was too exciting for them both, and too beautiful. Mrs Morel was full of joy and wonder. But he would have her walk with him more than she was able. She had a bad fainting bout. So grey her face was, so blue her mouth. It was agony to him. He felt as if someone were pushing a knife in his chest. Then she was better again, and he forgot. But the anxiety remained inside him, like a wound that did not close.

After leaving Miriam he went almost straight to Clara. On the Monday following the day of the rupture, he went down to the work-room. She looked up at him and smiled. They had grown very intimate, unawares. She saw a new brightness about him.

"Well Queen of Sheba!" he said, laughing.

"But why?" she asked.

"I think it suits you. You've got a new frock on."

She flushed, asking:

"And what of it?"

"Suits you—awfully! *I* could design you a dress."

"How would it be?"

He stood in front of her, his eyes glittering, as he expounded. He kept her eyes fixed with his. Then suddenly he took hold of her. She half started back. He drew the stuff of her blouse tighter, smoothed it over her breast.

"More *so*!" he explained.

But they were both of them flaming with blushes, and immediately he ran away. He had touched her. His whole body was quivering with the sensation.

There was already a sort of secret understanding between them. The next evening he went into the cinematograph with her for a few minutes before train time. As they sat, he saw her hand lying near him. For some moments he dared not touch it. The pictures danced and dithered. Then he took her hand in his. It was large and firm, it filled his grasp. He held it fast. She neither moved nor made any sign. When they came out his train was due. He hesitated.

"Goodnight," she said. He darted away across the road.

The next day he came again talking to her. She was rather superior with him.

"Shall we go a walk on Monday?" he asked.

She turned her face aside.

"Shall you tell Miriam?" she replied sarcastically.

"I have broken off with her," he said.

"When?"

"Last Sunday."

"You quarrelled?"

"No! I had made up my mind. I told her quite definitely I should consider myself free."

Clara did not answer, and he returned to his work. She was so quiet, and so superb!

On the Saturday evening he asked her to come and drink coffee with him in a restaurant, meeting him after work was over. She came, looking very reserved and very distant. He had three-quarters of an hour to train-time.

"We will walk a little while," he said.

She agreed, and they went past the Castle into the Park. He was afraid of her. She walked moodily at his side, with a kind of resentful reluctant, angry walk. He was afraid to take her hand.

"Which way shall we go?" he asked, as they walked in darkness.

"I don't mind."

"Then we'll go up the steps."

He suddenly turned round. They had passed the Park Steps. She stood still in resentment at his suddenly abandoning her. He looked for her. She stood aloof. He caught her suddenly in his arms, held her strained for a moment, kissed her. Then he let her go.

"Come along," he said, penitent.

She followed him. He took her hand and kissed her finger-tips. They went in silence. When they came to the light he let go her hand. Neither spoke till they reached the station. Then they looked each other in the eyes.

"Goodnight," she said.

And he went for his train. His body acted mechanically. People talked to him. He heard faint echoes answering them. He was in a delirium. He felt that he would go mad if Monday did not come at once. On Monday he would see her again. All himself was pitched there, ahead. Sunday intervened. He could not bear it. He could not see her till Monday. And Sunday intervened—hour after hour of tension. He wanted to beat his head against the door of the carriage. But he sat still. He drank some whiskey on the way home, but it only made it worse. His mother must not be upset, that was all. He dissembled, and got quickly to bed. There he sat, dressed, with his chin on his knees, staring out of the window at the far hill with its few lights. He neither thought nor slept, but sat perfectly still, staring. And when at last he was so cold that he came to himself, he found his watch had stopped at half past two. It was after three o'clock. He was exhausted, but still there was the torment of knowing it was only Sunday morning. He went to bed and slept. Then he cycled all day long, till he was fagged out. And he scarcely knew where he had been. But the day after was Monday. He slept till four o'clock. Then he lay and thought. He was coming nearer to himself—he could see himself, real, somewhere in front. She would go a walk with him in the afternoon. Afternoon! It seemed years ahead.

Slowly the hours crawled. His father got up—he heard him pottering about—then he set off to the pit, his heavy boots scraping the yard. Cocks were still crowing. A cart went down the road. His mother got up. She knocked the fire. Presently she called him softly. He answered as if he were asleep. This shell of himself did well.

He was walking to the station—another mile! The train was near Nottingham—would it stop before the tunnels?—but it did not matter, it would get there before dinner time. He was at Jordan's. She would come in half an hour. At any rate she would be near. He had done the letters. She would be there. Perhaps she had not come. He ran downstairs. Ah, he saw her through the glass door. Her shoulders stooping a little to her work made him feel he could not go forward; he could not stand. He went in. He was pale, nervous, awkward, and quite cold. Would she misunderstand him. He could not unite his real self with this shell.

"And this afternoon," he struggled to say. "You will come?"

"I think so," she replied, murmuring.

He stood before her, unable to say a word. She hid her face from him. Again came over him the feeling that he would lose consciousness. He set his teeth and went upstairs. He had done everything correctly yet, and he would do so. All the morning, things seemed a long way off, as they do to a man under chloroform. He himself seemed under a tight band of constraint. Then there was his other self, in the distance, doing things, entering stuff in a ledger, and he watched that far-off him carefully to see he made no mistake.

But the ache and strain of it could not go on much longer. He worked incessantly. Still it was only twelve o'clock. As if he had nailed his clothing against the desk, he stood there and worked, forcing every stroke out of himself. It was a quarter to one—he could clear away. Then he ran downstairs.

"You will meet me at the Fountain at two o'clock," he said.

"I can't be there till half past."

"Yes," he said.

She saw his dark, mad eyes.

"I will try at a quarter past."

And he had to be content. He went and got some dinner. All the time he was still under chloroform, and every minute was stretched out indefinitely. He walked miles of street. Then he thought he would be late at the meeting place. He was at the Fountain at five past two. The torture of the next quarter of an hour was refined beyond expression. It was the anguish of combining the living self with the shell. Then he saw her. She came! And he was there.

"You are late," he said.

"Only five minutes," she answered.

"I'd never have done it to you," he laughed.

She was in a dark blue costume. He looked at her beautiful figure.

"You want some flowers," he said, going to the nearest florist's.

She followed him in silence. He bought her a bunch of scarlet, brick-red carnations. She put them in her coat, flushing.

"That's a fine colour!" he said.

"I'd rather have had something softer," she said.

He laughed.

"Do you feel like a blot of vermilion walking down the street!" he said.

She hung her head, afraid of the people they met. He looked sideways at her as they walked. There was a wonderful close down on her face near the ear that he wanted to touch. And a certain heaviness, the heaviness of a very full ear of corn that dips slightly in the wind, that there was about her, made his brain spin. He seemed to be spinning down the street, everything going round.

As they sat in the tram-car, she leaned her heavy shoulder against him, and he took her hand. He felt himself coming round from the anaesthetic, beginning to breathe. Her ear, half hidden among her blonde hair, was near to him. The temptation to kiss it was almost too great. But there were other people on top of the car. It still remained to him to kiss it. After all he was not himself, he was some attribute of hers, like the sunshine that fell on her.

He looked quickly away. It had been raining. The big bluff of the Castle rock was streaked with rain, as it reared above the flat of the town. They crossed the wide, black space of the Midland railway, and passed the cattle enclosure, that stood out white. Then they ran down sordid Wilford Road.

She rocked slightly to the tram's motion, and as she leaned against him, rocked upon him. He was a vigorous, slender man with exhaustless energy. His face was rough, with rough-hewn features, like the common people's. But his eyes under the deep brows were so full of life, that they fascinated her. They seemed to dance, and yet they were still, trembling on the finest balance of laughter. His mouth the same was just going to spring into a laugh of triumph, yet did not. There was a sharp suspense about him. She bit her lip moodily. His hand was hard clenched over hers.

They paid their two halfpennies at the turnstile and crossed the bridge. The Trent was very full. It swept silent and insidious under the bridge, travelling in a soft body. There had been a great deal of rain. On the river levels were flat gleams of flood water. The sky was grey, with glisten of silver here and there. In Wilford church-yard the dahlias were sodden with rain, wet, black-crimson balls. No one was on the path that went along the green river meadow, along the elm-tree colonnade.

There was the faintest haze over the silvery dark water and the green meadow-banks, and the elm trees that were spangled with gold. The river slid by in a body, utterly silent, and swift, inter-twining among itself like some subtle, complex creature. Clara walked moodily beside him.

"Why," she asked at length, in rather a jarring tone, "did you leave Miriam?"

He frowned.

"Because I *wanted* to leave her," he said.

"Why?"

"Because I didn't want to go on with her. And I didn't want to marry."

She was silent for a moment. They picked their way down the muddy path. Drops of water fell from the elm-trees.

"You didn't want to marry Miriam, or you didn't want to marry at all?" she asked.

"Both," he answered. "Both!"

They had to manoeuvre to get to the stile, because of the pools of water.

"And what did she say?" Clara asked.

"Miriam? She said I was a baby of four, and that I always *had* battled her off."

Clara pondered over this for a time.

"But you have really been going with her for some time?" she asked.

"Yes."

"And now you don't want any more of her?"

"No. I know it's no good."

She pondered again.

"Don't you think you've treated her rather badly?" she asked.

"Yes! I ought to have dropped it years back. But it would have been no good going on. Two wrongs don't make a right."

"How old *are* you?" Clara asked.

"Twenty five."

"And I am thirty," she said.

"I know you are."

"I shall be thirty one—or *am* I thirty one—?"

"I neither know nor care. What does it matter!"

They were at the entrance to the Grove. The wet, red track, already sticky with fallen leaves, went up the steep bank between the grass. On either side stood the elm-trees, like pillars along a great aisle, arching over and making high up a roof from which the dead leaves fell. All was empty and silent and wet. She stood on top of the stile, and he held both her hands. Laughing, she looked down into his eyes. Then she leaped, her breast came against his, he held her and covered her face with kisses.

They went on up the slippery, steep red path. Presently she released his hand and put it round her waist.

"You press the vein in my arm, holding it so tightly," she said.

They walked along. His fingertips felt the rocking of her breast. All was silent and deserted. On the left the red wet plough land showed through the doorways between the elm-boles and their branches. On the right, looking down, they could see the tree-tops of elms growing far beneath them, hear occasionally the gurgle of the river. Sometimes, there below they caught glimpses of the full, soft-sliding Trent, and of water meadows dotted with small cattle.

"It has scarcely altered since little Kirke White used to come," he said.

But he was watching her throat below the ear, where the flush was fusing into the honey-white, and her mouth that pouted disconsolate. She stirred against him as she walked, and his body was like a taut string.

Half way up the big colonnade of elms, where the Grove rose highest above the river, their forward movement faltered to an end. He led her across to the grass, under the trees at the edge of the path. The cliff of red earth sloped swiftly down, through trees and bushes, to the river that glimmered and was dark between the foliage. The far below water-meadows were very green. He and she stood leaning against one another, silent, afraid, their bodies touching all along. There came a quick gurgle from the river below.

"Why," he asked at length, "did you hate Baxter Dawes?"

She turned to him with a splendid regal movement. Her mouth was offered him, and her throat, her eyes were half shut, her breast was tilted as if it asked for him. He flashed with a small laugh, shut his eyes, and met her in a long, whole kiss. Her mouth fused with his, their bodies were sealed and annealed. It was some minutes before they withdrew. They were standing beside the public path.

"Will you go down to the river?" he asked.

She looked at him, leaving herself in his hands. He went over the brim of the declivity and began to climb down.

"It is slippery," he said.

"Never mind," she replied.

The red clay went down almost sheer. He slid, went from one tuft of grass to the next, hanging on to the bushes, making for a little platform at the foot of a tree. There he waited for her, laughing with excitement. Her shoes were clogged with red earth. It was hard for her. He frowned. At last he caught her hand and she stood beside him. The cliff rose above them and fell away below. Her colour was up, her eyes flashed. He looked at the big drop below them.

"It's risky," he said, "or messy at any rate. Shall we go back?"

"Not for my sake," she said quickly.

"All right. You see I can't help you, I should only hinder. Give me that little parcel and your gloves. Your poor shoes!"

They stood perched on the face of the declivity, under the trees.

"Well, I'll go again," he said.

Away he went, slipping, staggering, sliding to the next tree, into which he fell with a slam that nearly shook the breath out of him. She came after cautiously, hanging on to the twigs and grasses. So they descended, stage by stage, to the river's brink. There, to his disgust, the flood had eaten away the path, and the red decline ran straight into the water. He dug in his heels and brought himself up violently. The string of the parcel broke with a snap, the brown parcel bounded down, leaped into the water, and sailed smoothly away. He hung on to his tree.

"Well I'll be damned!" he cried crossly. Then he laughed. She was coming perilously down.

"Mind!" he warned her. He stood with his back to the tree, waiting.

"Come now," he called, opening his arms. She let herself run. He caught her, and together they stood watching the dark water scoop at the raw edge of the bank. The parcel had sailed out of sight.

"It doesn't matter," she said.

He held her close, and kissed her. There was only room for their four feet.

"It's a swindle!" he said. "But there's a rut where a man has been, so if we go on I guess we shall find the path again."

The river slid and twined its great volume. On the other bank, cattle were feeding on the desolate flats. The cliff rose high above Paul and Clara, on their right hand. They stood against the tree in the watery silence.

"Let us try going forward," he said, and they struggled in the red clay along the groove a man's nailed boots had made. They were hot and flushed. Their barkled shoes hung heavy on their steps. At last they found the broken path. It was littered with rubble from the water, but at any rate it was easier. They cleaned their boots with twigs. His heart was beating thick and fast. Round the next corner he thought he remembered there was a little bay of level land. He went in front, she followed silently. Her shoes and skirt bottoms were covered with red earth. They climbed over a fallen tree. She stayed behind a moment because some clay had gone into her shoe. They were almost at the place. His heart beat thick and fast.

Suddenly, coming onto the little level, he saw two figures of men standing silent at the water's edge. His heart leaped. They were fishing. He turned and put his hand up warningly to Clara. She hesitated, buttoned her coat. The two went on together.

The fishermen turned curiously to watch the two intruders on their privacy and solitude. They had had a fire, but it was nearly out. All kept perfectly still. The men turned again to their fishing, stood over the grey-glinting river like statues. Clara went with bowed head, flushing; he was laughing to himself. Directly they passed out of sight behind the willows.

"Now they ought to be drowned," said Paul, softly.

Clara did not answer. They toiled forward along a tiny path on the river's lip. Suddenly it vanished. The bank was sheer red solid clay in front of them, sloping straight into the river. He stood and cursed beneath his breath, setting his teeth.

"It is impossible," said Clara.

He stood erect, looking round. Just ahead were two islets in the stream, covered with osiers. But they were unattainable. The cliff came down like a sloping wall from far above their heads. Behind, not far back, were the fishermen. Across the river the distant cattle fed silently in the desolate afternoon. He cursed again deeply under his breath. He gazed up the great steep bank. Was there no hope but to scale back to the public path?

"Stop a minute," he said, and digging his heels sideways into the steep bank of red clay, he began nimbly to mount. He looked across at every tree foot. At last he found what he wanted. Two beech trees side by side on the hill held a little level on the upper face, between their roots. It was littered with damp leaves, but it would do. The fishermen were perhaps sufficiently out of sight. He threw down his rain-proof and waved to her to come.

She toiled to his side. Arriving there, she looked at him heavily, dumbly, and laid her head on his shoulder. He held her fast as he looked round. They were safe enough from all but the small, lonely cows over the river. He sunk his mouth on her throat, where he felt her heavy pulse beat under his lips. Everything was perfectly still. There was nothing in the afternoon but themselves.

When she arose, he, looking on the ground all the time, saw suddenly sprinkled on the black wet beech roots many scarlet carnation petals, like splashed drops of blood. And red, small splashes fell from her bosom streaming down her dress to her feet.

"Your flowers are smashed," he said.

She looked at him heavily as she put back her hair. Suddenly he put his finger-tips on her cheek.

"Why dost look so heavy?" he reproached her.

She smiled sadly, as if she felt alone in herself. He caressed her cheek with his fingers, and kissed her.

"Nay," he said. "Never thee bother."

She gripped his fingers tight, and laughed shakily. Then she dropped her hand. He put the hair back from her brows, stroking her temples, kissing them lightly.

"But tha shouldna worrit," he said, softly, pleading.

"No, I don't worry," she laughed, tenderly, and resigned.

"Yea, tha does! Dunna thee worrit," he implored, caressing.

"No," she consoled him, kissing him.

They had a stiff climb to get to the top again. It took them a quarter of an hour. When he got onto the level grass, he threw off his cap, wiped the sweat from his forehead, and sighed.

"Now we're back at the ordinary level," he said.

She sat down panting on the tussocky grass. Her cheeks were flushed pink. He kissed her, and she gave way to joy.

"And now I'll clean thy boots and make thee fit for respectable folk," he said.

He kneeled at her feet, worked away with a stick and tufts of grass. She put her fingers in his hair, drew his head to her, and kissed it.

"What am I supposed to be doing," he said, looking at her laughing; "cleaning shoes or dibbling with love? Answer me that!"

"Just whichever I please," she replied.

"I'm your boot-boy for the time being, and nothing else."

But they remained looking into each other's eyes and laughing. Then they kissed with little nibbling kisses.

"T-t-t-t!" he went with his tongue, like his mother. "I tell you, nothing gets done when there's a woman about."

And he returned to his boot-cleaning, singing softly. She touched his thick hair, and he kissed her fingers. He worked away at her shoes. At last they were quite presentable.

"There you are you see!" he said. "Aren't I a great hand at restoring you to respectability? Stand up! There, you look as irreproachable as Britannia herself!"

He cleaned his own boots a little, washed his hands in a puddle, and sang. They went on into Clifton village. He was madly in love with her: every movement she made, every crease in her garments sent a hot flash through him and seemed adorable.

The old lady at whose house they had tea was roused into gaiety by them.

"I could wish you'd had something of a better day," she said, hovering round.

"Nay," he laughed. "We've been saying how nice it is."

The old lady looked at him curiously. There was a peculiar glow and charm about him. His eyes were dark and laughing, he rubbed his moustache with a glad movement.

"Have you been saying *so*!" she exclaimed, a light rousing in her old eyes.

"Truly," he laughed.

"Then I'm sure the day's good enough," said the old lady.

She fussed about, and did not want to leave them.

"I don't know whether you'd like some radishes as well," she said to Clara. "But I've got some in the garden—*and* a cucumber."

Clara flushed. She looked very handsome.

"I should like some radishes," she answered.

And the old lady pottered off gleefully.

"If she knew," said Clara, quietly, to him.

"Well, she doesn't know—and it shows we're nice in ourselves, at any rate. You look quite enough to satisfy an archangel, and I'm sure I feel harmless—so—if it makes you look nice, and makes folk happy when they have us, and makes us happy—why, we're not cheating them out of much."

They went on with the meal. When they were going away the old lady came timidly with three tiny dahlias in full blow, neat as bees, and speckled scarlet and white. She stood before Clara, pleased with herself, saying:

"I don't know whether—" and holding the flowers forward in her old hand.

"Oh how pretty—!" cried Clara, accepting the flowers.

"Shall she have them all?" asked Paul reproachfully of the old woman.

"Yes, she shall have them all," she replied, beaming with joy. "You have got enough for your share."

"Ah but I shall ask her to give me one," he teased.

"Then she does as she pleases," said the old lady, smiling. And she bobbed a little curtsey of delight.

Clara was rather quiet and uncomfortable. As they walked along, he said:

"You don't feel criminal, do you?"

She looked at him with startled grey eyes.

"Criminal!" she said. "No."

"But you seem to feel you have done a wrong."

"No," she said. "I only think—'if they knew.'"

"If they knew, they'd cease to understand. As it is, they do understand, and they like it. What do they matter! Here, with only the trees and me, you don't feel not the least bit wrong, do you?"

He took her by the arm, held her facing him, holding her eyes with his. Something fretted him.

"Not sinners, are we?" he said, with an uneasy little frown.

"No," she replied.

He kissed her, laughing.

("You like your little bit of guiltiness, I believe," he said. "I believe Eve enjoyed it, when she went cowering out of Paradise. And I guess Adam was in a rage, and wondered what the deuce all the row was about—a bit of an apple that the birds could peck, if they wanted to."

But there was a certain glow and quietness about her that made him glad. When he was alone in the railway carriage, he found himself tumultuously happy, and the people exceedingly nice, and the night lovely, and everything good.)

Mrs Morel was sitting reading when he got home. Her health was not good now. And there had come that ivory pallor into her face which he never noticed, and which afterwards he never forgot. She did not mention her own ill-health to him. After all, she thought it was not much.

"You are late!" she said, looking at him.

His eyes were shining, his face seemed to glow. He smiled to her.

"Yes—I've been down Clifton Grove with Clara."

His mother looked at him again.

"But won't people talk?" she said.

"Why? They know she's a suffragette and so on. And what if they do talk!"

"Of course there may be nothing wrong in it," said his mother. "But you know what folk are, and if once she gets talked about—"

"Well, I can't help it. Their jaw isn't so almighty important, after all."

"I think you ought to consider *her*."

"So I *do*! What can people say?—that we take a walk together. I believe you're jealous."

"You know I should be *glad*, if she weren't a married woman."

"Well my dear—she lives separate from her husband and talks on platforms—so she's already singled out from the sheep, and as far as I can see, hasn't much to lose. No—her life's nothing to her, so what's the worth of nothing? She goes with me—it becomes something. Then she must pay, we both must pay. Folk are so frightened of paying—they'd rather starve and die."

"Very well, my son—we'll see how it will end."

"Very well, my mother—I'll abide by the end."

"We'll see."

"And she's—she's *awfully* nice mother—she is really! You don't know!"

"That's not the same as marrying her."

"It's perhaps better."

There was silence for a while. He wanted to ask his mother something, but was afraid.

"Should you like to know her?" he hesitated.

"Yes," said Mrs Morel, coolly. "I should like to know what she's like."

"But she's nice, mother, she is! And not a bit common!"

"I never suggested she was."

"But you seem to think she's—not as good as—she's better than ninety nine folk out of a hundred, I tell you. She's *better*, she is! She's fair, she's honest, she's straight—there isn't anything underhand or superior about her—don't be mean about her."

Mrs Morel flushed.

"I am sure I am not mean about her. She may be quite as you say—but—"

"You don't approve," he finished.

"And do you expect me to?" she answered, coldly.

"Yes!—yes!!—if you'd anything about you, you'd be glad. Do you *want* to see her."

"I said I did."

"Then I'll bring her—shall I bring her here?"

"You please yourself."

"Then I *will* bring her here—one Sunday—to tea. If you think a horrid thing about her, I shan't forgive you."

His mother laughed.

"As if it would make any difference," she said. He knew he had won.

"Oh but it feels so fine, mother, when she's there—she's such a queen in her way—"

Occasionally, he still walked a little way from Chapel with Miriam and Edgar. He did not go up to the farm. She, however, was very much the same with him, and he did not feel embarrassed in her presence. One evening she was alone when he accompanied her. They began by talking books: it was their unfailing topic. Mrs Morel had said that his and Miriam's affair was like a fire fed on books—if there were no more volumes it would die out. Miriam, for her part, boasted that she could read him like a book, could place her finger any minute on the chapter and the line. He, easily taken in, believed that Miriam knew more about him than anyone else, so it pleased him to talk to her about himself, like the simplest egoist. Very soon the conversation drifted to his own doings. It flattered him immensely that he was of such supreme interest.

"And what have you been doing lately?"

"I—oh not much—I made a sketch of Bestwood from the garden, that is nearly right at last. It's the hundredth try—"

So they went on. Then she said:

"You've not been out then lately?"

"Yes—I went up Clifton Grove on Monday afternoon with Clara."

"It was not very nice weather," said Miriam, "was it?"

"But I wanted to go out—and it was all right. The Trent *is* full."

"And did you go to Barton?" she asked.

"No, we had tea in Clifton."

"*Did* you! That would be nice."

"It was! The jolliest old woman—she gave us several pom-pom dahlias, as pretty as you like."

Miriam bowed her head and brooded. He was quite unconscious of concealing anything from her.

"What made her give them you?" she asked.

He laughed.

"Because she liked us—because we were jolly, I should think."

Miriam put her finger in her mouth.

"Were you late home?" she asked.

At last he resented her tone.

"I caught the 7.30."

"Ha!"

They walked on in silence, and he was angry.

"And how *is* Clara?" asked Miriam.

"Quite all right, I think."

"That's good," she said, with a tinge of irony. "By the way, what of her husband? One never hears anything of him."

"He's got some other woman, and is also quite all right," he replied. "At least, so I think."

"I see—you don't know for certain.—Don't you think a position like that is hard on a woman?"

"Rottenly hard."

"It's so unjust!" said Miriam. "The man does as he likes—"

"Then let the woman also—" he said.

"How can she!—and if she does, look at her position!"

"What of it?"

"Why—it's impossible!—You don't understand what a woman forfeits—"

"No, I don't.—But if a woman's got nothing but her fair fame to feed on—why, it's thin tack, and a donkey would die of it."

So she understood his moral attitude, at least, and she knew he would act accordingly. She never asked him anything direct, but she got to know enough.

Another day when he saw Miriam the conversation turned to marriage, then to Clara's marriage with Dawes.

"You see," he said, "she never knew the fearful importance of marriage. She thought it was all in the day's march—it would have to come—and Dawes—well, a good many women would have given their souls to get him—so—why not him!—Then she developed into the 'femme incomprise,'—and treated him badly, I'll bet my boots."

"And she left him because he didn't understand her?"

"I suppose so. I suppose she had to. It isn't altogether a question of understanding, it's a question of living. With him, she was only half alive, the rest was dormant, deadened. And the dormant woman was the 'femme incomprise'. And she *had* to be awakened."

"And what about him?"

"I don't know—I rather think he loves her—as much as he can. But he's a fool."

"It was something like your mother and father," said Miriam.

"Yes, but my mother, I believe, got *real* joy and satisfaction out of my father at first. I believe she had a passion for him. That's why she stayed with him. After all, they were bound to each other."

"Yes," said Miriam.

"That's what one *must have*, I think," he continued; "the real, real flame of feeling through another person, once, only once, if it only lasts three months. See, my mother looks as if she'd *had* everything that was necessary for her living and developing. There's not a tiny bit of a feeling of sterility about her."

"No," said Miriam.

"And with my father, at first, I'm sure she had the real thing. She knows—she has been there. You can feel it about her, and about him, and about hundreds of people you meet everyday. And once it has happened to you, you can go on with anything, and ripen."

"What has happened, exactly?" asked Miriam.

"It's so hard to say—but the something big and intense that changes you when you really come together with somebody else. It almost seems to fertilise your soul and make it that you can go on and mature."

"And you think your mother had it with your father?"

"Yes—and at the bottom she feels grateful to him for giving it her, even now, though they are miles apart."

"And you think Clara never had it?"

"I'm sure."

Miriam pondered this. She saw what he was seeking: a sort of baptism of fire in passion, it seemed to her. She realised that he would never be satisfied till he had it. Perhaps it was essential to him—as to some men to sow wild oats. And afterwards, when he was satisfied, he would not rage with restlessness any more, but could settle down and give her his life into her hands. Well then, if he must go, let him go and have his fill—something big and intense, he called it. At any rate, when he had got it, he would not want it: that he said himself. He would want the other thing, that she could give him. He would want to be owned, so that he could work. It seemed to her a bitter thing that he must go. But she could let him go into an inn for a glass of whiskey, so she could let him go to Clara—so long as it was something that would satisfy a need in him and leave him free for herself to possess.

"Have you told your mother about Clara?" she asked.

She knew this would be a test of the seriousness of his feeling for the other woman. She knew he was going to Clara for something vital, not as a man goes for pleasure to a prostitute, if he told his mother.

"Yes," he said, "and she is coming to tea on Sunday."

"To your house?"

"Yes. I want mater to see her."

"Ah!"

There was a silence. Things had gone quicker than she thought. She felt a sudden bitterness, that he could leave her so soon and so entirely. And was Clara to be accepted by his people, who had been so hostile to herself?

"I may call in as I go to Chapel," she said. "It is a long time since I saw Clara."

"Very well," he said, astonished, and unconsciously angry.

On the Sunday afternoon he went to Keston to meet Clara at the station. As he stood on the platform, he was trying to examine in himself if he had a premonition.

"Do I *feel* as if she'd come," he said to himself, and he tried to find out. His heart felt queer and contracted. That seemed like foreboding. Then he *had* a foreboding she would not come! Then she would not come, and instead of taking her over the fields home, as he had imagined, he would have to go alone. The train was late. The afternoon would be wasted, and the evening. He hated her for not coming. Why had she promised then, if she could not keep her promise? Perhaps she had missed her train—he himself was always missing trains—but that was no reason why she should miss this particular one. He was angry with her—he was furious.

Suddenly he saw the train crawling, sneaking round the corner. Here then was the train, but of course she had not come. The green engine hissed along the platform, the row of brown carriages drew up. Several doors opened. No, she had not come!—No!—Yes, ah there she was, she had a big black hat on! He was at her side in a moment.

"I thought you weren't coming," he said.

She was laughing rather breathlessly as she put out her hand to him. Their eyes met. He took her quickly along the platform, talking at a great rate, to hide his feeling. She looked beautiful. In her hat were large silk roses, coloured like tarnished gold. Her costume of dark cloth fitted so beautifully over her breast and shoulders. His pride went up as he walked with her. He felt the station people, who knew him, eyed her with awe and admiration.

"I was sure you weren't coming," he laughed, shakily.

She laughed in answer, almost with a little cry.

"And I wondered, when I was in the train, what*ever* I should do if you weren't there!" she said.

He caught her hand impulsively, and they went along the narrow twitchel. They took the road into Nuttall and over the Reckoning House Farm. It was a blue, mild day. Everywhere the brown leaves lay scattered. Many scarlet hips stood up on the hedge beside the wood. He gathered a few for her to wear.

"Though really," he said as he fitted them into the breast of her coat, "you ought to object to my getting them, because of the birds. But they don't care much for rose-hips in this part, where they can get plenty of stuff. You often find the berries going rotten in spring-time."

So he chattered, scarcely aware of what he said, only knowing he was putting berries in the bosom of her coat, while she stood patiently for him. And she watched his quick hands, so full of life, and it seemed to her she had never *seen* anything before: till now, everything had been indistinct.

They came near to the colliery. It stood quite still and black among the corn-fields, its immense heap of slag seen rising almost from the oats.

"What a pity there is a coal-pit here where it is so pretty," said Clara.

"Do you think so?" he answered. "You see I am so used to it, I should miss it.—No, and I like the pits here and there. I like the rows of trucks, and the headstocks, and the steam in the daytime and the lights at night.—When I was a boy, I always thought a pillar of cloud by day and a pillar of fire by night was a pit, with its steam, and its lights and the burning bank—and I thought the Lord was always at the pit-top."

As they drew near home she walked in silence, and seemed to hang back. He pressed her fingers in his own. She flushed, but gave no response.

"Don't you want to come home?" he asked.

"Yes, I want to come," she replied.

It did not occur to him that her position in his home would be rather a peculiar and difficult one. To him it seemed just as if one of his men friends were going to be introduced to his mother—only nicer.

The Morels lived in a house in an ugly street that ran down a steep hill. The street itself was hideous. The house was rather superior to most. It was old, grimy, with a big bay window. And it was semi-detached. But it looked gloomy. Then Paul opened the door to the garden, and all was different. The sunny afternoon was there, like another land. By the path grew tansy and little trees. In front of the window was a plot of sunny grass, with old lilacs round it. And away went the garden, with heaps of dishevelled chrysanthemums in the sunshine, down to the sycamore tree, and the field, and beyond one looked over a few red-roofed cottages to the hills with all the glow of the autumn afternoon.

Mrs Morel sat in her rocking-chair wearing her black silk blouse. Her grey-brown hair was taken smooth back from her brow and her high temples, her face was rather pale. Clara, suffering, followed Paul into the kitchen. Mrs Morel rose. Clara thought her a lady, even rather stiff. The young woman was very nervous. She had almost a wistful look, almost resigned.

"Mother—Clara," said Paul.

Mrs Morel held out her hand and smiled.

"He has told me a good deal about you," she said.

The blood flamed in Clara's cheek.

"I hope you don't mind my coming," she faltered.

"I was pleased when he said he would bring you," replied Mrs Morel.

Paul, watching, felt his heart contract with pain. His mother looked so small, and sallow, and done-for, beside the luxuriant Clara.

"It's such a pretty day, mother!" he said. "And we saw a jay."

His mother looked at him. He had turned to her. She thought what a man he seemed, in his dark, well-made clothes. He was pale and detached-looking, it would be hard for any woman to keep him. Her heart glowed. Then she was sorry for Clara.

"Perhaps you'll leave your things in the parlour," said Mrs Morel, nicely, to the young woman.

"Oh thank you," she replied.

"Come on," said Paul, and he led the way into the little front room, with its old piano, its mahogany furniture, its yellowish marble mantel-piece. A fire was burning. The place was littered with books and drawing boards.

"I leave my things lying about," he said. "It's so much easier."

She loved his artist's paraphernalia, and the books and the photos of people. Soon he was telling her: this was William, this was William's young lady, in the evening dress, this was Annie, and her husband, this was Arthur, and his wife and the baby. She felt as if she were being taken into the family. He showed her photos, books, sketches, and they talked a little while. Then they returned to the kitchen. Mrs Morel put aside her book. Clara wore a blouse of fine silk chiffon, with narrow black and white stripes. Her hair was done simply, coiled on top of her head. She looked rather stately and reserved.

"You have gone to live down Sneinton Boulevard?" said Mrs Morel. "When I was a girl—girl, I say!—when I was a young woman *we* lived in Minerva Terrace."

"Oh did you!" said Clara. "I have a friend in Number 6."

And the conversation had started. They talked Nottingham and Nottingham people. It interested them both. Clara was still rather nervous, Mrs Morel was still somewhat on her dignity. She clipped her language very clear and precise. But they were going to get on well together, Paul saw.

Mrs Morel measured herself against the younger woman, and found herself easily stronger. Clara was deferential. She knew Paul's surprising regard for his mother, and she had dreaded the meeting, expecting someone rather hard and cold. She was surprised to find this little, interested woman, chatting with such readiness. And then she felt, as she felt with Paul, that she would not care to stand in Mrs Morel's way. There was something so hard and certain in his mother, as if she never had a misgiving in her life.

Presently Morel came down, ruffled and yawning from his afternoon sleep. He scratched his grizzled head, he podded in his stocking feet, his waistcoat hung open over his shirt. He seemed incongruous.

"This is Mrs Dawes, father," said Paul.

Then Morel pulled himself together. Clara saw Paul's manner of bowing and shaking hands.

"Oh indeed!" exclaimed Morel. "I am very glad to see you, I am, I assure you. But don't disturb yourself—no—no! Make yourself quite comfortable, and be very welcome."

Clara was astonished at this flood of hospitality from the old collier. He was so courteous, so gallant! She thought him most delightful.

"And may you have come far?" he asked.

"Only from Nottingham," she said.

"From Nottingham. Then you have had a beautiful day for your journey."

Then he strayed into the scullery to wash his hands and face, and from force of habit came onto the hearth with the towel to dry himself.

At tea Clara felt the refinement and sang-froid of the household. Mrs Morel was perfectly at her ease. The pouring out the tea and attending to the people went on unconsciously, without interrupting her in her talk. There was a lot of room at the oval table, the china of dark-blue willow-pattern looked pretty on the glossy cloth. There was a little bowl of small, yellow chrysanthemums. Clara felt she completed the circle, and it was a pleasure to her. But she was rather afraid of the self-possession of the Morels, father and all. She took their tone. There was a feeling of balance. It was a cool, clear atmosphere, where everyone was himself, and in harmony. Clara enjoyed it, but there was a fear deep at the bottom of her.

Paul cleared the table whilst his mother and Clara talked. Clara was conscious of his quick vigorous body as it came and went, seeming blown quickly by a wind at its work. It was almost like the hither and thither of a leaf that comes unexpected. Most of herself went with him. By the way she leaned forward, as if listening, Mrs Morel could see she was possessed elsewhere as she talked. And again the elder woman was sorry for her.

Having finished, he strolled down the garden, leaving the two women to talk. It was a hazy, sunny afternoon, mild and soft. Clara glanced through the window after him, as he loitered among the chrysanthemums. She felt as if something almost tangible fastened her to him. Yet he seemed so easy, in his graceful, indolent movement, so detached as he tied up the too-heavy flower-branches to their stakes, that she wanted to shriek in her helplessness.

Mrs Morel rose.

"You will let me help you wash up," said Clara.

"Eh, there are so few, it will only take me a minute," said the other.

Clara however dried the tea-things, and was glad to be on such good terms with his mother. But it was torture not to be able to follow him down the garden. At last she allowed herself to go. She felt as if a rope were taken off her ankle.

The afternoon was golden over the hills of Derbyshire. He stood across in the other garden, beside a bush of pale Michaelmas daisies, watching the last bees crawl into the hive. Hearing her coming, he turned to her with an easy motion, saying:

"It's the end of the run with these chaps."

Clara stood near him. Over the low red wall in front was the country and the far-off hills, all golden and dim.

At that moment Miriam was entering through the garden door. She saw Clara go up to him, saw him turn, and saw them come to rest together. Something in their perfect isolation together made her know that it was accomplished between them, that they were, as she put it, married. She walked very slowly down the cinder-track of the long garden.

Clara had pulled a button from a holly-hock spire, and was breaking it to get the seeds. Above her bowed head the pink flowers stared, as if defending her. The last bees were falling down to the hive.

"Count your money," laughed Paul, as she broke the flat seeds one by one from the roll of coin. She looked at him.

"I'm well off," she said, smiling.

"How much?—Pf!—" he snapped his fingers. "Can I turn them into gold?"

"I'm afraid not," she laughed.

They looked into each other's eyes, laughing. At that moment they became aware of Miriam. There was a click, and everything had altered.

"Hello Miriam!" he exclaimed. "You said you'd come!"

"Yes, had you forgotten?"

She shook hands with Clara, saying:

"It seems strange to see you here."

"Yes," replied the other, "it seems strange to be here."

There was a hesitation.

"It is pretty, isn't it?" said Miriam.

"I like it very much," replied Clara.

Then Miriam realised that Clara was accepted as she had never been.

"Have you come down alone?" asked Paul.

"Yes! I went to Agatha's to tea. We are going to Chapel. I only called in for a moment, to see Clara."

"You should have come in here to tea," he said.

Miriam laughed shortly, and Clara turned impatiently aside.

"Do you like the chrysanthemums?" he asked.

"Yes—they are very fine," replied Miriam.

"Which sort do you like best?" he asked.

"I don't know—the bronze, I think."

"I don't think you've seen all the sorts. Come and look. Come and see which are *your* favorites, Clara."

He led the two women back to his own garden, where the towzled bushes of flowers of all colours stood raggedly along the path down to the field. The situation did not embarrass him, to his knowledge.

"Look Miriam—these are the white ones that came from your garden. They aren't so fine here, are they?"

"No," said Miriam.

"But they're hardier. You're so sheltered. Things grow big and tender and then die. These little yellow ones I like. Will you have some?"

While they were out there the bells began to ring in the church, sounding loud across the town and the field. Miriam looked at the tower, proud among the clustering roofs, and remembered the sketches he had brought her. It had been different then. But he had not left her even yet. She asked him for a book to read. He ran indoors.

"What—is that Miriam?" asked his mother coldly.

"Yes—she said she'd call and see Clara."

"You told her then?" came the sarcastic answer.

"Yes, why shouldn't I?"

"There's certainly no reason why you shouldn't," said Mrs Morel, and she returned to her book. He winced from his mother's irony, frowned irritably, thinking 'Why can't I do as I like?'

"You've not seen Mrs Morel before," Miriam was saying to Clara.

"No—but she's *so* nice."

"Yes," said Miriam, dropping her head. "In some ways she's very fine."

"I should think so."

"Had Paul told you much about her?"

"He had talked a good deal."

"Ha!"

There was silence until he returned with the book.

"When will you want it back?" Miriam asked.

"When you like," he answered.

Clara turned to go indoors whilst he accompanied Miriam to the gate.

"When will you come up to Willey Farm?" the latter asked.

"I couldn't say," replied Clara.

"Mother asked me to say she'd be pleased to see you any time, if you cared to come."

"Thank you—I should like to—but I can't say when."

"Oh very well!" exclaimed Miriam rather bitterly turning away.

She went down the path, with her mouth to the flowers he had given her.

"You're sure you won't come in?" he said.

"No thanks."

"We are going to Chapel."

"Ha!—I shall see you then!" Miriam was very bitter.

"Yes."

They parted. He felt guiltily towards her. She was bitter, and she scorned him. He still belonged to herself, she believed. Yet he could have Clara, take her home, sit with her next his mother in Chapel, give her the same hymn-book he had given herself, years before. She heard him running quickly indoors.

But he did not go straight in. Halting on the plot of grass, he heard his mother's voice, then Clara's answer:

"What I hate is the blood-hound quality in Miriam."

"Yes," said his mother quickly. "Yes! *Doesn't* it make you hate her, now!"

His heart went hot and he was angry with them for talking about the girl. What right had they to say that? Something in the speech itself stung him into a flame of hate against Miriam. Then his own heart rebelled furiously at Clara's taking the liberty of speaking so about Miriam. After all, the girl was the better woman of the two, he thought, if it came to goodness. He went indoors. His mother looked excited. She was beating with her hand rhythmically on the sofa-arm, as women do who are wearing out. He could never bear to see the movement. There was a silence. Then he began to talk.

In Chapel, Miriam saw him find the place in the hymn book for Clara, in exactly the same way as he used for herself. And during the sermon he could see the girl across the chapel, her hat throwing a dark shadow over her face. What did she think, seeing Clara with him? He did not stop to consider. He felt himself cruel towards Miriam.

After Chapel he went over Pentrich with Clara. It was a dark autumn night. They had said Goodbye to Miriam, and his heart had smitten him as he left the girl alone. "But it serves her right," he said inside himself, and it almost gave him pleasure to go off under her eyes with this other handsome woman.

There was a scent of damp leaves in the darkness. Clara's hand lay warm and inert in his own as they walked. He was full of conflict. The battle that raged inside him made him feel desperate.

Up Pentrich hill Clara leaned against him as he went. He slid his arm round her waist. Feeling the strong motion of her body under his arm as she walked, the tightness in his chest because of Miriam relaxed, and the hot blood bathed him. He held her closer and closer.

Then: "You still keep on with Miriam," she said quietly.

"Only talk—there never *was* a great deal more than talk between us," he said, bitterly.

"Your mother doesn't care for her," said Clara.

"No—or I might have married her.—But it's all up—really."

Suddenly his voice went passionate with hate.

"If I was with her now—we should be jawing about the 'Christian Mystery', or some such tack. Thank God I'm not."

They walked on in silence for some time.

"But you can't really give her up," said Clara.

"I don't give her up, because there's nothing to give," he said.

"There is for her."

"I don't know why she and I shouldn't be friends as long as we live," he said. "But it'll only be friends."

Clara drew away from him, leaning away from contact with him.

"What are you drawing away for?" he asked.

She did not answer, but drew further from him.

"Why do you want to walk alone?" he asked.

Still there was no answer. She walked resentfully, hanging her head.

"Because I said I would be friends with Miriam!" he exclaimed.

She would not answer him anything.

"I tell you it's only words that go between us," he persisted, trying to take her again. She resisted. Suddenly he strode across in front of her, barring her way.

"Damn it!" he said. "What do you want now?"

"You'd better run after Miriam," mocked Clara.

The blood flamed up in him. He stood showing his teeth. She drooped sulkily. The lane was dark, quite lonely. He suddenly caught her in his arms, stretched forward, and put his mouth on her face in a kiss of rage. She turned frantically to avoid him. He held her fast. Hard and relentless his mouth came for her. Her breasts hurt against the wall of his chest. Helpless, she went loose in his arms, and he kissed her, and kissed her.

He heard people coming down the hill.

"Stand up—stand up!" he said thickly, gripping her arm till it hurt. If he had let go she would have sunk to the ground. She sighed, and walked dizzily beside him. They went on in silence.

"We will go over the fields," he said, and then she woke up.

But she let herself be helped over the stile, and she walked in silence with him over the first dark field. It was the way to Nottingham and to the station, she knew. He seemed to be looking about. They came out on a bare hill top where stood the dark figure of the ruined windmill. There he halted. They stood together high up in the darkness, looking at the lights scattered on the night before them, handfuls of glittering points, villages lying high and low on the dark, here and there.

"Like treading among the stars," he said, with a quaky laugh.

Then he took her in his arms, he held her fast in a long kiss. She moved aside her mouth to ask, dogged and low:

"What time is it?"

"It doesn't matter," he pleaded, thickly.

"Yes it does—yes—I must go."

"It's early yet," he said.

"What time is it?" she insisted.

All round lay the black night speckled and spangled with lights.

"I don't know."

She put her hand on his chest, feeling for his watch. He felt his joints fuse into fire. She groped in his waistcoat pocket, while he stood panting. In the darkness, she could see the round, pale face of the watch, but not the figures. She stooped over it. He was panting, till he could take her in his arms again.

"I can't see," she said.

"Then don't bother."

"Yes—I'm going," she said, turning away.

"Wait—I'll look—" but he could not see—"I'll strike a match."

He secretly hoped it was too late to catch the train. She saw the glowing lantern of his hands as he cradled the light, then his face lit up, his eyes fixed on the watch. Instantly all was dark again. All was black before her eyes, only a glowing match was red near her feet. Where was he?

"What is it?" she asked, afraid.

"You can't do it," his voice answered out of the darkness.

There was a pause. She felt in his power. She had heard the ring in his voice. It frightened her.

"What time is it?" she asked, quiet, definite, hopeless.

"Two minutes to nine," he replied, telling the truth with a struggle.

"And can I get from here to the station in fourteen minutes."

"No—at any rate—"

She could distinguish his dark form again, a yard or so away. She wanted to escape.

"But can't I do it?" she pleaded.

"If you hurry," he said, brusquely. "But—you could easily walk it, Clara—it's only seven miles to the tram—I'll come with you."

"No—I want to catch the train."

"But why?

"I do—I want to catch the train."

Suddenly his voice altered.

"Very well," he said, dry and hard. "Come along then."

And he plunged ahead into the darkness. She ran after him, wanting to cry. Now he was hard and cruel to her. She ran over the rough dark fields behind him, out of breath, ready to drop. But the double row of lights at the station drew nearer. Suddenly:

"There she is!" he cried, breaking into a run.

There was a faint rattling noise. Away to the right, the train like a luminous caterpillar was threading across the night. The rattling ceased.

"She's over the viaduct—you'll just do it."

Clara ran, quite out of breath, and fell at last into the train. The whistle blew. He was gone. Gone!—and she was in a carriage full of people. She felt the cruelty of it.

He turned round and plunged home. Before he knew where he was he was in the kitchen at home. He was very pale, his eyes were dark and dangerous looking, as if he were drunk. His mother looked at him.

"Well I must say, your boots are in a nice state," she said.

He looked at his feet. Then he took off his overcoat. His mother wondered if he were drunk.

"She caught the train then?" she said.

"Yes."

"I hope *her* feet weren't so filthy—where on earth you dragged her I don't know."

He was silent and motionless for some time.

"Did you like her?" he asked, grudgingly, at last.

"Yes—I liked her.—But you'll tire of her, my son, you know you will."

He did not answer. She noticed how he laboured in his breathing.

"Have you been running?" she asked.

"We had to run for the train."

"You'll go and knock yourself up. You'd better drink hot milk."

It was as good a stimulant as he could have. But he refused, and went to bed. There he lay face down on the counterpane, and shed tears of rage and pain. There was a physical pain that made him bite his lips till they bled, and the chaos inside him left him unable to think, almost to feel.

"This is how she serves me, is it," he said in his heart, over and over, pressing his face in the quilt. And he hated her. Again he went over the scene, and again he hated her.

The next day there was a new aloofness about him. Clara was very gentle, almost loving. But he treated her distantly, with a touch of contempt. She sighed, continuing to be gentle. He came round.

One evening of that week Sarah Bernhardt was at the Theatre Royal in Nottingham, giving *La Dame aux Camélias*. Paul wanted to see this old and famous actress, and he asked Clara to accompany him. He told his mother to leave the key in the window for him.

"Shall I book seats?" he asked of Clara.

"Yes. And put on an evening suit, will you? I've never seen you in it."

"But good Lord, Clara, think of *me* in evening suit at the theatre!" he remonstrated.

"Would you rather not?" she asked.

"I will if you *want* me to—but I s'll feel a fool."

She laughed at him.

"Then feel a fool for my sake, once—won't you?"

The request made his blood flush up.

"I suppose I s'll have to."

"What are you taking a suit case for?" his mother asked.

He blushed furiously.

"Clara asked me," he said.

"And what seats are you going in?"

"Circle—three-and-six each."

"Well I'm sure!" exclaimed his mother sarcastically.

"It's only once in the bluest of blue moons," he said.

He dressed at Jordan's, put on an overcoat and a cap, and met Clara in a café. She was with one of her Suffragette friends. She wore an old long coat, which did not suit her, and had a little wrap over her head, which he hated. The three went to the theatre together.

Clara took off her coat on the stairs, and he discovered she was in a sort of semi evening-dress, that left her arms and neck, and part of her breast bare. Her hair was done fashionably. The dress, a simple thing of green crape, suited her. She looked quite grand, he thought. He could see her figure inside the frock, as if that were wrapped closely round her. The firmness and the softness of her upright body could almost be felt as he looked at her. He clenched his fists.

And he was to sit all the evening beside her beautiful, naked arm, watching the strong throat rise from the strong chest, watching the breasts under the green stuff, the curve of her thighs in the tight dress. Something in him hated her again for submitting him to this torture of nearness. And he loved her, as she balanced her head and stared straight in front of her, pouting, wistful, immobile, as if she yielded herself to her fate because it was too strong for her. She could not help herself—she was in the grip of something bigger than herself. A kind of eternal look about her, as if she were a wistful sphinx, made him mad to kiss her. He dropped his programme, and crouched down on the floor to get it, so that he could kiss her hand and wrist. Her beauty was a torture to him. She sat immobile. Only, when the lights went down, she sank a little against him, and he caressed her hand and arm with his fingers. He could smell her faint natural perfume, and it drove him wild with hunger. All the time, his blood kept sweeping up in great white-hot waves, that killed his consciousness momentarily.

The drama continued. He saw it all in the distance, going on somewhere, he did not know where, but it seemed far away inside him. He was Clara's white, heavy arms, her throat, her moving bosom. That seemed to be himself. Then away somewhere the play went on, and he was identified with that also. There was no himself. The grey and black eyes of Clara, her bosom coming down on him, her arm that he held gripped between his hands were all that

375

existed. Then he felt himself small and helpless, her towering in her force above him.

Only the intervals, when the lights came up, hurt him expressibly. He wanted to run anywhere, so long as it would be dark again. In a maze, he wandered out for a drink. Then the lights were out, and the strange, insane reality of Clara and the drama took hold of him again.

The play went on. But he was obsessed by the desire to kiss the tiny blue vein that nestled in the bend of her arm. He could feel it. His whole life seemed suspended till he had put his lips there. It must be done. And the other people! At last he bent quickly forward, and touched it with his lips. His moustache brushed the sensitive flesh. Clara shivered, drew away her arm.

When all was over, the lights up, the people clapping, he came to himself and looked at his watch. His train was gone.

"I s'll have to walk home!" he said.

Clara looked at him.

"Is it too late?" she asked.

He nodded. Then he helped her on with her coat.

"I love you. You look beautiful in that dress," he murmured over her shoulder, among the throng of bustling people. She remained quiet. Together they went out of the theatre. He saw the cabs waiting, the people passing. It seemed he met a pair of brown eyes which hated him. But he did not know. He and Clara turned away, mechanically taking the direction to the station.

The train had gone. He would have to walk the ten miles home.

"It doesn't matter," he said. "I shall enjoy it."

"Won't you," she said, flushing, "come home for the night? I can sleep with mother——"

He looked at her. Their eyes met.

"What will your mother say?" he asked.

"She won't mind."

"You're sure?"

"Quite!"

"*Shall* I come?"

"If you will."

"Very well!"

And they turned away. At the first stopping place they took the car. The wind blew fresh in their faces. The town was dark, the tram tipped in its haste. He sat with her hand fast in his.

"Will your mother be gone to bed?" he asked.

"She may be—I hope not."

They hurried along the silent, dark little street, the only people out of doors. Clara quickly entered the house. He hesitated.

"Come in," she said.

He leaped up the step and was in the room. Her mother appeared in the inner doorway, large and hostile.

"Who have you got there?" she asked.

"It's Mr Morel—he has missed his train. I thought we might put him up for the night, and save him a ten-mile walk."

"Hm!" exclaimed Mrs Radford. "That's *your* look-out! If you've invited him, he's very welcome as far as I'm concerned. *You* keep the house."

"If you don't like me I'll go away again," he said.

"Nay-nay, you needn't! Come along in.—I dunno what you'll think of the supper I'd got her."

It was a little dish of chip-potatoes and a piece of bacon. The table was roughly laid for one.

"You can have some more bacon," continued Mrs Radford. "More chips you can't have."

"It's a shame to bother you," he said.

"Oh, don't you be apologetic, it doesn't *do* wi' me! You treated her to the theatre, didn't you—?" There was a sarcasm in the last question.

"Well—!" laughed Paul, uncomfortably.

"Well—and what's an inch of bacon! Take your coat off."

The big, straight-standing woman was trying to estimate the situation. She moved about the cupboard. Clara took his coat. The room was very warm, and cosy in the lamplight.

"My sirs!" exclaimed Mrs Radford; "but you two's a pair of bright beauties, I must say! What's all that get-up for?"

"I believe we don't know," he said, feeling a victim.

"There isn't room in *this* house for two such bobby-dazzlers, if you fly your kites *that* high," she rallied them. It was a nasty thrust.

He in his dinner jacket, Clara in her green dress and bare arms were confused. They felt they must shelter each other in that little kitchen.

"And look at *that* blossom!" continued Mrs Radford, pointing to Clara. "What does she reckon she did it for?"

Paul looked at Clara. She was rosy, her neck was warm with blushes. There was a moment of silence.

"You like to see it, don't you?" he asked. The mother had them in her power. All the time his heart was beating hard, and he was tight with anxiety. But he would fight her.

"Me like to see it—!" exclaimed the old woman. "What should I like to see her make a fool of herself for!"

"I've seen people look bigger fools," he said. Clara was under his protection now.

"Oh ay—and when was that?" came the sarcastic rejoinder.

"When they made frights of themselves," he answered.

Mrs Radford, large and threatening, stood suspended on the hearthrug, holding her fork.

"They're fools either road," she answered at length, turning to the Dutch oven.

"No," he said, fighting stoutly. "Folk ought to look as well as they can."

"And do you call *that* looking nice!" cried the mother, pointing a scornful fork at Clara. "That, that looks as if it wasn't properly dressed."

"I believe you're jealous that you can't swank as well," he said, laughing.

"Me! I could ha' worn evening dress with anybody, if I'd wanted to," came the scornful answer.

"And why didn't you want to?" he asked, pertinently.—"Or *did* you wear it?"

There was a long pause. Mrs Radford re-adjusted the bacon in the Dutch oven. His heart beat fast, for fear he had offended her.

"Me!" she exclaimed at last. "No, I didn't! And when I was in service, I knew as soon as one of the maids came out in bare shoulders, what sort *she* was, going to her sixpenny hop."

"Were you too good to go to a sixpenny hop?" he said.

Clara sat with bowed head. His eyes were dark and glittering. Mrs Radford took the Dutch oven from the fire, and stood near him, putting bits of bacon on his plate.

"*There's* a nice crozzly bit!" she said.

"Don't give me the best," he said.

"*She's* got what *she* wants," was the answer.

There was a sort of scornful forbearance in the woman's tone that made Paul know she was mollified.

378

"But *do* have some!" he said to Clara.

She looked up at him with her grey eyes humiliated, and lonely.

"No thanks!" she said.

"Why won't you?" he answered, caressively.

The blood was beating up like fire in his veins. Mrs Radford sat down again, large and impressive and aloof. He left Clara altogether, to attend to the mother.

"They say Sarah Bernhardt's fifty," he said.

"Fifty!—She's turned sixty!" came the scornful answer.

"Well," he said, "you'd never think it! She made me want to howl even now."

"I should like to see myself howling at *that* bad old baggage," said Mrs Radford. "It's time she began to think herself a grandmother, not a shrieking catamaran—."

He laughed.

"A catamaran is a boat the Malays use," he said.

"And it's a word as *I* use," she retorted.

"My mother does sometimes—and it's no good my telling her," he said.

"I s'd think she boxes your ears," said Mrs Radford, good-humouredly.

"She'd like to—and she says she will—so I give her a little stool to stand on—"

"That's the worst of my mother," said Clara. "She never wants a stool for anything."

"But she often can't touch *that* lady with a long prop," retorted Mrs Radford to Paul.

"I s'd think she doesn't want touching with a prop," he laughed. "*I* shouldn't."

"It might do the pair of you good to give you a crack on the head with one," said the mother, laughing suddenly.

"Why are you so vindictive towards me?" he said. "I've not stolen anything from you."

"No I'll watch that," laughed the older woman.

Soon the supper was finished. Mrs Radford sat guard in her chair. Paul lit a cigarette. Clara went upstairs, returning with a sleeping suit which she spread on the fender to air.

"Why I'd forgot all about *them*," said Mrs Radford. "Where have they sprung from?"

"Out of my drawer."

379

"Hm!—You bought 'em for Baxter, an' he wouldn't wear 'em, would he?"—laughing—"Said he reckoned to do wi'out trousers i' bed." She turned confidentially to Paul, saying: "He couldn't *bear* 'em, them pyjama things."

The young man sat making rings of smoke.

"Well, it's everyone to his taste," he laughed.

Then followed a little discussion of the merits of pyjamas.

"My mother loves me in them," he said. "She says I'm a Pierrot."

"I can imagine they'd suit you," said Mrs Radford.

After a while, he glanced at the little clock that was ticking on the mantel-piece. It was half-past twelve.

"It is funny," he said, "but it takes hours to settle down to sleep after the theatre."

"It's about time you did," said Mrs Radford, clearing the table.

"Are *you* tired?" he asked of Clara.

"Not the least bit," she answered, avoiding his eyes.

"Shall we have a game at cribbage?" he said.

"I've forgotten it."

"Well, I'll teach you again.—May we play crib, Mrs Radford?" he asked.

"You'll please yourselves," she said, "but it's pretty late."

"A game or so will make us sleepy," he answered.

Clara brought the cards and sat spinning her wedding ring whilst he shuffled them. Mrs Radford was washing up in the scullery. As it grew later Paul felt the situation getting more and more tense.

"Fifteen two, fifteen four, fifteen six, and two's eight——!"

The clock struck one. Still the game continued. Mrs Radford had done all the little jobs preparatory to going to bed, had locked the door and filled the kettle. Still Paul went on dealing and counting. He was obsessed by Clara's arms and throat. He believed he could see where the division was just beginning for her breasts. He could not leave her. She watched his hands, and felt her joints melt as they moved quickly. She was so near; it was almost as if he touched her—and yet not quite. His mettle was roused. He hated Mrs Radford. She sat on, nearly dropping asleep, but determined and obstinate in her chair. Paul glanced at her, then at Clara. She met his eyes, that were angry, mocking, and hard as steel. Her own answered him in shame. He knew *she* at any rate was of his mind. He played on.

At last Mrs Radford roused herself, stiffly, and said:

"Isn't it nigh on time you two was thinking o' bed."

Paul played on without answering. He hated her sufficiently to murder her.

"Half a minute," he said.

The elder woman rose and sailed stubbornly into the scullery, returning with his candle, which she put on the mantel-piece. Then she sat down again. The hatred of her went so hot down his veins, he dropped his cards.

"We'll stop then," he said, but his voice was still a challenge.

Clara saw his mouth shut hard. Again he glanced at her. It seemed like an agreement. She bent over the cards, coughing, to clear her throat.

"Well I'm glad you've finished," said Mrs Radford. "Here—take your things"—she thrust the warm suit in his hand—"and this is your candle. Your room's over this—there's only two, so you can't go far wrong.—Well—Goodnight—I hope you'll rest well."

"I'm sure I shall—I always do," he said.

"Yes—and so you ought at your age," she replied.

He bade goodnight to Clara, and went. The twisting stairs of white, scrubbed wood creaked and clanged at every step. He went doggedly. The two doors faced each other. He went in his room, pushed the door to, without fastening the latch.

It was a small room with a large bed. Some of Clara's hairpins were on the dressing table—her hair-brush; her clothes and some skirts hung under a cloth in a corner. There was actually a pair of stockings over a chair. He explored the room. Two books of his own were there on the shelf. He undressed, folded his suit, and sat on the bed, listening. Then he blew out the candle, lay down, and in two minutes was almost asleep. Then click!—he was wide awake and writhing in torment. It was as if, when he had nearly got to sleep, something had bitten him suddenly and sent him mad. He sat up and looked at the room in the darkness. Then he realised that there was a pair of her stockings on a chair. He got up stealthily, and put them on himself. Then he sat still, and knew he would have to have her. After that he sat erect on the bed, his feet doubled under him, perfectly motionless, listening. He heard a cat somewhere away outside—then the heavy, poised tread of the mother—then Clara's distinct voice:

"Will you unfasten my dress?"

There was silence for some time. At last the mother said:

"Now then—aren't you coming up?"

"No—not yet," replied the daughter, calmly.

"Oh very well then! If it's not late enough, stop a bit longer. Only you needn't come waking me up when I've got to sleep."

"I shan't be long," said Clara.

Immediately afterwards Paul heard the mother slowly mounting the stairs. The candle-light flashed through the cracks in his door. Her dress brushed the door, and his heart jumped. Then it was dark, and he heard the clatter of her latch. She was very leisurely indeed in her preparations for sleep. After a long time, it was quite still. He sat strung up on the bed, shivering slightly. His door was an inch open. As Clara came upstairs, he would intercept her. He waited. All was dead silence. The clock struck two.—Then he heard a slight scrape of the fender downstairs. Now he could not help himself. His shivering was uncontrollable. He felt he must go or die.

He stepped off the bed, and stood a moment, shuddering. Then he went straight to the door. He tried to step lightly. The first stair cracked like a shot. He listened. The old woman stirred in her bed. The staircase was dark. There was a slit of light under the stair-foot door, which opened into the kitchen. He stood a moment. Then he went on, mechanically. Every step creaked, and his back was creeping, lest the old woman's door should open behind him, up above. He fumbled with the door at the bottom. The latch opened with a loud clack. He went through into the kitchen and shut the door noisily behind him. The old woman daren't come now.

Then he stood, arrested. Clara was kneeling naked on a pile of white underclothing on the hearthrug, her back towards him, warming herself. She did not look round, but sat crouching on her heels, and her rounded, beautiful back was towards him, and her face was hidden. She was warming her body at the fire for consolation. The glow was rosy on one side, the shadow was dark and warm on the other. Her arms hung slack.

He shuddered violently, clenching his teeth and fists hard to keep control. Then he went forward to her. He put one hand on her shoulder, the fingers of the other hand under her chin, to raise her face. A convulsed shiver ran through her, once, twice, at his touch. She kept her head bent.

"Sorry!" he murmured, realising that his hands were very cold.

Then she looked up at him, frightened, like a thing that is afraid of death.

"My hands are so cold," he murmured.

"I like it," she whispered, closing her eyes. The breath of her words was on his mouth. Her arms clasped his knees. The cord of his sleeping suit dangled against her and made her shiver. As the warmth went into him, his shuddering became less.

At length, unable to stand so any more, he raised her, and she buried her head on his shoulder. His hands went over her slowly, with an infinite tenderness of caress. She clung close to him, trying to hide herself against him. He clasped her very fast. Then at last she looked at him, mute, imploring, looking to see if she must be ashamed.

His eyes were dark, very deep, and very quiet. It was as if her beauty and his taking it hurt him, made him sorrowful. He looked at her with a little pain, and was afraid. He was so humble before her. She kissed him fervently on the eyes, first one, then the other, and she folded herself to him. She gave herself. He held her fast. It was a moment intense almost to agony.

Then he loosed her, and his blood began to run free. Looking at her, he had to bite his lip, and the tears of pain came to his eyes, she was so beautiful, and so desirable. The first kiss on her breast made him pant with fear. The great dread, the great humility, and the awful desire, were nearly too much. Her breasts were heavy. He held one in each hand, like big fruits in their cups, and kissed them, fearfully. He was afraid to look at her. His hands went travelling over her, soft, delicate, discriminate, fearful, full of adoration. Suddenly he saw her knees, and he dropped, kissing them passionately. She quivered. And then again, with his fingers on her sides, she quivered.

She stood letting him adore her and tremble with joy of her. It healed her hurt pride. It healed her, it made her glad. It made her feel erect and proud again in her nakedness. Her pride had been wounded inside her, she had been cheapened. Now she radiated with joy and pride again. It was her restoration, and her recognition.

Then, as she watched him at his service of worship, he looked up at her, his face radiant. They laughed to each other, and he strained her to his chest. The seconds ticked off, the minutes passed, and still the two stood clasped rigid together, mouth to mouth, like a statue in one block.

But again his fingers went seeking over her, restless, wandering, dissatisfied. The hot blood came up wave upon wave. She laid her head on his shoulder.

"Come you to my room," he murmured.

She looked at him and shook her head, her mouth pouting disconsolately, her eyes heavy with passion. He watched her fixedly.

"Yes!" he said.

Again she shook her head.

"Why not?" he asked.

She looked at him still heavily, sorrowfully, and again she shook her head. His eyes hardened, and he gave way.

When, later on he was back in bed, he wondered why she had refused to come to him openly so that her mother would know. At any rate then things would have been definite. And she could have stayed with him the night, without having to go as she was to her mother's bed. It was strange, and he could not understand it. And then almost immediately he fell asleep.

He awoke in the morning with someone speaking to him. Opening his eyes, he saw Mrs Radford, big and stately, looking down on him. She held a cup of tea in her hand.

"Do you think you're going to sleep till Doomsday?" she said. He laughed at once.

"It ought only to be about five o'clock," he said.

"Well," she answered, "it's half past seven, whether or not. Here, I've brought you a cup of tea."

He rubbed his nose and his brown moustache, pushed the tumbled hair off his forehead, and roused himself.

"What's it so late for," he grumbled.

He resented being wakened. It amused her. She saw his neck in the flannel sleeping jacket as white and round as a girl's. He rubbed his hair crossly.

"It's no good your scratching your head," she said. "It won't make it no earlier. Here, an' how long d'you think I'm going to stand waiting wi' this here cup."

"Oh—dash the cup!" he said.

"You should go to bed earlier," said the woman.

He looked up at her laughing with impudence.

"I went to bed before *you* did," he said.

"Yes my Guyney!—you did!" she exclaimed.

"Fancy," he said, stirring his tea, "having tea brought to bed to me. My mother'll think I'm ruined for life."

"Don't she never do it?" asked Mrs Radford.

"She'd as leave think of flying."

"Ay—I always spoilt my lot—that's why they've turned out such bad uns," said the elderly woman.

"You'd only Clara," he said. "And Mr Radford's in heaven. So I suppose there's only you left to be the bad un."

"I'm not bad—I'm only soft," she said, as she went out of the bedroom. "I'm only a fool, I am."

Clara was very quiet at breakfast, but she had a sort of air of proprietorship over him, that pleased him infinitely. Mrs Radford was evidently fond of him. He began to talk of his painting.

"What's the good," exclaimed the mother, "of your whittling and worrying and twistin' and too-in' at that painting of yours? What *good* does it do you, I should like to know? You'd better be enjoyin' yourself."

"Oh but," exclaimed Paul, "I made over thirty guineas last year."

"Did you!—Well—that's a consideration, but it's nothing to the time you put in."

"And I've got four pounds owing. A man said he'd give me five pounds if I'd paint him and his missis and the dog and the cottage. And I went and put the fowls in instead of the dog, and he was waxy, so I had to knock a quid off. I was sick of it, and I didn't like the dog.—I made a picture of it.—What shall I do when he pays me the four pounds?"

"Nay, you know your own uses for your money," said Mrs Radford.

"But I'm going to bust this four pounds. Should we go to the seaside for a day or two?"

"Who?"

"You and Clara and me."

"What—on your money!" she exclaimed, half wrathful.

"Why not?"

"*You* wouldn't be long in breaking your neck at a hurdle race," she said.

"So long as I get a good run for my money—!—Will you?"

"Nay—you may settle that a-tween you."

"And you're willing?" he asked, amazed and rejoicing.

"You'll do as you like," said Mrs Radford; "whether I'm willing or not."

CHAPTER XIII

Baxter Dawes

Soon after Paul had been to the theatre with Clara, he was drinking in the 'Punch Bowl' with some friends of his, when Dawes came in. Clara's husband was growing stout, his eyelids were getting slack over his brown eyes, he was losing his healthy firmness of flesh. He was very evidently on the downward track. Having quarrelled with his sister, he had gone into cheap lodgings. His mistress had left him for a man who would marry her. He had been in prison one night for fighting when he was drunk, and there was a shady betting episode in which he was concerned.

Paul and he were confirmed enemies, and yet there was between them that peculiar feeling of intimacy, as if they were secretly near to each other, which sometimes exists between two people although they never speak to one another. Paul often thought of Baxter Dawes, often wanted to get at him, and be friends with him. He knew that Dawes often thought about *him*, and that the man was drawn to him by some bond or other. And yet the two never looked at each other save in hostility.

Since he was a superior employé at Jordan's, it was the thing for Paul to offer Dawes a drink.

"What'll you have?" he asked of him.

"Nowt wi' a bugger like you," replied the man.

Paul turned away with a slight, disdainful movement of the shoulders, very irritating.

"The aristocracy," he continued, "is really a military institution. Take Germany now. She's got thousands of aristocrats whose only means of existence is the army. They're deadly poor, and life's deadly slow. So they hope for a war. They look for war as a chance of getting on. Till there's a war, they are idle good-for-nothings. When there's a war they are leaders and commanders. There you are then—they *want* war."

He was not a favourite debater in the public house, being too quick and overbearing. He irritated the older men by his assertive manner, and his cock-sureness. They listened in silence, and were

386

not sorry when he finished.

Dawes interrupted the young man's flow of eloquence by asking, in a loud sneer:

"Did you learn all that at th' theatre th' other night?"

Paul looked at him. Their eyes met. Then he knew Dawes had seen him coming out of the theatre with Clara.

"Why what about th' theatre?" asked one of Paul's associates, glad to get a dig at the young fellow, and sniffing something tasty.

"Oh, him in a bob-tailed evening suit, on the lardy-da!" sneered Dawes, jerking his head contemptuously at Paul.

"That's comin' it strong," said the mutual friend. "Tart an' all?"

"Tart begod—!" said Dawes.

"Go on—let's have it," cried the mutual friend.

"You've got it," said Dawes. "An' I reckon Morelly had it an' all."

"Well I'll be jiggered!" said the mutual friend. "An' was it a proper tart?"

"Tart, God blimey—yes!"

"How do you know?"

"Oh," said Dawes. "I reckon he spent th' night—"

There was a good deal of laughter at Paul's expense.

"But who *was* she, d'you know her?" asked the mutual friend.

"I should *shay sho*," said Dawes.

This brought another burst of laughter.

"Then spit it out," said the mutual friend.

Dawes shook his head, and took a gulp of beer.

"It's a wonder he hasn't let on himself," he said. "He'll be braggin' of it in a bit."

"Come on Paul," said the friend. "It's no good—you might just as well own up."

"Own up what?—that I happened to take a friend to the theatre!"

"Oh well, if it was all right, tell us who she was lad," said the friend.

"She *was* all right," said Dawes.

Paul was furious. Dawes wiped his golden moustache with his fingers, sneering.

"Strike me—! One o' that sort!" said the mutual friend. "Paul boy, I'm surprised at you.—And do you know her Baxter?"

"Just a bit, like!"

He winked at the other men.

"Oh well," said Paul, "I'll be going!"

The mutual friend laid a detaining hand on his shoulder.

"Nay," he said, "you don't get off as easy as that, my lad. We've got to have a full account of this business."

"Then get it from Dawes," he said.

"You shouldn't funk your own deeds, man," remonstrated the friend.

Then Dawes made a remark which caused Paul to throw half a glass of beer in his face.

"Oh Mr Morel!" cried the barmaid, and she rang the bell for the 'chucker-out.' Dawes spat and rushed for the young man. At that minute a brawny fellow with his shirt-sleeves rolled up and his trousers tight over his haunches intervened.

"Now then!" he said, pushing his chest in front of Dawes.

"Come out, yer little sod!" cried Dawes.

Paul was leaning, white and quivering, against the brass rail of the bar. He hated Dawes, wished something could exterminate him at that minute. And at the same time, seeing the wet hair on the man's forehead, he thought he looked pathetic. He did not move.

"Come out, you— —," said Dawes.

"That's enough Dawes," cried the barmaid.

"Come on," said the 'chucker-out' with kindly insistence. "You'd better be getting on."

And, by making Dawes edge away from his own close proximity, he worked him to the door.

"*That's* the little sod as started it!" cried Dawes, half cowed, pointing to Paul Morel.

"Why what a story, Mr Dawes!" said the barmaid. "You know it was you all the time."

Still the 'chucker-out' kept thrusting his chest forward at him, still he kept edging back, until he was in the doorway, and on the steps outside. Then he turned round:

"All right," he said, nodding straight at his rival.

Paul had a curious sensation of pity, almost of affection, mingled with violent hate, for the man. The coloured door swung to. There was silence in the bar.

"Serve him jolly well right," said the barmaid.

"But it's a nasty thing to get a glass of beer in your eyes," said the mutual friend.

"I tell you *I* was glad he did," said the barmaid—"Will you have another, Mr Morel?"

She held up Paul's glass questioningly. He nodded.

"He's a man as doesn't care for anything, is Baxter Dawes," said one.

"Pooh—is he!" said the barmaid. "He's a loud-mouthed one, he is, and they're never much good.—Give me a pleasant-spoken chap if you want a devil."

"Well Paul my lad," said the friend. "You'll have to take care of yourself now for a while."

"You won't have to give him a chance over you, that's all," said the barmaid.

"Can you box?" asked a friend.

"Not a bit," he answered, still very white.

"I might give you a turn or two," said the friend.

"Thanks—I haven't time."

And presently he took his departure.

"Go along with him, Mr Jenkinson," whispered the barmaid, tipping Mr Jenkinson the wink. The man nodded, took his hat, said 'Goodnight all!' very heartily, and followed Paul, calling:

"Half a minute, old man. You an' me's going the same road, I believe."

"Mr Morel doesn't like it," said the barmaid. "You'll see, we shan't have him in much more.—I'm sorry, he's good company. And Baxter Dawes wants locking up, that's what he wants."

Paul would have died rather than his mother should get to know of this affair. He suffered tortures of humiliation and self-consciousness. There was now a good deal of his life of which necessarily he could not speak to his mother. He had a life apart from her—his sexual life. The rest she still kept. But he felt he had to conceal something from her, and it irked him. There was a certain silence between them, and he felt he had, in that silence, to defend himself against her. He felt condemned by her. Then sometimes he hated her, and pulled at her bondage. His life wanted to free itself of her. It was like a circle where life turned back on itself, and got no further. She bore him, loved him, kept him, and his love turned back into her, so that he could not be free to go forward with his own life, really love another woman. At this period, unknowingly, he resisted his mother's influence. He did not tell her things, there was a distance between them.

Clara was happy, almost sure of him. She felt she had at last got him for herself. And then again, came the uncertainty. He told her jestingly of the affair with her husband. Her colour came up, her grey eyes flashed.

"That's him to a 't'," she cried, "like a navvy! He's not fit for mixing with decent folk."

"Yet you married him," he said.

It made her furious that he reminded her.

"I did!" she cried. "But how was I to know!"

"I think he might have been rather nice," he said.

"You think *I* made him what he is!" she exclaimed.

"Oh no! He made himself. But there's something about him—"

Clara looked at her lover closely. There was something in him she hated, a sort of detached criticism of herself, a coldness which made her woman's soul harden against him.

"And what are you going to do?" she asked.

"How?"

"About Baxter."

"There's nothing to do, is there?" he replied.

"You can fight him if you have to, I suppose," she said.

"No—I haven't the least sense of the 'fist.'—It's funny—with most men there's the instinct to clench the fist and hit. It's not so with me. I should want a knife or a pistol or something to fight with."

"Then you'd better carry something," she said.

"Nay," he laughed. "I'm not daggeroso."

"But he'll do something to you—you don't know him."

"All right," he said. "We'll see."

"And you'll let him?"

"Perhaps—if I can't help it."

"And if he kills you?" she said.

"I should be sorry, for his sake and mine."

Clara was silent for a moment.

"You *do* make me angry," she exclaimed.

"That's nothing afresh," he laughed.

"But why are you so silly? You don't know him—"

"And don't want."

"Yes but—you're not going to let a man do as he likes with you—?"

"What must I do?" he replied, laughing.

"*I* should carry a revolver," she said. "I'm sure he's dangerous."

"I might blow my fingers off," he said.

"No—but won't you?" she pleaded.

"No."

"Not anything?"

"No."

"And you'll leave him to—?"

"Yes."

"You are a fool!"

"Fact!"

She set her teeth with anger.

"I could *shake* you," she cried, trembling with passion.

"Why?"

"Let a man like *him* do as he likes with you."

"You can go back to him if he triumphs—" he said.

"Do you want me to hate you?" she asked.

"Well—I only tell you," he said.

"And *you* say you *love* me!" she exclaimed, low and indignant.

"Ought I to slay him to please you?" he said. "But if I did, see what a hold he'd have over me."

"Do you think I'm a fool—!" she exclaimed.

"Not at all. But you don't understand me, my dear."

There was a pause between them.

"But you ought *not* to expose yourself—" she pleaded.

He shrugged his shoulders.

> " 'The man in righteousness arrayed
> The pure and blameless liver,
> Needs not the keen Toledo blade,
> Nor venom-freighted quiver—' "

he quoted.

She looked at him searchingly.

"I wish I could understand you," she said.

"There's simply nothing to understand," he laughed.

She bowed her head, brooding.

He did not see Dawes for several days. Then one morning as he ran upstairs from the spiral room he almost collided with the burly metal-worker.

"What the—!" cried the smith.

"Sorry!" said Paul, and passed on.

"*Sorry*!" sneered Dawes.

Paul whistled lightly, 'Put me among the Girls.'

"I'll stop your whistle, my jockey," he said.

The other took no notice.

"You're goin' to answer for that job of the other night."

Paul went to his desk in his corner, and turned over the leaves of the ledger.

"Go and tell Fanny I want order 097 quick," he said to his boy.

Dawes stood in the doorway, tall and threatening, looking at the top of the young man's head.

"—Six and five's eleven and seven's one-and-six—" Paul added aloud.

"An' you hear, do you!" said Dawes.

"*Five and ninepence!*"—he wrote a figure.—"What's that?" he said.

"I'm going to show you what it is," said the smith.

The other went on adding the figures aloud.

"Yer crawlin' little b—, yer daresn't face me proper."

Paul quickly snatched the heavy ruler. Dawes started. The young man ruled some lines in his ledger. The elder man was infuriated.

"But wait till I light on you, no matter where it is, I'll settle your hash for a bit, yer little swine!"

"All right," said Paul.

At that the smith started heavily from the doorway. Just then a whistle piped shrilly. Paul went to the speaking tube.

"Yes!" he said, and he listened.

"Er—yes!" He listened, then he laughed.

"I'll come down directly.—I've got a visitor just now."

Dawes knew from his tone that he had been speaking to Clara. He stepped forward.

"Yer little devil!" he said. "I'll visitor you, inside of two minutes. Think I'm goin' ter have *you* whipperty-snappin' round?"

The other clerks in the warehouse looked up. Paul's office boy appeared holding some white article.

"Fanny says you could have had it last night, if you'd let her know," he said.

"All right," answered Paul, looking at the stocking. "Get it off."

Dawes stood frustrated, helpless with rage. Morel turned round.

"Excuse me a minute," he said to Dawes, and he would have run downstairs.

"By God, I'll stop your gallop!" shouted the smith seizing him by the arm. He turned quickly.

"Hey!—hey!" cried the office boy alarmed.

Thomas Jordan started out of his little glass office and came running down the room.

"What's a-matter, what's a-matter!" he said, in his old man's sharp voice.

"I'm just goin' ter settle this little b—, that's all," said Dawes, desperately.

"What do you mean?" snapped Thomas Jordan.

"What I say," said Dawes. But he hung fire. Morel was leaning against the counter, ashamed, half grinning.

"What's it all about?" snapped Thomas Jordan.

"Couldn't say," said Paul, shaking his head and shrugging his shoulders.

"Couldn't yer—couldn't yer—!" cried Dawes, thrusting forward his handsome, furious face, and squaring his fist.

"Have you finished?" cried the old man, strutting. "Get off about your business, and don't come here tipsy in the morning."

Dawes turned his big frame slowly upon him.

"Tipsy!" he said. "Who's tipsy? I'm no more tipsy than *you* are."

"We've heard that song before," snapped the old man. "Now you get off, and don't be long about it.—Comin' *here* with your rowdying—"

The smith looked down contemptuously on his employer. His hands, large and grimy, and yet well-shaped for his labour, worked restlessly. Paul remembered they were the hands of Clara's husband, and a flash of hate went through him.

"Get out before you're turned out," snapped Thomas Jordan.

"Why who'll turn me out, yer fungussy little sod?" said Dawes, beginning to sneer.

Mr Jordan started, marched up to the smith, waving him off, thrusting his stout little figure at the man, saying:

"Get off my premises—get off!"

He seized and twitched Dawes' arm.

"Come off!" said the smith, and with a jerk of the elbow he sent the little manufacturer staggering backwards. Before anyone could help him, Thomas Jordan had collided with the flimsy spring door, it had given way, and let him crash down the half dozen steps into Fanny's room. There was a second of amazement. Then men and girls were running. Dawes stood a moment looking bitterly on the scene, then he took his departure.

Thomas Jordan was shaken and bruised, not otherwise hurt. He was, however, beside himself with rage. He dismissed Dawes from his employment and summoned him for assault.

At the trial Paul Morel had to give evidence. Asked how the trouble began, he said:

"Dawes took occasion to insult Mrs Dawes and me because I accompanied her to the theatre one evening. Then I threw some beer at him and he wanted his revenge."

"*Cherchez la femme!*" smiled the magistrate.

The case was dismissed after the magistrate had told Dawes he thought him a skunk.

"You gave the case away," snapped Mr Jordan to Paul.

"I don't think I did," replied the latter. "Besides, you didn't really want a conviction, did you?"

"What do you think I took the case up for?"

"Well," said Paul, "I'm sorry if I said the wrong thing."

Clara was also very angry.

"Why need *my* name have been dragged in?" she said.

"Better speak it openly than leave it to be whispered."

"There was no need for anything at all," she declared.

"We are none the poorer," he said indifferently.

"*You* may not be," she said.

"And you—?" he asked.

"I need never have been mentioned."

"I'm sorry," he said. But he did not sound sorry.

He told himself easily: 'She will come round.' And she did.

He told his mother about the fall of Mr Jordan and the trial of Dawes. Mrs Morel watched him closely.

"And what do you think of it all?" she asked him.

"I think he's a fool," he said.

But he was very uncomfortable, nevertheless.

"Have you ever considered where it will end?" his mother said.

"No," he answered, "things work out of themselves."

"They do, in a way one doesn't like as a rule," said his mother.

"And then one has to put up with them," he said.

"You'll find you're not as good at 'putting up' as you imagine," she said.

He went on working rapidly at his design.

"Do you ever ask *her* opinion?" she said at length.

"What of?"

"Of you—and the whole thing?"

"I don't care what her opinion of me is. She's fearfully in love with me, but it's not very deep."

394

"But quite as deep as your feeling for her."

He looked up at his mother curiously.

"Yes," he said. "You know mother, I think there must be something the matter with me, that I *can't* love. When she's there, as a rule I *do* love her. Sometimes, when I see her just as *the woman*, I love her, mother. But then, when she talks and criticises, I often don't listen to her."

"Yet she's as much sense as Miriam."

"Perhaps. And I love her better than Miriam. But *why* don't they hold me?"

The last question was almost a lamentation. His mother turned away her face, sat looking across the room, very quiet, grave, with something of renunciation.

"But you wouldn't want to marry Clara?" she said.

"No—at first perhaps, I would. But why, why don't I want to marry her or anybody? I feel sometimes as if I wronged my women, mother."

"How wronged them, my son?"

"I don't know—"

He went on painting rather despairingly. He had touched the quick of the trouble.

"And as for wanting to marry," said his mother, "there's plenty of time yet."

"But no, mother. I even love Clara, and I did Miriam. But to *give* myself to them in marriage—I couldn't. I couldn't belong to them. They seem to want *me*, and I can't ever give it them."

"You haven't met the right woman."

"And I never shall meet the right woman while you live," he said.

She was very quiet. Now she began to feel again tired, as if she were done.

"We'll see, my son," she answered.

The feeling that things were going in a circle made him mad.

Clara was indeed passionately in love with him, and he with her, as far as passion went. In the daytime he forgot her a good deal. She was working in the same building, but he was not aware of it. He was busy, and her existence was of no matter to him. But all the time she was in her spiral room, she had a sense that he was upstairs, a physical sense of his person in the same building. Every second she expected him to come through the door, and when he came, it was a shock to her. But he was often short and off-hand with her. He gave her his directions in an official manner, keeping her at bay. With what wits she had left she listened to him. She dared not misunderstand or fail to remember. But it was a cruelty to her. She wanted to touch his chest. She knew exactly how his breast was shapen under the waistcoat, and she wanted to touch it. It maddened her to hear his mechanical voice giving orders about the work. She wanted to break through the sham of it, smash the trivial coating of business which covered him with hardness, get at the man again. But she was afraid, and before she could feel one touch of his warmth, he was gone, and she ached again.

He knew that she was dreary every evening she did not see him, so he gave her a good deal of his time. The days were often a misery to her, but the nights and the evenings were usually a bliss to them both. Then, they were silent. For hours they sat together, or walked together in the dark, and talked only a few, almost meaningless words. But he had her hand in his, and her bosom left its warmth in his chest, making him feel whole.

One evening they were walking down by the canal, and something was troubling him. She knew she had not got him. All the time he whistled softly and persistently to himself. She listened, feeling she could learn more from his whistling than from his speech. It was a sad, dissatisfied tune, a tune that made her feel he would not stay with her. She walked on in silence. When they came to the swing bridge, he sat down on the great pole, looking at the stars in the water. He was a long way from her. She had been thinking.

"Will you always stay at Jordan's?" she asked.

"No," he answered, without reflecting. "No—I s'll leave Nottingham and go abroad—soon."

"Go abroad—what for?"

"I dunno! I feel restless."

"But what shall you do?"

"I shall have to get some steady designing work, and some sort of sale for my pictures first," he said. "I am gradually making my way, I know I am."

"And when do you think you'll go?"

"I don't know. I shall hardly go for long, while there's my mother."

"You couldn't leave her?"

"Not for long."

She looked at the stars in the black water. They lay very white and staring. It was an agony to know he would leave her. But it was almost an agony to have him near her.

"And if you made a nice lot of money, what would you do?" she asked.

"Go somewhere in a pretty house near London, with my mother."

"I see."

There was a long pause.

"I could still come and see you," he said. "I don't know.—Don't ask me what I should do, I don't know." There was a silence. The stars shuddered and broke upon the water. There came a breath of wind. He went suddenly to her, and put his hand on her shoulder.

"Don't ask me anything about the future," he said miserably. "I don't know anything.—Be with me now, will you, no matter what it is—."

And she took him in her arms. After all, she was a married woman, and she had no right even to what he gave her. He needed her badly. She had him in her arms, and he was miserable. With her warmth she folded him over, consoled him, loved him. She would let the moment stand for itself.

After a moment he lifted his head, as if he wanted to speak.

"Clara?" he said, struggling.

She caught him passionately to her, pressed his head down on her breast with her hand. She could not bear the suffering in his voice. She was afraid in her soul. He might have anything of her, anything. But she did not want to *know*; she felt she could not bear it; she wanted him to be soothed upon her, soothed. She stood clasping him and caressing him, and he was something unknown to her, something almost uncanny. She wanted to soothe him into forgetfulness.

And soon the struggle went down in his soul, and he forgot. But then Clara was not there for him, only a woman, warm, something he loved and almost worshipped, there in the dark. But it was not Clara. And she submitted to him. The naked hunger and inevitability of his loving her, something strong and blind and ruthless in its primitiveness, made the hour almost terrible to her. She knew how stark and alone he was. And she felt it was great, that he came to her. And she took him simply, because his need was bigger either than her or him. And her soul was still within her. She did this for him in his need, even if he left her. For she loved him.

All the while, the peewits were screaming in the field. When he came to, he wondered what was near his eyes, curving and strong with life in the dark, and what voice it was speaking. Then he realised it was the grass, and the peewit was calling. The warmth was Clara's breathing heaving. He lifted his head and looked into her eyes. They were dark and shining and strange, life wild at the source staring into his life, stranger to him, yet meeting him. And he put his face down on her throat, afraid. What was she. A strong, strange, wild life, that breathed with his in the darkness through this hour. It was all so much bigger than themselves, that he was hushed. They had met, and included in their meeting the thrust of the manifold grass stems, the cry of the peewit, the wheel of the stars.

When they stood up they saw other lovers stealing down the opposite hedge. It seemed natural they were there. The night contained them.

And after such an evening they both were very still, having known the immensity of passion. They felt small, half afraid, childish and wondering, like Adam and Eve when they lost their innocence and realised the magnificence of the power which drove them out of Paradise and across the great night and the great day of humanity. It was for each of them an initiation and a satisfaction. To know their own nothingness, to know the tremendous living flood which carried them always, gave them rest within themselves. If so great a magnificent power could overwhelm them, identify them altogether with itself, so that they knew they were only grains in the tremendous heave that lifted every grass-blade its little height, and every tree, and living thing, then why fret about themselves: they could let themselves be carried by life. And they felt a sort of peace each in the other: there was a verification which they had had together. Nothing could nullify it, nothing could take it away. It was almost their belief in life.

But Clara was not satisfied. Something great was there, she knew, something great enveloped her. But it did not keep her. In the morning it was not the same. They had *known*—but she could not keep the moment, she wanted it again, she wanted something permanent, she had not realised fully. She thought it was he whom she wanted. He was not safe to her. This that had been between them might never be again. He might leave her. She had not got him. She was not satisfied. She had been there, but she had not gripped the—the something, she knew not what, which she was mad to have.

In the morning he had considerable peace, and was happy in himself. It seemed almost as if he had known the baptism of fire in passion, and it left him at rest. But it was not Clara. It was something that happened because of her, but it was not her. They were scarcely any nearer each other. It was as if they had been blind agents of a great force.

When she saw him that day at the factory, her heart melted like a drop of fire. It was his body, his brows. The drop of fire grew more intense in her breast. She must hold him. But he, very quiet, very subdued this morning, went on giving his instructions. She followed him into the dark, ugly basement, and lifted her arms to him. He kissed her, and the intensity of passion began to burn him again. Somebody was at the door. He ran upstairs. She returned to her room, moving as if in a trance.

After that, the fire slowly went down. He felt more and more that his experience had been impersonal, and not Clara. He loved her. There was a big tenderness, as after a strong emotion they had known together. But it was not she who could keep his soul steady. He had wanted her to be something she could not be.

And she was mad with desire of him. She could not see him without touching him. In the factory, as he talked to her about spiral hose, she ran her hand secretly along his side and over his hips. She followed him out into the basement for a quick kiss. Her eyes, always mute and yearning, full of unrestrained passion, she kept fixed on his. He was afraid of her, lest she should too flagrantly give herself away before the other girls. She invariably waited for him at dinner time, for him to embrace her before she went. He felt as if she were helpless, almost a burden to him. And it irritated him.

"But what do you always want to be kissing and embracing for?" he said. "Surely there's a time for everything."

She looked up at him and the hate came into her eyes.

"*Do* I always want to be kissing you?" she said.

"Always! Even if I come to ask you about the work. I don't want anything to do with love when I'm at work. Work's work—"

"And what is love?" she asked. "Has it to have special hours?"

"Yes—out of work hours."

"And you'll regulate it according to Mr Jordan's closing time?"

"Yes—and according to the freedom from business of any sort."

"It's only to exist in spare time?"

"That's all—and not always then—not the kissing sort of love."

"And that's all you think of it?"

"It's quite enough."

"I'm glad you think so."

And she was cold to him for some time. She hated him. And while she was cold and contemptuous, he was uneasy, till she had forgiven him again. But when they started afresh, they were not any nearer. He kept her because he never satisfied her.

In the spring they went together to the sea-side. They had rooms at a little cottage near Theddlethorpe, and lived as man and wife. Mrs Radford sometimes went with them.

It was known in Nottingham that Paul Morel and Mrs Dawes were going together, but as nothing was very obvious, and Clara was always a solitary person, and he seemed so simple and innocent, it did not make much difference.

He loved the Lincolnshire coast and she loved the sea. In the early morning they often went out together to bathe. The grey of the dawn, the far, desolate reaches of the fen land smitten with winter, the sea-meadows rank with herbage, were stark enough to rejoice his soul. As they stepped onto the high-road from their plank bridge, and looked round at the endless monotony of levels, the land a little darker than the sky, the sea sounding small beyond the sand-hills, his heart filled strong with the sweeping relentlessness of life. She loved him then—he was solitary, and strong, and his eyes had a beautiful light.

They shuddered with cold. Then he raced her down the road to the green turf bridge. She could run well. Her colour soon came, her throat was bare, her eyes shone. He loved her for being so luxuriously heavy and yet so quick. Himself was light; she went with a beautiful rush. They grew warm, and walked hand in hand.

A flush came into the sky, the wan moon, half way down the west, sank into insignificance. On the shadowy land, things began to take life, plants with great leaves became distinct. They came through a pass in the big, cold sandhills, onto the beach. The long waste of foreshore lay moaning under the dawn and the sea. The ocean was a flat dark strip with a white edge. Over the gloomy sea the sky grew red. Quickly the fire spread among the clouds and scattered them. Crimson burned to orange, orange to dull gold, and in a golden glitter the sun came up, dribbling fierily over the waves in little splashes, as if someone had gone along and the light had spilled from her pail as she walked.

The breakers ran down the shore in long, hoarse strokes. Tiny seagulls, like specks of spray, wheeled above the line of surf. Their crying seemed larger than they. Far away the coast reached out and melted into the morning, the tussocky sand-hills seeming to sink to a level with the beach. Mablethorpe was tiny on their right. They had alone the space of all this level shore, the sea, and the upcoming sun, the faint noise of the waters, the sharp crying of the gulls.

They had a warm hollow in the sand-hills where the wind did not come. He stood looking out to sea.

"It's very fine," he said.

"Now don't get sentimental," she said.

It irritated her to see him standing gazing at the sea, like a solitary and poetic person. He laughed. She quickly undressed.

"There are some fine waves this morning," she said, triumphantly.

She was a better swimmer than he. He stood idly watching her.

"Aren't you coming?" she said.

"In a minute," he answered.

She was a white, velvet-skinned woman with heavy shoulders. A little wind, coming from the sea, blew across her body and ruffled her hair.

"OO!" she said, hugging her breasts between her arms, "it's cold!"

The morning was of a lovely, limpid gold colour. Veils of shadow seemed to be drifting away on the north and the south. Clara stood shrinking slightly from the touch of the wind, twisting her hair. The seagrass rose behind the white stripped woman. She glanced at the sea, then looked at him. He was watching her with dark eyes which she loved and could not understand. She gathered her breasts between her arms, cringing, laughing:

"OO, it will be so cold!" she said.

He bent forward and kissed the two white, glistening globes she cradled. She stood waiting. He looked into her eyes, then away at the pale sands.

"Go then!" he said quietly.

She flung her arms round his neck, drew him against her, kissed him passionately, and went, saying:

"But you'll come in?"

"In a minute."

She went plodding heavily over the sand, that was soft as velvet.

She was a rich, white body moving with heavy grace across the foreshore. He, on the sand-hills, watched the great, pale coast envelop her. She grew smaller, lost proportion, seemed only like a large white bird toiling forward.

"Not much more than a big white pebble on the beach—not much more than a clot of foam being blown and rolled over the sand," he said to himself. She seemed to move very slowly across the vast, sounding shore. As he watched, he lost her. She was dazzled out of sight by the sunshine. Again he saw her, the merest white speck moving against the white, muttering sea-edge.

"Look how little she is!" he said to himself. "She's lost like a grain of sand in the beach—just a concentrated speck blown along—a tiny white foam-bubble—almost nothing among the morning. Why does she absorb me."

The morning was altogether uninterrupted: she was gone in the water. Far and wide, the beach, the sand-hills with their blue marram, the shining water glowed together in immense, unbroken solitude.

"What is she after all?" he said to himself. "Here's the sea-coast morning, big and permanent and beautiful. There is she, fretting, always unsatisfied, and temporary as a bubble of foam. What does she mean to me, after all? She represents something, like a bubble of foam represents the sea. But what is *she*! It's not her I care for—"

Then, startled by his own unconscious thoughts, that seemed to speak so distinctly that all the morning could hear, he undressed and ran quickly down the sands. She was watching for him. Her arm flashed up to him, she heaved on a wave, subsided, her shoulders in a pool of liquid silver. He jumped through the breakers, and in a moment her hand was on his shoulder.

He was a poor swimmer and could not stay long in the water. She played round him in triumph, sporting with her superiority, which he begrudged her. The sunshine stood deep and fine on the water. They laughed in the sea for a minute or two, then raced each other back to the sandhills.

When they were drying themselves, panting heavily, he watched her laughing, breathless face, her bright shoulders, her breasts that swayed and made him frightened as she rubbed them, and he thought again: "But she is magnificent, and even bigger than the morning and the sea.—Is she?—is she?"

She, seeing his dark eyes fixed on her, broke off from her drying with a laugh:

"What are you looking at?" she said.

"You!" he answered, laughing.

Her eyes met his, and in a moment he was kissing her white, 'goose-fleshed' shoulder, and thinking: "What is she? What is she?"

She loved him in the morning. There was something detached, hard and elemental about his kisses then, as if he were only conscious of his own will, not in the least of her and her wanting him.

Later in the day he went out sketching.

"You," he said to her, "go with your mother to Sutton—I am so dull."

She stood and looked at him. He knew she wanted to come with him, but he preferred to be alone. She made him feel imprisoned, when she was there, as if he could not get a free deep breath, as if there were something on top of him. She felt his desire to be free of her.

In the evening he came back to her. They walked down the shore in the darkness, then sat for awhile in the shelter of the sandhills.

"It seems," she said, as they stared over the darkness of the sea, where no light was to be seen—"it seemed as if you only loved me at night—as if you didn't love me in the daytime."

He ran the cold sand through his fingers, feeling guilty under the accusation.

"The night is free to you," he replied. "In the daytime I want to be by myself."

"But why?" she said. "Why even now, when we are on this short holiday?"

"I don't know. Love-making stifles me in the daytime."

"But it needn't be always love-making," she said.

"It always is," he answered, "when you and I are together."

She sat feeling very bitter.

"Do you ever want to marry me?" he asked curiously.

"Do you me?" she replied.

"Yes—yes—I should like us to have children," he answered slowly.

She sat with her head bent, fingering the sand.

"But you don't really want a divorce from Baxter, do you?" he said.

It was some minutes before she replied.

"No," she said, very deliberately. "I don't think I do."

"Why?"

"I don't know."

"Do you feel as if you belonged to him?"

"No—I don't think so."

"What then?"

"I think he belongs to me," she replied.

He was silent for some minutes, listening to the wind blowing over the hoarse, dark sea.

"And you never really intended to belong to *me*?" he said.

"Yes I do belong to you," she answered.

"No," he said. "Because you don't want to be divorced."

It was a knot they could not untie, so they left it, took what they could get, and what they could not attain, they ignored.

"I consider you treated Baxter rottenly," he said another time.

He half expected Clara to answer him, as his mother would, "You consider your own affairs, and don't know so much about other people's." But she took him seriously, almost to his own surprise.

"Why?" she said.

"I suppose you thought he was a lily of the valley, and so you put him in an appropriate pot, and tended him according. You made up your mind he was a lily of the valley, and it was no good his being a cow-parsnip, you wouldn't have it."

"I certainly never imagined him a lily of the valley."

"You imagined him something he wasn't. That's just what a woman is. She thinks she knows what's good for a man, and she's going to see he gets it; and no matter if he's starving, he may sit and whistle for what he needs, while she's got him, and is giving him what's good for him."

"And what are you doing?" she asked.

"I'm thinking what tune I shall whistle," he laughed.

And instead of boxing his ears, she considered him in earnest.

"You think I want to give you what's good for you?" she asked.

"I hope so.—But love should give a sense of freedom, not of prison. Miriam made me feel tied up like a donkey to a stake. I must feed on her patch and nowhere else. It's sickening."

"And would *you* let a *woman* do as she likes?"

"Yes—I'll see that she *likes* to love me. If she doesn't—well, I don't hold her."

"If you were as wonderful as you say—" replied Clara.

"I should be the marvel I am," he laughed.

There was a silence in which they hated each other, though they laughed.

"Love's a dog in the manger," he said.

"And which of us is the dog?" she asked.

"Oh well—you of course."

So there went on a battle between them. She knew she never fully had him: some part, big and vital in him, she had no hold over; nor did she ever try to get it, or even to realise what it was. And he knew in some way that she held herself still as Mrs Dawes. She did not love Dawes, never had loved him. But she believed he loved her, at least depended on her. She felt a certain surety about him that she never felt with Paul Morel. Her passion for the young man had filled her soul, given her a certain satisfaction, eased her of her self-mistrust, her doubt. Whatever else she was, she was inwardly assured. It was almost as if she had gained *herself*, and stood now distinct and complete. She had received her confirmation. But she never believed that her life belonged to Paul Morel, nor his to her. They would separate in the end, and the rest of her life would be an ache after him. But at any rate, she *knew* now, she was sure of herself. And the same could almost be said of him. Together they had received the baptism of life, each through the other. But now their missions were separate. Where he wanted to go she could not come with him. They would have to part sooner or later. Even if they married, and were faithful to each other, still he would have to leave her, go on alone, and she would only have to attend to him when he came home. But it was not possible. Each wanted a mate to go side by side with.

Clara had gone to live with her mother upon Mapperley Plains. One evening, as Paul and she were walking along Woodborough Road they met Dawes. Morel knew something about the bearing of the man approaching, but he was absorbed in his thinking at the moment, so that only his artist's eye watched the form of the stranger. Then he suddenly turned to Clara with a laugh, and put his hand on her shoulder, saying, laughing:

"But we walk side by side, and yet I'm in London arguing with an imaginary Orpen—and where are you—?"

At that instant Dawes passed, almost touching Morel. The young man glanced, saw the dark brown eyes burning, full of hate and yet tired.

"Who was that?" he asked of Clara.

"It was Baxter," she replied.

Paul took his hand from her shoulder and glanced round. Then he saw again distinctly the man's form as it approached him. Dawes still walked erect, with his fine shoulders flung back, and his face lifted. But there was a furtive look in his eyes, that gave one the impression he was trying to get unnoticed past every person he met, glancing suspiciously to see what they thought of him. And his hands seemed to be wanting to hide. He wore old clothes, the trousers were torn at the knee, and the handkerchief tied round his throat was dirty. But his cap was still defiantly over one eye. As she saw him, Clara felt guilty. There was a tiredness and despair on his face, that made her hate him because it hurt her.

"He looks shady," said Paul.

But the note of pity in his voice reproached her, and made her feel hard.

"His true commonness comes out," she answered.

"Do you hate him?" he asked.

"You talk," she said, "about the cruelty of women—I wish you knew the cruelty of men, in their brute force. They simply don't know that the woman exists."

"Don't *I*?" he said.

"No," she answered.

"Don't I know you exist?"

"About *me* you know nothing," she said bitterly—"about *me!*"

"Not more than Baxter knew?" he asked.

"Perhaps not as much."

He felt puzzled and helpless and angry. There she walked, unknown to him, though they had been through such experience together.

"But you know *me* pretty well," he said.

She did not answer.

"Did you know Baxter as well as you know me?" he asked.

"He wouldn't let me," she said.

"And I have let you know me?"

"It's what men *won't* let you do—they won't let you get really near to them," she said.

"And haven't I let you?"

"Yes," she answered, slowly. "But you've never come near to me.

You can't come out of yourself, you can't. Baxter could do that better than you."

He walked on pondering. He was angry with her for preferring Baxter to him.

"You begin to value Baxter now you've not got him," he said.

"No—I can only see where he was different to you."

But he felt she had a grudge against him.

One evening, as they were coming home over the fields, she startled him by asking:

"Do you think it's worth it—the—the sex part—?"

"The act of loving, itself?"

"Yes—is it worth anything to you?"

"But how can you separate it?" he said. "It's the culmination of everything—all our intimacy culminates then."

"Not for me," she said.

He was silent. A flash of hate for her came up. After all she was dissatisfied with him, even there, where he thought they fulfilled each other. But he believed her too implicitly.

"I feel," she continued slowly, "as if I hadn't got you—as if all of you weren't there—and as if it weren't *me* you were taking—"

"Who then?"

"Something just for yourself. It has been fine, so that I daren't think of it. But—is it *me* you want, or is it *It*?"

He again felt guilty. Did he leave Clara out of count, and take simply woman. But he thought that was splitting a hair.

"When I had Baxter, actually had him, then I *did* feel as if I had all of him," she said.

"And it was better?" he asked.

"Yes—yes—it was more whole.—I don't say you haven't given me more than he ever gave me—"

"Or could give you."

"Yes—perhaps.—But you've never given me yourself."

He knitted his brows angrily.

"If I start to make love to you," he said, "I just go like a leaf down the wind—"

"And leave me out of count," she said.

"And then is it nothing to you?" he asked, almost rigid with chagrin.

"It's something.—And sometimes you have carried me away—right away—I know—and—I reverence you for it—but—"

"Don't 'but' me," he said, kissing her quickly, as a fire ran through him.

She submitted, and was silent.

It was true as he said. As a rule, when he started love-making, the emotion was strong enough to carry with it everything, reason, soul, blood, in a great sweep, like the Trent carries bodily its black-swirls and intertwinings, noiselessly. Gradually the little criticisms, the little sensations were lost, thought also went, everything borne along in one flood. He became, not a man with a mind, but a great instinct. His hands were like creatures, living; his limbs, his body were all life and consciousness, subject to no will of his, but living in themselves. Just as he was, so it seemed the vigorous, wintry stars were strong also with life. He and they struck with the same pulse of fire. And the same joy of strength which held the bracken-frond stiff near his eyes held his own body firm. It was as if he and the stars and the dark herbage and Clara were licked up in an immense tongue of flame which tore onwards and upwards. Everything rushed along in living beside him, everything was still, perfect in itself, along with him. This wonderful stillness in each thing in itself, while it was being borne along in a very ecstasy of living, seemed the highest point of bliss.

And Clara knew this held him to her, so she trusted altogether to the passion. It, however, failed her very often. They did not often reach again the height of that once when the peewits had called. Gradually, some mechanical effort spoilt their loving, or, when they had splendid moments, they had them separately, and not so satisfactorily. So often, he seemed merely to be running on alone. Often, they realised it had been a failure, not what they had wanted. He left her, knowing *that* evening had only made a little split between them. Their loving grew more mechanical, without the marvellous glamour. Gradually, they began to introduce novelties, to get back some of the feeling of satisfaction. They would be very near, almost dangerously near to the river, so that the black water ran not far from his face. And it gave a little thrill. Or they loved sometimes in a little hollow below the fence of the path where people were passing occasionally, on the edge of the town. And they heard footsteps coming, almost felt the vibration of the tread; and they heard what the passers-by said, strange little things that were never intended to be heard. And afterwards, each of them was rather ashamed, and these things caused a distance between the two of them. He began to despise her a little, as if she had merited it!

One night he left her to go to Daybrook station, over the fields. It was very dark, with an attempt at snow, although the spring was so far advanced. Morel had not much time; he plunged forward. The town ceases almost abruptly on the edge of a steep hollow. There the houses with their yellow lights stand up against the darkness. He went over the stile and dropped quickly into the hollow of the fields. Under the orchard, one warm window shone in Swineshead Farm. Paul glanced round. Behind, the houses stood on the brim of the dip, black against the sky, like wild beasts glaring curiously with yellow eyes down into the darkness. It was the town that seemed savage and uncouth, glaring on the clouds at the back of him. Some creature stirred under the willows of the farm pond. It was too dark to distinguish anything.

He was close up to the next stile before he saw a dark shape leaning against it. The man moved aside.

"Good-evening!" he said.

"Good-evening," Morel answered, not noticing.

"Paul Morel?" said the man.

Then he knew it was Dawes. The man stopped his way.

"I've got yer, have I?" he said, awkwardly.

"I shall miss my train," said Paul.

He could see nothing of Dawes' face. The man's teeth seemed to chatter as he talked.

"You're going to get it from me now," said Dawes.

Morel attempted to move forward. The other man stepped in front of him.

"Are yer goin' to take that top-coat off," he said, "or are you goin' to lie down to it?"

Paul was afraid the man was mad.

"But," he said, "I don't know how to fight."

"All right then," answered Dawes, and before the younger man knew where he was, he was staggering backwards from a blow across the face. The whole night went black. He tore off his overcoat and coat, dodging a blow, and flung the garments over Dawes. The latter swore savagely. Morel, in his shirt sleeves, was now alert and furious. He felt his whole body unsheath itself like a claw. He could not fight, so he would use his wits. The other man became more distinct to him. He could see particularly the shirt breast. Dawes stumbled over Paul's coats, then came rushing forward. The young man's mouth was bleeding. It was the other man's mouth he was dying to get at, and the desire was anguish in its strength. He stepped quickly through the stile, and as Dawes was coming through, after him, like a flash he got a blow in over the other's mouth. He shivered with pleasure. Dawes advanced slowly, spitting. Paul was afraid. He moved round to get to the stile again. Suddenly, from out of nowhere, came a great blow against his ear, that sent him falling helpless backwards. He heard Dawes' heavy panting, like a wild beast's. Then came a kick on his knee, giving him such agony that he got up and, quite blind, leapt clean under his enemy's guard. He felt blows and kicks but they did not hurt. He hung onto the bigger man like a wild cat, till at last Dawes fell with a crash, losing his presence of mind. Paul went down with him. Pure instinct brought his hands to the man's neck, and before Dawes, in frenzy and agony, could wrench him free, he had got his fists twisted in the scarf and his knuckles dug in the throat of the other man. He was a pure instinct, without reason or feeling. His body, hard and wonderful in itself, cleaved against the struggling body of the other man. Not a muscle in him relaxed. He was quite unconscious, only his body had taken upon itself to kill this other man. For himself he had neither feeling nor reason. He lay, pressed hard against his adversary, his body adjusting itself to its one pure purpose of choking the other man, resisting exactly at the right moment, with exactly the right amount of strength, the struggles of the other, silent, intent, unchanging, gradually pressing its knuckles deeper, feeling the struggles of the other body become wilder and more frenzied. Tighter and tighter grew his body, like a screw that is gradually increasing in pressure, till something breaks.

Then suddenly he relaxed, full of wonder and misgiving. Dawes had been yielding. Morel felt his body flame with pain, as he realised what he was doing. He was all bewildered. Dawes' struggles suddenly renewed themselves in a furious spasm. Paul's hands were wrenched, torn out of the scarf in which they were knotted, and he was flung away, helpless. He heard the horrid sound of the other's gasping, but he lay stunned. Then, still dazed, he felt the blows of the other's feet, and lost consciousness.

Dawes, grunting with pain like a beast, was kicking the prostrate body of his rival. Suddenly the whistle of the train shrieked two fields away. He turned round and glared suspiciously. What was coming? He saw the lights of the train draw across his vision. It seemed to him people were approaching. He made off across the field into Nottingham. And dimly in his consciousness as he went, he felt on his foot the place where his boot had knocked against one of the lad's bones. The knock seemed to re-echo inside him. He hurried to get away from it.

Morel gradually came to himself. He knew where he was and what had happened, but he did not want to move. He lay still, with tiny bits of snow tickling his face. It was pleasant to lie quite, quite still. The time passed. It was the bits of snow that kept rousing him when he did not want to be roused. At last his will clicked into action.

"I mustn't lie here," he said, "it's silly."

But still he did not move.

"I said I was going to get up," he repeated. "Why don't I!"

And still it was some time before he had sufficiently pulled himself together to stir. Then, gradually, he got up. Pain made him sick and dazed. But his brain was clear. Reeling, he groped for his coats and got them on, buttoning his overcoat up to his ears. It was some time before he found his cap. He did not know whether his face was still bleeding. Walking blindly, every step making him sick with pain, he went back to the pond and washed his face and hands. The icy water hurt, but helped to bring him back to himself. He crawled back up the hill to the tram. He wanted to get to his mother, he must get to his mother. That was his blind intention. He covered his face as much as he could, and struggled sickly along. Continually, the ground seemed to fall away from him as he walked, and he felt himself dropping with a sickening feeling, into space. So, like a nightmare, he got through with the journey home.

Everybody was in bed. He looked at himself. His face was discoloured and smeared with blood, almost like a dead man's face. He washed it and went to bed. The night went by in delirium. In the morning he found his mother looking at him. Her blue eyes!—they were all he wanted to see. She was there, he was in her hands.

"It's not much, mother," he said. "It was Baxter Dawes."

"Tell me where hurts you," she said, quietly.

"I don't know—my shoulder—Say it was a bicycle accident, mother."

He could not move his arm. Presently Minnie, the little servant, came upstairs with some tea.

"Your mother's nearly frightened me out of my wits, fainted away," she said.

He felt he could not bear it. His mother nursed him. He told her about it.

"And now I should have done with them all," she said quietly.

"I will, mother."

She covered him up.

"And don't think about it," she said, "only try to go to sleep. The doctor won't be here till eleven."

He had a dislocated shoulder, and the second day acute bronchitis set in. His mother was pale as death now, and very thin. She would sit and look at him, then away into space. There was something between them that neither dared mention. Clara came to see him. Afterwards, he said to his mother:

"She makes me tired, mother."

"Yes. I wish she wouldn't come," Mrs Morel replied.

Another day Miriam came. But she seemed almost like a stranger to him.

"You know, I don't care about them mother," he said.

"I'm afraid you don't, my son," she replied sadly.

It was given out everywhere that it was a bicycle accident. Soon he was able to go to work again. But now there was a constant sickness and gnawing at his heart. He went to Clara, but there seemed, as it were, nobody there. He could not work. He and his mother seemed almost to avoid each other. There was some secret between them which they could not bear. He was not aware of it. He only knew that his life seemed unbalanced, as if it were going to smash into pieces.

Clara did not know what was the matter with him. She realised that he seemed unaware of her. Even when he came to her, he seemed unaware of her. Always, he was somewhere else. She felt she was clutching for him, and he was somewhere else. It tortured her, and so she tortured him. For a month at a time, she kept him at arm's length. He almost hated her, and was driven to her in spite of himself. He went mostly into the company of men, was always at the 'George' or the 'White Horse.' His mother was ill, distant, quiet, shadowy. He was terrified of something. He dared not look at her. Her eyes seemed to grow darker, her face more waxen. Still she dragged about at her work.

At Whitsuntide he said he would go to Blackpool for four days, with his friend Newton. The latter was a big, jolly fellow, with a touch of the bounder about him. Paul said his mother must go to Sheffield to stay a week with Annie, who lived there. Perhaps the change would do her good. Mrs Morel was attending a woman's doctor in Nottingham. He said her heart and her digestion were wrong. She consented to go to Sheffield, though she did not want to. But now, she would do everything her son wished of her. Paul said he would come for her on the fifth day, and stay also in Sheffield till the holiday was up. It was agreed.

The two young men set off gaily for Blackpool. Mrs Morel was quite lively as Paul kissed her and left her. Once at the station, he forgot everything. Four days were clear—not an anxiety, not a thought. The two young men simply enjoyed themselves. Paul was like another man. None of himself remained—no Clara, no Miriam, no mother that fretted him. He wrote to them all, and long letters to his mother. But they were jolly letters that made her laugh. He was having a good time, as young fellows will in a place like Blackpool. And underneath it all was a shadow for her.

Paul was very gay, excited at the thought of staying with his mother in Sheffield. Newton was to spend the day with them. Their train was late. Joking, laughing with their pipes between their teeth, the young men swung their bags onto the tram-car. Paul had bought his mother a little collar of real lace, that he wanted to see her wear, so that he could tease her about it.

Annie lived in a nice house and had a little maid. Paul ran gaily up the steps. He expected his mother laughing in the hall. But it was Annie who opened to him. She seemed distant to him. He stood a second in dismay. Annie let him kiss her cheek.

"Is my mother ill?" he said.

"Yes—she's not very well—don't upset her."

"Is she in bed?"

"Yes."

And then the queer feeling went over him, as if all the sunshine had gone out of him, and it was all shadow. He dropped the bag and ran upstairs. Hesitating, he opened the door. His mother sat up in bed, wearing a dressing gown of old rose colour. She looked at him almost as if she were ashamed of herself, pleading to him, humble. He saw the ashy look about her.

"Mother!" he said.

"I thought you were never coming," she answered, gaily.

But he only fell on his knees at the bedside, and buried his face in the bed-clothes, crying in agony, and saying: 'Mother—mother—mother!' She stroked his hair slowly with her thin hand.

"Don't cry," she said. "Don't cry—it's nothing."

But he felt as if his blood was melting into tears, and he cried in terror and pain.

"Don't—don't cry," his mother faltered.

Slowly she stroked his hair. Shocked out of himself, he cried, and the tears hurt in every fibre of his body. Suddenly he stopped. But he dared not lift his face out of the bedclothes.

"You *are* late—where have you been?" his mother asked.

"The train was late," he replied, muffled in the sheet.

"Yes—that miserable Central!—Is Newton come?"

"Yes."

"I'm sure you must be hungry—and they've kept dinner waiting."

With a wrench, he looked up at her.

"What is it, mother?" he asked, brutally.

She averted her eyes as she answered:

"Only a bit of a tumour, my boy—you needn't trouble—it's been there, the lump has, a long time."

Up came the tears again. His mind was clear and hard, but his body was crying.

"Where?" he said.

She put her hand on her side.

"Here!—But you know, they can sweal a tumour away."

He stood feeling dazed and helpless, like a child. He thought perhaps it was as she said—yes, he reassured himself it was so. But all the while his blood and his body knew definitely what it was. He sat down on the bed and took her hand. She had never had but the one ring, her wedding ring.

"When were you poorly?" he asked.

"It was yesterday it began," she answered submissively.

"Pains!"

"Yes—but not more than I've often had at home.—I believe Dr Ansell is an alarmist."

"You ought not to have travelled alone," he said, to himself more than to her.

"As if that had anything to do with it," she answered quickly.

They were silent for awhile.

"Now go and have your dinner," she said. "You *must* be hungry."

"Have you had yours?"

"Yes. A beautiful sole I had. Annie *is* good to me."

They talked a little while, then he went downstairs. He was very white and strained. Newton sat in miserable sympathy.

After dinner he went into the scullery to help Annie to wash up. The little maid had gone on an errand.

"Is it really a tumour?" he asked.

Annie began to cry again.

"The pain she had yesterday—I never saw anybody suffer like it!" she cried. "Leonard ran like a madman for Dr Ansell.—And when she'd got to bed, she said to me 'Annie, look at this lump on my side—I wonder what it is'—And there I looked, and I thought I should have dropped. Paul, as true as I'm here, it's a lump as big as my double fist. I said, 'Good gracious, mother, whenever did that come.'—'Why child,' she said, 'it's been there a long time.'—I thought I should have died, our Paul, I did.—She's been having these pains for months at home, and nobody looking after her."

The tears came to his eyes, then dried suddenly.

"But she's been attending the doctor in Nottingham—and she never told me," he said.

"If I'd have been at home," said Annie, "I should have seen for myself."

He felt like a man walking in unrealities. In the afternoon he went to see the doctor. The latter was a shrewd, lovable man.

"But what is it?" he said.

The doctor looked at the young man, then knitted his fingers.

"It may be a large tumour which has formed in the membrane," he said slowly, "and which we *may* be able to make go away—"

"Can't you operate?" asked Paul.

"Not there," replied the doctor.

"Are you sure?"

"*Quite!*"

Paul meditated a while.

"Are you sure it's a tumour?" he asked. "Why did Dr Jameson in Nottingham never find out anything about it?—She's been going to him for weeks, and he's treated her for heart and indigestion."

"Mrs Morel never told Dr Jameson about the lump," said the doctor.

"And do you *know* it's a tumour?"

"No, I am not sure."

"What else *might* it be. You asked my sister if there was cancer in the family. Might it be cancer?"

"I don't know."

"And what shall you do?"

"I should like an examination, with Dr Jameson."

"Then have one."

"You must arrange about that. His fee wouldn't be less than ten guineas, to come here from Nottingham."

"When would you like him to come?"

"I will call in this evening and we will talk it over."

Paul went away, biting his lip.

His mother could come downstairs for tea, the doctor said. Her son went upstairs to help her. She wore the old-rose dressing gown that Leonard had given Annie, and with a little colour in her face, was quite young again.

"But you look quite pretty in that," he said.

"Yes, they make me so fine, I hardly know myself," she answered.

But when she stood up to walk, the colour went. Paul helped her, half carrying her. At the top of the stairs she was gone. He lifted her up and carried her quickly downstairs, laid her on the couch. She was light and frail. Her face looked as if she were dead, with the blue lips shut tight. Her eyes opened, her blue, unfailing eyes. And she looked at him, pleadingly, almost wanting him to forgive her. He held brandy to her lips, but her mouth would not open. All the time she watched him lovingly. She was only sorry for him. The tears ran down his face without ceasing, but not a muscle moved. He was intent on getting a little brandy between her lips. Soon she was able to swallow a tea-spoonful. She lay back, so tired. The tears continued to run down his face.

"But," she panted, "it'll go off—don't cry."

"I'm not doing," he said.

After awhile, she was better again. He was kneeling beside the couch. They looked into each other's eyes.

"I don't want you to make a trouble of it," she said.

"No mother—you'll have to be quite still, and then you'll get better soon."

But he was white to the lips, and their eyes, as they looked at each other, understood. Her eyes were so blue, such a wonderful forget-menot blue! He felt, if only they had been of a different colour, he could have borne it better. His heart seemed to be ripping slowly in his breast. He kneeled there, holding her hand, and neither said anything. Then Annie came in.

"Are you all right?" she murmured timidly, to her mother.

"Of course," said Mrs Morel.

Paul sat down and told her about Blackpool. She was curious.

A day or two after he went to see Dr Jameson in Nottingham, to arrange for a consultation. Paul had practically no money in the world. But he could borrow.

His mother had been used to go to the public consultation on Saturday morning, when she could see the doctor for only a nominal sum. Her son went on the same day. The waiting room was full of poor women, who sat patiently on a bench around the wall. Paul thought of his mother in her little black costume sitting waiting likewise. The doctor was late. The women all looked rather frightened. Paul asked the nurse in attendance if he could see the doctor immediately he came. It was arranged so. The women sitting patiently round the walls of the room eyed the young man curiously.

At last the doctor came. He was about forty, good-looking, brown-skinned. His wife had died, and he, who had loved her, had specialised on women's ailments. Paul told his name, and his mother's. The doctor did not remember.

"Number 46M." said the nurse, and the doctor looked up the case in his book.

"There is a big lump that may be a tumour," said Paul. "But Dr Ansell was going to write you a letter."

"Ah yes!" replied the doctor, drawing the letter from his pocket. He was very friendly, affable, busy, kind. He would come to Sheffield the next day.

"What is your father?" he asked.

"He is a coal-miner," replied Paul.

"Not very well off I suppose?"

"This—I see after this," said Paul.

"And you—?" smiled the doctor.

"I am a clerk in Jordan's Appliance factory."

The doctor smiled at him.

"Er—to go to Sheffield—!" he said, putting the tips of his fingers together and smiling with his eyes. "—Eight guineas?"

"Thank you!" said Paul, flushing, and rising. "And you'll come tomorrow?"

"Tomorrow—Sunday!—yes! Can you tell me about what time there is a train, in the afternoon?"

"There is a Central gets in at 4.15."

"And—will there be any way of getting up to the house—shall I have to walk?" The doctor smiled.

"There is the tram," said Paul. "The Western Park tram."

The doctor made a note of it.

"Thank you," he said, and shook hands.

Then Paul went on home to see his father, who was left in the charge of Minnie. Walter Morel was getting very grey now. Paul found him digging in the garden. He had written him a letter. He shook hands with his father.

"Hello, Son, tha has landed then?" said the father.

"Yes," replied the son. "But I'm going back tonight."

"Are ter beguy!" exclaimed the collier. "An' has ter aten owt?"

"No."

"That's just like thee," said Morel. "Come thy ways in."

The father was afraid of the mention of his wife. The two went indoors. Paul ate in silence, his father, with earthy hands and sleeves rolled up, sat in the arm-chair opposite and looked at him.

"Well, an' how is she?" asked the miner, at length, in a little voice.

"She can sit up—she can be carried down for tea," said Paul.

"That's a blessin'!" exclaimed Morel. "I hope we s'll soon be havin' her whoam then.—An' what's that Nottingham doctor say?"

"He's going tomorrow to have an examination of her."

"Is he beguy!—That's a tidy penny, I'm thinkin'."

"Eight guineas."

"Eight guineas!" The miner spoke breathlessly. "Well, we mun find it from somewheer."

"I can pay that," said Paul.

There was a silence between them for some time.

"She says she hopes you're getting on all right with Minnie," Paul said.

"Yes I'm all right—an' I wish as she was," answered Morel. "But Minnie's a good little wench, bless 'er heart." He sat looking dismal.

"I s'll have to be going at half past three," said Paul.

"It's a trapse for thee lad!—Eight guineas!—An' when dost think she'll be able to get as far as this?"

"We must see what the doctors say tomorrow," Paul said.

Morel sighed deeply. The house seemed strangely empty, and Paul thought his father looked, lost, forlorn and old.

"You'll have to go and see her next week, father," he said.

"I hope she'll be a-whoam by that time," said Morel.

"If she's not," said Paul, "then you must come."

"I dunno wheer I s'll find th'money," said Morel.

"And I'll write to you what the doctor says," said Paul.

"But tha writes i' such a fashion, I canna ma'e it out," said Morel.

"Well—I'll write plain."

It was no good asking Morel to answer, for he could scarcely do more than write his own name.

The doctor came. Leonard felt it his duty to meet him with a cab. The examination did not take long. Annie, Arthur, Paul and Leonard were waiting in the parlour anxiously. The doctors came down. Paul glanced at them. He had never had any hope, except when he had deceived himself.

"It *may* be a tumour—we must wait and see," said Dr Jameson.

"And if it is," said Annie, "can you sweal it away?"

"Probably," said the doctor.

Paul put eight sovereigns and half a sovereign on the table. The doctor counted them, took a florin out of his purse, and put that down.

"Thank you!" he said. "I'm sorry Mrs Morel is so ill. But we must see what we can do."

"There can't be an operation?" said Paul.

The doctor shook his head.

"No," he said, "and even if there could, her heart wouldn't stand it."

"Is her heart risky?" asked Paul.

"Yes—you must be careful with her."

"Very risky?"

"No—er—no—no! Just take care."

And the doctor was gone.

Then Paul carried his mother downstairs. She lay simply, like a child. But when he was on the stairs, she put her arms round his neck, clinging.

"I'm so frightened of these beastly stairs," she said.

And he was frightened too. He would let Leonard do it another time. He felt he could not carry her.

"He thinks it's only a tumour!" cried Annie to her mother. "And he can sweal it away."

"I *knew* he could," protested Mrs Morel, scornfully.

She pretended not to notice that Paul had gone out of the room. He sat in the kitchen, smoking. Then he tried to brush some grey ash off his coat. He looked again. It was one of his mother's grey hairs. It was so long! He held it up, and it drifted into the chimney. He let go. The long grey hair floated and was gone in the blackness of the chimney.

The next day he kissed her before going back to work. It was very early in the morning, and they were alone.

"You won't fret, my boy!" she said.

"No mother."

"No—it would be silly. And take care of yourself."

"Yes," he answered. Then, after a while, "And I shall come next Saturday, and shall I bring my father?"

"I suppose he wants to come," she replied. "At any rate, if he does you'll have to let him."

He kissed her again, and stroked the hair from her temples, gently, tenderly, as if she were a lover.

"Shan't you be late?" she murmured.

"I'm going," he said, very low.

Still he sat a few minutes stroking the brown and grey hair from her temples.

"And you won't be any worse mother?"

"No my son."

"You promise me?"

"Yes—I won't be any worse."

He kissed her, held her in his arms for a moment, and was gone. In the early, sunny morning he ran to the station, crying all the way, he did not know what for. And her blue eyes were wide and staring as she thought of him.

In the afternoon he went a walk with Clara. They sat in the little wood where bluebells were standing. He took her hand.

"You'll see," he said to Clara, "she'll never be better."

"Oh you don't know," replied the other.

"I do," he said.

She caught him impulsively to her breast.

"Try and forget it, dear," she said, "try and forget it."

"I will," he answered.

Her breast was there, warm for him, her hands were in his hair. It was comforting, and he held his arms round her. But he did not forget. He only talked to Clara of something else. And it was always so. When she felt it coming, the agony, she cried to him:

"Don't think of it, Paul, don't think of it my darling."

And she pressed him to her breast, rocked him, soothed him like a child. So he put the trouble aside for her sake, to take it up again immediately he was alone. All the time as he went about, he cried mechanically. His mind and hands were busy. He cried, he did not know why. It was his blood weeping. He was just as much alone whether he was with Clara or with the men in the 'White Horse.' Just himself and this pressure inside him, that was all that existed. He read sometimes. He had to keep his mind occupied. And Clara was a way of occupying his mind.

On the Saturday Walter Morel went to Sheffield. He was a forlorn figure, looking rather as if nobody owned him. Paul ran upstairs.

"My father's come," he said, kissing his mother.

"Has he?" she answered, wearidly.

The old collier came rather frightened into the bedroom.

"How dun I find thee, lass?" he said, going forward and kissing her in a hasty, timid fashion.

"Well—I'm middlin'," she replied.

"I see tha art," he said. He stood looking down on her. Then he wiped his eyes with his handkerchief. Helpless, and as if nobody owned him, he looked.

"Have you gone on all right?" asked the wife, rather wearily, as if it were an effort to talk to him.

"Yis!" he answered. "'Er's a bit behint-hand now and again, as yer might expect."

"Does she have your dinner ready?" asked Mrs Morel.

"Well—I've 'ad to shout at 'er once or twice," he said.

"And you *must* shout at her if she's not ready. She *will* leave things to the last minute."

She gave him a few instructions. He sat looking at her as if she were almost a stranger to him, before whom he was awkward and humble; and also as if he had lost his presence of mind, and wanted to run. This feeling that he wanted to run away, that he was on thorns to be gone from so trying a situation, yet must linger because it looked better, made his presence so trying. He put up his eyebrows for misery, and clenched his fists on his knees, feeling so awkward in presence of a big trouble.

Mrs Morel did not change much. She stayed in Sheffield for two months. If anything, at the end she was rather worse. But she wanted to go home. Annie had her children. Mrs Morel wanted to go home. So they got a motor-car from Nottingham—for she was too ill to go by train—and she was driven through the sunshine. It was just August, everything was bright and warm. Under the blue sky, they could all see she was dying. Yet she was jollier than she had been for weeks. They all laughed and talked.

"Annie!" she exclaimed. "I saw a lizard dart on that rock."

Her eyes were so quick, she was still so full of life.

Morel knew she was coming. He had the front door open. Everybody was on tip-toe. Half the street turned out. They heard the sound of the great motorcar. Mrs Morel, smiling, drove home down the street.

"And just look at them all come out to see me!" she said. "But there, I suppose I should have done the same.—How do you do Mrs Matthews—how are you, Mrs Harrison?"

They none of them could hear, but they saw her smile and nod. And they all saw death on her face, they said. It was a great event in the street.

Morel wanted to carry her indoors, but he was too old. Arthur took her as if she were a child. They had set her big deep chair by the hearth where her rocking-chair used to stand. When she was unwrapped and seated, and had drunk a little brandy, she looked round the room.

"Don't think I didn't like your house Annie," she said. "But it's nice to be in my own home again."

And Morel answered huskily:

"It is lass, it is."

And Minnie, the little, quaint maid, said:

"An' we glad t'ave yer."

There was a lovely yellow ravel of sunflowers in the garden. She looked out of the window.

"There are my sunflowers!" she said.

CHAPTER XIV

The Release

"By the way," said Doctor Ansell one evening when Morel was in Sheffield, "we've got a man in the fever hospital here, who comes from Nottingham—Dawes. He doesn't seem to have many belongings in this world."

"Baxter Dawes!" Paul exclaimed.

"That's the man—has been a fine fellow, physically, I should think. Been in a bit of a mess lately. You know him?"

"He used to work at the place where I am."

"Did he? Do you know anything about him? He's just sulking, or he'd be a lot better than he is, by now."

"I don't know anything of his home circumstances, except that he's separated from his wife and has been a bit down, I believe. But tell him about me, will you. Tell him I'll come and see him."

The next time Morel saw the doctor, he said:

"And what about Dawes?"

"I said to him," answered the other, "'do you know a man from Nottingham named Morel?'—and he looked at me as if he'd jump at my throat. So I said 'I see you know the name—it's Paul Morel.' Then I told him about your saying you would go and see him. 'What does he want?' he said, as if you were a policeman—"

"And did he say he would see me?" asked Paul.

"He wouldn't say anything—good, bad, or indifferent," replied the doctor.

"Why not?"

"That's what I want to know. There he lies and sulks, day in, day out—can't get a word of information out of him."

"Do you think I might go?" asked Paul.

"You might."

There was a feeling of connection between the rival men, more than ever since they had fought. In a way Morel felt guilty towards the other, and more or less responsible. And being in such a state of soul himself, he felt an almost painful nearness to Dawes, who was suffering and despairing too. Besides, they had met in a naked

423

extremity of hate, and it was a bond. At any rate the elemental man in each had met.

He went down to the isolation hospital, with Dr Ansell's card. The sister, a healthy young Irish woman, led him down the ward.

"A visitor to see you, Jim-crow," she said.

Dawes turned over suddenly with a startled grunt.

"Eh?"

"Caw?" she mocked. "He can only say 'Caw!'—I have brought you a gentleman to see you. Now say thank you, and show some manners."

Dawes looked swiftly with his dark, startled eyes, beyond the Sister at Paul. His look was full of fear, mistrust, hate, and misery. Morel met the swift, dark eyes, and hesitated. The two men were afraid of the naked selves they had been.

"Dr Ansell told me you were here," said Morel, holding out his hand.

Dawes mechanically shook hands.

"So I thought I'd come in," continued Paul.

There was no answer. Dawes lay staring at the opposite wall.

"Say 'Caw'!" mocked the nurse. "Say 'Caw', Jimcrow!"

"He is getting on all right?" said Paul to her.

"Oh yes! He lies and imagines he's going to die," said the nurse, "and it frightens every word out of his mouth."

"And you *must* have somebody to talk to," laughed Morel.

"That's it!" laughed the nurse. "Only two old men and a boy who always cries. It *is* hard lines! Here I am dying to hear Jim-crow's voice, and nothing but an odd 'caw' will he give."

"So rough on you," said Morel.

"Isn't it!" said the nurse.

"I suppose I am a godsend," he laughed.

"Oh—dropped straight from heaven," laughed the nurse.

Presently she left the two men alone. Dawes was thinner, and handsome again, but life seemed low in him. As the doctor said, he was lying sulking, and would not move forward towards convalescence. He seemed to grudge every beat of his heart.

"Have you had a bad time?" asked Paul.

Suddenly again Dawes looked at him.

"What are you doin' in Sheffield?" he asked.

"My mother was taken ill at my sister's in Thurston Street.—What are you doing here?"

There was no answer.

"How long have you been in?" Morel asked.

"I couldn't say for sure," Dawes answered, grudgingly.

He lay staring across at the wall opposite, as if trying to believe Morel was not there. Paul felt his heart go hard and angry.

"Dr Ansell told me you were here," he said coldly.

The other man did not answer.

"Typhoid's pretty bad, I know," Morel persisted.

Suddenly Dawes said:

"What did you come for?"

"Because Dr Ansell said you didn't know anybody here. Do you?"

"I know nobody nowhere," said Dawes.

"Well," said Paul, "it's because you don't choose to then."

There was another silence.

"We s'll be taking my mother home as soon as we can," said Paul.

"What's a-matter with her?" asked Dawes, with a sick man's interest in illness.

"She's got a cancer."

There was another silence.

"But we want to get her home," said Paul. "We s'll have to get a motorcar."

Dawes lay thinking.

"Why don't you ask Thomas Jordan to lend you his?" said Dawes.

"It's not big enough," Morel answered.

Dawes blinked his dark eyes as he lay thinking.

"Then ask Jack Pilkington—he'd lend it you.—You know him."

"I think I s'll hire one," said Paul.

"You're a fool if you do," said Dawes.

The sick man was gaunt and handsome again. Paul was sorry for him because his eyes looked so tired.

"Did you get a job here?" he asked.

"I was only here a day or two before I was taken bad," Dawes replied.

"You want to get in a convalescent home," said Paul.

The other's face clouded again.

"I'm goin' in no convalescent home," he said.

"My father's been in the one at Seathorpe, an' he liked it.—Dr Ansell would get you a recommend."

Dawes lay thinking. It was evident he dared not face the world again.

"The sea-side would be all right just now," Morel said. "Sun on those sand-hills, and the waves not far out."

The other did not answer.

"By Gad," Paul concluded, too miserable to bother much; "it's all right when you know you're going to walk again, and swim——"

Dawes glanced at him quickly. The man's dark eyes were afraid to meet any other eyes in the world. But the real misery and helplessness in Paul's tone gave him a feeling of relief.

"Is she far gone?" he asked.

"She's going like wax," Paul answered. "But cheerful—lively—."

He bit his lip. After a minute he rose.

"Well, I'll be going," he said.—"I'll leave you this half-crown."

"I don't want it," Dawes muttered.

Morel did not answer, but left the coin on the table.

"Well," he said, "I'll try and run in when I'm back in Sheffield. Happen you might like to see my brother-in-law. He works in Pyecrofts."

"I don't know him," said Dawes.

"He's all right. Should I tell him to come?—He might bring you some papers to look at."

The other man did not answer. Paul went. The strong emotion that Dawes aroused in him, repressed, made him shiver.

He did not tell his mother, but next day he spoke to Clara about this interview. It was in the dinner hour. The two did not often go out together now, but this day he asked her to go with him to the Castle grounds. There they sat while the scarlet geraniums and the yellow calceolarias blazed in the sunlight. She was now always rather protective, and rather resentful towards him.

"Did you know Baxter was in Sheffield hospital with typhoid?" he asked.

She looked at him with startled grey eyes, and her face went pale.

"No," she said, frightened.

"He's getting better.—I went to see him yesterday—the doctor told me."

Clara seemed stricken by the news.

"Is he very bad?" she asked, guiltily.

"He has been. He's mending now."

"What did he say to you?"

"Oh nothing. He seems to be sulking."

There was a distance between the two of them. He gave her more information.

She went about shut up and silent. The next time they took a walk together, she disengaged herself from his arm, and walked at a distance from him. He was wanting her comfort badly.

"Won't you be nice with me?" he asked.

She did not answer.

"What's the matter?" he said, putting his arm across her shoulder.

"Don't!" she said, disengaging herself.

He left her alone, and returned to his own brooding.

"Is it Baxter that upsets you?" he asked at length.

"I *have* been *vile* to him," she said.

"I've said many a time you haven't treated him well," he replied.

And there was a hostility between them. Each pursued his own train of thought.

"I've treated him—no, I've treated him badly," she said. "And now you treat *me* badly. It serves me right."

"How do I treat you badly?" he said.

"It serves me right," she repeated. "I never considered him worth having, and now you don't consider *me*.—But it serves me right.—He loved me a thousand times better than you ever did."

"He didn't," protested Paul.

"He did!—At any rate he did respect me, and that's what you don't do."

"It looked as if he respected you," he said.

"He did! And I *made* him horrid, I know I did. You've taught me that.—And he loved me a thousand times better than ever you do."

"All right," said Paul.

He wanted to be left alone now. He had his own trouble, which was almost too much to bear. Clara only tormented him and made him tired. He was not sorry when he left her.

She went on the first opportunity to Sheffield to see her husband. The meeting was not a success. But she left him roses and fruit and money. She wanted to make restitution. It was not that she loved him. As she looked at him lying there, her heart did not warm with love. Only she wanted to humble herself to him, to kneel before him. She wanted now to be self-sacrificial. After all she had failed to make Morel really love her. She was morally frightened. She wanted to do penance. So she knelt to Dawes, and it gave him a subtle pleasure. But the distance between them was still very great, too great. It frightened the man. It almost pleased the woman. She liked to feel she was serving him across an insuperable distance. She was proud now.

Morel went to see Dawes once or twice. There was a sort of friendship between the two men, who were all the while deadly rivals. But they never mentioned the woman who was between them.

Mrs Morel got gradually worse. At first, they used to carry her downstairs, sometimes even into the garden. She sat propped in her chair, smiling, and so pretty. The gold wedding ring shone on her white hand, her hair was carefully brushed. And she watched the tangled sunflowers dying, the chrysanthemums coming out, and the dahlias.

Paul and she were afraid of each other. He knew, and she knew, that she was dying. But they kept up a pretence of cheerfulness. Every morning, when he got up, he went into her room in his pyjamas.

"Did you sleep, my dear?" he asked.

"Yes," she answered.

"Not very well?"

"Well—yes."

Then he knew she had lain awake. He saw her hand under the bedclothes, pressing the place on her side, where the pain was.

"Has it been bad?" he asked.

"No—! It hurt a bit, but nothing to mention."

And she sniffed in her old, scornful way. As she lay, she looked like a girl. And all the while her blue eyes watched him. But there were the dark pain-circles beneath that made him ache again.

"It's a sunny day," he said.

"It's a beautiful day."

"Do you think you'll be carried down."

"I shall see."

Then he went away to get her breakfast. All day long he was conscious of nothing but her. It was a long ache that made him feverish. Then, when he got home in the early evening, he glanced through the kitchen window. She was not there. She had not got up.

He ran straight upstairs and kissed her. He was almost afraid, to ask:

"Didn't you get up, Pigeon."

"No," she said. "It was that morphia—it made me tired."

"I think he gives you too much," he said.

"I think he does," she answered.

He sat down by the bed, miserably. She had a way of curling and lying on her side, like a child. The grey and brown hair was loose over her ear.

"Doesn't it tickle you?" he said, gently putting it back.

"It does," she replied.

His face was near hers. Her blue eyes smiled straight into his, like a girl's, warm, laughing with tender love. It made him pant, with terror, agony and love.

"You want your hair doing in a plait," he said. "Lie still."

And going behind her, he carefully loosened her hair, brushed it out. It was like fine, long silk of brown and grey. Her head was snuggled between her shoulders. As he lightly brushed and plaited her hair, he bit his lip, and felt dazed. It all seemed unreal, he could not understand it.

At night he often worked in her room, looking up from time to time. And so often he found her blue eyes fixed on him. And when their eyes met, she smiled. He worked away again mechanically, producing good stuff without knowing what he was doing.

Sometimes he came in, very pale and still, with watchful, sudden eyes, like a man who is drunk almost to death. They were both afraid of the veils that were ripping between them.

Then she pretended to be better, chattered to him gaily, made a great fuss over some scraps of news. For they had both come to the condition when they had to make much of the trifles, lest they should give in to the big thing, and their human independence would go smash. They were afraid, so they made light of things and were gay.

Sometimes as she lay he knew she was thinking of the past. Her mouth gradually shut hard in a line. She was holding herself rigid, so that she might die without ever uttering the great cry that was tearing from her. He never forgot that hard, utterly lonely and stubborn clenching of her mouth, which persisted for weeks. Sometimes, when it was lighter, she talked about her husband. Now she hated him. She did not forgive him. She could not bear him to be in the room. And a few things, the things that had been most bitter to her, came up again so strongly, that they broke from her, and she told her son.

He felt as if his life were being destroyed, piece by piece, within him. Often the tears came suddenly. He ran to the station, the tear-drops falling on the pavement. Often, he could not go on with his work. The pen stopped writing. He sat staring, quite unconscious. And when he came round again, he felt sick, and trembled in his limbs. He never questioned what it was. His mind did not try to analyse or understand. He merely submitted, and kept his eyes shut, let the thing go over him.

His mother did the same. She thought of the pain, of the morphia, of the next day, hardly ever of the death. That was coming, she knew. She had to submit to it. But she would never entreat it or make friends with it. Blind, with her face shut hard and blind, she was pushed towards the door. The days passed, the weeks, the months.

Sometimes, in the sunny afternoons, she seemed almost happy.

"I try to think of the nice times—when we went to Mablethorpe and Robin Hood's Bay and Shanklin," she said. "After all, not everybody has seen those beautiful places. And wasn't it beautiful!—I try to think of that, not of the other things."

Then again, for a whole evening she spoke not a word, neither did he. They were together, rigid, stubborn, silent. He went into his room at last to go to bed, and leaned against the doorway, as if paralysed, unable to go any further. His consciousness went. A furious storm, he knew not what, seemed to ravage inside him. He stood leaning there, submitting, never questioning.

In the morning they were both normal again, though her face was grey with the morphia, and her body felt like ash. But they were bright again nevertheless. Often, especially if Annie or Arthur were at home, he neglected her. He did not see much of Clara. Usually he was with men. He was quick and active and lively, but when his friends saw him go white to the gills, his eyes dark and glittering they had a certain mistrust of him. Sometimes he went to Clara, but she was almost cold to him.

"Take me!" he said, simply.

Occasionally she would. But she was afraid. When he had her then, there was something in it that made her shrink away from him, something unnatural. She grew to dread him. He was so quiet, yet so strange. She was afraid of the man who was not there with her, whom she could feel behind this make-belief lover: somebody sinister, that filled her with horror. She began to have a kind of horror of him. It was almost as if he were a criminal. He wanted her—he had her—and it made her feel as if Death itself had her in its grip. She lay in horror. There was no man there loving her. She almost hated him. Then came little bouts of tenderness. But she dared not pity him.

Dawes had come to Colonel Seely's Home near Nottingham. There Paul visited him sometimes, Clara very occasionally. Between the two men the friendship had developed peculiarly. Dawes, who mended very slowly and seemed very feeble, seemed to leave himself in the hands of Morel.

In the beginning of November Clara reminded Paul that it was her birthday.

"I'd nearly forgotten," he said.

"I thought quite," she replied.

"No!—Shall we go to the seaside for the week-end?"

They went. It was cold and rather dismal. She waited for him to be warm and tender with her. Instead of which, he seemed hardly aware of her. He sat in the railway carriage looking out, and was startled when she spoke to him. He was not definitely thinking. Things seemed as if they did not exist. She went across to him.

"What is it, dear?" she asked.

"Nothing!" he said. "Don't those windmill sails look mono-tonous?"

He sat holding her hand. He could not talk nor think. It was a comfort, however, to sit holding her hand. She was dissatisfied and miserable. He was not with her: she was nothing.

And in the evening they sat among the sand-hills looking at the black, heavy sea.

"She will never give in," he said quietly.

Clara's heart sank.

"No," she replied.

"There are different ways of dying. My father's people are frightened, and have to be hauled out of life into death like cattle into a slaughter-house, pulled by the neck. But my mother's people are pushed from behind, inch by inch. They are stubborn people, and won't die."

"Yes," said Clara.

"And she won't die. She can't. Mr Renshaw, the parson, was in the other day. 'Think,' he said to her, 'you will have your mother and father and your sisters, and your son, in the Other Land.' And she said, 'I have done without them for a long time, and *can* do without them now. It is the living I want, not the dead.'—She wants to live, even now."

"Oh how horrible!" said Clara, too frightened to speak.

"And she looks at me, and she wants to stay with me," he went on monotonously. "She's got such a will, it seems as if she would never go, never—"

"Don't think of it," cried Clara.

"And she was religious—she is religious now—but it is no good. She simply won't give in. And do you know, I said to her on Thursday, 'Mother, if I had to die, I'd die. I'd *will* to die'—and she said to me, sharp, 'Do you think I haven't—do you think you can die when you like!'"

His voice ceased. He did not cry, only went on speaking monotonously. Clara wanted to run. She looked round. There was the black, re-echoing shore, the dark sky down on her. She got up terrified. She wanted to be where there was light, where there were other people. She wanted to be away from him. He sat with his head dropped, not moving a muscle.

"And I don't want her to eat," he said, "and she knows it. When I ask her, 'Shall you have anything?' she's almost afraid to say 'Yes.' 'I'll have a cup of Benger's,' she says. 'It'll only keep your strength up,' I said to her.—'Yes,' and she almost cried, 'but there's such a gnawing when I eat nothing, I can't bear it.' So I went and made her the food.—It's the cancer that gnaws like that at her.—I wish she'd die."

"Come," said Clara, roughly. "I'm going."

He followed her down the darkness of the sands. He did not come to her. He seemed scarcely aware of her existence. And she was afraid of him, and disliked him.

In the same acute daze, they went back to Nottingham. He was always busy, always doing something, always going from one to the other of his friends.

On the Monday he went to see Baxter Dawes. Listless and pale, the man rose to greet the other, clinging to his chair as he held out his hand.

"You shouldn't get up," said Paul.

Dawes sat down heavily, eyeing Morel with a sort of suspicion.

"Don't you waste your time on me," he said, "if you've owt better to do."

"I wanted to come," said Paul. "Here—I brought you some sweets."

432

The invalid put them aside.

"It's not been much of a week-end," said Morel.

"How's your mother?" asked the other.

"Hardly any different."

"I thought she was perhaps worse, being as you didn't come on Sunday."

"I was at Skegness," said Paul. "I wanted a change."

The other looked at him with dark eyes. He seemed to be waiting, not quite daring to ask, trusting to be told.

"I went with Clara," said Paul.

"I knew as much," said Dawes quietly.

"It was an old promise," said Paul.

"You have it your own way," said Dawes.

This was the first time Clara had been definitely mentioned between them.

"Nay," said Morel slowly, "she's tired of me."

Again Dawes looked at him.

"Since August, she's been getting tired of me," Morel repeated.

The two men were very quiet together. Paul suggested a game of draughts. They played in silence.

"I s'll go abroad when my mother's dead," said Paul.

"Abroad!" repeated Dawes.

"Yes—I don't care what I do."

They continued the game. Dawes was winning.

"I s'll have to begin a new start of some sort," said Paul. "And you as well, I suppose."

He took one of Dawes' pieces.

"I dunno where," said the other.

"Things have to happen," Morel said. "It's no good doing anything—at least—no, I don't know.—Give me some toffee."

The two men ate sweets, and began another game of draughts.

"What made that scar on your mouth?" asked Dawes.

Paul put his hand hastily to his lips, and looked over the garden.

"I had a bicycle accident," he said.

Dawes' hand trembled as he moved the piece.

"You shouldn't ha' laughed at me," he said, very low.

"When?"

"That night on Woodborough Road—when you and her passed me, you with your hand on her shoulder."

"I never laughed at you," said Paul.

Dawes kept his fingers on the draught-piece.

"I never knew you were there till the very second when you passed," said Morel.

Dawes moved his piece.

"It was that as did me," he said, very low.

Paul took another sweet.

"I never laughed," he said, "except as I'm always laughing."

They finished the game.

That night Morel walked home from Nottingham, in order to have something to do. The furnaces flared in a red blotch over Bulwell, the black clouds were like a low ceiling. As he went along the ten miles of high-road, he felt as if he were walking out of life, between the black levels of the sky and the earth. But at the end was only the sick room. If he walked and walked for ever—there was only that place to come to.

He was not tired when he got near home, or he did not know it. Across the field he could see the red firelight leaping in her bedroom window.

"When she's dead," he said to himself, "that fire will go out."

He took off his boots quietly and crept upstairs. His mother's door was wide open, because she slept alone still. The red firelight dashed its glow on the landing. Soft as a shadow, he peeped in her doorway:

"Paul," she murmured.

His heart seemed to break again. He went in and sat by the bed.

"How late you are!" she murmured.

"Not very," he said.

"Why what time is it?" The murmur came plaintive and helpless.

"It's only just gone eleven."

That was not true—it was nearly one o'clock.

"Oh," she said, "I thought it was later."

And he knew the unutterable misery of her nights that would not go.

"Can't you sleep, my pigeon?" he said.

"No—I can't," she wailed.

"Never mind, little," he said, crooning. "Never mind, my love. I'll stop with you half an hour, my pigeon, then perhaps it will be better."

And he sat by the bedside, slowly, rhythmically stroking her brows with his finger tips, stroking her eyes shut, soothing her, holding her fingers in his free hand. They could hear the sleepers' breathing in the other rooms.

"Now go to bed," she murmured, lying quite still under his fingers and his love.

"Will you sleep?" he asked.

"Yes—I think so."

"You feel better, my little, don't you?"

"Yes!" she said, like a fretful, half soothed child.

Still the days and the weeks went by. He hardly ever went to see Clara now. But he wandered restlessly from one person to another, for some help, and there was none anywhere. Miriam had written to him tenderly. He went to see her. Her heart was very sore when she saw him white, gaunt, with his eyes dark and bewildered. Her pity came up hurting her till she could not bear it.

"How is she?" she asked.

"The same—the same," he said. "The doctor says she can't last—but I know she will. She'll be here at Christmas."

Miriam shuddered. She drew him to her, she pressed him to her bosom, she kissed him, and kissed him. He submitted, but it was torture. She could not kiss his agony. That remained alone and apart. She kissed his face, and roused his blood, while his soul was apart writhing with the agony of death. And she kissed him and fingered his body, till at last, feeling he would go mad, he got away from her. It was not that he wanted just then—not that. And she thought she had soothed him and done him good.

December came, and some snow. He stayed at home all the while now. They could not afford a nurse. Annie came to look after her mother, the parish nurse, whom they loved, came in morning and evening. Paul shared the nursing with Annie. Often, in the evenings, when friends were in the kitchen with them, they all laughed together and shook with laughter. It was reaction. Paul was so comical, Annie was so quaint. The whole party laughed till they cried, trying to subdue the sound. And Mrs Morel, lying alone in the darkness, heard them, and among her bitterness was a feeling of relief.

Then Paul would go upstairs gingerly, guiltily, to see if she had heard.

"Shall I give you some milk?" he asked.

"A little," she replied plaintively.

And he would put some water with it, so that it should not nourish her. Yet he loved her more than his own life.

She had morphia every night, and her heart got fitful. Annie slept beside her. Paul would go in in the early morning, when his sister got up. His mother was wasted and almost ashen in the morning, with the morphia. Darker and darker grew her eyes, all pupil, with the torture. In the mornings the weariness and ache was too much to bear. Yet she could not, would not weep, or even complain much.

"You slept a bit later this morning, little one," he would say to her.

"Did I?" she answered, with fretful weariness.

"Yes—it's nearly eight o'clock."

He stood looking out of the window. The whole country was bleak and pallid, under the snow. Then he felt her pulse. There was a strong stroke and a weak one, like a sound and its echo. That was supposed to betoken the end. She let him feel her wrist, knowing what he wanted.

Sometimes they looked in each other's eyes. Then they almost seemed to make an agreement. It was almost as if he were agreeing to die also. But she did not consent to die—she would not. Her body was wasted to a fragment of ash. Her eyes were dark and full of torture.

"Can't you give her something to put an end to it?" he asked the doctor at last.

But the doctor shook his head.

"She can't last many days now, Mr Morel," he said.

Paul went indoors.

"I can't bear it much longer—we shall all go mad," said Annie.

The two sat down to breakfast.

"Go and sit with her while we have breakfast, Minnie," said Annie. But the girl was frightened.

Paul went through the country, through the woods, over the snow. He saw the marks of rabbits and birds in the white snow. He wandered miles and miles. A smoky red sunset came on slowly, painfully, lingering. He thought she would die that day. There was a donkey that came up to him over the snow by the wood's edge, and put its head against him, and walked with him alongside. He put his arms round the donkey's neck, and stroked his cheek against his ears.

His mother, silent, was still alive, with her hard mouth gripped grimly, her eyes of dark torture only living.

It was nearing Christmas; there was more snow. Annie and he felt

436

as if they could go on no more. Still her dark eyes were alive. Morel, silent and frightened, obliterated himself. Sometimes he would go into the sick room and look at her. Then he backed out, bewildered.

She kept her hold on life still. The miners had been out on strike, and returned a fortnight or so before Christmas. Minnie went upstairs with the feeding cup. It was two days after the men had been in.

"Have the men been saying their hands are sore, Minnie?" she asked, in the faint, querulous voice, that would not give in. Minnie stood surprised.

"Not as I know of, Mrs Morel," she answered.

"But I'll bet they are sore," said the dying woman, as she moved her head with a sigh of weariness. "But at any rate there'll be something to buy in with this week."

Not a thing did she let slip.

"Your father's pit-things will want well airing Annie," she said, when the men were going back to work.

"Don't you bother about that, my dear," said Annie.

One night Annie and Paul were alone. Nurse was upstairs.

"She'll live over Christmas," said Annie. They were both full of horror.

"She won't," he replied, grimly. "I s'll give her morphia."

"Which?" said Annie.

"All that that came from Sheffield," said Paul.

"Ay—do!" said Annie.

The next day he was painting in the bedroom. She seemed to be asleep. He stepped softly backwards and forwards at his painting. Suddenly her small voice wailed:

"Don't walk about Paul."

He looked round. Her eyes, like dark bubbles in her face, were looking at him.

"No my dear," he said gently. Another fibre seemed to snap in his heart.

That evening he got all the morphia pills there were, and took them downstairs. Carefully he crushed them to powder.

"What are you doing?" said Annie.

"I s'll put 'em in her night milk."

Then they both laughed together like two conspiring children. On top of all their horror flickered this little sanity.

Nurse did not come that night to settle Mrs Morel down. Paul went up with the hot milk in a feeding cup. It was nine o'clock.

She was reared up in bed, and he put the feeding cup between her lips, that he would have died to save from any hurt. She took a sip, then put the spout of the cup away, and looked at him with her dark, wondering eyes. He looked at her.

"Oh it *is* bitter, Paul!" she said, making a little grimace.

"It's a new sleeping draught the doctor gave me for you," he said. "He thought it wouldn't leave you in such a state in the morning."

"And I hope it won't," she said, like a child.

She drank some more of the milk.

"But it *is* horrid!" she said.

He saw her frail fingers over the cup, her lips making a little 'moue.'

"I know—I tasted it," he said. "But I'll give you some clean milk afterwards."

"I think so," she said, and she went on with the draught. She was obedient to him like a child. He wondered if she knew. He saw her poor wasted throat moving as she drank, with difficulty. Then he ran downstairs for more milk. There were no grains in the bottom of the cup.

"Has she had it?" whispered Annie.

"Yes—and she said it was bitter."

"Oh!" laughed Annie, putting her under lip between her teeth.

"And I told her it was a new draught. Where's that milk?"

They both went upstairs.

"I wonder why Nurse didn't come to settle me down!" complained the mother, like a child, wistfully.

"She said she was going to a concert, my love," replied Annie.

"Did she!"

They were silent a minute. Mrs Morel gulped the little clean milk.

"Annie, that draught *was* horrid!" she said, plaintively.

"Was it, my love?—Well, never mind."

The mother sighed again with weariness. Her pulse was very irregular.

"Let *us* settle you down," said Annie. "Perhaps Nurse will be so late."

"Ay," said the mother, "try."

They turned the clothes back. Paul saw his mother like a girl curled up in her flannel night dress. Quickly they made one half the bed, moved her, made the other, straightened her nighty over her small feet, and covered her up.

"There," said Paul, stroking her softly. "There!—now you'll sleep."

"Yes," she said.—"I didn't think you could do the bed so nicely," she added, almost gaily. Then she curled up, with her cheek on her hand, her head snugged between her shoulder. Paul put the long thin plait of grey hair over her shoulder, and kissed her.

"You'll sleep, my love," he said.

"Yes," she answered trustfully. "Goodnight."

They put out the light and it was still.

Morel was in bed. Nurse did not come. Annie and Paul came to look at her at about eleven. She seemed to be sleeping as usual after her draught. Her mouth had come a bit open.

"Shall we sit up?" said Paul.

"I s'll lie with her as I always do," said Annie. "She might wake up."

"All right—and call me if you see any difference."

"Yes."

They lingered before the bedroom fire, feeling the night big and black and snowy outside, their two selves alone in the world. At last he went into the next room and went to bed.

He slept almost immediately, but kept waking every now and again. Then he went sound asleep. He started awake at Annie's whispered 'Paul—Paul!' He saw his sister in her white night-dress, with her long plait of hair down her back, standing in the darkness.

"Yes!" he whispered, sitting up.

"Come and look at her."

He slipped out of bed. A bud of gas was burning in the sick chamber. His mother lay with her cheek on her hand, curled up as she had gone to sleep. But her mouth had fallen open, and she breathed with great, hoarse breaths, like snoring, and there were long intervals between.

"She's going," he whispered.

"Yes," said Annie.

"How long has she been like it?"

"I only just woke up."

Annie huddled into the dressing gown, Paul wrapped himself in a brown blanket. It was three o'clock. He mended the fire. Then the two sat waiting. The great, snoring breath was taken—held

439

awhile—then given back. There was a space, a long space. Then they started. The great, snoring breath was taken again. He bent close down and looked at her.

"Isn't it awful!" whispered Annie.

He nodded. They sat down again helplessly. Again came the great, snoring breath. Again they hung suspended. Again it was given back, long and harsh. The sound, so irregular, at such wide intervals, sounded through the house. Morel, in his room, slept on. Paul and Annie sat crouched, huddled, motionless. The great, snoring sound began again—there was a painful pause while the breath was held—back came the rasping breath. Minute after minute passed. Paul looked at her again, bending low over her.

"She may last like this," he said.

They were both silent. He looked out of the window, and could faintly discern the snow on the garden.

"You go to my bed," he said to Annie. "I'll sit up."

"No," she said, "I'll stop with you."

"I'd rather you didn't," he said.

At last Annie crept out of the room, and he was alone. He hugged himself in his brown blanket, crouched in front of his mother, watching. She looked dreadful, with the bottom jaw fallen back. He watched. Sometimes, he thought the great breath would never begin again. He could not bear it, the waiting. Then suddenly, startling him, came the great harsh sound. He mended the fire again, noiselessly. She must not be disturbed. The minutes went by. The night was going, breath by breath. Each time the sound came, he felt it wring him, till at last he could not feel so much.

His father got up. Paul heard the miner drawing his stocking on, yawning. Then Morel, in shirt and stockings, entered.

"Hush!" said Paul.

Morel stood watching. Then he looked at his son, helplessly, and in horror.

"Had I better stop a-whoam?" he whispered.

"No—go to work—she'll last through tomorrow."

"I don't think so."

"Yes. Go to work."

The miner looked at her again, in fear, and went obediently out of the room. Paul saw the tape of his garters swinging against his legs.

After another half hour, Paul went downstairs and drank a cup of tea, then returned. Morel, dressed for the pit, came upstairs again.

"Am I to go?" he said.

"Yes."

And in a few minutes Paul heard his father's heavy steps go thudding over the deadening snow. Miners called in the street as they tramped in gangs to work. The terrible, long-drawn breaths continued—heave—heave—heave—then a long pause—then Ah—Ah—h—h—h—h! as it came back. Far away over the snow sounded the hooters of the iron works. One after another they crowed and boomed, some small and far away, some near, the blowers of the collieries and the other works. Then there was silence. He mended the fire. The great breaths broke the silence—she looked just the same. He put back the blind and peered out. Still it was dark. Perhaps there was a lighter tinge. Perhaps the snow was bluer. He drew up the blind and got dressed. Then, shuddering, he drank brandy from the bottle on the wash-stand. The snow *was* growing blue. He heard a cart clanking down the street. Yes, it was seven o'clock, and it was coming a little bit light. He heard some people calling. The world was waking. A grey, deathly dawn crept over the snow. Yes, he could see the houses. He put out the gas. It seemed very dark. The breathing came still, but he was almost used to it. He could see her. She was just the same. He wondered, if he piled heavy clothes on top of her, it would make it heavier and the horrible breathing would stop. He looked at her. That was not her—not her a bit. If he piled the blanket and heavy coats on her.

Suddenly the door opened and Annie entered. She looked at him questioningly.

"Just the same," he said calmly.

They whispered together a minute then [he] went downstairs to get breakfast. It was twenty to eight. Soon Annie came down.

"Isn't it awful.—Doesn't she look awful?" she whispered, dazed with horror.

He nodded.

"If she looks like that—!" said Annie.

"Drink some tea," he said.

They went upstairs again. Soon the neighbours came with their frightened question:

"How is she."

It went on just the same. She lay with her cheek in her hand, her mouth fallen open, and the great, ghastly snores came and went.

At ten o'clock nurse came. She looked strange and woe-begone.

"Nurse!" cried Paul, "she'll last like this for days."

"She can't, Mr Morel," said nurse, "she can't."

There was a silence.

"Isn't it dreadful," wailed the nurse. "Who would have thought she could stand it.—Go down now, Mr Morel, go down."

At last, at about eleven o'clock, he went downstairs and sat in the neighbour's house. Annie was downstairs also. Nurse and Arthur were upstairs. Paul sat with his head in his hands. Suddenly Annie came flying across the yard, crying, half mad:

"Paul—Paul—she's gone!"

In a second he was back in his own house and upstairs. She lay curled up and still, with her face on her hand, and nurse was wiping her mouth. They all stood back. He kneeled down and put his face to hers and his arms round her:

"My love—my love—Oh my love!" he whispered again and again. "My love—oh my love!"

Then he heard the nurse behind him, crying, saying:

"She's better, Mr Morel, she's better."

When he took his face up from his warm, dead mother he went straight downstairs, began blacking his boots.

There was a good deal to do, letters to write, and so on. The doctor came and glanced at her, and sighed.

"Ay—poor thing," he said, then turned away. "Well, call at the surgery about six for the certificate."

The father came home from work at about four o'clock. He dragged silently into the house and sat down. Minnie bustled to give him his dinner. Tired, he laid his black arms on the table. There were swede turnips for his dinner, which he liked. Paul wondered if he knew. It was some time, and nobody had spoken. At last the son said:

"You noticed the blinds were down?"

Morel looked up.

"No!" he said. "Why—has she gone?"

"Yes."

"When wor that?"

"About twelve this morning."

"Hm!"

The miner sat still for a moment, then began his dinner. It was as if nothing had happened. He ate his turnips in silence. Afterwards he washed and went upstairs to dress. The door of her room was shut.

"Have you seen her?" Annie asked of him when he came down.
"No," he said.

In a little while he went out. Annie went away, and Paul called on
the undertaker, the clergyman, the doctor, the registrar. It was a
long business. He got back at nearly eight o'clock. The undertaker
was coming soon to measure for the coffin. The house was empty,
except for her. He took a candle and went upstairs.

The room was cold, that had been warm for so long. Flowers,
bottles, plates, all sick-room litter was taken away: everything was
harsh and austere. She lay raised on the bed, the sweep of the sheet
from the raised feet was like a clean curve of snow, so silent. She lay
like a maiden asleep. With his candle in his hand, he bent over her.
She lay like a girl asleep and dreaming of her love. The mouth was a
little open, as if wondering from the suffering, but her face was
young, her brow clear and white as if life had never touched it. He
looked again at the eyebrows, at the small, winsome nose, a bit on
one side. She was young again. Only the hair as it arched so
beautifully from her temples was mixed with silver, and the two
simple plaits that lay on her shoulders were filigree of silver and
brown. She would wake up. She would lift her eyelids. She was with
him still. He bent and kissed her passionately. But there was
coldness against his mouth. He bit his lip with horror. Looking at
her, he felt he could never, never let her go. No! He stroked the hair
from her temples. That too was cold. He saw the mouth so dumb
and wondering at the hurt. Then he crouched on the floor, whispering to her: "Mother—Mother!"

He was still with her when the undertakers came, young men who
had been to school with him. They touched her reverently, and in a
quiet, business-like fashion. They did not look at her. He watched
jealously. He and Annie guarded her fiercely. They would not let
anybody come to see her, and the neighbours were offended.

After a while Paul went out of the house, and played cards at a
friend's. It was midnight when he got back. His father rose from the
couch as he entered, saying in a plaintive way:

"I thought tha wor niver comin', lad."

"I didn't think you'd sit up," said Paul.

His father looked so forlorn. Morel had been a man without
fear—simply nothing frightened him. Paul realised with a start that
he had been afraid to go to bed, alone in the house with his dead. He
was sorry.

"I forgot you'd be alone, father," he said.

"Dost want owt to eat?" asked Morel.

"No."

"Sithee—I made thee a drop o' hot milk. Get it down thee, it's cold enough for owt."

Paul drank it.

"I must go to Nottingham tomorrow," he said.

After a while, Morel went to bed. He hurried past the closed door, and left his own door open. Soon the son came upstairs also. He went in to kiss her goodnight, as usual. It was cold and dark. He wished they had kept her fire burning. Still she dreamed her young dream. But she would be cold.

"My dear!" he whispered, "my dear!"

And he did not kiss her, for fear she should be cold and strange to him. It eased him she slept so beautifully. He shut her door softly, not to wake her, and went to bed.

In the morning Morel summoned his courage, hearing Annie downstairs and Paul coughing in the room across the landing. He opened her door and went into the darkened room. He saw the white uplifted form in the twilight, but her he dared not see. Bewildered, too frightened to possess any of his faculties, he got out of the room again and left her. He never looked at her again. He had not seen her now for months, because he had not dared to look. And she looked like his young wife again.

"Have you seen her?" Annie asked of him, sharply, after breakfast.

"Yes," he said.

"And don't you think she looks nice?"

"Yes."

He went out of the house soon after. And all the time he seemed to be creeping aside to avoid it.

Paul went about from place to place, doing the business of the death. He met Clara in Nottingham, and they had tea together in a café, when they were quite jolly again. She was infinitely relieved to find he did not take it tragically.

Later, when the relatives began to come for the funeral, the affair became public, and the children became social beings. They put themselves aside. They buried her in a furious storm of rain and wind. The wet clay glistened, all the white flowers were soaked. Annie gripped his arm and leaned forward. Down below, she saw a dark corner of William's coffin. The oak box sank steadily. She was gone. The rain poured in the grave. The procession of black, with its umbrellas glistening, turned away. The cemetery was deserted under the drenching cold rain.

Paul went home and busied himself supplying the guests with drinks. His father sat in the kitchen, with Mrs Morel's relatives, 'superior' people, and wept, and said what a good lass she'd been, and how he'd tried to do everything he could for her—everything. He had striven all his life to do what he could for her, and he'd nothing to reproach himself with. She was gone, but he'd done his best for her. He wiped his eyes with his white handkerchief. He'd nothing to reproach himself for, he repeated. All his life he'd done his best for her.

And that was how he tried to dismiss her. He never thought of her, personally. Everything deep in him he denied. Paul hated his father for sitting sentimentalising over her. He knew he would do it in the public houses. For the real tragedy went on in Morel in spite of himself.—Sometimes, later, he came down from his afternoon sleep white and cowering.

"I *have* been dreaming of thy mother," he said, in a small voice.

"Have you father?—When I dream of her, it's always just as she was when she was well. I dream of her often, but it seems quite nice and natural, as if nothing had altered."

But Morel crouched in front of the fire, in terror.

The weeks passed half real, not much pain, not much of anything, perhaps a little relief, mostly a *nuit blanche*. Paul went restlessly from place to place. For some months, since his mother had been worse, he had not made love to Clara. She was as it were dumb to him, rather distant. Dawes saw her very occasionally, but the two could not get an inch across the great distance between them. The three of them were drifting forward.

Dawes mended very slowly. He was in the convalescent home at Skegness at Christmas, nearly well again. Paul went to the sea-side for a few days. His father was with Annie in Sheffield. Dawes came to Paul's lodgings. His time in the Home was up. The two men, between whom was such a big reserve, seemed faithful to each other. Dawes depended on Morel now. He knew Paul and Clara had practically separated.

Two days after Christmas Paul was to go back to Nottingham. The evening before, he sat with Dawes smoking before the fire.

"You know Clara's coming down for the day tomorrow?" he said.
The other man glanced at him.

"Yes, you told me," he replied.

Paul drank the remainder of his glass of whiskey.

"I told the landlady your wife was coming," he said.

"Did you?" said Dawes, shrinking, but almost leaving himself in the other's hands. He got up rather stiffly and reached for Morel's glass.

"Let me fill you up," he said.

Paul jumped up.

"You sit still," he said.

But Dawes, with rather shaky hand, continued to mix the drink.

"Say when," he said.

"Thanks!" replied the other. "But you've no business to get up."

"It does me good, lad," replied Dawes. "I begin to think I'm right again then."

"You are about right, you know."

"I am, certainly, I am," said Dawes, nodding to him.

"And Len says he can get you on in Sheffield."

Dawes glanced at him again, with dark eyes that agreed with everything the other would say, perhaps a trifle dominated by him.

"It's funny," said Paul, "starting again!—I feel in a lot bigger mess than you."

"In what way, lad?"

"I don't know. I don't know. It's as if I was in a tangled sort of hole, rather dark and dreary, and no road anywhere."

"I know—I understand it," Dawes said, nodding. "But you'll find it'll come all right."

He spoke caressingly.

"I suppose so," said Paul.

Dawes knocked his pipe in a hopeless fashion.

"You've not done for yourself like I have," he said.

Morel saw the wrist and the white hand of the other man gripping the stem of the pipe and knocking out the ash as if he had given up.

"How old are you?" Paul asked.

"Thirty nine," replied Dawes, glancing at him.

Those brown eyes, full of the consciousness of failure, almost pleading for re-assurance, for someone to re-establish the man in himself, to warm him, to set him up firm again, troubled Paul.

"You'll just be in your prime," said Morel.—"You don't look as if much life had gone out of you."

The brown eyes of the other flashed suddenly.

"It hasn't," he said. "The go is there!"

Paul looked up and laughed.

"We've both got plenty of life in us yet, to make things fly," he said.

The eyes of the two men met. They exchanged one look. Having recognised the stress of passion each in the other, they both drank their whiskey.

"Yes begod!" said Dawes, breathless.

There was a pause.

"And I don't see," said Paul, "why you shouldn't go on where you left off."

"What—!" said Dawes, suggestively.

"Yes—fit your old home together again."

Dawes hid his face and shook his head.

"Couldn't be done," he said, and he looked up with an ironic smile.

"Why?—because you don't want?"

"Perhaps."

They smoked in silence. Dawes showed his teeth as he bit his pipe stem.

"You mean you don't want her?" asked Paul.

Dawes stared up at the picture, with a caustic expression on his face.

"I hardly know," he said.

The smoke floated softly up.

"I believe she wants you," said Paul.

"Do you?" replied the other, soft, satirical, abstract.

"Yes.—She never really hitched on to me—you were always there in the background. That's why she wouldn't get a divorce."

Dawes continued to stare in a satirical fashion at the picture over the mantel-piece.

"That's how women are with me," said Paul. "They want me like mad, but they don't want to belong to me.—And she *belonged* to you all the time. I knew—."

The triumphant male came up in Dawes. He showed his teeth more distinctly.

"Perhaps I was a fool," he said.

"You were a big fool," said Morel.

"But perhaps even *then* you were a bigger fool," said Dawes.

There was a touch of triumph and malice in it.

"Do you think so!" said Paul.

They were silent for some time.

"At any rate I'm clearing out tomorrow," said Morel.

"I see," answered Dawes.

Then they did not talk any more. The instinct to murder each other had returned. They almost avoided each other.

They shared the same bedroom. When they retired, Dawes seemed abstract, thinking of something. He sat on the side of the bed in his shirt, looking at his legs.

"Aren't you getting cold?" asked Morel.

"I was lookin' at these legs," replied the other.

"What's up with'em? They look all right," replied Paul, from his bed.

"They look all right—but there's some water in 'em yet."

"And what about it?"

"Come and look."

Paul reluctantly got out of bed and went to look at the rather handsome legs of the other man, that were covered with glistening dark-gold hair.

"Look here," said Dawes, pointing to his shin. "Look at the water under here."

"Where?" said Paul.

The man pressed in his finger-tips. They left little dents that filled up slowly.

"It's nothing," said Paul.

"You feel!" said Dawes.

Paul tried with his fingers. It made little dents.

"Hm!" he said.

"Rotten, isn't it?" said Dawes.

"Why?—it's nothing much."

"You're not much of a man with water in your legs."

"I can't see as it makes any difference," said Morel. "I've got a weak chest."

He returned to his own bed.

"I suppose the rest of me's all right," said Dawes, and he put out the light.

In the morning it was raining. Morel packed his bag. The sea was grey and shaggy and dismal. He seemed to be cutting himself off from life more and more. It gave him a wicked pleasure to do it.

The two men were at the station. Clara stepped out of the train, and came along the platform, very erect and coldly composed. She wore a long coat and a tweed hat. Both men hated her for her composure. Paul shook hands with her at the barrier. Dawes was leaning against the book-stall, watching. His black overcoat was buttoned up to the chin, because of the rain. He was pale, with almost a touch of nobility in his quietness. He came forward, limping slightly.

"You ought to look better than this," she said.

"Oh, I'm all right now."

The three stood at a loss. She kept the two men hesitating near her.

"Shall we go to the lodging straight off," said Paul, "or somewhere else?"

"We may as well go home," said Dawes.

Paul walked on the outside of the pavement, then Dawes, then Clara. They made polite conversation. The sitting-room faced the sea, whose tide, grey and shaggy, hissed not far off.

Morel swung up the big arm-chair.

"Sit down, Jack," he said.

"I don't want that chair," said Dawes.

"Sit down," Morel repeated.

Clara took off her things and laid them on the couch. She had a slight air of resentment. Lifting her hair with her fingers, she sat down, rather aloof, and composed. Paul ran downstairs to speak to the landlady.

"I should think you're cold," said Dawes to his wife. "Come nearer to the fire."

"Thank you, I'm quite warm," she answered.

She looked out of the window at the rain and at the sea.

"When are you going back?" she asked.

"Well—the rooms are taken until tomorrow, so he wants me to stop. He's going back tonight."

"And then you're thinking of going to Sheffield?"

"Yes."

"Are you fit to start work?"

"I'm going to start."

"You've really got a place?"

"Yes—begin on Monday."

"You don't look fit."

"Why don't I?"

She looked again out of the window instead of answering.

"And have you got lodgings in Sheffield?"

"Yes."

Again she looked away out of the window. The panes were blurred with streaming rain.

"And can you manage all right?" she asked.

"I s'd think so. I s'll have to!"

They were silent when Morel returned.

"I shall go by the 4.20," he said as he entered.

Nobody answered.

"I wish you'd take your boots off," he said to Clara. "There's a pair of slippers of mine!"

"Thank you," she said. "They aren't wet."

He put the slippers near her feet. She left them there.

Morel sat down. Both the men seemed helpless, and each of them had a rather hunted look. But Dawes now carried himself quietly, seemed to yield himself, while Paul seemed to screw himself up. Clara thought she had never seen him look so small and mean. He was as if trying to get himself into the smallest possible compass. And as he went about, arranging, and as he sat talking, there seemed something false about him, and out of tune. Watching him unknown, she said to herself there was no stability about him. He was fine in his way, passionate and able to give her drinks of pure life, when he was in one mood. And now he looked paltry and insignificant. There was nothing stable about him. Her husband had more manly dignity. At any rate *he* did not waft about with any wind. There was something evanescent about Morel, she thought, something shifting and false. He would never make sure ground for any woman to stand on. She despised him rather for his shrinking together, getting smaller. Her husband at least was manly, and when he was beaten, gave in. But this other would never own to being beaten. He would shift round and round, prowl, get smaller. She despised him. And yet she watched him rather than Dawes, and it seemed as if their three fates lay in his hands. She hated him for it.

She seemed to understand better now about men, and what they could or would do. She was less afraid of them, more sure of herself. That they were not the small egoists she had imagined them made her more comfortable. She had learned a good deal, almost as much as she wanted to learn. Her cup had been full. It was still as full as she could carry. On the whole, she would not be sorry when he was gone.

They had dinner, and sat eating nuts and drinking by the fire. Not a serious word had been spoken. Yet Clara realised that Morel was withdrawing from the circle, leaving her the option to stay with her husband. It angered her. He was a mean fellow after all—to take what he wanted and then give her back. She did not remember that she herself had had what she wanted, and really, at the bottom of her heart, wished to be given back.

Paul felt crumpled up and lonely. His mother had really supported his life. He had loved her, they two had in fact faced the world together. Now she was gone, and forever behind him was the gap in life, the tear in the veil, through which his life seemed to drift slowly, as if he were drawn towards death. He wanted someone, of their own free initiative, to help him. The lesser things he began to let go from him, for fear of this big thing, the lapse towards death, following in the wake of his beloved. Clara could not stand for him to hold on to. She wanted him, but not to understand him. He felt she wanted the man on top, not the real him that was in trouble. That would be too much trouble to her, he dared not give it her. She could not cope with him. It made him ashamed. So, secretly ashamed because he was in such a mess, because his own hold on life was so unsure, because nobody held him, feeling unsubstantial, shadowy, as if he did not count for much in this concrete world, he drew himself together smaller and smaller. He did not want to die, he would not give in. But he was not afraid of death. If nobody would help he would go on alone.

Dawes had been driven to the extremity of life, until he was afraid. He could go to the brink of death, he could lie on the edge and look in. Then, cowed, afraid, he had to crawl back, and like a beggar take what offered. There was a certain nobility in it. As Clara saw, he owned himself beaten, and he wanted to be taken back whether or not. That she could do for him.

It was three o'clock.

"I am going by the four twenty," said Paul again to Clara. "Are you coming then or later?"

"I don't know," she said.

"I'm meeting my father in Nottingham at 7.15," he said.

"Then," she answered, "I'll come later."

Dawes jerked suddenly, as if he had been held on a strain. He looked out over the sea, but he saw nothing.

"There are one or two books in the corner," said Morel. "I've done with 'em."

At about four o'clock he went.

"I shall see you both later," he said as he shook hands.

"I suppose so," said Dawes. "An' perhaps—one day—I s'll be able to pay you back the money as—"

"I shall come for it, you'll see," laughed Paul. "I s'll be on the rocks before I'm very much older."

"Ay—well—" said Dawes.

"Goodbye!" he said to Clara.

"Goodbye," she said, giving him her hand. Then she glanced at him for the last time, dumb, and humble.

He was gone. Dawes and his wife sat down again.

"It's a nasty day for travelling," said the man.

"Yes," she answered.

They talked in a desultory fasion until it grew dark. The landlady brought in the tea. Dawes drew up his chair to the table without being invited, like a husband. Then he sat humbly waiting for his cup. She served him as she would, like a wife, not consulting his wish.

After tea, as it drew near to six o'clock, he went to the window. All was dark outside. The sea was roaring.

"It's raining yet," he said.

"Is it!" she answered.

"You won't go tonight, shall you?" he said, hesitating.

She did not answer. He waited.

"I shouldn't go in this rain," he said.

"Do you *want* me to stay?" she asked.

His hand as he held the dark curtain, trembled.

"Yes," he said.

He remained with his back to her. She rose and went slowly to him. He let go the curtain, turned hesitating towards her. She stood with her hands behind her back, looking up at him in a heavy, inscrutable fashion.

"Do you want me, Baxter?" she asked.

His voice was hoarse as he answered:

"Do you want to come back to me?"

She made a moaning noise, lifted her arms, and put them round

452

his neck, drawing him to her. He hid his face on her shoulder, holding her clasped.

"Take me back!" she whispered, ecstatic. "Take me back, take me back!" And she put her fingers through his fine, thin dark hair, as if she were only semi-conscious. He tightened his grasp on her.

"Do you want me again?" he murmured, broken.

CHAPTER XV

Derelict

Clara went with her husband to Sheffield, and Paul scarcely saw her again. Walter Morel seemed to have let all the trouble go over him, and there he was, crawling about on the mud of it, just the same. There was scarcely any bond between father and son, save that each felt he must not let the other go in any actual want. As there was no one to keep the home on, and as they could neither of them bear the emptiness of the house, Paul took lodgings in Nottingham, and Morel went to live with a friendly family in Bestwood.

Everything seemed to have gone smash for the young man. He could not paint. The picture he finished on the day of his mother's death—one that satisfied him—was the last thing he did. At work, there was no Clara. When he came home, he could not take up his brushes again. There was nothing left.

So he was always in the town at one place or another, drinking, knocking about with the men he knew. It really wearied him. He talked to barmaids, to almost any woman, but there was that dark, strained look in his eyes, as if he were hunting something.

Everything seemed so different, so unreal. There seemed no reason why people should go along the street, and houses pile up in the daylight. There seemed no reason why these things should occupy the space, instead of leaving it empty. His friends talked to him: he heard the sounds, and he answered. But why there should be the noise of speech he could not understand.

He was most himself when he was alone, or working hard and mechanically at the factory. In the latter case there was pure forgetfulness, when he lapsed from consciousness. But it had to come to an end. It hurt him so, that things had lost their reality. The first snowdrops came. He saw the tiny drop-pearls among the grey. They would have given him the liveliest emotion at one time. Now, they were there, but they did not seem to mean anything. In a few moments they would cease to occupy that place, and just the space would be where they had been. Tall, brilliant tram-cars ran along the street at night. It seemed almost a wonder they should trouble to rustle backwards and forwards. 'Why trouble to go tilting down to Trent Bridges?' he asked of the big trams. It seemed they just as well might *not* be, as be.

The realest thing was the thick darkness at night. That seemed to him whole and comprehensible and restful. He could leave himself to it. Suddenly a piece of paper started near his feet and blew along down the pavement. He stood still, rigid, with clenched fists, a flame of agony going over him. And he saw again the sick room, his mother, her eyes. Unconsciously he had been with her, in her company. The swift hop of the paper reminded him she was gone. But he had been with her. He wanted everything to stand still, so he could be with her again.

The days passed, the weeks. But everything seemed to have fused, gone into a conglomerated mass. He could not tell one day from another, one week from another, hardly one place from another. Nothing was distinct or distinguishable. Often, he lost himself for an hour at a time, could not remember what he had done.

One evening he came home late to his lodging. The fire was burning low, everybody was in bed. He threw on some more coal, glanced at the table and decided he wanted no supper. Then he sat down in the arm-chair. It was perfectly still. He did not know anything, yet he saw, far away, the dim smoke wavering up the chimney. Presently two mice came out, cautiously, nibbling the fallen crumbs. He watched them as it were from a long way off. The church clock struck two. Far away he could hear the sharp clinking of the trucks on the railway. No, it was not they that were far away. They were there in their places. But where was he himself.

The time passed. The two mice, careering wildly, scampered cheekily over his slippers. He had not moved a muscle. He did not want to move. He was not thinking of anything. It was easier so. There was no wrench of knowing anything. Then, from time to time, some other consciousness working mechanically flashed into sharp phrases.

"What am I doing?"

And out of the semi-intoxicated trance came the answer:

"Destroying myself."

Then a dull, live feeling, gone in an instant, told him that it was wrong. After a while, suddenly, came the question:

"Why wrong?"

Again there was no answer, but a stroke of hot stubbornness inside his chest resisted his own annihilation.

There was a sound of a heavy cart clanking down the road. Suddenly, the electric light went out, there was a bruising thud in the penny-in-the-slot meter. He did not stir, sat gazing in front of him. Only, the mice had scuttled and the fire glowed red in the dark room.

Then, quite mechanically and more distinctly, the conversation began again inside him.

"She's dead—what was it all for—her struggle—?"

That was his despair wanting to go after her.

"You're alive."

"She's not."

"She is—in you."

Suddenly he felt tired with the burden of it.

"You've got to keep alive for her sake," said his will in him.

Something felt sulky, as if it would not rouse.

"You've got to carry forward her living, and what she had done, go on with it—."

But he did not want to. He wanted to give up.

"But you can go on with your painting," said the will in him. "Or else you can beget children.—They both carry on her effort—"

"Painting is not living."

"Then live."

"Marry whom?" came the sulky question.

"As best you can."

"Miriam."

But he did not trust that.

He rose suddenly, went straight to bed. When he got inside his bedroom, and closed the door, he stood with clenched fists.

"Mater, my dear—" he began, with the whole force of his soul. Then he stopped. He would not say it. He would not admit that he wanted to die, to have done. He would not own that life had beaten him, or that death had beaten him.

Going straight to bed, he slept at once, abandoning himself to the sleep.

So the weeks went on. Always alone, his soul oscillated, first on the side of death, then on the side of life, doggedly. The real agony was that he had nowhere to go, nothing to do, nothing to say, and *was* nothing himself. Sometimes he ran down the streets as if he were mad. Sometimes he was mad: things weren't there, things were there. It made him pant. Sometimes he stood before the bar of the public house where he had called for a drink. Everything suddenly stood back away from him. He saw the face of the barmaid, the gabbling drinkers, his own glass on the slopped, mahogany board, in the distance. There was something between him and them. He could not get into touch. He did not want them, he did not want his drink. Turning abruptly, he went out. On the threshold he stood and looked at the lighted street. But he was not of it or in it. Something separated him. Everything went on there below those lamps, shut away from him. He could not get at them. He felt he couldn't touch the lampposts, not if he reached. Where could he go? There was nowhere to go, neither back into the inn, or forward anywhere. He felt stifled. There was nowhere for him. The stress grew inside him, he felt he should smash.

"I mustn't," he said, and turning blindly, he went in and drank. Sometimes the drink did him good, sometimes it made him worse. He ran down the road. Forever restless, he went here, there, everywhere. He determined to work. But when he had made six strokes, he loathed the pencil violently, got up and went away, hurried off to a club where he could play cards or billiards, to a place where he could flirt with a barmaid who was no more to him than the brass pump-handle she drew.

He was very thin and lantern-jawed. He dared not meet his own eyes in the mirror, he never looked at himself. He wanted to get away from himself, but there was nothing to get hold of. In despair he thought of Miriam. Perhaps—perhaps—?

Then, happening to go into the Unitarian Church one Sunday evening, when they stood up to sing the second hymn, he saw her before him. The light glistened on her lower lip as she sang. She looked as if she had got something, at any rate: some hope in heaven, if not in earth. Her comfort and her life seemed in the after-world. A warm, strong feeling for her came up. She seemed to yearn, as she sang, for the mystery and comfort. He put his hope in her. He longed for the sermon to be over, to speak to her.

The throng carried her out just before him. He could nearly touch her. She did not know he was there. He saw the brown, humble nape of her neck under its black curls. He would leave himself to her. She was better and bigger than he. He would depend on her.

She went wandering, in her blind way, through the little throngs of people outside the church. She always looked so lost and out of place among people. He went forward and put his hand on her arm. She started violently. Her great brown eyes dilated in fear, then went questioning at the sight of him. He shrank slightly from her.

"I didn't know—" she faltered.

"Nor I," he said.

He looked away. His sudden, flaring hope sank again.

"What are you doing in town?" he asked.

"I'm staying at Cousin Anne's."

"Ha! For long?"

"No—only till tomorrow."

"Must you go straight home?"

She looked at him, then hid her face under her hat-brim.

"No," she said. "No! It's not necessary."

He turned away and she went with him. They threaded through the throng of church people. The organ was still sounding in St Mary's. Dark figures came through the lighted doors, people were coming down the steps. The large, coloured windows glowed up in the night. The church was like a great lantern suspended.—They went down Hollow Stone, and he took the car for the Bridges.

"You will just have supper with me," he said, "then I'll bring you back."

"Very well," she replied, low and husky.

They scarcely spoke while they were on the car. The Trent ran dark and full under the bridge. Away towards Colwick, all was black night. He lived down Holme Road, on the naked edge of the town, facing across the river meadows towards Sneinton Hermitage and the steep scarp of Colwick wood. The floods were out. The silent water and the darkness spread away on their left. Almost afraid, they hurried along by the houses.

Supper was laid. He swung the curtain over the window. There was a bowl of freesias and scarlet anemones on the table. She bent to them. Still touching them with her finger-tips, she looked up at him, saying:

"Aren't they beautiful?"

"Yes," he said. "What will you drink—coffee?"

"I should like it," she said.

"Then excuse me a moment."

He went out to the kitchen.

Miriam took off her things and looked round. It was a bare, severe room. Her photo, Clara's, Annie's were on the wall. She looked on the drawing board to see what he was doing. There were only a few meaningless lines. She looked to see what books he was reading. Evidently just an ordinary novel. The letters in the rack she saw were from Annie, Arthur, and from some man or other she did not know. Everything he had touched, everything that was in the least personal to him, she examined with lingering absorption. He had been gone from her for so long, she wanted to re-discover him, his position, what he was now. But there was not much in the room to help her. It only made her feel rather sad, it was so hard and comfortless.

She was curiously examining a sketch-book when he returned with the coffee.

"There's nothing new in it," he said; "and nothing very interesting."

He put down the tray and went to look over her shoulder. She turned the pages slowly, intent on examining everything.

"Hm!" he said, as she paused at a sketch. "I'd forgotten that! It's not bad, is it."

"No!" she said. "I don't quite understand it."

He took the book from her and went through it. Again he made a curious sound of surprise and pleasure.

"There's some not bad stuff in there," he said.

"Not at all bad," she answered gravely.

He felt again her interest in his work. Or was it for himself. Why was she always most interested in him as he appeared in his work?

They sat down to supper.

"By the way," he said, "didn't I hear something about your earning your own living?"

"Yes," she replied, bowing her dark head over her cup.

"And what of it?"

"I'm merely going to the farming college at Broughton for three months—and I shall probably be kept on as a teacher there."

"I say—that sounds all right for you! You always wanted to be independent."

"Yes."

"Why didn't you tell me?"

"I only knew last week."

"But I heard a month ago," he said.

"Yes—but nothing was settled then."

"I should have thought," he said, "you'd have told me you were trying."

She ate her food in the deliberate, constrained way, almost as if she recoiled a little from doing anything so publicly, that he knew so well.

"I suppose you're glad," he said.

"Very glad."

"Yes—it will be something."

He was rather disappointed.

"I think it will be a great deal," she said, almost haughtily, resentfully.

He laughed shortly.

"Why do you think it won't?" she asked.

"Oh, I don't think it won't be a great deal. Only you'll find earning your own living isn't everything."

"No," she said, swallowing with difficulty. "I don't suppose it is—"

"I suppose work *can* be nearly everything to a man," he said, "though it isn't to me. But a woman only works with a part of herself. The real and vital part is covered up."

"But a man can give *all* himself to a work?" she asked.

"Yes, practically."

"And a woman, only the unimportant part of herself?"

"That's it."

She looked up at him, and her eyes dilated with anger.

"Then," she said, "if it's true—it's a great shame."

"It is.—But I don't know everything," he answered.

After supper they drew up to the fire. He swung her a chair facing him, and they sat down. She was wearing a dress of dark claret colour, that suited her dark complexion and her large features. Still the curls were fine and free, but her face was much older, the brown throat much thinner. She seemed old to him, older than Clara. Her bloom of youth had quickly gone. A sort of stiffness, almost of woodenness had come upon her. She meditated a little while, then looked at him.

"And how are things with you?" she asked.

"About all right," he answered.

She looked at him, waiting.

"Nay," she said, very low.

Her brown, nervous hands were clasped over her knee. They had still the lack of confidence or repose, the almost hysterical look. He winced as he saw them. Then he laughed, mirthlessly. She put her finger between her lips. His slim, black, tortured body lay quite still in the chair. She suddenly took her finger from her mouth and looked at him.

"And you have broken off with Clara?"

"Yes."

His body lay like an abandoned thing, strewn in the chair.

"You know," she said, "I think we ought to be married."

He opened his eyes, for the first time since many months, and attended to her with respect.

"Why?" he said.

"See," she said, "how you waste yourself! You might be ill, you might die, and I never know, be no more then than if I had never known you."

"And if we married?" he asked.

"At any rate I could prevent you wasting yourself—and being a prey to other women—like—like Clara."

"A prey?" he repeated, smiling.

She bowed her head in silence. He lay feeling his despair come up again.

"I'm not sure," he said slowly, "that marriage would be much good."

"I only think of you," she replied.

"I know you do.—But—you love me so much, you want to put me in your pocket. And I should die there smothered."

She bent her head, put her finger between her lips, while the bitterness surged up in her heart.

"And what will you do otherwise?" she asked.

"I don't know—go on, I suppose. Perhaps I shall soon go abroad."

The despairing doggedness in his tone made her go on her knees on the rug before the fire, very near to him. There she crouched as if she were crushed by something, and could not raise her head. His hands lay quite inert on the arms of his chair. She was aware of them. She felt that now he lay at her mercy. If she could rise, take him, put her arms round him, and say 'You are mine,' then he would leave himself to her. But dare she? She could easily sacrifice herself. But dare she assert herself? She was aware of his dark-clothed, slender body, that seemed one stroke of life, sprawled in the chair close to her. But no, she dared not put her arms round it, take it up, and say 'It is mine, this body. Leave it to me!' And she wanted to. It called to all her woman's instinct. But she crouched, and dared not. She was afraid he would not let her. She was afraid it was too much. It lay there, his body, abandoned. She knew she ought to take it up, and claim it, and claim every right to it. But—could she do it? Her impotence before him, before the strong demand of some unknown thing in him, was her extremity. Her hands fluttered, she half lifted her head. Her eyes, shuddering, appealing, gone almost distracted, pleaded to him suddenly. His heart caught with pity. He took her hands, drew her to him, and comforted her.

"Will you have me, to marry me?" he said very low.

Oh, why did not he take her! Her very soul belonged to him. Why would not he take what was his! She had borne so long the cruelty of belonging to him and not being claimed by him. Now he was straining her again. It was too much for her. She drew back her head, held his face between her hands, and looked him in the eyes. No, he was hard. He wanted something else. She pleaded to him with all her love, not to make it *her* choice. She could not cope with it, with him, she knew not with what. But it strained her till she felt she would break.

"Do you want it?" she asked, very gravely.

"Not much," he replied with pain.

She turned her face aside. Then, raising herself with dignity, she took his head to her bosom, and rocked him softly. She was not to have him then! So, she could comfort him. She put her fingers through his hair. For her, the anguished sweetness of self-sacrifice! For him, the hate and misery of another failure. He could not bear it, that breast which was warm and which cradled him without taking the burden of him. So much he wanted to rest on her, that the feint of rest only tortured him. He drew away.

"And without marriage we can do nothing?" he asked.

His mouth was lifted from his teeth with pain. She put her little finger between her lips.

"No," she said, low and like the toll of a bell. "No, I think not."

It was the end then between them. She could not take him and relieve him of the responsibility of himself. She could only sacrifice herself to him, sacrifice herself every day, gladly. And that he did not want. He wanted her to hold him and say, with joy and authority:

"Stop now all this restlessness and beating against death. You are mine for a mate." She had not the strength. Or was it a mate she wanted, or did she want a Christ in him?

He felt, in leaving her, he was defrauding her of life. But he knew that in staying, stifling the inner, desperate man, he was denying his own life. And he did not hope to give life to her by denying his own.

She sat very quiet. He lit a cigarette. The smoke went up from it wavering. He was thinking of his mother, and had forgotten Miriam. She suddenly looked at him. Her bitterness came surging up. Her sacrifice then was useless! He lay there aloof, careless about her. Suddenly she saw again his lack of religion, his restless instability. He would destroy himself like a perverse child. Well then, he would!

"I think I must go," she said softly.

By her tone he knew she was despising him. He rose quietly.

"I'll come along with you," he answered.

She stood before the mirror pinning on her hat. How bitter, how unutterably bitter it made her that he rejected her sacrifice. Life ahead looked dead, as if the glow were gone out. She bowed her face over the flowers, the freesias so sweet and spring-like, the scarlet anemones flaunting over the table. It was like him to have those flowers.

He moved about the room with a certain sureness of touch, swift, and relentless, and quiet. She knew she could not cope with him. He would escape like a weasel out of her hands. Yet without him her life would trail on lifeless. Brooding, she touched the flowers.

"Have them!" he said, and he took them out of the jar, dripping as they were, went quickly into the kitchen. She waited for him, took the flowers, and they went out together, he talking, she feeling dead.

She was going from him now. In her misery she leaned against him as they sat on the car. He was unresponsive. Where would he go, what would be the end of him? She could not bear it, the vacant feeling where he should be. He was so foolish, so wasteful, never at peace with himself. And now where would he go? And what did he care that he wasted her? He had no religion—it was all for the moment's attraction that he cared, nothing else, nothing deeper. Well, she would wait and see how it turned out with him. When he had had enough, he would give in, and come to her.

He shook hands and left her at the door of her cousin's house. When he turned away, he felt the last hold for him had gone. The town, as he sat upon the car, stretched away, over the bay of railway, a level fume of lights. Beyond the town the country, little smouldering spots for more towns—the sea—the night—on and on! And he had no place in it. Whatever spot he stood on, there he stood alone. From his breast, from his mouth sprang the endless space— and it was there behind him, everywhere. The people hurrying along the streets offered no obstruction to the void in which he found himself. They were small shadows whose footsteps and voices could be heard, but in each of them, the same night, the same silence. He got off the car. In the country all was dead still. Little stars shone high up, little stars spread far away in the floodwaters, a firmament below. Everywhere the vastness and terror of the immense night which is roused and stirred for a brief while by the day, but which returns, and will remain at last eternal, holding everything in its silence and its living gloom. There was no Time, only Space. Who could say his mother had lived and did not live? She had been in one place, and was in another, that was all. And his soul could not leave her, wherever she was. Now she was gone abroad into the night, and he was with her still. They were together. But yet there was his body, his chest that leaned against the stile, his hands on the wooden bar. They seemed something. Where was he?—one tiny upright speck of flesh, less than an ear of wheat lost in the field. He could not bear it. On every side the immense dark silence seemed pressing him, so tiny a speck, into extinction, and yet, almost nothing, he could not be extinct. Night, in which everything was lost, went reaching out, beyond stars and sun. Stars and sun, a few bright grains, went spinning round for terror and holding each other in embrace, there in a darkness that outpassed them all and left them tiny and daunted. So much, and himself, infinitesimal, at the core a nothingness, and yet not nothing.

"Mother!" he whimpered, "mother!"

She was the only thing that held him up, himself, amid all this. And she was gone, intermingled herself! He wanted her to touch him, have him alongside with her.

But no, he would not give in. Turning sharply, he walked towards the city's gold phosphorescence. His fists were shut, his mouth set fast. He would not take that direction, to the darkness, to follow her. He walked towards the faintly humming, glowing town, quickly.

Appendix

Foreword to *Sons and Lovers*

John, the beloved disciple, says, 'The Word was made Flesh.' But why should he turn things round? The women simply go on bearing talkative sons, as an answer. 'The Flesh was made Word.'

For what was Christ? He was Word, or he became Word. What remains of him? Word! No flesh remains on earth, from Christ; perhaps some carpentry he shaped with his hands retains somewhere his flesh-print; and then his word, like his carpentry, just the object that his flesh produced, is the rest. He is Word. And the Father was Flesh. For even if it were by the Holy Ghost his spirit were begotten, yet flesh cometh only out of flesh. So the Holy Ghost must either have been, or have borne from the Father, at least one grain of flesh. The Father was Flesh—and the Son, who in himself was finite and had form, became Word. For form is the Uttered Word, and the Son is the Flesh as it utters the Word, but the unutterable Flesh is the Father.

And the Word is not spoken by the Father, who is Flesh, forever unquestioned and unanswerable, but by the Son. Adam was the first Christ: not the Word made Flesh, but the Flesh made Word. Out of the Flesh cometh the Word, and the Word is finite, as a piece of carpentry, and hath an end. But the Flesh is infinite and has no end. Out of the Flesh cometh the Word, which blossoms for a moment and is no more. Out of the Flesh hath come every Word, and in the Flesh lies every Word that will be uttered. The Father is the Flesh, the eternal and unquestionable, the law-giver but not the law; whereas the Son is the mouth. And each law is a fabric that must crumble away, and the Word is a graven image that is worn down, and forsaken like the Sphinx in the desert.

We are the Word, we are not the Flesh. The Flesh is beyond us. And when we love our neighbour as ourself, we love that word, our neighbour, and not that flesh. For that Flesh is not our neighbour, it is the Father, which is in Heaven, and forever beyond our knowledge. We are the Word, we know the Word, and the Word alone is ours. When we say 'I', we mean 'The Word I am.' This flesh I am is beyond me.

So that if we love our neighbour, we love that Word, our neighbour, and we hate that Lie, our neighbour, which is a deformity. With that Flesh, our neighbour, We, the Word-Utterer, have nothing to do. For the Son is not greater than the Father. And if we love and subserve that Flesh, our neighbour, which is the Father, it is only by denying and desecrating the Father in ourselves. For the Flesh is the Almighty. The Flesh will feel no pain that is not upon itself, and will know no hurt but its own destruction. But no man can destroy the Almighty, yet he can deny Him. And pain is a denial of the Father. If then we feel the pain and suffering of our neighbour's flesh, we are putting destruction upon our own flesh, which is to deny and make wrathful the Father. Which we have done. For in loving our neighbour, the Flesh, as ourself, we have said 'There is no Father, there is only the Word.' For it is the Word hath charity, not the Flesh. And it is the Word that answereth the cry of the Word. But if the Word, hearing a cry, shall say 'My flesh is destroyed, the bone melteth away', that is to blaspheme the Father. For the Word is but fabric builded of the Flesh. And when the fabric is finished, then shall the Flesh enjoy it in its hour.

But we have said 'Within this fabric of the word the Flesh is held.' And so, the Son has usurped the Father. And so, the Father, which is the Flesh, withdraws from us, and the Word stands in ruins, as Nineveh and Egypt are dead words on the plains, whence the Flesh has withdrawn itself. For the lesser cannot contain the greater, nor the son contain the Father, but he is of the Father.

And it is upon the head of that nation that shall deny the Father. For the Flesh will depart from that collective Word, the nation, and that great nation shall remain as a Word in ruin, its own monument.

For who shall say, 'No child shall be born of me and my wife. I, the Word, have said it'? And who shall say—'That woman whom my Flesh, in its unquestionable sincerity, cleaveth toward, shall not come unto my flesh. But my Word shall come unto her. I, the Word, have said it'? That is to usurp the flesh of my neighbour, and hold governance over it by the word. And who shall say 'That woman shall be Flesh of my Flesh. I, the Word, have said it'? For either the woman is Flesh of my Flesh, or she is not, and the Word altereth nothing, but can only submit or deny.

And when we burned the heretic at the stake, then did we love that Word, our neighbour, and hate that Lie, the heretic. But we did also deny the Father, and say 'There is only Word.' And when we suffer in our flesh the pangs of those that hunger, then we do deny the Flesh, and say, it is not. For the Flesh suffereth not from the hunger of the neighbour, but only from its own hunger. But the Word loveth its neighbour, and shall answer to the cry of the Word,

'It is just, what thou asketh.' For the Word hath neither passion nor pain, but lives and moves in equity. It has charity, which we call love. But only the Flesh has love, for that is the Father, and in love he begets us all, of love are we begotten. But it was spoken 'They shall be one flesh.' Thus did the Word usurp the Father, saying 'I unite you one flesh.' Whereas the Word can but confirm. For the twain are one flesh, whether the Word speak or not. And if they be not one twain, then the Word can never make them so, for the Flesh is not contained in the Word, but the Word in the Flesh. But if a man shall say 'This woman is flesh of my flesh,' let him see to it that he be not blaspheming the Father. For the woman is not flesh of his flesh, by the bidding of the Word; but it is of the Father. And if he take a woman, saying in the arrogance of the Word 'The flesh of that woman is goodly,' then he has said 'The flesh of that woman is goodly as a servant unto the Word, which is me,' and so hath blasphemed the Father, by which he has his being, and she hath her being. And the Flesh shall forsake these two, they shall be fabric of Word. And their race shall perish.

But if in my passion I slay my neighbour, it is no sin of mine, but it is his sin, for he should not have permitted me. But if my Word shall decide and decree that my neighbour die, then that is sin, for the Word destroyeth the Flesh, the son blasphemeth the Father. And yet, if a man hath denied his Flesh, saying 'I, the Word, have dominion over the flesh of my neighbour,' then shall the Flesh, his neighbour, slay him in self defence. For a man may hire my Word, which is the Utterance of my flesh, which is my work. But my Flesh is the Father, which is before the Son.

And so it was written: "The Word was made Flesh," then, as corollary, "And of the Flesh was made Flesh-of-the-Flesh, Woman." This is again backward, and because the Son, struggling to utter the Word, took for his God the accomplishment of his work, the Uttered Word. Out of his flesh the word had to come, and the flesh was difficult and unfathomed, so it was called the servant. And the servant of the servant was woman. So the Son arranged it, because he took for his God his own work when it should be Accomplished: as if a carpenter called the chair he struggled with but had not yet made, God. But the Chair is not a God, it is only a rigid image. So is The Word a rigid image, parallel of the chair. And so the end having been chosen for the beginning, the whole chronology is upside-down: the Word created Man, and Man lay down and gave birth to Woman. Whereas we know the Woman lay in travail, and gave birth to Man, who in his hour uttered his word.

It is as if a bit of apple-blossom stood for God in his Wonder, the apple was the Son, as being something more gross but still wonderful, while the pip that comes out of the apple, like Adam's rib, is the mere secondary product, that is spat out, and which, if it falls to the ground, just happens to start the process of apple-trees going again. But the little pip that one spits out has in it all the blossom and apples, as well as all the tree, the leaves, the perfume, the drops of gum, and heaven knows what else that we never see, contained by miracle in its bit of white flesh: and the tree, the leaves, the flowers themselves, and the apple are only amplifications of this little seed, spent: which never has amplified itself enough, but can go on to other than just five-petalled flowers and little brown apples, if we did but know.

So we take the seed as the starting point in this cycle. The woman is the Flesh. She produces all the rest of the flesh, including the intermediary pieces called man—and these curious pieces called man are like stamens that can turn into exquisite coloured petals. That is, they can beat out the stuff of their life thin, thin, thin, till it is a pink or a purple petal, or a thought, or a Word. And when it is so beaten out, that it ceases to be begetting stuff, of the Father, but is spread much wider, expanded and showy: then we say, 'This is the Utmost!'—as everybody will agree that a rose is only a rose because of the petals, and that the rose is the utmost of all that flow of life, called 'Rose.' But what is really 'Rose' is only in that quivering, shimmering flesh of flesh, which is the same, unchanged for ever, a constant stream, called if you like Protoplasm, the eternal, the unquestioned, the infinite of the 'Rose', the Flesh, the Father—which were more properly, the Mother.

So there is the Father—which should be called Mother—then the Son, who is the Utterer, and then the Word. And the Word is that of the Father which, through the Son, is tossed away. It is that part of the Flesh in the Son which is capable of spreading out thin and fine, losing its concentration and completeness, ceasing to be a begetter, and becoming only a vision, a flutter of petals, God rippling through the Son till He breaks in a laugh, called a blossom, that shines and is gone. This vision itself, the flutter of petals, the rose, the Father through the Son wasting himself in a moment of consciousness, consciousness of His own infinitude and gloriousness, a Rose, a Clapping of the Hands, a Spark of Joy thrown off from the Fire to die ruddy in mid-darkness, a Snip of Flame, the Holy Ghost, the Revelation. And so, the eternal Trinity.

———

And God the Father, the Inscrutable, the Unknowable, we know in the Flesh, in Woman. She is the door for our in-going and our out-coming. In her we go back to the Father: but like the witnesses of the Transfiguration, blind and unconscious.

Yea, like bees in and out of a hive, we come backwards and forwards to our woman. And the Flowers of the World are Words, are Utterance—"Uttering glad leaves," Whitman said. And we are bees that go between, from the flowers home to the hive and the Queen; for she lies at the centre of the hive, and stands in the way of bees for God the Father, the Almighty, the Unknowable, the Creator. In her all things are born, both words and bees. She is the quick of all the change, the labour, the production.

And the bee, who is a Son, comes home to his Queen as to the Father, in service and humility, for suggestion, and renewal, and identification which is the height of his glory, for begetting. And again the bee goes forth to attend the flowers, the Word, in his pride and masterfulness—his new strength and new wisdom. And as he comes and goes, so shall man for ever come and go: go to his work, his Uttering, wherein he is masterful and proud; come home to his woman, through whom is God the Father, and who is in herself, whether she will have it or not, God the Father, before whom the man in his hour is full of reverence, and in whom he is glorified and hath the root of his pride.

But not only does he come and go: it is demanded of him that he come and go. It is the systole and diastole of the Heart, that shall be. The bee comes home to the hive, and the hive expels him to attend the flowers. The hive draws home the bee, the bee leaps off the threshold of the hive, with strength, and is gone. He carries home to the hive his essence of flowers, his joy in the Word he has uttered; he flies forth again from the hive, carrying to the flowers the strength and vigour of his scrambling body, which is God Almighty in him. So he fetches and carries, carries and fetches.

So the man comes home to woman and to God, so God the

Father receives his Son again, a man of the undying flesh; and so the man goes forth from the house of his woman, so God expels him forth to waste himself in utterance, in work, which is only God the Father realising himself in a moment of forgetfulness. Thus the eternal working. And it is joy enough to see it, without asking why. For it is as if the Father took delight in seeing himself for a moment unworking, for a moment wasting himself that he might know himself. For every petalled flower, which alone is a Flower, is a waste of productiveness. It is a moment of joy, of saying 'I am I.' And every table or chair a man makes is a selfsame waste of his life, a fixing into stiffness and deadness of a moment of himself, for the sake of the glad cry 'This is I—I am I!' And this glad cry when we know, is the Holy Ghost the Comforter.

So, God Eternal, the Father, continues, doing we know not what, nor why: we only know He is. And again and again comes the exclamation of joy, or of pain which is joy—like Galileo and Shakspere and Darwin—which announces 'I am I.'

And in the woman is the eternal continuance, and from the man, in the human race, comes the exclamation of joy and astonishment at new self-revelation, revelation of that which is Woman to a man.

Now every woman, according to her kind, demands that a man shall come home to her with joy and weariness of the work he has done during the day: that he shall then while he is with her, be re-born of her; that in the morning he shall go forth with his new strength.

But if the man does not come home to a woman, leaving her to take account of him, but is a stranger to her; if when he enters her house, he does not become simply her man of flesh, entered into her house as if it were her greater body, to be warmed, and restored, and nourished, from the store the day has given her, then she shall expel him from her house, as a drone. It is as inevitable as the working of the bees, as that a stick shall go down stream.

For in the flesh of the woman does God enact Himself. And out of the flesh of the woman does He demand: 'Carry this of Me forth to utterance.' And if the man deny, or be too weak, then shall the woman find another man, of greater strength. And if, because of the Word, which is the Law, she do not find another man, nor he another woman, then shall they both be destroyed. For he, to get that rest, and warmth, and nourishment which he should have had from her, his woman, must consume his own flesh, and so destroy himself: either with wine, or other kindling.—And she, either her surplus shall wear away her flesh, in sickness, or in lighting up and illuminating old dead Words, or she shall spend it in fighting with her man to make him take her, or she shall turn to her son, and say, 'Be you my Go-between.'

But the man who is the go-between from Woman to Production is the lover of that woman. And if that Woman be his mother, then is he her lover in part only: he carries for her, but is never received unto her for his confirmation and renewal, and so wastes himself away in the flesh. The old son-lover was Œdipus. The name of the new one is legion. And if a son-lover take a wife, then is she not his wife, she is only his bed. And his life will be torn in twain, and his wife in her despair shall hope for sons, that she may have her lover in her hour.

D. H. Lawrence

Gargnano. Jan. 1913.

EASTWOOD
and surrounding villages, c. 1900

Pinxton
Station
Pinxton
Station

Mansfield

Selston

Annesley

Hall

Bagthorpe

Annesley
Park

Underwood

Crossley
Banks

Selston Colliery

Pond

New Brinsley

Brook

Haggs
Farm

Felley Mill

River Erewash

Willey
Spring

Felley
Mill Farm

Yewtree Inn

Moor Green
Reservoir

Ford

Misk Hill

High
Park
Wood

Beauvale
Priory

Robin Hood's
Well

Hucknall
Torkard

Willeywood
Farm

Oakes
Farm

Brinsley

Brinsley Colliery

High Park
Colliery

Willey Lane

New Inn

Lower Pond

Coneygrey
Farm

Barber Walker & Co.

Watnall
Colliery

Plumptre
Colliery

Beaggarlee
Works

Bunker's Hill
Junction

Moor
Green
Colliery

Private Railway

Langley
Mill

Beauvale Brook

Newthorpe
Grange

MoorGreen

Eastwood and
Langley Mill Station

Board
School

Castle
Greasley

Station

The
Breach

Church

Eastwood

Beauvale

Castle
Farm

Hill
Top

New London
Colliery

Watnall
Chaworth

New Eastwood

Reckoning
House

Watnall
Cantelupe

Erewash Valley Line

Windmill

Watnall
Station

Bulwell

Shipley Gate
Station

River Erewash

Chalk
Hill

Stn

Station

Midland Railway

Viaduct

Kimberley

Nuthall

N

Cotmanhay

Great Northern Railway

Cinderhill

2 miles

1

0
1   2   3 km

EASTWOOD c. 1900

Cocker Lane
Colliery Railway
Engine Lane
Thorn Tree Inn
Nether Green
Newthorpe Grange
Meadow
Beauvale Brook
Greenhills Road
Cricket Ground
Pavilion
Sheep-bridge
Mansfield Road
B.W.& Co Offices and Grounds
Palmerston Arms
(No. 28 – Lawrence Family Home)
The Breach
Garden
Road
Whitecross
The Squares
No. 3 – Lawrence Family Home
Walker St
Lynn Croft
Croft Road
Board School
Langley Mill Lane
Derby Rd.
Three Tuns Inn
Beauvale
St Mary's Church
Nottingham Road
Three Tuns Road
(No. 97 – Lawrence Family Home)
Ivy Lane
Eastwood
Hill Top
Church Street
Cemetery
New Eastwood
Nottingham Canal
G.N.R. Pinxton Branch
Erewash Canal
Newmanleys Mill
Weir
Shipley Lock
Shipley Boat Inn
Shipley Gate Station
Footbridge
R. Erewash

0   1   2 miles
0   1   2   3 km
======= Footpaths

THE SQUARES

Mansfield Road
Princes Street
Primitive Methodist Chapel
Mechanics' Hall
Miners' Arms
Victoria Street
Scargill Street
Hospital Ground
Congregational Chapel
Statutes Ground
Market Place
Nottingham Road
Wellington Street
Derby Road
Church Road
Lord Nelson
Co-op Reading Room

Explanatory Notes

5 To Edward Garnett DHL suggested dedicating the novel to Garnett on 19 November 1912 before he knew Garnett would cut it. This dedication appeared in the first edition.

9:8 Charles II Charles II reigned 1660–85.

9:12 stockingers Poor weavers who produced stockings in their cottages.

9:13 Bestwood DHL's fictional name for Eastwood. Maps of this part of Nottinghamshire appear before the Explanatory Notes. DHL used actual place-names in the Nottingham area but gave one or sometimes two fictional names to locations in and around Eastwood, as follows (actual names in brackets): Aldersley (Annesley), Beggarlee pit (Brinsley pit), Boathouse Station (Shipley Gate Station), Bottoms (Breach), Bretty (Brinsley), Bunker's Hill pit (Plumptre pit), Chalk Knob (Chalk Hill), Greenhill Lane (Greenhills Road), Keston (Kimberley), Lethley Bridge (Langley Mill), Minton (Moor Green), Nethermere (Moor Green Reservoir), Nuttall pit (Watnall pit), Scargill Street (Walker Street), Selby (Selston), Shepstone (Shipley), Spinney Park pit (High Park pit), Strelley Mill (Felley Mill), Swineshead Farm (probably Swinehouse Farm), Tinder Hill (Cinder Hill), Willey Farm (Haggs Farm), Willey Water (Moor Green Reservoir), Woodlington (perhaps Wood Linkin).

9:17 Carston, Waite and Co. Based on the Erewash valley mining firm, Barber, Walker & Co.

10:28 Mrs Morel The novel's Morel family consists of Mrs Gertrude Morel, her husband Walter (11:1) and their children William (11:5), Annie (11:6), Paul (42:40) and Arthur (64:11). They are a radically adapted recreation of Lawrence's family: his mother, Lydia Lawrence, née Beardsall (1851 to 9 December 1910, see 437:6); his father, John Arthur Lawrence (1846–1924); and their five children: George Arthur (b. 26 September 1876), William Ernest (b. 22 July 1878), Emily Una (b. 21 March 1882), David Herbert Richards (b. 11 September 1885) and Lettice Ada (b. 16 June 1887). In the novel DHL based the eldest son, William, on William Ernest (always known as Ernest); Annie on both Emily and Ada; Paul on the artistic side of his own character; and Arthur on George, Ada and himself.

11:39 horses Merry-go-rounds.

13:23 full as he could carry Full of beer, drunk.

15:26 **independents ... Colonel Hutchinson** [15:27]   Congregationalists
... Colonel John Hutchinson (1615–64), an Independent, was Governor
of Nottingham Castle during the Civil War (1642–9).

15:28 **grandfather ... George Coppard** [15:30] **... her mother**
[15:33]   Both Lydia Lawrence's grandfathers were lace-makers. George
Coppard is based on Lydia Lawrence's father, George Beardsall (1825 to
27 June 1899). Mrs Coppard is based on Lydia Lawrence's mother, Lydia
Beardsall, née Newton (1828–1900).

15:37 **favoured**   Resembled, looked like.

16:30 **stiff necked**   Proud and stubborn; interested in wealth rather than
religion (Exodus xxxii. 9).

18:12 **Roger de Coverley**   A popular country dance, in which the dancers
stand in two rows.

19:28 **pledge**   Promise to drink no alcohol.

24:36 **the spear through the side**   John xix. 34.

31:12 **'Lead Kindly Light.'**   DHL exploits the hymn (1833) by John
Henry Newman (1801–90) for comic effect: 'Lead, kindly Light, amid the
encircling gloom,/ ... The night is dark, and I am far from home,/ ...
Keep Thou my feet; I do not ask to see/ The distant scene; one step
enough for me.'

31:15 **'Geneviève'**   Popular song 'Sweet Genevieve' (1876) by George
Cooper (1840–1927) whose words echo Mrs Morel's nostalgia (17:6): 'The
days may come, the days may go,/ But still the hands of mem'ry weave/
The blissful dream of long ago.' (DHL's added French accent was an
error which was removed by Duckworth's printers.)

40:6 **Hose**   Worker for the hosiery trade, who distributed unsewn stockings
to women outworkers so that they could stitch the back seam at home for
piece-work.

40:14 **trap**   A small, two-wheeled, horse-drawn cart.

45:22 **the Wedding at Cana**   John ii. 1–11.

48:10 **cascara**   A laxative.

50:11 **Joseph**   Genesis xxxvii. 5–8 and xlii. 6. Joseph dreamed that his
brothers' corn sheaves bowed to his own. Years later he became ruler of
Egypt and his brothers bowed to him.

56:23 *The Child's Own*   *The Child's Own Magazine*, published by the
Sunday School Union.

61:33 **clubs**   Local mutual-aid societies. Cf. 'on the club' (114:29) – living
on benefit based on regular payments to a club.

65:14–15 **'We shall ... to roll—'**   The yeast-seller combines two hymns:
'Shall we meet beyond the river,/ Where the surges cease to roll?' and
'We shall meet beyond the river,/ By and by.' The river (Jordan)
symbolizes the boundary between life and death.

66:1 **'At the Cross at the cross, where I found—'**   The chorus of the
hymn 'Alas and did my saviour bleed' is close to this: 'At the cross, at the

478

cross, where I first saw the light,/ And the burden of my heart rolled away . . .'

66:9 **Solerman—** Solomon: Matthew vi. 28–9 and I Kings iii–x.

66:37–40 **'Adam an' Eve . . .'** Children's rhyme with many variations ('bade' means 'bathe').

69:18 **Women's Guild** 'The Women's Co-operative Guild', founded in 1883 as the 'Women's League for the Spread of Co-operation'.

69:19 **Co-operative Wholesale Society** A movement begun in 1844 to encourage self-help among working people.

72:7 **'A rose would smell as sweet—'!** *Romeo and Juliet* I. v. 42–3.

72:15 **Joseph's-Coat** Genesis xxxvii. 3.

73:11 **Mechanics' Hall** Mechanics' Institutes were a movement started in 1823 to provide 'mechanics' (manual labourers) with facilities for self-education.

73:29 **'Postle** Short form of 'Apostle', Paul's nickname (see also pp. 454–9).

73:31 **dead gone on me** Infatuated with me.

73:35 **no cop** No good.

74:22 **Mater** Mother (Latin).

76:31 **Nicholas Nickleby** *The Life and Adventures of Nicholas Nickleby* (1838–9) by Charles Dickens (1812–70).

76:34 *King Solomon's Mines* Popular novel (1886) by Sir Henry Rider Haggard (1856–1925).

77:17 **Black Watch** The 42nd Highland regiment of the British Army (from 1739) whose name came from their dark tartan.

78:17 **board school . . . High School in Nottingham** [78:18] Schools providing free education for children from five to thirteen, and managed by School Boards, were established by the Elementary Education Act of 1870 . . . Nottingham High School was a fee-paying grammar school (see 142:14) which offered scholarships for poor children.

80:19 **as rich as Croesus** Croesus, king of Lydia in Greece *c.* 560–546 BC, famous for his wealth.

80:20 **Lafayette** French name well-known in Britain at the turn of the century because of the fame of the French general and politician, Marie-Joseph, Marquis de Lafayette (1757–1834), who fought in the American War of Independence and was prominent in the French Revolution.

80:27 **'Transpires'—oh yes!** The original meaning, 'escapes by evaporation', began to alter *c.* 1800 in the USA to 'happens, takes place', at first considered wrong in Britain, but slowly accepted after 1900.

82:14 **lerky** A version of hide-and-seek.

83:15 **Band of Hope** Youth clubs founded (*c.* 1847) to teach Christianity and temperance (abstinence from alcohol).

87:24 **scotch** Impediment, brake, 'spanner in the works'.

88:22 **iron goose** Anvil in the shape of a goose's neck.

88:30 **moleskin**   Thick, velvety cotton cloth used for pit-trousers.

91:16 **kicking against the pricks**   Rebelling (Acts ix. 5).

92:13 **knits the sleep**   An echo of *Macbeth* II. ii. 38 (see also 171:36).

96:33 *de haut en bas*   Condescendingly (French).

98:35 **tip**   Hat ornament made from a feather or fur tail.

101:38 **the moon should be turned to blood**   A sign that Judgement Day is near (Joel ii. 31, Revelation vi. 12).

102:6 **'My shoes ... in milk.'**   A ring game (see 101:2) with many versions, some of which ended: 'Here we go around, around, around,/ Until we all touch the ground.'

104:11 **Spanish tarts**   Small jam tarts.

111:9 **there's the fever and the mortification**   'There's the danger of fever and gangrene to consider.'

112:33 **Disability Fund**   From 1897 collieries were obliged to compensate miners injured at work.

114:6 **this world's gear**   Possessions, material necessities.

114:29 **'on the club'**   See note on 61:36.

116:21 **girl**   DHL's fictionalization of his elder brother Ernest's girl-friend, Louisa Lily Western 'Gypsy' Dennis (b. 1879).

117:6 **Thomas Jordan**   Based on the firm of J. H. Haywood where DHL worked for three months late in 1901. Mr Jordan's daughter (139:36) is based on Emily Flintoff Haywood, whose work was included in the exhibitions by local artists at the Castle Museum and Art Gallery, Nottingham.

118:13 **one and eleven three**   One shilling and eleven pence three farthings (a farthing under two shillings).

119:2 **scaffold**   Charles I (1600–1649), king of England and Scotland (1625–49), was beheaded on such a raised wooden stage.

119:12 **norfolk suit**   Fashionable suit with knee breeches and a loose pleated jacket with a belt.

123:8 **Keep's**   An art shop in Angel Row, Nottingham.

123:11 **sable brush**   A watercolour brush.

129:18 **chlorodyne**   Narcotic and painkiller containing chloroform, morphine and other substances.

133:9 **'Two Little Girls in Blue.'**   Popular song (1893) by Charles Graham about a mistaken accusation of infidelity.

133:40 *Au revoy*   *Au revoir*, goodbye (French).

137:1 **Elaine in the *Idylls of the King***   See Book Seven of the poem (1859) by Alfred, Lord Tennyson (1809–92).

138:37 **'There is a Tavern—.'**   Popular song: 'There is a tavern in the town,/ And there my dear love sits him down,/ And sips his wine mid laughter free,/ And never, never thinks of me.'

140:33 *Arabian Nights*   A collection of Arabic tales (fourteenth to sixteenth century) supposedly told each night by Scheherezade to the Caliph of Baghdad.

148:40 **Mr Leivers** The novel's Leivers family consists of Alfred, his wife
Mrs Leivers (149:1), their daughters Agatha (207:6) and Miriam (154:11)
and their sons Edgar, Geoffrey, Maurice (155:18–20) and Hubert (183:35).
DHL modelled them on Edmund Chambers (1863–1946), his wife Sarah
Ann Chambers (1859–1937), their daughters Muriel May Chambers
Holbrook (1883–1955) and Jessie (1887–1944), and their sons Alan Aubrey
(1882–1946), Hubert (1888–?), Bernard (1890–?) and Jonathan David
(1898–1970). The family were tenants (1898–1910) of Haggs Farm (see
Willey Farm, 149:40, 153:6).

156:32 **'The Lady of the Lake'** Poem (1810) by Sir Walter Scott (1771–
1832).

156:39–40 **'Not such . . . silently'** Not identified.

160:1 **foulard** Light material made of silk and cotton.

160:33 **Annie Swan's** Pen-name of a best-selling writer of romantic fiction,
Mrs Burnett Smith (1872–1943).

164:32 **Goose Fair** Annual fair unique to Nottingham, held for three or
four days early in October.

166:16 **erysipelas** A bacterial skin disease, often fatal before the discovery
of antibiotics.

169:33 **my son—my son** Cf. 2 Samuel xviii. 33.

173:19–20 **Ediths . . . Guy Mannerings** Characters from works by Sir
Walter Scott. Edith is heroine of *The Lord of the Isles* (1815); Lucy
Ashton is heroine of *The Bride of Lammermoor* (1819); Rowena and Brian
de Bois-Guilbert are characters in *Ivanhoe* (1819); Rob Roy is the outlaw
hero of *Rob Roy* (1817); Guy Mannering is a colonel in *Guy Mannering*
(1815).

174:6 **'Colomba' or the *Voyage Autour de ma Chambre*** *Colomba* (1841)
by Prosper Merimée (1803–70). *Voyage Autour de ma Chambre* (1794) by
Xavier de Maistre (1763–1852).

176:15 **King Cophetua's beggar maid** The painting *King Cophetua and
the Beggar Maid* (1884) by Sir Edward Burne-Jones (1833–98) was
inspired by Tennyson's poem, 'The Beggar Maid' (1842).

178:19 **'the other cheek' . . . spat on her** [178:23] **. . . proud humility**
[178:24] Matthew v. 38–9 and Luke vi. 27–9 . . . Matthew xxvii. 30
(RV) . . . see 'Epithalamion' (1595) ll. 305–6, by Edmund Spenser
(1552?–99).

180:14 **'les derniers fils d'une race épuisée.'** 'The last sons of a worn-
out family' or 'The last descendants of a dwindling race' (French).

183:6 **ponder these sayings** Luke ii. 19.

184:22 **women who went with Mary** Luke xxiv. 1–10.

193:12–13 **sparrow falling—and hairs of the head** Matthew x. 29–30;
Luke xii. 7.

199:28 **Glories of the Snow** Scilla, a spring-flowering bulb.

202:26 **letters of the Law** Exodus xx–xxxiii.

205:4 **rampant** 'Rearing' (of an animal in heraldry) and 'uncontrolled' or 'unrestrained'.

205:8 **Mary Queen of Scots** Mary Stuart (1542–87) spent several periods of imprisonment in Wingfield Manor.

205:33 **where no help came** Psalm cxxi. 1.

207:12 **Veronese's 'St Catherine.'** DHL's description fits a painting by Paolo Veronese (1528–88), *The Vision of St Helena*. St Catherine of Alexandria was patron saint of girls.

208:11 **serpent in her Eden** Genesis iii.

208:35 **died for the souls of men** Based on 1 John iii. 1, 16.

209:31 **Platonic friendship** Non-sexual love for someone of the opposite sex, an ideal once attributed to the Greek philosopher Plato (*c.* 429–347 BC).

212:2 **Jean Ingelow** 'The High Tide on the Coast of Lincolnshire, 1571' (1863), popular poem by Jean Ingelow (1820–97) about a milkmaid (Elizabeth) drowned by floods at Mablethorpe.

212:22–3 **'The Flowers of the Forest'** A lament for Scottish deaths at the battle of Flodden, by Jane Elliot (1727–1805), included in Palgrave's *Golden Treasury* (see note on 263:34).

214:31 **Coons** White minstrel singers dressed as Negroes.

215:3 **sad Botticelli angel** Sandro Botticelli (1444–1510) painted angels with drooping eyelids to represent mystic ecstasy. In 'Study of Thomas Hardy' DHL wrote, 'Perhaps there is a melancholy in Botticelli, a pain of Woman mated to the Spirit' (*Study of Thomas Hardy*, 67:4–5).

215:5 **Come down Lover's Lane** Popular song (1906) by Arthur J. Mills (lyrics) and Bennett Scott (music).

215:14 **gothic arch** Norman arches were rounded and were built from the eleventh to the thirteenth century; gothic arches were pointed and were built from the twelfth to the sixteenth century.

218:16 **proprietously** 'Courteously' (from 'propriety') rather than 'possessively' (from 'proprietor'). The word was perhaps invented by DHL.

219:10 **taken the King's Shilling** Joined the army, by accepting a shilling from a recruiting officer (in use *c.* 1700–1900).

221:21–2 **exhibition of Students' Work in the Castle** The Castle Museum and Art Gallery in Nottingham held annual displays of work by local artists which were reported nationally. Paul's successes (see also 295:3) are not based on DHL's experience.

223:1 **Dawes** Clara Dawes was probably created out of DHL's experience chiefly of Alice Dax (1878–1959), but also of Louie Burrows (1888–1962) to whom he was engaged from December 1910 to February 1912, Helen Corke (1882–1978) with whom he collaborated on *The Trespasser*, and Frieda Weekley (1879–1956) whom he married in July 1914. It is unlikely that Baxter Dawes was based on Alice Dax's husband, Henry Dax (1873–1962). The name Dawes may be based on Dax; but DHL also puns on the bird, daw: raven (271:22), crow (424:5–27) and Jack[daw] (449:20).

223:32 **women's rights** Women had no vote (until 1918, and then only if over thirty years old); women also campaigned against low pay and for state maternity benefit.

227:2 **Verlaine** Paul Verlaine (1844–96), a lyrical symbolist French poet.

228:16 **Orion** Constellation named after a giant huntsman in Greek mythology killed by the goddess of the moon (see also 233:27–38). His 'jewels' (233:28) are the three stars of his belt, and his 'dog' (228:17, 233:28) is Sirius the dog-star. DHL was influenced by Tennyson's 'Locksley Hall' (1842, see lines 7–8), and mentioned Orion in *The White Peacock* (88:3, 260:30), *The Rainbow* (132:14), *Women in Love* (408:32) and 'Hymn to Priapus' (*Collected Poems*, i. 198).

230:30 **lived and moved and had her being** Acts xvii. 28.

232:6 **Michael Angelo** See 345:11 and note.

234:21 **Balzac** Honoré de Balzac (1799–1850), French novelist.

241:12 **Liberty's** London store, founded in 1875, specializing in fabrics inspired by pre-Raphaelite painting; it had a policy of accepting designs from freelance artists.

245:1 **King Alfred burned the cakes** According to legend this happened when Alfred the Great (AD 849–901), King of the West Saxons (AD 871–901), was sheltering from invading Vikings in AD 878 in the home of a swineherd.

245:25 **Solomon's baby** I Kings iii. 16–28.

246:40–247:6 **'Ce matin ... si clair——'** '"This morning the birds woke me," he read. "It was still half-light. But the little window in my bedroom was pale and then yellow, and all the birds of the wood burst out in a lively resonating song. The whole dawn vibrated. I had been dreaming of you. Do you see the dawn, too? The birds wake me nearly every morning, and there is always a touch of fear in the cry of the thrushes. It is so clear——'

247:13 **agrees with the direct object when it precedes** The past participle 'eveillé' (246:40) refers to Miriam and should be feminine: 'eveillée'.

248:5 **Baudelaire's 'Le Balcon.'** A poem from *Les Fleurs du Mal* (1857) by Charles Baudelaire (1821–67).

248:13–17 **Behold her ... like a nun—'** 'Fair Ines', a poem by Thomas Hood (1799–1845). The quotations are from William Wordsworth (1770–1850), 'The Solitary Reaper' (1807), ll. 1–2, 'Behold her, single in the field . . .' and an untitled sonnet (1807), ll. 1–2, 'It is a . . . and free,/ The holy time is quiet as a Nun.' Both poems can be found in Palgrave's *Golden Treasury* (see note on 263:34).

251:17–18 **Herbert Spencer** In a stream of internationally best-selling books published from 1851 to 1893, Spencer (1820–1903) applied the theory of evolution to biology, psychology, ethics and sociology, and developed an agnostic-evolutionary philosophy. Paul's interest in Spencer is shown in his discussions of 'protoplasm' (183:5), 'gravitation' and 'proportion' (240:27–9), 'the race of sparrows' (193:15), and in the related topic of ethics (293:1). DHL's interest is also shown in the use of the words 'force' (181:28), 'particle' (182:23) and 'phosphorescence' (464:35).

256:6 **Primitive Methodist Chapel** A fundamentalist section of the Methodist Church, which broke away in 1812.

263:15 **Who hath believed** Isaiah liii. 1.

263:23 **Mary loved at Bethany** John xi–xii, Luke x. 38–9. DHL saw Mary of Bethany as the 'almost neutral' woman who wanted a 'spiritual marriage, bodiless' (*Study of Thomas Hardy* 114:32, 115:1).

263:34 **Palgrave's** *Golden Treasury* *The Golden Treasury of the Best Songs and Lyrical Poems in the English Language* (1861), edited by Francis Turner Palgrave (1824–97), contains some poems referred to in this novel (212:22, 248:13–17, 272:14, 313:23).

263:38 *Tartarin de Tarascon* Satirical novel (1872) by Alphonse Daudet (1840–97).

265:29 **purpose, no anchor of righteousness** A blend of Shakespeare and the Bible: 'Infirm of purpose!' (*Macbeth* II. i. 54); 'Which hope we have as an anchor of the soul, both sure and stedfast' (Hebrews vi. 19); 'Stand therefore . . . having on the breastplate of righteousness' (Ephesians vi. 14).

267:8 **Circe** A sorceress in Homer's *Odyssey*, who turned her visitors into pigs.

267:8 **Tippoo** Tippoo Sahib, sultan of Mysore (1749–99) and an enemy of the British in India.

267:31 **the Renan** *Vie de Jésus* **stage** The *Life of Jesus* (1863; English version 1864) by Ernest Renan (1823–92) was the biography of an ordinary man who founded a religious sect.

268:12 **chapter of St. John . . . the verse** [268:20] John xvi. 21.

270:18 **Margaret Bonford's meeting** Based on the radical suffragist Margaret Bondfield (1873–1953), who was Assistant Secretary of the Shopworkers' Union (1898–1908); itinerant lecturer (1908–12) for the Women's Trade Union League, the Independent Labour Party and the Women's Labour League; and founder president (1905) of the 'Adult Suffrage Society', which campaigned for full democratic rights for all women. Later, she was the first woman chairman of the Trades Union Council (1923), a Labour MP (1923) and, as Minister of Labour (1926), the first woman cabinet minister.

271:22–3 **the Raven that quothed 'Nevermore'** 'The Raven', poem by Edgar Allan Poe (1809–49).

272:14 **'Mary Morrison'** Poem by Robert Burns (1759–96) which became a popular song, included in Palgrave's *Golden Treasury*.

273:29 **Queen Boadisca** Boadisca, Boudicca or Boadicea (d. AD 62) led the Britons into battle against the invading Romans, but lost.

273:29–30 **Song of the Shirt** Poem about a poor seamstress (1843) by Thomas Hood (1799–1845).

Explanatory Notes

273:31 **lay his head** Parody of Matthew viii. 20.

274:19 **Deirdre or Iseult** Irish heroines from early romances: Deirdre from 'The Sons of Usnach' (Irish, first century BC); Iseult (or Isolde) from 'Sir Tristrem' (French, pre-1300; Tristan and Isolde was a German version).

274:21 **pavilion** A medieval knight's tent.

274:24 **broidery** Embroidery: vocabulary from Tennyson's 'The Princess' and 'Idylls of the King' (see 137:2).

274:26 **W.S.P.U.** The Women's Social and Political Union, a suffragette pressure group founded in 1903 by Emmeline Pankhurst. Green, purple and white were the movement's colours.

274:33 **shadow** *The Dog and the Shadow* (1826), a painting by Sir Edwin Landseer (1803–73), shows a dog looking at its reflection ('shadow') in water.

274:36 **let *me* be clever** Parody of a line from 'A Farewell to C.E.G.' by Charles Kingsley (1819–75), 'let who can be clever'.

279:18–19 **'ashes . . . the devil must'** Popular parody of the Burial Service in the *Book of Common Prayer*: 'We therefore commit his body to the ground; earth to earth, ashes to ashes, dust to dust; in sure and certain hope of the Resurrection to eternal life.'

280:35 **couchant** Lying down with its head raised (like 'rampant', 205:4, a term describing animals in heraldry).

286:4–5 **'A son's my son . . . whole of my life.'** Proverb, often ending, 'whole of her life'.

293:1 **Manual of Ethics** A textbook (1893) by the idealist philosopher John S. Mackenzie (1860–1935).

293:23 **Omar Khayyam** The *Rubáiyát* of the Persian poet Omar Khayyám (d. 1123), translated into English in 1859 by Edward FitzGerald (1809–83).

293:27 **The Blessed Damosel** Poem (1850) by Dante Gabriel Rossetti (1828–82).

297:16 **vest** Waistcoat.

299:29–30 **a divine discontent** Charles Kingsley, in *Health and Education* (1874), popularized the idea that a feeling of discontent was really a desire for knowledge and virtue.

301:19 **done in carbon** Carbon drawings made from photographs.

301:36 **jenny** A winding-machine, often called a 'spinning-jenny'; DHL's verb, 'jennying' (303:30), is unusual.

303:32 **sweated . . . force ourselves into the labour market** [303:34] 'Sweated labour': long hours, hard work and poor pay . . . The Nottingham lace industry's prosperity owed much to a large, low-paid workforce of women, many working at home.

304:19 **Juno dethroned** The queen of the (Roman) gods, Juno, was often depicted as enthroned and statuesque.

307:6 *Lettres de mon Moulin* 'Letters from my Mill' (1866), stories by Alphonse Daudet (1840–97).

308:16 'The Rose and the Tomb.' From *Les Voix Interieurs* (1837) by Victor Hugo (1802–85).

309:6 **Penelope** Penelope, in Homer's *Odyssey*, spent twenty years weaving while she waited for her husband Odysseus to return from the Trojan war.

312:21 **the Queen of Sheba** 1 Kings x. 1–2. Proverbial both for her pride and her magnificent appearance (see 347:19).

313:23 **Bulk only** A reference to a poem by Ben Jonson (1572–1637), ten lines of which were included in Palgrave's *Golden Treasury* under the title 'The Noble Nature', beginning 'It is not growing like a tree/ In bulk, doth make Man better be.'

314:1–2 **remorseful angels** Angels driven out of heaven with Lucifer after his failed rebellion against God: Revelation xii. 9 and *Paradise Lost* (1667) by John Milton (1608–74).

314:6 'The optimist by intention!' Deliberate optimist, who bases a belief in social progress on a blend of Christianity and the theory of evolution.

314:30–31 **like two cherubs in the sky** Parody of the nursery rhyme 'Twinkle, twinkle little star' ['. . . Like a diamond in . . .'].

315:9–10 **gave with the right** Parody of Matthew vi. 3.

324:39 **Sir Thomas More says one can marry at twenty four** Paul has misremembered the prescription in *Utopia* (1516) by Sir Thomas More (1478–1535): 'The woman is not married before she be 18 years old. The man is four years elder before he marry.' (English translation by Ralph Robinson 1551; reprinted by Everyman, 1910.)

327:18 **in the Gretchen way** i.e. the risk of pregnancy. In *Faust* (Part I, 1808) by Johann Wolfgang Goethe (1749–1832), Gretchen is seduced and made pregnant by Faust.

331:14 *not-to-be* *Hamlet* II. ii. 56. See also *Letters*, i. 504.

345:10 **impressionists ... Michael Angelo's people** [345:11] Impressionists emphasized light rather than shape (see Paul's remarks at 183:1–5) and formed a school of painting which began in France in 1874 and dominated European art for many years ... Michelangelo Buonarrotti (1475–1564).

346:32 **Venus of Milo** A second-century marble statue of Venus in the Louvre, Paris, famed as representing female beauty.

349:30 **unite** The sentence 'He could not ... this shell,' was added by DHL on the proofs, which are now lost. It seems likely that the first printers misread DHL's 'unite' as 'write'. That is the version that was printed until Keith Sagar edited the novel for Penguin Classics and conjectured that DHL wrote 'unite'.

349:37 **chloroform** Anaesthetic used by dentists.

353:1 **little Kirke White** In his poem 'Clifton Grove' (1803) the Nottingham poet Henry Kirke White (1785–1806) described his boyhood enjoyment of the Grove.

358:13–15 **Eve . . . bit of an apple** Genesis ii–iii.

361:25 **the 'femme incomprise,'** The woman who is not understood (French).

364:24–5 **pillar of cloud . . . by night** Exodus xiii. 21–2.

371:17–18 **the 'Christian Mystery'** The theory that the truth of Christianity is revealed by God and cannot be tested scientifically.

374:22–3 **Sarah Bernhardt . . . *La Dame aux Camélias*** Sarah Bernhardt (1844–1923), a French actress, appeared at the age of sixty-three at the Theatre Royal, Nottingham, in *La Dame aux Camélias* by Alexandre Dumas (1824–95), where DHL saw her (15 June 1908).

378:15 **Dutch oven** A pot used for cooking meat over an open fire or kitchen range.

380:9 **Pierrot** A character in French pantomime with whitened face and loose, white, trousered costume.

387:9 **bob-tailed** 'With its tail cut off', i.e. Paul wore a dinner jacket (see 377:36) and not a long-tailed evening jacket.

387:9 **on the lardy-da** Dressed flashily for a dissolute evening.

387:14 **had it** i.e. sex.

390:23 **not daggeroso** Not the dagger-carrying type.

391:23–6 **'The man in righteousness . . . quiver—'** A lighthearted translation by American President John Quincy Adams (1767–1848), of a satirical ode (Book i. 23) by Horace (65–08 BC).

391:38 **'Put me among the Girls.'** Comic Music Hall song by Clarence W. Murphy and Dan Lipton (1907).

394:6 *Cherchez la femme* 'Look for the woman' (French), i.e. a woman is the cause of this trouble.

405:37 **Orpen** Sir William Orpen (1878–1931), portrait painter.

414:10 **Central** The private railway company.

424:5 **Jim-crow** Pun on Dawes (see note to 223:1). Also 'street clown' in rhyming slang because it rhymes with 'saltimbanco', Italian for 'acrobat'.

429:23 **veils that were ripping** As at Christ's death, e.g. Luke xxiii. 45. See also 451:14–15.

430:15–16 **Mablethorpe and Robin Hood's Bay and Shanklin** Only the first and last are described in the novel (211:30, 347:7).

432:21 **Benger's** Benger's Food, a powder which could be mixed with water to make a liquid food for invalids.

437:5–6 **The miners . . . before Christmas** 3,650 Eastwood miners were on strike from 15 June to 24 November 1910 over the introduction of coal-cutting machines.

438:14 **moue** Pouting grimace.

445:26 *nuit blanche* Sleepless night (French).

448:15 water   Dawes has oedema – excess fluid in the body – a symptom of poor health, high blood pressure or low kidney function.

464:21 ear of wheat   John xii. 24.

464:35 phosphorescence   Light given off by plants, insects, sea creatures and the bacteria of putrefaction: the word is associated both with something luminous and with decay.

Further Reading

Biographical Studies

Chambers, Jessie, *D. H. Lawrence: A Personal Record by 'E.T.'*, Frank Cass & Co. Ltd., 1935. (*A memoir of Lawrence's early years which treats* Sons and Lovers *as an attempt at a historical record and accuses Lawrence of inaccuracy.*)

Nehls, Edward, ed., *D. H. Lawrence: A Composite Biography* (3 volumes), University of Wisconsin Press, 1957. (*An anthology of memoirs and other documents relating to Lawrence's life.*)

Worthen, John, *D. H. Lawrence: The Early Years 1885–1912*, Cambridge University Press, 1991. (*The definitive treatment of the* Sons and Lovers *period.*)

Critical Studies of the Complete Sons and Lovers

Baron, Helen, 'Lawrence's *Sons and Lovers* versus Garnett's', *Essays in Criticism*, October 1992, Vol. xlii No. 4, pp. 265–78. (*Discusses those passages showing Lawrence's interest in the theory of evolution which were cut by Garnett.*)

Black, Michael, *D. H. Lawrence: Sons and Lovers*, Cambridge University Press, 1992. (*Full account of the novel's genesis and relation to other literature, plus an original and helpful discussion of its imagery.*)

Critical Studies of the Version Abridged by Garnett

Draper, R. P., ed., *D. H. Lawrence: The Critical Heritage*, Routledge & Kegan Paul, 1970. (*Reprints eight of the first reviews.*)

Finney, Brian, *D. H. Lawrence: Sons and Lovers*, Penguin Critical Studies, 1990. (*Readable discussion of the main categories of critical approach.*)

Harvey, Geoffrey, *Sons and Lovers—The Critics' Debate*, Macmillan, 1987. (*Helpful survey of the critical debate, with useful reading list.*)

Kermode, Frank, *Lawrence*, Fontana, 1973. (*pp. 16–23 are devoted to* Sons and Lovers *and provide an economical and stimulating survey of the literary issues.*)

Littlewood, J. C. F., 'Son and Lover', *The Cambridge Quarterly*, Autumn/Winter 1969/70, pp. 323–61. (*Treats* Sons and Lovers *as an attempt at*

Further Reading

historically accurate self-analysis and judges it untruthful in comparison with Jessie Chambers's memoir.)

Murfin, Ross C., *Sons and Lovers: A Student's Companion to the Novel*, Twayne, 1987. (*A study of conflict and division in the characters and their contemporary society.*)

Sklenicka, Carol, *D. H. Lawrence and the Child*, University of Missouri Press, 1991. (*Chapter 2, pp. 36–55, is devoted to* Sons and Lovers, *which is discussed in terms of the mother–son relationship and Lawrence's later criticisms of Freud.*)

Tedlock, E. W., ed., *D. H. Lawrence and 'Sons and Lovers': Sources and Criticism*, New York University Press, 1965; University of London Press, 1966. (*Useful collection of older critical essays.*)

Widdowson, Peter, ed., *D. H. Lawrence*, Longman Critical Readers, 1992. (*Contains many interesting and some classic studies, including ones by Kate Millett and Terry Eagleton.*)

Worthen, John, *D. H. Lawrence and the Idea of the Novel*, Macmillan, 1979. (*Chapter 3, pp. 26–44, is devoted to* Sons and Lovers, *and uses the history of composition as a critical tool for analysing the development of Lawrence's art.*)

Glossary of Dialect Forms

Page and line references are to first occurrences only.

a' (27:40) All; 'an' a'': and all, really, then; 'what's a' on you': what are all of you.

'a (130:21) Have.

'ae-penny (12:13) Halfpenny.

agate (220:28) Afoot, happening.

allers (39:34) Always.

'appen, happen (39:13) Perhaps.

arena ter (15:13) Aren't you.

as (66:12) That; 'a lad as': a boy that, a boy who.

'as (220:31, 275:9) Has; have.

ash-pits (10:21) Lavatory sheds without plumbing, where ash was used to cover the contents of the closet.

a-whoam (418:40) At home.

ax, axin' (91:33) Ask, asking.

bacca (89:27) Tobacco.

badly (95:3) Ill.

barkled (47:4) Clogged, choked.

beguy (296:27) By God.

bent (278:1) Reedy grass.

be-out (11:17) Without.

bested (96:28) Arrived before (see kested).

bezzle (32:11) Guzzle, drink immoderately; squander, waste.

blab-mouthed (25:21) Too talkative, indiscreet.

bob (130:20) God; 'strike my bob' probably from 'strike me, God'.

bobby-dazzler, bobby-dazzlers (151:21, 377:33) Eye-catching, fashionable garment; fashionably dressed people.

b'r a (15:1) But a.

breeks, britches (70:2, 72:10) Breeches, trousers.

browght, browt (15:5) Brought.

butty (25:40) Leader of a team of miners working a stall.

cadin' (89:24) Tame, affectionate; 'that cadin'': so tame.

canna (18:37) Can't.

carfle (167:14) Coal wagon, coal truck.

'casions (39:7) Occasion, reasons, need; 'tha's no 'casions ter': you've no need to.

catamaran (379:14) Argumentative woman (dialect); raft.

chair (42:14) Container which carried coal and miners between coalface and surface.

chelp (83:27) Insolence.

chunterin' (52:9) Muttering, grumbling, complaining.

clap thysen into (236:36) Quickly put yourself into, suddenly dress in.

clapped eyes on (58:22) Caught sight of, saw, noticed.

clout (46:36) Dishcloth, floorcloth.

clunch (25:28) Solid clay.

cobbler (66:35) Horse chestnut, conker.

copperful (40:11) Copper bowl full of hot water and laundry.

cossed (25:29) Cursed.

cowd (236:23) Cold.

crozzly (378:36) Cooked hard, crunchy, crisp.

curl (18:33) Pretence; 'taking the curl out of me': undermining my attempts at cleverness.

daresn't (392:13) Dare not.

day-man (238:39) Miner hired by the butty and his team on a daily basis, casual worker, irregular, extra.

didna (58:21) Didn't.

dingin' (47:26) Hammering, beating.

doesna (287:32) Thou dost not, you don't.

doo-er (51:39) Door.

dossn't (83:26) Daren't.

dot (259:6) Hit, punch.

druv (275:25) Driven.

d'st, dost (25:26) Do you.

dun, dunna (19:15) Do, don't.

dunno (235:20) Don't know.

durs'na, dursn't (156:28) Durst not, daren't.

eddish (11:38) A field of stubble and grass where cattle graze.

'er's (421:23) She's, she is.

fawce (89:16) Cunning, false.

feyther (167:3) Father.

flig (102:31) Eager, in a hurry.

flush (27:1) Well-paid, having plenty of cash to spend.

flybie-skybie (82:14) A thoughtless, flighty person.

fol-de-lol (125:11) A useless ornament; vapid, showy person.

fridging (29:17) Chafing, wearing away by rubbing, fraying.

frumenty (92:37) Dessert of wheat cooked in milk and sugar.

fun (25:34) Found.

Fuzzball (204:29) Puffball fungus or dandelion in seed.

gabey (59:10) Fool, baby, fusspot.

gaffer (25:24) Boss.

gallivant (98:8) Go out looking for fun.

gawp (39:30) Fool, simpleton.

gen (15:1) Given.

ger (33:10) Get; 'ger out on't': get out of it.

gi'e, gi'ein' (15:13) Give, giving.

gin-close (38:34) Small pasture overlying former gin-pit.

gin-pit (9:6) Shallow mine using a rope-drum winch ('gin'), rotated by horses or donkeys, to hoist coal to the surface.

gleg (308:26) Furtive look, peep.

guttle (239:27) Guzzle, drink heavily.

Guyney (384:40) God; variant of Notts dialect 'My Guy'.

ha', ha'e (20:6) Have.

hadna (104:31) Hadn't.

ha'ef (105:30) Half.

hae'f-crown (15:1) Half-crown – two shillings and sixpence.

ham (15:14) Am.

han (43:14) Have.

ha'porth (66:3) Halfpennyworth.

happen (42:2) Perhaps; 'tha'll happen': perhaps you will.

hash (41:14) Serve chopped-up leftovers.

Hey-up theer (41:39) 'Hey-up, there': Hey, you over there.

h'ice-'ouse (235:14) Ice-house.

hing (89:39) Hang.

hisn (32:18) His ones.

holer (26:3) Collier who undercuts the coal-seam.

holled (103:12) Hurled, thrown.

how'r'yer (130:17) How are you.

hurtle (236:3) Huddle, shrink.

hutch up (204:33) Move closer together.

h'yer (130:21) Have you.

ikey (281:26) Proud, superior, cocky.

I'n (39:7) I've.

I'ne (143:27) I'm, I am.

isn't the' (12:8) Aren't there.

issen (220:39) Himself.

jiggered (387:15) Astonished (but here vulgar: buggered).

jockey (83:27) Cheeky young man, upstart.

jowl (98:39) Strike, knock, push.

kested (198:34) Arrived before.

knivey (288:1) Mean, tormenting, teasing.

leading (239:5) Charge for coal bought by miners at special rates at the pithead.

let on (143:22) Alighted on, came across, found, caught (past tense of 'light on', see below).

letn (102:29) Have let, have allowed to.

light on (392:16) Come across, find, catch.

loose-a', loose-all (41:19) Stop-work (signal at the end of a shift or day).

'lowance (13:10) Allowance, free drinks in payment for serving behind the bar.

ma'e, may yer (15:16, 58:29) Make, make you.

mardy (62:17) Spoilt, petted, over-indulged; soft, timorous.

marrain (402:17) Sea reed or bent grass.

mashed the tea (295:34) Brewed the tea.

milord (53:23) My lord, Sir (ironical).

mind (15:14) Inclination; 'ter's a mind': you'd like to.

misdoubt (296:33) Doubt, deny.

moudiwarp (19:12) Mole.

mucky (15:21) Messy, untidy; 'mucky little 'ussy': worthless cheeky young woman.

mun (19:16) Must.

nesh (52:1) Delicate, weak.

niver (46:25) Never; 'tha niver says!': you don't mean it.

nobbut (208:7) Nothing but, only.

nobby (77:17) Smart, optimum.

none, non (67:36, 70:10) Not.

nowt (15:1) Nothing.

n'r (236:6) Nor, than.

off'n (65:24) Off from, i.e. off.

on (15:14) Of; in phrases 'which on 'em' (15:14), 'get out on it' (33:8), 'none on yer' (52:10), etc.

oppen (235:1) Open.

'oss (52:11) Horse.

owd (208:8) Old.

owt (47:11) Anything.

paddle (57:8) Make puddles.

panchion (31:18) A large, shallow, earthenware bowl.

pap (224:14) Baby-food; weakling.

pay the b— out (52:16) Revenge myself on the bitch.

pedgilling (32:29) Laboriously picking over bits to make a living; working hard, struggling.

peen (61:20) Pain.

penn'orth (100:25) Penny-worth.

pick-haft (46:27) Handle of a pick-axe.

podded (366:25) Shuffled about, padded, pottered.

ponching (29:37) Pounding laundry with a wooden implement.

pore fing (289:4) Poor thing.

pulamiter (236:7) Whiner.

raked (15:25) Added coal to make the fire burn slowly all night (23:20).

ring (101:2) Game in which children form a circle and sing.

rip (72:8) Wildly energetic boy.

rip along (40:27) Work fast, speed along.

road (88:21) Way; 'out of my road': out of my way; 'this road': in this direction.

robinet (136:30) Robin.

run the rig (287:1) Run riot, live wildly or dissolutely.

runnin' (275:10) In a row; 'three days an' runnin'': three days in a row, three consecutive days.

safe working (41:24) Coal seam free from dangerous gases.

scrattling (99:13) Scratching a living, poor, mean.

s'd (109:17) Should.

seed (13:6) Saw.

sen (19:17) Self: in 'thysen', 'mysen', etc.

setts (109:11) Cobble-stones, road surface of rough stones.

shifting-trousers (236:30) Spare trousers, leisure trousers.

sholl, shollt (73:20, 57:11) Shall, shall you?

shonna (27:37) Shan't.

shouldna (356:7) Shouldn't.

a sight afore (70:13) Long before.

sithee (70:32) See thou, i.e. look.

sixpenny-hop (73:12) Inexpensive public dance.

slive up (89:23) Sneak up.

s'll, s'lt (20:6) Shall, shalt.

sluther (27:34) Shuffle.

smite (76:30) Mite, tiny bit, an atom.

snap, snap-bag (36:23) Lunch, snack; lunch bag, snack bag.

snied wi' (89:36) Infested with, full of.

snipey (67:33) Scolding, sharp-tongued.

soaking (99:28) Baking thoroughly.

soft water tub (27:39) Rain water butt.

somethink like (295:22) Really something, very impressive.

spin of toffee (12:6) Twist of toffee (from a machine).

spoon (197:13) Kiss; '*spoon* and do': kiss and cuddle, etc.

spooney (311:25) Someone who likes kissing and cuddling.

sprottle (204:35) Sprawl.

stall (25:24) Length of coal-face allocated to a team of miners.

stir a peg (39:7) Move a leg, do anything at all.

stool-harsed (70:1) Stool-arsed, someone who sits down to work; 'stool-harsed Jack': office boy.

stoppage, stopped (95:35) Deduction, deducted.

'Strewth (236:8) God's truth.

summat (104:31) Something.

sweal (414:23) Cause to wither and disappear.

tack (371:18) Stuff, rubbish.

ta'e, ta'ein', ta'en (15:14) Take, taking, taken.

team (283:30) Teem, pour.

tear, in a (298:22) In a temper, irritated.

ter (12:12, 15:8) To *or* thou, you.

tha (46:25) Thou, you.

Tha'lt (69:10) Thou shalt, you will.

tha'rt (69:10) Thou art, you are.

the' (12:8) There; 'isn't the'': aren't there.

thorns, on (312:20) Eager.

thronged (22:5) Crowded with people.

tidy (76:39) Moderate; well enough, quite well; 'tidy size': good size, well padded; 'tidy step': long distance; 'tidy penny': large sum of money.

toe-rag (213:6) Fool, beggar.

tomorror (126:26) Tomorrow; 'come again tomorror': say that again (I can't believe it!).

tr'a (67:11) To have.

trapse (194:13) Trudge a long way.

truck-end (70:6) Bottom, seat.

tweedle (156:30) Whistle.

twistin' and too-in' (385:15) Twisting and turning, i.e. struggling, labouring, wrestling.

twitchel (364:2) Narrow passage between two walls or hedges.

'ud (19:23) Would.

un (89:16) One.

us (237:17) Our.

'ussy (15:21) Hussy, literally 'housewife', woman; frequently in sense 'cheeky, assertive young woman' (see **mucky**).

wagging on (39:19) Being active, busy, continuing to work.

wakes (11:2) Annual holiday and fair.

wash with (346:20) Impress.

waxy (385:24) Angry.

ways, come thy (418:14) Come, come along, come with me.

we glad (422:27) We're glad.

well-set-up (17:10) Standing up straight, upright.

wessel-brained (161:23) Empty-headed, confused.

wha 'r' (32:8) What are.

Wha's (87:5) What does.

What's (89:25) What dost thou, what do you.

whipperty-snappin' (392:27) Acting like a cheeky youngster.

whittle (239:35) Fret, worry, bemoan.

whoam (33:9) Home.

wik (70:6) Week.

winder (61:7) Shock, something amazing, a knock-out blow (pronounced with 'i' as in 'window').

wizzen-hearted (28:25) Hard-hearted, mean.

wizzening (11:35) Whining.

wor, worn't (25:29) Was, wasn't.

worrit (356:7) Worry.

wunna (41:37) Won't.

yarning (67:28) Telling tales.

y'ave ter (12:12) You have to.

y'ead (87:16) Head.

yer (15:16) You.

yi, yis (19:12) Yes.

yit (105:32) Yet.

yo' (87:5) You.

Edward Garnett's Editing of
Sons and Lovers

This is a list of the passages which were altered or cut out of the first edition of *Sons and Lovers* (Duckworth 1913) as a result of Garnett's editing of the manuscript and further censorship of the proofs. These passages have only been printed in the Cambridge University Press edition (1992) and this Penguin Twentieth-Century Classics edition (1994).

Page:line	Passage
12:38–13:1	'Well!' she said, . . . gave him his tea.
13:12–16	The children were . . . went to bed.
18:39–19:4	'Aren't you . . . He seemed quaint.
21:29–33	Being of a . . . they liked her.
23:12–26	William, the baby, . . . together downstairs.
26:5–15	A butty is . . . his own fault.
26:21–3	to the pits . . . a pit going.'
29:36–30:7	Mrs Morel was depressed . . . best of things.
30:30–31:5	Mrs Morel always said . . . yellow heads again.
31:39–32:9	'Well you've been . . . woman—eh?—what?'
32:17–31	' "Let 'im look . . . Nottingham carousing—'
33:2–6	'I'd smite you down . . . hate of him.
34:28–32	She looked round her . . . stir and ripple.
38:31–9	He always left . . . simply and naturally.
39:22–40:5	Mrs Kirk was a thin . . . laughed heartily.
44:19–45:11	The mother lay in bed . . . aside and fumed.
45:32–46:18	'No,' she said aloud, . . . for her to begin.
47:28–48:16	'Needn't he—oh . . . a glass,' said Mrs Morel.
48:40–49:21	It was about this time . . . side against him.
51:34–52:16	'You have no need . . . meaning his wife.
52:24–9	She did not trust . . . let any woman tell.
52:30–31	*Garnett changed* 'I know . . . said pitiably to herself, *to* 'But I know . . . added to herself.
57:18–36	But the next evening . . . answered Mrs Morel.
59:23–40	She went up with her coal . . . went to bed.
63:23–64:2	So, having to get . . . afraid of the child.
65:5–17	One morning Mrs Morel . . . ha'porths of barm.
65:17–18	*Garnett changed* Mrs Morel *to* she

65:22–66:11	Mrs Anthony did not . . . indignant than ever.
68:38–69:16	'No, you've done it . . . Mrs Morel to her son.
70:28–73:2	The children of the Bottoms, . . . and she him.
73:14–36	'Waltz!' exclaimed . . . fair as a lily—'
74:13–26	Mrs Morel hated . . . replied his mother.
75:4–23	'Yes.' . . . own up—'
76:11–78:7	He never knew how . . . some shallow hussy.
79:30–80:15	'That's Jockey Club . . . Grand—
97:26–34	'An' they say . . . your own fault.'
113:36–114:2	He had not the faintest . . . invariably replied:
115:33–116:4	His letters . . . writing to you.——'
117:39–118:3	And suddenly she turned . . . people could hear!
122:6–10	Should we buy . . . some proper dinner.'
125:3–126:6	'Well, you never . . . for Saturday morning.'
135:16–25	He told her everything . . . ignominious for him.
137:9–24	'What are you making?' . . . each other, laughing.
138:2–9	'What yer been . . . quite cheerfully.
138:15–38	'Come Paul, my darling . . . sketch I'm doing.'
138:39	*Garnett changed* Then *to* Often
139:36–9	Mr Jordan's daughter . . . interest in the boy.
140:33	but much duller,
149:5–150:7	'If you won't . . . How he must feel—!'
150:19–151:9	'But you've done . . . nuisance!' she exclaimed.
155:24–156:8	'Have you had . . . that stuff,' said Geoffrey.
158:39–159:17	And as he lay . . . I go like this.'
159:18	again
161:5–15	'Be quiet, William,' . . . through a few lines.
162:23–9	They remained . . . still, staring across the room.
164:8–18	'You know,' . . . a long way off.
185:4–23	Often they walked . . . discussion of books.
186:19–36	'Did *you* want . . . her the touchstone.
188:14–32	'Tell me what seems . . . more accurately than he.
190:30–194:18	In Bestwood was . . . too cross to condescend.
203:12–24	In the church-yard . . . his wide mouth.
204:4–205:4	'Isn't this all right!' . . . made Miriam laugh.
211:23–9	He went out before . . . another letter.
212:34–213:9	'I think "Elizabeth" . . . your grandeur.'
213:39–214:6	'That stinking . . . the look of him.'
232:22–233:14	'Then how can I . . . 'At any rate,'
233:14–17	'not now. You . . . veritable torture.—
240:16–35	'And you like it?' . . . till it was done.'
243:30–40	'None of those . . . I won't,' she answered.
263:10–37	Over tea he . . . Her heart sank.
263:37	*Garnett changed* She *to* After tea she

266:20–30	And yet, he . . . suffered rather badly.
273:2–34	The conversation . . . She was indignant.
291:34–292:3	'Must I write . . . and flounder.
292:12–24	When I talk to you, . . . to dissipate?
292:31–293:11	I might marry in . . . now, in my heart.
293:24–294:6	'—You will find . . . "us", is it not?
294:8–14	I must play . . . radically different. So
294:20–23	Now I must balance . . . run away from——'
308:3–31	For several days . . . said the other girls.
314:6–40	'The optimist . . . smell as sweet etc.".'
320:5–17	'I tell you . . . he!' she sneered.
323:14–22	All the talk, . . . he and Miriam.
333:30	naked
333:32	*Garnett changed* hips *to* body
333:34–5	and threw off his things.
333:35	*Garnett changed* And then, *to* but
334:18	very
346:5–347:2	'And then you talk . . . when she comes.'
353:16	regal
358:13–16	And I guess Adam . . . if they wanted to.
372:18	, in a long kiss
375:19	*Garnett changed* thighs *to* limbs
375:31	natural
375:31	and it drove him wild with hunger
381:33–6	Then he realised . . . erect on the bed
382:28	naked
383:20–30	Then he loosed her, . . . sides, she quivered.
384:27	*Garnett changed* his nose and his brown moustache *to* face
385:38	and rejoicing
399:22	and over his hips
401:19	*Garnett changed* a white, velvet-skinned woman *to* white and velvet skinned
401:22–3	'OO!' she said, hugging . . . 'it's cold!'
401:29	*Garnett changed* gathered *to* hugged
401:32–3	the two white glistening globes she cradled.
402:1–2	She was a rich, . . . across the foreshore.